HEDGE FUND GRANNIES

Gerard A. Herlihy

Copyright © 2014 by Gerard A. Herlihy
Cover Illustration by Shelly J. Cox

ISBN: 0692241744
ISBN 978-0692241745
Library of Congress Control Number: 2014912040
Gerard A. Herlihy, West Palm Beach, FL

PRINTED IN THE UNITED STATES OF AMERICA

First United States Edition

CHAPTER 1

APRIL 22, 2011

Allie handed the clipboard to Chris Reilly, the day shift supervisor at Holy Name Medical Center. Every morning following the graveyard shift in the intensive care unit, Allie jumped out of her superhero nurse's uniform and into her civvies. Today her outfit was a simple medium-blue silk dress, a string of white beads, and black flats.

Allie was pretty, athletic, perky and smart. She was also very single and for now uninterested in dating. She was too busy as a single mom trying to keep her teenage boy from getting into further trouble.

She tore through the backroads toward Ben's Deli. At a stoplight, she applied some lip gloss, dabbed on a little eyeliner, and poofed her hair. She always took the local route free of speed traps: along Queen Anne Road, across the train trestle, take Windsor to Woodbine to Front Street until she arrived at Ben's in Bergenfield, New Jersey.

Allie loved connecting with her friends before they left for their New York banking and lawyer gigs. It was an hour filled with intellectual conversation and lots of laughs. Every morning was different. It provided needed relief from her hectic activities of work and raising her rebellious kid.

In an hour, she would head home and beg her son to go to school, try to get five hours of sleep, then wake up, clean the house and make dinner. Breakfast at Ben's was Allie's daily oasis.

CHAPTER 2

APRIL 22

"Look at zie pig. She is beautiful!" cried Albert Schneider in his thick German accent. Albert was Pierre Beauty Products' fifty-year-old chief scientist.

"Do you really think she's pretty? Come on, Albert," chuckled Steven Button, Pierre's young health and beauty business unit manager.

"Not zie pig," Albert said still admiring the friendly animal. "Look at its vonderful hair. It eez perfect."

"Albert, I hope you tested the shampoo on humans," said Steven teasingly. He and Albert had worked together on this project since inception and knew every detail of its progress.

"Of course," said Albert. "You know ve have tested on many vomen. But, if I can make zie pig's coarse hair zoft and manageable, imagine vhat I can do for zie vomen of zie world. She is zie prettiest piglet in all zie vorld. I am done. Ve must get zie chairman to approve our project. Zis vill revolutionize zie beauty business!"

Steven admired the happy little pink-potbellied oinker and thought, *She really is the prettiest pig I've ever seen. And with four shampoos and brushings a day, she certainly has to be the happiest and the cleanest.*

CHAPTER 3

APRIL 22

Ben's Deli was packed as usual at six in the morning on Good Friday. Normally, Ben's would be filled with executives on their way to New York financial jobs alongside construction workers and landscapers getting a hot meal before their outdoor jobs started. But today, everyone was a golfer. Good Friday officially opens the golf season in the Greater New York City area.

Ben's was a good place to begin the day. The service was quick, food was always fresh and hot, and coffee was high-test-caffeinated. After the commuter rush ended, local store owners, students and housewives took turns at the counter. Eventually, job hunters joined the scene for free Wi-Fi and java.

Entering Ben's Deli, you passed through a corridor of two large tables guarding the dining area, like Patience and Fortitude, the marble lions defending the entrance to New York City's Public Library. Bergenfield's Mayor, Hector Alvarez, chaired the Patience table presiding over the general dining area. Dealing with hundreds of daily issues facing town management required patience.

JB, Bergenfield's restless resident retired executive, presided over the Fortitude table. His table had a panoramic view of the noisy side of the dining area where the food line, juke box and cash register stood. Fortitude, or courage while facing adversity, would be a great description for JB who often helped friends in need. Mischievous when idle would be the less flattering label for JB. He had salvaged the boardroom table as part of his retirement package from ITT. When the deli was barely open for business and Ben was struggling five years ago, JB convinced Ben to replace three badly cracked Formica tables with this imposing piece of furniture. It now dwarfed the surrounding booths.

Wall Street closed the trading and banking offices on Good Friday. Much of the rest of the country worked. Decker, Bret and Buyout sat with JB waiting for their 10:00 AM tee time at Ridgewood Country Club. Decker owned Decker's Doors and Millwork, a struggling casualty of the real estate collapse. Bret was an overworked Wall Street M&A lawyer. Buyout, JB's unpaid early morning assistant, was a first-year financial analyst just graduated from the Wharton MBA program.

Not everyone had the day off. At 7:00 AM, Michael Li joined JB's table as he did most days before opening the doors as the branch manager of Consolidated Northern Bank. Allie joined minutes later, cool, calm, and showing no signs that she had broken three traffic laws on her way to the deli.

This morning, Mayor Hector Alvarez sat with his municipal posse including the chiefs of the police and fire departments. In an hour, Hector would be playing fire and rescue for a two dollar Nassau at the slightly downscale Rockleigh Golf Course, the local muni club. No valet parking. No locker room attendant. No driving range. Grass on the greens would be a luxury this early in the year. Under the rules of golf, snow on a putting green was a loose impediment and could be swept from the line of your putt. Enforcement of the rule occasionally came in handy during April.

Ben's hummed like a kitchen symphony. The cooking crew served breakfast from the serving line. Diners filled travel mugs with Starbuck's dark roast coffee. Ben rang the register. Twelve tables and another dozen booths seated ninety. Inexpensive Americana memorabilia hung from the walls. Diners watched STCK-TV closed caption daily financial news reports from a half dozen flat screen TVs placed at the register and around the dining area. Occasionally, Ben would crank up the juke box to announce the arrival of a favorite guest. Ben was a Deli Maestro!

This week, everything had been normal. Same old, same old. Wake up. Shower. Go to Ben's. Get breakfast while watching STCK-TV. Rush to work. Work like a dog. Crawl home. Tomorrow, wake up. Shower. Go to Ben's. But today was Good Friday and a day of rest. Because today was golf.

Ruining the serenity of the moment, former mayor Gilbert Gilchrist burst into Ben's followed by a gust of bad karmic wind. A minute later, Gilbert's guest made a more timid entrance. Mayor Hector and JB looked up at the startling entrance. At Ben's, daily routines were well known to the regular crowd. Everyone knew that Gilbert never made it to Ben's this early in the morning. Something was definitely up. More importantly, Gil never carried anything more than the local newspaper. Today he was toting a leather briefcase that served as his standard bearer of authority. Gil looked armed and ready for trouble.

Gilbert had employed an assortment of tactics to antagonize Hector since being unseated as mayor four years ago. Gil was friendly with the town managers, the police officers, the shop owners and the school board. He used every opportunity to seed discontent and undermine Hector. It wasn't his style to resort to physical attacks. Besides, Gilbert's guest didn't look the bodyguard type, weighing in at 150 pounds at most, at least fifty graying years old, and not more than five-and-a-half feet tall.

If Gilbert's guest wasn't a bodyguard, then he had to be part of the arsenal. Something was definitely up, as foretold by the wide grin that Gilbert proudly wore.

CHAPTER 4

APRIL 25, 2011

Thirty-five miles South of Ben's on the Garden State Parkway and five miles west across Route 24 are the Morristown, New Jersey offices of Pierre Beauty Products. Pierre was the top selling high-end, hair-product company and a leader in perfume and cosmetic products. Albert Schneider began his presentation to Olivier Gaillard, Pierre's Chairman, and a handful of financial and operating executives.

Albert stood and reported in his heavy German accent: "Herr Gaillard, ve haf spent over two years testing zis new material. It's zie best natural product aufailable to replace zie harsh degreasing chemical in our shampoo."

Albert hesitated for a few seconds respectfully awaiting Olivier's nod to continue. At fifty years old with a full head of white hair, Albert looked like a nice grandpa. In real life, he was a brilliant scientist and a leading floral chemist as well. He had what the industry called a "nose" for identifying scents. Unfortunately, he was so wrapped up in devising new formulas and fragrances that he never developed great social skills.

Olivier tried to put Albert at ease, saying, "Albert, please sit down. And call me Olivier. We have worked together for twenty years. Surely you know me well enough to use my first name. And you really have to slow down when you speak and try to enunciate in English. Try not to say the word 'zie'. Please proceed."

Albert was slightly embarrassed and sat sheepishly, his head slightly bowed. "As you are avare, our shampoo is not 100 percent all natural. For years, ve haf been trying to identify a replacement material for zie shampoo degreaser, sodium laureth sulfate. Zie orange peel based degreasers are not conducive to shampooing. Ve haf been tasked vith replacing zis degreaser with a natural ingredient zat delivers zie same result. It must remove zie natural oils and dirt from your hair during shampooing."

Albert looked up briefly over his reading glasses, then continued, "I von't repeat zie details zat are explained in your printed materials. Zere is a grassy plant growing in Bergen County, New Jersey zat has a very high concentration of a natural chemical zat can replace sodium laureth sulfate. Zie plant creates a product zat is a natural derivative of cleansing compounds."

Albert grew excited at the unveiling of his discovery. This could be the single most important development ever at Pierre. He clenched his fists as he spoke, and his voice pitched higher. He proudly said, "Vie discovered it quite by accident when ve observed der fuel depot manager and maintenance manager arguing. Zie head of maintenance vuz trying to apply a veed-killing chemical to zie crabgrass near zie depot. Ve asked zie fuel depot manager vhy he was defending zie weeds. He said zat zie crabgrass breaks up zie soil and decomposes zie oil around zie oil tanks.

"After learning zat crabgrass broke up oil deposits, ve tested our local crabgrass. Our plants haf characteristics of zie degreaser chemical, but zie concentrations are too small to be commercially profitable. In our investigation, ve talked to the research team at Jake's Seed & Supply who had manufactured zie crab grass killer. Zere director is a colleague auf mine. He pointed us to zere specialized veed killer vhich vuz formulated to kill resilient crabgrass in a small commuting town named Bergenfield."

Albert methodically went through the excruciating details leading to his discovery. Chairman Olivier already knew the story, but gave Albert the few extra minutes of airtime to enjoy his triumph. Albert plodded on, "Zis Bergenfield crabgrass over a long time mutated and grew more resistant to Jake's veed killer. Each year, zhey developed a stronger formula. Each year, zie grass grew even more resistant. And zie natural degreaser chemical in zie plant became more powerful. We decided to nickname zie veed 'formidable firma' because it cannot be killed."

Albert laughed at his play on words, but no one joined in. Albert's wife had suggested that he use more humor in the office to offset his stern appearance. Albert thought the table would get a kick out of the subtle joke substituting formidable for terra firma. Olivier smiled politely, but totally missed the intended pun. Albert began sweating. Once again, Albert failed to be one of the regular guys.

Albert continued nervously, "Vie quietly obtained samples of this Bergenfield plant, and through a variety of processes and mixing vith certain other natural ingredients, ve vere able to replicate zie degreasing characteristics of sodium laureth sulfate. In other vords, it's natural, it vorks and is safe.

"Our problem is zat ve haf not been able to grow zis plant in other areas or even in a hothouse environment. Grown elsevhere, the chemical concentration greatly diminishes. The plant must haf mutated over zie last three hundred years to acclimate to the local conditions and soil. Therefore, ve haf concluded that ve need to develop a vay to secure our supply from zie local townspeople of Bergenfield. Ve will be basically asking zem to grow crabgrass for profit. Many already involuntarily grow it because it's too hard to eliminate."

Olivier already knew the plan of action. However, he wanted his management team to improve their decision-making and leadership skills. Olivier was a handsome fifty-year-old executive with a hint of French aristocracy. He was impeccably dressed in an Yves Saint Laurent gray herringbone suit, a Hugo Boss shirt, gold cuff links and a dark polka dot tie. Olivier said, "I can see many issues here. I know that you have thought them through. What do you recommend?"

Albert was still reeling from his failed standup comedy routine. He recovered slightly. The chairman was asking for his opinion on something other than science and chemistry. He said, "I recommend ve develop zis highly fragmented supply source and introduce it into our product. Simultaneously, ve must continue to vork on finding another location vere ve can grow zis plant zat is more suitable to larger scale farming methods. I recommend zat ve pay homeowners to grow our organic degreaser. I also believe zat I haf identified zie person who can help us organize zie supply source for us. He is zie former mayor of the town. I had breakfast vith him last Friday."

Olivier changed his tone to that of a coach instructing a quarterback to lead his team down the field. "Okay. Go talk to him again. We want optionality until we are sure of the commercial success of this product. If you're successful, we will present this to Eva."

CHAPTER 5

APRIL 26, 2011

It was forty-five degrees this morning outside Ben's which meant that it would hit the mid-fifties by noon. Commuters shed the black comforters disguised as winter coats and wore lighter trench coats for the chilly April weather. Early signs of spring surfaced in the form of daffodils and tulips on town lawns.

Over the last five years, Ben's Deli developed into a convenient launching pad to midtown in New York City. From Ben's, you drove twenty minutes to the Secaucus Junction. At Secaucus, you jumped aboard a train for the last five-mile, thirty-minute commute into the Big Apple.

JB positioned himself strategically where he could greet patrons, unofficially serving as Maître D. JB was a retired ITT executive who could not restrain his commentary on how to improve anything and everything. Once, he told Ben how to serve food faster. Ben didn't treat the suggestion kindly. Another time, JB gave mayor Hector an elaborate plan to improve downtown traffic patterns. JB had a burning itch to fix things, and couldn't help himself from sharing his recommendations.

Today, on JB's right sat twenty-six-year-old Lattimer Barrymore Oglethorpe. Everyone deserves a nickname, but this was a tough one. What do you call him? Laddy? Oggie?

JB at first called him by his initials, LBO, which on Wall Street was the acronym for leveraged buyout. The name was unanimously disapproved by the table. Eventually, the group settled on Buyout.

Buyout acted primarily as JB's morning number cruncher and research analyst. A graduate of the Wharton School, Buyout was learning real life finance in pre-work hours. At 7:30, he would head to work on Wall Street as a junior financial analyst in investment banking. He had plenty of time before the managing directors straggled in. Buyout worked until midnight most nights, but was always raring to go at 6:00 AM.

To JB's left sat Bret Wolfman. Bret was one of several general counsels at Montauk & Malibu. Bret was the typical deal lawyer on Wall Street who worked ridiculous hours, often staying until after midnight four days a week. Bret was JB's straight man, providing a stream of setups for his witty but sarcastic cracks.

Jonathon Decker sat next to Bret. Decker's door manufacturing plant was a mile from Ben's near the railroad tracks on New Bridge Road. The real estate and home improvement market was still reeling from the 2008 crash, and Decker was shouldering all of the company's troubles. He remained cheerful on the outside, but the pressure was increasingly noticeable.

Michael Li was a homegrown product of Bergenfield. He went to work at the local bank immediately after high school and earned his college degree at night. The small bank owned by the town merchants had been swallowed by larger and larger banks until it was finally bought by Consolidated Northern Bank.

Each time the bank was purchased, the new owners quickly recognized that Michael was the bank's best asset. He was smart and knew his customers well. His Asian background and language skills attracted the local Chinese, Korean and Filipino residents to the bank. More importantly, he kept the bank's loan losses low and avoided the mortgage, stock market and commodities busts of 2008 and 2009.

Business news on STCK-TV aired continuously at Ben's every morning. Occasionally, the juke box interrupted the audio portion of the entertainment. When Ben bought the deli out of bankruptcy, the juke box was part of the property. The Wurlitzer was stained and old, but the records from the sixties were still in place. A metal tag identified a company in Fort Lee as the previous juke box owner. The company was now extinct. The owners had never been by to collect the money or to change the records. Ben guessed that either they forgot about it, or they may be doing twenty in Rahway Prison, but no one knew for sure.

JB said with feigned exasperation, "I'm having post-Easter traumatic stress syndrome. The chocolate is gone, and I have nothing to improve my mood. Everyone's in Florida this week. I have no one to entertain."

Michael Li: "Thanks a lot JB. What am I, chop suey? You can entertain me!"

Bret: "Excellent use of the mixed metaphor, Michael. That is a four-star pun, which is an excellent rating for a slow week!"

JB looked startled when Ben's front door practically came off its hinges as Gilbert barreled in followed by three guests. "I don't know about you guys, but something is definitely up in Gilbert land. That's twice he's made the emperor's entrance into Ben's in a week. Last week, he had one guest. Today he brought the whole gang."

Decker: "I'm betting a buck that he found a loophole in the town bylaws. Maybe there's a no-Filipino clause buried somewhere. He's gonna steal the mayor's office from Hector!"

JB: "Nope, you're wrong. I detect the distinct aroma of financial greed and opportunity. Gilbert smells money. Being mayor again may be the unintended result. But Gilbert is either buying something cheap or selling something overpriced. Those guys are his meal ticket."

"Oops, Gilbert is definitely looking for trouble. He just sat in the mayor's booth. Hector's gonna be ripping mad when he gets here. Call 911!"

CHAPTER 6

APRIL 26

While there was no official reserved seating, it was generally acknowledged that the mayor's booth was off-limits. Gilbert knew the rules of etiquette at Ben's, and his slight appeared intentional.

Gilbert was still sore over losing the election to Mayor Alvarez. He blamed the election loss on the huge Filipino voter turnout. Most voters would say he lost because downtown Bergenfield continued to deteriorate and the town council did nothing to fix it.

Gil's guests were unavoidably conspicuous. Steel rimmed glasses, gray hair, and comfortable shoes were not an unusual look. The pocket protectors and pen assortment were slight hints that they might be scientists or engineers. What raised an eyebrow was that they acted secretively. Olivier had told Albert to keep a low profile, and Albert's team was overdoing the spy routine. The more they tried to act inconspicuous, the more obvious they became. They scanned the deli as if paranoid that they would be discovered.

JB was constantly bored and ever in need of amusement. His ten years of retirement after being a big shot at ITT presented a constant challenge to keep himself occupied. Sometimes, he acted the role of Saint Jude, the patron saint of lost causes. JB was known to help people and small businesses get through some tough times with advice and sometimes even a few bucks.

More often, JB's alter ego took control like the prick of a thorn from a dead rose bush. If JB was bored, he might just needle a target a little too much. That was JB's daily agenda. He had to stay productively busy. Spending the early morning with the gang at Ben's was good medicine for JB's bore-a-phobia. After they left for work, JB had to find eight more hours of entertainment to fill his day.

JB eyed his next victims at Gilbert's table. He sauntered over to say hello. Gilbert knew enough to remain friendly with JB and he was courteous but circumspect when JB greeted them. The three visitors looked very uneasy as JB sat uninvited at the booth and tossed out a few harmless probing questions.

JB raised an eyebrow and said, "I see that you researchers are from Morris County. Why are you such a long way away from home? You guys aren't opening an R&D center here, are you?"

JB disarmed them with his insight. It wasn't that hard for him to guess that the guests were scientists. Their Ford Explorer SUV reeked of science lab. White lab coats hung over the back seat. Empty vials and beakers scattered around. Pierre Beauty product samples in an opened cardboard box in the rear compartment. An instruction manual for a $100,000 electron microscope. These were not trinkets found in a soccer dad's car.

The scientists were nonplussed but Gilbert remained calm and said, "Albert and his two guests are golf buddies of mine. Last week we played their Morris County course, Flanders Valley. It's a top 100 public golf course, you know? Today we're playing the Railside at Great Gorge. But you always amaze me. How'd you know where Albert's from?"

JB said coyly, "If you really want to keep your visit a secret, first, hide the Pierre samples in the back of your Ford Explorer. Second, never wear sunglasses indoors unless you are Johnny Depp. Only Johnny can wear sunglasses in a deli. But third, the last place to keep a secret is Ben's Deli. This is the Grand Central Station of gossip traffic."

JB let loose a grin. "Gil, your secret is safe with me. But if you don't want to antagonize the townspeople, I wouldn't sit in the Mayor's booth. He should be along any minute. And tell Olivier I said hi."

JB stood, spun on his heels, and walked back to his table. The scientists immediately moved to the adjacent unoccupied table. Albert's assistant removed his sunglasses. Gilbert did not want to move. He wanted to make a point and show Mayor Hector he was back in power again. But he also wanted to lock in the consulting contract, so he reluctantly shifted over to Albert's new table.

Albert nervously said, "Gilbert, ve need to keep zis under control. Until ve are ready to lock up zie supply, ve haf to keep zis very confidential. How does zis man know ve work for Olivier?"

Gilbert did his best to dismiss their concerns, saying, "JB's harmless…he's just mischievous. Underneath he's a great guy, but he's been known to stir the pot 'cause he needs some excitement. He might be doing a little of both with you guys. Let's get back to business."

JB rejoined his chairman's table laughing. "The guys with the bad case of paranoia are chemists with Pierre Beauty Products. I have no idea what they are doing here, but they must think ol' Gilbert will help them get some sort of town approval they need. I saw them getting out of their car and there were boxes of Pierre shampoo and crème rinse products in the back. They were very secretive about who they were, but I think I disarmed them enough."

JB saw Mayor Hector arrive at Ben's with two local shopkeepers unaware of Gilbert's attempted table takeover. He said, "Rats. We could have had a real dust-up if Hector had been on time."

CHAPTER 7

APRIL 26

Minutes later, the conversation abruptly ended at the board table as the juke box played *Pretty Woman* by Roy Orbison. The song often signaled Allie's entrance into Ben's. The jukebox played the New Jersey version from the *Roy Orbison - Black and White Night* album. Halfway through the song, Asbury Park's own Bruce Springsteen could be heard battling lead guitars with James Burton.

Walter Harrigan, the local record store owner, had made a vinyl recording of this Grammy winning song for the juke box. Long ago, Ben and Walter bypassed the juke box lock so they could change records. Customers couldn't see the names of the songs through the stained yellow plastic front of the Wurlitzer. That was fine with Ben. He'd rather have a random record play than have someone impose their taste on the eatery.

Walter Harrigan joined JB's group occasionally. More often, he slept in late. Walter was the resident hippie and owner of Bergenfield Records and Recording. While his competitors at the Paramus malls over the years had converted to CDs and DVDs and iPod download services, Walter still sold vinyl records alongside the newer mediums. Vinyl records were making a nostalgic comeback. CD and DVD stores in Paramus were going out of business.

Walter's other specialty was creating vinyl records for DJs. He owned a Vinyl Recorder T560 and converted music to records on 45s and 33s. DJs from around the Northeast needed vinyl to produce sound effects in discos and at Bar Mitzvahs. Walter worked the hours of an owl to produce the special discs.

JB's table turned as Allie entered. She was Ben's favorite customer and the town sweetheart. The married guys were flattered when she harmlessly flirted with them. Allie made everyone feel good about themselves for a few minutes a day.

Her full name was Susan Allison Bertrand, but everyone knew her as Allie. She was warm and friendly to everyone. She wasn't a threat to most of the women, probably because she had been a single mom for the last twelve years with no visible sign that she intended to change her marital status. Every year Allie was named 'nurse of the year' at Holy Name Medical Center, the birthplace of many of the locals. No one came a close second.

Allie: "Hello JB! Hi guys! How are the handsome and famous today?" She wasn't really asking for a response. This was her normal friendly greeting.

JB answered for the group. "Our day just got better. Do you see Gilbert's guests over there? We think they need a Bergenfield Welcome Wagon starter kit. They're from Pierre Beauty Products. Do us a favor and ask them if they need a tour or some brochures on your way out."

Allie could be thirty-five years old but neither admitted nor denied the number. Her son was fifteen, so guessers could triangulate from that. She could pass for thirty and could be forty or even older for all anyone knew. She had shoulder-length brunette hair which had a natural wave and curl as it landed on her shoulders. No gray was yet showing, and you could tell this was her natural hair color. She had a tendency to flip her hair with a smile that disarmed people during conversations.

Allie never wore her nurse's scrubs to Ben's. She always changed into a nice skirt and blouse or dress and looked like she was heading to an office job. Few locals knew and no one could tell that Allie sewed her collection of modest, barely-above-the-knee pleated skirts and A-line dresses. She had put her high school sewing and home economics courses to good use. She was saving her money in the hope that one day her son might come out of his funk and decide to enter college.

Allie had complained to JB one day, "Men have it so easy. One day you wear a gray suit. The next day you wear navy. Women have to wear a different outfit every day or they are classified as either poor or fashion-challenged."

Allie was an athletic size 8 and 5'8" tall with the long thin calves of a long distance runner. Allie had run track in high school, and still pounded a few miles a day on the treadmill. Allie stood six feet in high heels, a perfect height for a date with a confident man if you had the fortune to be in her company at a cocktail hour.

But Allie wasn't dating and hadn't for a while. Allie didn't share the details, but her husband left when their son Marty was three. It was a mystery why he left, but JB heard a story that Allie threw the guy's clothes on the lawn, and then staked them into the ground with his broken golf clubs. He was never to be seen around Bergenfield again.

Now, raising Marty was a chore that grew increasingly more difficult as he worked his way through his teens. Allie had to work full-time to pay the bills. And Marty was always angry and always in trouble. A few years ago, Allie switched to the night shift at Holy Name to spend more time with her son. Clever Marty snuck out after midnight and got into more trouble.

After Allie purchased her Starbucks and bagel, she passed JB's table and gave her signature hair flip. "I can't stay today. Gotta go. Have a good day, guys. Everyone, get back to work now or the economy will crash. You're my last and only hope," she ordered with mock authority. Then Allie winked at JB and said, "Watch this!"

She sauntered over to Gilbert's table, eyed the scientists, ran her hands through her hair, and asked, "Mayor Gil, do you think I need a new hair color or just a new shampoo?" Albert and his team were visibly flushed.

Allie turned to Albert. "It's okay, boys. Your secret is safe with me. But to be sure, maybe you should hand out some Pierre samples to keep the crowd on your side." Allie flipped her hair once more, turned and left. The scientists were disarmed by her gently swaying hips, and alarmed that she knew their secret identities.

After Allie left the deli, Albert spoke quietly, "She is very beautiful and charming. Now two people know vhy ve are here. How do zhey know so much? Ve haf to keep zis quiet."

Gilbert dismissed the episode, saying, "JB's just having some fun with you. Everything will be fine. Let's discuss the contract and get to work. First, I've gotta have the $100,000 up front because I have expenses, you know. Second, if I don't deliver a thousand homes to you in ninety days, I'll return a pro rata share of the fee.

"However, I do have a new request. I need a deal for up to a hundred houses where you contract to take a hundred percent of the product instead of the twenty-five percent that we are guaranteeing to everyone else. I need this spiff to convince the community leaders to accept the deal."

Albert did his best to act like he had the upper hand in the negotiation. "It sounds like a lot auf money, and zis project is not a 'go' yet. I need corporate approval, but I might be able to push it through. Is zere a chance zat you could get a sample number auf houses to agree preliminarily to zie proposal? If ve had evidence zat even a few dozen vill agree to such a proposition, it vould help us convince our board."

Gilbert nodded solemnly. "I can deliver two dozen house contracts ready for you to sign by next Friday. I know this town. These are hardworking people moving their way up the middle-class ladder. Two thousand a year with a chance at four times that number's a big deal to these people. It'll pay a big part of a year's college tuition. It's their American dream."

Albert wrapped up the discussions. "Okay, Gilbert, if you deliver two dozen agreements by next Friday, I vill present our recommendation to zie board during zie week. Our general counsel vill draft a simple commodity purchase and option agreement for zem to sign. Also, Mr. Gilchrist, ve can probably agree to zie hundred houses at a hundred percent, but remember, zis is at $15 dollars per pound before processing fees. If zie price rises, everyone has to take a reduction. Let's meet here again next Friday."

Albert had quickly determined that the community leaders were most likely Gilbert and a few cronies on the town council. But that didn't matter. He just needed to get the deal done. They all shook hands, got up and left.

JB watched them exit. Apparently he had found a new activity to while away the time – Gilbert watching. Mayor Alvarez smelled nothing but trouble.

CHAPTER 8

APRIL 26

A few dozen towns away and at twice the average Bergenfield housing price sat Morristown at the heart of Morris County, New Jersey. The area was home to a few dozen large U.S. Corporations including ATT and a few of the big pharmaceutical, drug and cosmetic companies like Pfizer and Colgate Palmolive. The chemical and pharmaceutical industries were big in New Jersey employing large numbers of scientists, chemists and engineers. R&D was big business in New Jersey, thanks to Thomas Alva Edison, who gave research a head start in Menlo Park in the late 1800s.

Hidden among the manufacturing plants, research and development centers and corporate offices of Viagra and Bayer aspirin, nestled the unassuming eight-acre facility of Pierre Beauty Products.

Pierre's top-selling, high-end shampoo was marketed as a natural product with no chemical additives. The small lettered disclaimer said "whenever possible". The top salons sold Pierre. The hair stylists to the stars all raved publicly about Pierre's magical products. The stars were paid well to rave, but the products really were the best. Not everyone could afford Pierre, but everyone knew it was number one.

All-natural shampoo was becoming the new battleground in consumer marketing. A half-dozen start-ups had created new formulations of chemical-free hair products. Despite claims to the contrary, so far none were quite as effective as the chemical versions. However, it was just a matter of time before someone made the discovery that would change the industry. It was important to Pierre management that they be the first to become 100% all natural.

At Pierre's research center, Albert Schneider met with Olivier Gaillard and his team. Albert was excited and very proud of his progress dealing with Gilbert, and was anxious to report his results. Albert said, "Herr Gaillard, yesterday ve met with our primary contact. He is zie former mayor of Bergenfield and is vell connected and vell liked among zie townspeople and business owners. He is extremely close vith zie entire town council, who vill haf a lot auf say and sway over our endeavors.

"Vie believe he has zie connections and leverage to assist us in accomplishing our goals. In fact, he has assured us zat ve can secure an adequate supply of zie plant materials to launch our new product line."

"Albert, please call me Olivier in such small company," the chairman said casually. Olivier kept his poise, but he was clearly frustrated. His attempts to mentor Albert sometimes showed little results. Albert just didn't know how to soften his rough edges.

Olivier paused and then continued making his point. "This is a very important decision for the company. We're not used to taking big risks with such an unusual supply chain. At the same time, we're also the leading natural cosmetic and beauty-products company, and this finding of yours could be a disruptive biotechnology. Let's hope that our competitors haven't made the same discovery."

Albert interjected, "Vie are sure zat zhey haf not."

"Albert, you cannot be certain. Nevertheless, my main concern is locking up the supply without taking on huge commitments. We could delay this. No one knows our secrets. Then we could develop a more dependable supply source. But so far we haven't been able to identify similar growing conditions. It's a freak of nature how this stuff grows in this isolated area. It's like the edelweiss of New Jersey," Olivier said, referring to the unique flower growing high in the Alps.

"At the same time, if this secret does leak, we have lost our advantage. I think the best course is to lock up this fragmented supply chain for a few years, keeping it low profile, and hopefully develop a more secure source. I want Eva to be part of this decision. Go prepare your PowerPoint slide show and have my assistant help you. Maybe she can pretty things up a little."

Olivier hid his excitement over the developments until Albert left the meeting. Negotiating the development path would be critical. How do you secure the product supply and keep your competitors at bay? How do you keep this discovery secret for at least a year or two? How the heck do you sign up a thousand homeowners and convince them to grow weeds for a living?

And what would he do with Albert? Albert was a great scientist. He was extraordinary as a floral chemist. Moreover, this discovery was totally out-of-the-box. Ninety-nine percent of chief technology officers would have never pursued this odd biochemistry. But Albert had, and not only that, he seemed to have developed an actual human relationship with another person. Olivier allowed himself a slight chuckle. Perhaps Albert's contact wasn't human after all. Perhaps his friend Gilbert was a mechanical robot!

Albert's rough social skills were the primary reason that Olivier kept his CEO, Eva Marteen, from the technology meetings. Besides, Eva was the marketing and branding expert, and Olivier typically chaired technology development. But that wasn't the reason to keep Eva hidden from view. Albert was scared to death around normal women, but in front of Eva he lost his ability to speak. Olivier kept Eva fully informed, but Eva agreed that she'd stay in the shadows until the right time.

Olivier contemplated his options. Should he let Albert continue to develop this opportunity, or should he bring in his Harvard MBAs to take over? Olivier rarely relied on gut instinct, but this time he decided to let Albert run with the ball. Besides, the MBAs might scare away the townspeople. It was time for Albert to prove he was more than a great scientist.

CHAPTER 9

APRIL 27, 2011

Bergenfield, New Jersey was one of the first stops for Bronx and Brooklyn residents wanting to move from the city. Fifty years ago, the migration was Irish, Italian, German, Greek and Jewish. Today, Chinese, Latinos and Filipinos also make Bergenfield their new home. No matter what nationality, they all had the same goal – to improve their lot.

Bergenfield was half affordable. Nothing near New York City was cheap. But the town was an easy commute to the City for work. It was a place with two- and three-bedroom homes that sat on 4,000 square feet of building lot. It was Jersey strong and Jersey tough. It was a good place to raise kids. It had good but crowded schools and little serious crime.

Teens could be city-tough when they first arrived, but the gang attitude softened over time. For some, it took longer than others.

The surrounding towns to the east and north had a higher standard of living. Richer residents in towns like Alpine and Tenafly had a few extra zeros in their bank accounts. People living closer to the Holland Tunnel had maybe one less zero in their bank account. Bergenfield was smack in the middle of the two poles.

The town was six miles from the mall center of the universe spread along Routes 4 and 17 in Paramus. Bergenfield had a mile of shops and stores stretching along Washington Avenue from Teaneck to Dumont. The stores had seen more prosperous times. Almost everyone shopped at the malls and big box stores.

It was the Wednesday after Easter, schools were out, and a few residents who could afford it were vacationing in Florida. Spring fever ran high. JB, Michael Li and Decker shared the executive table. Michael was dressed casually. It was unusual to see him in anything but a suit and tie.

JB looked outside where five older ladies were walking toward the knitting store like a gaggle of nuns on their way to morning prayer. Auntie Ev, the unofficial leader, had named the group Nanny Grannies because they babysat for their grandchildren often enough to be full-time nannies. JB observed Auntie Ev's troop, and said, "I wish I were that happy. They're so content. If I knitted for four hours straight, I'd stab myself with the needle and end it all."

Michael gave his standard Confucius-influenced response: "Knitting is just another form of meditation. Some people meditate with a mantra, like *Om*. Some meditate through prayer. Some find inner peace through music. It's just a good process to clear your mind and find contentment."

JB laughed. "You know how I find inner peace? Hitting a decent drive and making a thirty-foot birdie putt! By the way, Michael, you always wear a suit and tie. Why the casual Wednesday?"

Michael was the town banker. He was a tall, handsome, Chinese-American who became a successful businessman by staying at home in Bergenfield. He might be the most respected person in town. He gave sage advice. He helped families finance their first home purchase. He steered them from bad investments. Furthermore, being a regular member of JB's board table elevated Michael's status even higher. Not only was he a good businessman and advisor, he hung out with the cool guys.

Michael responded, "Everyone is on vacation this week in Florida except Auntie Ev and me. So I declared spring break week in Bergenfield. No business suits!"

A few tables away, Bret was sitting at a small booth with Catherine Mulcahy, better known as Panama Blonde. Not many knew the origin of the name, but Catherine got hissy if anyone called her Panama Blonde to her face. Catherine was fortyish years old, had light Irish skin, and was tall, blonde and top-heavy. She had a beautiful face and great hair, but the first thing most guys noticed when they saw Panama was the fantastic chest!

Panama Blonde and Bret were having an intense conversation about something, but it wasn't romantic. She was seeking free legal advice. After she left the deli and Bret came over, JB teased him: "Does Panama have goo-goo eyes for our boy?"

Bret shrugged off the insinuation. "Her husband went missing at sea five years ago. Apparently he was sailing around the world in some misguided midlife crisis adventure. The boat's satellite transponder stopped sending signals off the coast of Chile."

"He left her with nothing but the house, a mortgage, a few stocks and cash. She wants to have him declared legally dead. This is a little far afield from my mergers and acquisitions area of expertise, but how can you refuse such an attractive woman's plea for help?" Bret gave a sly smile while twisting his imaginary Snidely Whiplash moustache.

Gavin Kelleher asked, "Isn't the time limit seven years? I saw that in a Cary Grant movie once with Irene Dunne. I think it was called *My Favorite Wife*." Gavin was a turnaround consultant partner at a Big Four CPA firm in New York. Gavin occasionally joined JB's table when he found himself tending to troubled clients in New Jersey.

Bret gave a quick lesson on death in absentia: "Most countries and states use the seven year rule, but it's a common law rule. If there is evidence that the person is likely dead, like in a plane crash where you cannot identify the bodies, but there's proof that the person was on board, then the court can immediately declare the person dead. A boat transponder going dead off the coast of Chile probably doesn't qualify. However, it's a well-known pirate area, and it could meet the test of being exposed to 'imminent peril'.

"The estate isn't much except for the house and small liquid assets. Right now, the house is in their joint names, and legally she can't sell it. I advised her to file the motion if she's in a hurry to get remarried – but otherwise, why pay the expense?"

JB laughed and quipped, "No big trust fund? That takes her off my list of eligible women in the area." Everyone knew JB was kidding, of course. He was happily married to Wanda, his high school sweetheart from Cape Cod, Massachusetts.

The jukebox began playing *The Wanderer* by Dion, a New Jersey anthem. JB turned to Buyout and said in an exaggerated tone. "Buyout, this is the most important thing you will ever do. It's even more important than graduating from Wharton. Every time a song plays on the jukebox, you fill in this Bingo card with the song and artist. There are a hundred songs on the jukebox and a hundred squares on this card. We have to identify the songs and submit a completed card to Ben before anyone else to win. The jukebox cover is so yellowed that you can't see the song title. So the only way to fill in the blanks is to hear the song and get the number. You understand?"

Buyout nodded. The task could be considered demeaning for most Wharton graduates, but Buyout was willing to tolerate pledging activities to hang around his mentor. JB was legendary on Wall Street for his manufacturing turnaround skills.

JB became surprisingly serious. "It's very important to me that we win this game. A lot of prestige goes with the prize. Whoever wins gets a life-sized poster hung behind the cash register. Diners will have to stare at it for a month. I want that poster to be a picture of me.

"Now, a lot of these songs are oldies, so you may not know the name. You can use Shazam to identify any songs that you don't know. It's a web app for the iPhone that ID's songs and singers."

JB looked up and saw the scientists sit with Gilbert at a more discreet table near the rear of Ben's Deli. He watched Gilbert deliver a stack of legal-sized documents to the scientists; then raised his arms as if awaiting applause for the victory that had been secured.

JB was again intrigued. Something was definitely up. It wasn't likely an illegal or shady activity. Gilbert wasn't like that. But tossing signed documents around with Pierre executives was just an unusual event for Ben's, a modest place to get a cup of Joe. Big deals might get signed in New York City at restaurants like Nobu or perhaps under the famous blue elephant head hanging from the walls of the Harvard Club. At Ben's, until now the biggest deal-signing might have been for a new magazine subscription. But here was Gilbert raising his arms in victory. What did he just win?

CHAPTER 10

APRIL 27

Gilbert was sociable with Albert, but a little too glib. He was overconfident, bordering on obnoxiousness. "I don't know where Ben's Deli came from. This was a hole-in-the-wall dump five years ago, and now it's the most prosperous spot in town, except for the Dello Russo Laser Vision Center by Main Street."

Gilbert sipped his Starbucks dark-roasted coffee supercharged with caffeine. Who needs Monster Energy drinks when you have Starbucks?

Ben had found out the hard way about selling the famous brand. The company was nice enough, but Ben had to get a license to use the name when he sold its coffee. He paid a little extra, but it was worth it. The deli offered help-yourself coffee urns filled with Starbucks Italian or French dark roast. Mid-morning and mid-afternoon, someone manned the espresso machine and made lattes, cappuccino and espresso. No specialty drinks were served during busy periods.

During espresso hour, Ben's rule was that your order could only have two adjectives and one size. No Vente-Grande-Machiatto-Frapacino-Latte-Soy-Chai with Cinnamon at Ben's. The barista was born in Costa Rica, and if you confused him, he'd just give you a coffee with milk.

So the order was, "I'll have a cappuccino with skim milk." Or "I'll have a latte with regular milk." If you wanted a double espresso, order two espressos. If you wanted iced coffee, go grab a cup of ice and pour your coffee into it.

Albert turned to Gilbert and did his best to act like he had a strong poker hand, but he figured this shouldn't be a hard negotiation. "Did you bring zie two dozen agreements? Ve are not going forward unless ve see evidence zat ve can get zie town's cooperation."

Gilbert smiled, opened his weathered, leather briefcase, and pulled out four legal binders full of papers. "Actually, I signed up a few more 'n you required. Here's seventy-five signed agreements. They include half of the town council, thirty-five business owners, eight firemen and police officers, the high school principal, a dozen teachers and a lot of other very influential townsfolk. How'd I do?" Gilbert leaned back, clearly enjoying himself.

Albert responded as coyly as possible, but Gilbert had delivered. He looked at the master list and saw that the mayor wasn't among the signed participants; but just about everyone else was. "How did you do zis so quickly?"

Gilbert gave his impression of a magician waving a magic wand. "Presto! It's magic. I told you I know these people. I also said I needed to give some people a contract for a hundred percent of their production. Well, this stack of contracts includes fifty homes at a hundred percent. The other twenty-five were done at twenty-five percent to prove we could sell at that rate too. I'm reserving the remaining 100 percent option deals to use as I need them. And I will need them."

Albert repeated himself, a little louder this time. "No. I mean how did you get zie people together to sign zo quickly?"

Gilbert snorted. "It's easy. I called a meeting at Tommy Fox's, the local favorite watering hole, and bought everyone a Guinness or glass of wine. I told them in strictest confidence, and they all signed. No one declined. I can round up the thousand you need in about a month. The town council could help with that. But it goes public at that point, you know. There's no keeping this a secret for long."

At that moment, Albert realized that he had made a friend, perhaps his first real friend ever. He honestly liked Gilbert. More than that, Gilbert promised and delivered. Gil was the key that could open the door for Albert's greatest creation.

Albert had seen the move in dozens of buddy-cop movies. Unrehearsed and certainly never before attempted, Albert threw his arm around his new buddy's shoulder. "Okay, Gilbert, you did a great job. I vill give you an answer tomorrow. Let's meet here at Ben's. Zis place is starting to grow on me."

CHAPTER 11

APRIL 27

Albert paced around Pierre Beauty Products' executive conference room nervously awaiting her arrival. For three years, Chairman Olivier Gaillard had been championing the technology phase of Albert's project. Today, Eva Marteen, Pierre's CEO, would be asked to approve a decision that might change the shampoo industry – and risk a few million dollars in the process.

Eva was the beautiful face behind Pierre's products and the brains behind its luxury-product marketing strategy. She scared the living crap out of Albert.

Albert stood at attention as Eva glided into the conference room with the poise of a Vogue fashion model. She was six-feet tall in stockings. In high heels, she towered over New York's fashion executives.

Eva kept her auburn hair in a classic bob with a sharp slant from back to front. It accented her cheekbones and her long neckline. Her skin was flawless; her makeup was impeccable. Today, she wore a simple yellow silk dress with a slight V-neck and a string of pearls to match her earrings. The outfit was nothing extravagant, but it looked positively glamorous on Eva. Christian Dior would be proud.

When Eva was twenty-five years old, considered ancient for a high-fashion model, she had cornered Olivier, who had been attending her photo shoot. She convinced him to hire her in the Pierre management training program where she started in a low-level marketing job.

On a typical Monday, she might be a fashion model on a photo shoot posing for Pierre's products for a national ad campaign. On Tuesday, she'd return to her corporate cubicle and write copy for a Pierre magazine advertisement.

Twenty years later, with the help of Olivier's mentoring, Eva had developed into a top CEO. She ran the company focused on representing and maintaining the Pierre brand.

Eva took the seat at the head of the conference table and quietly chatted with Olivier while Albert Schneider nervously searched through his presentation. Albert fumbled the fifty-page slide deck onto the floor. Papers flew everywhere. Albert had an IQ of 150 and a PhD in biochemistry, but he was a physical wreck when he had to deliver a formal management presentation.

Eva was aware that Albert was nervous around her, but so were most men. She also knew that he was a great scientist and she needed to make him feel he was an important part of the team that made Pierre so successful. Seeing that Albert was in trouble, Eva spoke with a sweet, calming voice. "Albert, it's okay. Don't worry about the handouts. I don't like paper anyway. Just use the overhead projector."

Olivier nodded his agreement. Albert pushed the mess of papers aside and began his presentation, clearly flustered. "Danke, Mademoiselle Eva. Pardon zie mess.

"I understand zat Monsieur Gaillard has kept you informed about zie technology developments. It has been a real success. Today, ve vill propose a solution how to obtain control of zie supply.

"Let me provide a brief background on zie technology. Zat squeaky sound zat your hair makes after shampooing is not zie sound of cleanliness. In fact, it's zie sound of a degreaser, sodium laureth sulfate. It's an effective cleaner, but it's harsh on zie hair. Every major shampoo manufacturer uses it."

Albert advanced to a slide of a duck covered in crude oil being washed in a soapy mixture. "You haf seen zie advertisements recently vhere plain dishwashing liquid is used to clean oil from birds harmed by zie oil spill. Zat soap contains zie same chemical zat is in your shampoo – sodium laureth sulfate."

Eva laughed. "Thank you for the image. I won't be ordering the duck at Maxim's in Paris this weekend."

Her laughter helped Albert regain his composure. Olivier's secretary had convinced Albert to use the duck slide, and it had worked. Albert managed a smile and advanced to the next slide. "Five years ago, ve vere tasked to replace zis chemical vith a natural ingredient zat vould still remove zie oil and dirt from your hair during shampooing. Ve identified such a chemical in a local veed."

Albert was getting more excited and began pacing around the room. "Zis local crabgrass strain has an unusually high concentration of zis chemical. Apparently, it mutated and grew stronger to fight veed-removal chemicals. Through a variety of processes and combining vith certain other natural cleansers, ve vere able to replicate zie degreasing characteristics of sodium laureth sulfate. Ve have tested zie product for over a year. It vorks extremely vell."

Eva interrupted politely with her slight French accent, "Albert, how many slides did you prepare? I already know about the chemical and also your test results. And I admire your relentless perseverance to discover this magical ingredient. You have done a magnificent job. Tell me what I don't already know from your reports. Also, in the end, we have to ask the same question of all of our new products. Do we keep women beautiful?"

Albert blanched. "I apologize again, Mademoiselle. I vill skip zie old material."

The chief scientist opened a green trash bag and plopped a large sample of crabgrass on the conference table. "Zis is it. Zie scientific name is Sanguinalis, or hairy grass. Ve now believe zat zis strain of crabgrass vas imported into New Jersey by Dutch settlers during zie tulip craze along vith zie black tulip bulbs. After zie tulip market collapsed, zie veed continued to grow unchecked in zis area for three hundred years."

Eva interrupted. "Okay, now this is interesting from a marketing perspective. What are black tulips? I never heard of such a flower."

Albert felt like a ping-pong ball. First he fumbled the slide deck. Then he recovered. She'd laughed at a slide. Then she complained. Now he was in her good graces again.

He advanced the presentation to a photograph of a field of dark-colored tulips in Holland. Thank goodness for Olivier's assistant. She insisted on pretty pictures to keep the audience interested.

Albert walked to the front of the room and pointed at the flowers on the screen. "In the mid-1600s, zere vas a speculative fever for tulip bulbs in Holland. Zie darkest-colored flowers vere zie most expensive. Tulip bulb prices reached thousands of dollars.

"It's one of zie first known commodity price bubbles. Zie market eventually collapsed, and many people lost zere fortunes. Alexandre Dumas wrote a story about it – *The Black Tulip.*"

Eva leaned toward Olivier. "What a great name for our new mascara line – The Black Tulip. Okay, so let's get back to our weed. Why are they still growing it?"

Albert advanced the presentation to a photo of a bag of Jake's weed killer. "Zhey aren't growing the veeds, not intentionally anyvay. Zhey haf been trying to get rid of it for years. Every spring it sprouts and every year homeowners treat it vith zis specialty chemical. Zie crabgrass germinates hundreds of times and keeps reseeding zie lawn.

"By zie end of June, lawns look like camouflage helmuts!" Albert had forwarded to a slide of an army helmet sitting on a patched lawn. The colors looked remarkably similar.

"Let me emphasize something further. As far as vie know, it really only grows in a very small region. Zie adjacent towns successfully removed zie veeds years ago. Vealthier neighborhoods banded together, tore up zere lawns and planted sod. They burnt zie old grass to keep it from spreading.

"Zie Bergenfield townspeople haf never conceded defeat. Every year zhey buy zie new improved version of veed killer. Zie following year, zie veed returns even stronger. It covers about eighty percent of zie town. Ve also discovered some small growth in Dumont, zie town just north of Bergenfield."

Eva said, "So let me summarize. This magical chemical comes from a weed that no one wants and grows in small quantities on eight thousand lawns. So what is our plan to lock up sufficient supply so we can change our shampoo formula? How are you going to convince so many homes to grow an unattractive weed in their front yards? This is something that cannot fail, or our reputation will be ruined."

Albert stiffened, "Vith Monsieur Gaillard's permission, ve developed a relationship vith an important local official in Bergenfield. In less zan forty-eight hours, he vas able to sign up seventy-five homes to sell us zere veeds. Zis is strong evidence zat he can sign up many more.

"Zie question is how much supply ve vant to lock up, and at vhat price. At some price, zie less affluent families vill participate. Zis is a middle-income town, and many vere hurt by zie housing price collapse in 2008."

Eva looked encouraged. "How many homes do you need to start production?"

Albert advanced the slide and aimed his laser pointer at a table of numbers. "Vie believe zat it's prudent to move slowly and create a special product line until zie customer accepts it. Therefore, ve recommend zat ve contract vith a thousand homes. Ve vill agree to purchase a fourth of zere annual output vith an option to purchase all of it. Ve also believe zat a price of $15 dollars per pound vill be enough of an incentive. At zis price, it vill be haf zie price of sodium laureth sulfate.

"Under zis scenario, our maximum commitment is $2 million dollars. Each family vould make about two thousand dollars. Zat is a lot of money to zese families.

"Assuming zat our product line does vell, ve can increase to all of zie homes and buy all of zere production. Zat adds up to nearly five million pounds vich is more than ve could ever use. Zat vould be enough to make a billion dollars of shampoo, vich is much higher than our existing sales.

"Last zhting. Ve will need assistance signing up homes. Zis is vere our local consultant enters zie picture. Ve are asking you to approve his consulting fee of $100,000."

"And of course," Eva said factually, "you are investigating biotechnology solutions to clone this chemical, correct?"

Albert nodded. "Yes, but so far zie chemical has been difficult to replicate, and I vouldn't expect progress for several years."

Eva removed her high heels and strolled in her bare feet at the head of the table. "This is a very risky decision. The dilemma that we face is the following: How do we control the supply with a minimum financial commitment until we are sure of market acceptance, while at the same time keeping a low profile? We don't know if the market will accept this product. Our competitors' all-natural products are having a difficult time increasing sales, but their products aren't that good. We have tested the shampoo on small population samples, but we won't know for a long while how the product will be accepted by a broad population of users.

"My board will not allow me to risk large capital on this venture under these constraints. We will have to prove to the board that we can prosper under this unusual supply arrangement until a better alternative is developed. I agree with you. We should develop this source incrementally, which your proposal appears to achieve.

"At fifteen dollars a pound, you accomplish one of the goals, which is to keep costs in line. If the price goes above thirty dollars a pound, this will affect our gross margins. I don't believe we can raise shampoo prices very much. While women might pay a little extra, we risk losing the men's market. A lot of men might like the idea of a chemical degreaser in their hair. It sounds macho.

"Despite all of the obstacles and hurdles that we face, if you are confident that you can deliver the thousand contracts at this price, you can safely assume approval at today's board of directors meeting.

"Of course, we will give you all of the corporate assistance you need, including access to our internal legal and commodity trading teams to round up the contracts."

Eva closed her leather folder and pulled on her shoes. She stood to leave. "Albert, get this magical friend of yours to arrange for the rights to buy this magical crabgrass so we can make magical shampoo and then make magical returns for our shareholders. Last point. We will not mention the word crabgrass. This is now an organic cleansing agent.

"Vielen dank und viel glück. Keep me posted." Eva had wished him luck in German, one of five languages that she spoke fluently.

Albert walked from the meeting beaming. He called Gilbert and left a message on his phone. "Gilbert, ve haf a deal. Let us meet tomorrow morning at Ben's. 7:30 sharp!"

CHAPTER 12

APRIL 28, 2011

The following morning, Gilbert Gilchrist casually strolled into Ben's Deli just after 8:00 AM. He wore gray slacks and a tan windbreaker. He waved to Albert as he walked to the food counter to order his toasted bagel with cream cheese and dark-roast coffee. Then he stopped and chatted with Ben at the cash register. Gilbert was well-liked around town. He was a professional mayor-type who fully enjoyed shaking hands and kissing babies. He missed the interaction with the public and the power he'd felt as mayor when he helped the voters.

Gilbert was an athletic, six-feet tall. He carried an extra fifteen pounds, but maintained a decent physical shape for a man in his sixties. He combed his full head of white hair straight back from a gently receding widow's peak.

Albert tried to appear patient as he waited in a booth reading *The Record* for the third time. While he watched Gilbert schmooze around the deli, Albert realized that it had been a mistake to ask Gilbert to arrive so early. Albert was growing more comfortable around Gilbert. He even dressed more casually, giving up the lab coat and tie for a pair of khakis and a blue checkered shirt.

Gilbert sat down and handed Albert a coffee and sweet bun. "Albert, I'm really sorry that I'm late. One thing you should know about me. No meetings before eight. Okay?"

Albert smiled and handed Gilbert an envelope. "Zat's okay, Gilbert. Meine schuld. I'm sorry. I meant my fault. I understand. Here's zie signed consulting agreement and a check for zie $25,000 retainer. Ve should start planning zie next phase and decide how to contact zie homeowners."

Gilbert took a sip from his coffee, but didn't open the envelope. A hundred thousand dollars total was a lot of money, but Gilbert needed two things to make this deal sweeter. First, he needed the entire fee in advance so he could start the wheels turning on his plan. Second, he needed to delay Albert's "next phase" for at least two weeks.

Gilbert handed the envelope back to Albert. "I'm not trying to be a prick or anything. I really need the full amount up front. Please go back and speak to your bosses. I have another meeting to attend. We can speak again later."

Albert thought for a moment. Was Gilbert threatening to go to Pierre's competitors? Gilbert didn't seem to be that type of man, but here he was turning down a $25,000 check. Albert couldn't be sure. He already had the authority from Pierre to pay the whole retainer, so why take the risk?

Albert pushed the envelope back into Gilbert's hand. "Okay Gilbert. I vill send you another check. I need to get back to vork. Ve can discuss zie execution of zie plan later. Congratulations. You just made a lot auf money!"

Gilbert used a fake, whiney voice. "Albert, can't you wire the money today? Here, I wrote the wire instructions down."

Albert looked at the scribbling on a piece of scrap paper. "Let me see vhat I can do. Give me a few minutes."

Albert walked outside and called Pierre's treasury department to initiate the wire. A maze of internal approvals was required. After a frustratingly, unsuccessful twenty minutes, he called Olivier and begged him to bypass the approval process.

A frazzled Albert returned to Gilbert's table and said, "Zie money vas sent. I haf to get back to zie office and sign away my life. Then I'm going to hide in my lab and take a nap. Zis is exhausting."

After Albert left, Gilbert took a minute to enjoy the first step in his victory. Investing the $100,000 fee in foreclosed homes could make him a millionaire several times over. Property values would probably improve dramatically with the Pierre deal. The town might even want to make him mayor again. With his new wealth, he just might turn the mayor job down. Instead, he'd settle for a nice statue on the lawn of Town Hall. Yep, Gilbert Gilchrist would look good in bronze with a raised sword on horseback.

Mayor Alvarez sat down at Gilbert's table and jostled him from his daydream. "Gil-baby, let's have a chat. I heard that you've been wheeling and dealing. I'm guessing you ain't up to any good. Now what are you planning? I hope it's your retirement in Florida."

Hector wore a brown suit with a brightly-colored, flowered tie and a matching pocket handkerchief. Hector was medium height and slightly husky. He had a full head of dark hair that he wore parted on the side. His moustache was full, but straight-lined – no handlebar, no Fu Manchu. Forty-year-old Hector and his wife had five children spread through Bergenfield's middle school and high school. They enthusiastically attended all of their children's sporting, marching band, and theater events.

Gilbert gave a haughty laugh. "Hardy-har-har! Good joke, future ex-mayor. How's that downtown improvement project going? I see lots of for-rent signs on Washington Avenue. Are you planning to fill the stores with a bunch of Filipino groceries and Korean restaurants?"

Hector scowled, "I'm the mayor and will be unless the voters say otherwise. If you plan to do anything, I mean any single thing, to affect the commerce of this town, you had better make me and the town council part of the conversation. There's a rumor that you plan to open a nightclub in town. Forget it. You won't get a permit to wash your car unless I say so."

Gilbert glared at Hector. "We'll see about that. Besides, I use the Clinton Car Wash. Joe would have been out of business today if your council had its way. He's my friend forever. And by the way, do I look like the kinda guy who would open a disco? Good grief."

Hector was not getting through to Gilbert. He changed to a conciliatory tone and tried to argue logic. "This town has 9,000 homes and hundreds are still in default from the housing crash. People are hurting. Some are out of work. Most lost a lot in their retirement savings. We should be working together to help improve their lives. If you want to help, that's one thing. But don't impede our progress, or I'll make life difficult."

Gilbert smiled wryly. "I'll take care of your housing crisis for you, Hector."

Hector rose to leave. "Gilbert, I have always extended an olive branch to you, and you always refuse it. If you want to do battle, then let's take off the gloves and have a real contest. You'll have heart failure before the opening bell."

Gilbert imitated a boxing bell. "*Clang! Clang! Clang!* I'm still standing!"

Hector walked away shaking his head. Gilbert's phone pinged. First Second Third Bank had sent a text message that a wire had been deposited into his account. Gilbert quickly left Ben's. The heck with Hector.

CHAPTER 13

APRIL 28

Gilbert chewed on an unlit cigar, race-walked three hundred yards up Washington Avenue, and entered the near-empty banking floor of the First Second Third Bank. He deposited the Pierre check at the merchant's express window and walked to David Elliot's corner office.

For fifty years, Redstone Bank was a sleepy, small-town bank that serviced merchants and local residents. Then, the housing real estate boom began. First Second Third Bank, the nation's largest home mortgage mill, acquired Redstone in 2007 during the go-go banking years. Locals now called it "One-Two-Three." Passersby could be heard whistling the old Len Barry tune with the same name. Redstone had been bought at the top of the housing boom and at the peak of its earnings. It had gone straight downhill ever since.

1-2-3 wasn't the only bank in trouble. Nearly every bank in America had joined the mortgage lending frenzy. Real estate prices had been rising rapidly. Banks willingly lent an ever increasing percentage of an ever increasing home value.

The lower and middle class had not shared in the country's prosperity during the last three decades. Wages had stagnated as jobs moved offshore to Asia. Clever workers maintained their lifestyle by borrowing against their rising home values. As home prices skyrocketed, many families bought expensive houses far above their means. They paid for the homes by borrowing with zero-principal-payment and low, variable-interest-rate mortgages.

Banks all over the country packaged the high-risk mortgages and sold them to Wall Street. These Mortgage Backed Securities were known on the trading floor as Ginnie Maes because Ginnie Mae, a quasi-government corporation, guaranteed the loans backed by federally insured programs.

Then the mortgage defaults came. Large numbers of borrowers missed their mortgage payments. Ginnie Mae values crashed. Bear Stearns, an investment bank and leading packager of Ginnie Maes, collapsed. The value of homes, the banks that had lent to them, and the bond market that had financed them, toppled like a stack of dominos.

Millions more homeowners defaulted on their mortgages. The stock market collapsed as investors discovered that all sorts of non-bank companies had ventured into the mortgage investment business. Investment banks had bought protection and made a few side bets with naked credit default swaps, and the insurance companies that had written the swaps went broke. The United States government had to bail out the banks, Wall Street, the auto industry and the insurance industry to keep the world from going broke.

The ability to finance a home purchase had evaporated virtually overnight.

Across New Jersey, 1-2-3 had thousands of problem mortgages; a few hundred sat in Bergenfield. The Federal bank examiners had staked permanent residence in the bank's conference room. It was only a matter of time before the FDIC took over the bank.

David Elliot, one of the bank's fifty senior vice presidents, had lived through the boom years and was now paying the price. He didn't receive many friendly visitors these days. He was glad to see Gilbert at the teller window. David looked at his computer screen and saw the $75,000 wire that had hit Gilbert's account. Apparently, Gilbert had come into a little money.

The two had a long relationship. Gilbert had given David's bank most of the town's banking business while he was mayor. In return, David approved some adventurous loans for Gilbert's investments, which so far had worked out.

David was in his forties but the bank's workout problems had accelerated his aging process. The new flecks of gray hair nicely matched David's steel-rimmed eyeglasses. He wore the bank officer's standard issue uniform – a navy, pin-striped suit with pleated trousers, a white shirt and a navy and gray wide-striped tie. An American-flag pin adorned his suit coat lapel.

Gilbert handed David two Starbucks espressos and sat in front of the large mahogany banker's desk. David looked quizzically at Gilbert, and asked, "Thanks, but why two coffees?"

Gilbert said, "Ben's rules. No exceptions. Pour them together to make a double espresso. How y'all doing? It's pretty quiet out there."

David chuckled. "Well, my deposits are up this month, thanks to you."

Gilbert laughed. "Don't count on that money staying in free checking too long. David, my good friend, I'm here to change your life. But it's not by making a teeny little deposit. Tell me, how many bad foreclosures do you still have?"

David was grim. "Gil, all foreclosures are bad. Some are worse than others. I can't tell you the number, but we have more than we like."

"It's okay, Dave," Gilbert shrugged. "The records are easily available. I already know there are four hundred loan defaults in town and another four hundred coming soon. That's the number of houses not paying real estate taxes today. I'm guessing that your bank has half of them. I also know that your bank is under bank supervision and will collapse if you don't get these mortgages off your books. I heard the bank has six months to live, unless depositors make a run on the bank earlier.

"I'm going to make your day. I want to take some of your defaulted mortgages off your hands. I'll buy the houses in a short sale. I'll talk to the residents and convince them to forgo the foreclosure process.

"It's gonna take you another two years to get rid of these squatters. They're paying you nothing right now, and the bank has to pay the real estate taxes and insurance. Each house must be costing you ten grand a year."

Dave reacted coolly. On one hand, these homes were an albatross around the bank's neck. The two-year-old battle had exhausted his bank loan officers who'd spent the last three years chasing deadbeats and caretaking the defaulted properties. A hundred Wall Street vulture funds had already pored over 1-2-3's books and concluded the loans were unsalvageable.

Gilbert wasn't doing charity work here, but what could he do that the best and brightest on Wall Street couldn't?

"What's the catch?" David eyed him warily. "Why do you want these houses now? And at what price?"

Gilbert leaned forward and placed his forearms on David's desk. "You must have some mortgages that are not too badly under water. You already took a loan loss reserve to what, two hundred thousand bucks?"

David said, "Try one-fifty."

Gilbert continued, "That's even better. So, your problem is that a few hundred families did strategic defaults knowing that they could live for free for two years. And you guys can't find the right documents or prove title, so you can't foreclose. You and every other bank in the country thought you were saving a few hundred bucks by using that MERS system to record deeds. How'd that work out for you guys?"

David groaned. "I fought that MERS system, but the guys in corporate mandated that we use it. For three hundred years, buyers filed deeds in the county courthouse, and it always worked. This MERS thing. Ugh!"

"Let's forget MERS," Gilbert said casually. "We'll use the county courthouse for this deal. Here's my offer, and it's only good for a week. I want to buy fifty homes that are in default. My investor group will put up $600,000. That's twelve grand per home."

David looked surprised and sat up. He expected Gilbert to try to buy a home or two. Fifty was a big number.

Gilbert smiled broadly. "I see that I have your attention. We'll offer $2,000 to each seller to move. We'll give $2,000 per home to the town if they write off the delinquent real estate taxes. The bank gets the rest – eight grand per home. Not to mention, $8 million dollars of your problem loans become good overnight.

"In return, your bank will provide a mortgage to us for the value of the home. I also want a $200,000 home improvement line of credit so we can fix up the houses."

David interrupted, "The town will never write off that much in taxes."

"I'm highly confident that they will," Gilbert countered. "Let's just say that I have some influence in that area. Let me go on.

"The houses will appraise for a buck-seventy-five. Your insolvent bank will report a profit of twenty-five big ones on each house. How's that sound?"

David spoke with a banker's cautionary tone. "Gilbert, there's no doubt that these homes are a problem to the bank. But you have never dealt with these people. Their personalities have changed. They have the protection of the courts. They're living rent free. They beat the system.

"I'll go further. It's not just home mortgages. It's luxury car loans. It's boat loans. What a mess! Our workout bankers spend all week searching Barnegat Bay for our boat collateral. When we find a boat, they move it to another dock before a sheriff can seize it. We can't keep up with them without the help of a satellite tracking system for loans. Worse yet, they still go boating on the weekend. It's criminal!"

David concluded, "I appreciate your enthusiasm, but I'm skeptical that even you can pull it off."

Gilbert looked David in the eye. "I can deliver on my side. All I ask is that you go to your borrowing committee and get preapproval for the line. If I don't convince the homeowners to deal, you've lost nothing. What do you say?"

David thought out loud. "I guess the worst that happens is that you don't close, and we've lost nothing. Or, you deliver and then default again, which leaves us with another defaulted mortgage problem."

Gilbert leaned forward. "Yeah, maybe. But, if I default, you won't have a squatter on your property. You can foreclose immediately. I'll sign a confession of judgment if you want. And you'll have eight grand in your pocket and another eight grand in forgiven real estate taxes. You'll be way ahead."

Gilbert knew how to close a sale. He'd already turned the corner. He was past the point of asking for a loan. He acted as if David had already agreed, which he probably had. "Let me go through your default listing. I bet I can identify fifty prospects."

"Who's your investor group?" David said hastily. "I have to do a background check on everyone, including criminal record and credit history."

Gilbert smiled. "Well you saw my money this morning. I'm the general partner. Four of the investors are town councilmen. Now you know how I'm getting the unpaid taxes written off. The rest of the investors are wealthy guys that are clean as a whistle."

David twirled his pen and leaned back in his chair. "Okay, Gilbert. Maybe we can do this. If the town approves the tax write-off. If the homeowners agree to a short sale. Those are big ifs. Then and only then will I approve the sale and new mortgages.

"I have local-lending-authority for $5 million specifically to restructure this crap. That doesn't buy you fifty houses. At most, it would finance about thirty. I could sign a non-binding term sheet today. If you want approval for fifty, I will have to go to corporate for approval. That could take weeks."

Gilbert raised his arms in mock surrender. "No time for bank bureaucracy. Let's do thirty homes. Actually, that will make this easier. You draft the term sheet, and let me look at the defaulted list."

David added, "I understand what you're doing, but the bank isn't doing anything illegal here. What you do in the town council meetings is your problem."

David had a moment to think. If Gilbert succeeded, David could get rid of half of his workout group. He led Gilbert downstairs to the bowels of the bank where George Daniels presided over a table of unhappy bankers poring over loan documents while contemplating new careers other than in banking.

David said, "George, stand up and meet Gilbert, the retired mayor of Bergenfield. He is going to take thirty mortgages off your hands. Gilbert, George is in charge of nonperforming assets."

George shook his hand. "It's a true pleasure to meet you, Saint Gilbert. How can I help you help me?"

Gilbert was in a hurry and didn't want to chit-chat. "I want a list of the homes in default, the mortgage balance, the name and address and phone number of the homeowners, and the amount of past-due taxes and insurance."

"We have a master list here. All insurance is paid. The taxes are about two years behind on each home," George replied.

Gil said, "I'll be back to you in a few days. You have to keep this confidential except to discuss with Mr. Elliot. Understood?"

"Understood," George nodded.

Gilbert thanked David and quickly left the bank carrying the printout and the commitment letter. He called Johnny from his cell phone. No answer at the hardware store. Then he called Trudy at the beauty salon. The voice message answered; it wouldn't open for an hour. He called Chris at *The Bergenfield Valley News*. He was with a customer. At least he was working. Gilbert called Howie Bergman. His secretary claimed the lawyer was in a meeting about a client's neck brace.

Gilbert was getting frustrated. He walked to Johnny's store. He'd wait out front until Johnny arrived. Then he'd make Johnny change the sign that lied about the store's opening hours.

CHAPTER 14

APRIL 28

The *California Gurls* ringtone blared from Johnny's cellphone. Katie Perry sang; then Snoop Dogg joined in a rap. Ben had heard enough. He yelled from the cash register, "Johnny, either answer the phone or turn off the ringer. You're scaring away my customers."

Oblivious-to-the-world Johnny looked at the caller ID and declined the call. Gilbert could wait until he finished his coffee.

Across the deli, JB sat alone reading *The New York Times*. At 9:30 AM, a parade of gas-guzzlers screeched to a halt at the bus stop outside Ben's. The candy-apple-red Ford F350 Crew Cab 4x4, black Cadillac Escalade, Ford Explorer and Porsche Cayenne averaged 5,000 pounds of steel and 400 horsepower. Bully power!

Kimberly, Rosemary, Barbara and Carlie strutted from their soccer-mom, child-shuttles. The women had formed a gal-group three years ago and since had grown inseparable. In the beginning, they spent weekends at joint kids' activities. Then they added group yoga and spinning classes to their calendars. Last year, their families vacationed together for a week in Port St. Lucie, Florida. The husbands took the kids to the Mets' spring training games while the girls drank mojitos and tanned at the beach.

One day, after a couple of strong cocktails, Kimberly suggested that they form an underground sorority, sans the secret handshake. They named themselves Iota Mu Eta, which, properly slurred, morphed into "I ordered a mojito!"

A month ago, the girls discovered a new joint activity – online Texas hold 'em poker on the Zynga web site. Three husbands and a serious boyfriend had been abandoned for two hours every night. The men were not happy.

The Mojito girls grabbed breakfast and sat with JB. Kimberly bragged, "JB, I lost a million dollars on Zynga last night. Thank goodness it's not real money. I might have to buy poker chips if this keeps up!"

Kimberly's poker name was River, which is the term for the last communal poker card turned face up. She was thirty-five, 5'8" with brown hair, hazel green eyes and the soft curves and fluttering eyelashes of Marilyn Monroe. River was a supermom who shuttled her five boys to sporting events.

Rosemary said, "Norma Jean, you're too busy chatting with Big Bucks! The guy is probably broke and just released from Alcatraz." Rosemary was a forty-year-old, 5'7" blue-eyed, blonde-haired nurse with three lacrosse-playing girls. Her poker name was Charmer.

Barbara lamented, "I thought that Fold-Em was sending me secret code texts. Find out he's a keyboard stutterer – he can't type." Barb was a brown-eyed blonde with Norwegian and English blood.

JB laughed. "How do you know that these players aren't teenagers? How do you know if they're even guys? Or obese? Or bald?"

Carlie said, "We don't, but who cares? We think Big Pair is a real D Cup. My fave is Chance Allure. You know, like chancellor. He texts with a British accent. Cheerio and all that rot." Carlie's poker avatar was Shark Diver. She worked for a nonprofit that protected wildlife and deep-sea-dived among sharks in her spare time. Born in Germany, she also had the beautiful face and blonde hair of Heidi Klum.

River said, "My husband warned me to cut down on my poker play or he'll take my iPad away. I quit playing by ten, unless he's out cold. Then I sneak back on."

The girls laughed as the wind from a human tornado, better known as Misty, blew napkins and swizzle sticks to the floor. River looked up and cried, "Watch out, Vanya the Hun is coming through! JB, if you want to get her goat, use her real name, Giovanna."

River got a table full of laughs as she stretched the name – Gee-Oh-Vannnn-Ya. Misty heard the group laughing as she passed by the table. She paused, gave River a nasty scowl, and walked to the food line.

River laughed. "I'm in trouble now. We'd better go, JB. I'm not up for a fight today. Misty is too much to handle. See you tonight on Zynga!"

CHAPTER 15

APRIL 28

Giovanna Francella hated her birth name. At the age of thirteen, she heard the Johnny Mathis song and strong-armed her friends into calling her Misty. She had no idea that Misty would one day become the preferred stage name of thousands of strippers across America.

Misty was an olive-skinned, Sicilian beauty with short, wavy brown hair and deep, dark brown eyes. Two hours a day, seven-hundred-thirty hours a year, Misty perfected her outer beauty. It took an hour every morning to fix her hair and perfectly apply the makeup, mascara and lip gloss. It took another hour to remove the mask at night.

Misty maintained the bounce of the head cheerleader at a high school pep squad, which she once was. She was perky and pretty and could be mean as a snake to anyone who crossed her.

Every weekday, she wore a dress and matching silk scarf. She was petite and stood barely five-feet tall before a lift from four-inch, high-heeled espadrilles. She claimed to be a marketing executive, which was a slight stretch of the truth from her job as a sales assistant at Mackie's Used Cars on Route 17.

Her enemies generally agreed that Misty had missed her calling. The job for which she was most qualified was inspector at a mirror factory.

Misty was born in Cresskill, the town kitty-corner northeast of Bergenfield. She was back living with her parents after three failed marriages at the age of thirty-five. The first marriage to her high school boyfriend ended in less than a year. He'd lost his job, and Misty wasted little time finding a replacement provider.

Hubby number two had lots of fancy assets. Misty discovered soon after the wedding that he had even fancier debt including IRS liens on his home, two boats and three sports cars.

Number three was definitely rich. Misty had hired a private investigator to make sure. Unfortunately, the couple never celebrated their first anniversary. Misty installed a dead-bolt lock on the bedroom door in a battle over who was going to be boss and control the checkbook. The pre-nup left Misty with next-to nothing. She was infuriated and broke.

Misty was plotting her revenge against the poker moms as she reached Ben at the cash register. "Ben, sweetie, I know I'm early, but may I have a vente caramel latte with skim milk, no foam and extra cinnamon? I want the natural brown sugar. And put the fancy lid on it with that little green insert so it doesn't spill while I'm driving."

Ben exhaled in exasperation and shook his head. "Misty, every day you ask for a specialty coffee. Every day I tell you that we don't make specialty drinks until 10:00 AM, which is still fifteen minutes away. We don't make Local Mocha Locos here either. We haven't changed the rules today. Here's your coffee. Add your milk and sugar over at the condiment table, please."

Vainglorious Misty ignored Ben's rejection and examined her mascara in her compact mirror. She pulled a manila budget envelope from her purse and spilled some crumpled bills and a few coins on the counter.

It was the Misty accounting, budgetary, financial management and control system. She kept a separate envelope for every conceivable expenditure – breakfast, car insurance, eyeliner, gasoline, lunch, lipstick, vacation, and mascara – twenty envelopes in all. Whenever she paid for a purchase, the world stopped rotating while she rifled her purse for the appropriate envelope.

Ben rolled his eyes and drummed his fingers as she counted $3.12 in exact change. Ben scribbled an unreadable number on an order ticket for her receipt. Misty wasn't finished.

She carefully entered the amount into a journal, added to a new subtotal, and placed the receipt in the envelope.

Ben dismissed her with an impatient cry. "Next," he pleaded. It was enough to ruin his day. The line of impatient customers now numbered six.

JB watched in total amazement as the little female Napoleon commandeered Ben's and brought all productive activity to a halt. It was her daily five minutes of fame. She wanted attention and demanded that people witness her presence.

Misty stopped briefly at JB's table and appeared to be looking for Kimberly. She reached for the front door, and Gilbert rushed in, nearly knocking her over. He muttered a quick "Excuse me," and rushed to Johnny's table.

Gilbert stood over Johnny and yanked out his ear buds. "Why aren't you answering your phone?"

Johnny started to protest, but Gilbert pulled his chair from the table. Johnny stood, and Gilbert grabbed his elbow and pulled him out the door.

Ben called over to JB. "Looks like Gilbert's taking Johnny to the woodshed. Ya know, he's been holding a lot of meetings here lately. Maybe I should charge office rent? Whadaya think?"

CHAPTER 16

APRIL 28

Gilbert dragged Johnny True Value along Washington Avenue like a teenager on his way to detention. His anger at Johnny's slight was subsiding. Johnny was Johnny, and never would change. He softened his tone. "We need to get to work. David agreed to our deal. Everyone has to meet right away. Like now!"

Johnny pulled his arm away, and said, "Okay, okay. I got it. Stop it! You're rippin' my jacket. Gimme a second and I'll ping Trudy and Chris to join us."

Trudy and Chris arrived at the hardware store fifteen minutes later. Johnny locked the door and flipped the "closed" sign to keep the unlikely customer away. They sat at a faux butcher-block table that had no chance of being sold.

Trudy D'Angelo owned a hair salon that specialized in the poof cut. It was a unique, Jersey-girl hairstyle in vogue since the sixties that created a two-inch bob of hair at the crown of the head. Snookie, the star of *Jersey Shore,* had created a poof renaissance on the MTV drunken-reality-television-show that aired from the Seaside Heights bars and boardwalk.

Chris Bloom owned *The Bergenfield Valley News,* the town's shopper weekly. Business had been weak for nearly three years because the dwindling number of downtown merchants had cut their advertising spending. Chris picked up some slack by printing mailers, greeting cards and posters. He was barely paying the bills.

Gilbert waved a handful of documents in the air. "Here's the bank's commitment letter to buy thirty homes and a list of two hundred homes in default. All we have to do is get the town to write off the taxes and convince the squatters to do a short sale. We have one week to get it done.

"Johnny, call an emergency town council meeting for next Thursday. Howie will help you. The rest of the town council probably won't go for this. Hector might be swayed. But Doug the CPA will vote no because it's too much money. Lori the librarian votes with Doug.

"We have $360,000 of partner equity. I'm putting up a hundred. You each put up fifteen because you have work to do. It's what they call sweat equity. A few silent partners will kick in the rest.

"Chances to make this much money don't come around very often. If this works out, you could make ten times your money in two years. Maybe twice that. No one, and I mean no one, is to know about this deal. If anyone learns, we're all in big trouble. Are we understood?"

The group nodded their solemn agreement.

Gilbert: "Your contribution depends on the size of the tax write-off. We're asking them to forgive almost $200,000. If the town approves less, you're gonna have to put up more money. Then it starts to be painful."

Trudy: "I don't have that type of extra money hangin' around the parlor. We better get the full write-off."

Chris: "I agree. But, what will the other investors get?"

Gilbert: "Every limited partner gets eight percent of the profits. The same as you. Their units just cost more. I'm the general partner and get sixty percent. That's six LP units for forty-eight percent plus a free twelve percent as GP."

Johnny: "That sounds fair, but I wouldn't want to rub it in their faces that we paid less. Let's keep this among ourselves."

Gilbert was still miffed at Johnny for not answering his phone. Now Johnny was acting like he was in charge. Gilbert wanted to dress him down, but thought better. No disharmony. Get the deal done. Still, he couldn't avoid adding a little sarcastic tone. "Thanks, Johnny. Let me explain how it works. We're buying the houses in a short sale. You've read about these in the papers. The people in these homes haven't paid a mortgage or tax payment in two years. A short sale is essentially selling the house for less than the mortgage and taxes, but everyone contractually agrees to the sale so you don't have to foreclose in court."

Gilbert said emphatically, "Squatters stop short sales! We're going to pay them to leave."

Johnny said, "Yeah. I know a buncha these people. They refinanced their houses, put the money in the bank and then did this strategic default thing, whatever that is. It sounds like dine-and-dash at a restaurant – have a nice meal and sneak out the back door. Now they're livin' free until whenever."

Gilbert nodded. "You're right. And you guys happen to know most of the squatters on this list. Your job is to convince them to take our deal before next Tuesday. We'll pay them $2,000 up front and let them stay in the house for up to two years – no rent for the first year and then $1,000 a month in year two if they decide to stay. That's cheap rent for a home.

"I need thirty names to agree. If each of you signs up ten homes, we'll have forty to choose from."

Trudy looked dazed. "Gilbert, you're makin' my head spin with all of these numbers. Okay, you want fifteen thousand dollars. I can rustle that up by Tuesday.

"Next, you want me to find ten cousins or friends on the list and go convince them. That's easy. I'm looking at this list. I see at least two dozen. The Martini extended family did a strategic default and then had a closing party. They taped the foreclosure notices to the wall. Everyone rented tuxes and drank champagne. I had a lot of fun from what I can remember.

"But what makes you think these houses are gonna go up? The housing market's a mess. Nothin' is sellin' in this horrible market."

"Trudy," Gilbert smiled knowingly, "that's a good question. This is insider information. Only one person in town knows what's about to happen – me. You cannot breathe a word about this even to your husband."

CHAPTER 17

APRIL 28

Trudy raised a scapular of Saint Anthony that she was wearing around her neck and made the sign of the cross. "I swear I won't tell nobody, but I gotta tell my husband. I never keep anythin' from him."

Gilbert laughed. "Okay, Trudy, you can tell Paulie. I'm just making a point. If word gets out, the squatters won't agree to sell.

"There's a very good reason the houses are gonna go up in value. A company is about to pay a thousand homes in Bergenfield to grow crabgrass on their lawns. Not just any crabgrass. Our town is sitting on a high-potency species of oil-eating weed. We hit a gusher – an oil guzzling gusher. And I'm their advisor and get to choose which houses get the deal."

Chris laughed. "Pay me! I can't get rid of the stuff. I tried to plant sod, and it lived one year. The crabgrass seeds come from everywhere. You can't fight it."

Gilbert continued, "Be glad you lost the battle, Chris. This is why your cousins can't know about this, Trudy. If they discovered that they were about to make ten grand a year, they'd never agree to the short sale. Which is why we want them to sign quickly."

Gilbert handed everyone a photocopy of rough projections handwritten on a piece of legal paper. "I scratched out rough estimates. The mortgage, insurance and taxes will be covered by the crabgrass sales. We'll be near breakeven in the first year and cash flow positive next year. Your cousins agree to move out at the end of the lease so we can sell the house. If anyone squats on the property, one of your other cousins can take care of them, if you know what I mean.

"The best part is that the home value should go up a hundred thousand at least. Thirty homes equal three million of profit. You'll make about $300,000 – double that if homes sell for $375,000.

"Let's discuss our next steps. Johnny, after you put these foreclosures on the town agenda, try to convince Hector to vote for the deal. It'll just make everything easier."

"I think I can convince him, but we might need to sweeten the pot. We also might need more money to pay the homeowners," Johnny insisted. "Maybe another two thousand?"

Gilbert had had it with Johnny. He was lazy and took credit for other people's work. If he didn't need Johnny's vote next Thursday, he'd show him the door. Gilbert stood up and spoke sternly. "Okay Johnny-big-bucks, but that means you have to put up another eight grand. Is that what you want to do? Fine with me. But your negotiating pressure is the ticking clock. If the town doesn't approve this right away, the buyers move on to another town.

"As for the homeowners getting another two grand, two thousand a home is $60,000 that we don't have. Really, do you folks want to come up with more money? Or buy fewer houses? Let's get real here."

Johnny looked offended that Gilbert hadn't endorsed his ideas. Gilbert felt that he'd exercised unusual restraint by not calling him an idiot, moron and imbecile. Gilbert sat again and lowered his voice. "Back to Hector. It would be nice if he voted for this. But I wouldn't worry about him. I'd worry about the district attorney and sheriff. They'll be fitting you for orange jumpsuits if the town discovers that you forgave your own real estate taxes."

"I don't look good in orange," Chris said, making a sour face. "But I'm not sure that this is illegal. It's more like kinda dishonest, you know, by not disclosing our interest in the transaction, right? I think that the worst that can happen is they throw us off the town council.

"But Gil, I can see why the others are investors. What do you need from me other than ten names and a vote?"

Gilbert laughed out loud. "Why, Chris, you're my one-man, public relations team! You're going to print a front-page headline in tomorrow's paper to scare the squatters into signing our deal so we can steal their homes.

"And I want big, bold letters. We're gonna tell them that the courts are ending the mortgage mess. Strategic defaults are toast! The banks are about to throw them into the street!

"Just quote unnamed sources and speculation. There are plenty of quotes on the Internet. Just google it. I just saw an interview with a judge in Hackensack. He complained about homeowners gaming the system. Quote him."

Chris looked uncomfortable. Trudy patted him on the shoulder and said, "You can do it, Chris. You're good at this creative writing stuff."

Gilbert examined the faces of his three partners. Trudy was the hardest worker and had heart, courage and brains. She'd be great. Johnny was wacky and greedy. He was the loose cannon. Chris was meek and mild. Hopefully he wouldn't suffer a nervous breakdown. Gilbert would have to deal with it on their trip to Oz. "Are we all agreed? Everyone look at this list and give me ten names that you can call. I'll get Howie to do the same."

Gilbert turned on the charisma that had won three mayoral elections. "Guys, your ship has come in. The chance to get into a deal like this is why local business people join the town council. Let's go make some money.

"I have one last administrative detail. I formed a company in Florida to buy the houses and named it Bergen Development Company. It's an LLC, or limited liability company. I'm using my buddy's law offices for the corporate address in Miami. The board and officers are hired guns. You're going to be investors in the LLC, but you can't use your real names.

"Go online and set up a front company in Florida to act as your investor. It takes twenty minutes and $300. Also, use the name of someone you can trust as the registering officer. We don't want Mayor Hector to trace this to you. If you have any problems, ask Howie to help."

Everyone nodded agreement and began to look at the list for relatives, cousins, family and friends who were either conning the system or maybe legitimately defaulted on their mortgage. Chris looked up from the list and said, "This may be easier than we think. I found three schlubbs on the first page. We may not need Howie."

Gilbert didn't have the heart to dress down Chris. He'd save his energy for Johnny the freeloader. "Chris, we do need Howie – we need his money, his vote, and his free legal work. It would cost us another $60,000 to close deeds on thirty homes. That is, unless you want to put up more money... Chris?"

Chris sheepishly said, "No thanks, Gil. You know best. But trouble seems to find Howie somehow. You know what I mean."

"I agree, but we need him," Gilbert pointed out reluctantly. "Howie is drafting a lease and short sale agreement for the squatters to sign. It'll be ready in an hour. You have four days to sign up ten sellers. Let's meet at my house Tuesday night at six to see where we are. I'll buy pizza and beer.

"Chris, go draft the newspaper article! I'll come by tomorrow morning to approve it. The paper has to be delivered tomorrow if we're going to get these squatters to sign by Tuesday.

"Guys," Gilbert clapped his hands like a football coach before the big game. "We have a lot of work to do. Try your best. If we only get ten houses, it's still worth it. But thirty is three times better, right?"

CHAPTER 18

APRIL 29, 2011

JB, Michael, Allie and Bret sat together at the Ben's Deli board table. Allie looked remarkably fresh for someone who'd just finished working the midnight shift at the hospital.

JB leaned back in his chair and proclaimed his scheme of the day. "I've invented a new way to lose weight – the raw liver diet!"

Michael and Bret dropped their bagels in unison with a look of disgust. Allie contorted her face. "Yuck! That's revolting! Besides, if you eat too much liver, don't you get an overdose of iron?"

"I'm not eating raw liver," JB laughed. "I'm going to lose twenty pounds in my liver. I'm cutting out wine for two months. I read that they did an autopsy on some guy who was a heavy drinker. His liver weighed forty pounds! I'm sure my belly is from an overweight liver."

"That's silly," Allie snorted. "What's more ludicrous is the chance that you could go a day without drinkin' a glass of wine. But, you know what they say: 'Do everythin' in moderation and nothin' to excess.' I might cut back myself."

Allie looked at her watch. "I gotta go before my son sets the house on fire cookin' breakfast. I just can't keep up with him."

JB raised an eyebrow. "How can you set fire to cereal?"

"Marty can do it," Allie sighed miserably. "He used a butane torch to toast his Cheerios, and the napkin caught fire. He's home from school this week. Suspended again.

"He's really angry, and I'm tryin' so hard to get through to him. He wants a father, and I don't have the right plumbing. I don't know what to do. When I worked day shifts, he cut school. When I worked night shifts, he was drunk by nine. When I switched to the graveyard shift, he snuck out at midnight. He just wants to get into trouble. And he's a smart kid. He'd have good grades if he didn't get suspended all the time."

"There's a dozen men right here who would leave their wives to marry you. Not me, of course," Michael clarified. "Why not find him a new father?"

Allie laughed. "You know that Groucho Marx joke about not wantin' to join a country club that would have him as a member? Well, I don't want a husband who'd divorce someone to have me as his wife."

Gilbert overheard the diet conversation while paying for his breakfast. He stopped at the table and rested his hand on JB's shoulder. "Good morning, voters. Sorry to eavesdrop, JB, but I have to argue against your liver diet. Just remember: Researchers discovered that red wine is good for your heart. And more people die from heart disease than from obesity. So whatever you do, don't stop drinking."

As Gilbert walked away, JB said, "Now that's why Gil was such a great mayor. He's a genius at making voters happy!"

Gilbert left Ben's Deli and walked toward the *Bergenfield Valley News* offices. Twenty years ago, the fifty small store fronts on Washington Avenue were homes to retail stores: an ice cream parlor; a stationery store; a hobby shop; a sporting goods store.

Much of the retail business had left downtown. Some of the stores were occupied by small businesses: a civil engineer; a tax preparation service; a real estate agent who was visibly idle. The Palace Theater and Tommy Fox's stood their ground, but it was a battle for most retailers to thrive in downtown Bergenfield.

Gilbert walked behind the counter and handed Chris the customary Starbucks. He began to review the draft of the front-page article. "Chris, the article is good, but we need to scare the crap out of them with the headline. Let's make it really big type – FORECLOSURE MESS OVER? Then have a second smaller headline – JUDGE RULES ON MORTGAGES. That should get 'em."

Chris faltered. "Aren't we going to get in trouble for this? Those headlines aren't entirely accurate?"

Gilbert spoke with the raised voice of a benevolent Dutch uncle. "Chris! First, the question mark covers your ass. Besides, when did newspapers ever let facts get in the way of a good story? Second, you're going to make $300,000. That's more than you make in five years from this wannabe newspaper. Third, there is nothing in your article that is factually incorrect.

"And fourth, fifth and sixth, no one reads the damn articles anyway. They just read the headlines and then hunt for coupons and garage sale notices. But if you are not cool about this, now is the time to get out. We'll still be friends."

Chris shook his head. "I'm in. I need the money. This place is killing me. Today I'm typesetting birthday invitations for $75. What a job!"

"Okay Chris, good decision," Gilbert chuckled. "Now, let's talk about delivery. You usually use the post office to deliver these on Monday, right?"

Chris nodded his head while he edited and enlarged the headline wording.

"We can't wait until the mail gets delivered," Gilbert continued. "I'll hire some day workers that hang around the Teaneck Armory. They can hand-deliver the papers to our targets and their fifty neighbors. We need something extra to make them look at the paper. What are those Phil's Pizza flyers in that stack over there?"

Chris turned to where Gilbert was pointing. "Those are promotional flyers that we printed this morning. They're going in a Value Pack mailer."

Gilbert rubbed his chin while he thought. "They'll have to do. Stick one on every paper just below the headline. Phil isn't going to mind getting an extra thousand ads for free.

"I'll be back in four hours to pick them up. Do a short run of a thousand papers. We'll put extra papers in the stores, library, post office and corner newspaper boxes. I'll see you at one."

Gilbert drove to the Teaneck Armory and picked six day workers who were somewhat presentable. He offered them $100 apiece to deliver the papers and gave them bus fare to travel the mile to the *Bergenfield Valley News* offices. Gilbert was careful that his activities didn't draw attention. There were enough gossipers in town who would ask why a crew rode in the back of his pickup truck.

It was now time for Howie to start pulling his weight.

CHAPTER 19

APRIL 29

Gilbert entered the disheveled law offices of Howie Bergman. Boxes filled with legal papers from decade-old unsettled lawsuits decorated the hallway. Cardboard dust filled the air. Howie thought the files made his office look busy. In fact, it only made him look sloppy and disorganized.

Howie was a personal injury lawyer on his good days. He wasn't particularly ambitious and was not at all good at chasing ambulances. Unwilling to pay for billboard advertising, he was content to handle cases that managed to walk into his office without tripping.

He made a little money handling contracts and real estate closings and wrote an occasional will. The town paid him a $2,000 monthly retainer for legal advice. Without the town contract, Howie would be practicing bankruptcy law – on himself!

Frizzy brown hair circumnavigated below the crown of Howie's head. The top of the globe was as bald as a hard-boiled egg. He carried an electric shaver at all times to trim his four o'clock shadow which regularly arrived before noon. Today, he wore an inexpensive brown suit and beige shirt, but his uninspiring tie would soon be hanging at half-mast. He was a crumpled mess who perfectly matched his musty office.

Gilbert greeted Howie with a Starbuck's latte. Howie pushed the coffee aside. He leaned back in his chair, folded his arms in defiance, and raised the edge of his voice in a Jersey-tough-guy voice. "You think you can buy my services for the price of a cappuccino? Fuggedaboudit. You're really startin' to piss me off.

"I'm the lawyer doin' all of the work around here. And you have me as an equal partner with Trudy, Johnny and Chris. It's not fair. Worse, I'm the one who gets disbarred if this deal goes bad."

Gilbert knew that Howie-maintenance was a big part of his job. Howie's legal work would be critical for the next ten days. It wasn't just the legal fees that Howie was saving. Any honest lawyer could prepare a bunch of deeds. Gilbert needed Howie's less-honest skillset to handle the somewhat gray areas of this transaction.

Howie-maintenance: Act I – *Don't bark back.* Gilbert remained remarkably polite. "Howie, please calm down. You don't need to get tough with me. We've known each other a long time. I appreciate that you have some work to do initially. After the closing in a week, you'll coast and collect a nice fat check in two years."

Howie stood his ground. "I ain't doin' it. There's no way a beautician, a hammer sales-man and a paperboy get the same share as me. You want me to do all the dirty work and thirty real estate closings in one week, and I'm gettin' nothin'. Go find yourself another lawyer."

Howie-maintenance: Act II – *Threaten to take away his Milk Bone.* Gilbert's voice was calm. "Okay, Howie. I have another lawyer willing to do the work. Thanks for considering it. I thought I was doing you a favor knowing how tough business is for you. You must have come into a big caseload since we last spoke. I thought you had some free time. We'll catch you on the next deal."

Gilbert stood to leave. Howie jumped from his chair and beat him to the door. "Wait a minute, Gil. There must be some middle ground here. I'll do the deal, but you gotta pay me my standard rate. This just ain't fair."

Howie-maintenance: Act III – *Threaten to hit Howie with a newspaper.* Gilbert stood four inches taller than Howie. He looked down and poked his finger in Howie's chest. "You know what isn't fair? Any one of you getting a dime more than the other. You all are taking a big risk, and you all have work to do. Trust me on this. Trudy is delivering twenty houses.

That's two or three million in profit. If anyone should get a bigger share, it's Trudy. But I don't hear her griping. That girl is a saint. Your legal work is an overvalued commodity. I can get any lawyer in town to close a bunch of deeds and file them in the courthouse.

"I'll add something else, you ungrateful piece of crap. When I was mayor, I gave you a contract with the town that pays you two thousand a month. After fifteen years, you know what I got from you? Nada. Nothing. Zilch. Squat. Not even a Christmas card.

"Speaking of which, including you in this deal is yet another gift. I'm giving you the opportunity to make some big money, which by the looks of this dump, you need badly. I don't need you, Howie. You'd probably screw up the closing anyway."

Howie tried to usher Gilbert back to his seat. "Jesus, Gilbert. That's a little rough. I'm sorry. I'm really sorry. I just didn't understand, I guess. Can you at least cover my expenses?"

Howie-maintenance: Act IV – *Throw the dog a bone.* "Howie, I'm not sure that you deserve this, but I'll pay you $300 per home, but only if you close on time by next Friday. Let's get back to work."

Howie-maintenance: Final Act – *Don't rub the dog's nose in it.* Proceed like nothing ever happened. Howie scampered like a puppy to his swivel leather chair. Gilbert inspected Howie's large solid-oak desk covered in coffee stains and cigarette burns. It had once been a magnificent piece of furniture. All it needed was a little sandpaper and varnish, and it would be worthy of PBS's *Antiques Roadshow*. Howie treated it with the respect of a TV tray.

Gilbert sat on the front edge of the client chair carefully avoiding the broken wicker caning. "We need everyone's investment money no later than Tuesday before the town meeting. That's five days. Make sure everyone sets up their front companies. You can charge them a couple of hundred for that. They won't have enough time to establish offshore bank accounts, so they'll send the money to you. Put the money in an escrow account to hide the trail."

Howie, now the team player, said, "I have an unused escrow account at David's bank. I'll just change the name on the account."

Gilbert smiled. "Good. I knew you'd find a way to get this done. Closing costs should be minimal, but I'll try to get Elliot to pay for most. You draft the deeds. We shouldn't need title insurance. We'll get a representation from the bank and the sellers that they have good title."

Howie protested, "I usually make money on the title opinion. I own the surety company…"

Gilbert held up a hand, stopping Howie's protest. "Howie, not this time. There's no money in the budget. Every $10,000 I pay you is one less house we buy. You have to sacrifice.

"David will send you a master loan and mortgage agreement. It should be standard documents. It's important that we get this done quickly. Capische? You have any more issues or complaints?"

Howie raised his hands in surrender. "No, no, no. I'm good, Gilbert. Are we good? I was just makin' the point that I was earnin' my way. You're bein' more than generous."

"Make sure you sign up ten homeowners, too," Gilbert ordered. "You must have some shady clients on that list. Otherwise, I'm giving your share to Trudy. And don't ever cross me again."

Gilbert stood and spun on his heel. "I'll see you Tuesday at my house at six."

CHAPTER 20

MAY 3, 2011

On Tuesday evening, the four councilmen and soon-to-be vulture investors sat with Gilbert in his large, comfortable den. At one end, a large sofa and two leather chairs formed an amphitheater around a large screen TV and sound system. At the other end of the den, four wooden seats surrounded a bridge table lit by a Tiffany lamp.

A case of Budweiser was chilling on ice. Uncle Frank's Pizzeria from neighboring Dumont had just delivered three sausage and mushroom pizzas. Trudy grabbed the first slice, took a big bite, and said, "This is good! Jersey pete-zer is better than anything in New Yawk! They use fresh moots-a-rell. Ya know what I'm sayin'? Mangia, guys! Eat!"

The New Jersey unofficial, unabridged, dialect dictionary provides an interpretation of Trudy's food review. Don't pronounce the vowel at the end of food, like mozzarella or prosciutto. Pizza is always pete-zer. And don't forget the twenty-seventh letter of the alphabet – the silent 'g'. However, contrary to stereotypes portrayed in television sitcoms, people from Jersey never say Joisey.

Trudy was five-foot-five, one hundred twenty pounds of pure Italian charm. Tonight, she used a French barrette to keep her dark, shoulder-length hair behind her ears to display large, gold hoop earrings. Trudy had big brown eyes, beautiful long eyelashes and a wide smile. She was in a permanent state of happiness. Tonight Trudy wore tight Levi's jeans, a black silk blouse and running sneakers – Bergenfield casual elegance.

Chris and Gilbert sat at the bridge table with Trudy. Howie and Johnny ate their pizza in front of the big screen television and watched the Mets get trounced by the Phillies again. There would likely be another thrashing in in a few hours in the second game of the doubleheader. The Mets stunk, and the Phillies had their number, but Bergen County rooted for them anyway.

Trudy tallied up the contracts between bites. "Gilbert, I got good news and I got bad news. Da good news is that we have too many houses. I count thirty-five yesses and five maybes. Da bad news is that a dozen of them banded together and demanded more money. Vinnie Martini called me as their chief negotiator and demanded $6,000 per home to sign our deal."

Howie glared at Trudy and yelled from across the den. "Forget the Martinis. We don't need those crooks. We'll just buy fewer houses."

Trudy yelled, "Watch your mouth, Howie. That's my cousins you're disrespectin'. If Vinnie heard you, he'd put you in one of your client's wheelchairs – permanently!"

Howie maintenance never ended. Gilbert spoke like an exasperated father of fighting teenagers. "Hey! Calm down – both of you. Howie, every home that we don't buy costs us a hundred grand in profits. Without the Martini clan, we only have twenty-three houses. Do you really want to give up a million dollars of profit?

"We can deal with the Martinis, but not in an up-front payment. Maybe we could pay it a little later, like in a year when we have more money. I could ask the bank to sell the houses cheaper. Or lend us more money. As a last resort, we could ask the town to take a bigger haircut. There's a dozen ways to tackle this issue."

Johnny spoke after wolfing down a slice of pizza. "I wouldn't want to ask the town for more. The last thing we need is a closer look by Hector or Doug. And by the way, it looks like Hector may vote for the tax write-off."

Gilbert grabbed a second slice of pizza and opened a beer. "Johnny, you're right. I was thinking out loud. Trudy, call Vinnie. Ask him if he'll take two thousand now, two thousand next July and the rest in a note that he'll get in two years. I'll check with David. He may have some wiggle room."

Trudy called Vinnie Martini from her cell phone and started walking to the far side of the room. "Vinnie, it's your cousin, Trude. Whatcha' doin' to me? You're givin' me a heart condition!"

Gilbert dialed David Elliot from the speaker phone while the rest of the group listened in. "David. Gilbert here. You'll be happy to hear that the squatters are going for our deal. But a few people are costing a little more than we expected. I need some help from you. Can you reduce the house price by a few thousand to make this work?"

David answered, "Gilbert, you have a great deal already. I can't reduce the price, and I definitely cannot increase the mortgage loan. Besides, I already sent the signed term sheet to corporate. If we change anything, this will get held up. I thought you wanted to do this fast."

Gilbert pleaded, "David, we're tapped out. I'll have to buy fewer houses, if that's what you want."

David lowered his voice. "Gil, get off the speaker phone."

Gilbert picked up the phone handset, and said, "I'm sorry, David. Everyone here can be trusted."

David said sternly, "The fewer people who witness our conversation, the better. I don't want you to buy fewer houses. I actually prefer that you buy more. Headquarters likes the deal. They gave me authority to lend another $2 million. But I can't increase the mortgage amount per home. Those hundred percent financing days are over."

Gilbert said nonchalantly, "The $2 million won't help unless we find a way to increase the loan per home. I'll just have to cut back to twenty homes."

David protested, "No, no, no! Don't cut back. I'll get you the money. But there's a little catch. I wouldn't mind if you gave me a small fee to close this deal. When I say me, I mean me and not the bank.

"The bank will provide you a small home improvement credit line to help pay for some extra houses. For that, I think it would be fair if I earned a small percentage ownership in your little company, say twenty percent?"

Gilbert thought for a moment. It sounded like David was about to violate bank policy, if not the law. But Gilbert's hands were clean. He'd just have to find a way to route David's investment so that he could deny any involvement.

Gilbert walked down the hallway out of earshot. "I can sell you one LLC unit, which is the same as everyone else. It's closer to eight percent than twenty. But it's free to you only if we get this deal done and make the property transfers by next Friday. If I give you any more, the others will figure it out, and I don't think you want anyone to know about your involvement."

Gilbert spoke gravely, "Dave, so far, forgiving real estate taxes might be considered a petty offense. Maybe Johnny loses his council seat and gets his hand slapped. But this is a hanging sentence for you if you get caught. You understand?"

David said coolly, "Gilbert, save the lecture. I know what I'm doing. You don't get anything done by next Friday without me. I don't want to be greedy. Give me three units, and I will guarantee you close on time."

Gilbert ran the numbers in his head. The home improvement loan would help, but they were still short. They still needed Vinnie's cooperation to get to thirty homes. The two free partnership units given to Dave would cut into everyone's share of profits. However, David was absolutely guaranteeing that they would close the purchases by next Friday. David was also insinuating that they would not close without him.

With or without Vinnie's help, Gilbert had to deal with David. "I can do two units, and that's my final offer. You're gonna make a lot of money if this thing works."

David moaned and complained but eventually agreed to take two partnership units. Gilbert wasn't happy. David wasn't happy.

"David, you have to hide your ownership. Set up an LLC and offshore bank account. You know how. Don't use Howie. He'll figure out that you're in for free.

"Next, we'll make this look like you paid for your units. Howie is already moving everyone's money into an escrow account. When the money moves from escrow, I'll slip your ownership in. Does that work?"

David said, "Great minds think alike."

Gilbert returned to the den and spoke loudly, "David, I understand that Howie and your lawyers are progressing. If everyone works through the weekend, we can close next week. Thank you for acting so quickly."

Gilbert hung up the phone and started dancing an Irish jig. Across the room, Trudy was making animated hand gestures on her call with Vinnie. "Of course I'll send you manigott on Sunday. You know I make the best homemade gravy. I'll call you back in ten minutes."

Trudy hung up, and said to Gilbert, "Vinnie wants in."

Gilbert stopped dancing. "What exactly does 'in' mean?"

"Vinnie smelled a deal," Trudy said. "Your newspaper headline tipped him off. He said that until yesterday, the biggest headline had been FALL LEAF PICKUP THIS WEEK. I didn't tell him nothin', I swear. Said he wants in on the same terms as everyone else. I told him it was $15,000 a unit. He said he wants one unit for himself and one unit for his workers. He's payin' in cash – twenty dollar bills. Also, if you let him in, your proposal to pay the Martini clan $2,000 next year is okay."

Gilbert added it up. "The larger this group gets, the bigger the chance that we're gonna have a leak. Between Vinnie's and David's new deals, we can buy all thirty-five houses. Plus, Vinnie is muscle if we ever need it."

"Vinnie don't talk," Trudy said resolutely. "He's family. But, he said he wants to be awarded any home improvement projects for the houses. He has a buildin' contractor business, you know."

Gilbert looked at the group as if in thought. This decision required drama. "Okay, tell Vinnie he's in for two units. Same drill – set up an LLC in Florida and an offshore bank account. I'd run those twenties through the washing machine before cashing them. Call Vinnie and welcome him to the party."

Trudy interrupted with a laugh. "Vinnie isn't givin' you drug money, silly. He gets paid cash for certain construction jobs. It's his rainy-day money. I can deposit the cash in my business. The banks won't notice. You guys can do the same."

Gilbert smiled to himself. The bank might not notice an extra twenty grand deposited in Trudy's account. She had a good business. But the bank would be shocked if Howie or Chris deposited a fifth of that much.

Half of the battle had been won by signing up thirty-five short sales. That alone was a miracle. Now, the limited partners of Bergen Development had to act normal for two days until the town council voted on the tax abatement. Gilbert's job was to keep the troops calm. Seven partners had to act like nothing was happening.

"Everyone, I cannot stress enough the importance of keeping a low profile," Gilbert said. "We still have to win the battle at the town council. And we still have to get the bank to keep it together until we buy the homes. Please, keep quiet. Don't raise suspicions. And, Trudy, you're in charge of miracles. Go to church and pray that the news about Pierre doesn't leak."

The partners left Gil's home in a great mood – except Johnny. He looked at today's victory a bit differently. If Pierre's plans expanded, Johnny could go broke. Eighty percent of his store profits came from selling Jake's crabgrass killer concoction. And he had a warehouse full of it. A thousand customers were about to disappear in the next two weeks, and a $100,000 of sales would evaporate with it.

Gilbert could warn Johnny about keeping quiet until he was blue in the face. Johnny had to take care of Johnny first. As he drove home, he made two decisions. First, he would dump as much of Jake's crabgrass killer as possible in the next week. Second, he would sell the store to some sucker who would underestimate the Pierre impact. He had been planning for a long time to move to his bay-front cottage in Lavallette. This would just step up the timeline.

CHAPTER 21

MAY 4, 2011

Gilbert was in such a great mood that he decided to walk to Ben's for breakfast. It was springtime. The sun was shining. Birds were chirping. Tulips and daffodils were blooming.

Gilbert took a shortcut through the St. John's parking lot where grade school children wearing plaid uniforms played while waiting for classes to start. As he turned the corner in front of the church entrance, Gilbert saw Chris across the street on a ladder hoisting a wide sale banner over Johnny's storefront.

SUPER SALE ON JAKE'S WEED KILLER

Gilbert hustled across the street, grabbed the sign from Chris's hand and burst into the store.

"What are you doing?" Gilbert screamed. "The town council meeting is tomorrow night. Which part of 'keep a low profile' did you not understand? Do you want everyone to know?"

"I'm just puttin' up some sale signs," Johnny said defiantly. "I gotta unload this stuff before the Pierre deal goes public. Nobody's gonna connect the two."

Gilbert lowered his voice to preteen admonishment level. "They absolutely will connect the dots, you idiot. How do you think it looks when a town councilman sells his entire weed killer inventory two days before a town council meeting and a week before Pierre signs a thousand homes? Next, they'll be scrutinizing the tax write-off. Your sale ends now! This minute!" It wasn't a request. It was an order.

"Gilbert, I'm ruined if I don't get rid of this stuff," Johnny pleaded. "I got $250,000 of it sittin' in my warehouse. I gotta move it or I'm broke. And then I gotta sell this dump of a store, too."

A quarter million was a big number. Gilbert appreciated Johnny's issues, but had to keep him calm until they closed the purchase with the bank. The store was a rat trap, and Johnny had done nothing to improve it for ten years. Johnny used the old funeral parlor business strategy – people only shopped at Johnny's because they had to.

Gilbert said, "Alright, Johnny. I understand. Hold off on the sale signs until the town council meeting is over. The first order of business is to forgive the real estate taxes. Otherwise, you have to come up with more money. Agreed?"

Johnny gave a reluctant nod.

"Johnny, take my advice. When you finally start your sale, don't advertise like you're going out of business. Do the opposite. Tell everyone there's a shortage this year and that they have to get their orders in quick. No one cares about saving twenty bucks, but everyone cares about getting shut out in a panic.

"Also, if you give me two weeks, I think I can help you sell this place. I know someone who might be interested."

Johnny got excited. "Who is it? Someone I know?"

Gilbert had no intention of disclosing Allie's name. Johnny would call her within ten minutes and scare her away. "Just give me some time. Do you have Hector lined up for tomorrow's vote?"

Johnny calmed down a little. There was no doubt that Gilbert was connected in town. He said, "Hector was askin' a lotta questions, but I'm pretty sure he'll vote for it. He wanted to check the backgrounds of the buyers, but I told him it was a private hedge fund located in the Cayman Islands.

"Luckily, David Elliot is out on business today, or Hector woulda spoken to him. Regardless, he's convinced the federal government is never gonna fix the housing crisis, and we have to cure this locally."

"Okay Johnny. Just keep your cool. We'll sell your stuff and your store," Gilbert said calmly. He could have been mistaken for the character Ice in *West Side Story*. The only thing missing was the snapping of two dozen fingers behind him.

CHAPTER 22

MAY 4

The month of May marks the beginning of New Jersey's brutal six-month hay fever season. Bart sat at Ben's armed with a box of tissues, a can of saline spray and a half dozen hay fever and cold remedies. He wheezed, "I'm sure that medicine companies fertilize the Meadowlands to increase the pollen count. And I also think they're using genetic engineering to breed more potent pollen, too!"

JB and Bret groaned. Michael, Decker and Allie ignored him.

Bart was a physically unimpressive 150 pounds of thirty-year-old accountancy hiding behind a bushy moustache. He was the town pessimist and conspiracy theorist. Unfortunately, every once in a blue moon, one of Bart's theories proved true, which just encouraged him more. Bart was a bank auditor, a job custom-fit for his persistent paranoia.

"You guys never listen to me," Bart said in a pouty voice. "This time I'm sure I'm right. I saw crop dusters spraying over Secaucus last week. What else could they be spraying? And ask yourself – Why would the New Jersey legislature designate this mess as an ecosystem? The cold medicine companies must've lobbied them."

Commuters to New York City drove the New Jersey Turnpike past the Meadowlands swamp every day. Football fans recognize the name for the stadium that was home to the Giants and Jets. However, not far outside the stadium walls amid a dozen industrial towns sits 8,400 acres of heavily polluted muck populated by reeds, mosquitos, and old tires. The state and federal EPA had been trying to clean up the toxic soil for thirty years.

JB snickered, "Bart, did you think that they just might be spraying for mosquitos?"

It was a rhetorical question, but Bart began to respond. JB halted him and said, "I will grant you one thing. Fifty years ago they could have developed the Meadowlands into waterfront property. Instead, they declared it a sacred wetland. And they made it worse by creating the reservoir up in Oradell. Now the water doesn't flow south anymore. It's a tidal pool of toxicity."

Decker cheerfully chirped, "I was hiking one of the Meadowlands trails last month and saw an Osprey. The birds must like it!"

JB laughed derisively. "Decker, only you would take joy on a nature walk through one of the most uninhabitable areas in America.

"You know, most of South Florida in the sixties looked just like the Meadowlands. Instead of rats, Florida had gators and snakes. Real estate developers filled in the swamp and created a bunch of lakes. Now, Palm Beach County has a hundred golf courses. And one thing that Bergen County needs more than anything else is golf courses."

Steve Allen, the town pharmacist, joined the table. Known as Shorty, he was blond, handsome and very tall – nearly six-and-a-half feet, which perfectly explained the nickname. He was also an extremely eligible single dad in his fifties. "I heard you guys. Hay fever and head colds are worse than ever. The line in my store is ten deep to buy Clariton, Sudafed, nose spray, tissues, you name it. I can't keep the stuff in stock. It's a sniveling fraternity. Kappa Kappa Achoo!"

Johnny leaned over from the adjacent table. "You know, it ain't the Meadowlands. Cattails don't shed a lot of pollen. That crabgrass on your lawn is the biggest source of hay fever in town. It germinates hundreds of times a year.

"By the way, I haven't announced it yet, but I'm having an early season sale on crabgrass killer in two weeks. Jake's Seed & Supply has a newer stronger formula this year, but they expect a limited supply. Get your orders in fast before we run out!"

Gilbert could make Johnny take down the sale sign, but he couldn't stop his door-to-door sales pitch. Johnny was so busy pushing chemicals that he missed the voluptuous and beautiful Panama Blonde walking by the table and winking at Bret. She wore a light gray skirt and white pleated blouse under a navy, cotton cardigan sweater. However, no amount of material could conceal Panama's busty figure. Fifty sets of eyes tried to act nonchalant as they followed Panama to her table next to the juke box.

Bret joined Panama, and the wandering eyes returned to their meals. The calming hum of breakfast being served returned to the air. Within minutes, the peace was broken as Misty reached the cash register and began her daily harassment of Ben. She demanded her latte. She complained. She rolled her eyes. She created yet another drama scene with manila budget envelopes. Every day – it was the same routine.

Satisfied that she had ruined Ben's day, Misty walked to JB's table. "Who's tarantula talking to?"

"By tarantula, I presume that you mean the lovely Catherine Mulcahy?" JB said. Most patrons kept a safe distance from Misty. JB, however, considered Misty an occasional source of entertainment and controversy. It broke up the boredom. At times, he even encouraged her bad behavior.

Misty laughed. "Lovely, my ass. Anyway, who's the cute guy she's talking to?"

JB flashed his devilish grin. "Ah, you're here earlier than usual today. That's Bret, our resident Wall Street M&A lawyer. He works at Montauk & Malibu. Please don't destroy his life by introducing yourself."

Misty fluttered her eyelashes in her best imitation of Scarlett O'Hara. "Why, JB, you flatter me. Why would sweet, little ol' Misty ruin such a pretty boy's life?"

Misty took a seat at a small booth with direct line-of-sight to Bret's table. Fifteen minutes later, Panama left the deli, and Misty leapt across the room and landed with soft catlike feet in Bret's booth. From across the room, Misty could be seen smiling, posing, laughing, leaning in and acting utterly charming. After several minutes, she handed Bret her card and left with a swivel of her hips. She turned and caught Bret watching her ass.

Bret returned to the board table dazed by Misty's arrow. JB teased, "Bret, I didn't know that Ben's Deli served sweet and sour on its menu."

The table sang a low chorus of *heh-hehs* and *tee-hees*. Bret blushed. "Misty was just asking for a little friendly advice over an inheritance she received. She wants to meet me at Tommy Fox's tonight to talk about how to manage the money. I told her I didn't get home until eight, and she said that was perfect. Said her yoga class ended then."

"That girl is truly amazing." JB shook his head in disbelief. "That's a new Ben's record —three total fabrications in three minutes. I can assure you the following: first, there is no inheritance; second, there is no money to manage; and third, she definitely doesn't do yoga.

"I know that there's no money because her ex-husband stiffed her in a pre-nup. She's living at home with mommy and daddy. And there's no way she's doing yoga in a heated roomful of women with hairy legs. The humidity would ruin her makeup.

"No, my dear friend. That's a husband-reconnaissance drone, and she has targeted you as number four."

Allie counseled, "Bret, listen to JB. She's more trouble than you can handle."

Bret took the punishment. "Hey, I'm a big M&A lawyer on Wall Street. Surely you don't think I can be manipulated by a small-town girl. You lovelorn advisors have a nice day. I have to get to work before gridlock hits the Holland Tunnel. See you guys tomorrow."

Allie moved into Bret's seat. She asked quietly, "JB, have you heard about any businesses for sale? I'm getting' desperate. I looked at a few business broker listings. It's all gas stations, failed franchises and machine shops. I thought that if I bought a downtown retail business, Marty could come straight to the store after school."

"Retail? You're kidding, right? You'll work more hours than you do now," JB warned.

"I've thought that through," Allie said. "No one will die if I leave a cash register for an hour. But, I can't get away from the hospital during my shift. Ever. I work in critical care.

"The school called me three times this year to deal with Marty problems, and I couldn't leave my post. When I moved to the night shift, his behavior got worse. Marty's my first priority. I hafta to help my kid get through these issues he's havin'. He needs me around him during the day. They're threatenin' to throw him out of school, and they mean it."

"Okay. I can try to help you," JB sighed. "Do you have any money saved?"

"I think I have enough," Allie replied. "My 401k is pretty decent. Holy Name matched my contributions all of these years. Luckily, I was outta the stock market when it crashed.

JB, I don't wanna own a candy store, either. It has to be somethin' that I can expand with creative ideas."

JB nodded. "Okay, Allie, I got it. No gift shops or greeting card stores. And I'm guessing you don't want to buy a bar. I'll corner Hector and see if he knows anything for sale. He should be back today for the town council meeting. He's looking for entrepreneurs to reinvent downtown. And we have enough lawyers and accountants around here to give you advice on how to buy a company."

Allie said thanks and left. Gilbert had overheard the conversation and thought, *I just need her to stay out of Johnny's sight for another week, and then I can convince her to buy Johnny's headache.*

CHAPTER 23

MAY 4

Traffic was light as Bret headed home through the Lincoln Tunnel. By the time he reached the turnpike entrance, he had decided to accept Misty's invitation. What was there to lose? It was a harmless cocktail.

Then JB's and Allie's warnings reverberated through his head. As he reached the Teaneck Road exit, he changed his mind. Misty was too much drama. Way too much trouble.

But at the Memorial Field stop sign, he declared himself undecided.

Minutes later, his Audi drew near the rear entrance of Tommy Fox's. He tapped the brakes, thought for a minute, and bravely turned into the parking lot. Maybe he needed a little drama in his life. Her invitation was noncommittal. How much trouble can there be in sharing a drink or two? He was a half-hour late. She probably wouldn't even be there. He hadn't eaten yet, anyway.

Misty was sitting in a booth in the dining room out of sight from the bar. She sipped a near-empty glass of wine and pretended to be texting on her cell phone. One thing about Misty, she was always glammed. Her hair and makeup were perfect. She was covered in gold jewelry – love-knot earrings, a necklace with a large gold heart, a wrist full of gold bangles, and a Movado gold watch. Misty may be poor, but she *never* dressed the part.

Misty feigned surprise when Bret approached her table. She instantly became charming, bubbly, smart and witty. The waitress refilled Misty's wine glass and brought Bret a glass of Johnny Walker Black with a splash of water.

She didn't trash a single person. Misty spoke highly of Bret's friends at Ben's. She loved JB's wit and sarcasm. Michael was delightful. Decker was a gentleman. Allie was a sweetheart. She asked Bret about his job and what he liked. They both ordered the Penne Vodka and shared a bottle of chardonnay.

Bret talked about the football Giants. Misty said she loved sports and always watched the games on Sunday.

Bret said he had tickets to the symphony, but rarely had time to go. Misty said she loved the symphony, but didn't have a box this year.

Bret talked about planning a President's Day ski weekend in Vail. Misty said she loved the outdoors and often skied at Hunter Mountain.

Bret said that he might move into the city one day because the daily commute was tough. Misty said she loved the city and liked to stroll in Central Park on Sunday afternoons after visiting the Metropolitan Museum.

At ten o'clock, she touched his hand affectionately and said, "Bret, I need to go. I have an early meeting tomorrow. It was wonderful talking with you." She refused an escort to her car, telling Bret to finish his dinner.

Despite his appearance as a sophisticated, thirty-five-year-old Wall Street executive, Bret wasn't very experienced when it came to women. As handsome as he was, he'd never had time for relationships. He worked a constant 80-plus hours a week. Developing a normal relationship with a normal girl wasn't in the cards. He dated here and there, but not many women in New York were tolerant of an absentee boyfriend, even if he did make a lot of money.

Also, Bret was not a blueblood, Harvard-educated lawyer at the greatest investment bank in the world. Bret was a hard-working, middle-class guy who worked his way through law school and joined a third-tier bank.

He succeeded at Montauk & Malibu because he was incredibly efficient at creating work product, and was the fastest contract writer in a team of forty lawyers. He'd never make partner. His last name was not Morgan or Pierpont or Merrill. Bret was destined to be a general counsel at some corporation somewhere some day after the firm had squeezed all remaining life from his soul and turned him into a tired sack of bones.

Bret thought the dinner went rather well. It seemed that they had a lot in common. Misty had a terrible reputation around Ben's, but that crowd could be rough on someone they didn't like. Three divorces was a lot of baggage, but he was no catch either with his ridiculous work schedule.

But there was definitely one overwhelming, overriding reason to date Misty. She was one great-looking girl. Plus, she was no wallflower.

Misty laughed as she drove away in her squeaking 2001 Geo Metro. She hated skiing, hated sports, and detested the Giants. The last time she sat through a symphony, it had been performed by her high school orchestra. And it would be a cold day in July in Hell before she moved into the city.

Bret knew his way around Wall Street and billion-dollar mergers and high-stakes finance. He knew nothing about high-stakes romance. He had no immune system. He'd never learned adult-relationship survival skills. He had no ability to fight unsuspecting attacks. He had no counterpunch.

This was Misty's area of expertise. In the world of women and relationships, Bret was essentially an animal raised in captivity. He had been released into the wild, defenseless against female predators.

None of these childish men's hobbies matter, thought Misty. *This is just the courting ritual. Eventually, all men need to be told what to do, how to dress, and what to do with their free time and their money. And that's what I'm really good at!*

By the time she was done with him, Bret would hate football, abhor skiing, loathe the symphony, and detest the idea of living in New York. Bloomingdale's and antique shopping are the only ways to spend Sunday afternoons.

CHAPTER 24

MAY 5, 2011

On Thursday evening at 7:00 PM, Hector stood behind the podium flanked by six town councilmen. The first few rows were filled by two dozen local business owners. A hundred town residents were scattered throughout the high school auditorium.

Hector was losing the battle of downtown and had resorted to cheerleading to revive the once prosperous shopping area. Hector called the meeting to order. "I've invited you, our most prominent local businessmen and women, to this meeting to encourage you to work with the town council to improve the enterprise zone. We must attract shoppers to town and continue to improve business and housing property values."

The town had created an enterprise zone to battle the decline, but the Paramus malls had inflicted their damage long ago. People rarely shopped for anything but convenience items in town. Bergenfield was six miles from the heartland of American malls, and every conceivable type of luxury and sale-priced merchandise was a fifteen minute drive away. Shopping was a sport in Paramus. It was drudgery in Bergenfield.

The town had commissioned a strategic study of the town's retail options. Hector waved the report as he spoke. "You cannot compete with the big box stores at what they do best. Instead, create market niches! Sell something that they cannot get at the mall. Let's build a reputation in Bergenfield as the place to buy really cool stuff. Our downtown is accessible. It has lots of parking. You're blessed with traffic. Your potential customers drive past your stores every day. We've given you all the zoning variances you need. Now it's your turn. Make that traffic want to stop. Invest a little. Improve your storefronts. Change your product offerings.

"Look at Ridgewood. Their shopping district looks quaint. Fifty years ago, those stores looked exactly like ours. They just spent a little money to improve the facades." Hector had absolutely no idea what the upscale Ridgewood stores looked like fifty years ago.

Harvey Wendell, the town baker stood up. "Hector, we rent our stores. Real estate partnerships own the space and they haven't put a dime into these stores in decades. Plus, the paths from the parking lots to the street are downright frightening."

"I understand, but you have long-term leases," Hector countered. "You should make the improvements. Band together and create a theme. I'll make a deal with you. If you commit to improve the storefronts, I'll get the town to create a strolling mall with no vehicle traffic from Clinton Avenue to Church Street.

"And Harvey, I agree with you about the entranceways. Our consultants concluded that the alleys scare the heck out of shoppers. I'll work on a plan to create a shopping walkway connecting the parking lots to the main road. We'll put in pavers and trees, and it'll be a nice place to stroll and shop.

"But somehow, you're going to have to convert these low-end stores into higher-value cafes, boutiques and specialty stores. Downtown real estate has been so cheapened that a group of women could afford to rent a valuable storefront to form a knitting club. They don't even sell anything there."

Bobby Middleman stood in mock protest. "How dare you! The Dangerous Knitter is my store. Ironic name, don't you think?"

The crowd gave a hearty laugh. "Hector, you're missing the boat," Bobby chided. "Knitting is a retirement sport, and half of this town is near retirement. If you want shoppers strolling downtown, then quilting, knitting and needlepoint should be your biggest attractions. You should visit Sisters in Oregon. Every weekend, it's crawling with thousands of quilt fanatics."

Hector calmed the room. "Okay Bobby, maybe you have an idea. Let's work on this together and come up with a plan. And let's invite the real estate owners in on this, too."

This discussion continued for another half hour, and Johnny True Value was growing impatient. Hector was goading the bakery into developing French pastries. He suggested that someone should open an old-fashioned ice cream parlor like they used to have at Jahn's on Route 4. He asked Walter to add video games to his record store. Everyone booed.

"Gamers play online, Hector," shouted Walter.

Finally, the pitch came to an end and the room cleared except for the town council. The meetings were televised on the local cable network. Gilbert watched anxiously from home.

Hector opened the discussion about the short sale. "As I understand the proposal, this buyer is asking us to forgive $6,000 of the $8,000 per home in past due real estate taxes on thirty-five homes that are in default.

"They'll pay us $2,000 per home. We'll receive $70,000 this year, and the houses will start paying taxes regularly. However, the town has to write off $200,000. That's a lot of money. However, if we wait a year, the homes will be another $100,000 behind on payments. This will never fix itself unless we agree to take action.

"Moreover, there's an intangible at stake. These homes are depressing the value of the other houses in the market. The defaulters are not taking care of their properties. If we wait too long, we could be living in a ghetto.

"Johnny explained to me that First Second Third Bank is writing off a substantial amount of mortgage balance to get this done. It's always nice to have good company when you make a decision. David Elliot is a respected banker.

"I'm not aware of any covenants in our municipal bond agreements that prevent us from doing this. I'm inclined to approve this. However, I'd like to meet the buyers and talk with David, too."

Johnny stood and spoke from his table. "As I told you, the buyer's a hedge fund from the Cayman Islands. It's a small deal for them, and they gave us a take it or leave it proposal for tonight's meetin'. If we don't approve it, they'll go on to the next town."

Gilbert let loose a sigh of relief. Johnny was performing well.

Hector nodded. "Johnny, I think I agree with you. This is an opportunity if we act quickly. The town council has reviewed the written proposal from Bergen Development Fund. Is there any discussion?"

Doug Pearson was a CPA and the council's authority on finances. He argued, "The town has a priority lien. No one can sell their house without paying us. I really think we should turn down the offer. It's too much money to concede."

"Doug, you're partly right," Hector responded. "We do have a priority lien. At the same time, these houses will never be sold if we all stick to our guns. The bank is writing off a lot of mortgage balances to get his done. They know that if they clear out this mess, the rest of their portfolio will improve and all of their customers will be better off.

"There are millions of homes in America in the same situation. Only short sales solve the problem. We should take the same attitude that David Elliot is taking. Let's fix this mess and put it behind us. But you should vote with your conscience. Does anyone else have something to say?"

Hector paused for thirty seconds. No one spoke up.

"Okay, discussion is over," Hector continued, "Let's put this to a vote. All in favor of the proposal to participate in a short sale of up to thirty-five homes to be named and write off up to $6,000 per home in real estate taxes, say aye!"

Four councilmen said aye; Doug abstained. Trudy had conspicuously left the room before the vote. Hector declared, "The resolution passes. Howie, please provide a legal opinion that this doesn't violate our charter or any of our loan agreements. If there is no other business, I declare the meeting closed."

Following the meeting, Trudy, Howie, Johnny and Chris met Gilbert at Tommy Fox's. After the waitress took the drink order, Howie started to complain. "They're asking for legal opinions. I'm going to lose my license over this."

Trudy chided Howie, "Stop being a big baby. You're not givin' an opinion dat you're a crook. You're only sayin' da town is allowed to do this. Am I right, or am I right?"

Howie wasn't calming down. "Yeah, but I'm writing all of the documents and setting up your LLCs for you. I'm the most exposed here."

Chris said quietly, "Howie, your license is the last thing you have to worry about if this gets out. We're all going to burn for this. They'll run us out of town. Drink up your beer, and start dreaming about how you're going to spend your profits in two years. Me, I'm buying a sailboat."

Gilbert reflected on the moment. They had accomplished two incredible feats in less than ten days. He'd feel a lot better in a week when the sale was complete.

As they relaxed, the band played *I Shot the Sherriff* by Bob Marley. The moment was not lost on the table.

CHAPTER 25

MAY 6, 2011

Ben's Deli was bustling with energy. Eggs were frying. Bacon was sizzling. Rye bread was toasting. High test caffeine was percolating.

Ben's was not quite a diner. A New Jersey diner is a revered institution where highly-efficient waitresses serve hot meals and great desserts to customers in booths equipped with individual juke boxes. A deli, on the other hand, is a place to order takeout tuna, hot corned beef or pastrami sandwiches accompanied by a fantastic tasting pickle and German potato salad. Hold the pig's feet and pickled eggs with that tuna on rye! Ben's was a deli-diner – great hot food, one huge classic juke box, and tables but no waitresses.

Ten years ago, Ben had used his life savings to purchase a bankrupt cafe. It was a rough start, but Lady Luck found her way to his doorstep. New Jersey Transit built a transfer station in Secaucus for New York commuters. Ben's Deli was Point A on the path from Bergen County to the transfer station. Business boomed, and eventually Ben hired a crew of hardworking Central Americans from Costa Rica and Nicaragua to cook while he ran the register and entertained customers.

Ben quickly recognized the changes in his customer base and added creature comforts to keep the crowd happy. Five flat screen televisions played STCK-TV, CNN and FOX Business Network. Wi-Fi service was free. Starbuck's coffee was in demand. Eight glass front refrigerators carried over a hundred varieties of beverages and bottled water. You could still get an egg cream at Ben's Deli, for those who remember what an egg cream was. The ten-cent plain cost a dollar, however. Prices have gone up.

After the morning crowd had left, Gilbert and Albert grabbed breakfast and sat in a booth. Albert ignored his food and anxiously began the conversation. "Gilbert, haf you made any progress? It's over a veek now since I paid you. I must see an action plan! How are you going to deliver contracts on 1,000 homes? How do you plan to do zis?"

Gilbert knew the question was coming. He needed to stall Albert for another week until they closed the purchase.

"There are three ways to get this done," Gilbert said, keeping his tone calm. "First, the slower and more secretive way is to use our network to contact individuals they know. Think of it like a Bergenfield viral network. This could take two months."

"Zat is too long!" Albert pleaded.

"Well, second, we could advertise to the town," Gilbert said. "We can place an article in the front page of the *Bergenfield Valley News* and announce a recruiting meeting. Then we have our army help persuade each homeowner to sign the paperwork. Unfortunately, this would raise some objections, particularly from the mayor. He'll be against this project, I can assure you."

"No, no. No ads!" Albert protested. "Not yet. After ve sign up zie homes, it vill be okay to tell people who ve are. But not yet. Vhat is alternative three?"

Gilbert had held his preferred solution to the end. "The third way is more discreet, but it costs money. I have a team of workers ready to go. You pay them $100 per home to sign up sellers. They can do it quickly, perhaps in two weeks. It won't be in the papers. These guys know the townsfolk and have a great way of talking with the people. They're very convincing. You can take the $100 out of the $500 advance payment to the homeowners, so it won't cost you anything."

Albert considered the plans and agreed to option three. He left Ben's slightly bewildered as to why more progress had not yet been made. Gilbert thought as Albert walked away, *Vinnie Martini and his family are going to make more money than any of us on this deal the way this is going.*

The big, organized mob was long gone in New Jersey, but small pockets existed everywhere. They had moved from the rackets to Internet gambling. They still controlled the ports and the waste disposal businesses. Loan sharking still persisted. But to most people, they were out of sight except for movies and television shows.

People still thought that guys like Vinnie Martini were connected. It was a macabre romantic fantasy. There are mafia wannabes all over the Jersey Shore during the summer. You didn't want to cross the one who was actually in a family, or "made". If you were smart, you stayed clear of all of them. But connected or not, Vinnie and his cousins were excellent at organizing and getting things done, especially when a nice fee was involved. Gilbert would talk with Vinnie after the homes were safely purchased and not a second sooner.

CHAPTER 26

MAY 6

Gilbert gave a disapproving glance at Averill Winthrop as he left his meeting with Albert. Averill had set up shop for the day at a table out of sight from Ben's register. He was meeting with one of his stock brokerage clients.

If a person could wear a look of covetousness, it was Averill. He stared at a person's wallet like Casanova looked at a woman's body. He wanted your money and was figuring how to get it.

He wasn't particularly unattractive, but he wasn't handsome either. He stood five-feet-eight and weighed maybe a hundred sixty pounds. Averill had a full head of brown hair with all of the style of a two-dollar haircut. He constantly played with his pride and joy, a handlebar moustache which fortunately cloaked his stained teeth. He wore a suit, but the shirt was frayed at the collar, and the pocket on his suit pants had a small tear. In summary, Averill looked like somebody who endeavored to dress up and had failed miserably.

Averill was a broker at Long, Mopey, North, Oscar and Penn, better known as LMNOP. The penny stock brokerage firm rented a small office at the end of Wall Street for the sole purpose of putting "Wall Street" on its letterhead. However, Wall Street had long ago become a business rather than a place, and most investment banks had moved uptown or to the West Side years ago.

Averill was the lone broker at the Bergenfield branch of LMNOP. His compliance supervisor worked across the river and had no intention of ever visiting the shabby office. The furniture was scarred and broken. The rugs had been worn through. The offices had an odd rank smell and were so embarrassing that Averill met his clients at Ben's.

This morning, Averill sat with a middle-aged Filipino client and gave his sales pitch. "Mrs. Suarez, I know that Apple at $350 per share is a lot of dollars, but you shouldn't think like that. The company could easily split the stock ten-for-one and it would be $35 a share. But this stock is going to $500 soon."

Averill had inherited four hundred accounts from a retiring stockbroker whose clients had all owned Apple stock in the 1980s. The accounts were dormant. The customers never called Averill because they had no idea who he was. Averill never called the customers because he couldn't make any money on accounts that didn't actively trade.

A month ago, Averill had received a call from a customer asking if her mother should sell her Apple stock. Averill had been irritated that a dead account was distracting him from surfing the web. Averill told her to sell so at least he could earn a commission. When the stock jumped five percent the next day, the former customer gave Averill an earful. "Why did you tell me to sell? You oaf!"

Averill looked at the dormant accounts and realized he had hundreds of new cold-calling targets. His customers were sitting on $50 million of Apple stock ready to trade and earn commissions. Most of them had probably forgotten about the shares when Apple's stock price slid to the low teens.

He studied the Apple stock price history. Everyone was jumping on the iPod band-wagon. Business news shows talked nonstop about the iPhone, the hottest technology in the consumer marketplace.

Averill was at his cold-calling best that day four weeks ago. Averill dialed an account and read from a script. He turned the phone's earpiece away so he couldn't hear any cus-tomer protests. It was a tactic taught to him by an old vacuum cleaner salesman.

"Hello, Mrs. Elmira. This is Averill Winthrop. I'm the new senior financial advisor on your brokerage account. I see that you continue to hold Apple stock. That has been a very smart decision. Our firm has come out with a revised buy recommendation. We believe this stock could go to a thousand dollars. We recommend that you use your margin buying power and double down on this fantastic stock. How many shares would you like to buy today?"

Everything that Averill said in the phone calls was untrue. His firm had no research department, so it had no recommendation. Not even his name was true. He had adopted Averill as his first name because it sounded like someone who would work at JC Montague. His real first name was Barry, and he hated it.

Mrs. Elmira owned 500 shares that she had bought for $20,000 in 1985. Now the stock was worth $175,000. Averill convinced her to buy another 500 shares on margin. He then asked for a referral for another customer.

At the end of four weeks, Averill had convinced half of the revived accounts to increase their Apple holdings. He convinced the other half of the customers to sell Apple and buy other stocks. Either way, he was intent on making a commission. He called the hundreds of new referrals and sold them more Apple. Apple fever had come to Bergenfield!

CHAPTER 27

MAY 11, 2011

The loan closing and home sale was being held in the First Second Third Bank basement conference room. Hundreds of boxes containing the old defaulted mortgage documents sat outside the conference room. No wonder the banks couldn't foreclose on a bad loan. It could take months to find the right promissory note and deed.

Early in the day, the teams quickly suffered paperwork fatigue and nearly conceded defeat. It was hopeless finding the existing notes and deeds for each home. Gilbert and David agreed that they could still close if the bank guaranteed title.

Scattered around the floor of the conference room were thirty-five separate loan closing binders each with two hundred pages of new notes, deeds, affidavits, quitclaims, contracts, rental agreements, waivers and estoppels.

It was total chaos. The bank lawyers and Howie were overwhelmed, but the closing process was not really the bailiwick of lawyers. Betty, the paralegal and notary, was clearly in charge. She had hired two temporary paralegals for the day from an online staffing agency. The temps did their best to make copies and organize the binders.

Howie went outside every half hour to smoke a cigarette. The bank lawyers felt equally helpless and joined Howie in the alleyway.

After six hours of shuffling paper and signing documents, the mountain of paper on the conference table was still growing. Gilbert watched the organized chaos, looked at his watch, and his eyes laser-beamed toward Howie.

"Has David signed the deeds yet?"

Howie was a disheveled, frantic mess. "I have to sign the rental agreements and quit-claims first. We have to create filing binders. The bank won't release the deeds until we transfer the money. We'll never close today!"

Gilbert put his hand on Howie's shoulder to calm him. "Howie, I need you to focus. Once we have a signed deed, we own the property. Nothing else matters. Transfer the deeds, get them recorded, and deal with this other stuff later.

"Don't worry about the leases. If our new tenants cashed our check, they are bound. If they don't sign, we evict them. Just get to the county courthouse before it closes. Give David Elliot instructions to transfer the money. Then he'll hand you the deeds. Go. Now, Howie!"

A dazed Howie stood and left the conference room to find David Elliot.

CHAPTER 28

MAY 11

Not more than two minutes later, Howie returned to the conference room white as a ghost. He whispered to Gilbert, "We have a problem. You'd better go talk with David."

Gilbert hustled up the stairs and entered the corner office. He took the seat across from David, who sat smugly chewing on an unlit cigar. "Howie says there's an issue," Gilbert frowned. "Is the bank reneging on the deal?"

David displayed a sinister grin. "Yeah, we might. There's no way we're closing today, and maybe not this week either. I'm not sure that we like the terms anymore."

Gilbert didn't bother to protest. On the surface, David was the nice town banker. But he had a darker side, and Gilbert had dealt with that too. "Okay, David, what does the bank want? I told you that we have limited capital. If you guys want more money for each house, we just buy fewer homes."

David leaned forward. "The bank is fine. I told you in our meeting that I wanted three partnership units, and you squeezed me to two. Well, now I want four. Or we don't close."

Gilbert looked at his iPhone. Time was running out if they were going to record the deeds today. "David. That is beyond outrageous. It's forty percent of the company. I'll go to your bosses. They'll close the deal. And they'll run you out of the bank!"

David shot him an evil look. "How do you know which boss to call? Maybe they're in on this, too. Why do you think I need the extra units? Besides, if you do anything to hurt me, I'll blow your cover. The citizens will be running you out of town with pitchforks. I suggest that you give me the units and be glad I didn't ask for more."

Gilbert began to think. It wasn't the first time he'd faced a shakedown. In the end, greed was often the motivator to get deals done. Gilbert made a quick calculation. He knew his way around partnership agreements. He could easily redefine the partnership terms anyway he wanted including what a unit was. He would just double everyone's number of units. Trudy and the council would now get two units, and David wouldn't know until it was too late to complain. That's what he gets for not asking for a copy of the partnership agreement.

"Okay, David. You and I can threaten and bluff all we want," Gilbert said in a faux defeated voice. "In the end, neither of us is going public. There's too much money at stake. I'll give you three units. I can't do four."

David gave a creepy smile and fanned the stack of signed deeds in the air. "Gilbert, this is my last hurrah. This bank won't be paying me much longer the way things are going. I don't want to be greedy. Three units will do. However, I'm taking a small fee out of the escrow account for my personal time and expenses. Let's say ten thousand dollars is fair."

Gilbert decided that it wasn't fair, but he took the offer. He signed the wire transfer authorization and grabbed the signed deeds from David's hands. He did not shake hands or say goodbye. Their friendship was over.

CHAPTER 29

MAY 11

Gilbert rushed from David's office and looked at his phone again. It was nearly 3:00 PM. He called downstairs and told Howie to hurry to the front entrance. Howie ran outside with Betty the paralegal in tow. Gilbert was holding the signed deeds standing next to a black Lincoln MKX.

"Here's your ride. The driver is going to take the New Bridge Road route to Hackensack. After you cross the Hackensack River, you'll be ten minutes from the county courthouse. Now hurry up and good luck! If there's traffic, get out of the car and run the last mile! You have to record these today before David shakes us down again."

Howie and Betty jumped in the car and were flattened against the back seat as the driver sped south on Washington Avenue. After turning right on Clinton, the driver mounted a flashing red light on the dashboard. Cars parted like the Red Sea believing they were yielding to an unmarked police car. The SUV crossed the railroad tracks in mid-air and turned left on Woodbine Road on two wheels. Twenty-five minutes later, Howie rushed into the deed recording office at One Bergen County Plaza.

The staff at the clerk's office allowed Howie and Betty to stay past the four o'clock closing time. Howie slumped in a chair while Betty and the county staff began to process the deeds.

At five o'clock, the homes were officially held in the name of Bergen Development Company. Howie was exhausted. He called Gilbert. "We made it, but I'm not done. We have a week's worth of paperwork to finish. I'm going back to the bank."

Gilbert was in a festive mood. "Howie, stop! You're not filing paperwork tonight. You're meeting us for a closing party at Tommy Fox's. Get your ass over here!"

A half hour later, Howie entered the private party room at Tommy Fox's Public House. Johnny True Value handed him a glass of burgundy and gave the first of a succession of toasts on their newfound prosperity.

After a few drinks and much backslapping, Trudy stood and clinked her wine glass to get everyone's attention. "Howie, we never coulda closed this deal without you. I know you feel unappreciated, but we love you, sort of."

Trudy handed Howie an envelope. Howie was shocked to find a gift certificate from Jos. A. Banks. Trudy squeaked, "They're havin' a two-for-one suit sale this week. Gilbert and I are gonna help you shop. Somethin' other than brown. Okay?"

The table took turns cracking jokes at Howie's expense. They had considered other gifts: a membership in Hair For Men; a vacuum cleaner for his office; a larger yarmulke; a lifetime supply of shoe polish. Howie enjoyed the ribbing, perhaps for the first time in his life. He was genuinely affected by the kindness. He couldn't remember the last time someone had bought him a gift.

Gilbert sipped his Bass Ale and smiled. In three weeks, the small team had pulled off a financial miracle. They owned $8 million worth of homes that they bought at a nice discount for a $6 million dollar mortgage and a few hundred thousand of equity. David Elliot got greedy, but in the end it wouldn't matter. Plus, he did get the deal done. Finding Vinnie Martini was a stroke of luck. The stars had been aligned perfectly.

In the end, the vision to see the impact of Pierre's plans was the driving force. Now Gilbert turned his attention to the small tasks of signing up a thousand homes for Pierre and helping Johnny sell his hardware store.

CHAPTER 30

MAY 12, 2011

Johnny crawled into the store well past opening hours. As usual, no line of customers waited to greet him. The dark glasses did little to shield his eyes from a blazing sun as he attempted to raise the sale sign over the store awning.

He had an awful, pounding headache. Gilbert had picked up the tab and had encouraged everyone to celebrate heartily. Johnny obliged and ordered several glasses of very expensive forty-year-old Macallan single-malt Scotch whiskey. It certainly tasted smooth going down followed by a few pints. Now Johnny was paying for it, but he didn't care.

Chris had done a favor for Johnny and wrote a front-page article in *The Bergenfield Valley News* about the expected record year for weed growth. There might be a shortage of Jake's weed killer. Johnny might have to allocate orders to customers. Johnny had also mailed an advertising flyer three days ago that would be arriving in mailboxes today.

Johnny nursed a quart container of iced tea. Feed a cold – starve a fever – drown a hangover. The word about the weed killer sale had apparently spread quickly, and a handful of customers entered the store. Johnny considered delaying the sale due to a hangover day, but decided to fight through the pain.

Mid-morning, Gilbert walked into the store and handed Johnny a wrapped gift. Johnny tore through the gift wrapping and laughed at the contents – a bottle of aspirin. "Thanks, I needed that," he said. "That was a great night last night. Let's never do it again."

Gilbert spoke quietly. "We'll do it again. The day we sell those homes and make everyone rich. Let's make sure everyone keeps doing their part. But that isn't why I'm here. I'm going to talk to JB. He's very close with Allie, and she's your best potential buyer. How much do you want for this place?"

"I gotta think about it." Johnny pondered the question. "Ten days ago I had a quarter mil of weed killer inventory. I put up a sale sign and already sold a hundred bags in the last hour. If this keeps up, I just might get rid of the stuff. That'll make it easier to sell this dump. But if this Pierre deal takes off, this business is in trouble. Without those weed killer sales, this store makes nothin'."

"Hold on a minute!" Gilbert raised his hand. "Don't ever say that again. Not when you are trying to sell this gold mine. You don't know for sure that this Pierre weed business is going to be successful. Right now, they only want a thousand homes. That means eight thousand homes still need your stuff."

"But we do know, don't we?" Johnny protested. "Otherwise we wouldn't have bought those houses, right? So I gotta sell. Like now!"

"Johnny, man up," Gilbert lectured. "You sound desperate. Let the buyer decide how big the Pierre business will be. It's not your job to warn her of the risks.

"Okay, let's get back to your asking price. You make $200,000 a year pre-tax, or EBITDA, which means Earnings Before Interest Taxes Depreciation and Amortization. They use it to value companies. It's basically pre-tax, pre-interest cash flow. You have no bank debt; your balance sheet looks okay. I'm assuming you'll take care of the payable to Jake's with that money, correct?"

Johnny was planning otherwise, but recalculated his response. "If I gotta. Or maybe just pay it down to normal terms."

Gilbert scribbled numbers on a pad of paper. "Okay, eight times EBITDA is $1.6 million. That's the highest possible price. Four times EBITDA is $800,000. I'm guessing you'd take it. I'll start the negotiations with the $1.6 million asking price. Agreed?"

Johnny objected, "This place should be worth a million at least!"

Gilbert shook his head disapprovingly. "Johnny, let me get this straight. You think the place is going to pot, but you want someone to pay you a million. Sometimes I just don't understand the new math they're teaching kids today.

"Forget about the price for now. Just don't do anything crazy for a few days and let's see what I can do. I'm going to find JB."

CHAPTER 31

MAY 12

JB had just finished charming a table of housewives with funny stories of corporate mismanagement. Gil sat and handed JB his signature calling card – a coffee and sweet bun. JB begged off. "I won't be able to putt straight if I have another one."

JB was dressed for golf, wearing khakis and a Pebble Beach golf sweater. Gilbert was a tinge jealous that he wasn't joining him. "Which *Golf Digest* top 100 course are you playing today? Baltusrol or Winged Foot?"

JB scoffed, "I don't play those high profile courses unless I'm coerced. They're too easy. Manicured greens. Short rough. Caddies to find your lousy drive. I'm a muni golfer at heart. I learned to play at Ponkapoag in Massachusetts where you teed off from a patch of dirt with half a tee marker.

"My life's goal is to shoot par on courses with fairways worn thin by the play of a hundred thousand rounds a year. Today, my destination is Bey Lea in Toms River. You can't find a course with much more play than that! And twenty-five mile per hour winds in the afternoon make it very interesting when you get to the sixteenth hole."

"I'm with you on that point. There are a lot of great muni golfers around here." Gilbert wasn't here to talk golf. He tried to turn the conversation. "Anyway, JB, you said that Allie might be interested in buying a local store. I might be able to help."

JB cocked his head suspiciously. "She's looking at a few stores, but none make enough money for a single mom to live on. What do you have?"

"I heard Johnny True Value might sell his store at the right price," Gilbert said with considerable understatement. "He's looking to buy something down the Jersey Shore. Do you think Allie could run a hardware store? It takes a lot of knowledge to help customers."

"Allie?" JB proclaimed. "How hard can it be to sell nails after you've been a nurse in heart surgery? You know, she rebuilt half of her house. Put in new kitchen cabinets. Installed a bathroom shower. Rewired her den. That's a heckuva lot more than Johnny can do, I assure you."

"That's for sure," said Gilbert. "Besides, I'm sure Johnny can train her for a short period until she knows the products.

"The store did over a million last year and his operating profit was $350,000. It'll be lower this year. Maybe $250,000. Is that too steep for Allie?"

JB thought for a moment. "Those numbers don't make a lot of sense looking at the square footage of the store. The best of stores generate sales of $300 per square foot max, and hardware stores are probably half of that number. His store has no more than two thousand square feet. That equals $600,000 in sales. How does he sell a million-five? There must be something unusual about his product mix that makes that statistic odd. He's not selling a bunch of John Deere tractors in Bergenfield. What's the big sales item?"

Gilbert gave a puzzled look. In thirty seconds, JB had fully analyzed the store operations and asked the singular question that Gilbert didn't want to answer. That might explain why he was so successful running a division of ITT.

"Well, I think the outdoor garden inventory turns over pretty quickly. But still, you can look at the financials and figure it out. I'm guessing that she could borrow a million from the bank, but she'd need $500,000 in equity to close the deal."

JB had thought that Gilbert was usually a pretty savvy negotiator, but the look on his face gave away Johnny's negotiating position. Johnny wasn't going to get anywhere near a million-five. He said, "Okay, we'll look at it, but your numbers are off by at least half. The banks only lend fifty percent against inventory and seventy-five percent against receivables. Since Johnny sells for cash and credit card, there shouldn't be any receivables. We might squeeze a half million from the banks. But let me talk to Allie and see if she wants to take a peek."

Gilbert tossed out, "Between us guys, Johnny under-managed the store except for a few high volume items. Allie could do a lot to improve sales. Also, you should know up front Johnny is expecting a slightly down year. He'll still do well, but he wants to move near the beach. Allie should be able to negotiate a better price. This is confidential, of course."

"Of course, but we'd have figured it out eventually," said JB matter-of-factly. "Anyway, if I help Allie, I'm not going to waste my time chasing information. I've closed a hundred acquisitions in my life, and I know what I want for due diligence. These are my minimum requirements before we start.

"I'm assuming he doesn't have audited financials. We'll let him certify his financials and provide a personal guarantee for any materially incorrect numbers. I want monthly and annual income statements for the last three years. No cash-based financials. We want an accrual-based balance sheet and his signature on the liabilities. Don't bother with any funny accounting like derivatives. All that does is screw up reality."

JB was unstoppable. He ran through his demands in rapid fire. "Tell Johnny to provide copies of the store's income tax and sales and use tax returns for the last three years, copies of the bank statements, an inventory listing, an accounts payable aging, any loan agreements, and a schedule of sales by product code. And we're not standing over a copy machine. Tell Johnny to make the copies. You seem to know the drill. But this is a starting point."

Gilbert raised his hands in mock surrender. "JB, you exhaust me. I'll relay the information, but I don't envy Johnny over the next three months with you at the table."

JB snorted, "Envying Johnny sounds like unexplored territory. Gilbert, what do you get out of this? I'm not begrudging you, but if there are any fees, they need to be paid by the seller."

"You know, I never discussed it with Johnny," Gilbert said. "I'm just making an introduction and have no intention of doing all of that groundwork. Doug Pearson will provide all of that accounting stuff. He keeps Johnny's books and tax returns. And Doug is a straight shooter. Let's just say that Johnny owes me one if this works out."

Gilbert said his goodbyes to JB and headed to the door. He looked at his phone. It was near noon and time to meet Vinnie. Hopefully, Vinnie had a good plan to sign up a thousand homes for the Pierre deal.

CHAPTER 32

MAY 12

Vinnie had nixed Gilbert's suggestion to meet at Ben's Deli. "I think da place is bugged. Plus, that schifoso stockbroker creeps me out. Let's meet at da Italian American Club and grab a hero."

Gilbert joined Vinnie who had already started on a veal parmesan sub. Gilbert ordered a cold antipasto. "Vinnie, our next step to prosperity is to sign up a thousand homes for Pierre Beauty Products. The homeowners are guaranteed $2,000 a year for three years, but…"

Vinnie interrupted, "I know all about da Pierre deal. Whadaya think? I'm stupid or somethin'? I've already thought dis through and got a plan. My cousins and I looked around town when we were pickin' up junk da other day. Dare's some areas where da houses are – let's be kind – not in da best shape. The good news is, dey got da most weeds.

"You can fuggedabout da homes in da eastern end near Tenafly. Dey got real lawns. So's da people up on da hill near Teaneck. Plus, I don't want no neighborhood of mine goin' downhill, so my block is out.

"Da closer ya get to da center of town, da easier it'll be to sign up people. Plus, dare's four hundred rental units in town, and we know mosta da landlords. We do a lotta dare maintenance and repair work. So if your goal's 1,000, it'll be easy as pie if youse got da money 'cause I got da people."

Indeed, Vinnie could organize and get things done when it came to making money. Gilbert started the bidding. "Pierre will pay the homeowners $500 in advance for their order. I talked to their team, and they have authorized me to use fifty bucks of that advance to pay a finder's fee. On a thousand homes, your guys'll make fifty grand."

"I know youse got more to give, but I don't wanna be greedy," said Vinnie as he took another bite of the hero. "Here's da deal dat you're gonna give me: I'll take a hundred bucks a home, but we get paid on every home Pierre signs up, not just da first thousand. Call 'em up. If dey agree, I promise we'll be done in a week. If dey don't agree, I doubt dey'll get another hundred homes to sign. Capisce?"

Gilbert excused himself from the table and called Albert from his cell phone. Albert quickly ran the proposal by Olivier, who gave his approval. Ten minutes later, Gilbert returned to the table. "Pierre said it's a deal. They'll send over a contract for you to sign tomorrow."

Vinnie cut Gilbert off. "We don't need no contract. Your handshake's your word. Youse won't back out on me – of dis I'm absolutely sure. Gimme da forms and my guys'll start visitin' people tonight. Tell Pierre to send signed contracts 'cause I don't wanna lose nobody over one-a your paperwork fiascos. We got a reputation to uphold."

"Pierre insists on a written agreement," said Gilbert. "I'll deliver enough agreements to start this afternoon. The rest will be tomorrow. It's a pleasure doing business with you."

"Deliver 'em here. We'll use my club as headquarters. And it's a pleasure doin' business wit you, too. Had I known youse back den, I would've voted for ya last election," Vinnie said with a wry smile.

Gilbert left the meeting and called Trudy from his cell phone. Trudy stopped shampooing a customer's hair to take the call. "Trudy, are you sure that your cousin isn't in the mob?"

"Who, Vinnie? No way," Trudy laughed. "I already told ya. Dare's no big mob anymore. They jailed all-a dose guys in the seventies. But I'll tell you two things. One, if dare's a job to get done dat requires hard work and muscle, Vinnie's da guy. He ain't afraid to get his hands dirty. And two, don't never cross him. He's put a few guys in the hospital, and none-a dem pressed charges for dare own good."

CHAPTER 33

MAY 14, 2011

Two days later, Gilbert received a text message from Vinnie to meet him at the Italian American Club. Vinnie was taking a big bite of a meatball parm hero when Gilbert arrived. Gilbert acted wary. He asked, "Is there a problem?"

Vinnie looked insulted. "Problem? Dare's no problem. I just wanna deliver da first three hundred agreements. We signed up all-a da landlords last night. We had 'em here for a free Chianti and spaghetti dinner. Dey thought it was a great idea. A few of them're thinkin' bout buyin' up some-a dose foreclosures around town. I gave 'em Elliot's number. And we had Joey notarize everyone's signature to make it nice and legal."

"You can't use Joey to notarize!" Gilbert stiffened. "You need an official notary!"

"What? You tink we're country bumpkins or sumpin?" Vinnie joked. "Joey's a notary. He passed da exam and everything. You know, we got businesses too, and I'll be damned if I'm gonna run to da bank and get a notary every time I sign sumpin'.

"Now I'll trust youse on dis, but we wanna a check for dese landlords tomorrow. And a check for our hard work wouldn't hurt matters. And last thing, we added a line on da form for dare tax ID number. Dey gotta pay taxes on dis, right?"

Gilbert was amazed at Vinnie's ability to talk like a tough guy and act like a CEO. He started grinning. "Vinnie, maybe we should use you as the attorney. You seem to know this stuff better than they do."

Vinnie finished his last bite of the hero and wiped his hands with a napkin. "You'd never get dese deals done if I didn't pay attention. Look, my guys're all sucking wind wit da construction downturn and all. Dey need dis money. So do your best to get it here tomorrow. My wire instructions are on da top of da page. And oh, by da way, here's my bill for da dinner. Surely youse don't expect me to pay dat outta my fee. Am I right? Fifty people, thirty bucks a head. You can't beat dese prices."

Vinnie was at a minimum entertaining. He got work done. He didn't take any grief. He was on a roll, and Gilbert was enjoying the show.

Somebody at Pierre was equally appreciative of his efficiency. A courier delivered a parcel to Vinnie the next morning. It contained checks for Vinnie, the landlords, and the Italian American Club.

CHAPTER 34

MAY 24, 2011

Vinnie Martini's crew cleaned up. They showered, shaved, donned sports jackets and splashed on a little aftershave. Martini's office assistant called targeted homeowners and set up appointments for Vinnie's army. They looked positively official holding metal clipboards as they visited their clients.

Socially presentable, they quickly met their quotas. Word about the Pierre deal spread fast; residents waited at their front doorsteps to sign their agreements. Someone, somewhere, had underestimated how much $2,000 meant in this horrible economy. The Martini crew earned $100,000 and deserved every penny of it.

Not yet Memorial Day, Gilbert had delivered a full month ahead of schedule. Albert greeted him in Pierre's small conference room. Eva made a quick appearance and thanked Gilbert personally. He'd been around many famous people in his lifetime, but had to work hard not to act starstruck in front of the CEO beauty.

Albert beamed. "Thank you so much. You haf done vunderful vork. Ve haf collected enough material to produce a sample run for zie salon schools. Zese schools provide free haircuts for people villing to risk zere hairlines."

Albert slapped his knee and laughed uncontrollably. Gilbert politely smiled after he finally understood the attempted humor. Albert was trying so hard to improve his delivery. It was one thing to tell a good joke. It was quite another to tell a joke well. It would be a long time before he was ready for the comedy club circuit.

Albert wiped the laugh tears from his eyes and took a deep breath to regain his composure. "Maybe if you saw some of zie haircuts, you vould get zie joke better. Anyvay, back to business. If zis experiment is successful, ve may need to sign up more homes."

"I suggest you start early," Gilbert said. "When we go to the nicer neighborhoods, it could be a tougher sell. Also, people start to spray their lawns about now. Doesn't that herbicide stuff make the weed unusable?"

"Ve haf studied zis," Albert said. "Zhey are doing it all vron, vrong, um backwards! Zhey should use pre-emergent herbicide to kill zie seeds. Zhey wait until zie veeds are nice and bushy and zen try to kill zhem. It's too late! And za stupid ones vater zere lawns after zhey spread zie chemicals. Zhey vash zie chemicals avay!"

Gilbert had to contain his laughter. Albert couldn't pronounce "wrong" but recovered well. When Albert became animated, his hard German accent flooded his sentences.

"If zie first crop isn't so great, zie plants spread hundreds auf seeds, so by August, ve vill haf lots of thick plants."

"Okay, Albert," Gilbert smiled. "You're the scientist. I still think we should choose the houses with the most weeds. Kinda funny concept, if you think about it. Let me know when you want to start. Vinnie is ready."

Gilbert was in a great mood heading back to Bergenfield. He lowered the windows as his Cadillac Escalade reached Washington Avenue. It was a beautiful, sunny day. The air smelled like fresh spring flowers. Birds were chirping. Squirrels were flirting and chasing each other. Young mothers pushed baby strollers and chatted with girlfriends about weekend plans. Everything was quiet. Blissful.

Gilbert entered Ben's wearing a big smile. Hector jumped from his table and stood in his way. He raised his voice. "Gilchrist! Who the hell gave you the right to decide who gets a contract? And who the hell gave you the authority to promote this? Do you have a permit? 'Cause you won't get one from me. I have a mind to declare these weeds a public nuisance. You'll ruin real estate values in this town. The place will look like a garbage dump."

Diners looked up, surprised at Hector's outburst. Gilbert backed up two feet. "Whoa, Hector! Down boy. I didn't do anything wrong. I didn't even select the houses. Who told you I did?"

Hector reddened further with anger. "I know you're behind it. We saw you meeting with those scientists. Your friends in town got a good deal."

Gilbert didn't want to antagonize Hector today. Life was just too good. "Hector, I had nothing to do with it. Pierre hired Vinnie Martini, and he made the decision. I think he picked the homes with the best crabgrass, or worst according to whose perspective.

"Listen, the Pierre execs just told me there'll be more houses, so your voters can get in on the next round. I'll talk to Vinnie and make sure they get contracts first. And the town can sell crabgrass from municipal lawns, too."

Gilbert had unintentionally poured jet fuel on the fire. Hector was incensed. "I don't want any of this crap on town property. This is a blight! And there isn't a Filipino family on Martini's entire list. Everyone should have the right to a contract. This is a lot of money. What about the rest of the town?"

"Which one is it, Hector?" Gilbert said with bemusement. "Everyone gets a contract, or no one can? Make up your mind.

"These people need this income. Homes are financially underwater from the real estate collapse. Everyone's making less money, assuming they still have a job. No one's getting any overtime pay. Kids are moving back home with their parents. It sounds like you don't want to win the next election, Hector. With your attitude, I'll bet you that even I could win the Filipino vote."

Hector saw customers observing the battle and lowered his voice. He was still visibly angry. "This isn't about elections. It's about improving the value of our homes and our image. We'll be the laughing stock of the country. You're ruining everything we've done for the last three years."

Hector turned and walked to his table. He slammed his chair and spilled coffee everywhere. No truce had been declared. Gilbert went to the food counter, grabbed a Danish and a cup of Starbucks and sat next to JB.

"No good deed goes unpunished around here," Gilbert sighed.

JB offered some solace. "Hector thinks making the town prettier will improve home values. It usually does. But this time he might be wrong. Home prices won't see those price levels for another ten years. That was a crazy time. If you bought at the top, you're screwed.

"A thousand people got lucky and hit the Martini lottery. Everyone else is probably pissed. A battle line is forming, and Hector just fired the first shot.

"Why did Pierre sign up a thousand homes? Why are they buying this stuff? Are they building a chlorophyll factory? I doubt it. Chlorophyll absorbs light, but I don't think there is much commercial use for it. Don't tell me they created a perfume that smells like crabgrass!"

JB was laughing, but Gilbert was absorbed in thought. He remained circumspect without any facial expression. He and his vulture partners might be the only people outside of Pierre who knew what the real purpose was.

"Gilbert, you're thinking too hard," JB kidded. "Anyway, how is Johnny coming along with Allie's documents?"

"Johnny's at his beach house. Doug is preparing the information for you, but he needs a few days," replied Gilbert.

JB gave his signature devious smile. "Well, I guess Johnny isn't in a rush to sell. That's okay. We have other options."

CHAPTER 35

MAY 26, 2011

Misty sat in a booth a safe distance from the board table and waited for Bret to bring her breakfast. Ben was relieved. A day not serving Misty added a day to his life span.

JB watched Bret and asked the table, "Should we rescue ol' Bret now, or let him crash and burn on his own?"

Buyout looked up from his laptop and silently studied Bret. Decker observed, "It would be cruel to let this go on too long, but he hasn't gotten this much in his entire life. Let it go for the summer." Decker sang sotto voce, *See You in September. Bye-bye. So long. Farewell!*

"You have to admit," JB chortled, "Misty has been on her best behavior for two weeks now. Maybe she just needed to meet the right guy!"

Misty's hard edge had disappeared. She was sweet and friendly to everyone. Her wardrobe had improved too. Misty had met Bret's work crowd and quickly realized conservative dress was de rigueur. She had considerably toned down the splashy colors and styles. Today she wore a simple tan poplin skirt and jacket.

This was a new source of entertainment for the board table. Bret and Misty were going well beyond the social rules for public displays of affection. They were holding hands. They were nose-rubbing for cripes sake. Rubbing noses in Ben's! Call the health inspector!

Panama Blonde entered Ben's looking fabulous in a mint-green linen pantsuit with white sandals. She walked past the smitten couple and politely said hello to Bret. Misty snarled, "Tarantula, can't you see we're busy here? We're having a private conversation."

JB heard the growl, looked up and said, "Looks like Ben's hosting the Memorial Day fireworks early."

Panama Blonde tried to maintain decorum and ignored Misty. She said politely, "I apologize for interrupting, Bret. Would you call me later about the legal issue we were discussing? Thanks."

Panama Blonde walked to the counter and ordered her breakfast. As she stood on line to pay her bill, Misty maneuvered in front of her carrying a tall hot chocolate. When she was in range, Misty whipped around and spilled the drink covering Panama Blonde's brand new outfit. It was a perfect drenching. For the final blow, Misty inconspicuously tilted the cup and tapped the few remaining drops onto Panama's open-toed sandals. Panama Blonde was a chocolate and marshmallow mess.

Ben should have immediately offered a cloth to clean the mess. However, he first had to memorialize the moment. He reached below the counter, pressed a button, and the juke box played Elton John's *Saturday Night is Alright for Fighting*.

Buyout began taking pictures with his cell phone camera. Other patrons joined in the photo op. Michael was aghast. Decker was shocked. JB was beside himself in laughter. He cried, "Oh the humanity! The ruination! The devastation!"

JB turned to Decker and said, "My money is on the blonde in the third round. She has seven inches and twenty pounds on the mouse."

Decker nodded. "I'll take that bet. Misty can inflict some real damage with those nails. They may be cyanide-tipped. Besides, I think Catherine is too nice to hit back."

Tears welled up in Panama's eyes. She turned and glared at Misty while Ben tried to clean her once-beautiful outfit. Misty gave Panama Blonde the *Who me?* look.

Panama Blonde pushed away Ben's hand. "Don't bother. The suit is ruined. As for you, Misty, there's an old saying. Revenge is a dish best served cold. I'll have my turn another day."

"I don't know what you're talking about," Misty said sweetly. "It was an accident. You hit my arm. You should watch where you're going."

Misty leaned over and whispered, "Between us girls, stay away from Bret. You're out of your league."

Panama Blonde walked toward the exit with the most dignity you could maintain in a hot-chocolate-and-marshmallow-covered, mint-green pantsuit. She stopped as she reached Bret and said, "I really need your advice, Bret. If you're not allowed to call me, I understand. But watch out for Little Miss Alley Cat. She'll rip your heart out."

Misty had refilled her hot chocolate and could be heard arguing with Ben. "I shouldn't have to pay for the first cup. The witch knocked it out of my hand!"

Bret grinned at JB and Decker. Out of Misty's hearing range, he said, "Life is great! Now I've got two women fighting over me?"

JB called back, "You think that's the fight? It's just the warm-up!"

In the tiny window of two weeks, Misty had gone from town terror, to Ben's Deli sweetheart, to Muhammad Ali. Life with Misty sure was exciting.

Allie stepped around Miguel as he cleaned the chocolate drink from the floor and walked to the food counter. She wore a simple navy dress with tiny white polka dots. She passed Misty and shook her head in disapproval.

When she reached the register with her order, Ben played one of his Allie-greeting songs, *The Girl from Ipanema.*

"*… when she passes, each one she passes goes – ah.*"

Allie handed Ben a ten-dollar bill for the coffee and egg sandwich and said, "Thanks for the song, Toots!"

"Allie, you're the only woman who doesn't waste time rifling her purse for exact change," Ben complimented her.

Allie flipped her hair. "Ben, it's the Allie Bertrand economic theory on the circulation of the money supply. Men pay with paper money and receive change. Men leave change on their dresser. Wives see change and refill their purses.

"Therefore, it's entirely men's fault when women take so much time findin' exact change at the register. As for me, unfortunately, I don't have an eligible man to leave me money, so I pay with paper. My piggy bank at home overflows with hundreds of quarters."

Ben offered, "I'm an eligible man, you know."

Allie laughed and dismissively waved her hand. "You're happily married, Ben. I see your wife at St. John's every Sunday prayin' for your soul. But thanks for the offer."

Allie sat with JB and Decker, and took a sip of her coffee. "You know, I saw Misty acting strangely and cuttin' to the front of the line. She looked like a jungle cat sneakin' up on a helpless animal. Too bad I missed mosta the fight. The photographers blocked my view. Any blood spilled?"

JB nodded toward the victor's table. "Misty won the first round. Estimated damage had to be $200 at least. Those were nice threads."

"That stain's not comin' out," Allie said. "One good thing about wars of attrition is both sides kill each other. I couldn't think of two more despicable creatures to battle it out. Next fight, we should sell seats and make some money. Ben could install a webcam and hook it to the Internet. My kid can do it for free!"

"You'd better hold the fight soon. I'm moving to Florida next year," JB announced. "I know it's hot down there in the summer, but they don't have this horrible allergy season."

"There's no pollen at the shore," Allie quipped. "Go to Manasquan for the summer."

"Speaking of the beach," JB raised an eyebrow, "Johnny went away for the weekend. Doug's doing the prep work. On Tuesday, I'll take you over to his office and help you with the due diligence.

"Take my words of advice. You should ask for a three month lock-up to give you time to see how his business is doing. He'll want to close yesterday. You want to close in September. Let's ask Bret to draft a letter of intent. If Johnny doesn't sign it, we call off the project. For now, you and your son should take the weekend and get away. Everyone else is."

Allie said, "I'm takin' Marty and three of his friends to Great Adventure to ride some stand-up roller coaster. One of his friends is a girl. He isn't sayin', but I think maybe she's his girlfriend."

"What possible trouble could he get in with a girlfriend?" JB laughed loudly. "At least he isn't using a butane torch to cook his breakfast anymore!"

CHAPTER 37

MAY 27, 2011

Memorial Day weekend weather was fantastic. The shore-bound traffic on the Garden State Parkway moved swiftly. E-ZPass had installed a hundred-foot-wide, overhead-toll-card-swipe that only helped drivers to attempt new land speed records on their way to the beach.

The Jersey Shore had a little bit of something for everybody. It was an interesting mix of extremely wealthy mansions down the road from family bungalows and weekly rentals; near-private beachfronts next to crowded boardwalks. Sailboats were in the minority; stink potters ruled the bays!

The northernmost beach on the Jersey Shore was Sandy Hook. It was a rolling stone's throw from Rumson, home to Jersey rockers Jon Bon Jovi and Bruce Springsteen. A dozen miles south was where Bruce got his start at Asbury Park's Stone Pony.

Mile-long wooden promenades offered carnival games, entertainment, and comfort food at the famous boardwalks. Asbury Park, Seaside Heights and Park, Atlantic City, and Wildwood hosted millions of visitors every summer.

Buyout sat in Ben's listening to music through his iPod earphones. He was waiting for his ride and had already dressed for the beach. He wore a Yankee's baseball cap, aviator sunglasses, a Tommy Bahama flowered shirt, surfer jams and sandals.

Buyout was headed to his rental beach house a block from the beach in Sea Girt. For three days, he and his twelve roommate buddies would drink and chase girls all night at the clubs, play two-man volleyball on the beach, and crawl back to work exhausted on Tuesday.

JB heard the distinguishable BMW honk as a white, convertible three series pulled up to the curb. He flipped Buyout's cap. "Your ride's here. Stay out of trouble!"

Buyout ran for the door.

CHAPTER 38

MAY 27

Cute-looking Misty sat in Ben's wearing a yellow flowered sundress and red floppy straw beach hat with matching tote bag. Mean Misty was nowhere to be seen.

Bret brought her breakfast, which she quickly devoured. The ocean was calling; no time to waste. Bret stood to leave and gave JB a pretend *Save me!* look. JB smiled and waved good-bye. Allie shook her head and looked away.

Misty had planned a special weekend getaway in Cape May. It's the southernmost beach town in New Jersey and a full eighty miles south of the Atlantic City gambling casinos. She had booked a room at the romantic Virginia Hotel, a quaint historic landmark. Misty was leaving no chance Panama Blonde or one of Bret's friends would interrupt their romantic stay. She was having Bret all to herself and planned to keep Bret happily occupied in a fuzzy alcohol daze.

Bret and Misty checked into the hotel after the three-hour drive. A chilled bottle of champagne greeted their arrival. Bret had barely taken a sip when Misty shoved him onto the bed and jumped on top of him. It was the start of an hour-long, sweaty, acrobatic, sheet-tearing, Kama Sutra redefining, pretzel-twisting, love fest. They found themselves exhausted lying on the mattress, which somehow had slipped to the floor. Bret and Misty jumped into the pool, returned for champagne and ordered cold lobster salad.

Misty sat astride Bret and round two started. It would be a long weekend. He could forget the stack of legal work he'd brought with him.

CHAPTER 39

MAY 27

Gavin Kelleher and his family headed to their three-bedroom, bay-front brick beach house on Chadwick Beach Island. Every week for fifteen straight weeks of summer, the Kelleher family hosted a dozen friends, relatives and children. The children slept on bunk beds and air mattresses. It was camping on the bay.

Chadwick was on Route 35, north of Seaside Heights and south of Belmar. Gavin took a local shortcut, the Route 70 exit on the Parkway. On Hooper Avenue, he passed Action Pest Control's 'Pest of the Month' sign. This month's pest was slugs.

Gavin stopped at La Bella Abruzzi on Fisher Boulevard to pick up sausage and meatballs for Saturday night's dinner. They crossed the Barnegat Bay on the old Tunney Bridge.

From the top of the bridge, you can see the lights from the Seaside Heights Casino Pier at the northern end of the boardwalk and the Seaside Park Ferris Wheel at the southern end. In between was a mile of food stands, amusement rides, Skee Ball, carnival games and an antique carousel surrounded by funhouse mirrors. It was a time machine to a century past.

The men took the teens crabbing early Saturday morning. They steered the Boston Whaler in the shallow waters. The Intracoastal Waterway was twenty feet wide and barely distinguishable from the shallower bay; if you had a deep keel, the chances of running aground were high. The crabbers raised the pots from the water and pulled out a dozen large keepers. They released the smaller crabs and a couple of pregnant females back into the bay.

Early Saturday evening, Gina Kelleher served spaghetti with marinara and crabs. Bottles of Chianti, loaves of Italian bread and plates of meatballs and sausage filled the table. It was loud. It was fun. Everyone laughed. The kids told exaggerated stories about the crabbing expedition.

Dessert would be served on the boardwalk. Gavin and Gina drove their guests to Seaside Heights. The small children, grandparents and Gina headed to the carousel and kiddie rides. The men took the older children to the Jet Star roller coaster. It wasn't the biggest roller coaster in the world, but it was rickety and scared the heck out of riders who clung to the cars careening around the hairpin turn over the ocean.

The next ride was the Himalaya. The cars went pretty fast, and it was a teenager favorite because it played loud, popular rap and rock music. More importantly, it attracted other teens and was the most popular hangout on the Casino Pier.

After a few battles in the bumper cars, they headed to the Kohr's stand where Gina's entourage was already licking thick custard from sugar cones. Kohr's custard is Haagen Daz on steroids.

After finishing their ice cream, the kids played a few games of chance. Five-year-old Brooke sunk a free throw and won a pink basketball. Instant replay wasn't available to award the assist to the barker.

To cap off the night, Gavin bought a few bags of deep-fried, powder-sugar-coated zeppoles to eat on the way home. Nothing beats a Jersey Shore boardwalk with the family on a warm summer's eve.

CHAPTER 40

MAY 31, 2011

Sunburnt diners moved gingerly through Ben's Deli following the Memorial Day weekend. Buyout was bright red and in deep pain. He applied multiple large dollops of green aloe gel to his bald forehead.

Most everyone was tanned or burnt except Bret, who had spent the weekend indoors. JB teased him in an Irish brogue. "Bret-me-lad, was it rainin' all weekend in the Cape of May? What sunblock do ye use? Hawaiian Tropic SPF 1000? Where's yar tan?"

Bret said sheepishly, "We shopped a lot, I guess."

JB busted a gut. "Shopped for what? Engagement rings?"

After breakfast, JB and Allie walked two blocks to Doug Pearson's offices diagonally across from the Roy W. Brown Middle School. It was time to take a peek at Johnny's books.

Roy W. Brown was straight from a page of the Americana handbook. The school had a beautifully manicured lawn on a slight hill, wide front steps leading to the auditorium on one side and the girl's gymnasium on the other. An American flag flew from a fifty-foot pole. It looked serene.

Doug's secretary, Dottie Freemont, greeted Allie and JB and escorted them to the client conference room. The offices were everything Doug – conservative, pragmatic and nicely furnished but modest in taste. A few simple frames on the wall displayed his CPA certificate, college diploma and several photographs from awards ceremonies.

Two copies of the due diligence files were awaiting review. Each pile had numerous reports and documents over a foot high. JB looked at the files for no more than ten minutes. "Johnny is doing alright," JB said with a little surprise in his voice. "He made $350,000 last year on sales of $1.1 million.

"Doug does nice work. He made this easy to see the quick picture. Allie, look at this sales-by-product analysis. Seventy percent of the revenues are from one product – weed killer. Now, look at Doug's analysis of profitability-by-product line. Johnny is making most of his money on this stuff."

Allie groaned, "JB, I could never afford to buy this place. I had no idea his hole-in-the-wall made so much."

JB consoled Allie. "Don't quit on me so early. Johnny is selling for a reason, and I don't believe 'moving to the Jersey Shore' is it. If I were to guess, he's scared this weed killer business is in danger. He just lost a thousand customers. That's a hundred thousand of sales right there. Who knows? You might be able to buy this cheap."

JB talked to himself. "Does this guy know he's losing money on practically every item he sells? He made so much money selling weed killer he neglected the rest of the business."

"Maybe he had to," Allie offered. "The hardware store is a front for weed killer. Think about it. If he didn't sell crabgrass killer, would anyone shop there?"

"I wouldn't ascribe any mad scientist theory to Johnny's store management," JB said and they laughed. "He has moderate intelligence. I'd label him a C student. My guess is True Value gave him a model floor plan, and Johnny stuck to it. When some items didn't sell, he stopped merchandising.

"Regardless, I don't think you're gonna find the solution until you own the store and see how customers react. I can tell you Johnny ignored this business. He did very little to offer new products. His place is a crap heap. Go to any True Value store in the area. They're filled with updated merchandise and they offer friendly help. Here all you get is weed killer. If you could sell dust for a living, he'd make a fortune.

"Let's keep looking at the numbers, but you don't have to pay full price for this place. I'm guessing you pay him some cash. Some of the price has to be tied to future performance. The best structure from your vantage point is in the form of an earn-out. An earn-out pays only if you make the profits. Also, you can pay part of the price in a promissory note."

JB and Allie continued to look at the files. Allie had been browsing in the store two days earlier. JB had told her to look for old or obsolete items. The store shelves were covered in grime. A bottle of wood glue had cemented to the shelving. An old package of ant killer had yellowed.

Doug had also provided a slow-moving inventory report. The spreadsheet highlighted $50,000 of inventory that hadn't sold a single unit in over a year.

"JB, look at this," Allie said. "These items gotta be thirty years old. Look! Christmas lights from 1965 on the books for $5,000. They hafta be a fire hazard."

JB said, "Assuming they're in inventory. Don't worry – we'll count everything at closing."

After poring through the stack of reports, JB said to Allie, "Let's talk numbers. First, there's a lot of risk buying this place. But if it were well-run, you couldn't afford it. You have to believe you can fix this business and run it profitably.

"Next, you should assume the weed killer business will drop by twenty or thirty percent, not the ten percent you know for sure. I heard Gilbert tell Hector that Pierre might sign up another thousand homes.

"You should pay a multiple of three or four times historical cash flow at most for this type of business. He wants eight times, but that multiple is used for big buyouts with high growth rates. This business is not growing.

"Assuming current crabgrass killer sales drop by a third, profits will drop to $150,000 on the chemicals. You'll make another fifty on the rest of the store. If I calculate this on a back of an envelope, at a multiple of four times cash flow, the price would be $800,000 dollars.

"Johnny's dream is probably to get the million dollar retirement number. There's your rough range of values. You'll pay something in the middle. At what price you arrive will be a test of your negotiation skills and how willing you are to walk away from the deal."

JB called Bret at his office and gave him a quick summary of the economics. JB said quietly on his cell phone, "He's not shopping this around yet, and he wants to sell quickly. I was hoping you could draft a ninety day LOI for Allie in your spare time.

"There's another issue, Bret. Johnny wants to sell stock and not assets. Maybe you can educate Allie on the issue."

JB put his cell phone on speaker. Bret said, "Hi, Allie. I can whip up an LOI tonight and have it to you before tomorrow.

"Let me explain this stock versus assets issue. If you buy the common stock of a company, you get everything – all of the assets and liabilities and all of the unknown warts and hidden liabilities. You particularly have to worry about exposure to litigation or a product liability claim.

"You also inherit the tax basis of the assets. Johnny doesn't have a lot of equipment, so that doesn't matter."

"If you buy assets instead of stock, you only buy the specific assets and liabilities you choose and nothing else. You don't become liable for the unknown, although some court cases have pierced the concept.

"A seller usually prefers to sell stock because he'll pay lower taxes at the capital gains rate. In an asset deal, the corporation first pays taxes on the sale. Then the owner pays taxes a second time on the distribution from the company. There are some complicated ways to avoid the double tax.

"Allie, there's your lesson and more than you need to know. Johnny owns the store in a limited liability company. I already checked the state records. So the tax issue is irrelevant. An LLC doesn't pay corporate taxes on the sale.

"True Value is not a franchise operation – it's a cooperative. So the question of transferability of the True Value name is not an issue. You have to ask yourself why he wants to sell his LLC instead of the assets.

"I'd guess Johnny's advisors are telling him to sell his LLC so he has a clean break. No more exposure. No more liabilities. That puts the onus on you to ferret out any exposure during your due diligence check.

"With a hardware store, you never know. Could he have product liability exposure out there for a defective lawn mower or snow blower? Are these chemicals toxic? Did he have a spill? Are they an environmental hazard? Did someone slip and fall in his store? We'll ask for representations from him that there are no known issues and demand an indemnity agreement at closing."

Allie said seriously, "He couldn't have any liability for a defective lawn mower. He never sold any."

Bret and JB chuckled. Allie managed a polite smile realizing she had made a joke. Her head was spinning with all of the financial, legal, accounting and tax issues. All she wanted to do was simply buy a store.

Bret continued, "Allie, it's your call if you want to push back on this. Either way, we'll paper the deal to protect you. Johnny can be a little weasel, so I recommend you be careful."

"I hear you, Bret," Allie said. "Thanks for taking our call. I think it's time to visit Michael and find out how much the bank can lend. Then we'll know how much I can pay."

CHAPTER 41

JUNE 6, 2011

Allie had fifteen minutes to kill and paced nervously along Washington Avenue on her way to Consolidated Northern Bank. When she entered the building, Michael Li was finishing a meeting with an attractive, well-dressed, gray-haired woman.

"Well, you know why I'm here," Allie confessed as she sat across from Michael. "The sum total of my borrowin' experience is a credit card which I always pay off, a car lease and a home mortgage. I'll need a bank loan if I'm goin' to buy Johnny's business."

There. She said it. Her pulse was racing. Her hands were sweating. She had just asked a banker to lend her a boatload of money. It didn't matter that she had known Michael since they were in high school. She was way out of her comfort zone. She was scared out of her mind, but did her best to appear calm and composed. No bank was going to lend to an idiot or someone who can't handle themselves.

Michael looked the perfect picture of a hometown banker. He wore a navy suit, a crisp white shirt, a striped tie and a carnation in his suit lapel. Michael sensed Allie's nervousness, but most first-time borrowers were understandably uneasy.

"Well, Allie, you've come to the right place. You know banks make money by lending to good customers right?"

"Why Michael, I never thought of that," Allie said with a gleam in her eye. She was clearly more comfortable kidding with her breakfast buddies. "I read you big banks make money speculatin' in swaps, whatever they are."

Michael reacted defensively. "Allie, we're a small bank and never enter into in fancy speculative derivative transactions. Most of our customers are local businesses, so we rarely have a need to hedge a loan. At most, we might provide an interest rate swap to provide a fixed interest rate to a customer. Also, foreign currency futures are technically a derivative, and many businesses use them to protect their foreign exposure."

"Stop, Michael!" Allie raised her hands. "Stop defendin' yourself. I was just ribbin' you. Everyone knows your bank is conservative and well run.

"Anyway, JB and Bret have been helpin' me look at Johnny's books. I think we have a good understandin' of his business. The big question is how much I can afford to pay compared to how much Johnny wants.

"I plan to invest $200,000 from my 401k. That'll leave me $100,000 in reserve. I must be lucky. The stock market made me nervous and I sold everythin' before the crash.

"Also, I can refinance my home mortgage for another $100,000. I never borrowed during the crazy real estate market either. Lucky again, I guess."

"Luck has nothing to do with your good fortune," Michael counseled. "You work hard and save. You don't take unnecessary risks. I have hundreds of former customers asking me to refinance their defaulted mortgage. There isn't much I can do when they borrowed against their home equity and spent the money.

"Let me put you at ease and tell you that you have the character of a good borrower. Plus, I will serve as your reference. Let's get back to you. Tell me what the numbers look like."

Allie spent the next half hour explaining the due diligence, the sales and profit numbers, the inventory including the thirty-year-old Christmas lights, and the weed killer issue.

"Based upon what you're telling me, you could borrow against inventory," Michael spoke analytically. "There is good cash flow, but you expect it to decline. Typically, the bank would lend $350,000. I can increase the inventory advance ratio slightly. Subject to documentation and the results of your due diligence, I will find a way to increase the loan to $450,000. I have local lending authority to commit to the loan today, if you wish."

"I didn't know it was so easy to get a loan," Allie quipped.

"It isn't, Allie," Michael affirmed. "Ninety percent of new businesses that request loans are rejected. Most fail because of insufficient collateral. Some fail because of a poorly thought-out business plan. Others have character issues. We know you, and we know the store you're buying. That's two things in your favor.

"Also, to be quite frank, banks are receiving criticism from the government that we're not lending enough. Under these circumstances, you make an excellent candidate who happened to come in the door at the tight time. Please understand that the commitment is based on your reputation and goodwill. I don't expect you to let me down.

"Allie, you may find a banker willing to lend you more. I prefer to keep this conservative and keep some reserve to help you when you're in need."

"No, Michael," Allie said sweetly. "The other banks won't know me. I prefer someone I can trust. I'll just take it out of Johnny's hide and make a lower offer. With your loan and my equity, it looks like the most we can pay Johnny in cash is $750,000. He won't like it."

Michael warned, "Don't pay too much and use all of your resources. Keep some of the money for a rainy day when times get tough. Sellers almost always take a promissory note for some of the purchase price.

"I can provide you a loan commitment letter if you'd like."

"Thank you Michael," Allied said. "I guess that's what I need. Bret is drafting the LOI tonight. I'll track down Johnny."

Allie left the bank so excited she wanted to skip down Washington Avenue. If Bret finishes the LOI, she could hand-deliver it to Johnny the next morning.

CHAPTER 42

JUNE 10, 2011

With Bret's LOI in hand, Allie called Johnny at the store. He never returned the call. Matt Miller, the white-haired store manager, told her he was with customers.

She called again on Thursday and heard the same story. Allie drove to the store. Johnny was nowhere to be found.

Allie pressed Matt for Johnny's whereabouts. Lying wasn't his strong suit. Finally, the gentleman whimpered from behind the register. Johnny hadn't returned yet from his weekend at the beach. In exasperation, Allie called Doug, who promised to have Johnny at his offices the next morning.

On Friday morning, Allie and JB sat in Doug's conference room. They kept themselves busy studying the extensive due diligence files while waiting for Johnny's arrival.

Johnny unapologetically waltzed into the room an hour late. He'd tanned well, and was dressed too laid back for such an important meeting. He raised his sunglasses, and said, "Lousy Jersey Shore traffic."

Johnny was carrying a real attitude. He was smug, obnoxious, full of himself and down-right disrespectful.

Allie was no wallflower. She stared Johnny in the eyes and raised her voice. "What's up, Johnny? You left town to get a tan? You're too busy to answer my calls? Why are you wastin' my time? Why are you wastin' Doug's time?"

"Um, er, uh," Johnny stuttered. "I thought Doug was takin' care-a you. Doug, weren't you answerin' their questions?"

JB watched in awe and admiration. The town sweetheart had Johnny True Value on the ropes in round one.

Doug refused to be the fall guy. He gave Johnny a stern look. "I told you on Tuesday Allie wanted to deliver an offer letter in person. Why didn't you call her back?"

Johnny was rattled. This conversation wasn't going in the right direction. He said, "Gee, Allie. There must be some miscommunication. Course I'm interested. Lemme see the offer."

Johnny reached for the LOI, but Allie held onto it. She was polite but curt. "Johnny, the amount of cash I have from my savings and the bank loan is a solid number. It's not increasin'. I've read your files and concluded your business is deterioratin'. That makes it risky. I think I can fix it, but it's gonna take some additional investment on my part."

Johnny reached for the letter once again, and Allie placed it on the table out of his reach. She said, "I'm willin' to sign this ninety-day letter of intent to buy your business based upon a formula. It's subject to a few conditions. You hafta maintain your business in good financial condition and not do anythin' to hurt its value. There can be no material adverse change in the business or the balance sheet from where it stands today. And you hafta bring all of your obligations current."

Allie had memorized the passages from the LOI with Bret's help. She continued, "Your business made $350,000 dollars last year. Based upon the formula in the letter of intent, you'll get your million dollars eventually. However, I need cash to fix this place up. I'm willin' to pay you $500,000 in cash at closin'. I'll pay you another quarter million in a note payable in three years. The last quarter million will be paid in an earnout over five years.

"Under the earnout, you'll be paid up to $50,000 a year for five years if the store profits exceed $250,000. If we earn the $350,000 you claim you make, you'll get the full earnout."

Johnny wasn't about to be bullied by a 120 pounds of smart and pretty. He raised his voice. "You're crazy. You think you can buy my business for only $500,000 in cash. I'm not sellin' for less'n a million in cash up front."

"Johnny, you made a lot of money," Allie said with a subtly sarcastic tone. "That's 'made', as in the past tense of 'make'. You're about to make a lot less unless you improve the place. Your weed killer business is goin' to hell. You and I both know it. Still, I'm willin' to buy your place and take the risk of fixin' it.

"Otherwise, we can end this discussion. I know how much I can afford to pay. I know how much the bank will lend. And I know how much it will cost to upgrade the place so customers'll return. I have to gut the store, buy new shelving, fixtures and lightin', replace all of the store signs, and buy a new awning. I also have to buy $200,000 in new inventory that True Value told you to add a year ago."

Johnny cried defensively, "Don't listen to 'em. It'll never sell in this town. I've tried it before. Hammers and nails is all they want. Not pretty flower-covered waste baskets."

Allie said firmly, "If you're right, I might have to reduce my offer. Regardless, we can disagree on what the customers might want. Here's the offer letter. Meanwhile, you have ninety days until closin' to try to improve operations so it doesn't fall apart the day after I buy it. The earnout is really in your hands."

Johnny looked at Doug. His eyes were pleading for help. He'd get his million, but only if the business didn't collapse. This wasn't how he saw it playing out. Doug nodded to Johnny to follow him to his office.

CHAPTER 43

JUNE 10

Johnny paced the room. Doug sat and folded his arms. Johnny would be a former client as soon as he sold the business. Doug was doing his best to remain professional despite Johnny's slithery behavior.

Doug finally spoke, in the tone of a trusted financial advisor, "Even though Allie is offering a sizable cash payment, you'll find a better buyer if you take your time and shop around. With your cash flow, someone will be willing to pay the million you want.

"Also, you probably should hire a business broker to sell it for you. They'll find the highest offer out there. Last, I strongly advise you to hire a lawyer, not just rely on a free legal tip from a guy you met at the Aztec Hotel bar."

"I talked to them effin brokers," argued Johnny. "They want twenty grand in advance to prepare some fancy sellin' book and then get paid a huge success fee. And they said it could take six months or more to find a qualified buyer.

"I don't have six months. This Pierre deal is gonna kill my sales, and it can only get worse. Allie is here and now. I just have to convince her to give me more cash. It was just her first offer, I'm positive."

Johnny didn't look so sure. Doug said, "You're probably right about the cash part. It was her first offer. However, it appears Allie has a pretty good understanding of what's happening to your business. If your sales are about to drop, the earnout won't be worth anything. Again, I recommend you hire a business broker, or you'll be leaving money on the table."

"JB kept his mouth shut the entire meetin'," Johnny said. "But there ain't no way a nurse knows all this stuff. He's gotta be behind this stupid offer structure. Whoever heard of a freakin' earnout?"

Doug said, "Sorry, but if I were Allie's advisor, I would have recommended the same structure. This is very typical when a seller believes there's a big upside and the buyer won't pay for it unless it happens."

"Whose side you on?" Johnny said impertinently. "Never mind. Let's get back in there. I wanna sell, and I wanna sign this deal today. But no earnout! And stop takin' her side!"

CHAPTER 44

JUNE 10

Allie sat quietly with her hands folded as Doug and Johnny returned to the room. JB was in the corner on his cell phone booking an afternoon round of golf.

After JB ended his call, Johnny looked directly at Allie and put on his charming disguise. "I think you're the best buyer for my store. I really care about its future, and I think it'll do best in your hands. If we can move the cash and note around a little, we might be able to cut a deal today. Increase the cash to $850,000 and reduce the note to $150,000. Then we have a deal. I'm not doin' an earnout."

Allie did not twitch a muscle nor say a word. JB gave Allie a signal with his eyes that was indiscernible to Doug or Johnny. Allie returned a brief glance to JB, and said, "Johnny, I got a little more cash to give, but I was countin' on the money to fix up the store. I can stretch to $600,000. The rest of my offer is half-note, half-earnout. If you want a million dollars, some of the price has gotta be an earnout. Otherwise, no deal."

Johnny perked up. Negotiations had begun. Allie had counteroffered. It was a good sign. She had wiggle room. She was willing to meet somewhere, but where?

The offers and counteroffers continued for ten minutes. Allie didn't budge further on the cash. Johnny refused to accept any earnout. Allie offered to increase the note and reduce the earnout slightly. Johnny again refused. Allie stayed firm on the cash component of the offer.

Doug took notes and watched the discussions intently but quietly. JB played with his new iPhone 4, a never-ending source of entertainment and amusement.

Exasperated, Johnny said, "Ya know, I could run the business for a year, take home another $350,000, and sell it for a million next June."

Allie barked, "Hah! Go right ahead. You won't make half of that, and next year you'll be lucky if someone paid you half a million. And I won't be around to bid on it."

Johnny was out of ammunition and looked defeated. They both knew the business was going to have a tough year. Did Johnny have the patience to spend the next year trying to find a stupid buyer who didn't see the problems? Or did he ink a deal with Allie who was ready to sign a check?

Allie sensed Johnny was weakening. It was time to deliver her best terms. "Johnny, this is goin' nowhere. You're not givin' on any point. Here's my final offer. You don't hafta tell me now. Think about it. I have things to do today.

"I'll increase the cash to $650,000. I'll agree to reduce the earnout to $125,000. I'll give you a note for $200,000, but half of the note will be due in five years instead of three."

"Allie, you've reduced the offer," cried Johnny. "It's less than a million now."

Allie was adamant. "Yeah, but the cash increased. That's what you wanted. From the looks of it, I have to dine on cat food for the next three years just to pay you to sit on the beach. I'm not sure I'm doin' the right thing. Let me know by tomorrow night. Otherwise, I'll find another business."

Allie began to collect her papers acting like she was preparing to leave. Johnny quickly thought through the terms. He had Allie and her money, and he knew better than to let her leave the room.

Under the worst case, assuming the earnout was worthless, Johnny was selling for $850,000. He thought he could pull another $100,000 out of the business by selling down inventory before the sale. It was close enough to his million dollar target.

"Okay, Allie. I accept your offer." Johnny feigned sincerity. "I think you're gettin' the better of me, though."

JB looked up from his iPhone and spoke for the first time. "Johnny, I just want to be clear about this LOI. First, it contains a no-shop provision. Second, there can be no material deterioration in the operations or financial condition of the company. If the balance sheet materially changes, the purchase price gets adjusted. And my third and last point: you'll have to provide reps, warranties and indemnifications. There's a list of the items on the last page of the LOI."

Johnny started to read the small print in the LOI for the first time. He whined, "What's this no-shop provision? What if I get a better offer? I'm not signin' this."

Allie looked Johnny squarely in the eyes, and said sternly, "I'm investin' a lot of time and money in this deal. The no-shop protects me. If you don't agree, the deal is over."

Johnny growled, "What if you can't get financin' from the bank?"

Allie pulled Michael's loan commitment letter from her folder and showed it to Johnny. "I have financin'. Here's proof."

Johnny scanned the letter for the dollar amount, but didn't read the fine print. "Alright, let's get this deal done," Johnny said, rubbing his hands together.

Johnny quickly signed the two copies and handed one to Allie. Sir Johnny the Charming said, "I have complete confidence in you, Allie."

Allie stuffed the LOI in her folder. "Why don't I believe you? JB, let's go."

Allie and JB walked outside into the warm June breeze. A dirty, ten-year-old, dented Ford F150 pickup truck drove past filled with crab grass. Dirt and weeds spilled from the truck and left a trail on the way to its destination. JB snapped a photo with his cell phone.

"I believe you have just witnessed the first official delivery of crabgrass to Pierre," JB observed with a near solemn tone. "Even if it's not, I'm declaring it. I'm sending this pic to *The Record*!"

Allie laughed, "You traitor, you! Send it to Chris at *The Bergenfield Valley News* for Pete's sake. The guy hasn't had a scoop in years. Remember! From now on, support your local business!"

CHAPTER 45

JUNE 13, 2011

It was two weeks to harvest time! Pierre was scrambling to organize a small collection effort. They weren't quite ready. Initially, they had promised to buy the June production from a small group of homeowners. But the word had spread, and it was too late to back out. Pierre would have to make do and keep their thousand conscripted mini-farmers happy.

Not a single homeowner had a clue what to do. Do we pull the weed from the ground? Or do we just cut the green part? Do we shake the dirt? Do we wash it first? Our neighbors walk their pets here, you know. Where do we deliver it? Can we send it UPS? How do we weigh it?

On a micro level, would anyone reimburse Mrs. VanWyck for her rose shipping boxes? Rose boxes?

Emily VanWyck had harvested early. She was a retired widow and winner of several American Beauty Rose awards, so she knew a thing or two about growing. Emily didn't care about lawns, only roses, so clipping crabgrass for profit was a bonus. Petite, white-haired and finicky about details, she had expected Pierre to provide specific detailed instructions on how to correctly harvest her crabgrass and how to package and deliver it. Nothing but silence!

Emily, anxious to collect her first check, decided to send the crabgrass to Pierre the only way she knew how. She carefully cut the grassy part of the crabgrass and placed it into twenty long stem rose boxes. She sent them UPS to Albert's offices along with an eye-popping bill for shipping.

Albert was a scientist, not a farmer. At the last minute, Eva assigned James McHeath and Andrew Berg, two thirty-year-old Harvard MBAs in Pierre's management training program to save Albert.

Pierre's lawyers had ruled out entering people's properties to collect the crabgrass. They dreamed up hundreds of ways they could possibly be sued. No, the thousand homeowners would have to cut and deliver the weeds to some central area for processing. In three weeks, people would start delivering their crop.

Jim and Andy concluded they'd have to create a temporary receiving and processing area that caused as little disruption as possible. They had no employees trained to handle ag products. They needed to hire laborers to receive and sort the goods. They also needed supervisors who knew agriculture. Luckily, they found a few aggie students on summer break from Rutgers University to help with the project.

Where should they collect the product? Does everyone plop two hundred pounds of cut weeds into the back of a pickup and drive it to Morristown? Would Pierre provide security passes to a thousand drivers to get through the compound gates? Part of the Pierre complex was performing scientific experiments for the federal government. Would everyone need a federal security clearance?

The MBAs met with Albert in Pierre's small conference room. Jim wore a Brooks Brothers navy pinstripe suit, a heavily-starched, white button down shirt, red striped tie and black tasseled loafers. His gold rimmed glasses recalled the image of an early twentieth-century banker. He had sternly and frequently declared in the offices that he would never change his style to accommodate the fashions of the day.

Jim began the presentation. "Albert, you started too late to develop an efficient system. This is an unmitigated disaster waiting to happen. For this first harvest, we have to do the best we can and accept the cost of large crop losses."

Andy sat next to McHeath. He wore a gray herringbone suit from J. Press, a blue pencil-striped shirt and medium-blue foulard tie. Andy stood and advanced the presentation to the next PowerPoint slide. "Albert, please don't be alarmed by McHeath," he said reassuringly. "He likes to scare people. We can and will fix this for you."

Andy resumed the slide presentation. "For the present, we have prepared a plan to organize, establish the technical parameters for an acceptable product, build a system of procedures for harvesting, create short-term logistics plans, educate the homeowners on how to reap and deliver, and implement an electronic payment system. In Phase Two, we will deliver to you a formal plan to handle larger crops in the future."

"We attempted to hold an educational seminar at the high school auditorium," Jim interjected, "but the mayor vetoed it. Luckily, we convinced Lawrence Silverman, the school superintendent, to overrule the mayor. The school is apparently outside the mayor's jurisdiction.

"We're holding three seminars this week at Roy W. Brown Middle School and rebroadcasting it on our Internet site. We'll also deliver a hard copy of the presentation to each home."

Andy tried to act sympathetic to Albert's anxiety. "It's logistically impossible to collect the plants at every home, but the lawyers ruled that out from the get-go. We were hoping to use the fields near the town pool as a transfer station, but the mayor successfully vetoed the idea.

"Mr. Silverman then agreed to let us use the school fields as the staging area for a few months. How did we do this? We appealed to his financial interests. For a fee of fifty cents a pound, or an estimated $100,000, you can use the soccer field behind Roy W. Brown Middle School.

"The school will use the money to install an irrigation system and plant grass on the soccer field. The teams have been playing on dirt for years. The superintendent creatively suggested we call it a gift to the school which will generate a lot of positive goodwill.

"In summary, our interim logistical solution is to ask homeowners to transport their crop to the school at their appointed time where we will sort and weigh the crop. Our staff will provide the sellers an electronic receipt. We've contracted with a local truck company to ship the sorted product to Morristown."

Jim warned, "We believe the mayor will be an impediment to smooth operations. We suggest you initiate a governmental relations effort to influence his attitude. We don't think campaign contributions will work. We have to convince him this is beneficial to the townspeople. Mad is too mild a word to describe hizzoner. Rather, the words outraged and gone ballistic come to mind."

Andy ran through the remaining slides and concluded the presentation. "We'll get through this, but eventually you'll need a transfer station and processing plant locally near Bergenfield. Otherwise, this is going to cost you twenty dollars a pound to deliver."

After the MBAs left the conference room, Albert slumped in his chair in thought; farming would never be his strong suit. He desperately wanted to return to his lab.

CHAPTER 46

JUNE 24, 2011

To paraphrase Plato, necessity is the mother of invention. And Americans sure know how to invent.

Baby boomers learned how to start a business early in life. Entrepreneurship was part of early television comedy. Moe, Larry and Curly took stabs at opening a detective agency, running a plumbing repair service, and cutting hair at a barber shop in episodes of *The Three Stooges*. Abbot and Costello concocted unusual ways to earn money to pay Mr. Fielding the back rent. And, Ralph Kramden and Ed Norton hatched a weekly get-rich-quick scheme on *The Honeymooners*.

In late May, Kenny Fradella had observed a woman wrestling crabgrass. Kenny was the high school metal shop teacher who often won teacher-of-the-year awards. He had an uncanny ability to tell fantastically funny tales about the most mundane events. He was fifty years old and had back problems for the last ten. He sympathized with the woman as she bent over, pulled the crabgrass upward, and cut the plant with a garden scissor. She repeated this process on every plant for over three hours. It was tough work.

Kenny thought there had to be a better way. He returned to the shop and designed a Rube-Goldberg-looking contraption that cut the crabgrass from a standing position. A noose grabbed the weed by the throat, and a hand lever swung a scythe to cut above the plant roots.

The beta version was very complicated, unwieldy and dangerous. It nearly cut through Kenny's steel-toed safety work boots. Version 1.1 added a safety shield.

Ms. Harriet Wilson, the chemistry teacher and Kenny's school hall buddy, offered to help. Harriet had taught at the school for nearly thirty years and had managed to win a handful of teacher-of-the-year awards, too. Around the halls, she wore a lab coat and kept safety glasses around her neck. At school, she always wore her long brown hair in a bun – not for style – but to keep it from catching fire in one of her student's experiments gone wrong.

She studied Kenny's gizmo and suggested some improvements. First, she added a small lithium-ion, battery-operated motor to operate the scythe. Harriet then added a two-dollar tilt sensor that activated a brake; it stopped the blade if the scythe angle became too steep. Now, no one would lose a toe if they raised the scythe off the ground.

Kenny and Harriet redesigned the machine several more times to make it work simpler. The final touch was adding a slip-proof rubber handle and a self-cleaning function. Voila! The teachers had created a lawn and garden crabgrass reaper in less than a month. It cost $312 and a hundred hours to build the first prototype. Eat your heart out, Eli Whitney!

Kenny and Harriet tested their product at a few volunteer homes after school hours. The first few tests were a little rough on the crabgrass, but the leaves were still saleable. After a few minor adjustments, the contraption worked pretty well. Basically, it was a combination weed whacker, tree trimmer and lawn mower bag on wheels.

They filed a utility patent for their invention online and agreed to split the $70 Patent and Trademark electronic filing fee.

Neither teacher wanted to be personally liable for someone's improper use of the product. The machine was a consumer device with dangerous moving parts. To protect their personal assets, they established a New Jersey limited liability company. It cost $125 to file a Certificate of Formation on the New Jersey Department of the Treasury web site. They named their new enterprise Crab Baby LLC.

Two weeks before the final crop delivery date, Harriet spent a half day applying for a business license at town hall. In the afternoon, they began making Crab Babies in Kenny's garage.

Woodrow Schaeffer, the BHS wood shop teacher, was Kenny and Harriet's third musketeer. Woody was the junior varsity basketball coach, and at six-foot-two, he could still beat most of his players in a game of one-on-one. He was ten years younger and looked up to his two friends like a kid brother. He had a summer to kill like most teachers, and he wanted to join the party. Woody offered cheap labor and badly needed startup capital to help the team.

At teacher's salaries, they needed Woody's money badly. Woody kicked in $3,000 to buy parts, which was a lot of money to a teacher and a lot of risk. It was exciting just the same, and at worst, tax deductible.

Each day, the Crab Baby management, manufacturing, marketing, sales and finance executives rushed to Kenny's garage and worked out the kinks in the production process. Every night at nine o'clock, they called it a day. Although school still came first, Harriet gave her summer school students a temporary reprieve from written homework assignments. She had little time to grade papers.

Next, they had to find inexpensive parts in bulk. Woody purchased two-by-twos and made handles on a machine lathe. Harriet bought motors on the web, battery packs at Radio Shack, a tilt sensor at a Newark supply store, and wiring and other parts at Home Depot.

Kenny found a thousand scythe blades on EBay from a lawn and garden company that was going out of business. He bought a hundred. Crab Baby was already out of cash and would have to bootstrap the business until they had more capital. The team figured they would sell the first hundred units and use the money to buy parts to manufacture the next hundred.

On the first day, the team produced three Crab Babies and ruined the parts for another five. Day by day, the process improved. By week's end, they increased production to two per hour. Scrap rates were declining, and they managed to salvage parts from bad production runs.

By the second week, the company had sold twenty Crab Babies for $199 apiece. They grossed almost $4,000 at a small profit. If they broke fewer parts during assembly, they'd make money. Ms. Wilson opened a bottle of Freixenet champagne and they toasted to their success.

Crab Baby needed money to grow. The executive team wrote a ten-page business plan using a template from the Small Business Administration web site. It took half a week to write and rewrite the plan to look presentable. The appendices included color photographs of the Crab Baby in action, a copy of the patent filing and letters from satisfied customers.

Armed with five copies of the plan, they visited Michael Li at Consolidate Northern Bank to ask for a loan. Michael cautioned them about growing too rapidly. What if your first design fails in the field? What if Pierre stops buying? Perhaps you'll find better or cheaper parts and you regret purchasing too much of the wrong inventory? It was good advice.

It would take months to get approval for a Small Business Loan, but they started the application process. In the interim, Michael approved a $5,000 overdraft credit line for each of the teachers.

The team figured they could make about 100 machines a week if they hired some part-time workers to work on weekends. There was no shortage of willing bodies in the high school ranks, and five of their favorite students joined the Crab Baby workforce.

The three teachers taught: Safety First! The scythe was very sharp and could easily cut off a finger. Mrs. Wilson kept an old glove box unit in her basement which she used for chemistry experiments. The glove box stood eight feet high; it was basically a pair of industrial rubber gloves poking through a plastic protective window so the operator wouldn't get splashed with chemicals. In this case, the glove box would serve to prevent injuries.

Harriet designed a mechanical robot arm to attach the scythe to the rotating couple which could be operated safely inside the glove box. OSHA would have been proud of the safety conscious design.

At the end of the week, payday came. The company nearly ground to a halt. Kenny, Harriet and Woody looked at each other. No one knew how to figure out the complex payroll tax forms and myriad of regulations. They had created this incredible engineering feat in less than two months, and they were about to be foiled by government bureaucracy.

They opened the federal and state welcome kits. Some welcome! There were federal income tax, FICA social security tax, Medicare tax, state income tax, federal unemployment tax, state unemployment and disability tax, and worker's compensation insurance. It was an administrative nightmare.

Fortunately, Woody's nephew was an accountant; he agreed to set up the payroll system the next week. Meanwhile, they paid the students in cash under the table.

Refusing to be crushed by the government burden, Crab Baby became a humming assembly operation. A high school art student created a logo of an animated weed with bulging eyes. The scythes went out the door as soon as they were assembled.

The word had spread. Two hundred bucks seemed like a lot of money, but the first buyers raved about the machine. The waiting list grew to three hundred.

Crab Baby could potentially sell a unit to every house with a Pierre contract. A thousand units at $200 was $200,000 in sales for the startup business. The teachers estimated they would make $50,000 from the venture, which was a nice addition to their teacher salaries. Harriet and Kenny awarded Woody a 25% profit interest which wasn't too shabby.

Besides the money, it was truly exciting to begin a new business.

CHAPTER 47

JUNE 30, 2011

The first crabgrass harvest went as well as could be expected. The Harvard MBAs donned preppie farmer clothes – khakis, Ralph Lauren Polo shirts, Sperry Topsiders and aviator glasses. The Rutgers aggie grad students wore the more practical jeans, tee shirts, work boots and safari hats to protect against the sun.

At Gilbert's suggestion, they hired a dozen temporary nonunion farm workers who were between crops. They had a free month until New Jersey blueberries ripened. They needed little training to learn how to sort the material and separate the good vegetation from unwanted roots and soil.

Immediately, Team Pierre saw a problem. The crabgrass seeds were going airborne toward the soccer field. Once they germinated, they would become unstoppable. The Aggies designed a collection unit from one of Pierre's spare environmental dust bag devices. Temporary tarps would have to make do. It wasn't the hundred percent solution.

By the end of the week, twenty tons of crabgrass and a ton of seeds had been trucked to Morristown for extraction and storage. The trucks left deep ruts in the parking lot, which Pierre would have to repave. They weren't just being generous good citizens. They needed the soccer field for at least two more crops until they found an alternative transfer station.

The Martini lottery winners received more good news – Pierre agreed to buy all of their August and October production. It was a financial windfall for the lucky ones with contracts.

Neighbor jealousy festered. The unfortunate unchosen raised their voices at the monthly town council meeting. "There's a trail of weeds and dirt snaking through the streets. We demand fines! We demand jail time!" A month in the chair on low voltage would be too light a sentence for these profiteering monsters.

The Star Ledger ran an online blog about the growing anger in the cozy community. Twenty protestors at the town meeting could hardly be considered deep resentment, but it was a slow news week in the July heat.

Eva read the story as the weed dream team sat quietly at Pierre's headquarters. Joining Steven and Albert was Ed Krick, the shampoo business unit manager. Eva wore elegant chic business attire – a white linen jacket covering a navy silk shell. It looked positively summery.

"To begin, I want to congratulate you on the success of your first mission," Eva said enthusiastically. "You did a fabulous job under difficult circumstances.

"How-ev-er," she stretched the word for emphasis, "we don't want to become farmers. We'll manage the process as best as possible for a brief time until the long-term solution is finalized. We also must maintain the good reputation of Pierre. It's getting a little tarnished lately. It looks like the complaints are from people who want to be in on the money. Right?"

Ed Krick said, "I can definitely handle more inventory if you want to increase production. Customer reaction has been overwhelmingly positive. Students at the beautician schools are trying to buy extra samples for relatives. In less than four weeks, an underground movement has formed. The buzz is all over the Internet.

"It's a little early, but I'd bet we got a hit on our hands. We're recommending a quick production run to offer small sizes for sale at the schools. Our product managers have been talking to the deans, and they're ready to sell it if we hit a low price point. If we cut the size to six ounces, we can retail it for $5 dollars. We wholesale at $3 dollars and make a margin of fifty percent.

"The market is small, but still a good entry vehicle. We also considered producing a black market version to create buzz, but I'm guessin' Pierre won't go for it."

"Hold the rest of the marketing presentation for later discussion," Eva said politely. "I'm in the middle of holiday promotions for our fragrance and cosmetics launches. You boys are getting way too ahead of the plan here. I'm just not ready to deal with launching the product until January.

"What about the upset homeowners? Do they really care about the mess, or is it about the money?"

Steven said, "I went to the town hall meeting. A handful are making noise, but they're working for the mayor. I'd say most people are upset they didn't get a contract. It's becoming a lot of money. And don't forget the bragging rights."

"Okay, I get it," Eva smiled. "However, we don't want to buy from the entire town at full capacity. I just cannot imagine using five million pounds of crabgrass anytime in the next few years. It takes far too long for markets to develop. It's very rare for a new product introduction to go national and penetrate the market as quick as you guys are suggesting. So, what are your ideas to spread the wealth in town?"

"Vonce ve process zie plant and extrakt zie chemical," Albert thumped his notebook in cadence with his delivery, "zie materials haf a good shelf life. As long as ve haf space in zie warehouse, I vould not object to shtocking extra inventory."

"Why offer contracts at all?" Ed asked. "Just agree to buy a hundred pounds from anyone living in town. It's still $1,500 per household. That'll calm your protestors."

"We could try, but our biggest problem is logistics until the processing plant is built," Andy asserted. "A thousand deliveries of two hundred pounds is one thing. If four thousand homes deliver a hundred pounds each, we'd have to expand the delivery window to three weeks. More expense. More opportunity for problems. More effect on the neighborhoods.

"Also, we won't outwit the mayor next year. He's not a happy puppy."

"Vell, you might not find zo many homes. Zhey sprayed veed killer in May before zhey realized zis vas valuable. It's a good thingk zat zhey didn't use pre-herbicide. Zat vould have killed zie seeds. Zie veeds vill come back soon. It's very poverful, povver, um, strong. You might haf three thousand homes at most for zie August crop."

Andy spoke in proverbs. "Well, good fortune sometimes is just dumb luck. The seeds were going airborne at the transfer site. The aggies designed a machine to catch the seeds and a screening system to remove the dirt. We've got a ton, I mean literally one ton – two thousand pounds, of seed. We could sell it to anyone who needs it."

"By the time you figure out how to package the seeds and comply with whatever laws we don't know about, the season will be over," Eva mused. "Give them away. Use the Italian guy who signed up the contracts to distribute them.

"Okay, boys. I see a plan forming. First, I want out of the farming business as soon as possible. Let's focus on the transfer station start-up. Second, keep the townspeople happy by agreeing to buy everyone's crabgrass. Ed, you'll have three or four hundred thousand pounds to make shampoo. No more. You'll have to live with it. Andy, that's small enough to handle your logistics problem at the transfer station. Increase the delivery window to ten days. Talk to our Marlon Brando about spreading the seeds. He seems to be a popular guy in town."

Andy and Ed chuckled at the reference to Vinnie Martini. Albert looked befuddled. Wasn't Brando deceased?

"Last item," Eva said. "Albert and Steven, go visit the mayor and ask him to help us. Find out what his trigger point is. You know the town has a tax problem. Our project should raise property values and help him resolve those suits seeking tax abatement.

"Meanwhile, tell your friend Gilbert we'll open purchases to other homeowners. Meeting over. Good luck!"

CHAPTER 48

JULY 11, 2011

July Fourth week was a write-off. Anyone not on vacation was subconsciously body surfing at the beach. A temporary secretary worked the mayor's phones, but he was unavailable. The mayor was clearly intentionally not returning Pierre's calls.

In exasperation, Albert and Steven asked Gilbert for his help. The three of them settled in at a very quiet Ben's Deli.

"I see you have some growing pains. Pardon the pun," Gilbert joked. He had dressed for the summer heat wearing an ivory-colored Don Johnson sports coat and a light peach collarless shirt with the top two buttons undone. He wore shoes with no socks for the full Miami Vice look.

Steven said defensively, "It's a start-up. We expect a few bumps in the road. We think the first harvest went quite well. Now we have a plan to build a more permanent solution to the collection process, but Mayor Alvarez isn't cooperating. He won't see us. I'm guessin' we can't use the junior high after the summer."

"If I were mayor, I'd put a time limit on your stay, too," Gilbert said. "The kids need the fields by September for soccer and gym. No, I think you have to find another place."

"Did you look at the plans we sent you?" asked Steven. "It's a $200 million dollar central processing plant and transfer station. We're beginning to look for sites."

"Yeah, I saw it. Looks fantastic!" said Gilbert. "Any mayor around our area would love to have it built in their town. Well, not the rich towns, but most of the middle-class areas would. And the county and state will be happy too. They'll give you lots of tax abatements if you add employment. But not Hector. He's sticking to his guns."

Steven said earnestly, "Mr. Gilchrist, Pierre is also increasing its purchasing to cover the whole town. It might calm the citizens."

Gilbert didn't have the capital to buy more houses, not that there were any cheap homes left. The landlords in town had already scoffed up the remaining foreclosures in town. Each of Bergen Development's properties was worth at least $50,000 more. That added to nearly $2 million in profits, and half of it was Gilbert's.

"I suggest you meet with Alvarez as a courtesy," Gilbert counseled. "I'll sneak you in through his secretary. He'll probably toss you outta his office, but at least you tried. Then ask the town council to approve the proposal over Hector's objection. Let's just say the council is friendly to your cause.

"I heard you were gonna tear down some warehouses on Front Street to build the facility. No need. The town owns ten acres in Prospect Park. It's at the end of Harrington Street. At $500,000 an acre, the town should be willing sell it to you. That's $5 million dollars for you math whizzes. Don't bother pulling out your HP calculators."

"Very funny," Steven snorted. He decided Gilbert was a good guy and was encouraging a little teasing. "Only old geezers over forty use an HP. We calculate in our head until it's a complex second derivative.

"So why do you think the town would sell? It's not like the town has a lot of ball fields."

"There are two reasons, kid," Gilbert spoke with his Bogart voice. "First, they don't have the money to maintain the grounds. Someone's gonna get hurt playing there. The only thing growing there is your crabgrass. Ironic, huh?

"Second, and more important, the town has a budget problem because of the big drop in real estate values. Yeah, house prices may be up this quarter, but they're still down two hundred grand since 2008. A thousand homes are fighting their assessment value. If they win, the town is really screwed.

"The money from the sale will plug the gap. The mayor can't say no. Well, actually he can and will say no. But the town council will overrule him.

"Go meet Hector, get tossed. Then I'll arrange a meeting with Johnny Carrera on the town council. Albert, you've met Johnny. They call him Johnny True Value in town."

CHAPTER 49

JULY 15, 2011

The business section front page in the Sunday edition of *The Record* blared:

FIRST SECOND THIRD BANK REPORTS LOWER LOAN LOSSES

"The First Second Third Bank reported a $100 million decline in loan losses during the quarter due primarily to short sales of 400 foreclosed properties. The buyers included a real estate partnership, a number of multiple housing owners and a Real Estate Investment Trust.

Sources said the buyers were looking to capitalize on income from sales of a locally grown plant which can be used for pharmaceutical purposes. While the balance sheet improvement is substantial, the bank still holds over $1 billion of foreclosed mortgages in New Jersey and remains under Federal Bank supervision."

David Elliot read the article and thought, *It was my deal, and I'm not getting a dime for it. Not even a pat on the back. No atta boy. Not even a freakin' lunch. The Feds banned all bonuses. I'm losing my job after they shut this mortgage mill down. Well, screw them. I own a few units of Gilbert's partnership. It's not F-U money, but it certainly helps.*

CHAPTER 50

JULY 18, 2011

Albert and Steven sat outside Hector's offices in the old municipal hall on North Washington Avenue. Hector had stalled for a week. He made them cool their heels another hour in the foyer. After a sufficient time of insult, Hector allowed them into his office.

The Pierre men wore deferential suits and ties. No flying ducks. No waddling penguins. No bright colors. Just navy suits and dark foulard ties.

"There's no need to introduce yourselves," Hector barked. He sat with his arms folded across his chest, sweat soaking though the tan suit. Lesser men would have opened a top button and removed the tie. Not Hector.

"Albert's been sneaking around town since April. You, kid, I can tell by your clothes you must be the Pierre MBA. You're not welcome here, but I'll give you ten minutes only 'cause my secretary mysteriously allowed you on my calendar."

Steven deflected the personal attack. It was the second time he had been called kid in two hours. The word contained two totally different meanings: one was an endearment; one was an insult. "Perhaps we got off on the wrong foot. We were trying to keep it quiet until we finished testing the materials. The rumor is that we intentionally excluded Filipinos. I assure you we didn't redline the town. Our agents selected the homes and apartments which were the easiest to sign up. In the next round, we'll include more homes."

"Not if I have anything to do with it!" Hector snapped. "Do you understand what you're doing to our town? The place will be a mess. We'll be the laughing stock of the country. Not just the county. Not just the state. THE WHOLE DAMN COUNTRY!" he yelled. His face reddened.

Steven considered withdrawing peacefully. However, Gilbert had made a good suggestion: "You know Hector is going to say no. Speak to him and grab some sound bites. I'd love to hear him say he doesn't care about how much money the Filipinos make."

Steven stiffened his posture knowing he was about to provoke another blow. "You know, house values are up nicely in the last two months. People are going to make some decent money. Maybe you should embrace it. You could market your town as the home of a wonder plant."

The Mayor's light brown skin was turning purple with anger. "Wonder plant, my ass! You're destroying my town, and I'm gonna make you pay for it. I have legal counsel reviewing our options to sue you for diminution of the value of our homestead.

"It's not just housing, either. Downtown businesses will suffer. I'm working my ass off and asking the shops to improve their frontage. You guys come along, and no one wants to spend a dime anymore."

Steven had enough damaging quotes from the mayor. He delivered the final dagger. "If our product does what we think it does, we could be purchasing over $10 million a year, which is a lot of income to your voters. Do you really want to be the one to tell them they can't improve their standard of living?"

Hector stood and pointed to the door, his face contorted in rage. "Out of my office, now! I want you out of our damn town. You go one bleeping mile over the speed limit, my officers will ticket you. If you leave one blade of grass on the street, we'll fine you for littering. You may have Gilbert helping you, but I'm still the mayor here. Oh, yeah, by the way, don't bother asking. We're not planting crabgrass at my town hall or in any of my parks."

"Last time we looked at the ownership records, they're the *town's* buildings and parks, Mayor, not yours." Steven stood and left. Albert meekly followed.

CHAPTER 51

JULY 18

A policeman followed Steven's car as he drove under the speed limit and parked behind Ben's Deli. Steven needed a sugar rush following the beating. Gilbert and Johnny True Value were already seated at a booth.

Albert: "Mayor Alvarez vas not very velkoming, vwelkom, um friendly."

Steven: "Like you predicted, Gilbert. He threw us out of his office."

Gilbert: "Well, you did the right thing and asked."

Steven: "Hector's words were pretty damaging. I wish I had a recorder."

Gilbert: "A recorder would make you look like the bad guy. For the record, we can now say Hector rejected a proposal which could make millions for our townspeople. Let's focus on the next steps. Johnny, you call another emergency meeting of the town council to approve the plan."

Steven: "Mr. Carrera, our needs are rather simple but big. We want to build a transfer station and processing plant on the Prospect Park fields with the town backing of an industrial revenue bond. The town must provide a full-faith guarantee of the bond. Hackensack has already indicated they want the project and are willing to guarantee a bond if we build it there. Having another town compete usually helps you sell the guarantee to your detractors.

"We'll structure the deal and form the company to operate the facility. We'll also provide the equity investor to fund the operating company. However, we need the town approval. In return, we will increase our offer to at least a hundred pounds a year from everyone in town. That's $1,500 a house."

Johnny tried to act nonchalant, but he always sat in Gilbert's shadows. It was time to establish he was the boss in these negotiations. "You already know you gotta have town council approval. I can deliver enough votes. I'm a hunnerd percent sure. Dougie and Hector won't go along, but we don't need their votes.

"But I may hafta grease the wheels a little. Just so there's no money paper trail, I suggest Pierre buy ten thousand pounds from companies controlled by me. I'll deal with takin' care of the right people with the money."

Gilbert almost fell off his chair. It was the most blatant demand for a bribe he had ever witnessed. In twenty years of public service, Gilbert had never asked for money. He saw a few tickets to Giants games, but he never received a gift large enough to raise eyebrows or influence his decisions. Johnny was about to have his head handed to him. He wouldn't be the one to tell him.

Steven kept his poise. Pierre had trained its executives how to deal with this type of advance. "Mr. Carrera, we're a public company. We cannot make improper payments to any government or one of its officials. It's a criminal offense. Not only would Pierre pay a fine, but the officers involved would go to jail.

"If you asked us to purchase product from the town as part of a contract which is fully disclosed, we could do it. But mind you, the mayor refused such an offer not more than an hour ago. If the payment is to you, I'm afraid we cannot approve such a deal."

Gilbert leaned away from him. Johnny sat uneasily and alone. He backpedaled. "Of course I meant the town. Not me. That'd be a bribe. I just think it'd be good if the town sold crabgrass from its properties. I was suggestin' we include it on the agenda at the town council meetin'. Hector's alone. The rest of us are behind you."

Steven sat silently for a full minute to let the moment soak into Johnny's tiny moral conscience. "As long as we're clear," Steven said. "Let's discuss the process. First you and your legal counsel should meet with the investment banks who are raising the money to build the plant.

"We estimate you'll need $150 million to build the transfer station and another $50 million of operating capital. We included an estimated $5 million to pay the town for the Prospect Park fields. The funding for the equity of the operating company has also been arranged.

"This deal is too small for our investment bankers. Instead, a smaller bank, Mexican Chartered Financial has agreed to manage the offering. They can raise the $200 million within three months assuming you have qualified financial staff and the markets continue to be favorable. It also assumes your town council approves the bond.

"When can the bankers meet your council?"

CHAPTER 52

AUGUST 10, 2011

The town council crowded into the New York City conference room overlooking the West Side Promenade. Mexican Chartered wasn't a household name, but they sure didn't skimp on furnishings. Doug attended despite his objection to the bond. Someone had to protect the town's interests. Hector was a no-show.

The rest of the town council was there. Howie wore a new suit. Trudy and Chris wore near-business attire. Johnny felt the deal was a lock and the investment bank was already decided. He wore a tie, but kept it loosely around his neck. He slouched in the chair and feigned interest.

The investment bankers from the municipal finance division began the presentation. They looked like any other Wall Street banker. Belinda, the sole woman on the team, was a pretty, thirty-year-old blonde who carried twenty pounds too many due to long hours and excessive travel. She wore an expensive navy suit from Bloomingdale's, a gold and navy silk scarf, and a gold brooch. The two men wore European cut suits and bright colored ties.

The bankers handed out a mocked-up prospectus cover on top of an old bond offering Bergenfield had financed. The $200 million on the cover looked like an impressive number. Equally impressive were the $4 million in banker fees and commissions.

Belinda spent the next hour going through the details. She explained how the bank marketed and sold the deal. She discussed the need for limited dog and pony shows where management would meet with potential investors. The investors would be primarily large municipal bond mutual funds. Ten percent of the offering would be sold to individual retail investors. It would be a registered deal, and the bonds would be listed and tradable.

The investment bank had done its homework. The details of the plan were intense. Belinda said, "The use of proceeds is to build the proposed transfer station on the old Prospect Park fields. The operating company would reserve $50 million for working capital. As is customary, a guarantee from the town of Bergenfield would be required. The interest rate will be four percent, tax-free. No principal payments will be due until the third year of the bond, and would thereafter be amortized over the remaining seven years of the term."

The senior suit with the lime green tie and matching suspenders took over the presentation. Tall and handsome with blond hair and tortoise-shell glasses, he looked like someone with a name like Chip from Greenwich, Connecticut.

He said, "My name is Chip Thurstwell. I work in the private equity area of the bank. An operating company will be established and staffed with industry personnel. The operating company is necessary to manage the crop receiving, processing and transfer operations. Pierre does not want to remain as the operator.

"We have identified a hedge fund willing to fund the company. They historically have funded agriculture and biofuel start-ups which have tolling revenue guarantees. The hedge fund, Oenotropae Funding Corp, will invest $5 million dollars in equity capital to run the station. They insist on an exit plan where they sell their equity preferably at a profit within three years."

Howie googled and laughed to himself. Oenotropae was the name of three Greek goddesses who can, among other things, change grass into wheat. How karmic! Now, they'll be changing crabgrass into silver!

More than a few hedge fund managers had named their funds after mythical gods. There were very few good names left from which to choose. Jupiter, Neptune, Mars and Apollo were taken long ago. Roman, Greek, Egyptian, Scandinavian. All gone. They had to search really hard for Oenotropae.

Chip the prep continued, "We located a temporary agribusiness management team from Chicago to run ops until a permanent team can be hired. We have retained a search firm, The Oxbridge Group, which has a history of Wall Street searches but also has ties to the ag community through its Lake Forest connections. Nina Swift is in charge of the search and is standing by on Skype. Nina?"

Nina appeared on the TV screen. She was a pretty blonde with a freckled nose. She looked like she was in her thirties, but her bio on the screen implied an extra decade. She sounded every bit of the Philadelphia Main Line where she undoubtedly lived.

"Gentlemen, thank you for having me. Normally, we wouldn't conduct a search without an engagement letter from the client. However, we understand the critical nature of your search. We identified the three candidates to run your facility. They're all available on a short-term contract. You'll have to reimburse them for living expenses.

"Also, the hiring window is narrow. Offer positions quickly or they will likely go elsewhere. Furthermore, they're very experienced representing companies to investors on your road show.

"The next issue is hiring permanent management in a few months. We are concentrating on the president search. We believe it is important you hire a local person who is familiar with the townspeople and is politically connected."

Johnny sat up straight and fixed his tie. He'd just heard his next calling in life – President.

"He must have a good general business background having successfully run a $50 million dollar business," Nina added.

Johnny thought he could get past the experience requirement. It was time to act like a company president and pass the first interview.

"I totally agree with Ms. Swift's assessment," said Johnny, obviously kissing ass. "Let's first conquer this bond financin' and then conduct the search. I'll be the point man on this project. I look forward to workin' with Oxbridge."

Nina nodded. "Thank you, Mr. Carrera. I have one last issue if you don't have questions. Our firm will receive a fee of one-third of management's total compensation, which is standard in the business."

Johnny said, "You've done great work. Of course we'll pay your fee."

Nina signed off Skype. Chris started complaining about the fees and high salaries.

Howie snapped, "How are you gonna get the deal done without experienced people? Who's gonna run the place?"

Chris said, "I can manage it easily! There's nothin' to it."

Howie countered, "You? And how much money do you think the bank will raise with you in charge?"

Trudy patted Chris on the shoulder and he became quiet.

The third team member stood and took over the presentation. "My name is Javier Maria Santiago Blohm Louis Mendez. I'm a vice president in the Municipal Finance Group. You can call me Javier.

"The bond covenants require a certain level of guaranteed revenue funding for repayment. It's called a tolling arrangement. Pierre has agreed to commit to a fee no less than $3 a pound and a minimum of one million pounds. That covers operating expenses and half of the interest. You can make up the shortfall in the early years from the working capital reserve. If the production increases to the full town capacity, the total fee would increase to $14 million.

"According to our projections, the project will make money in year two. This assumes you will hire low-cost seasonal nonunion workers during processing. The bond covenants allow you to buy and sell the commodity to balance your production and reduce your risk. Typically, this translates into profits on commodity trading."

The presentation continued for another hour. In excruciating detail, the bankers laid out the potential investors, their sales and marketing plan, the timing of the due diligence, document preparation, road show and closing. Every task was planned – even lunch for the Saturday drafting session. The menu from Fraunces Tavern on 54 Pearl Street in lower Manhattan was attached to the planning schedule. George Washington had said farewell to his Continental Army there a tad more than two centuries ago.

At the end of the presentation and after a few minor questions, Howie stood and spoke. He was wearing his new suit bought by his Bergen Development partners as a gift. Despite Trudy's protests, he had purchased three brown suits, one in each shade. Today, he wore a dark brown vested suit with a snazzy blue and brown striped tie.

"As you all know, the mayor is not in favor of the bond offering. He also is against growing crabgrass for profit despite its overwhelming benefit to our townspeople.

"He informed me in writing the bond offering requires his approval and a town referendum. I reviewed the town charter with our outside counsel, and we have concluded the town council can approve the bond offering with a two-thirds majority vote. Let's proceed, but follow protocol."

Everyone but Doug nodded their heads. Doug said, "I just heard the same presentation you heard. This project's going to lose money in the first year. I heard nothing to lead me to believe it'll get any better. I think Pierre should provide more tolling guarantees if this stuff is so important to their future."

Belinda looked up from her Blackberry. "The tolling agreement was negotiated between Pierre and the representatives from the largest bond investors. They don't require full tolling coverage."

Doug was alone in his argument. "Maybe the bond investors are happy, but we have to give the guarantee. Speaking for the town, I'm not satisfied."

Johnny interrupted, "Look, Doug. We know you and Hector are against this huge opportunity for our townspeople. You've had your turn tryin' to sabotage it. This crabgrass is the best thing to happen to people in this town in a hunnerd years. And you two guys aren't goin' to stop it. Now, the bank said the tollin' agreement is good 'nough and if it's good 'nough for them, it's good 'nough for me. Let's finish this up and let the bank raise the money. Right guys?"

Trudy, Howie and Chris mumbled their assent. Doug restrained his anger. He and Hector would have to battle it out in the town council meeting.

CHAPTER 53

AUGUST 15, 2011

Howie brought outside legal counsel to the town council meeting. He expected a battle and got one. For over an hour, in front of a dozen citizens and the town Internet TV camera, Mayor Alvarez argued the bond was illegal and threatened to sue the town council if they approved it. The lawyers continued to cite the sections of the town charter which proved him wrong. Hector was championing a lost cause.

Hector rose and spoke into the microphone. "We've worked hard together these last three years to rebuild our town. We're making progress improving the enterprise zone. The real estate collapse is behind us; home prices are rising. I'm pleading with you. You're risking our solvency. You're putting us on the hook for a $200 million dollar bond guarantee. Your miracle plant may not turn out as good as you hope. You could be stuck with an expensive building, a huge debt obligation and no playgrounds. I truly believe guaranteeing the bond is a bad idea.

"Nevertheless, I know the rest of the council is voting for the proposal. I'm asking you to let the townspeople speak. Hold a town meeting and hear the voice of the people. If they're in favor of your plan, I'll step aside and let you approve the bond."

Johnny True Value read a text message from Gilbert, who was watching the meeting on the town television station. Johnny rose. He thought the headhunter might be watching on the Internet so he had to dress and speak like an executive. He wore his best solid navy blue interview suit. He took a crash public speaking course by watching a few company CEOs deliver investor presentations on the Internet. The lesson: look at the camera, speak slowly, smile, use hundred dollar words and don't argue with anyone!

"Hector, I know you're impassioned about this issue, as are we. This is real money for the citizens of our humble town. The rest of the town council believes it's time to stop acting parsimoniously. We should do what's right for the people, not what's right for us as individuals. Regardless, I'm open to a forum to let the people speak. Of course, this must be arranged posthaste. If no one else objects, we'll hold a town meetin'…I mean meeting at the high school gymnasium on Thursday night at 7:00 PM."

A surprised Hector stared at Johnny and thought, *Who the heck taught Johnny to use words reserved for a prep school English teacher? Has any human being ever used parsimoniously or posthaste in the same speech? And who dressed him this morning?*

CHAPTER 54

AUGUST 18, 2011

Nearly a thousand people packed the Bergenfield High School gymnasium bleachers. Another hundred spectators stood in the SRO section at the end of the basketball court. The doors to the gym were opened for ventilation, which only let the August heat in.

It quickly became a social event reminiscent of a sophomore sock hop – the guys on one side and the girls on the other. Moms talked about their kids. Dads discussed manly things like the Yankees and the Mets. The crowd was loud but not rowdy.

The town's Internet television camera aimed at the podium. Mayor Hector Alvarez wore a navy sport coat and an all-American red, white and blue tie. He looked tired and beaten. He barely managed his official mayoral greeting smile. A few supporters gathered near him in a protective cocoon.

Vinnie Martini was enjoying his rock star status. The word was out. He controlled the Pierre contract awards. The Bergenfield Don sat on the corner bleacher while his patrons paid homage. He was friendly and affable but publicly denied his influence. "Guys, guys, c'mon. I'm not da boss here. Just helpin' where I can. Youse all know me," he said with a big wink.

Mayor Alvarez stood and asked for quiet. "I want to thank you all for coming tonight. This issue is important. We want everyone to have their opinion heard.

"I will speak first and give my viewpoint against the bond offering. Johnny Carrera will speak for the proponent's side. Then we'll open the mike for comments from the audience. After the meeting, the town council will move to a separate room and vote.

"First, let me explain the facts. Pierre Beauty Products wants the town to build a $200 million dollar transfer station and processing plant. That equals $7,000 dollars of debt for every man, woman and child in the town! That's $22,000 dollars for every home!

"They want us to provide a bond guarantee, but they're not guaranteeing anything in return. Why aren't they at least agreeing to buy enough crabgrass to support the facility? Why? 'Cause they're not sure the miracle plant is performing miracles just yet. That's why.

"They don't care about you or your kids. They want to take away our baseball fields which serve as a source of recreation to our townspeople. I don't have to tell you spare land is not a plentiful resource in our town.

"Those issues alone are enough to make you vote against the deal. But it gets worse. Yeah, you might see some temporary income from selling crabgrass if you're lucky enough to win the Pierre sweepstakes. But turning our town into a weed terrarium will destroy your property values. Any chance of improving our shopping district will be lost. People will move. Families will leave our schools. It will be a downward spiral. It's a horrible thing for our community.

"I repeat what I told the council earlier. We've worked hard together these last three years to rebuild our town. We're making progress. Home prices are improving. Please give us more time. I'm pleading with you. You're risking the solvency of the town. It's the worst idea ever.

"Assuming you approve it against my best advice, you gotta ask yourself. Who profits? Did you get a contract from Pierre? Is the wealth distributed fairly?"

A voice from the crowd yelled, "Communist!" Gilbert's shills were seated around the audience; they catcalled, hissed and booed throughout the Mayor's speech.

Hector ignored the insults. "Why doesn't the money from crabgrass sales reduce your real estate taxes instead? You know the town has a budget problem. Hundreds of homes stopped paying taxes 'cause they got financial problems. I have to pay overtime to our dedicated municipal workers who have to clean up after the Pierre deliveries.

"Talking about fairness. I learned some of you were awarded full contracts from Pierre while some only received twenty-five percent deals. You have to ask why a hundred people got treated special. Worse, eight thousand homes didn't get any contract. Yes, Pierre is trying to calm you down by buying a small amount. Will they stop as soon as the plant is built? Suppose Pierre decides to issue more contracts. Who gets them? Friends of Gilbert Gilchrist? Do you have to grease the palm of some corrupt politician to get your fair share?

"What if you don't want crabgrass? The weed germinates hundreds of times every summer. Once it spreads, it's impossible to eradicate. Those of you who have nice lawns will lose them if the bond measure passes. Maybe the lawn lobby has a right to sue the crabgrass growers?

"And why is this weed worth fifteen dollars a pound? What's to stop Pierre from dropping the price as soon as the plant is built? For that matter, why shouldn't the contracts go to the cheapest seller? You might have some neighbors willing to sell for five dollars a pound."

The crowd gave a Bronx cheer. Marty Thompson stood and yelled, "I'm not selling my plants for less than $15 a pound. Anyone undercuts me is gonna get a visit from my buddies. Ya know what I mean?" The crowd roared in laughter.

Nicholas Anderson, the Republican Party local leader yelled, "Why don't you confiscate everyone's lawns to pay for increased government spending? You democrats eventually do it anyway."

Someone yelled, "Dem's fightin' words." The crowd gave a collective "Whoa!"

The mayor had to wait until the ruckus died down. The open forum wasn't going well. He pleaded his last argument. "Look at the mess they left in June. Our roads were dirty and covered with weeds. The crabgrass grew all over the soccer field at Roy W. Brown. It's now unplayable."

Of all of the arguments, it was the least convincing. The mayor said in a dejected voice, "Here's my last point."

The crowd cheered the oncoming end of the speech.

"If for only one reason alone," the mayor said, "you should save our ball fields so our kids have a place to play. I turn the podium over to Johnny Carrera."

A voice from the standing-room-only section yelled, "You can't play on those ball fields. They're a mess. Plus, they're full of valuable weeds!" The crowd laughed again.

Sally Brulecki quickly stepped up to the microphone. She was one of the town hotties, a slender divorced mom in her early forties wearing tight jeans and a provocative V-neck sweater. She asked, "How much more could you ruin the town? I need the money to pay my daughter's college tuition!"

The men's section cheered Sally with moral support. "Yeah! Yeah! Heh-heh!"

Johnny True Value walked to the podium. The crowd quieted. Johnny was well liked in a harmless sort of way like all hardware store owners. They greeted you at the store. They helped you find something obscure. They patted your grandchildren on the head. It was hard to be controversial in hardware.

However, the True Value smock was missing. Johnny was dressed for a funeral, perhaps Hector's. However, words like parsimonious wouldn't work with this crowd. He had to speak like the Johnny they all knew.

"Let's respect the Mayor's point of view. He wants what he thinks is best for the town. He really does mean well. But this time he might be wrong. You're lookin' smack in the face of a chance to make some money, and it could get much bigger. You may never see an opportunity like this again in your lifetime."

Gilbert had written Johnny's talking points. It was a blatant appeal to the populist pocketbook. The crowd cheered every word. The small group against the bond referendum kept quiet. They were outnumbered.

"First, I have some new information about Pierre's plans. The mayor already hinted at it. They agreed to buy crabgrass from any homeowner within the town limits. A minimum hundred pounds a year for the next three years. You can make fifteen hundred bucks a year if you want."

The crowd applauded. Several stood clapping. "So, if you want, and I'm certainly not tellin' you what to do. If you want, you all can grow a small plot of crabgrass in your backyard outta sight." Johnny tossed a thumb over his shoulder. "This way you make a little money and you still keep your front lawn nice. What's wrong with that? What's wrong with that?"

More cheers and applause filled the gym. "And oh, not to mention, you guys can keep on buyin' Jake's crabgrass killer so I can pay my bills."

One of the stooges yelled, "What if you're Mickey? How's he gonna get paid? He can't grow a thing with dat black thumb of his?"

Mickey McCaffrey laughed at the ribbing. He was the Pony League baseball coach and had taught hundreds of kids in town how to steal a base and hit the cutoff man.

"Well, Mickey, you're just gonna hafta learn," Johnny joked. "Look at Billie. His lawn is covered in weeds, and I'll bet he doesn't do a thing to make 'em grow. Right Billie? Maybe he can give you gardnin' lessons."

Billie stood in the front row and pointed his huge beer belly toward the crowd. "Right! I'm givin' gardnin' lessons at those adult education classes Thursday nights. Hunnerd bucks to learn my secrets!"

The bleachers shook as the throng stomped their feet and laughed. It was louder than a wrestling team pep rally.

Hector sat alone on the dais and stared at the crowd. Johnny was turning the meeting into a big circus. The bond guarantee was serious business, yet no one was taking it seriously. Even his Filipino brethren couldn't restrain their laughter.

If the headhunter was watching on the Internet, Johnny was passing the job interview with straight A's. The crowd was behind him, and Johnny appeared immensely popular in town.

"Okay kids, quiet down," Johnny said half-seriously. "Next thing. We don't really need the Prospect Fields for baseball. We looked at the schedules. There's plenty of room for the Bronco League to play their games at the other fields in town. They'll play some games under the lights, but most kids I know love ta play at night.

"Anyway, too many people get hurt playin' on the old sandlot. There's no soil left. So we did a quick study. It would cost the town $200,000 dollars to fix the fields with new grass and irrigation. We certainly don't have that kinda money around here.

"So the mayor's point is incorrect. We're not taking away valuable playgrounds.

"The third point the mayor made is the mess we got on the roads. Well, if you ask me, he's givin' you a good reason to approve the transfer station. The mess can be isolated and easier ta clean up.

"And let's not forget. Pierre's been a good citizen. You know they gave us two hundred grand to build a new soccer field. For five years, Hector vetoed the funds to fix the fields. The kids are playin' on dirt. We need Pierre, if you ask me."

The crowd stood and applauded. Johnny had made his point. The battle was over. He didn't need to embarrass the mayor any further.

"If anyone wants to speak, just step up here to the mike."

Gilbert gave a hand signal to his troops to stay seated. Old Mrs. Farnswick walked to the podium. Johnny pulled up a stand so she could see over the podium. She cleared her throat and said, "I think we should censor the computers in the library. The things they show on the Internet are a disgrace."

People bent over in laughter. Johnny called for quiet. "Thank you, Mrs. Farnswick. I'll personally log onto the computers and see what they're lookin' at."

The audience laughter became uncontrollable. A voice from the front row joked, "Johnny's monitoring porn sites. Hey, you gonna give us a written report on your findings?"

"No, no report," Johnny smiled. "Okay, anyone else? No one? Okay, you had your chance. The council is gonna meet in the library. You can stay and watch on the big screen TV. Or you can switch to ESPN. Subway Series! The Yanks are playin' the Mets tonight! Let's go vote."

A group of men grabbed the TV controls and searched for the game on Sports Network. Johnny led the council to the library. Hector sat for a minute with Doug. He was outnumbered and the citizens had spoken.

The town council held the meeting and approved the bond offering. Hector and Doug voted no.

After the TV cameras were turned off, Hector was ungracious in defeat. "I wash my hands of this mess. The place will be a dump. You guys clean it up. When I first moved here, someone told me Jersey was the armpit of the nation. Well, all you're doing is feeding that horrible reputation. You'll never recover."

Hector stomped out of the room. Doug started to follow, but stopped and turned to the council. "I hope you guys know what you're doing."

Johnny returned to the room and reported the voting results to the remaining crowd. Allie sat high up in the bleachers and assessed the damage to the estimated weed killer market. On one hand, Johnny had made the point that people can keep their front lawns and still grow a small plot in the backyard. A lot of people in the audience seemed to nod when they heard the idea. He even encouraged them to buy the weed killer. Allie overheard conversations as she moved through the crowd. Indeed, people liked the idea of keeping their lawns while still making money. On the other hand, Pierre was building a very large transfer station.

She started calculating in her head. The town would produce a million pounds if the thousand homes sold everything and a couple of thousand homes sold a hundred pounds. It was an eighth of the town capacity. Two million pounds was a quarter of the town. She was now pretty sure the hardware store would lose up to a quarter of weed killer sales. She could live with the decline as long as she paid Johnny the right price.

Tomorrow she'd check on the store again and see if sales were holding up.

CHAPTER 55

AUGUST 22, 2011

Allie dropped by the store while Johnny was away, which nowadays was often. Johnny had been running an end-of-season sale for the month of August. Johnny got motivated when he realized Allie wasn't paying for the old junk. Someone had dusted the shelves and removed the old glue bottle.

Allie watched shoppers buying items seemingly out of production since the Civil War. Matt Miller was ringing up a sale of tarnished brass hasps, a set of glass door handles, a package of unusual cabinet knobs and an antique shower rod, slightly bent. It took a final clearance sale to motivate. Who knows? You never know when you might need one of these whatchamacallits. Plus, they're cheap!

Matt knew Allie was snooping, not shopping. However, she was about to become his new boss, and he wanted to put on a good show. He smiled from behind the register, pushed back his white hair and offered to help. Matt was a retired telephone worker who put in two days a week to supplement his income. He had become a full-timer this summer now that Johnny was hanging at the beach.

Allie held up a pound of two-inch aluminum nails on sale for four dollars. "Matt, what do you usually sell these nails for?"

"Well, Ms. Bertrand, we don't usually sell them by the pound," allowed Matt. "Johnny thought of that last month when he started the sale. People don't buy bulk nails here. They go to Home Depot or Loews for big purchases. We usually sell 'em a few at a time for a quarter. There are a hundred nails in a pound, so I'd guess we got about $25 dollars a box."

Allie's first thought was Johnny was dumping inventory below-cost to take cash out of the store. She held up a Baggie filed with rusted and used nails priced at $10. "You're kiddin' me, right?"

"Oh no, Ms. Bertrand. I've sold a lot of those. People buy really old nails and screws for antiquing. I found boxes of old rusted hardware and screws in the basement. They're sellin' pretty well."

Allie looked around the garden area. "Where's all of the Jake's weed killer? I saw a delivery truck unloading bags last week."

"Delivered to customers while I was on vacation last week, Ms. Bertrand," Matt said politely.

Good news thought Allie. "Okay Matt, you can call me Allie from now on. My mother was Mrs. Bertrand.

"I guess you know I'm takin' over here in a few weeks. I'll be visiting a lot. Tryin' to get the feel of the store, ya know. Plus, I've ordered some new items to freshen up the place. And we're shuttin' the store a few days for renovations too. Anyway, if you have any ideas on items which would sell well or somethin' the customers have been lookin' for, let me know."

Allie thanked Matt and headed home. She was still working the night shift at Holy Name, but buying Johnny's store was taking a lot of time. Michael had sent her loan documents to review. Bret had sent her a folder of acquisition documents. The store had a web site, but Allie wanted to add an online store. Her son was fiddling with the project, but he said she needed integrated software to run the online store properly. Maybe she needed to wait a little. She was clearly taking on more than she could handle in the short time left until closing.

She needed a nap. The documents could wait. Besides, she didn't understand the archaic language anyway. She'd just ask Michael and Bret to decipher them at her new temporary office in Ben's.

CHAPTER 56

AUGUST 23, 2011

Panama Blonde found a new set of dining friends far from JB's and Bret's tables. She was keeping a safe distance from Mistyland. She also started wearing a light waterproof trench coat to protect her from any more accidental cocoa spills.

She figured sitting fifteen feet from Bret and on the other side of the dividing wall was far enough. If cocoa flew over the wall, everyone had to consider it a toss and not an accidental spill. Even by JB and his biased judges. The sportscaster announced, "Here are the scores. Misty got a nine, a nine, and a three from the Bolivian cocoa judge! It's unfair. Something has to be done about the South American judges in the cocoa tossing event. They'll ruin the sport!"

Misty hadn't arrived yet. Bret was sitting alone reading *The Wall Street Journal.* Panama Blonde looked around and decided it was safe to approach. After speaking for less than a minute, she returned to her table out of Bret's sight.

Misty caught Panama Blonde's movements through the deli window. She rushed into the deli and beelined for Panama's table. Misty pulled her up by her arm and dug in her fingernails.

"I told you to stay away from Bret," she spat angrily. "Do you really wanta mess with me, bitch?"

Misty scraped her four-inch stiletto heels across Panama's open-toed sandals and drew blood.

Panama pulled free and grabbed her bleeding arm while hopping on her good leg. "What kind of animal are you? You hurt me! I was just asking Bret a question. You don't own him. Besides, I have no intentions on him. I'm still married, in case you didn't know."

Misty backed Panama against the wall near the front door. She snapped, "We all know your husband ran away from you, you heartless witch. He's not lost at sea. He's hidin' from you.

"This is your last warning. If I ever see you talk to Bret again, I will do more than draw a little blood. And some words of advice. I'd wear construction boots around here."

Panama wasn't accustomed to physical confrontations. Even though she had seven inches on Misty, she was forty years old and would never think about doing anything but retreating from an attack. She wasn't sure how to react, but she had a bloody arm and her foot hurt like hell. She stared at Misty for a second, turned and limped to her car.

Misty walked around the corner and sat with Bret. He said, "What happened to Panama, honey? You two aren't fighting again, are you?"

"Oh, it was just friendly girl chat. Nothing serious. I think she had to go home and change her shoes." Misty smiled.

Bret looked across the room and saw Allie chatting with Michael and JB. Michael was leafing through a set of documents and explaining them to her.

Misty was babbling some nonsense about fashion or Hollywood or television. Bret couldn't be less interested. He ignored her and read the closed captioning on the morning's financial news.

STCK-TV reported home sales were horribly low and nowhere near a rebound. Yearly new-home starts were under 300,000 homes – 20% of the normal build. Mortgage interest rates were low, but very few buyers qualified for the new tough restrictive terms.

The reporters asked for a comment from a trader on the New York Stock Exchange. He gave an impish smile wearing his medium blue trader's jacket and picture ID card above his shirt pocket. "If you wanna end the housing crisis, you gotta either increase the demand, and we know that ain't gonna happen anytime soon, or reduce the supply. The best way to reduce the housing supply is to bulldoze a million homes in California, Arizona, Nevada and Florida. Then home prices'll pick right up. Trust me. So our stock of the day is Caterpillar. We think bulldozer demand is gonna go up."

The announcers laughed. The stock recommendation wasn't taken seriously. Traders had a million puns. Airline stocks are taking off. Garbage stocks are picking up. Elevator stocks are up and down. Soup stocks are hot. It was Wall Street corniness to pass the day.

Other stories passed by on the closed-capture banner. The interest rate on short term treasury securities was near zero. Bond traders were arguing with economists over the right amount of stimulus to pull the economy from the crash. Would the United States default on its debt like Tea Party Congressmen were threatening?

And then, breaking news! A weather map commandeered half of the TV screen. Hurricane Irene was threatening the New York and New Jersey area. It was still hundreds of miles away and would land Friday or never. Today was Tuesday. The weekend was a lifetime away. Hurricanes didn't hit the Northeast often. They usually turned out to sea or headed inland after battering the Outer Banks in North Carolina. The arrow on the TV map pointed straight at Ben's Deli's front door.

CHAPTER 57

AUGUST 28, 2011

Irene was downgraded to a Category One Hurricane when it bounced back to sea after a ten-hour pummeling of the Outer Banks. It was heading north toward New Jersey.

NOAA predicted a storm surge at high tide and major flooding. New Jersey declared a state of emergency and mandatory evacuations for Atlantic City and low-lying areas east of Route 9. New York City did likewise and shut the subway system in anticipation of flooding. The governments were taking the threat seriously.

Irene landed in Little Egg Inlet, New Jersey at 5:35 AM on Sunday. A few hours later, it smacked Coney Island. Irene's hurricane winds did their usual damage – pruning trees, leveling signs, tearing shingles and roof tiles. Her greater wrath wasn't wind, it was water.

Flooding was extreme after eleven inches of rain were dumped on the state at high tide. There was no place for the water to go. The Hoboken train stations were submerged. A lane of the Holland Tunnel closed. Felled trees blocked roads everywhere. Millions lost power. Paterson, New Jersey looked like the lost underwater city of Atlantis.

And the water kept coming long after the storm subsided. Guess where all the rain in New York State goes? Downhill to New Jersey.

Irene flooded Bergenfield and drowned the crabgrass crop. Streets near Cooper's Pond had become waterfront property. Homeowners tried dredging their lawns, but the water returned. The crabgrass on higher ground fared slightly better. The plants in the low end of the valley were mush.

Although the crop yields would be low for August, the rivers of water spread crabgrass seeds to every home in town. The next harvest in October could be spectacular.

The hurricane was good news for Johnny True Value. In the three days before Irene landed, he sold every hurricane lamp, battery, saw, hammer, diesel generator and nail in the store. The sale was over. He charged full price for every item. *Someone keeps watchin' out for me*, he thought. Just in time for the sale to Allie.

CHAPTER 58

SEPTEMBER 1, 2011

The critical issue for Allie was weed killer sales. She wanted to canvas the neighborhood to get a feel for how people were leaning. Did they want to join the weed growers? Was it worth their while?

Following Irene, Allie had to conserve gasoline for the daily drive to Holy Name. Most gas stations were closed; there was no electricity to run the pumps. Allie used the surrounding chaos as an excuse to conduct a backyard survey. Many people were home from work due to the lack of petrol. She canvased the three blocks near her house.

Her neighbors' attitude about Pierre was equally divided and highly correlated to the state of their lawns. If they had nice grass, they were anti-Pierre. If they had a lawn of uncontrollable weeds, they were pro-Pierre. And a third was noncommittal; they'd withhold judgment until they saw how things worked out for the others.

However, even the best gardeners were going to let just a little crabgrass grow for the money. What could it hurt?

Annie Fowler said, "I'm not a weed snob. John won't mind if I grow crabgrass out of sight. But I'd better not let the stuff get outta control. It's gonna be a real trick. The stuff is nasty. It spreads like wildfire."

By Thursday, the gas stations had reopened and Allie visited the store. It didn't take a genius to see the store inventory was way down. In the face of a natural disaster, homeowners found uses for every hardware item, even grommets. Matt Miller sat idly behind the register.

Allie: "Nice smock, Matt. When do I get mine?"

Matt: "I'd give ya one, but Johnny doesn't keep any extras around. My apron hasta be five years old."

Allie: "You guys must've sold a lot of product before the storm hit."

Matt: "Record week, I reckon. People actin' crazy. There's not a single roll of duct tape or twine left."

Allie: "Good for Johnny, I guess. When do you expect your next delivery?"

Matt: "We usually get one 'bout now, but who knows with all the problems due to the storm. Anyways, I don't do the orderin'. Johnny does. There must be a copy of the purchase order 'round here somewhere, but I couldn't find it. I'll ask Johnny when I see him."

Allie: "Thanks. Don't bother. Besides, what's the chance you'll see him?"

Allie did a three-sixty survey, said goodbye and left the store. There was only so much tire-kicking she could do before closing. Besides, in ten days, Doug would provide final numbers.

CHAPTER 59

SEPTEMBER 12, 2011

The pressure was on. The closing was in three days. JB and Allie had a meeting scheduled at Doug's offices in an hour to review the financial statements and reports from July and August. Bret and Allie sat in Ben's and reviewed the final purchase documents two seats from JB, who sat calm as a Barnegat Bay clam in December.

Misty snuck up and surprised Bret with a kiss on his cheek.

Bret: "Hi, honey. I thought you were going straight to work today."

Misty: "I was, but I just couldn't live without seeing you even one second."

JB made a gagging sound.

Misty: "JB, I'm kidding. You of all people should understand sarcasm. Anyway, Bret, dear, I forgot to mention it the other night. We're having dinner with my family tomorrow might. My mom's making lasagna. Plus my two sisters and their families will be there."

Bret: "Misty, you know I can't. Allie is buying the store Wednesday, and JB and I are helping. We'll have to do it another time."

Misty, ignoring Allie sitting two seats away: "You what? You can't! My mother is already preparing. She told her friends. You'll insult my father. You HAVE to come. Tell Allie to pay for her own lawyer!"

Bret: "Sorry, Misty, but I've committed for months now. You heard me talking about it. You had to know."

Misty, in her sweet, manipulative voice: "Allie dear, you don't really need Bret for the closing, do you?"

Allie, as if Misty weren't sitting two chairs away: "Bret, you'd be putting me in a difficult position. I can't change lawyers on two-day notice. You do what you have to do. I'll delay the closing if your girlfriend won't let you help a friend."

Bret: "No, Allie. We're good. Misty, ask your parents to reschedule. They'll understand."

Misty hissed like a snake: "The inseparable Musketeers, huh? You guys deserve each other, you losers. Bret, can't you see these friends of yours are just trying to break us up. They don't want you to be happy."

Bret: "Please don't be upset. We can see your parents over the weekend."

Misty, her face turning dark and evil: "No, Bret. We won't be seeing my parents over the weekend. Didn't I tell you? I'm going to the Berkshires with my girlfriends. Surely you remember."

Bret looked confused. Vain Misty stood without saying another word and walked toward the food counter with her head facing high.

Bret: "Jeez. What was that about? I think I would have remembered if she said she was going on a girl's weekend. I'm sorry you guys have to hear our dirty laundry."

Allie: "Don't fall for it, Bret. She's using emotional blackmail. She wants you to think she's with other men to punish you so you won't defy her again. You've been dating, what? Six months? And she's playing this kinda game?"

JB: "I don't know psychology, but I do know a psycho when I see one. That look on her face had Norman Bates written all over it."

Allie: "Don't be silly. She's not a slasher. I took a lot of psychology classes in nursing school. It's called triangulation. She threatened an affair to make you jealous."

JB: "I thought triangulation was how life guards locate swimmers who start drowning."

Bret: "C'mon, JB. This is serious. What am I supposed to do?"

Allie: "The only cure for any problem is adult conversation. However, she may need therapy if this is imbedded behavior. You got the time? She might need years of counseling."

JB: "Don't cure her yet. I want to meet that other person she's got hiding in there. Did you see the Bride of Frankenstein look when she left? Priceless!"

Allie: "Okay guys. Joke all you want. JB, I have to run some errands. I'll see you in an hour. Good luck Bret."

CHAPTER 60

SEPTEMBER 12

Misty psycho-walked to the food line and poured an extra-large drink from the soda fountain. She was fiddling with her budget envelopes at the cash register when she saw Allie stand and start toward the door. Misty threw the payment on the counter and swiftly crossed the expanse.

Allie caught the movement from the corner of her eye. Misty faked tripping and lunged toward Allie, soda first. Allie sidestepped and the contents of the drink floated through the air. Allie's foot was just far enough in the aisle to catch Misty's heel. Misty did a face-plant into a thirty-two ounce puddle of grape soda and ice. She was a purple mess. Allie's assist was elegant yet unseen to casual observers. It was a work of art.

Phone camera flashes popped. Bret and JB looked on in shock. Ben played *Smoke on the Water* on the jukebox. He shrugged his shoulders toward JB. "Deep Purple is the best I could do."

Allie grabbed a handful of napkins and threw them on Misty, clearly not trying to be helpful. She stepped over her, careful not to get wet. Turning to JB, Allie smiled and said innocently, "I'll see you at Doug's."

Purple Misty sat in the puddle unable to stand. Miguel started mopping the floor around her. Bret, half in fear, offered her a hand.

"Get away from me, you bastard! It's all your fault!"

She stared angrily at Allie who was smiling as she sashayed out the door. This battle was just beginning.

CHAPTER 61

SEPTEMBER 12

JB walked through the foyer to Doug's conference room and caught Dottie and Allie laughing at something on her iPhone. It was a pic of the battle at Ben's. Bergenfield's social media had already posted pictures of Misty online. They named it the "Grape Scrape". No one could find a good rhyme for purple.

Dottie hid her phone, slightly embarrassed she was caught gossiping. JB smiled. "Don't worry, Dot. I won't tell Doug as long as you send me a copy. I'm making a collage for Christmas."

Dottie showed them into the conference room where they faced another foot-high stack of carefully-prepared due diligence files.

JB and Allie studied the reports. July and August financial statements. Sales by product code. Accounts payable aging. Inventory detail listing. The final balance sheet.

JB: "Johnny sure did step in it. Sales were over $300,000 in August – more than double the normal volume."

Allie: "Like I told you. Store inventories are way down. Matt Miller said they had record sales 'cause of Irene."

JB: "It's not just Irene. Weed killer inventory is zero. It was $300,000 when you signed the LOI."

Allie: "Isn't that a good thing? It means people are still buying the weed killer. Matt said a truckload came in August and was already delivered to customers."

JB: "It's good going forward, I guess. But your borrowing base is way down. You needed the inventory so you could borrow from the bank."

Allie: "What am I gonna do? I can't pay him $650,000 in cash if I can't borrow from the bank."

JB: "Don't get discouraged. The LOI says we get to adjust the purchase price. Johnny thinks he's pulling a fast one, but he can't get away with it. Keep looking."

Allie sounded defeated. JB sounded reassuring.

JB: "Yup, there it is. Johnny stopped paying his vendors. His past-due payables are almost a hundred grand. I'm guessin' Johnny pulled $400,000 dollars of cash from the store in the last forty-five days. He's diabolical. If only he used his genius for good, the world would be a better place."

Allie: "How can you be making jokes at a time like this? I can't buy the store now."

JB: "Allie, don't you trust me? Of course you can and will buy the store. Remember, the LOI did two things. First, it gave you an option, meaning you can but don't have to buy the place. Second, the LOI says Johnny has to keep the balance sheet exactly the same or we adjust the price. He has to put the money back."

Allie: "Who's gonna tell him? Oh, I see the look, JB. I don't know how to bargain. What do I say?"

JB put a comforting arm around her shoulders. "Allie, I'm going to tell you a top corporate secret. At work, when a crisis formed, when the world seemed to be ending, when there were no answers in sight, when all hope was lost, we went to the one place where miracles appeared. We went where magical solutions became clear as day. We went to lunch!"

They thanked Dottie and walked down Washington Avenue to Tommy Fox's. JB was about to teach Allie the next step in negotiating tactics.

CHAPTER 62

SEPTEMBER 14, 2011

It took Doug two days to find him. Johnny had turned off the ringer on his cell phone while fishing in Lavallette. He finally returned Doug's call and said he planned to stop by the closing, sign a few docs, collect the check and hand over the keys. Doug told him to get his ass up to Bergenfield before the deal fell apart.

He cruised the eighty miles back to Bergenfield in his new red Cadillac Seville paid for with the cash he had pulled from the store. An unshaven and unkempt Johnny entered the conference room an hour late and smelling slightly like fish. Ten o'clock had become Johnny's new nine.

JB had counseled Allie on how to deal with Johnny. Be tough. Deliver the message. Be willing to walk away. Don't let him think your offer is negotiable. And if things aren't going well, toss out a personal insult to throw him off.

Allie understood. She also had been a nurse for twenty years administering TLC and had her limitations on how tough she could act. She didn't have manly tough-guy red ties and suspenders in her wardrobe to look mean. She made do with a beige linen blouse and jeans. No makeup. No jewelry except a runner's watch. Nothing girly or frilly.

"Johnny, looks like you had a nice summer," Allie opened. "It smells like you've been fishing."

"I heard you've been by the store," said Johnny. The insult about his odor passed undetected. "Sales 've been great. You're buyin' at just the right time. I'm kinda sorry to be sellin', ya know."

Allie was extremely nervous. She focused on JB's advice and took a deep breath. "Johnny, I'm still interested in buyin' your store, but we need to have a conversation. Under the terms of the LOI, you were required to maintain your inventory levels and keep your debts current.

"To be exact, your inventory declined $400,000 in the last two months. You wiped out all of the weed killer stock and you drew down the store inventories without replenishing them. Have you reordered inventory in the last two weeks?"

Johnny hesitated. "Lemme think. I'm not sure the PO was sent. We've been busy with the hurricane and all."

"Hurricane shmurricane. You haven't been inside the store in a month," Allie sneered. "I'm not done. You also didn't pay your bills on time. Your past-due payables are now a hundred grand. So, before we close, you need to restore the inventory and pay your bills, or we have to adjust the purchase price dollar for dollar."

Doug looked at Johnny and shook his head disapprovingly. Johnny had bled the business dry during the ninety days before closing. No wonder he could afford the Caddy.

Johnny removed his sunglasses and acted shocked. "That's ridiculous. I read the language. It doesn't mean what you say. It means I hafta maintain inventory which means I hafta keep the inventory in good condition. Not at the same dollar level. That'd be crazy. Did your Wall Street boyfriend tell you to pull a fast one at closin'?

"And, Miss Smarty Pants. I always pay my vendors fifteen days late, so they ain't past due accordin' to my business practices.

"So, lemme tell you how it's gonna be. We got a contract for a million bucks, and either you close or I'm gonna sue you," Johnny said, baring his teeth. "Dammit. Dammit. Dammit! I knew I should've looked for other buyers."

Allie called up the spirit of the woman who found the nerve to throw her husband out on the street for being a philandering jerk. "Exactly what other chump would buy this rat's nest? I'm the only dumbass stupid enough to believe I can fix it. Your weed killer business is going down forty percent. The rest of the store does diddly squat."

Johnny leaned forward and pounded the table. "This store is worth a million bucks, and I'm not takin' a penny less. You either come to the closin' on Thursday with a check, or I'm filin' the lawsuit on Friday. Think you can outsmart me, huh?"

"I tried to outsmart you? Are you kidding me?" challenged Allie. "You raided the balance sheet. You dumped inventory below cost. I'll be lucky to sell a single nail in the next year. Now, do you want to live up to your obligations under the LOI, or do we hafta go to court."

"You're not going to court," he screamed. "I am! I WANT MY MILLION DOLLARS ON THURSDAY!"

Doug motioned with his hands to calm down. "Both of you need to cool it. My neighbors can hear you through the walls."

Allie took a deep breath and said calmly, "Johnny, I have an option to buy. You have to sell if I exercise the option. You can sue me. This is America. Any schmo can sue. But you'll lose. I, on the other hand, can sue you and win. I'll own your store for free if you wanna go to court.

"Here's a letter from my attorney statin' the adjustment in the purchase price resultin' from your actions. There's also a document exercisin' the option and buyin' at the new price. The closin' papers have all been updated and the $500,000 dollar adjustment is being applied against the cash component. I'm delivering a check in the amount of $150,000 dollars at closing. I'll see you Thursday."

Johnny crumpled the attorney letter and threw it at Allie. "I'm not sellin' to you at any price. Don't bother comin' to the closin' cause there ain't gonna be one."

Allie pushed the papers back to Johnny. "I'll leave the documents with you in case you change your mind. Otherwise, we shouldn't waste each other's time. Let the judge decide."

Allie left the conference room doing her best to appear strong and steady. Johnny turned to Doug. "Do you believe her? The nerve!"

Doug maintained his professional composure. "Johnny, she happens to be right on the LOI. You can't just sell the inventory and not pay your bills. Also, she has an option to buy. If she exercises it, you have to sell."

Johnny said sarcastically, "Once again, you take Allie's side. Are you guys sleepin' together?"

Doug grabbed his papers and stood. "I'll ignore your last comment. I told you before to get a lawyer, but you wanted to save money. Now you're up a creek, aren't you? I'll go further. You knew you couldn't pull this stunt, but you thought Allie would just give in. Your biggest mistake, buddy, was thinking Allie was stupid. She's not."

CHAPTER 63

SEPTEMBER 14

Allie met JB at Tommy Fox's to commiserate over lunch. She did what she had to do, but didn't feel good about it. Playing hardball was not her natural suit, and she felt stressed out.

JB asked, "How's the world of big time negotiating treating you? You're not backing out, are you?"

Allie looked pale. "I feel horrible. I can't believe I talked to another person like that. I told him he smelled like a fish. Some demon was inside me moving my lips. Maybe I'm not paying enough for the store. He's pretty insulted. He's gonna sue me. I'm depressed."

"You did the right thing," JB consoled. "Were you insulted when he pillaged the balance sheet? No. So why should he be insulted when you adjust the price? Allie, negotiations take time. He doesn't have another buyer, and we know he's lazy. It's too much work. Just give this some time to settle in. I can assure you he's talking to Doug, and Doug knows the LOI. He'll talk some sense into Johnny."

Allie eyed JB cannily. "Who's got what in the pool?"

"Michael bet you'll close on Wednesday. Bret has Tuesday. Decker thinks you go to court. Ben and I both picked Monday which is unfair 'cause I have undue influence. I'm pretty sure Misty didn't bet."

Allie managed to laugh. "Oh my God. Misty. I forgot about her. Bret must think I intentionally tripped her. Maybe I am evil."

JB laughed. "You're kidding me. You deny you tripped Misty?"

Allie feigned a look of innocence. "JB, I'll never admit to the crime. Believe what you must.

"Back to your bet. You think I'm gonna change the closing date so one of you can make five bucks? No way. I'll close whenever that jerk calls me."

"Here comes lunch. I ordered red meat so you can stay angry," said JB.

Allie took a big bite of the hamburger and washed it down with iced tea. "JB, I'm in trouble. I was so sure we were gonna close. I already resigned from my job. I can't go back. They hired my replacement. Worse, I tapped out my credit cards to order inventory for my gala opening. If we don't close this deal, I'm screwed."

"Just do like I said. Don't answer the phone if it's Johnny. Make him sweat." JB lifted an eyebrow. "At least until Monday so I win the bet."

CHAPTER 64

SEPTEMBER 15, 2011

Allie didn't want to hang with the crew on the should-have-been closing day. She waited until mid-morning and sat alone in Ben's. She was thinking through her options when Panama Blonde's big boobs bounced past. It pushed Allie over the edge.

She looked up from her drink. "Why are you so cheerful, Miss Bleached-Barbie-Doll-with-the-silly-implants?"

Panama Blonde looked at Allie in total surprise. She wiped something from her eye and scurried around the corner to a table of one, then hid behind a newspaper.

Allie immediately regretted her attack. This wasn't like her. She bought two cherry cheese Danishes at the counter and sat at Panama's table.

"Here, peace offering. I'm sorry, Panama. I'm having a very bad day and you just set me off."

Panama pushed away the offering without taking a bite. Her voice quivered. "Allie, I didn't do anything to deserve this. We don't know each other. I don't know why you hate me.

"I've never done anything to hurt you. I guess you and Bret are friends, but I'm not interested in him romantically. I have a legal problem and he helped me a little.

"I just don't know what I've done to get on your table's bad side. I've even found a new group of friends to avoid you. What do I have to do to stop getting assaulted around here by Misty and you?"

Allie raised her palms. "Whoa! Panama. You really know how to insult a girl. Don't put me in Misty's cell block."

Panama relaxed and let out a breath. "Sorry. She's a piece of work, isn't she?"

Panama took a bite of the pastry. "If we're actually gonna be friends, my name's not Panama Blonde. It's Catherine. Panama is a horrible name Misty gave me going back fifteen years now. It's a long story. But I'd appreciate it if you'd call me Catherine. Catherine Mulcahy is my full name."

"I'm sorry Pan… um, I mean Catherine," Allie said in a gentle tone. "I heard your husband went missing at sea. That's terrible."

"He was kind of a jerk," Catherine shrugged. "I didn't miss him when he took off, and I didn't feel sad when I heard he'd disappeared. I know I sound cold, but he really abandoned me. I mean, he has this stupid mid-life crisis. He hops on a thirty-foot sailboat, which I hear is way too small to sail around the world. We didn't discuss it. He told me he was leaving, and poof, he was gone. And I barely heard from him once he left. Three years later the boat transponder stopped sending signals off the coast of Chile where I hear dangerous pirates hang out.

"He was selfish. He left no money that I know of. He ran a cash business in the garment center in the City. I'm guessin' he took the cash with him on his dick cruise. Plus I'm bettin' he met a couple of girlfriends along the way.

"I don't want him back. I want my life back. We don't have any kids. I've got a good career in the auction business and can support myself. Unfortunately, I'm stuck in limbo until the courts declare him dead, which they won't. Bret is advising on this, not about anything else."

"It looked like you and Misty were fightin' over Bret. I saw the catfight. You know, she threw the cocoa on you intentionally. We all saw it," Allie said.

Catherine laughed. "It wasn't funny. She cost me three hundred dollars. But I'll get my revenge. I heard about the grape soda. I wish I'd seen it. Nice going!"

"Thanks. Call it a favor." Allie let herself smile, then gave a look of remorse.

"I'm sorry for attacking you. Bad-hair day. I'm trying to buy Johnny True Value's store, and he's so sleazy. I'm risking my life savings. If this doesn't work, I'm unemployed."

Catherine said, "Sounds like bigger problems than the stitches I had to get in my foot from little Miss Goosestep. She punctured my foot."

Allie offered a handshake and said, "Okay. Truce. We have a common enemy. The little female Napoleon is too much for just one of us. So why is your nickname derogatory? I always thought it was cute. I think everyone does."

"First things first," Catherine said. "My boobs aren't fake. They're just big. I was thinking about reduction surgery, but I don't wanna go under the knife."

Allie laughed and said, "Honey, every woman wishes she had your problem. Leave 'em alone."

"Well, the puppies do get in the way and guys are always starin' at me." Catherine gave the tiniest jiggle and her breasts tried to find freedom. "See, they have a mind of their own.

"Anyway, Panama Blonde is a name biologists use for a blonde-colored hairy tarantula. I played basketball in high school and had a good game in the state tourney. The paper said I had a gargantuan game.

"Misty was a cheerleader for one of the teams in the bracket. It takes an evil mind to create tarantula from the word gargantuan. They didn't have Google back then, you know. She even created a cheer for me. Somethin' about defending me required a razor and gallon of shaving cream.

"Here it is twenty-three years later, and this Misty creature is back in my life. My husband moved us here, and I couldn't believe my bad luck to run into li'l Miss Pep Rally. She's just a horrible person."

"If I were you," Allie said with her voice rising, "I wouldn't just accept the Panama Blonde name, I'd embrace it. I'd wear Panama hats. I'd make up Panama Blonde business cards. I'd even put a picture of a hairy spider on the back. It'd make that little brat so angry."

"Actually," Catherine confided, "my plan of revenge is a little more sinister. If my spy network is correct, I think Christmas Eve around 12:20 AM is D-day."

Allie looked intrigued. "Tell me. Tell me. What's the plan? How can I help? I love adventures."

Catherine said in a low voice, "You gotta' keep this top secret. No one can know – especially Bret. I know how to burn Giovanna."

Catherine and Allie huddled, and for the next fifteen minutes, they masterminded the details of the Christmas Eve midnight massacre.

CHAPTER 65

SEPTEMBER 16, 2011

Johnny called Howie for advice and Howie confirmed Doug's conclusion. Allie had properly exercised the option and Johnny had to sell. Technically, Johnny was in default and Allie could sue for damages.

Johnny concluded Howie was an idiot and hired a lawyer from a big Hackensack corporate law firm who told Johnny the same thing. Johnny immediately fired him and put a stop payment on the thousand dollar retainer.

Two more lawyers and two thousand-dollar retainers later, the vote was unanimous. Johnny had tried to pull a fast one and got caught. Jay, the third lawyer, told him, "If you were in a court of law, a judge could conclude your behavior was very bad. Worse, Allie was a single parent who left her job to buy the store, and a jury would be very sympathetic to her."

Johnny was not taking the advice seriously. "How much can the damages be? It's not like she lost anything except a little time."

"How does a nice round sum like a million dollars sound?" Jay warned with a contemptuous smile. "If they proved fraud, it could be trebled.

"I suggest that you get back to her, act nice, and try to close as fast as possible. Also, I heard you visited two of my lawyer buddies down the block. We're a close community, you know. So be warned. If you put a stop payment on my retainer, I'll file criminal fraud charges against you. And I have lots of relatives who are judges in town."

Johnny tried to call Allie. He could not believe she had changed her voice message. He had to listen to forty-five-seconds of nauseatingly cheery crap before he could leave a message.

He waited an hour. No return call. He called again. And again. He had to listen to the stupid forty-five second greeting each time.

He pleaded with Doug for help.

Allie picked up Doug's call on the first ring. "Hey! Good thing I have your number in my caller ID. I was gonna let it go to my message box again if creepy called. What can I do for you?"

Doug embellished the story. Johnny was truly sorry and misunderstood the LOI. He's ready to close on Monday.

Allie was particularly feisty. JB and Ben were going to win the pool. "Okay, Doug. We'll hold the closing at the bank offices. And tell penguin to shower and show up on time. If he smells like fish again, I'm walkin'. And oh, by the way, I hope he enjoyed my new phone greeting. I made it 'specially for him."

Doug laughed. "I heard."

CHAPTER 66

SEPTEMBER 19, 2011

Allie and Johnny True Value barely acknowledged each other from the opposite ends of Consolidated Northern Bank's large conference table. Johnny had hired a new lawyer who had become familiar with the documents over the weekend. Bret had taken a vacation day to handle Allie's legal work.

Lawyers shuffled papers. Allie and Johnny signed acquisition documents. Michael handed Allie loan documents to sign. What the heck was an estoppel certificate? What was subrogation of rights? The personal guarantee was easy enough to understand. If the loan defaulted, the bank owned her.

The smallest thing became a monster headache. Where were the extra keys for the door locks? What's the alarm code? How do we change the web site password?

Allie entered into an intense battle with Johnny over the representations, warranties and schedule of assumed liabilities. "This was part of the LOI, Johnny. You hafta sign this appendix which says there are no unrecorded liabilities. Also, under no circumstances am I gonna assume any liability for customer returns. You sold a whole buncha stuff in August, and I have no idea what's comin' back at me. You've gotta pay for any returns."

Johnny whined, "I'm tired of this. The LOI's a bunch of crap. I'm startin' to think you defrauded me. Anyway, what's stoppin' you from acceptin' returns and stiffin' me with the bill? For example, sweetheart, no one has the right to return weed killer. If they break a shovel, that's their problem. I never took back a return."

Allie ignored the sweetheart comment. She was near the finish line. JB recommended they come up with a number. After a lot of haggling, they agreed that Johnny would be responsible for the first $50,000 of returns.

Michael Li had handled hundreds of loan closings in his career and anticipated everything. First, he opened a lock box bank account to handle daily receipts. Next, he opened a credit card account to process customer purchases. Small things like check books and deposit slips were all prepared.

Just before five o'clock, Allie signed the last document, and Michael wired the money to Allie's account. The money was immediately transferred to Johnny no-longer True Value's bank account.

JB entered the room, ceremoniously uncorked a bottle of Perrier Jouet champagne and filled four glasses. Michael, Bret and JB toasted the town's newest entrepreneur, Susan Allison "Allie" Bertrand.

"Thank you, guys," Allie gushed. "You really are the best friends a gal could have."

She looked at her watch. "Oh my goodness, I don't have to work tonight. You have no idea how great it'll be to wake up at sunrise."

At the other end of the table, Johnny had been arguing with his attorney about the bill. It wasn't pretty. He angrily scribbled off a check, said something about damn lawyers and left it on the table.

He slithered by Allie's celebration and shot her a nasty look.

CHAPTER 67

SEPTEMBER 20, 2011

Johnny no-longer True Value didn't wait long for the ink to dry on the closing documents. He called Steven Button at Pierre. Steven was still recovering from his meeting with the mayor.

Johnny said, "I've got an idea that'll benefit Pierre and help the town. I'm sure you know I've been championin' your cause to the town council and the people. I got you your vote. You're lookin' for a president of the transfer and processin' company who has good people skills and is connected with the local community. Who'd be better than me?"

Steven didn't say yes and didn't say no. Johnny certainly had helped Pierre win approval of the bond offering and the purchase of the Prospect Park fields. He came across well liked at the podium where he allowed the mayor to leave with some dignity.

Steven checked with Eva, Albert and Olivier. He explained that hiring Johnny would almost assure the project start-up would be successful. The temporary agribusiness team from Chicago would run the facility, so Johnny couldn't do any damage to operations.

Eva was wary. "Like I said, I want to be out of the agriculture business. We're not running this plant. This isn't our decision to make. Get approval from the hedge fund and the investment bankers."

Oenotropae Funding Corp concluded that paying Johnny $100,000 a year was a good investment if it helped ensure the project would succeed. They hired him and gave him his first task – hiring an experienced controller with SEC experience.

Oeno planned to take the tiny company public someday so they could make a ridiculously high return on their $5 million investment. They wanted a financial executive who knew the complex rules and regulations of the Securities Exchange Commission.

The company would also need a catchy corporate name and stock ticker symbol that stock brokers could pick up easily. A Wall Street sound bite. It helped if the name gave a vision of an exciting company with hyperbolic sales growth. Software, technology and gaming stocks were sexy and loved by the top fund managers. Automobile companies and utilities were treated like dogs. It was a battle of sexy growth versus boring stability.

After considerable thought, which in the fast world of hedge funds was several minutes, the managing director of the project concluded Nano technology was burgeoning. He also recognized bio fuels were a hot sector. Also, anything Internet related still attracted investors despite the crushing collapse of the dot-com boom barely ten years earlier.

The chemical in the crabgrass was Nano, sort of. It was a bio fuel, sort of. And for sure, they would have an Internet presence even if it was only a web site. Based on these important considerations, Nano Bio.Com was formed to operate the transfer plant. The charter was filed in Delaware, the favorite place to incorporate because its laws are codified and protected companies from crazy consumers and investors.

Johnny rented a one-room furnished office in town. The landlord provided phone, Internet and receptionist services to the six companies renting offices in the building.

He had to find a controller. Doug Pearson told him to search on Monster.com. In twenty-four hours, he had received six hundred resumes. After reviewing twenty, Johnny sat exhausted. He decided against interviewing all newbies and oldies. Everyone looked smart and promising on paper. He didn't want a kid who knew nothing. And he didn't want a senior citizen who knew too much.

Johnny struggled through several brief phone interviews. He had no idea what to ask and had no answers to questions about the company. He quickly grasped Nano Bio.Com was a start-up and 90% of the candidates wanted things like stability, benefits and corporate structure. Nano offered none of these.

Somehow, sixty-year-old Justin Gelfar slipped through the oldie filter and answered Johnny's prayers. Justin was experienced in start-ups and taking companies public. Johnny fabricated answers to Justin's questions during the interview and told him it was his job to develop the policies after he joined.

Justin wore a solid navy suit when he started work the following Monday. By Tuesday, he wore the more practical khakis and denim work shirt. This was not going to be a formal office. During his interview, he never thought to ask where his office would be. For the first few days, he shared the far side of Johnny's desk. This job would require all of the entrepreneurial skills that Justin could recall. A week later, GE leasing services delivered a temporary office building to the Prospect Fields site.

Justin studied the banker presentation and the town's charter. At lunch, Johnny told Justin, "We're gonna take over the processing from Pierre this month. It's over $2 million in fees, which we could use 'round here. The Chicago guys are plannin' for it. They're gonna hire some immigrant workers to do the work and pay 'em cash."

It wasn't the first time in his life Justin heard the suggestion. "Johnny, you cannot hire just anyone. You have to get documentation that they are citizens and have them complete immigration form I-9 and withholding tax forms. Quite frankly, we're not ready for this. You either should hire a human resources manager or outsource this to an employee leasing company."

Johnny didn't want any more complications. He said to Justin, "Employee leasing it is. Let 'em figure out this bureaucratic nightmare. Go find someone to handle our temporary workforce."

Justin returned to the trailer and searched online for temp agencies that provided manual laborers. He thought, *What exactly does Johnny do at work? I should be working on the bond financing, not hiring weed pickers. The bankers are badgering me for the company's plans, and the company has nada. What have I gotten myself into?*

CHAPTER 68

SEPTEMBER 20

Allie closed the store for renovations. Her first symbolic act was to move the faux butcher block table away from the shopping area. The unpaid invoice inbox officially turned it into office furniture.

The store was a decent size – 2,000 square feet. Johnny had wasted half of the floor space to store weed killer. Allie moved the storage pallets to the basement and spent half the day removing years of weed killer dust from the wooden floors. One stack of ten bags nicely displayed should be plenty.

Johnny's paint section had rarely seen a customer. Ironically, the area badly needed a new coat of paint. He had been offering a downscale no-name brand no one wanted. The inventory was old, and the cans were tarnished and rusty. Allie donated the paint to Goodwill, which was a helluva lot easier than complying with waste disposal rules.

Allie built a new paint center with bright track lighting so shoppers could compare the colors. She switched to Benjamin Moore for interior house paint and Valspar for bathrooms and kitchens. Benjamin Moore offered its retailers an online storefront service so shoppers could browse from home. Allie was going virtual!

Allie decided she couldn't compete with the big box stores on commodity items. If her customers wanted a hundred pounds of bulk nails, they could find them on Route 4, preferably in a store and not on the road. She was going to sell decorative yet functional home and garden improvements. You could still purchase a hammer or screwdriver, but at a fair price and profit.

Johnny had a small office at the back of the store which looked as professionally built as a *Little Rascals* clubhouse. Allie tore it down and replaced it with wood and glass displays. This would be her bath accessory area. Stores at the malls were making a killing selling upscale handles, towel holders and accessories. Allie was going to save them the trip and help customers beautify their homes one knob at a time.

She reserved an area by the front display window for Allie's Corner – a space for locally-made home and garden items. It was Allie's R&D area, a place for new product ideas. If items sold, she'd order more. If they sat, she'd try something else. For sure, she wouldn't die slowly selling commodity items at little profit until the store went broke.

She convinced a handful of local high school home economics and crafts teachers to create a few one-of-a-kind products. People loved frogs, rabbits and squirrels in their gardens as long as they were ceramic and didn't eat the flowers. One teacher made miniature scarecrows in farmer clothes. Another made a stack of decorative appliques. Bird feeders, flowered watering cans and an Americana rocking chair filled the rest of the corner.

Mrs. Wilson showed up with a small load of Crab Babies. At first, Allie politely refused to take them as a matter of principle. It would be treason. Mrs. Wilson was persistent though, and at a 30% mark-up, Allie couldn't say no.

It took every minute of ten days to rip out the old, install the new, clean, paint and stock shelves. She was exhausted. Saturday was the grand opening. It was only one day, but it was the first day of her new life.

CHAPTER 69

OCTOBER 1, 2011

"GRAND OPENING!" The bright red, white and blue banner hanging over the store front announced. The sign over the awning proudly announced the new owner – "ALLIE'S" in big letters. Below in smaller letters, it said, "A True Value Hardware Store."

Allie and Matt had worked until two in the morning stocking shelves and cleaning. They were back at seven making last-minute adjustments. It wasn't perfect, but it looked nice. No one would recognize it as old Johnny's place.

Just before the opening, her son Marty knocked on the front window. Allie opened the door and gasped, "Oh no. What's wrong?"

"Nothing, Ma," Marty grimaced. "I came by to help. If you don't want me here, it's okay. I'll leave and hang out with my friends."

Allie grabbed his hand and proudly led him to Matt. "Mr. Miller, meet your new sales assistant. Teach him everything you know. For starters, explain the cash register so he can ring up sales."

She wanted to watch her son's first steps in a hardware store, but she had too much to do. She was rearranging Allie's Corner and turned around to see Marty at the register wearing an Allie's True Value apron. What the heck just happened?

At 9:00 AM, Allie unlocked the front door to a small group of shoppers waiting to enter. The first person through the door was Auntie Ev followed by a brigade of Nanny Grannies. Gertie, the grayest of the Grannies, opened a card table and covered it with a red-checkered cloth. She placed a huge tray of homemade cookies and three jugs of ice cold lemonade on the table.

Auntie Ev put her arm around Allie. "We gals have to support each other, you know."

Dozens of customers wandered in and browsed. Auntie Ev said, "I cannot believe what you've done to this place. You know, Johnny was never nice to my girls. Oh my. Look at Allie's Corner. It's so adorable."

Auntie Ev grabbed the arm of a customer and walked her to the indoor picket fence. The Nanny Grannies acted like unpaid salesgirls. For hours, they hustled merchandise and gushed to anyone who'd listen what a marvelous job Allie had done.

Ben came by with a large canister of Starbucks coffee. Michael Li dropped by with a tall gift tray wrapped in red cellophane. JB wandered in mid-morning with a bouquet of flowers from Broderick's Florist.

By early afternoon, the store opening calmed to a nice welcoming party. The Grannies had left, but customers kept arriving. Word had spread, and it was a nice day to go shopping. The register was busy.

Near six o'clock, as the store quieted, Allie surveyed the store. People were amazed at the store transformation. Most customers made courtesy purchases as a welcoming gesture. Antique drawer handles were a big hit. Portable drills with longer-lasting, lithium-ion batteries sold well. The Crab Babies were gone before noon. Allie's Corner needed a major restocking except for the rocking chair, which seemed to take up too much room. All they want is hammers and nails, Johnny? My ass!

Allie concluded she needed new merchandise ideas, more items in Allie's Corner, and some big ticket items besides Crab Babies. It would take a helluva lot of decorative drawer knobs to replace 18,000 bags of weed killer sales.

None of this mattered. Today was a grand success of a grand opening, and she was tired in a positively grand way.

Matt had finished tallying the days register receipts and woke Allie from her daydream. "Marty left you a message earlier."

Allie gasped for the second time today. "Oh, no! What did he do? Is he okay?"

Matt laughed. "Nothing's wrong. You gotta let up on the kid, Allie. He bought dinner on the way home. Burgers and beans."

Allie smiled. "Okay, wise guy. Let's see how you deal with a sixteen-year-old with too much energy and way too many hormones."

Allie grabbed the canvas bag with a $1,000 from the day's cash collections. Store sales were $25,000, although Crab Babies made up nearly half of the total. Regardless, it was an overwhelming success, and Allie felt both relief and happiness.

"I'll drop this in the night depository. Matt, we did great today. More importantly, you were wonderful with Marty. Thanks for teaching him the register. See you on Monday."

CHAPTER 70

OCTOBER 2, 2011

The Monday morning business development meeting was in progress at Den-Ken Commodities' offices in downtown Chicago. Identical twins Denny and Kenny Delong always met with their staff of traders and analysts before the markets opened. They had both wrestled for Iowa State and kept a jock-friendly atmosphere at the firm. Den and Ken had learned ground floor how to trade wheat and soybeans twenty years ago. They had come a long way at forty-five years old to own one of the more respected trading firms in Chicago.

Typically the meetings focused on developing new customers. There was always a hedge fund or pension fund getting into commodities. Occasionally, they considered opening a desk to trade an emerging market, like Brazilian palm oil. Den and Ken were careful with capital, but were known for taking gambles on new ventures.

"What's this magic plant Pierre Beauty Products has been harvesting?" asked Ken. "The story hit the Jersey newspapers over the summer. My buddies now are telling me it's heating up. The town's building a $200 million dollar plant. That ain't peanuts.

"Maybe Pierre made a mistake by not locking up the futures contracts when they had the chance. Is it too late for us to get into this market? How big is it? Can we make money? Amnon did a study and will provide all the answers. Whadaya got, Amnon?"

"Please open your electronic books," commanded Amnon. He stood six feet tall and was a muscular 200 pounds. He looked strong and sounded authoritative, a skill he had learned as a tank commander and captain in the Israeli army.

Den-Ken's commodity research analyst opened the presentation on the 60-inch TV screen. The brokers opened the 200 page electronic document stored on the company's intranet. Paper presentations were a no-no in the twenty-first century.

"You may find this difficult to believe," Amnon said, "but Pierre Beauty Products is extracting a degreasing chemical from crabgrass growing in a town in North Jersey. The extract replaces the sodium laureth sulfate, which is a chemical in shampoo that cleans your hair.

"Sodium laureth sulfate isn't necessarily terrible. In fact, it's in ordinary dish detergent. But it's not natural, and Pierre's been converting all of its products to all-natural ingredients. If this stuff gains acceptance, they'll have a huge advantage over the competition.

"Pierre tested the new shampoo in beauty school salons, and it looks like a game changer. I obtained some samples, and the stuff really works, as you can tell by my beautiful wavy hair this morning." Amnon ran his hand through his short hair like a Clairol TV model. The table had a good laugh.

"It's early, but there's definitely an underground buzz. I found chat rooms talking about it. Samples are selling on eBay at double the retail price. It's appearing on the top of the Google search lists.

"Pierre did a decent job keeping this quiet, but I think this is gonna go public pretty quickly. However, if we found out about it, the competition can't be far behind. This stuff is growing five miles from the George Washington Bridge, yet not a peep has been heard on Madison Avenue.

"The data supporting our investigation is in your electronic notebooks. This crabgrass produces a concentration of this natural degreaser that is a hundred times stronger than plants grown outside this tiny area. Pierre has unsuccessfully tried to grow it in a hothouse, on farmland and in the tropics. So far, no good!

"We estimate the annual supply is $80 million if every house produced at an average capacity of six hundred pounds a year and sold to Pierre at their established market price of $15. We believe ten percent of the homes in the wealthier areas will not participate at these prices, but might at much higher prices.

"There are three crops – June, August and October. The crabgrass germinates hundreds of times a year. So each crop could deliver 5.4 million pounds annually, or 1.8 million pounds per contract.

"There are two other significant factors. The town is building a $200 million dollar transfer station and processing plant, so they believe this is going to be big. And Oenotropae invested $5 million in a company to manage the facility, which they intend to bring public. Oeno is one of our clients. We got a lot of our information from an investor document they had prepared."

Den stood at the head of the table. "Thanks, Amnon. To summarize, we have a niche product which could increase in value if other shampoo companies join the fray. Or maybe non-cosmetic companies can find a use for this stuff. We have a limited supply, which is great for commodity prices. We have a fragmented group of suppliers, which is also good for trading.

"The market is small for now, but does it have the potential to become very large? Better yet, can we control the market? Right now, Pierre has set the price artificially low if you ask me. If we corner the market properly, do we get to set the price?

"Ask yourself. Is this commodity like the rubber market which trades sideways? Is it like platinum with great volatility and price swings? Or is it like the diamond market which trades at a high premium?"

Ken threw up his hands. "Which one is it guys and gals? Is it boring like rubber or wild and crazy like platinum?"

The nine partners tossed the idea around for fifteen minutes, which is a lifetime for a commodity trader. The consensus was they had an opportunity with unknown size and a lot of risks. They'd be developing an embryonic market. They'd have to find customers, buyers, sellers, and maybe even new users for the product. Every market started like this. Even Texas Intermediate Oil trading had a beginning.

Den and Ken huddled privately. Den popped back up and fist-bumped his twin. "We've made a decision. We'll allocate a million dollars of firm capital to develop the trading market for this plant. We'll file a listing application on the MERC to begin trading three contracts a year and three years of futures.

"Amnon, it's your job to find investors to buy $5 million dollars of limited partnership units to trade in the contract. Go to our usual list. Get started on the private placement document today!"

Ken turned to Becca Gilman, the pretty, first-year marketing assistant who supported new account openings for broker-salesmen. A star lacrosse player at TCNJ, she fit right in with the traders at Den-Ken.

"Becca, you're in charge of marketing. I want every beauty products company to be inundated with pretty flyers about this new wonder plant. I want this in the newspapers. I want this in social media. When someone googles natural shampoo or crabgrass, I want our trading platform to be top of the search list. We're going to create crabgrass hysteria. You have a budget of $25,000 to get started. Is everyone in?"

It was like a Chicago Bears' tailgate party without the bratwurst. The adrenaline was pumping. Ken stood and grabbed his billfold. "Okay, twenty dollar pool for naming rights. What do we call the contract?"

Traders threw their antes into the M&M-filled center piece bowl. The partners shouted possible names. WEED? No. It sounds like an illegal drug. GRASS. Nope. Same thing. And it has too many letters. Keep it to four letters. NOIL? They'll confuse it with oil.

Amnon yelled out, "LAWN?"

"Are you kidding me?" Den chortled. "There won't be any lawns left after we trade this thing! DIRT would be more appropriate." He got a tableful of laughs.

Becca's eyes lit up. "Why not just CRAB? Traders will have a riot with that name."

Den looked around the table and yelled, "Hold the phones! We have a winner! Becca, you just won a hundred eighty bucks. Now you gotta buy lunch for the table."

Becca stood and took several bows. "Alright guys, we're ordering from Manny's Deli. Anyone not ordering corned beef gets corned beef."

CHAPTER 71

OCTOBER 21, 2011

Mid-October was the time to watch the fall colors change. It's pretty, but highly overrated. How many times have you heard someone from New Jersey say, "I love the seasons, especially the change in colors?" The colors are awesome, but they only last a week. Two days of fantastic reds and four days of fading yellows are followed by brown, colorless brown. Brown leaves. Brown dirt. Brown tree trunks. Brown, brown, brown!

Pierre wanted out of the agri-business and formally advised Nano Bio.Com to start controlling the crabgrass collection process. Nano announced it would accept early deliveries at the Prospect Park fields. Tom McInerney, the general manager, saw a problem and halted deliveries before noon on the first day.

Tom was a seasoned Ag executive from Illinois who had worked his way up the ladder, from hay baler on a farm as a kid, to receiving clerk at Towson Grain during college summers, to general manager of a $100 million silo operation. At forty years of age, he was a modern farmer with a master's degree, still wearing steel-toed work boots but now carrying the management clipboard.

"Johnny, we got a problem out in the receiving area," Tom said breathlessly. "There are fifty cars in line and more arriving every minute. People think Pierre's gonna stiff them. One of the guys told me he heard Pierre was taking the first thousand sellers and no more. Did you hear about this?"

Johnny leaned back in his chair wearing a devilish smirk. "Hear 'bout it? Who do you think started the rumor? Tommy, you've never run a sale in your business, have you?"

"What are you talking about? Pierre hasn't put any limits on us," exclaimed Tom.

"Listen, Tommy," said Johnny. "I read your employment agreement. It looks just like mine. If we make plan, we get a fifty percent bonus. If we exceed plan, the number goes up. I have every intention of makin' plan and gettin' paid. The more we process, the more fees we get from Pierre, and the more likely we make bonus."

Tom said, "I spoke to the Pierre guys. They're counting on two thousand homes, three thousand max. They haven't agreed to anything in writing. What happens if we take in too much and Pierre doesn't buy it?"

"Don't worry. I got that covered," Johnny said totally in control. "We have five million bucks in the bank, and we're allowed to buy crabgrass for our own account. We'll buy any extra crabgrass and then sell it to Pierre in June. In the meantime, we make bonus. Are you in?"

Tom scratched his chin and thought for a moment. "I guess it's alright. How do we handle this? I mean, what are the ground rules? You're creating a little hysteria with your rumor, you know."

Johnny said, "Pierre's good for the first three or four hundred thousand pounds, for sure. We gotta process five hundred thousand to beat plan. So, for the next two weeks, we buy a little more than what Pierre formally agreed. Once we hit our number, we cut back. Make sense?"

Tom nodded in agreement. "One more thing. We gotta put in some quality control systems so we don't buy unqualified product."

"I already thought about it," Johnny replied. "Everyone who sells hasta prove they live here. That way we know the crabgrass is the real stuff. Second, any crabgrass got blue and white beads on it ain't no good. Those beads are Jake's weed killer chemical. If they get in our warehouse, they're gonna contaminate the place."

"One of the sorters seems to know good weeds from bad," Tom smiled. "Name's Pedro. He already rejected some deliveries 'cause they weren't the right type of plant. I wanna hire him full-time and make him my foreman. He can train the others. Also, I'll need to hire a few more workers. And authorize overtime. I'm taking deliveries until nine at night. Otherwise, we'll never process all of it."

Word spread quickly around town. It's okay to deliver an extra forty or fifty pounds. Buy a Crab Baby and you'll be done in half the time.

CHAPTER 72

OCTOBER 31, 2011

Allie watched from the Halloween display in her store window as a convoy of cars slowly drove by with trunks half-open and filled with crabgrass. It reminded her of a funeral procession and certainly didn't make her more excited about the prospects for selling Jake's weed killer.

On the positive side, Allie had become the informal exclusive distributor for Crab Babies. They sold as fast as they arrived. The rest of the store had decent results, not too bad for a new store.

The Crab Babies were put to good use. For the last two weeks of October, residents cut and hustled their crabgrass to Prospect Field. Their lawns looked ravaged. Houses had large swaths of bare dirt with crabgrass roots protruding.

Some homes tried to mask the mess. Sally Spencer planted shrubbery high enough to hide the scarred earth. Mary Beth Sirocco displayed her lawn Christmas nativity scene with life-sized statues a month early. Harry Gold used a little humor. He built a miniature golf course including Lego windmills through the remaining crabgrass clumps.

However, the streets bore the truth of what Mayor Hector Alvarez had warned. When you drove through town, it was not a pretty sight. Dirt and weed leaves were strewn everywhere. Hector gave strict orders to his head of sanitation. Do not clean up this disaster. Let the town see what they have done.

CHAPTER 73

NOVEMBER 7, 2011

It took a mere three weeks for Amnon to raise $5 million for CRAB FUND, LLC, a limited liability company formed to trade CRAB. Ten hedge funds invested a half million apiece. Den-Ken took a 6% commission on the funds which it reinvested in the deal.

A week later, CRAB became officially listed by the MERC and open to trade. The MERC was officially called the CME, but traders still called it the old name, which was short for the Chicago Mercantile Exchange. It was part of the CME Group which ran the four big exchanges: CME or the MERC, CBOT, NYMEX and COMEX. Combined, they traded over a quadrillion dollars of contracts annually.

The listing committee scratched their heads over this one. For the last ten years, most new listings were financial products like exchange-traded funds (ETFs) or derivative contracts. Agricultural commodity listings were reserved for the big dogs – like corn, wheat, soybeans and cocoa.

Many commodities are not listed and traded for a simple reason. A commodities contract must have standardized terms such as quantity, quality and location. A quantity might be 5,000 bushels of corn or one troy ounce of gold. They also must be deliverable at a place to the buyer: wheat in Chicago; West Texas intermediate crude at Cushing, Oklahoma; or CRAB in Bergenfield.

Fruit, for example, doesn't trade on an exchange because it perishes. One day you own plums, the next day you have prunes. CRAB didn't have these problems. Pierre had already set the standardized terms, and the chemical in the CRAB didn't perish. CRAB could be stored like bales of wheat.

Nevertheless, Den and Ken had to appeal to the MERC to convince them that a real market opportunity existed. The MERC granted the listing with some hesitation, but finding new listings was tough, and Den-Ken was a reputable and well-capitalized firm.

Den-Ken placed a ceremonial order to sell one contract at $15 to start trading. CRAB FUND, LLC bought the contract. The next contract sold at $17, a 13% gain for the day. A few floor brokers noticed the trade. However, the spread of West Texas Intermediate oil to Brent Crude was widening, and traders were too busy placing their bets. CRAB could wait a few days.

The futures agreement filed with the MERC stated that the delivery point was at or near the town of Bergenfield, which gave Den-Ken some options. Preferably, Nano Bio. Com would act as the processor and perhaps even agree to store excess inventory occasionally. Otherwise, they'd have to find a suitable alternative.

It wasn't hard to sell Johnny and Tom on the proposal. Tom made a few calls to his Chicago commodity buddies to get a bead on Den-Ken's plans. Until today, they believed their fortunes were tied solely to Pierre. Now someone else liked their crabgrass.

The Pierre deal paid Nano Bio.Com a $3.00 per pound processing fee. Den-Ken offered to pay the higher of $3.00 or 10% of the CRAB price up to a maximum of $10.00. The deal also offered to pay demurrage and storage fees of 20 cents a pound to store crabgrass.

Johnny signed the contract without the advice of legal counsel. It looked like legal boilerplate, but who the heck knew what a commodity futures contract boilerplate was?

CHAPTER 74

NOVEMBER 8, 2011

Den and Ken plotted strategy to wrest price-setting power from Pierre. Their objective was to control the market supply and force Pierre to buy on the exchange. As a first step to undermining the Pierre option agreements, Den-Ken planned to convince Bergenfield homeowners to open commodity accounts and sell their CRAB through the exchange.

Then they would have to find a way to stop Pierre from going around Den-Ken. Tarnish Pierre's image just a little. Maybe plant a seed of mistrust. *No matter how much more they want to pay you, it's not enough!*

Five Den-Ken trader-salesmen descended on Bergenfield the day after the MERC listing was approved. The young guns knocked on doors and gave their spiel. "Don't sell to Pierre for only $15. Open a commodity account with Den-Ken and sell your CRAB futures at the market. It'll definitely trade higher."

The salesman opened his iPad and showed the housewife the current trading price on the screen. "Pierre pays when you deliver, which could be a year from now. If you open an account with us, you get a $17 credit when you sell.

"Pierre is only buying a hundred pounds from each home. With a Den-Ken account, you can sell a thousand pounds if you want. You can't lose. And the margin requirement is only twenty-five percent."

They signed up two hundred homes in ten days, but faced diminishing returns for their efforts. Door-to-door salesmen were rare in the twenty-first century. It was hard work. People had to be both home and willing to answer the doorbell.

Cold calling on the phone wouldn't work, either. Success rates on phone solicitations were about one percent. Unsolicited calls met hang-ups and cuss words. Plus there were always those pesky do-not-call laws to circumvent.

A direct marketing campaign made sense. Nowadays, a company can buy cable TV spots for as little as $20 a spot during the daytime. Plus, you could target just the Bergenfield viewers. Dentists and chiropractors had perfected localized ads years ago.

Den-Ken hired a local small market advertising agency to develop fifteen- and thirty-second spots. It showed a handsome elderly couple enjoying their affluent lifestyle with profits from CRAB. "Open your account and trade CRAB at Den-Ken today!" They bought cheap spots whenever they became available on the financial news networks and morning shows like *Perry Mason, Murder, She Wrote* and *The Price is Right.*

Lining up the sellers was only half of the equation. They needed buyers too. It would take time to develop the environment for a hot-trading commodity. If they wanted traders to become interested in the market, CRAB trading would need to have increasing liquidity and high volatility. Liquidity came from large trading volume which allowed traders to get in and out of markets quickly. Volatility, or large daily price swings, gave traders a chance to make money.

Den-Ken was providing some liquidity with trading by the CRAB FUND. They needed others to join in.

Traders love a good story, something that they can sell to their clients. Even better was an attention grabber, a front page newspaper headline to start the frenzy.

War, pestilence, floods and famine were great for grain and oil prices, but probably not much help to crabgrass. Where was the next shampoo company willing to use this magical ingredient? Would some government agency declare sodium laureth sulfate harmful to humans? Would New Jersey declare crabgrass the state flower? Would a prominent professor declare this crabgrass plant a miracle? Would it cure cancer? End poverty? Make children behave better?

What unforeseen act of God or man would benefit CRAB?

CHAPTER 75

NOVEMBER 19, 2011

Pierre warily watched Den-Ken's activity. For a month, they hoped for a quick fizzle. A couple hundred new accounts at Den-Ken weren't enough to disrupt Pierre's plans. Who was going to buy crabgrass besides Pierre? No one, at least not yet.

Eva looked up from her desk to the muted television on her office wall. Den-Ken was running ads on STCK-TV. "Open your account and trade CRAB at Den-Ken today!"

Eva's jaw dropped. She quickly assembled her management team and issued new marching orders: "Offer contracts to the whole town. Lock up everyone in sight with an option agreement! Give them a $200 signing bonus against their first sale."

Pierre hand-delivered eight thousand mailers announcing they would hold a signing day the Saturday before Thanksgiving. A form contract was enclosed with terms identical to the earlier deal. Pierre would pay $15 per pound and agree to buy no less than 25% of a home's crabgrass production. It was a lot of money to most homeowners.

The contract signing was being held in the Friend's Meeting Room in the basement of the Bergenfield Public Library. An orderly group of 70 people sat and patiently waited their turns to hand over the signed forms and get their signing bonus. More were pouring into the building every minute. Eric Winderman and two Pierre assistants sat at the front table. Eric called the first number.

A burly man in his fifties jumped ahead of Danny Park, the first on line. He handed Eric a stack of 200 contracts. "I'm not waitin'. This is from my neighborhood, all signed and sealed. You can mail 'em the bonuses."

Eric wasn't going to argue. They would review the contracts later to make sure they were properly completed. Eric called, "Next!"

Danny Park approached the table shaking his head at the rudeness. The Den-Ken team lay in wait. Amnon came from around the corner and stood in his path. He commanded, "Do NOT sign those agreements!"

Behind him were five Den-Ken traders. Camera flashes came from the side of the room. Paparazzi had been hired to record the event and blast it all over the Internet.

Amnon demanded, "Your crop is worth much more than what Pierre is paying. The CRAB contract was worth $20 a pound yesterday. Why are you selling to Pierre at $15?"

The traders walked around the room handing out business cards and commodity account applications. The young Pierre team was unequipped for an uprising. Two paralegals and a senior accountant thought they'd have a nice leisurely day sitting at a desk helping people sign forms. Eric left the room and frantically called Steven Button. "We got a problem."

It took Steven a half hour to drive to the library. All hell had broken loose. Another two hundred people had arrived and spilled over to the first floor of the library. The Den-Ken salesmen were blocking the desk. The paparazzi were taking pictures and video. A few of the elderly left the fray and wandered upstairs.

A man in the audience saw Steven arrive at the table and pegged him as management despite his dress in jeans, a Polo shirt and sneakers. "Why should we sign your agreement? Are you guys trying to con this town again?"

Steven tried to calm the crowd. "We're not tricking anyone. We've paid decent money to people in town. We opened up the buying to everyone in October. I think we've been very fair."

Amnon stood five feet from Steven. "If it's so fair, why're they paying twenty-five percent below market?"

Steven appraised Amnon for a brief second. Who was this guy? He had to be from Den-Ken, but was he a trader or a bodyguard?

Steven had to raise his voice over the noise, but still appear calm. "Listen, only one contract traded hands at $20. It's not a real market. Try to sell ten contracts and see how far the price drops.

"Let's talk about this. If you sign with us today, you have a multi-billion dollar company behind the agreement. You know you'll get paid year after year. You'll never sell less than the minimum, no matter what happens to the market.

"If you sell through a commodity account, you don't know what money you'll get. Den-Ken is a small, highly-leveraged commodity trading outfit. They're the type of firm who almost destroyed this country two years ago by speculating in derivatives and credit default swaps. Are they willing to guarantee you $20 a pound? Do they have the money to back their guarantee?"

Amnon acted offended. "We're NOT a financial speculator. We're the backbone of the agriculture industry. Thousands of independent farmers trade with us every year. We trade agriculture futures, which happens to be what this crabgrass is.

"I'll ask you a simple question. Why did Pierre decide $15 a pound was a fair price? Because they say so? Why not let the market decide what is fair? We think it could be worth a hundred dollars a pound in a few years.

"I guarantee you this. If you open an account and offer to sell the next contract on Monday, you'll get $20 per pound."

The crowd noise strengthened. Steven argued louder. Amnon spoke louder still. Lori Keeler, the tiny, sixty-year-old head librarian, came down the stairs and pushed her way through the doorway. The usual "Shhhh!" wouldn't work today.

"My goodness! What in the world is going on here?" Lori waved her finger at Steven. "I was told you were holding a book signing today. Who are you people?"

Steven tried to explain. Amnon yelled over him. He wanted disruption and had no intention of letting anyone calm the crowds. You want frenzy? Here's frenzy!

Amnon stood between Steven and the librarian. "They're holding an illegal contract signing here on municipal property," Amnon said in a raised voice. "They're trying to steal from widows and orphans. The town needs to stop this barbaric act. They should be arrested."

Amnon hammed it up, but even the librarian looked at him funny when he used barbaric.

Finally, Lori called the police department and summoned help. Chris Bloom from *The Bergenfield Valley News* was taking pictures when Mike the Cop walked in. A home-grown Bergenfield boy, thirty-year-old Mike stood an imposing six-feet-two with his cap on. He blew his police whistle and rapped his nightstick on the front table. Everybody froze.

Mike pointed at Amnon and Steven and said, "You and your cohorts have one minute to disperse. Anyone here after one minute is gettin' a citation for disturbin' the peace."

The Den-Ken team magically disappeared with their paparazzi. Steven argued, "We have this room reserved today. They were intruding!"

Mike looked at his watch. "You now have thirty seconds to leave! Twenty-nine, twenty-eight. . ."

The Pierre team quickly grabbed their papers and the stack of signed contracts and left.

Two hundred contracts in hand were nowhere near the thousands Pierre had hoped for. Pierre had shown up for a signing; Den-Ken came for a fight.

The townspeople were slow to leave. Small groups gathered to discuss what to do. Gilbert stood with Chris and watched in utter amazement. Gilbert chuckled, "Boy, Mike really knows how to spoil a party."

Chris scrolled through the pictures on his digital camera and said, "I could run a hundred front pages with these. Look at Mrs. Magill pumping her fist at the Pierre guy. It's too bad I don't charge for this paper. I could sell a bunch. You don't think this is going to hurt our real estate deal. Do you?"

"Hurt? Are you kiddin'? You just witnessed a doubling of the value of Bergen Development," Gilbert chuckled. "Those Chicago guys are trying to corner the market."

Gilbert's wheels began turning. "Chris, it might not be a bad idea to help Den-Ken. Think about it. If the price of crabgrass goes up to thirty bucks, Pierre will probably have to match it. We'll make double the money.

"What we need now is good old-fashioned investigative journalism. Run one of your crazy pictures on the front cover of the *Bergenfield Valley News*. Give it a big title. FIGHT BREAKS OUT AT BERGENFIELD LIBRARY. Show the photo of Mike the Cop blowing his whistle.

"Tell your readers the market was $20 and Pierre tried to sign elderly couples at $15 before they found out. Give people instructions on how to open a Den-Ken account and their phone and fax numbers. Make Pierre look evil and Den-Ken like a savior. I saw a picture of Den on their web site. He looks trustworthy.

"If you want to make an extra hundred grand on your housing investment, work the weekend and have the paper on our doorsteps by Monday morning. We want everyone to sell their crabgrass through Den-Ken!"

CHAPTER 76

NOVEMBER 22, 2011

On Monday morning, *The Bergenfield Valley News* was the hottest newspaper in Bergenfield and on LaSalle Street in Chicago. Den-Ken paid Chris to run an extra ten thousand copies. They were mailing the front page to all of its customers.

The Record ran a half-page picture of Mike the Cop tooting his whistle with the headline: *Battle in Bergenfield!* The wire services picked up the story which began to spread through online media. A video posted on YouTube got 10,000 hits the first day. The story was heating up.

Bergenfield residents searched their wastepaper baskets for the discarded Den-Ken business card and commodity account application. In three days, Den-Ken opened hundreds of new accounts.

Timid homeowners dipped their toes in the water. Kevin Dunne who lived on First Street asked his Den-Ken broker to sell one CRAB futures contract for delivery in June. The sale appeared the next day in his statements as a credit for $2,000. It worked!

The CRAB FUND was the principal buyer for most of the first thousand contracts. They kept a floor bid of $20 per pound. When the commodity daily news rags picked up the story, commodity brokers smelled an opportunity and began buying.

By ten o'clock, the price of CRAB futures rose to $22, up 10%. Trading would be closed on Thanksgiving and barely be open a few hours on Friday. If a trader wanted a position, he had to buy before the holiday.

Traders got the thing they loved most – volatility! The intraday price swung $2 up and down, 10% moves. When the market closed at noon on Friday, the CRAB contracts for June, August and October 2012 delivery each had an open interest of over two thousand contracts and closed at an average of $25. At 100 pounds per contract, the value exceeded $5 million. It wasn't pork bellies, but it wasn't horse manure either.

CRAB FUND, LLC was showing a nice paper profit. Den thought through the elements that could make CRAB prices take off. It was a new commodity where the value wasn't fully known to everyone. It had a very narrow area of production and to date couldn't be replicated. The ultimate buyers of the commodity had large operating margins and could easily pass on price increases.

Pierre had made a mistake by dipping its toe in the water. It had the opportunity to sign up the entire town and didn't do it. Also, no legacy group was fighting the technology. Sodium laureth sulfate had no lobbying group like coal to fight solar, or pig farmers to fight corn ethanol.

Den and Ken called in Amnon. "Prepare a prospectus for CRAB FUND II. This time, raise $50 million. Every day we wait is money lost."

CHAPTER 77

NOVEMBER 30, 2011

"Is our nightmare over," asked Eva, "or has it just begun?"

Eva, Steven, Albert and Stephane met in Pierre's technology conference room. Stephane was the head commodity trader for Pierre. He was a tall, bilingual, handsome Frenchman working in Pierre's purchasing and trading offices in Philadelphia. He primarily traded physicals but on occasion hedged with futures on the exchanges.

Eva said, "I'm not sure we made a mistake. At the time, we didn't have certainty. It would have been imprudent to contract for more than we did.

"However, these commodity fellows in Chicago smelled an opportunity and have outsmarted us for now. My back channel sources tell me Den-Ken did a study and concluded we would need a lot more material because of the demand for our new formula shampoo. They were right.

"This market got away from us, and we just have to deal with it. Steven, please begin."

Steven stood by the laptop and launched the presentation on the television screen. Somehow, the pre-holiday beating at the library hadn't taken a toll on Steven. He looked fresh and sharp, wearing an Armani suit and a subdued paisley tie.

"We estimate we can pay more than double the current market without affecting the price of our shampoo," Steven began. "These numbers are early estimates but can only improve. We still don't know how much product we can extract from a pound of plants. Today, our extraction methods are rather crude.

"At most, 8,000 homes could eventually produce the plant. At 600 pounds per home, total annual production could reach 4.8 million pounds. That yields 16 million bottles of shampoo. At a retail sales price of $25 dollars, the shelf value is $400 million in sales.

"Every $10 dollars per pound we spend on CRAB translates into costs of about ten percent of sales. Our breakeven today compared to using sodium laureth sulfate is $60 per pound. We think we can double the yield easily, and also increase the yield by changing the shampoo formula. Therefore, eventually we could afford to pay as high as $120 per pound once Albert does his magic on improving the yield. Also, don't forget we already have contracted 1,200 hundred homes and locked in a price of $15 per pound."

Steven ran through the rest of the presentation, but the deciding point had already been made. They could pay more and would.

Eva said, "CRAB is trading between $25 and $30 dollars, which won't last long. Speculators are entering the market and will drive up prices. Den-Ken has one investment fund and is forming another.

"For now, we'll table the idea of signing more option agreements. The town hates us despite everything we did for them. We look like the evil empire.

"Okay. We can afford to pay more. The market wants our product badly. My board is telling me to concentrate on sales growth. There's plenty of profitability. I'm moving up the launch of our all-natural shampoo to this spring. Stephane, we want you to begin cautiously purchasing contracts.

"Use our French subsidiaries and brokerage accounts at our lead investment banks. They'll keep our activity quiet. During the next twelve months, I want to buy sufficient material to supply our three-year marketing plan. We have option agreements with homeowners to buy 700,000 pounds in place. You're authorized to buy up to one million pounds a year at current prices."

CHAPTER 78

DECEMBER 5, 2011

No one was thankful two weeks after Thanksgiving. Bergenfield homeowners who had signed Pierre contracts grumbled. Selling to Pierre at $15 per pound sounded like a good idea at the time. Now their neighbors were getting nearly twice that.

A personal injury lawyer stopped chasing ambulances long enough to organize a class action suit against Pierre claiming Force Majeure. Under this "act of God" provision, contracts could be broken in certain circumstances, like when a tornado destroyed a factory or a flood destroyed a crop.

In the 1980s, natural gas pipelines broke their contracts to purchase high-priced natural gas under Force Majeure claiming God had created the supply-demand imbalance. The suit against Pierre claimed a similar legal theory – only God could know that weeds would one day be valuable.

Pierre sent a nice letter to its household suppliers. It pleaded for rational behavior. Don't get caught up in the speculative fever. These are momentary price swings. You have the benefit of security. You have a contract. Pierre is the only real user of this product. We have offered a fair price. You're making $9,000 a year with little effort. Don't look a gift horse in the mouth.

The attorney amended the suit to include slander. It now claimed that Pierre, through its letter, implied the residents were stupid.

Pierre tried a different tack. It mailed each homeowner a check for $9,000 in advance for the 2012 production. Attached to the check was a standard release of claims form. If they cashed the check, their participation in the lawsuit ended.

It's pretty hard to tear up such a large check. Do you put much-needed money in the bank? Or do you join in the suit? It was a split decision. Half cashed the check; the rest pressed forward with the lawsuit.

Newly emboldened homeowners who were legally obligated to sell their crop to Pierre felt otherwise. They opened commodities accounts at Den-Ken and sold their 2012 estimated production at $30 per pound, even though Pierre had rights to it. Possession is nine-tenths of the law. It would take at least three years before the case came to trial. Putting $18,000 in the bank made a lot of sense.

A quarter of the town warmed up to the idea and opened commodity trading accounts with Den-Ken. Not everyone was sure the crabgrass would return this summer. The crabgrass always seemed to grow every year, but maybe the last dose of Jake's weed killer had finally worked. How can you sell a contract on the commodities exchange if you weren't sure you could deliver?

One homeowner, Kiley Draco, decided not to open an account with Den-Ken. He could sell commodities in his Morton Sprague broker account and save on commissions. He sold a hundred CRAB contracts believing it totaled a hundred pounds. He was shocked when his online statement showed that he sold 10,000 pounds. Kiley received an urgent message from his broker. It read:

You have taken a short position in a commodity and have lost $50,000 in less than a week. We hereby request that you provide sufficient documentation to prove that you are sophisticated in commodity trading. Otherwise, we will sell your position and close your account.

Kiley collapsed in his chair, logged onto his account and closed out the position. It was an expensive loss. He thought, *If only I had traded through Den-Ken, perhaps this wouldn't have happened?*

CHAPTER 79

DECEMBER 11, 2011

A bitter winter cold front plunged the wind chill factor to a toasty ten degrees. The town's Christmas decorations were holding onto lampposts for dear life during twenty mph gusts. A kitchen worker manned Ben's front door full-time to keep it from flying off its hinges when customers entered.

True Value Allie proudly wore her green and white New York Jets woolen hat. Her pony tail bobbed up and down as she chatted away. She was eating a hearty breakfast of ham and eggs to fight the cold. Allie was an official early bird regular now that her store opened at eight o'clock.

The table was preoccupied. Buyout was googling something on the Internet. Michael was reading the business pages. Decker was drinking his coffee gazing off into space.

Allie asked, "Hey Bret, are you still plannin' on goin' to Midnight Mass at St. John's with your honey? Just wonderin'."

Bret was morose. "Yes we're going, and I'm not too happy about it. Next topic."

Allie was her usually feisty self. "Thanks Grump. I'll talk to JB. Hey JB, I'm thinkin' of launchin' a crabgrass counteroffensive. I was gonna rent a crop duster and spray the town with weed killer. You suppose it's legal?"

"You may want to think about that one," said JB. "At least do it at night."

"Okay," shrugged Allie, "forget the crop duster. What if I snuck the chemical into the garden hoses?"

Bret looked slightly shocked.

"C'mon guys," Allie winked. "I'm kiddin'. You all lost your sense of humor?"

"I really need new ideas. New product lines. This store is like a shark. If it stops swimmin', it drowns. Speakin' of sharks, Bret, we haven't seen much of your girlfriend lately. What's up?"

"Um, I don't know." Bret shrugged. "I guess we're taking a sort of break. We've had a few dinners, but she hasn't stayed over since the incident. Then again, I haven't pushed the issue either."

Allie wrinkled her nose. "No nookie, Bret? Sounds like she's still punishin' you. Don't give in!"

Allie looked up abruptly. "Whoa! Oh my God. What do we have here?"

JB and Bret turned to the front door and saw Misty make an entrance that would have made Vivian Leigh proud. As she neared the table, her black overcoat fell open to display a stunning outfit.

Misty was dressed for a cocktail party. A tight black miniskirt clung to her thighs alluringly well above her knees. Her legs were strangled in black lace stockings. A black sheer top barely covered a revealing low-cut, V-neck silk blouse. All of this teetered atop a pair of hot red stiletto heels.

Misty did the catwalk to Bret's table, leaned over to show her teeny cleavage, and gave him a whiff of her Angel perfume. She sat next to him, practically on his lap.

Allie muttered to JB, "Looks like Bret's outta the doghouse."

"Bret," Misty mewed, "we haven't talked about our New Year's Eve plans yet. I have some great ideas."

Bret looked like a trapped rat. *Where do I hide? How do I escape? I need to find a dark corner.* He stammered, "Um, er, oh, I don't usually celebrate New Year's. Bad timing sort of thing you know, working on Wall Street. Um, er, um."

Misty cooed, unflustered. This time would be different. She had every intention of showing off her Montauk & Malibu Wall Street investment-banker-lawyer prize to her old entourage.

"Bret, you need a break. No one should work on New Year's Eve except bartenders, bands and parking valets.

"Now don't you worry about a thing. Your little Misty took care of all the plans. I made reservations at the Rainbow Room. Also, the restaurant may be able to get us seats in the grandstand in Times Square to watch the ball drop. It would be so romantic. Don't you think?"

Bret wouldn't be caught dead in Times Square on New Year's Eve where a million revelers stood toe-to-heel for hours to watch a disco ball finally drop 141 feet in ten seconds. Also, as a Montauk & Malibu executive, he could probably get a seat in the Mayor's Stand if he really wanted.

But most of all, Bret was concerned he might run into his co-workers. He had conveniently not told Misty about the Montauk & Malibu Christmas party extravaganza held the prior evening at the Metropolitan Museum of Art. A thousand executives and wives wore evening gowns and black tie, sipped champagne and tasted caviar. Bret wasn't willing to risk bringing Misty to the party. She might toss a chocolate mousse on the chairman's wife!

Bret delivered a truthful excuse. "Misty, I'm closing several deals. They have to be filed before the thirty-first or they lose their tax benefits. We talked about this. It happens every year. My buddies and I gave up on New Year's Eve plans long ago. We celebrate Russian New Year on January sixth. It's much better. Smaller crowds."

Misty gave a tiny impetuous stamp of her feet. "We HAVE to go! Please? My friends want to meet you."

Bret feared another Misty spectacle. He said sincerely, "I can't commit. Maybe if the deals close early, we can go. Unfortunately, these things have a way of closing at the last second."

Misty stamped her foot too hard. One of the stiletto heels broke, barely connected by a tiny flap. Misty became flustered and attempted to remove the heel, but it was caught.

"Think about it. I'll come over and make dinner. We can talk then, okay honey?" She stood to leave on one foot. She walked to the door dragging the broken heel along the floor. She'd looked a lot hotter during her entrance.

CHAPTER 80

DECEMBER 11

Poor Bret watched Misty struggle out the door. He shook his head. "This is getting to be too much. Is drama a requirement for dating?"

Allie smiled. She had no compassion for Misty after her last encounter. "Bret, Misty is what she is. You can't change a skunk into a cat by paintin' its stripe black. Not to speak badly, but she has a legendary trail of hurt men in her life and three ex-husbands to prove it. Have you said the L word yet?"

"Absolutely not!" Bret declared. "I'm a lawyer and an officer of the court. I'm scared to death of getting caught in some legal contract by saying the word. But she's hammering me for a ring.

"She claims I have a fear of commitment. I do have fear, but it isn't commitment. It's fear of who's on the other side of the abyss. Nice Misty or that other crazy person who makes an appearance?"

JB crossed his legs and counseled in his Viennese psychiatrist accent. "You know, Herr Volfman, zie term 'Fear of Commitment' vas made up by vomen to get men to commit. Vhat many men really haf is fear of insolvency."

Allie laughed and said, "Doctor Freud, don't forget zie fear of entrapment!

"Bret, girls use that line all the time to force guys to the altar. But I hafta tell you, as far as relationships go, you're the least experienced forty-year-old guy I've ever met. We like you, so please take this as advice coming from a friend.

"A lotta guys have a fear. They're scared to death someone is gonna take half their assets in a divorce settlement. I know you didn't grow up with a lot."

Bret said defensively, "I never used money as an excuse. It never held me back. But I'd say it'd be hard for anyone around here to out-poor my childhood."

"Bret, I'm no shrink," said Allie. "I've never even been to one, unless you count watchin' Frasier on Cheers. I'm also not your mother. People confuse nurses as mother figures. We're not maternal. We're healers. We bring you back to health. But if you're lookin' for another mother, look elsewhere.

"Anyway, only you can answer these questions. But I'm guessin' your natural instinct is to protect yourself from predators. You paid your way through college and worked full-time in the pot sink at the cafeteria. You didn't have much money to date girls, right?"

Bret protested, "I dated a few girls in college. I'm human, you know."

Allie laughed. "I'm not sayin' you were celibate. I'm sayin' the lack of funds interfered with your normal growth in relationships. As soon as the relationship threatened your wallet and jeopardized your ability to finish school, you found a reason, maybe subconsciously, to 'fire' your girlfriend. How many times did you pass up on a normal relationship with a woman 'cause of the funds issue? Am I right?"

Bret sat uneasily. "I hope the reasons were a little deeper than that. But there were a few girls who were more materialistic than others. They didn't last long."

"Again," Allie said in a sympathetic tone, "I'm not your psychiatrist, but you and I have similar experiences. I got married at eighteen and pregnant at nineteen, and was left alone with a child at twenty-two. I went to nursing school while my mother raised Marty. There was no money for anythin' other than food and tuition. And when I say food, I mean it in the simplest of menu choices. No restaurants. In the beginnin', my son and I ate on eight bucks a day.

"Protectin' your assets is part of who you are. It doesn't matter how much money you saved. You still feel poor. Think of it as being like someone who survived the Depression and continues to save old thread even though they're immensely wealthy. It's a natural mechanism."

JB had been sitting quietly during the counseling. He said, "Bret, the only money you spend on yourself is for clothes. I'll bet you have twenty suits in different shades of gray and blue. You own thirty different colors of Polo shirts. Clothes don't bring happiness. You probably don't realize it, but you don't do anything for yourself. You kind of need a breakthrough. I highly recommend taking up golf."

"Stop it with the golf," Allie bristled. "JB, you've got a wife, kids, grandkids, and a lot of friends. Okay, and you've got golf.

"Bret, if we're hittin' nerves, please tell us to stop. But our hearts are in the right place. JB is right. You don't try to find happiness. I'll bet the hour you spend with us at Ben's is the best part of your day. You have friends here. And JB can be entertainin' in a sarcastic, witty sort of way.

"Okay, so here is the point I am makin'. Just because you're finally ready to find happiness and conquer this fear of intimacy or insolvency or entrapment, whatever this fear is. Just because you're ready to enjoy life, it doesn't mean you have to conquer it with the first women who OD'd on you in the sack. She's usin' the bedroom to do exactly what you've been tryin' to prevent."

JB added, "Bret, if we all liked her, we'd tell you to get past it and tie the knot. Everyone has little spats. Yours aren't so little. Your friends here want you to be happy, but find somebody else, please."

Bret shook his head sadly, "Thanks for the advice, guys, but it's a little more complicated than that. Misty isn't half as bad as you think. We have a really nice time together when we're alone. She can be very sweet and extremely funny. I'd say she's territorial and a fighter, but I think all of that goes away if she were happily married and secure about her surroundings. Look at it from her perspective. Three guys dumped her, and she considers any woman near her boyfriend a threat. I don't blame her.

"But she sure does make a scene, though," Bret conceded with a laugh. "Listen, I gotta go before the Lincoln Tunnel turns solid."

A few minutes after Bret left, Panama Blonde took a seat at the table. JB gave her a surprised look. Allie beamed a big smile and said, "Hi Catherine, how're you today?"

"My word!" JB declared. "Al Gore was right. Global warming exists! When did you two girls melt the ice?"

Allie laughed, flipped her pony tail, and said, "My enemy's enemy is my friend. We have a common foe. You can officially welcome Catherine Mulcahy to our table.

"And Catherine, I have confirmation. All systems are a go for Christmas Eve."

CHAPTER 81

If it's on the Internet, it has to be right, right? Truth in media is an oxymoron, like a smoothie that provides roughage.

Ocean crabs crawl sideways. CRAB climbed higher. The daily volume was nice. Prices hovered in the low thirties. The open interest had climbed a few thousand contracts. Homeowners became more comfortable selling their future production through their Den-Ken accounts.

The commodity firm pounded the virtual media. They tweeted. They Facebooked. They LinkedIn. They developed authentic looking web sites dedicated to this new mysterious crabgrass with incredible qualities. They used their networkers who clicked on their pages and moved them up the Google page rankings. If you searched for "all-natural", a website about CRAB was near the top of the page along with the names of five tiny startup shampoo companies. The buzz grew louder.

You didn't have to search far for negative stories about sodium laureth sulfate. They were already in abundance, mostly planted by the tiny all-natural companies. Den-Ken's media department made it easier to find by linking them to the CRAB page.

The big question began appearing on the Pierre search page. What was this mysterious material Pierre was using to replace sodium laureth sulfate? Den-Ken's press release on the start of CRAB trading was a few search items lower. It was a start, but viral work takes time.

Hired bloggers did a viral swarm around the major shampoo companies. On Solarity Shampoo's website, they asked: *When are you switching to all-natural ingredients? Why are you using harsh chemicals? Why aren't you using the all-natural degreaser that Pierre uses?* The questions were repeated on every competitor's site.

Eva called Stephane into her office. "Look at this. Why is everyone hearing about our top secret material? Some secret. It's only a matter of time before these little companies start buying CRAB. How many contracts have we bought so far?"

"It's only been three weeks," explained Stephane. "We're trying not to move the market higher. We've bought a hundred contracts a day on average, or 150,000 pounds at an average price of $26 per pound. But those contracts are spread out over two years. The contracts for June delivery are $31 today. Only a third of our contracts are for 2012 delivery."

"Okay, Stephane," Eva said with urgency. "You're following instructions. However, this stupid class action lawsuit has me concerned. My sources tell me the lawyers are seeking an injunction to stop us from taking any crabgrass under the option agreements. Counsel tells me they might win unless we can prove irreparable harm.

"That means we can't be sure we have the 700,000 pounds we thought we had. How would you suggest we buy more futures without driving the price too high?"

"It's very simple," Stephane said. "You place an order of size in the market. But I wouldn't put in a market order. The price would take off. I'd get our broker to contact Den-Ken directly. They might sell you some of the contracts held by the CRAB FUND."

"Oh, mercy," wailed Eva. "I'd be trading with the enemy."

Stephane shrugged, "You might want to start thinking of them as a middleman, not an enemy. In some respects, they serve a valuable purpose by providing a market place to buy what you need.

"With your permission, I'll instruct our broker to make an institutional purchase of 2,000 contracts at a premium to the market. I suggest $34."

"Okay, Stephane," Eva sighed resignedly. "You have my authority. Let me know. And Joyeux Noel!"

"Merci beaucoup, Mademoiselle. Joyeux Noel!"

CHAPTER 82

DECEMBER 24, 2011

It was closing time on Saturday night. Allie rushed to wrap a gift for the last customer. Her store was one of the few in downtown Bergenfield that remained open this late on Christmas Eve.

After closing the shop, she raced through town blurring the nostalgic glow of the holiday lights hung over Washington Avenue. The new bulbs looked like the real 1950 originals but were less likely to burn down the town.

Bergenfield's main avenue presented a diversified holiday message. One lamppost hosted a cheery Saint Nick. Another held two elves who took turns hitting a hammer to make toys. Chanukah candles and a Jewish star were strung above the avenue. This year the town added a kinara for Kwanzaa, which held seven candles – three red, three green and a black candle in the center.

Allie was in a terrible rush. She had to pick up Marty's present, a MacBook laptop, at the Garden State Plaza, grab a pizza on the way home and get ready for Midnight Mass at St. John's church. Panama Blonde would be waiting.

CHAPTER 83

DECEMBER 24

Allie met Panama Blonde at 11:00 PM in front of the True Value store, diagonally across from the church. It was important to their plan to arrive well before Midnight Mass began. Any later, there was a good chance they'd be routed to the downstairs service. They sat in the last row and tried to be as inconspicuous as possible. In order for their scheme to work, everything had to be perfect.

At half past eleven, Allie nudged Catherine as Bret and Misty found a pew halfway to the altar. Bret carried Misty's overcoat presumably so she could show off her outfit. She wore a dark double-knit maxi skirt over black leather mid-calf boots. She added the saintly touch with a long white lace scarf over her head. She played with a three-strand pearl necklace which looked like this year's Christmas present. Bret wore the usual dark gray suit and dark tie.

Hundreds of forlorn sinners came out of the woodwork on Christmas primarily to socialize with old friends and take in a little religious spirit. By midnight, St. John the Evangelist Roman Catholic Church was standing room only. Priests in white vestments with gold trim began the mass.

Allie had attended St. John's grammar school thirty years earlier and knew a few of the nuns who still taught there. She said to Catherine, "Wait here. Let me do the talking."

Allie walked up the side aisle to the front vestibule where the nuns were seated. She spoke to Sister Helena in private for several minutes, pointed out Misty, and returned to the rear of the church. The side aisles were so crowded that she escaped unnoticed by Bret and Misty. After Allie sat, Catherine couldn't restrain her giggling. Allie elbowed her to keep quiet.

Midnight Mass was said in Latin. *Dominus Vobiscum. Et Cum Spiritu Tuo.* The words quieted the restless crowd standing in the aisles. Deacons patrolled the area to keep order.

At 12:30 AM, the priest began serving Holy Communion. Knowing Misty as they did, Allie and Panama Blonde were absolutely sure she'd jump to the front of the line. Their plan counted on it. Misty was an "I go first!" gal – a prima donna who demanded to be catered to before the less-worthy mass of humanity.

Hundreds filled the aisle to receive the sacrament at the altar. But Misty never budged. If she didn't try to receive communion, it would ruin their plan. Panama Blonde looked down dejectedly. Allie comforted her. "Don't give up yet."

After an endless fifteen minutes, the line finally subsided to a few dozen parishioners. Allie thought for a moment about doing something drastic. Maybe she could prod Misty to the altar if she pushed her buttons. She could join the communion line and say hi to Bret and Misty on the way. Invite her, perhaps. Anything to get Misty to move from her seat. Allie held back. She wanted to be far away if and when the fireworks started.

Allie whispered to Panama Blonde, "I'm sorry, Catherine. It didn't work. I was so sure."

"I was sure, too. Don't worry about it," Catherine whispered back. "There's always a next time."

At the last possible moment, Misty looked around the church to make sure no one else was coming. She stood and joined the end of the procession. There were a dozen people ahead of her. Her hands were folded in angelic prayer.

They had it all wrong. Misty didn't want to be first in line. She wanted to be last. She wanted the whole church to adore her outfit and admire her handsome Wall Street lawyer boyfriend as she returned to their pew.

As she neared the altar, Sister Helena moved in front of Misty and quietly spoke to her. Two other nuns stood behind the Sister. Gasps could be heard from the front rows. Were they preventing Misty from receiving the sacrament?

Sister Helena was trying to avoid a scene, but Misty was visibly upset. She started to step around the nuns. Sister Helena stood in her path and put a firm hand on Misty's shoulder. The two younger nuns motioned their arms to the side of the church. Misty conceded defeat and followed them to the vestibule. Sister Helena stopped to genuflect as she passed the statue of the baby Jesus and returned to her pew.

Misty hurried out the side door. Half of the church was in shock. Half was amused. Everyone was whispering. Bret sat all alone, not knowing what to do. The priests, slightly flustered, returned to the altar to begin the concluding rites.

Allie and Catherine had to leave the church before they burst out laughing. They walked the 200 yards down Washington Avenue to Tommy Fox's for a victory cocktail.

CHAPTER 84

DECEMBER 25, 2011

Allie raised her wine glass to Catherine and said, "Merry Christmas! Here's to our conspiracy! May no one ever learn of its members."

"Tchin! Tchin!" Catherine returned, touching her glass to Allie's. "If Bret ever found us out, we'd be outcasts. But maybe, just maybe, this'll enlighten him enough to ditch the trash. I mean really, how'd she ever land a Wall Street lawyer?"

"You and I both know how she landed him… in the sack," Allie giggled. "It should've worn off by now. She must have some powerful stuff."

A sizable crowd swelled Tommy Fox's Public House following Mass. A band was playing Irish songs on fiddle and guitar. Churchgoers not a few minutes earlier, they now sipped on Guinness or gin. The bar was in a festive mood.

Allie overheard Mrs. Hennessy talking about the excitement at church. The story grew bolder. The latest version described Misty being dragged by both ears.

Mrs. Hennessey took a sip of her neat gin and said in her strong Irish brogue, "She should be ashamed o' herself, she should. Divorced three times, oi hear. Far as Rome is concerned, she's excommunicated. It's a bloody sin to receive th' sacraments if ye've been banned from th' blessed church."

Bill O'Malley, behind bar tapping a glass of Guinness, said, "Perhaps oi should offer Sister Helena a position on weekends. We need extra door staff to handle th' likes of ye lads!"

Timothy Kern was sitting at the bar closest to O'Malley. The barkeep grabbed his friend's ear and gave his best imitation of a nun bouncer. "Now little Timothy, sneakin' into Tommy Fox's underage, are ye? Didn't oi give ye enough ruler on yer wrist in th' sixth grade? Does ye really want moire?"

The loud laughter drowned out the music. Decker walked in looking sideways at the boisterous bar crowd. He sat with Allie and Catherine. "What just happened?"

The girls acted innocent. Catherine said, "Well, we don't know all the details, but Bret's squeeze tried to storm the altar and receive communion, which is a no-no for excommunicated sinners. Anyway, that's what they're saying at the bar."

Bret entered the bar a minute later and sat with the gang, totally clueless. "I'm mortified. What was she thinking? Fighting a nun in church? I'm not Catholic, but that's gotta be a bad thing, right?

"I looked for her in the parking lot, but she was gone. She must've walked home. I'll leave her alone tonight, but how do I deal with this tomorrow on Christmas Day in front of her family?"

"Why Bret, I'm surprised you don't know," said Allie. "Misty's the ultimate chauvinist. She celebrates all victories and ignores all defeats. She won't even mention this in the mornin'. It'll be like it never happened."

Bret shook his head. "It's like she has three egos."

Allie asked, "You mean three personalities, don't you?"

Bret replied, "No, three egos. Me, me, and me. Last week, I was talking to her about how hard it was working late every night. She stopped me mid-sentence and snapped, 'That's enough about you and your work. That's all you talk about. What about me? What about my needs?' I was flabbergasted."

Decker joked, "I'm sorry, Bret. I thought dating one Misty was tough...but three? Is at least one of them kind?"

"Aw, that's not nice, Decker," teased Catherine. "Bret's in pain. Everybody! A toast to the holiday. Merry Christmas!"

They clinked their glasses. Decker caught a glimpse of Allie winking at Catherine. He smelled a conspiracy.

The violinist and guitar player rested onstage as an Irish colleen sang a cappella. The bar grew quiet. The song was *Silent Night* sung in Gaelic.

Oíche Chiúin, oíche Mhic Dé,
Cách 'na suan, dís araon...

CHAPTER 85

DECEMBER 27, 2011

Closing the $200 million industrial revenue bond was a paperwork struggle. At the behest of Mexican Charter Bank, Bergenfield hired its first treasurer to handle its end of the prospectus and represent the town in negotiations.

Suzanne Pettigrew was 35 years old and recently married. After ten years in municipal finance at Merrill Lynch, she'd been passed over for promotion to managing director. It was time to find a career away from the hundred hour workweek of an investment banker and find a more normal, less stressful position.

Suzanne looked like she already regretted her decision. She lived in expensive digs on the Upper West Side. Starting today, she reverse-commuted across the George Washington Bridge and the Palisades into Bergen County.

Suzanne accompanied Justin to Ben's Deli for a breakfast meeting her first day of work. Wearing a Bergdorf Goodman designer outfit and black pump shoes, she was a bit overdressed for the crowd of landscapers and local businessmen.

JB called to Justin and invited them to sit at the board table. Justin said, "Suzanne, you may not want to join that crew on your first day. That's a tough crowd."

Suzanne shrugged off Justin. "I'll make mincemeat out of 'em if they try to get too funny."

Justin sat warily at the far end of the table. Suzanne grabbed the seat next to JB.

Justin: "Everyone, meet Suzanne. She's the new town treasurer."

JB: "What brings a lovely, sophisticated city girl like you to our village?"

Suzanne: "They told me this town is filled with charming, intelligent gentlemen filled with sparkling conversation and wit. Where are they hiding?"

JB, noticing the wedding ring on Suzanne's left hand: "Touché. This table is filled with happily-married captains and former-captains of industry. All except for poor Bret-boy here whose significant other is possessed by the antichrist. You have any girlfriends wanting to save a soul?"

Suzanne, teasing: "I might know one or two. He looks respectable. I'm not sure about the friends he keeps."

JB: "Touché again. I think he sits with us because he's under some community service court order. He's a big-time, general counsel at Montauk and Malibu, you know. Makes decent bucks."

Suzanne: "What's a big Wall Street lawyer doing in this ghost town?"

Bret laughing: "You guys talk about me like I'm not here. I have feelings, you know. We're just having a problem locating them. As for why I'm here, isn't it obvious? It's for the climate and fresh air."

JB: "Suzanne, welcome. Even though it's your first day, I think we can safely add you to Ben's favorites list. You should pick your song for the juke box."

Suzanne: "That thing works?"

JB: "Yup, and don't insult it too loudly. Some think it may be human. Anyway, Ben sometimes plays a song to greet his favorite customers."

Suzanne: "Why would I pick any other song than *Suzanne* by Judy Collins?"

JB: "Done."

Suzanne: "Well it was nice meeting you all, I think. Off to the coal mines. We're drafting documents for this bond, and I have to make sure it doesn't implode and ruin your lovely town."

CHAPTER 86

DECEMBER 31, 2011

Justin and Suzanne managed to close the industrial revenue bond with an hour to spare before the federal wire system closed for the day. The money had already been raised and was sitting in escrow at Mexican Chartered waiting for the filing. They had worked twelve-hour days to paper the transaction and file the prospectus with the SEC. The bankers claimed that they had to raise the money before year-end due to "market conditions". The more likely reason was they wanted to add to their year-end bonuses.

Suzanne and Justin collapsed at Tommy Fox's for a one-drink closing party. She said, "You know, I left Wall Street to work less hours and spend more time with my new hubby. So much for that concept. What's in store for me next?"

Justin gave an exhausted smile. "It should be a lot easier from here."

Bret worked New Year's Eve until eight o'clock getting three tax deals closed before year-end. The oil companies "broke ground" to start drilling the wells, which was required to qualify for the $20 million of intangible drilling cost tax deduction.

Bret took a private car at the company's expense through the Holland Tunnel as revelers passed in the opposite direction heading for Times Square. Bret had no intention of calling Misty. She exhausted him.

Misty had made other plans anyway. She joined three girlfriends for a New Year's party at an Atlantic City casino. Both suspected this was going to end ugly.

CHAPTER 87

JANUARY 3, 2012

Making good on his only New Year's resolution, Ben visited Walter at the Bergenfield Record Store during the mid-morning lull. "I need you to burn a 45 of *Suzanne* by Judy Collins."

Walter Harrigan looked up from an old *Rolling Stone* magazine and peered through his John Lennon glasses. "You know, *Suzanne* was released as a single in 1972. It was the B side to *Someday Soon*. I have an original in stock, but it may be a little scratchy. Ten bucks."

Walt was a solid six feet topped by a curly sandy blond mop of hair. He wore a navy Wallace Beery shirt with the sleeves pushed above his elbows. He was near sixty, but could pass for fortyish. Ben and Walter were the same age, but Ben could easily be mistaken for his father.

Walter was sole proprietor of the Bergenfield Record Store and the town's living relic of the sixties' music movement. He had encyclopedic knowledge of vinyl records having spent much of his youth at the Fillmore East rock concert hall. His competitors at the Paramus malls over the years had moved on to CDs and DVDs and eventually closed their doors when the iPod took over the music business. Walter kept selling records, which became collectibles. Antique records had made a big nostalgic comeback.

Ben said, "Scratchy won't do. It's going in the jukebox. Just rip one on your machine from the digital version. It's a greeting card for a new member. JB recruited her, and she's a real cutie."

Ben inspected an old album cover of *Dear Mr. Fantasy* by Traffic. "Can you make any money selling this stuff?"

"I make enough to pay the bills and afford a nice glass of wine with dinner. I mean, it's not Ben's Deli money, but I get by," joked Walter.

"This humble store sells trips down memory lane with album covers in decent shape that people hang up in their dens. An old Beatles or Stones Album. Hendrix or Cream. Sex Pistols. Even the Carpenters. They all sell, and I make a markup on the picture frame. It's a great business at Christmas.

"Walt, thanks for the favor, again. I owe you one. I'll buy you a cappuccino upon delivery."

Ben crossed the street back to the deli. The kitchen workers had figured out Ben's jukebox override system and were playing *La Bamba* while they cleaned the grills.

CHAPTER 88

JANUARY 13, 2012

Misty never discussed her New Year's Eve with Bret. She hadn't given up on him just yet, but he was obstinate about the silliest things, like work. She had too much time invested. Perhaps he could still be tamed. She just needed to ramp up the offensive a notch.

Bret was exhausted at the young age of 40. He longed for a night at home eating take-out. Dining out every night took all the fun out of eating. Worse, Misty called him five times a day to plan their activities. He couldn't get any work done. This morning he skipped breakfast at Ben's just to have an hour of freedom.

Misty stood in line at Ben's in a red wool coat and matching scarf over her head. With her breakfast in hand, she pulled out her cash envelopes to pay the $3.87 bill with two dollar bills and eight quarters. Ben sighed. *Here goes another wasted four minutes of my life.*

She looked around the corner to make sure Bret wasn't nearby. "Ben, would you add a song on the juke box for Bret and me?"

Ben tried to look puzzled. "Misty, I don't know what you're talking about. You have to speak to the juke box owners. I think their name is on the back. You need quarters to play a song."

Misty sweet face disappeared. She scolded him like a nineteenth century schoolmarm. "Ben, quarters have nothing to do with playing that old Victrolla. YOU control the juke box and YOU play songs for your favorite customers."

Ben ignored her, handed over the change, and called, "Next!"

Sweet Misty returned. "Why can't you play a song for Bret and me? It's a very popular song among couples. You know," she half sung, "*Feelings. Nothing more than feelings.*"

Ben said, "First, I don't know what you're talking about. Second, that song is a serious buzz kill. If it was on the jukebox, I'd use a sledgehammer on it."

Misty counteroffered, "Alright Ben. It doesn't have to be *Feelings.* Let's compromise. How about *Anticipation* by Carly Simon?"

Ben shook his head and sputtered his lips. Everything with Misty had to be a negotiation. Nothing was ever done out of the kindness of your heart or generosity of spirit.

He was losing his patience. "No. That's the ketchup commercial song. Do you want me to lose every customer I have? The next thing you'll want is Glenn Miller. Misty, I'm just not doing it. Don't ask again!"

"Sorry. You DO play songs for customers," Misty said angrily. "You always play something for Nurse Cratchit over there. Whatever do you guys see in her? She wears no makeup. Her hair has never seen a roller or hair spray. Her clothes aren't even store bought. Ben, I'm asking you nicely for the last time."

Ben laughed and said, "*Nurse Cratchit?* You mean Nurse Ratched from *One Flew Over the Cuckoo's Nest. Bob Cratchit* was a character in *A Christmas Carol,* and if anyone could learn a lesson from that story, it would be you."

Misty was getting very angry. She demanded, "I insist that you play *Feelings* when Bret and I make our entrance."

The line grew five customers long. Danny Adler threw down a twenty dollar bill to pay for a three dollar breakfast. "You can give me my change next time, Ben. I have to make a flight to Europe."

Ben had to placate Misty to move the line. He offered, "I'll ask the juke box owner next time he's in. But I make no promises."

Misty said, "I have a question. How does the juke box contain 45s of songs that are only ten years old? They don't make 45s anymore."

Ben ignored her. "Next!"

CHAPTER 89

JANUARY 27, 2012

Late January in North Jersey was always gray, cold and dreary. Today, a heat wave of 90 degrees surprised everyone. Men wore polo shirts. Women wore shorts and miniskirts. The weather was getting downright wacky. In the last eight months, the Northeast had experienced Hurricane Irene, horrible flooding, an earthquake in Virginia, tornados and now summer weather in January.

Ben's air conditioners were running full blast. Bart, the town pessimist and conspiracy theorist, hadn't been seen in a while. He panhandled the table for spare change to buy a coffee. He once again claimed he had left his wallet at home. The table ignored him, but JB reached into his pocket for a couple of bucks.

JB: "Bart, you missed your calling in life."

Decker: "What, as a beggar?"

JB: "No, as a monk. It seems our Bart here pledged a vow of poverty."

Bart: "I'm sorry JB. My wife won't let me turn on the lights in the morning to get dressed. I can't see a thing. I thought I grabbed my wallet, but I must've dropped it before I left."

JB: "It's okay Bart. You'd think your wife would be a little more supportive of the breadwinner. Why isn't she up when you're getting ready? Does she at least make the coffee?"

Bart: "Make coffee? Are you kidding? She sleeps until ten. Then she beats the crap out of me when I get home from work. All I hear is what a failure I am. And I'm on an allowance. It barely pays for lunch. My life sucks."

JB: "Sorry, man."

Suzanne reached the cash register. Her new song played on the old jukebox. She thanked Ben and laughed as she joined the table. "I thought you guys were joking, or I would've put more thought into my selection."

"Don't worry. He won't play it every day, but he always seems to sense the day you need cheering up," said Allie.

JB stood and banged his spoon against his coffee mug. "May I have the men's attention? Before you head off to work, I have a proposal which requires board table approval. It'll be fun and save you money. This Valentine's Day, I recommend we hold a lingerie exchange!"

The table of twelve groaned. It was another of JB's crazy plans. Allie cried out, "You perv!"

"No girls allowed, Allie!" said a mock-serious JB. "This'll save you guys big money. Every year you spend three or four hundred bucks on this ridiculous day created by restaurants, chocolatiers, florists and lingerie stores. It's time we fought back."

Decker said, "There's no way we spend four hundred bucks."

JB countered, "Add it up. Roses – $75 dollars. Candy – $25. Restaurant – $200. And lingerie is another $100. Well, I have a way to save you the cost of the unmentionables.

"Look in your wife's dresser drawer. How many pairs of panties, nighties and camisoles still have the original price tag? They've never been worn. Every year, you're obligated to buy something, and every year it goes in the 'drawers' drawer."

"Maybe your wives would wear it if you guys stopped buying trashy and started buying classy," said Allie.

Ben stood over the table. He said, "I gotta side with JB on this one. If you don't buy lingerie, you're not romantic. If you do buy it, she won't wear it. It's a ritual or something. Every woman has the drawer. It's like a sacred burial ground for undies."

"You're right, Ben!" said JB. "Listen, this'll be fun. Here's the deal. Everyone bring in an item of your wife's lingerie that's never been worn. To be safe, it has to have been sitting for, let's say, at least three years in the 'no-no' drawer. The store tags have to be intact.

"We'll exchange among ourselves and re-gift it to our wives or significant others. She'll never know. It's going straight to the drawer anyway."

Gavin: "My wife has a twenty-year inventory. Never been worn. JB, I hate to admit it. The idea is brilliant."

Michael: "My wife also has such a drawer. However, a contest to save a hundred dollars sounds like a risk far outweighing the rewards. Would lose face if caught."

Decker: "Michael, you sound like a Confucius banker. It's not about saving the hundred bucks. It's the thrill of the game. Unfortunately, I'm not dating anyone right now, so I'm out."

Buyout: "I am dating someone, but I don't have anything to exchange."

JB: "I got you covered, Buyout. I have plenty extra."

Justin: "I can say with some legal authority that this event is a tax-free lingerie exchange. As long as you're swapping for like-kind panties."

Walter, laughing: "And they said accountants don't have a sense of humor. I'm definitely in. Sally may have an old baby doll nightie from the sixties sitting around."

JB: "No way, Walter. It has to be reasonably current."

Allie: "This is unfair. I want in."

Ben: "Not only am I in, hold the panty exchange here at Ben's on the thirteenth. It's a Monday. I'll buy coffee and bagels. You gotta show the goods to eat for free, though."

Decker: "Free breakfast? Okay, I'll exchange for the hell of it."

Allie: "It's gonna be a riot to see what you guys bought your wives."

JB: "I'm not kidding, Allie. No girls allowed."

Michael: "Okay, if everyone else is in, I'm in too. I hope this doesn't backfire."

Suzanne rose and said, "Thanks for the entertainment. You guys are lot of fun, but construction on the transfer station starts today. I have to shovel the first dirt. The mayor refuses to attend the groundbreaking.

"Two weeks until the lingerie show. I can't wait."

CHAPTER 90

FEBRUARY 13, 2012

Ben had set a feast of bagels, bialys, melon and carafes of coffee. The table was full of men including a few who weren't regulars. The idea had spread.

Allie, Panama Blonde and Suzanne sat at the adjacent table. JB chaired the lingerie exchange. "Okay, everyone has to present their scanties. If the majority of the table agrees, it goes in the grab bag."

It was a fashion show without live models. Michael Li went first and unfurled a blue and white Chinese floral chemise. Allie remarked, "That isn't unwearable. It's cute."

"It isn't the item that makes the ritual. She must reject it to keep her sense of honor," said Michael solemnly. "If she had purchased the item, she would wear it every night. But I purchased it, and she must reject it."

JB interrupted, "Michael, it's too recognizable. One of the other women might figure it out. Do you have anything else?"

Michael knew the item wouldn't fly. He sprung his real contribution, a nasty looking dark red bustier and panty item. "How's this?"

Allie said from exile, "Now *that* I wouldn't wear!"

The twelve took turns showing red and black thongs, string bikinis, a rather tame camisole, teddies, mesh stockings, a push-up bra, and bunny ears with furry panties and matching high heels. The collection was an embarrassing indictment of male fantasies.

JB held up a pair of huge white nylon granny panties. "Here's my contribution!"

Walter: "Wait! My wife loves those. They're like magic underwear!"

Decker, scowling: "How embarrassing! If I saw you shopping for those, I would've asked the police to tail you home."

JB: "Buyout was my secret shopper. They're just a gag gift. Here's my real delicate."

JB held a tiny string bikini, garter belt and stocking set all in shocking pink. The string looked extremely uncomfortable.

Gavin: "No wonder women don't wear this stuff."

Decker stood and held high three small triangles of blue cloth held together by a long complex of elastic strings. He said triumphantly, "Beat that!"

Walter grabbed the web of cloth from Decker and fiddled with the contraption trying to determine exactly how one would climb into or out of such an item.

Gavin: "That's not the top, Walter. That's the bottom!"

Decker: "There's no top or bottom. It's not designed to be worn for long. It's meant to be torn off."

The girls were rolling their eyes at the chauvinist display. Ben leaned over to their table and handed Allie a box wrapped in silver foil with red hearts. "Here, Allie, a gift from your BFFs on Valentine's Day."

Allie opened the package and gushed as she held up a Joe Namath New York Jets football jersey. "I can't believe you guys did this. You're so sweet."

JB: "They're on sale. No one wants to be seen in a Jets jersey."

Gavin: "I played golf with Namath once at Bear Lakes in West Palm. Great guy. Super competitive."

Allie: "I love the Jets. They're so human the way they keep tripping over themselves. Thank you, guys. I love all of you."

JB: "Enough of the Jets. Alright, you've seen the items. Everyone pick a number and grab your gift. Good luck. Whatever you do, don't tell your wife where you got it. You'll blow everyone's cover. Happy Valentine's Day!"

CHAPTER 91

FEBRUARY 14, 2012

Useless entropy is the unaccountable loss of energy in Einstein's theory of relativity. Valentine's Day is the unaccountable loss of time and energy every February 14.

V-Day landed on a Tuesday this year, which doomed millions of American men into heroic attempts at romantic behavior. If it had occurred later in the week, say on a Thursday, a husband could beg off the restaurant experience. "Let's do it Saturday when it's less crowded." Not to mention lower prices. But Tuesday was too far from the weekend.

There's nothing romantic about an overcrowded restaurant with unhappy patrons, besieged waiters and angry, overworked cook staff. Restaurants squeezed in far too many extra tables. Menu choices were limited. Diners were pressured to finish quickly and cede their table to the next couple waiting in line. It was just too many people cramming a well-intentioned rite into too little space and time. Are you getting this, Mr. Einstein?

CHAPTER 92

FEBRUARY 15, 2011

JB scrolled through his iPhone while Allie sat proudly in her Namath football jersey munching on a bagel with cream cheese.

Walter joined the table with a worried look. "I'm in big trouble. I picked the Spencer Gifts scanty teddy at the Valentine's Day exchange. My wife tried it on and it's five sizes too big. We had a huge fight. How was I supposed to know size 14 is large? She wants to return it. I'm screwed!"

"Of course you got caught," Allie snickered. "Women are way too smart for you guys."

Justin said, "Well E=mc squared. Your loss is my gain. Dorothy thinks the size six thong is the greatest gift ever. She wore it all day. And she IS a size 14."

"These are minor inconveniences," said JB. "I think the panty exchange was an overall success, except for Walter, who has to learn women's sizes. Walter, look in the leftover bag and pick a new item. The trick is to always buy a size eight or less. They'll exchange it later. It's a well-known statistical fact that a hundred fifty percent of all clothing gifts are returned by women for a different size."

"If your stats are true, that would mean women are returning more than once," Decker observed.

JB made a wry face. "Correct, Decker. It lets women shop more. Anyway, this event was so successful that we might want to do this again at Christmas. We're going to put Victoria's Secret out of business."

Gavin nudged JB and pointed to a table of four young guns eating breakfast. "I think those are the commodity guys. It's going to be an interesting year."

CHAPTER 93

FEBRUARY 15

Battle lines were being drawn. Mayor Hector Alvarez, Allie, and a thousand residents with nice lawns were on one side. They wanted the craze to end. Den-Ken, the partners of CRAB FUND I and II, and 4,000 homeowners sat opposite. Pierre was in the middle of a fragile alliance. They wanted the crabgrass, but at a better price. Four thousand homes sat undecided. At what price were they willing to join the fray?

A group of angry residents living in the nicely landscaped homes near Fairleigh Dickinson filed a lawsuit against the town. They named themselves The Teaneck Border Patrol. The suit claimed the town did not have the proper authority to approve the industrial revenue bond. The court ruled against them in a summary judgment.

Their second lawsuit claimed the weed was a nonnative invasive plant species which was disrupting the regional fauna and flora. It postulated that the Dutch inadvertently brought the invasive crabgrass into the United States when they imported tulip bulbs, which was probably true. Therefore, the crabgrass was a foreign species.

The judge threw the suit out based upon the statute of limitations. The judge wrote that the state and its residents had more than three hundred years to bring the action and had declined to do so in a timely fashion.

Desperate for a court win, the Teaneck Border Patrol filed a third suit based upon interference with property rights. The weed seeds travelled by air and spread hay fever. The judge fined them for filing a nuisance suit. He admonished them, "Find a better legal theory, or find a better lawyer!"

Mayor Hector Alvarez spoke loud on the issue but was drowned out by the sound of coins hitting piggy banks. He appealed to his Filipino community who had helped him get elected. They liked Hector, but they liked the large checks even more.

Hector opened a Twitter account and started tweeting daily about the downside effects of the crabgrass blight. In his profile, he wrote PROUD MAYOR and H8ER of WEEDS. His Filipino community politely followed him on Twitter, but no one retweeted his posts.

Hector preached moderation on the town web site. Keep our town clean. Beware of booms. They're temporary.

He started the CARE program – Crabgrasses Are the Real Enemy! The mayor's viral campaign wasn't working. The start of the growing season was a month away.

CHAPTER 94

FEBRUARY 29, 2012

Leap Day, the 29th of February. Cartoonist Al Capp created Sadie Hawkins Day in his *Li'l Abner* comic strip. It was a time every four years when girls were allowed to ask men to marry them. Based upon centuries-old Irish and English folk traditions, the rules have since changed. Now there are no rules.

Gilbert called a meeting of Bergen Development Company. Johnny declined because he was too busy. As a courtesy, Gilbert invited David Elliot, partner-non-grata. He never responded.

Gilbert laid it on the line to Vinnie, Trudy, Chris and Howie. "Of the thirty-five homes, seven need major repairs – two roofs, a boiler and at least four washing machines or dryers needed replacement. After we pay these bills, we've nearly run out of money.

"The reason we have a problem is because our crabgrass is disappearing from the lawns. We should've netted a hundred thousand dollars in October. We got half of that. Our renters are stealing our crabgrass and selling it."

Vinnie was angry. "Gilbert, gimme the names. I'll get da money. Dey'll either pay, or dey'll be livin' on da street."

Vinnie drove to Nano Bio.Com's makeshift offices. He wore all black – a leather jacket, double knit shirt and pressed slacks. He walked into Johnny's office like he owned the place.

"Johnny, here's da list of our homes. You should know dis. You're part owner, but I failed ta see ya at da meeting yesterday. Wha? Ya too busy nows ya got a fancy job?"

All week long, Johnny felt important. He was the president of a company with dozens of productive employees. Then Vinnie showed up and made him feel tiny as a pea.

Vinnie continued, "Lemme ask you a question. You guys bought any crabgrass from any of dese guys?"

Johnny was clueless. He grabbed the list and left the room to ask Justin. He returned and handed Vinnie a sales report marked in red ink. "I don't how this slipped by us. It was pretty hectic back in October. It's kinda late now. We already paid 'em."

Vinnie took a quick look at the report and threw it back at Johnny. "You gumba, why'd you do dis? You don't buy from nobody 'less dey are da rightful owner of da property, you hear? You got a thousand rental properties in town. How many of dose did you screw up? Huh?"

Johnny squirmed.

"I'll tell ya what I'm gonna do. I'm gonna do ya a favor and visit dese crooks and politely ask for my money. If any of 'em don't pay up, I'm coming ta you for payment. Ya got it?

"And next time Gilbert calls a partner meeting, I'd better see dat ugly puss of yours dare, ya hear me?"

CHAPTER 95

MARCH 1, 2012

Eva studied the printout and looked up at Stephane. "What does this mean?"

Stephane said, "That's the source of a lot of your pricing pressure. Den-Ken filed a Form D last month with the SEC. CRAB FUND II raised $50 million and has been buying for a month. My back channels tell me the investors included some state pension funds and corporate treasury departments. It's not just hedge funds this time."

Eva calculated in her head. "At $35 a pound, they could buy a million and a half pounds. The whole town can't produce three million pounds yet. These guys are trying to corner the market."

"Multiply that number by four Eva," Stephane explained. "There's only a 25 percent margin requirement on CRAB. And it's not just them. There are others. Orders are coming from the big trading desks.

"CRAB closed at $38 yesterday. That's up 50 percent since November. We're in the middle of the winter when you wouldn't expect prices to move very much. Imagine what'll happen during the growing season."

Eva asked, "Why do you say that?"

"Think of it this way," Stephane said. "Heating oil futures are quiet most of the year. When winter comes, the prices swing based upon weather and usage. Another example would be corn. Prices don't move much in the winter. In the summer, it can trade widely particularly if we face a drought or a bumper crop."

"I understand," said Eva. "You're saying the price could jump this summer. What's our current inventory and futures position?"

Stephane handed her the inventory report. "We have a quarter of what we need. I've been able to buy a little of the 2013 futures without affecting the market, but the 2012 market is very tight."

Eva said, "Our customers are supposed to deliver 700,000 pounds under the option agreements. They're getting more litigious. The grapevine says some of them sold their 2012 futures even though they're obligated to sell to us.

"Let's assume we are able to buy half of the optioned amount. You'd still need to buy another million pounds from June through October."

Eva put down the report. "Marketing tells me our preorders are very high. Any forecasts they gave you are wrong by at least double. We should do two things. First, Albert has to accelerate his program to increase the product yield. Second, you're going to buy on every dip. Somehow, you have to buy another million pounds at $35."

"Eva, there are no dips. CRAB is going linear. Just hope it doesn't go parabolic. If I put in orders to buy another million pounds, CRAB could go to a $100!" said Stephane.

Eva narrowed her eyes. "Stephane, if they have $60 million in partnership funds, couldn't we just buy from them as we need it? You know. Get out of the trading market."

"Eva, this is dangerous territory," Stephane said, grim-faced. "All of the fundamentals are pointing higher. Technicals are higher, too. I suggest we build our position before the June delivery. We said we could buy up to $60 and not affect our shampoo margins. I recommend that we increase our bid price and lock in our supply. Also, I'd add to our 2013 and 2014 futures positions. Those are a little cheaper. The speculators are buying the most current delivery dates."

Eva left the room and spoke to Olivier in the hallway. She returned and said with a sigh, "Alright, Stephane. Our boss just said to worry about sales growth. He reminded me that we're still making a lot of money.

"Here's the new marching orders. Buy another million pounds before June for $60 or less. Go do it. Bon chance!"

CHAPTER 96

MARCH 2, 2012

Following a month of brutal cold, early March was unseasonably warm. Late winter temperatures typically averaged in the low fifties. Then Mother Nature smacked New Jersey with one harsh cold snap before spring to remind you who was in charge. But not this year. Today it was sixty degrees, and winter coats stayed in the closet.

Averill Winthrop bought breakfast for Johnny no-longer True Value. He played with his gold pocket watch chained to the fob pocket of his suit vest.

"Johnny, tell me what's new at the transfer station? How's construction going? How're your finances?"

Even though the meal was free, Johnny was annoyed at the questioning. He replied between forkfuls of huevos rancheros, "Oenotropae wants its money back early. We're what they call an orphan deal – got no banker at the firm supportin' us. The partner who was overseein' the investment resigned from the firm. Oeno originally thought we could go public, but their investment bankers told 'em the deal's too small and the markets aren't very receptive. They claimed the IPO market had the shakes from the financial meltdown…whatever that means. Oeno is gonna try to find another way to exit from the investment."

Averill looked intrigued, and twisted his handlebar moustache. "I can take you public. There's a different path for small companies. Silverheels or Montague won't touch this deal. You need me."

Johnny looked askance. "How do you know 'bout IPO's? You don't work on Wall Street."

Averill faked a look of hurt. "Johnny, you offend me. Of course I work on Wall Street. It's a virtual street. Brokerage firms have offices all over the world. Almost no one is physically located on Wall Street anymore.

"I'm an investment banker. I raise money for small cap companies all the time. At my firm, we cater to smaller companies. We wear all hats. Let me work on this a few days and get back to you."

Johnny didn't care. Averill had picked up the six dollar breakfast tab.

Averill left and returned to his mess of an office. The furniture was old. Desks had twenty-year-old smears and marks. Tears in the vinyl couch cushions revealed sprouts of foam rubber. Dusty legal file boxes were stacked against every available wall space. This place needed a maid. Or an arsonist.

Averill thought for a minute. *The investor is already unhappy and wants to get out quickly. They think they made a mistake investing in Nano. They're no dummies. They'll sell but still want to get paid a decent price.*

Nobody wants to control this company, despite the fact that it's sitting at the porthole to some crazy emerging commodity craze. If I orchestrate this properly, I could control the company's finances, make a bunch of fees and make even more trading the stock.

Management was clueless about finances. Averill needed their backing if he was going to convince Oeno about the plan. He could buy their allegiance with employee stock options so they could make some money. The board was a bunch of old guys doing as they were told by Oeno. Buy them with stock options, too.

CHAPTER 97

MARCH 2

Averill juggled five balls with two hands and no money. Get management to back him. Convince Oenotropae to go public through a reverse merger. Buy a shell. Convince the half-dead Board of Directors they were important. Last, but not least, raise $10 million. Sounded easy.

Johnny didn't realize he guarded the entrance to the NBCI vault. Averill knew. For now, Johnny was a caretaker, an administrator. If Nano went public, he would become the senior officer with the most power in the company. He'd control the checkbook, dole out management compensation including stock options, and hire and pay ridiculous fees to the company's investment bankers. Averill wanted to be that banker. So far, Johnny could be bought for the price of a cheap breakfast.

Buying a shell would cost money that Averill didn't have, yet. He searched through a box of old business cards until he found the name of a securities lawyer from Miami he had met at a penny broker conference. His name was Louie DiSosa, but people called him the Shell King.

Louie bought companies in bankruptcy for very little money. The companies had no assets which is why the SEC called them shell companies. They had the outside of a shell; nothing was inside.

That was the beauty of a shell. They usually had a large number of shares outstanding which had last traded for less than a penny per share. You could merge your company into the shell and become public virtually overnight.

Louie made his money by cleaning shells. He was a Florida financial oyster shucker. After he took control of the float of outstanding common stock of a bankrupt company, he brought their SEC accounting filings current, which allowed it to be traded on an exchange again. A shell provided instantaneous float of a thousand disgruntled shareholders.

After a few months, Louie sold the shell. The going price these days was a half million dollars plus a piece of the action.

Unless you had a big investment bank raising you hundreds of millions of dollars, reverse merging into a shell was faster and cheaper. The alternative for a small company was too expensive and onerous. Microcap companies just didn't have the resources and legal and accounting talent to respond to the arcane and intense questions from the SEC during the registration process. Moreover, their bank accounts dwindled as they endured months of cryptic comments and questions from the SEC about disclosures and wording.

The SEC disliked shells for good reason. Although some shells became owned by legitimate companies with real prospects, many more were fronts for stock promoters trying to swindle investors.

Averill called Louie, and the conversation was brief. Averill needed a shell. Louie had one for $500,000 and 20% of the float. The shell for sale had been in the business of selling prepaid phone cards and check cashing services to under-documented immigrant workers in South Florida. It still had the original name, Teléfonos Para Turistas. That didn't matter to Averill. The business stopped operating two years ago.

Next, Averill planned to line up management behind the plan.

CHAPTER 98

MARCH 2

Averill was a stock broker, not an investment banker, at LMNOP. The difference between the two titles meant little to the 500 penny brokers in the firm. They all considered themselves quasi bankers. Their job was to hatch and latch.

First, you hatch an idea why some microcap company was severely undervalued, whether or not it made sense to the company's management. Then you built a position for yourself, promoted the stock to your clients, and did everything you could to make the stock price rise.

If successful, you latched on to the company. You convinced management you were the reason for the stock rise and should be entitled to fees and perhaps some extra information about the company's prospects. Why was that any different than what any investment banking department did?

Penny brokers and tiny companies had a symbiotic relationship. Wall Street neglected the micro market. Rules were stacked against tiny companies. Brokers at big firms were forbidden by internal rules from recommending any stock selling for less than $5.00 per share.

CEOs and CFOs at microcap companies welcomed penny brokers for good reason. No one else would follow them and recommend and buy their stock.

Averill was latching onto Nano Bio and would not be letting go. He drove to Nano Bio.Com's construction site and sat with his meal ticket. "Johnny, this company needs financial leadership. Oenotropae doesn't see the vision. This place could make a lot of money if it went public.

"First, let's take care of you," Averill said. "As president of a public company, you deserve more. You should receive a handsome management stock option award. Stock options align your interests with the shareholders so you hopefully make the right decisions. All the big companies have option programs."

Johnny played cautious. "Right now, Oenotropae is butterin' my bread. I have a $50,000 dollar bonus comin' to me. Until they say otherwise, and until I get my bonus, Oeno is my boss and I'm followin' their plan."

"Of course you'll get your bonus," Averill promised. "It's a contractual right. That's chump change. The options are worth a lot more. How does a million shares sound to you if we go public? And your management team gets options too."

The conversation continued for fifteen minutes. At first, Johnny was suspicious. Averill kept expanding the vision. Then he clinched it. Averill said, "Johnny, it's the million dollar check you didn't get to cash when you sold your store. If you back my plan, I promise you. You'll be rich."

The fact that the get-rich promise came from a guy wearing a suit with stripes disappearing halfway down the pant leg didn't seem to faze Johnny. What could possibly go wrong?

Johnny called his management team into his cramped office. The three managers wore overalls, plaid wool shirts and construction boots covered in dirt and grass stains. It was a dirty job managing the receiving dock.

Averill made his pitch. "I've been hired by Oenotropae to raise $10 million dollars and take your company public. It's important we lock up the management team to raise the money. The investors will want to see that you guys buy into the plan. If you each agree to two-year employment agreements, I'll award each of you stock options to buy a half-percent of the company when it goes public."

The management team was pretty excited. They were hired guns who were between jobs when Nano signed them. There was no risk tossing their hat into the ring on the chance that the plan might work. If it didn't work, they'd head back to Chicago. Nothing lost.

Johnny kept quiet while Averill lied. He thought, *Averill hasn't been hired yet by Oeno. He probably hasn't even met 'em. Maybe this is how bankers work. Little white lies to get deals done. Maybe not. But if Averill pulls this off, I'm goin' to make a million buckaroos, and for now, it seems like a good idea.*

For Averill, the hard part would be to convince Oenotropae to allow a nobody broker from Bergenfield, New Jersey to take a company public with no operating history, a transient management team, and an octogenarian board of directors. He'd go visit their offices, stick his foot in the door and sell them like an old-time vacuum cleaner salesman. He'd been thrown out of better places than Oeno plenty of times before. There was no harm in trying.

CHAPTER 99

MARCH 2

Averill called Oenotropae on his office speaker phone and told the receptionist he was Johnny Carrera from Nano Bio.Com. He hammered on his desk with his shoe heel to give his best imitation of construction site noise. She transferred the call to Lawrence Sipriani, vice president. NBCI was the smallest of a hundred portfolio companies that Lawrence managed.

Averill knew enough to keep his pitch under thirty seconds. Investment guys hated long conversations. "Good afternoon. I have a proposal for you. Johnny's management team and I want to take NBCI public in a reverse merger. We'll buy out your $5 million dollar investment and let you have a free ride of ten percent. We can close a $10 million private placement in thirty days. Do you want to meet?"

Lawrence was angry. "My receptionist said Johnny was on the line. Who the hell are you and how did you get through to my office?"

"My name's Averill Winthrop. I'm a vice president in investment banking at Long, Mopey, North, Oscar and Penn. The management team and I…"

Lawrence interrupted him with a laughed. "You work at LMNOP, huh? Since when do investment bankers do impersonations to get past a receptionist?"

Averill scrolled through his mental lying checklist. *Aha, there's a good one.* "I apologize. It's very noisy around the plant due to the construction. I didn't say I was Johnny. I said I was calling from Johnny's office. I just met with the management team."

The VP paused for nearly a minute, and Averill knew enough to keep quiet. "LMNOP, huh? That really is scraping the bottom. Come to think of it, you might just be the perfect piece of crap banker to take over this piece of crap investment.

"Alright, I'll meet you. First, give my secretary your personal information. No one gets into my office without a background check. And don't waste my time, bud. I want a solid proposal, not some crazy-ass scheme."

Averill tried to hide his excitement. "Thank you, sir. I won't waste your time."

He sat at his desk and scribbled his ideas on a sheet of paper. Oeno wanted a written proposal. He had studied a hundred penny stock offerings. The deal terms ranged all over the place. Starting with the facts, the shell had 20 million shares outstanding, and the Shell King said he was getting another 10. Avy had to raise $10 million. He would sell 100 million shares at ten cents per share. Averill would write in 5 million banker warrants for himself. NBCI would repay Oeno and have $5 million in the bank plus all of that money it still had from the bond offering.

He'd raise the money through a Regulation D private placement sold to wealthy investors and 35 not-so-wealthy allowed under the rules. His clients had the money he needed with all of their Apple stock winnings. It was just a matter of coaxing them to part with a hundred grand apiece.

Averill was always near broke. He fantasized about his share of the money. If he raised the $10 million, he'd earn an 8% commission. His firm would get half, but $400,000 was like eight years of pay in this post-apocalypse stock market. It had been a tough time, and his threadbare suit proved it.

Averill played with the numbers. Why should LMNOP get half of his commissions? They weren't doing any work. There had to be a way to get more shares in the company before the reverse merger took place. The NASD rules limited his commission percentage, but Averill wanted more.

This was no time to show his cards to LMNOP or Oeno. His proposal would be on the up-and-up. He'd sneak his extra comp into the deal near closing.

CHAPTER 100

MARCH 5, 2012

Oenotropae's New York City offices occupied four stories of a loft building in SoHo. The small lobby contained a life-sized granite statue of three Greek goddesses standing in a fountain making wine, wheat and olive oil. Oeno had purchased the building when it was relatively cheap. SoHo was no longer affordable to anyone but art dealers and restaurants.

Averill climbed two stories of stairs and was ushered into a conference room adjacent to the trading floor. Thirty young men sat in front of multiple large computer screens crammed with technical data and charts. This wasn't a wild trading floor with brokers yelling "Buy, buy, buy!" This was far more cerebral.

Lawrence Sipriani entered the room and sat without shaking hands. He wore a white oxford shirt with his sleeves rolled up to his elbows. The hedge fund manager didn't appear to be a day over thirty. He looked skeptically at Averill's business card.

Lawrence grabbed a bottle of Fiji water without offering one to Averill. "Okay, you've got five minutes to convince me why I should let you take this freakin' weed wacker public.

"And by the way, I didn't make this investment. One of our partners committed to the deal and then left the firm. Now I have to make something out of it along with a hundred other of his brilliant ideas."

If Averill had any sense, he'd have realized he was out of his league. As a long-time penny broker hustling to make a living, he looked at this meeting as just another chance to make a buck. He handed the hedge fund manager a typed term sheet. Lawrence quickly studied the paper.

Averill said, "We have a local presence in Bergenfield and know the management team very well. At LMNOP, we believe it's too costly for NBCI to go public by traditional means. It's too small. We also know you want to divest within the next year. We conveniently control a clean shell.

"We propose that NBCI go public through a reverse merger into our shell. LMNOP will be the investment banker and be retained to complete a $10 million dollar private placement. If you sign the term sheet, I'll retire your investment of $5 million in May. You'll own five million shares of the company free and clear."

The Oeno executive committee didn't like the looks of the micro-cap market. They had considered a reverse merger themselves, and here it was all wrapped up with a tidy bow.

Lawrence asked, "What's the cap table look like?"

Averill replied, "The shell has a thirty-five million share hangover. We're pricing a hundred million shares at ten cents in the private placement. We're taking our fees and half of our commission in stock. We get five million warrants. That adds up to eleven million. Management and the board are getting seven million stock options. Then there's your five million."

Lawrence studied the sheet and said, "That isn't a lot of shares for our risk to date. Let me talk to my partners and see what they think. My assistant can get you a soft drink if you want to wait."

Averill declined the drink, and sat patiently for the next hour. He looked at his blue-gray polyester blend suit and felt vastly inferior to the traders outside the conference room. The floor was eerily quiet. The traders whispered.

Lawrence returned and sat across from Averill. The term sheet was covered in scribbling. He said, "We're surprised at how far you progressed on this deal. We aren't saying no. But we need to see assurances that you can raise the money. Here is our counteroffer.

"If you can prove you control the shell and you line up firm commitments for the ten million, we'll take stock for forty percent of our investment. In other words, we want forty million shares, not five million. The good news is you only have to give us three million in cash. You close by mid-May or the deal is off."

Averill whined, "But you would be getting shares cheaper than the founders. The new money is paying ten cents a share. You'll only be paying five."

Lawrence lectured, "Averill, you seem like a nice guy, and you've done some nice first-year associate work here, but remember this. WE are the founders, not YOU. If you want to take time to think this over, go ahead. I'm going to Jackson Hole for a two week vacation tomorrow and will be unavailable. If you want to do the deal our way, I can have my assistant revise the term sheet and sign it today. Let me know."

Averill backpedaled quickly. "That's okay. I don't need any time. You're right. You're the founders and put up the risk capital."

An hour later, they signed the revised term sheet, which now had five full pages of legal mumbo jumbo that fully protected Oenotropae. Lawrence called a car service and had the driver take Averill back to the Secaucus transfer station where his car was parked.

He had until mid-May to raise $10 million from his relatively middle class and substantially aged client base. But first, he had to borrow a half million in a bridge loan to buy the shell.

CHAPTER 101

MARCH 9, 2012

Evelyn Marpease browsed around Allie's store midafternoon. Her hair was wound in a tight bun. Knitting needles peeked from her pocketbook. Auntie Ev was the perfect name, although no one knew for sure if she was an aunt. She was definitely a grannie, but Grannie Ev just didn't flow. She approached the cash register with a basketful of items.

Auntie Ev: "Allie, if there is anything I can do to help you, please let me know."

Allie: "Not unless you know how to end this crabgrass craze."

Auntie Ev: "I can tell you honestly, the Nanny Grannies are joining the crowd to earn some extra income. Times have been tough these last few years. Those fools on Wall Street practically destroyed my girls' retirement savings."

Allie: "I understand. I knew sales would be down. I thought people might grow a little and make money. But this is much bigger than anyone thought. A few thousand homes are still sittin' on the fence."

Auntie Ev: "Your store is pretty quiet. It could use more women shoppers. Lord knows the men don't come here anymore. Allie's Corner looks a little empty. My girls might be able to help you if you're interested."

Allie: "I'd love some new items, but I can't pay much in advance."

Auntie Ev: "Girl, we don't do this for profit. We're taking over the world one quilt at a time. We can do this on consignment. You can pay us when you sell it. Good enough?"

Allie: "I don't know what I've done to deserve your generosity. But thank you."

CHAPTER 102

MARCH 9

As Auntie Ev left the store, Brian, the delivery truck driver from Jake's Seed & Supply, walked in. He bellowed, "Got a delivery. Where do ya want it?"

"What?" Allie acted surprised. "I haven't ordered anything. Let me see that."

Allie examined the bill of lading. It stated 6,000 hundred pound bags of weed killer. It was a partial delivery under a blanket purchase order to buy 18,000 bags a year.

Allie knew about the open PO with Jake's, but was sure she had to place an order before it was delivered. She asked the driver to wait on the receiving dock, went into the back room, and frantically started searching for the original PO.

Allie's son passed the truck on his way into the store with schoolbooks in hand. He wore torn jeans and a Nirvana tee shirt. Marty saw the terrorized look on his mother's face and quickly guessed there was a situation.

He walked back to the dock and asked Brian, "That your truck? You're spillin' hazardous chemicals all over the parking lot. You better move it before the Feds show up."

Brian said, "I'm delivering an order. They ain't hazardous and there ain't no spill."

"That's a hazardous material sticker on your truck, isn't it?" Marty pointed. "What's those numbers in the blue and white boxes mean? You're delivering chemicals. You want me to call the EPA?"

Brian looked at the sticker on the truck. "Them stickers are always on the truck. They got nothin' to do with this load."

Marty was a lanky 160 pounds. His clothes didn't portray a lot of authority. Worse, his voice was changing and tended to crack during stressful situations. In his best Danny DeVito imitation, he forced his voice an octave lower and said. "Tell it to the cops."

Brian was just under six feet tall and a solid two hundred pounds. His arms were covered in tattoos, and his biceps spoke weightlifter. "You're a kid. I'm unloadin' this baby. Get outta of my way."

Marty followed Brian to the truck. There was a white powder trail spilling from the rear of the truck. The driver rolled opened the truck door. A pallet of Jake's Weed Killer was leaning on its side and several bags had broken.

Brian said, "C'mon son, cut me some slack. Lemme deliver the other pallets, and we'll adjust the bill for the shortage."

Marty bluffed, "Before I was kid. Now I'm son? No deliveries today, Brian. Today's Friday. We never accept deliveries on Fridays. The store's too busy.

"Besides, I'm not signin' that piece of paper, whatever it is. I'll give you a hand to straighten that stuff on the truck so you don't pollute anymore, but you gotta leave. Tell your boss he's got a problem."

Allie looked out the back entrance and saw her son standing in Brian's path with his arms folded defiantly. The driver was flailing his arms at Marty who stood resolutely. The driver abruptly closed the truck loading door and drove away.

She put her arm around Marty's shoulder when he reentered the store. "Thanks. I didn't know what to do. But he'll be back. I'd better call Bret or JB and ask for help. Can you mind the store?"

A half hour later, JB walked in the front door. "Refusing delivery won't stop them," he said. "It does give you some temporary leverage. What's the open PO amount?"

Allie said, "Eighteen thousand bags a year for the length of the contract. That's three more years. Right now, I have six thousand bags costing $180,000 at my doorstep. Do I have to buy it if I can't sell it?"

JB said, "The blanket PO doesn't obligate you until you place an order. It looks like Johnny signed an order a few months before you bought the store to lock in a fixed price. The schedule in the store acquisition file might have been confusing, but I think they disclosed it properly.

"It looks like you have to buy the 2012 and 2013 orders. Thirty-six thousand bags at thirty bucks. Over a half million a year."

Allie started scribbling on a pad and punching numbers into a calculator. "I know for sure I still have two thousand customers. There's three or four thousand people who are undecided. So let me press enter, times, equals... voila! I'm screwed.

"If the five thousand homes bought the usual two bags, I'd just have enough to pay Jake's. If only three thousand buy, I'm two hundred thousand in the hole. I don't make enough from the rest of the store to make up the shortfall."

What JB didn't say was *I told you so.* During due diligence, he had asked Allie to check out the open PO and make sure there was no liability.

"Allie, you have three main options," counseled JB. "One is to try to rescind the purchase with Johnny. You can ask Bret, but I think you lose in court. The PO is clearly listed on the liability schedule. Also, it'll take a year to litigate, and Jake's won't wait.

"Another option is to litigate with Jake's. You can try to sue to cancel the PO. They're a company with lots of money and a big legal department. They'll outspend you in litigation until you're broke. Bret's been able to help you a little so far, but I'm pretty sure he doesn't have the time to handle litigation. You'll spend a hundred grand easily on either of these suits. If you sue and lose, game over. You pay Jake's and no one else."

Allie's shoulders slumped. "What's option three? Leave town with no forwarding address?"

JB frowned. "No can do, Allie. Michael is counting on you to meet your bank obligations.

"Option three is working out a deal with Jake's that matches your expected cash flow with the payments. You are a decent-sized customer. They don't want to lose you. Let's guess they have a forty percent gross margin on this chemical. That's kind of standard in the industry.

"So collecting $300,000 is their break-even this year. That equals sales to three thousand homes. Somehow, we have to convince Jake's to give you extended payment terms. It's been done before, believe me. Sometimes the customer is so big, the vendor can't fire them."

"Okay, option three sounds better than court. But I got another problem," said Allie. "The bank loan has an obsolete inventory restriction. If inventory gets too stale, it comes out of the borrowing base. Then I have to repay the bank."

JB thought for a moment. "We can ask Jake's to hold off on the next two deliveries until you need them, but no later than December. They would still get to book the sale this year, and your one-year counting period with the bank won't start until then.

"Tell them we want a meeting, and make it next Saturday so Bret can be here."

CHAPTER 103

MARCH 12, 2012

Nursing her coffee at Ben's mid-morning, Misty was noticeably late for work. She kept glancing at the front door waiting for someone to arrive. Her smirk spelled trouble.

The regular ten o'clock group of Filipino ladies were saying goodbye to Ben at the register. An elderly gentleman in a navy suit and comfortable shoes entered and approached the counter. He asked Ben to meet privately. Ben led him to a table in the main dining area where he could keep an eye on the kitchen. After they sat, Misty moved to a seat two tables closer and within hearing range.

The visitor said, "Mr. Singleton. That's your name, correct?"

Rarely had anyone used his last name. He said, "That's right, but most people know me as Ben. How can I help you?"

The visitor said, "My name is Herman Cooper. I'm the auditor for JLO, the Jukebox Licensing Office. We collect music royalties on behalf of artists. We received a report that you have in your possession a juke box that has evaded paying the required royalties for fifteen years. If true, this is a serious offense punishable by a fine of no less than $750 per occurrence. Is that old Wurlitzer your jukebox?"

Ben saw Misty peeking over her iPhone and quietly giggling. He remained calm. "I don't own the juke box. The owner's name is on a metal tag. I can get it for you."

Herman said, "We know whose name is on the tag. We've also been told they haven't owned it for some time. Our informer claims you've been collecting the money."

Ben said, "I never collected a dime. Exactly who's telling you this misinformation?"

Misty could no longer restrain herself. She called from her table, "Now, Ben we know that's not true. People put quarters in there every day. I've seen you open the jukebox lots of times. You must have the money."

It became immediately clear to Ben why Misty had been hanging around this morning. She was the rat. She must have reported Ben as revenge for not playing her song. The $50,000 reward might be a motive, too.

Ben had a brief idea of spanking Misty over his knee like a terrible two-year-old. He temporarily rejected the notion and said to Herman, "Honestly, I've never collected money from the jukebox. But how much I collect shouldn't matter to you. You just need to know the royalties were paid, correct?"

"That's correct," Herman said, "but we've audited the royalty account for the old owners. Nothing's been paid. If you've been collecting the money, then it is in fact your machine and you therefore are delinquent."

Misty gave her best impression of Marv Albert announcing a Knicks game. She yelled, "YES! I knew he was up to something illegal. This will serve you right, Ben! Next time, play my song!"

Herman turned to Misty and said, "Lady, please stay out of this. We don't know anything yet. And Mr. Singleton has every right to explain himself. I respectfully ask you to stop eavesdropping on our conversation. Mr. Singleton, should we discuss this someplace more private?"

Ben said, "No, let's do this here so Misty can listen. I wouldn't want her to miss out on the excitement.

"Let's resolve the first issue. I don't own the juke box and never collected any money. No one has. Let's go look."

Ben fetched the key to the Wurlitzer from behind the counter and Herman watched him open the juke box. A crowd had formed behind Ben, and a dozen patrons were now witnessing firsthand how their beloved, honest Ben had allegedly cheated the man.

Inside the juke box was a large metal crate. It was filed to the brim with what had to be 10,000 old quarters. Herman looked amazed. Misty stood and looked at the stash.

"Mr. Cooper, the juke box was here when I bought the store out of bankruptcy," claimed Ben. "I heard the guys who owned it weren't the type that you wanted to cross. If they ever showed up, I'd just give them the money.

"When the quarters started overflowing, I had a metal shop make that box to hold the coins. There's three more in the back. Probably ten grand in quarters in total. I've never taken a dime."

Herman said, "I've never seen anything like that in my thirty years of audits. Okay, I understand. That still doesn't account for the nonpayment of royalties. Your customers still listened to music without compensation to the singers."

Misty jumped from her chair, and yelled, "See Ben. This is what happens when you aren't nice to your customers. I think I'll buy this place with my reward money." She laughed derisively.

Herman was an experienced auditor. He had learned long ago not to jump to conclusions in sensitive situations. He turned to Misty and said, "Lady, shut up and sit down. This is none of your business."

Misty didn't sit. This was thrilling.

Ben walked behind the counter, grabbed a ledger, and handed it to Herman. "I knew the jukebox owed royalties. Doug Pearson is my accountant. He set up a beneficiary account to pay royalties when I bought the store. You won't find it in the name of those guys on the tag. It's in an account called Trust f/b/o Ben's Deli. I have a record of every song played for five years. Here it is."

Herman scanned the ledger briefly, opened his laptop and dialed into his company's network. He found the royalty account. He quickly looked at Ben's spreadsheet.

Herman said, "Well, Mr. Singleton, I'll have to spend a little time to check your numbers, but this looks okay. I truly am sorry to bother you like this."

"That's okay. Let me buy you a late breakfast," offered Ben.

Herman politely protested with a raised hand. "Sorry Ben. I'm an auditor. Can't accept gifts. But thanks anyway. And I'd have to guess those quarters are legally yours."

Ben shook his head. "No way. The money was pledged to three churches and a synagogue in town a long time ago. I'll let 'em know they can have it now."

Misty bolted out the side door before Ben had a chance to throw her out.

CHAPTER 104

MARCH 15, 2012

After the Oeno meeting, Averill spent the next ten days working on borrowing a half million to buy the Telefonos Para Turistas corporate shell. Louie DiSosa gave Averill a list of possible bridge loan investors who provided fast money in exchange for large returns. Most of them lived overseas. Averill had met none of them.

Twenty years ago, the rich got richer by investing in Regulation S deals, which were small-company desperation financings. Reg S offerings were sold only to foreign investors and legally escaped onerous SEC registration statement requirements.

The buyers usually shorted, or sold, the stock in the market before the offering and drove the price down. After the deal closed, they repurchased the stock at lower prices and locked in 100% gains. The company might have been successful in raising needed money, but the deals destroyed its value and scared away new investors.

Ten years later, the Reg S door shut, and the Euros moved on to the next sure thing. They invested in unregistered convertible bond deals, known as PIPEs. This time, hedge funds joined the party. Once again, they shorted the stock before the offering and covered the shorts after they had driven the stock price down. Many small companies regretted the financing but had little choice.

The Euro speculators also dabbled in bridge loans with guaranteed hundred percent returns. Averill didn't really care how much the investment cost. It was the price of getting started. The terms for a private bridge loan were simple. An investor got his money back in a short period of time and received an equal amount of stock or warrants. That's double your money in two months.

At first, Averill thought it would be easy. Get five big hitters to put up a hundred grand each. He'd carve out a piece for himself as a carried interest. As long as the hot money was repaid, who'd be the wiser?

He underestimated how important $100,000 was to just about anyone. Averill spent the next ten days calling his list of speculator clients. A handful committed $25,000 each, but no money was changing hands until the order book was filled. Averill was referred to other potential investors who referred him to more potential investors. It was a big club, and they all knew each other.

Today, he was ready to close. Louie DiSosa prepared the legal documents for a fee of $25,000. Averill had lined up two dozen investors. A few of these characters might not be the most reputable players around. Averill had no intention of conducting background checks.

Andrei Yakovich had appointed himself as the group's financial representative. The terms got steeper an hour before closing. Investors demanded a 150% of their money back and penny stock warrants worth $500,000.

Averill whimpered, but he was in no position to say no. He had to prove to Oeno that he controlled the shell. He raised an extra $100,000. When no one was looking and the reverse merger was done, Averill thought he could grab the extra money as a fee.

CHAPTER 105

MARCH 16, 2012

If Oenotropae approved the reverse merger, Averill didn't really need the board's blessing. Technically, the board would hold a meeting and okay the transaction, but it was a mere formality. They would rubber stamp anything Oeno asked them to do.

Averill had a more selfish use for the board. His plan was to take Nano Bio.Com public and get Oeno to sell its stock as quickly as possible. Once Oeno was gone, Nano would be free of any silly corporate governance or hedge fund oversight. Averill intended to give the board stock options and pay them generous meeting fees so they would bless his deals in the future.

Averill visited Johnny at the transfer plant. In two months, an amazing amount of construction had been completed. The cement floor had been poured during the brief January heat wave. Forty-foot girders were connected to frame the building. Corrugated sheet siding and roof was stacked and ready to be installed.

"Johnny, I bought the shell company," bragged Averill. "I told you I'd deliver.

"The next part requires your skills of persuasion. We want the board to become more active in the company affairs, to appear independent to the public. You know, Oeno is going to be gone one day, and you're going to be the boss. You need a board that supports you. We also need to convince them that it's their idea to take care of your management compensation."

Johnny looked lost. "I'm gonna have to wake 'em up. Those guys all retired twenty years ago. Every time I call 'em, they're taking a nap. How am I gonna get 'em to approve anythin' when they need full-time nurses? Why are they gonna approve my options?"

Averill smiled, "Easy. Because the board gets stock options, too. They'll cooperate.

"Here's what you do. Approach Roland McPherson, the chairman, and he'll convince the others. I'm sure he's done this before. We'll grant the board members a few hundred thousand options each. That'll keep them happy. Your management team gets a half million each. You got a raise. You now get two million. Fair enough?"

Johnny, slightly bewildered, said "Two million, huh? Can you do all of this? I mean, it's gotta be harder than the way you explain it."

Averill said, "Johnny, trust me. Once Oeno is out of the way, we can do anything we want. This is a marionette board. I'll call Oeno and get their okay. It'll take me thirty days to raise the $10 mil. Your job is to get board approvals for the stock option plans and my retainer agreement. That includes my warrants and stock."

Johnny looked puzzled. "What warrants and stock?"

Averill said, "This is all standard terms on Wall Street. Oeno already okayed it. My firm gets an eight percent commission. Instead of taking all cash, which you guys need, we're taking the commission half in stock and half in cash. We also get an unaccountable spending allowance to cover my marketing expenses.

"I can't receive stock options like you guys because I'm not an employee. I should get treated the same as you, so my firm gets warrants to buy five million shares. I get half of those. Also, because I believe in the company's future, I'm willing to buy another ten million shares with a million dollar note. I'll type this up in a term sheet and send it to you."

This was way over Johnny's head. He couldn't tell if these stock awards and Averill's commissions were standard in the industry or not. He had to rely on Oeno. They should know. Averill was pretty slick. But he was doing the right thing by taking care of management.

Averill's investment banking department was more virtual than a real department. The executives running LMNOP approved small private placements as a formality. They didn't have a large investment banking group with seasoned bankers structuring deals. Averill would tell his firm about the commissions and the marketing allowance. He'd send them an early draft of the private placement document. They might read the whole document, but probably wouldn't get past the first page that said how much money the firm would make. They surely wouldn't read the final document which disclosed in small type Averill's note shares.

CHAPTER 106

MARCH 17, 2012

Jake's Seed & Supply sent a team of one, Benny Walsh, the regional sales vice president. Benny was a tall fifty-year-old man with a full mane of gray hair. He proudly wore a dark green sports jacket with a Jake's logo sewn onto the breast pocket and a matching green shamrock tie in honor of St. Pat's.

The meeting didn't start well. Benny demanded that Allie accept the merchandise. "We have a legally binding purchase order with you. It's a contract honored under any court. And there are two more shipments in July and October."

JB was standing by, along with Bret. He said, "We don't know how you managed to screw this up, but your chemical doesn't work anymore. The formula changed so much it's ineffective. The whole town conceded defeat. Your product is obsolete. We aren't buying it. Let's go to court."

Benny said, "Now hold on a minute. There's nothing wrong with our product. Your customers didn't start growing weeds 'cause of our chemicals."

JB shrugged. "We'll let a jury decide."

This banter went on for another fifteen minutes and little progress was made. Benny had only one objective – deliver the weed killer.

JB called for a sidebar with Bret and Allie. He said in a low voice, "I think Jake's has a problem. He let it slip they buy this stuff in one batch and have a year's worth of inventory.

Also, they have to book a sale by year-end. Allie, is there any chance that you can pay for the first shipment this year?"

"Yeah, spread over the year I can, but that's about it."

"They sent a salesman, and all he cares about is sales," said JB. "He seems open to delayed payment terms. Allie, you have a problem with this PO. Let's negotiate a truce."

They rejoined the Jake's executive and JB made his offer: "Here's the deal. We'll accept delivery of this shipment, but not the opened bags. You send a cleanup team to remove any chemicals spilled in our receiving dock. After you clean this up, we'll pay you on extended terms until this weed craze is over. We agree we owe you $180,000 dollars for this delivery. We'll pay you $60,000 in October and every six months until paid in full.

"Don't ship anything else until December 31. We have no place to put the stuff. We require eighteen month payment terms for the December delivery. And last thing. We're cancelling the PO for 2013. The blanket PO stays, but you can't deliver any more unless we order."

Benny said, "That's a one-way street. I get nothing, and you get forever to pay me. Why would I do this? And where's my collateral?"

"You get to book the sale this year," JB said. "I understand Jake's sold out to an LBO group last year. How will it look to your banks that you lost a big customer and have a half million of chemicals you can't sell? And you can have a security interest in the bags of weed killer if you want collateral."

Benny balked, and said, "First, you gotta take at least half of the 2013 order. I can't cancel a whole year. We already ordered the chemicals.

"Next, if I were open to your deal, and I say *if*, I hafta have some collateral. We own the store if you fail to pay. I can live with the payment terms, except the first payment is due in thirty days. I'm not waiting until October."

Allie, JB and Bret conferred. Bret said the best time to litigate was now. JB said she needed more time for the weed killer business to come back. Neither solution was perfect.

Allie thought it through, and said, "Guys, thanks for your advice, but this is my mistake and it's a doozy. What I need is time, and this is givin' me time. If I fight this in court and lose, I've lost my life savings and never even started the business. I hafta do this. Somehow, I hafta make this place profitable with a much smaller weed killer business."

After JB and Benny left, Bret offered to lend Allie money to get through the first payment. Allie shook her head no. "I'll have to get through this the old-fashioned way. I'm gonna stretch payments to my vendors until this ordeal ends."

CHAPTER 107

MARCH 19, 2012

Misty was an outcast following the juke box incident, but she managed to sneak into the deli occasionally when Ben was away from the register. Bret was done with Misty and didn't want to see her this morning. When he saw her slink into Ben's, Bret slid lower in his seat.

Misty tapped Bret on the shoulder and asked him to sit with her for a few minutes. He begrudgingly walked with her to a nearby table. He looked trapped. If only Ben had a funeral dirge on the jukebox.

Misty started sweetly. "Bret, you may not want to hear this, but I have your best interests in my heart. I just hate to see you so affected by that crowd. They aren't your friends. They're not good for you."

As a lawyer, he had learned to hear out the arguments of the opposing counsel. Misty continued, "I know how relationships work. You aren't as experienced in this area. That table is filled with emotional wife beaters. They're cheaters and misogynists.

"I have an idea. I think that we should go to premarital counseling and work this out. I have the name of an old professor of mine who does this. I made an appointment for us."

Bret unfolded his arms from across his chest and said sternly, "If you're finished, I'm not doing premarital *anything* with you. I'm certainly not going to couples counseling where your friend is the arbitrator. Do you think I'm an idiot? Misty, we should have this talk somewhere else, but you chose the forum. I want to stop seeing you."

Misty scowled. "How dare you do this here? How insensitive can you be? Look at your friends enjoying this scene. Are you showing off for them?"

"You know, public fighting isn't appropriate," Bret said calmly. "If you want to talk out an issue, let's do it at home. Everything with you is always so dramatic. It's like living on the Dr. Phil show.

"You're alienating all of my friends for what purpose? So you can have me to yourself. You badmouth everyone in the room, and now you've attacked Ben. Where the heck are you going to go in the morning now that Ben has banned you?"

Misty acted the victim and pleaded for pity. "Don't you care that I'm hurting inside? Why am I the only one to suffer any pain in this relationship? Your friends all hate me because you want to spend time with me."

"Hate's a strong word," said Bret. "I don't think they hate you. They think you're a ridiculous mess."

Misty dabbed at a fake sympathy tear. "I'm not a mess. How can you say such a horrible thing to me? If you really loved me, you'd see these people are trying to keep us apart. They dream up bad things to say about me to sway you. Don't you love me?"

Bret remained stoic. "Well, I will admit they did warn me about you. But they never said 'don't date Misty'. They said that you left a lot of bodies on the battlefield. You have to admit that you've broken a few hearts over the years."

Misty counterpunched, "Who's saying these terrible things about me? JB? Allie? Panama? These people are a bunch of children, sitting around every morning making wisecracks about anyone who walks past."

Misty paused a minute and softened her tone of voice. "Bret, honey, we have to choose the right way to behave in an adult relationship. It's important we spend time alone with each other and away from the influence of your friends. It's the best way to get to really know each other."

Bret maintained calm, not wanting to incite another outburst in public. No man came out ahead in a street fight. Referees only see who threw the last verbal punch, which was usually the guy losing his cool.

He said, "I think we've spent enough time alone together. Quite frankly, it's suffocating to be with you."

Misty gasped, "You don't mean that. Any decent person would agree with me and disagree with JB. He's a woman hater. Do you want to become a woman hater? You're already forty. Do you want to stay a bachelor? Then keep hanging out with your silly chums and spend your time abusing me and any other attractive female that enters this hellhole of a diner."

"You know, JB has been happily married to his high school sweetheart for forty years," Bret countered. "I've never heard him talking negatively about women. In fact, most women around here find him quite charming."

Misty said angrily, "I just knew you'd defend him. He's a bully, and you and everyone else around here are scared of him. Well I'm not!"

Bret rolled his eyes. "Is there anyone else around here you don't like? How about Decker? I know you've had a few run-ins with Catherine. I understand you started her Panama Blonde nickname. And Allie appears to be on your assassin's list, but you wouldn't dare take her on face-to-face. She'd beat you to a pulp…literally and verbally.

"And you tried to get Ben arrested for jukebox royalty payments, but you failed at that one, didn't you? You know, the only person you haven't maligned around here is Father Leonard, but attacking a priest is too low even for you, isn't it?"

Misty was losing the battle, and needed to exit carefully. Having it out at Ben's was a bad idea. "Bret, I love you. I thought you wanted a happy relationship with me so we could build a future together. Don't you want to be happy? Don't answer. We can talk about this another time."

"Don't go anywhere," Bret said sternly. "There's no other time. Of course I want to be happy, but I'm not happy with you. Let's end this peacefully and go our separate ways."

Misty was bordering on rage. Nine months invested. She thought Bret would give in like all of her previous men. Well, if you're losing a chess match, counterattack the flanks.

"Bret, first of all, I only get coffee here in the morning to be with you. I go out of my way to be here at six in the morning just so we can be together. Isn't that a sacrifice worthy of some compassion? I love you and only want what's best for you.

"Can't you see…these people aren't your friends? These women are vicious and have tried to make me look horrible. They only want to hang with you so they can say they have a powerful friend at Montauk & Malibu. They aren't sincere. They know you love me, and I'm in the way of their little sorority. Believe me. I have our best interests in mind. Now let's kiss and make up."

Bret sat calmly and carefully composed his response. He needed to end this misery and start getting some sleep at night. "Misty, I'm convinced we're not good for each other. Our lives are not intersecting. I work too many hours, and I know I'm not anywhere near ready for marriage. And you are. So I think you should spend your time finding someone to make you happy who enjoys the lifestyle and relationship that you want."

There. He took the high road. No drama in this conversation!

Misty raised her voice and everyone within three tables could hear. "Those aren't your friends. They're vicious and mean and want to keep us apart. You need to trust me. I know how relationships work. They require a lot of give and take…"

Bret interrupted, "Stop right there. You're a three time loser in the marriage department. Maybe I don't have a lot of experience in some ways, but your experience certainly isn't exemplary. Would I hire a CEO with three bankruptcies on his resume to run a new business? Never! This conversation is over. Please don't make this any more difficult."

Misty squeezed out a real tear. "How can you break up with me in a diner? How heartless are you?"

"It's not a diner, it's a deli," Bret said in exasperation. "Aren't you from New Jersey? Don't you know the difference? And you chose the arena for the fight, not me. I'm leaving. I have work to do." Bret grabbed his coat and promptly exited.

A few minutes later, Allie followed Misty out the front door. From inside Ben's, it looked like a meaningful conversation although one-sided in Allie's favor.

CHAPTER 108

MARCH 19

Allie stood on the sidewalk and waved her finger at Misty. She said in her toughest voice, "You've done enough damage to Bret. He's a really good guy, and you don't deserve him. Please leave him alone. Find another victim to fall for your line of BS. Are we understood?"

Misty wiped away a real tear. "You just saw Bret break it off. I've lost him forever. Are you trying to rub it in? Are you happy now?"

"I'm glad I could be of help," Allie said sarcastically as she ignored the tear. She walked inside Ben's and returned to her table.

Misty stood on the street outside Ben's and clutched her chest. She gasped for breath and bent over. Then she dropped to the ground. Ben saw Misty collapse, picked up the phone, dialed 911, and ran outside to help.

He yelled to a policeman down the block who was writing a parking ticket. Minutes later, the EMTs arrived with full sirens blaring. They lifted Misty onto a gurney and placed an oxygen mask over her mouth. They checked her vitals as the ambulance rushed her to the ER. Ben returned to the cash register and just shook his head. It was no time to play a song on the juke box. Misty might be seriously ill.

CHAPTER 109

MARCH 20, 2012

The following morning, one of the EMTs stopped at Ben's for coffee before work. JB sincerely asked how Misty was doing.

The EMT laughed and said, "She was pretty rough on the medical staff. The doctor said she had a heart of granite. He joked that they brought in a geologist to interpret her electrocardiogram.

"She refused admittance to Holy Name Medical Center because 'some witch named Allie used to work there.' Only she used something stronger than the *witch* word. She cursed every one of you guys all the way to Englewood Hospital. Anyway, it was a panic attack, not a heart attack.

"One more thing. When we tried to wheel her into the ER, she made us wait until she fixed her makeup. You know, we're volunteers. We don't get paid for this. That girl is crazy."

JB politely said, "Despite her shortcomings as a person, I still wouldn't wish her any physical harm. I'm glad to hear she's okay."

Decker dropped his bagel. "You're kidding, right? The woman hates you and everyone here."

JB laughed and said, "Decker. *Om!* I'm studying Indian philosophy and Karma. I don't want to come back as a cockroach, so I have to be kind to everyone."

Averill Winthrop had witnessed Misty's tirade the previous day. When Misty collapsed, Averill rose from his chair for a second. He wasn't concerned about her welfare. The crowd was blocking his view of a STCK-TV report on Apple's stock.

CHAPTER 110

MARCH 23, 2012

Allie stared at the pile of invoices and felt overwhelmed. Dealing with the small stuff in a store sometimes just wasn't much fun. Paying hundreds of small bills, ordering replacement inventory, filing payroll taxes. Ugh. Then there was the standing on your feet all day although she had done this most of her working life as a nurse. And dealing with the long periods of quiet during weekday lulls was sometimes challenging.

However, the good outweighed the bad. Allie loved talking with customers, helping them find new ideas, and, of course, totaling the receipts at the end of the day.

And she had a great local support group. Their leader, Auntie Ev, walked into the store wearing a red cotton turtleneck sweater, gray knee-length skirt and a moonstone necklace. She always seemed to be starting a new adventure, which was why she had such a large following among the ladies in town.

Ev placed a large bag on the counter and pulled out a huge folded quilt. "Here you go, courtesy of the Nanny Grannies."

Allie unfolded the quilt and held it against the wall. It was an eight-foot-square tapestry of rabbits peeking through tulips and daffodils. "Auntie Ev, it's beautiful. Maybe I'll keep it for myself."

"Now, now. You'll never make money that way," lectured Auntie Ev playfully. "It's perfect for spring, and Easter Sunday is in a few weeks. Don't let me tell you how to run your business, but if I were you, I wouldn't sell it. I'd use it for marketing.

"Think about it this way: If you sold it in this town, at best you might get a few hundred dollars. A quilt stitched by the Amish over in Lancaster Pennsylvania might get two or three times as much.

"My idea is to hold a raffle with the proceeds going to some popular charity. It could be for CYO basketball team uniforms. If you want, I'll ask Father Burke to announce it at church the next two Sundays."

"Brilliant idea," Allie said. "It should draw shoppers into the store. Thank you so much."

Auntie Ev smiled benevolently. "You probably know this already, but people love rabbit, frog, pig and turtle knickknacks around the house. Some love cats, but I'm not a cat person. We could make a quilt a month with cute little animals. Next month could be rabbits for the boy's CYO basketball team. Then the girls' softball team. Then something for the Little League."

Auntie Ev left the store and Allie stared again at the stack of invoices. She pushed them aside. Her first and only priority was to sell enough weed killer to people who still cherished nice lawns.

The first payment was due to Jake's in less than three weeks.

CHAPTER 111

APRIL 11, 2012

Any ideas about selling weed killer at a profit were sacrificed to cash flow demands. Allie had to move product, and customers loved a bargain. She had a short window to raise $60,000 to pay Jake's and live another day.

She created a four-color sales flyer to send to her target customers along the Teaneck and Tenafly borders. The area was generally more affluent, had the nicest properties, and so far had turned down the money they could make from selling crabgrass.

If she mailed the flyer, it would take a week and get lost in the pile of junk mail. Plus it would cost postage and envelopes. Allie and Marty hand-delivered the flyer inside the front door of each home, where it would only be competing with the menu from the Panda House Chinese restaurant.

Allie offered a special deal. A one-year supply for a customer was typically two bags at fifty dollars a bag. The flyer offered thirty percent off on a minimum purchase of four bags.

Allie ran into Janet Novak on Thames Boulevard near the Teaneck border. Janet grabbed a handful of flyers from Allie. "Give me those. I'll take care of my block for you. The neighbors all know me. I'll make sure they see this."

Allie filled the store's delivery van to the roof and parked it on Dover Court, the shortcut everyone took to avoid the light on New Bridge Road. Whatever she and Matt sold during the day, Marty and two high school friends delivered after school for a buck a bag plus tips.

With three days to spare, Allie sold enough to pay off Jake's. The last truckload was sold below cost to a generous soul. It was hard work. There had to be a better way.

Most people were taking a wait-and-see approach. To weed or not to weed, that is the question. Until now, Allie thought she had 2,000 weed-killer customers for certain. Now even they were in doubt. Where would she get the money to pay for the rest of this junk?

Allie had another problem. After filling up the store basement, she had 2,000 bags left and no place to put them. The rental storage unit in town refused to take chemicals. Father Burke at St. John's Church cleared out his garage to make room. It was a temporary solution. Worse, Allie had an even bigger shipment coming in December and nowhere to store it.

CHAPTER 112

APRIL 14, 2012

Summer was weeks away, but warm winds felt like the middle of summer after a very cold winter. Higher temperatures meant a healthy crabgrass crop along with the accompanying hay fever. The entire New York metropolitan area had the sniffles.

Old man Jorgen shuffled into the deli. Ben gave a Norwegian "God dag!" Ben could say good morning in a dozen languages, which he had learned as a cook in the Marines.

Henrik Jorgen was happily looking forward to retirement three years ago when his son moved back home. Henrik Jr. was sitting on top of the world in 2007 making six figures and trading up to bigger homes every year until he finally owned a McMansion. The 4,000 square foot house had six bedrooms, four baths, and a three car garage.

A year later, Junior lost his job. Not long after, he defaulted on his million-dollar, floating-rate mortgage. In a final show of support and eternal love, his wife divorced him. Henrik was lending his son money to help pay the bills, but cut him off after Junior bought a 60 inch LED television and Xbox. Bankrupt, Junior moved home.

Then, Henrik's 28-year-old daughter, Ingrid, called off her wedding. Well, actually, her fiancé called off the engagement after he checked her credit report. She owed a small fortune on student loans to attend a fancy liberal arts college where she studied art history. Henrik had urged her to pursue a more practical education at an affordable state college, but was overruled by the family. Ingrid was barely paying rent with her meager wages at an unheralded New York museum and hadn't made a loan payment in two years. Henrik was now out the wedding costs including hall rental. Ingrid also moved home.

Recently, Henrik couldn't figure out why he had difficulty getting an Internet connection. Then he discovered his son was playing the Call of Duty video game online. Henrik established a new rule. The kids had to go to the library during the day and conduct a job search. He was sure the librarians wouldn't let them play video games, right?

Ingrid and Junior were part of the Boomerang Generation. Henrik was a member of Generation GZ. As in Geeze, how did this happen to me? Or, Gee Whiz! I thought I was supposed to be playing golf in Florida at my age. All across the country, sixty-something couples anticipating retirement were besieged on all fronts and flanks.

Good citizens like Henrik saved for retirement and paid off their mortgage early instead of refinancing every few years to buy a new fancy car or a boat. But everyone, Henrik included, saw parts of their dreams evaporate in an eighteen month collapse of housing prices, the stock market and interest rates.

At one time Henrik had calculated he could downsize his living space with a move to Florida and pocket the $200,000 difference in housing costs.

Since then, his house value had declined thirty percent, his 401k had plummeted forty percent, and his kids controlled the TV remote. The government was now threatening to reduce his social security and Medicare benefits after forty years of faithful contributions.

To seal his fate, his wife insisted they support their children until they got back on their feet.

Nowadays, the only peace Henrik had in the morning was visiting Ben's to wait out the bathroom shower line at home.

CHAPTER 113

APRIL 20, 2012

Allie's Home Center was quiet as usual during mid-morning. Auntie Ev had just dropped off a second quilt for auction. This was a baseball theme using patches of New York Mets tee shirts, banners and jackets. The Easter auction had been a big success netting over $800 dollars for the CYO basketball team. The Nanny Grannies refused any payments. Fame was worth more than money to them.

Mrs. Knutson, a regular customer in her early forties, brought a small basket of lightbulbs to the counter. She was searching her pocketbook for correct change when she discovered a crumpled receipt. She handed it to Allie and said, "Dearie, I totally forgot about this. I paid Johnny in advance for Jake's crabgrass killer. He ran out of stock, and I left a deposit. Can I get a refund instead of taking the two bags?"

Allie almost fell off her chair and asked, "I don't know anything about this. Why would you prepay?"

"It was in July last year," Mrs. Knutson said somewhat flustered. "You remember? Johnny ran a big sale. We all rushed to buy thinking there was going to be a shortage. That was before anyone knew about this whole Pierre deal. It's not just me. A lot of people left deposits."

Mr. Forstman, the retired high school teacher, overheard the conversation and said, "Come to think of it, I prepaid too. I was going to ask Johnny about it, but then you bought the store."

Allie thought, *Here we go again.* She told Mrs. Knutson, "I can deliver the bags to you, but I'm afraid I can't provide cash refunds. You might want to ask Johnny for your money back."

Mr. Forstman said not to worry. Mrs. Knutson left in a huff without her lightbulbs. Allie hung the gone-to-lunch sign on the door, locked the store and hurried down to Ben's. She hoped to find JB there.

Ben stayed busy after the rush hour by offering specialty coffee drinks and bakery goods. The women in town took over Ben's for the late breakfast shift. Five thousand Filipinos lived in Bergenfield, and Ben catered to them by serving Barako Filipino coffee, tocino bacon and eggs.

Allie rushed into the deli and politely waved Ben off as she sat with JB. Everyone had left for work, and he was reading his third paper of the day. "What's up Allie? You look upset."

Allie was trembling but tried to keep her composure. "Johnny took deposits on Jake's weed killer when he ran out of stock last July. Customers want their refunds. If I don't pay them, I'm going to lose my reputation. What do I have to do? Sue Johnny?"

JB stood up. "Let's go see Doug. He should know what happened."

They walked to Doug Pearson's accounting offices. Across the street, children on morning recess stood near the front doors to the Roy W. Brown Middle School.

After hearing the story, Doug said, "I'm really not aware of any prepayments. I prepared Johnny's financial statements for the closing. There was no record of this. And I reconciled his bank statements, so I would have known if he'd received cash and not reported it. Unless he didn't deposit it. What did the receipt look like?"

Allie replied, "It was handwritten on a piece of Johnny's store stationary. It definitely wasn't a cash register receipt."

Doug asked Johnny to visit his office, and he arrived a half-hour later. Doug kept JB and Allie out of sight in the conference room. When Doug asked Johnny about the deposits, he fumbled through a few concocted explanations, but it was hard to fool Doug. Johnny finally admitted taking deposits without acknowledging the amount. Doug ushered him into the conference room and they sat with JB and Allie.

Johnny matter-of-factly declared, "You bought the common stock. You didn't buy the assets. You got what's on the balance sheet and all of the contingent liabilities. My lawyers told me so. That's the deal, and you know it. You got what you paid for. There ain't no more money comin', so don't ask."

"Johnny, exactly how many of these prepaid bags did you sell?" JB calmly asked. "Maybe this is a small problem and we can find a way to settle."

Johnny hardened. "I ain't settlin' nothin'. I've had enough of you shysters, you…"

JB cut him off, "It's true Allie bought the stock and not the assets. However, you prepared the financial statements and provided an officer's certificate stating the statements were true and accurate. I didn't see any liability for prepayments from customers. I'm asking you again. How much did you take?"

Johnny said, "They aren't liabilities. I got no debt to customers. This is Allie's problem. She shoulda checked the books better."

Allie went to speak, but JB held her back. "Johnny, advances from customers ARE liabilities. Ask Doug. He's your accountant."

Doug said, "Johnny, JB is right. I asked you before we issued the financials to Allie if there were any deferred revenues or advances. You answered no on the questionnaire. I have it right here."

JB maintained a neutral tone. "I'll ask you one last time. How much did you get from customers as advanced payments?"

Johnny remained defiant. "The answer's a lot. So you're Allie's tough guy, huh? Go ahead and sue. You ain't gettin' a dime from me."

JB leaned back in his chair and said, "In accordance with the terms of the acquisition agreement, the financial statements you submitted are materially incorrect. Therefore, Allie is exercising her right to rescind the agreement and is demanding the return of the cash, the note, and the earnout. She's also demanding damages of a million dollars plus $100,000 per month for the five months she labored at the store. Fair statement, Allie?"

Allie took the cue and said, "If he agrees to the damages in this meeting. But I gave up a great job and was defrauded. After today, the damages go up."

Johnny turned to Doug. "They're kiddin', right? They don't have the right to rescind this deal, do they? I don't want the store back."

Doug let out a sigh of reproof. "Johnny, I'm not your lawyer. And as of this moment, I'm no longer your accountant. This is not good behavior. If you received advances, they're a liability. You certified the financial statements were accurate. I just filed your tax returns based upon wrong information. I want you to tell me exactly how much you received in advance."

Johnny sat uncomfortably in his seat. "I dunno. Maybe a hundred thousand. Allie owes me more than that on the earnout. Let's swap the two and call it even."

Doug absorbed the magnitude of the number and said, "Where's the cash if you didn't deposit it in the bank?"

Johnny sheepishly answered, "It's home in a wall safe."

JB laughed. "My word, Johnny, you're a professional crook. You stole money from your own company AND you evaded income taxes. Not only will Allie get her money back, you're going to jail. Do you know who prepaid?"

Johnny realized he was outplayed. He said in defeat, "I have copies of the receipts with all of the names, but I never added it up. I can get 'em to you."

JB conferred with Allie privately in the hallway. "First, if Johnny turns the deposits over to you, you probably can't rescind the transaction. It was just a threat to get him to stop dawdling. However, even if Johnny pays you, you can't afford to give refunds. You're going to have to take a tough stance with customers. You need that money to make the next payment to Jake's."

They returned to the room and JB said, "If you deliver the stolen cash and the associated records, we won't rescind at this time. There'd better not be any more issues like this."

Johnny agreed to the terms. He left Doug's offices and returned an hour later with a briefcase stuffed with tens and twenties. He was short $15,000 and wrote a check for the difference.

After Johnny left, JB turned to Allie and said, "This is your lucky day."

Allie looked baffled. "Why? I'm still barely getting by, and you said this money goes to Jake's to pay for the weed killer."

"Well, you just cut a deal with Jake's to pay on extended terms," JB pointed out. "You just received a bunch of money to run your business. And your little storage problem just got smaller. After you deliver those two thousand bags, poor Father Burke can park his car in the garage again.

"Wait until you explain to Michael why you're depositing this much cash. He's going to get a kick out of this. For now, this is the money you needed to expand your product line."

CHAPTER 114

MAY 1, 2012

MAYDAY! MAYDAY! Averill had fifteen days left to meet Oenotropae's deadline to raise $10 million for NBCI. He was pretty confident they'd give him an extension, but Averill wanted to close as quickly as possible. Too many things could go wrong, and he needed the commission.

The Shell King had papered the transaction for his customarily excessive $50,000 fee. Averill didn't care. NBCI was footing the bill. Louie DiSosa knew his way around the SEC regulations and was worth every penny if it meant Averill was going to get paid.

DiSosa drafted a private placement memorandum by plagiarizing a biofuel company's selling document filed on the SEC.gov web site. Louie changed the name, rearranged a few sentences, inserted NBCI's logo and attached NBCI's audited December financial statements as an exhibit. Averill exaggerated the backgrounds of the management team and board of directors and wrote about the never ending possibilities of growth for this startup. Louie topped it off with forty pages of standard risk factors warning investors they could lose everything, including things they didn't even own.

Kinko's printed 1,000 pretty books with thick blue paper covers no investor would read. Averill used a local service to hand-deliver the books to every one of his current customers no matter how rich or poor they were. Under SEC rules, a company could raise money from an unlimited number of rich folks in a Regulation D private placement. They were limited in how much they could sell to the less fortunate.

Such rules never stopped Averill. If investors were willing to represent in writing that they earned over a quarter million a year, who was he to challenge them? The fact that they were driving a ten-year-old Ford Taurus and living in an old dilapidated house meant nothing to him. Maybe they kept their savings in a mattress?

The first half million was easy. When the bridge-loan investors learned Oenotropae was taking shares in exchange for part of their investment, they took a shot. They rolled their loan into the NBCI stock offering.

Averill now had to convince a hundred customers to invest $100,000 each into a risky new venture with no operating history, no balance sheet to speak of, and $200 million in debt. This investment would be processing the until-now-worthless weed for a brand new beauty product that a leading cosmetics company thought might sell. This was such an easy deal to market. Yeah, right!

He called the first of his Apple-stock-rich clients. "Buenos Dias, Senor Arturo. Como esta usted?"

Averill always tried to greet his mostly foreign-born clientele with a few words in their home language. He didn't know five words of Spanish and would be doomed without the help of Google Translate.

He switched to English. "You must be happy with the return on your Apple investment. Luckily we got in early. It's what you have to do on big opportunities. You have to get in early."

Arturo had become an expert on Apple stock, Apple products, Apple iTunes, Apple apps and Apple accessories. He owned an iPod, an iPhone and an iPad. He boasted to his friend's neighbors and relatives about his successful investment. Arturo was the king of Wall Street prowess. He bent Averill's ear for a full five minutes, and Averill kept his phone on mute so Arturo couldn't hear him surfing the web.

After Arturo sucked all of the room's oxygen through the phone line, Averill interrupted politely and said, "It's really satisfying to hear a great success story. You know, you live less than a mile from the ground floor of another great opportunity. You heard about it, but what you don't know is Nano Bio.Com is about to go public.

"We're raising a small private placement with selected qualified investors to fund this company. We'll take it public within a few weeks. The minimum investment is $100,000 dollars, which you can easily afford by borrowing against your Apple stock. You have plenty of excess equity. How many units would you like to buy, Arturo?"

Arturo had just finished bragging about how great an investor he was. How could he back down? He subscribed to a full unit.

It didn't hurt Averill's pitch when the price of CRAB increased to over $50 a pound during the week of his calls. The crabgrass phenomenon was a front-page story, and the whole town was caught up in the excitement.

In two weeks, Averill oversold the deal. Relatives of his customers wanted a stock allocation. Teachers and firemen wanted in. Grandmothers demanded shares.

In the end, he had 200 willing buyers and had to cut back the unit size to accommodate everyone. He told his slightly disappointed customers, "Just buy $50,000 in the private placement. I'll get you more stock in the aftermarket."

Technically, not more than two dozen investors were qualified according to SEC rules. It didn't matter. All of the investors signed the precompleted questionnaires professing their financial acumen. They all checked the box assuring LMNOP they were qualified investors and had either a net worth of a million dollars or had annual earnings of at least $250,000.

Johnny and Justin were more than surprised when Averill called and said he had raised the money. Averill was a little astonished himself.

CHAPTER 115

MAY 14, 2012

After working furiously all weekend, the closing was set for the end of the day Monday. Nano Bio.Com would be reverse-merging into the shell. The company name would be changed to NBCI. No more having to explain the silly Nano Bio.Com name again.

The Shell King plagiarized the legal filing documents, this time from an SEC filing by Frederick's of Hollywood which had recently swapped shares in a reverse merger. Ironically, one of their corsets had been swapped at the Valentine's Day panty exchange held at Ben's. Under SEC disclosure rules, everyone including Frederick's had to show their underwear when they went public.

Today, money would change hands. The merger documents and a "Super 8-K" would be filed with the SEC. Poof! Magic! NBCI would become publicly traded. By the end of the day, you could buy a share of NBCI under its new stock symbol, ROOT.

The closing was a frantic drafting of legal documents, document signing, share issuing and money moving.

Louie DiSosa had obtained a new CUSIP number for the ROOT stock certificates. A CUSIP is a unique national securities identifying number for every common stock. A new number was issued whenever a stock changed its name or moved to a new stock exchange.

The company was leaving the stock-market hinterlands of OTC-Pink, better known to brokers as the pink sheets. ROOT wasn't exactly moving into a ritzy financial neighborhood. Until it earned its keep as a trusted public company, it would have to hang around the slightly less-outcast region of the OTCBB, the Over-The-Counter Bulletin Board.

The transfer agent had long ago stopped servicing the shell because it hadn't paid its bills. Transfer agents keep track of a company's shareholders and issue new shares when properly instructed. Louie DiSosa sent Justin the last known hard copy of the stock listing from two years ago. It was the closest they would get to an accurate share count.

A new transfer agent would be starting the day after ROOT went public. In order to close the private placement, they had to issue shares the old-fashioned way. Louie ordered 500 NBCI stock certificates from IntraBankNote.com and had them shipped to Averill. Averill drove to the home of Roland McPherson, the 82-year-old chairman and CEO, who signed the blank shares. Names and share amounts would be filled in later.

Averill found an old typewriter and created a certificate for his 200 new investors in the private placement. He typed out two million shares to each of Oenotropae's twenty managing partners, 7.5 million shares to the bridge note investors, and finally, the private placement commission shares – two million to LMNOP and two million to himself. It seemed like an awful lot of shares.

Averill stared at the remaining stack of blank stock certificates all signed and free to be issued. This was his last chance.

There was this void of governance surrounding the company. Oeno was exiting and more concerned about getting its money out quickly. He had mentioned his five million warrants to Oeno, and they never blinked an eye. He had written the warrant description into the private placement. No one said a word.

The NBCI board barely mattered. The Shell King was creating all of the legal documents to take NBCI public, but Louie was mostly making sure he got his money and shares at closing.

As president, Johnny should be watching closely, but he didn't know any better. Justin was so overworked preparing the SEC filings that he didn't have the spare time to verify anything.

The LMNOP executives were pretty excited that Averill was generating some big cash and stock commissions. They inspected the documents to make sure they were getting their fair share, but little more. They did ask for their half of the warrants, though.

Averill thought, *It's a classic Chinese fire drill. Everyone's running around the car, but no one is driving. They're all looking out for number one to make sure they get paid. Who's watching the store? I told Johnny about the ten million shares I'm getting in exchange for a note payable. The board hasn't approved them, but they wouldn't remember it if they had. Justin's asking me for the final tally on the shares to insert into the Super 8-K. He's relying on me of all people to give him the number. What's the worst that could happen? They make me give the shares back?*

Averill created a stock certificate for ten million shares in the name of Barry Winthrop and placed it in his briefcase.

Seeing as no one was looking, he decided to issue an extra two million shares to Tuxedo Investments, which was Averill's new offshore Cayman Islands company. Well, it wasn't exactly a Cayman Islands company just yet, but he'd set it up it when he had the time. All of the big hedge fund managers had offshore companies. Why shouldn't he?

Averill stamped the back of each stock certificate with a special restrictive legend. Essentially, the shares could not be sold for six months. The legend read:

THESE SECURITIES HAVE NOT BEEN REGISTERED UNDER THE SECURITIES ACT OF 1933 AND MAY NOT BE SOLD OR OTHERWISE DISPOSED OF UNTIL REGISTERED UNDER THE ACT OR THE COMPANY HAS RECEIVED AN OPINION OF COUNSEL THAT SUCH REGISTRATION IS NOT REQUIRED.

Averill decided not to stamp his note shares or the Tuxedo shares.

Averill emailed: "Dear Justin, here's the final share tally for the Super 8-K. The total shares after closing will be 194.5 million. The 'note' shares were issued as an incentive to the PPM investors. Johnny knows about them. You should book a note receivable in the amount of $1 million. The total warrants are exercisable into 5 million shares with a five-year term and ten-cent exercise price. LMNOP and I each get half. The bridge note lenders also receive 5 million of penny warrants under the same terms. I reserved a million shares for Rockland IR. They are an investor relations firm to help promote the stock. You'll need them now that you are public. Johnny will explain."

The final shares outstanding will be:

Existing shareholders	20,000,000
Louie DiSosa, Esq.	10,000,000
Private placement	100,000,000
Partners of Oenotropae	42,000,000
Bridge note lenders	7,500,000
Commissions on PPM	4,000,000
Rockland IR	1,000,000
Private placement note shares	10,000,000
TOTAL	194,500,000

The numbers were neatly wrapped with a pretty ribbon. Justin entered the amounts into the pro forma financial statements and filed them as an exhibit to the Super 8-K. They would be gospel numbers until someone proved otherwise.

CHAPTER 116

MAY 14

The commodity price continued higher. Pierre was clearly the big dog in the market buying large quantities of CRAB. CRAB PARTNERS I and II were trading in and out of their positions and making a ton of money. Speculators entered the market. This crazy price run-up was not lost on the financial news media.

Ben turned up the volume as financial news network STCK-TV showed a video of downtown Bergenfield and the transfer station construction site. Jay McCall, the news anchor, was interviewing Ken Delong of Den-Ken Commodity Brokers.

Ken said, "I've never in my lifetime been so close to such an opportunity. We've barely seen the tip of the technology. It's like watching Edwin Drake drill the first oil well in Pennsylvania in 1859, which you all know was the start of the oil industry.

"CRAB has legitimate analogies to oil. It's a limited resource. The greatest concentration of it comes from a single geography, like oil from the Middle East. It has fantastic powers just like gasoline does. There's potential for millions of new products, just like oil spawned the chemical and plastics industries. New uses are being found every day. This is the ground floor."

After Ken signed off, Dickie Tribecca appeared on the screen live from the floor of the Chicago Board of Trade. Dickie was an old-time, seasoned government bond trader who touted zero inflation policies over growth. He always wore a dark suit, white shirt and a dark tie with indiscernible patterns.

"You know, and I've said this many times before, but these crazy, low interest rates are fueled by the U. S. government's easy money policy. They are much to blame for the soaring commodity prices around the world. And soaring commodity prices lead to inflation. People can speculate in oil and wheat and corn and now crabgrass because there's no borrowing cost when treasuries are sold at zero-percent interest rates. This insanity has got to stop!"

Les Stevens, STCK-TV's handsome, balding economics newscaster, sat at the news roundtable in New York. "Well, for once I agree with Dickie about the low interest rate effect on most commodities like wheat and oil. But not for crabgrass. The interest rate could be twenty percent and people would still be speculating in it.

"Let me tell you why. CRAB is already becoming a boon to the local economy. This Bergen County area had been particularly hard hit by the recession. The town is home to thirty thousand, second- and third-generation immigrants who lost their life savings to housing and stock market crashes. They're getting a second chance, and quite frankly, it's kinda nice to see.

"But on a national scale, this commodity could be a disruptive biotechnology to replace sodium laureth sulfate, or SLS. SLS is soap and a detergent degreaser. It's cheap, it works, and it's in everything we touch: shampoo, dish washing soap, and even toothpaste. For some people, it is an irritant to the skin and can cause mouth ulcers, particularly the SLES version which some believe might be a carcinogen.

"I'll finish with this. This is just the beginning. It's only a matter of time before the other companies learn Pierre's secret formula."

Jay McCall sat with a wide grin preparing to crack one of his many wisecracks of the day. He was a fifty-year-old handsome and funny host who had learned the Wall Street world as an MIT-rocket-scientist turned stock-picker. He joked, "Les, do you think they'll sell this herb at licensed weed stores like they do in California? Of course this weed is a lot cheaper at only $50 dollars a pound?"

Les sounded like a disapproving schoolteacher. "No, Jay. It's not that type of weed."

Jay kept jibing. "Do they need a state referendum to sell it? Oh yeah, let me not forget to ask. Is Obama going to tax it to pay for all of his liberal programs?"

The camera turned to Betsy Sands, the beautiful and brilliant host with fantastic blonde hair. Betsy was an on-air personality who backed up her opinions with advanced degrees from Ivy League schools. "Enough, guys. As a consumer, this can only be a good thing, right? I don't want a chemical degreaser in my hair. It makes my hair brittle. That squeaking sound during shampooing isn't what I thought it was. It's car-engine degreaser. Disgusting!"

Announcer Cal Bonita said, "You guys are joking now, but the company who processes this stuff is going public today through a reverse merger. Guess what the symbol is – ROOT!"

Cliff Lenihan was a big personality on STCK-TV. He had a rare combination of Jersey-boy rough-and-tumble packaged with the intellectual refinement of a Harvard MBA education. Every day, he interpreted complex financial events to average Americans. At night, he hosted a show which gave tried-and-true lessons about investing.

Cliff said, "Reverse merging is usually a terrible way to go public. There's a graveyard full of failed public companies that went down this path. You're public but you trade by appointment only. The SEC is also warning investors about these deals. This was probably in reaction to a bunch of Chinese companies who wanted to get around disclosure requirements.

"However, ROOT did something very unusual with this deal, despite all of the heavy dilution and starting off with some inherited disgruntled shareholders. They raised $10 million and now have plenty of money. And the hedge-fund guys from Oenotropae stayed in the deal. I'm gonna keep my eye on this one. For now, be careful until I've completed my research!"

The stock began trading at 3:45 PM just before the market closed. A few shares changed hands. Averill ceremoniously bought a thousand shares at the end of the day at $0.11 cents for a ten percent daily gain. It cost him $110. Averill's firm served as the lone market maker required for listing on the OTCBB.

CHAPTER 117

MAY 16, 2012

The blue TV screen announced the upcoming story:

REVERSE MERGERS - GOING PUBLIC?
OR GOING TO THE FINANCIAL GRAVEYARD?

The likeable STCK-TV reporter, Cal Bonita, asked his guest, a former SEC commissioner, "Should these horrible financings even be allowed? Aren't they almost always bad deals for investors?"

The gray-haired, bespectacled official replied, "Companies have the right to go public in this manner if they follow the rules. However, the SEC has been raising red flags. Just last year they issued an investor bulletin cautioning investors about reverse mergers. And now they have new "seasoning" requirements meant to discourage these deals.

"However, despite these impediments, I do expect reverse mergers to continue because they are substantially cheaper than registering through an IPO. The fact of the matter is small companies have a hard time raising capital. Wall Street has for the most part abandoned them."

Next to Cal, a split screen appeared. On the right, Simon Gupta, a senior investment banker at Silverheels and Penny, argued, "If you don't have a major investment bank overseeing the transaction, the offering has no integrity. Who's counting the money? Who's getting cold-comfort from the auditors? Who's determining if the price is fair to investors?

"Aside from honesty and fairness, reverse mergers don't deliver the most important goal – the broadly-held distribution of the company's stock by enthusiastic shareholders. In fact, it does the opposite. In the case of ROOT, when it went public, ten percent of it was owned by disgruntled shareholders who lost money on their previous investment. Most of them still aren't aware the stock is trading because it had gone dormant and now has a new name. As they become aware over time, the public relations nightmare will continue for years."

Greg O'Houlihan, the affable Chairman and the "O" in penny broker LMNOP, appeared in the third panel of the split screen. "While we prefer small firms use IPOs, a reverse merger is still a legitimate method to go public. It's very fast. ROOT went public in thirty days. It costs very little. Root's transaction costs were less than $100,000. And they have a legitimate business model.

"Registering your stock in a traditional IPO is so cost-prohibitive that small companies simply cannot afford it. We embrace these entrepreneurial start-ups and often support them with post-IPO trading activity. Full disclosure. My firm raised $10 million in a private placement for ROOT to coincide with their transaction."

Simon argued, "ROOT has no friendly float. The only shares that are registered and allowed to trade are the shares held by the guys who hate you. They became public technically. But they went to the prom and there're no classmates. There's no band. There isn't even any food. It's a bad date. And it takes years to get over it."

Greg smiled and said, "I'm sorry you had to relive your unhappy teens. Many of us enjoyed our senior proms.

"Companies can develop a following after they go public. It all comes down to their strategic business plan. If they have a good business model, they'll succeed. And ROOT has one. One more thing. LMNOP has plenty of dry powder in its musket for any disgruntled shareholders who want to dump their stock."

The panelists were both right. Small companies without solid plans were doomed. But big companies without solid plans were doomed too. Investment bankers defended the gates of going public and decided which business plans were worthy. Only good companies shall pass. Occasionally, a bad deal would get by. Those that failed would receive a call from a class action lawyer.

CHAPTER 118

MAY 17, 2012

Averill tested the market by placing a "bid" to buy a thousand shares of ROOT "at the market" with a "limit" of eight cents. No one nibbled. He raised the offer a penny. No bites. At ten cents, the order was filled. He examined the trade carefully.

The "ask" had been from a tiny brokerage firm in Miami. The OTCBB computer screen showed layers of sell orders – five thousand shares for sale at ten cents, ten thousand at eleven cents and fifty thousand at twelve cents, all from the same firm. In the next column, layers of buy orders from seven-to-nine cents from several small firms filled the screen.

Someone had also entered a buy order for a million shares at a penny and a sell order for an identical amount at ten dollars. They were hoping to make some quick money from a stupid trader who had entered a "market" order. In heavily traded stocks, a market maker kept orderly trading during the day to prevent exactly this bottom fishing. In a thinly traded stock like ROOT, the only market maker so far was Averill, and he wasn't risking his own capital to keep the markets steady.

The seller of the thousand shares could have been one of the original shareholders, but was more likely the Shell King.

Averill called Louie DiSosa. "King, how are you? You did a fantastic job for us. I'm just calling to thank you."

"Well, we're not done yet," said Louie in an irritated voice. "You guys are keeping me busy. You know, I make a lot less money filing paperwork with the SEC than I get from selling shells. Anyway, what can I do for you in thirty seconds or less? The clock's running."

"I just wanted to talk to you about your plans," said Averill. "I saw you sold a few shares this morning. You don't wanna sell them too fast. You'll hurt the market. Let me round up some buyers and take them off your hands."

"Averill, if you find a buyer to take my shares today, fine," replied Louie. "Otherwise don't bother me. I hafta sell 'em before your boys slam the market in July."

Averill acted surprised. "We can't sell for six months. Why are you so worried?"

"I can see you didn't read the documents," Louie laughed. "Oeno has a registration-rights agreement. ROOT has to file a registration statement in thirty days and then respond to the SEC comments in fifteen. Which means, bub, Oeno's and everyone else's shares could be tradable by July 1 unless the SEC gets tough with their review. But I gotta tell you, your controller knows what he's doing. I'm anticipating minimal comments from the SEC. Which means, I'm selling now."

Averill thought for a brief pause. He was no expert on the rules. After the SEC had relaxed the holding period rule to six months, the issue about registration rights agreements had gone away. If Oeno had demanded a registration statement, it meant it was planning to sell forty million shares as early as possible. It would absolutely kill the stock price.

"Okay, King," Averill said all chummy. "Gimme me a week. I don't mind if you sell a little above ten cents. But don't spook my investors. I have plenty of buyers, but if they think ROOT is going south, they'll let it collapse before they jump in. I'll get you ten cents for your ten-million shares, okay?"

"What, are you nuts?" Louie said, insulted. "If you want to lock up a big block, you gotta pay a premium. I want fifteen cents a share.

"Oh, and by the way. Oenotropae told me they want to keep a safe distance from the company. They don't wanna be in possession of material nonpublic information. They're cutting off all lines of communication. No more internal reports. Don't bother calling them. And they told me to hold an official election of the board of directors. Right now, everyone on the board is an Oeno-appointee. I'm drafting the proxy as we speak."

Averill thought through what Louie was telling him. Corporate governance was never good for insiders. Real board meetings. Audit committees. Compensation committees. What about the options he promised to the board and management team?

On the other hand, he had wanted Oeno out of the picture so they wouldn't be watching so closely. He'd tackle the Oeno problem later. It would take about $6 million to buy their shares in July.

"Louie, I'll get you twelve or thirteen cents, but you gotta stop selling and putting pressure on the price every day. My investors have to think they're getting a bargain."

"In return, I need you to do me a favor. Make sure you put the management and board stock option plans into the proxy. I promised those guys I'd take care of them."

Louie said, firm and final, "I'll take fourteen cents if you close by next Friday.

"As for the proxy, I'm not sure I can help you. Oenotropae only told me to draft a proxy to elect the board. I'm not allowed to even ask them about anything else. They don't want to make decisions anymore. Let me think for a sec. You know, Justin disclosed the options in the private placement docs as possible plans. If you get the board to approve them quickly, I'll put them in the proxy."

Averill said, "I'll take care of this. I'll get the chairman to hold a meeting and email you the approval. And I'll buy your shares next Friday. Okay?"

Averill had Johnny call Roland McPherson to explain the issue. Roland called an emergency board meeting and approved the option plans without any argument. Why would they object to awarding themselves options?

CHAPTER 119

MAY 17

Averill was in unfamiliar territory. Had he gone legit? For ten years, he had scrounged a living by selling made-up stories about unknown cheap stocks to small-time investors who bought the dream. Young first-time investors were prime targets because they didn't have enough savings to buy a hundred shares of IBM for $10,000. But they could afford to buy a thousand shares of Newfangled Nuts for a hundred bucks.

Then, last year, Averill won the golden-goose, Easter-egg-roll contest when Apple's stock price went crazy. Hundreds of Averill's near-dormant accounts suddenly became valuable. Remarkably, people thought Averill had something to do with their newfound wealth.

In April, Averill snagged the rights to lead a big private placement for ROOT. Averill had for the first time legitimately and honestly served a valuable purpose when he raised capital for ROOT. He earned a lot of money to boot. It was a lifetime opportunity for most small brokers. If you could just get your hands on one deal, you'd be set. You could relax a little. Not Averill. He wanted more.

LMNOP took half of Averill's commissions as the usual and just compensation for providing a shanty office and crackling phone line. The house always gets paid. LMNOP took its share of his warrants, too. After taxes, net-net, Averill he had a paltry $80,000 of cash but a ton of stock which he couldn't sell until it was registered with the SEC.

Well, not everything was legitimate. He had ten million shares which he supposedly paid for with a million-dollar promissory note. Johnny knew about them, but he had understood from Averill that Oeno had approved them. If Johnny had mentioned them to the board, Averill was sure he would have received some pushback on the number. He assumed the board knew nothing about them. Justin thought they were approved because Johnny had told him so. Averill decided he would have to maneuver his way around this little "approval" technicality.

The two million shares entered in the name of Tuxedo Investments, however, were outright theft.

This just needed a little curing time until memories got foggy.

CHAPTER 120

MAY 17

Averill wasn't built like other people. He had no family. Actually, he had a family, but they shunned him. His mother and father hadn't spoken to him since he was in college.

He was always involved with some get-rich-quick scheme. In his freshman year, he started a chain letter and made a few bucks. Then he ran a small Ponzi scheme for some mystery company paying big referral fees to people who joined for a small fee. The first dozen investors made money; the rest never saw a dime. A few of his victims discovered he was behind the ruse and beat him to a pulp. His parents paid ten grand to get Averill out of trouble before the police got involved.

In his senior year, Averill ran numbers for the local bookie. Every week, students picked ten football teams to win or lose. For a buck, they had a chance to make a thousand. Students rarely won. He started clipping the bookie's action and kept twenty percent of the bets for himself. Averill had a bad week when a dozen bettors asked for their winnings. His parents once again bailed him out. It was then they said their final goodbyes.

It didn't bother him when his parents had abandoned him. He didn't care much for them anyway. His life was built around creating fantastic tales that could lead to satisfying his insatiable greed. He wanted what others had.

Coveting was how he had lost his first job on Wall Street. He convinced a wealthy widow to open a brokerage account and trade stocks. It was only a matter of time before Averill began churning the assets. He traded over and over again generating commissions until the account was near-empty. She sued Averill and the firm, and they fired him after they lost the arbitration hearing.

Averill had zero success with women for similar reasons. He could be nice-looking enough, if he had bothered to clean up a tiny bit. But his single-minded purpose of making millions left no room for things like love, affection, caring, warm feelings and concern for his fellow man. He had the loyalty of an alley cat. His DNA was missing the code sequence for compassion.

After a rare date, he never asked the girl up to his apartment to see his etchings. He asked her to open a brokerage account and buy stock.

Love was elusive to lonely Averill.

CHAPTER 121

MAY 18, 2012

Misty peeked around the corner to see if the coast was clear. JB was sitting with Michael and called over, "Ben's gone to the bank. You're safe for ten minutes."

"Thanks, JB. If Ben saw me here, he'd crucify me." Misty regarded him warily. "You're kinda hard to figure out. Are we friends or enemies today?"

"Misty, I had nothing to do with your breakup," said JB. "You may want to look in the mirror on that one. However, I have an inside tip for you if you want. Someone around here just made a big commission check and I'm absolutely sure he isn't dating."

Misty said with mild curiosity, "Who? Decker? He's kinda cute but a little too outdoorsy for my tastes."

"No, this person may require some of your special skills in makeovers," said JB with a huge grin. "You know the broker who calls himself Averill? He raised ten million for the processing plant and made a half million in fees. I'm sure you can help him find a way to spend it. Don't say I never did anything for you."

"Ugh, him?" Misty groaned. She paused for a few seconds and said, "A half million, huh? I have to think hard about this one. I gotta go. I'm on double secret probation still. Put in a good word for me. This is the only place to get a good meal around here."

Misty skipped the hot-food line and bought a coffee to go. She went to pay Miguel at the register, looked up, and saw a picture mounted in a frame behind the register. She dropped the change and gave a guttural, shocked sound of disgust. "Oh, no. You DIDN'T do that!"

She grabbed her coffee and fled. Misty brushed past Allie in the doorway.

Allie was not her usual happy self when she wandered through the breakfast line. As she approached a bewildered Miguel, still at the register, Ben walked in and took over. Ben said, "Look up, Allie. Do you notice anything different?"

Allie said, "Sorry Ben. I'm havin' a bad-hair month. There's not much you can do to cheer me up unless you wanna buy a few thousand bags of useless chemicals."

Ben stepped to the side, and pointed behind him. Hanging on the wall was a photo of Allie in a picture frame. Below was a sign declaring her "Customer of the Month".

He said, "Congratulations, Allie. The coffee's free."

Allie laughed and caught JB and Decker snickering like a couple of teenage pranksters. "Oh my! So that's why Misty went runnin' outta here. What a hoot!"

Ben looked betrayed. "Misty? In here? How'd she get served? She's on permanent time-out. Miguel, Miguel, get back up here!"

Allie's mood snapped back into form, and she hugged JB and Michael before sitting at the table.

CHAPTER 122

MAY 18

Averill faced an unusual problem. Most pump and dump schemes bought and sold stock in companies long on story and short on results. It was all he knew. ROOT was a real company with actual prospects. How would he sell such a strange animal?

NBCI had a $200 million plant near completion. It had thousands of customers driving to its front doors every few months dropping off a newly-hot commodity. Averill calculated if NBCI processed at the current town capacity, revenues could exceed $20 million a year. NBCI could actually make money. And lots of it.

Something dawned on him no one else yet seemed to appreciate. CRAB was now $50 a pound. No homeowner was going to turn down $30,000 a year to grow CRAB. Crabgrass didn't look that horrible. Heck, he had read about Oregonians raising llamas on the front yards of their mega-mansions to escape property taxes. They claimed they were ranchers. Surely, a little crabgrass was less offensive than smelly South American camels.

There was more evidence of a tightening market. It was clear Pierre had thrown in the towel and given up on signing new option agreements. They were buying CRAB on the commodity exchange. And so were a bunch of other interested parties. CRAB was headed way higher.

Averill only knew one way to sell stock – the hint of inside information. He called Johnny for confirmation of his new hypothesis.

Averill: "I'm working on the proxy statement with Louie. Do you know what your revenues are going to be this quarter?"

Johnny: "How the hell would I know? All of the deliveries happen in the last week of the month. We won't know till it happens."

Averill: "Well, is it safe to say, based upon your knowledge of the trading patterns, you guys will process two million pounds in June? Give me your best guess. There's open contracts for six million pounds already, and at least a third of those are going to take delivery, don't you think?"

Johnny: "Averill, I got no idea. It can't be two million. We think a million-six is the most the town could produce. You'd have to ask Pierre what they're gonna take."

Averill: "And if you processed 1.6 million pounds, you get three bucks for the Pierre contracts and ten percent for everything else. Add it up. If the CRAB closing price was $50 dollars, wouldn't you say your revenues would be like seven or eight million?"

Johnny: "Averill, that's too hypothetical. My guys ran a spreadsheet. The range of possible revenues is between three and ten mil. At 1.6 million pounds, revenues would be seven mil, but…"

Averill hung up mid-sentence. That was the sound bite he needed.

CHAPTER 123

MAY 25, 2012

Averill called Arturo, his favorite Apple, iPhone and self-proclaimed stock market expert.

Averill: "Arturo, Como esta? This is Averill Winthrop at LMNOP. You made a great investment in ROOT. I'm sorry you got cut back to $50,000 in the private placement. I want to make it up to you."

Arturo, bragging: "Well, I wanted a lot more. You know I'm a player."

Averill: "That's why I'm calling you first. I just got wind ROOT is about to have a record quarter. A little birdie told me revenues will be $7 million and could be as high as ten. The market's only expecting four or five mil. My firm is recommending customers buy shares up at a price of up to fifteen cents. How many shares do you want?"

Arturo: "You got this from an insider?"

Averill: "My sources are the best. This stock's going up. Here's your chance to make some real money."

Arturo: "Okay, you can get me another ten thousand bucks worth. You're sure about this?"

Averill: "I'm sure, Arturo. Here's the plan. We're going to buy up the loose shares in the market and close the deal next week. You and a dozen of my choicest clients are going to join together. I know where I can buy a block of five million shares next Friday for fourteen cents a share. This is a rare insider deal. You sure you don't want more? This is your last chance to increase your participation in this truly fantastic opportunity."

Arturo: "Okay, make it $25,000."

Averill: "OK, Arturo. You're the man. Twenty investors max. Don't tell anyone about this. You'll see some small trades hit your account this week. Then we'll buy the five million next Friday. Last time. Keep this secret."

Those were magic words. In April, Averill had concluded Arturo was the head grape in the Bergenfield grapevine. Whatever he told Arturo came back to him from Luis or Pedro or Jose a few hours later heavily embellished.

As Averill cold-called the rest of his clients, Arturo told his buddies, "I got this from a reliable source. ROOT's gonna have a muy grande earnings quarter. Get in now before the market finds out."

By the time Averill reached the second page of his list of prospects, the rumor had grown. Pedro called Averill and said, "Mi amigo me dijo que el tiene, how you say, um, insider info? ROOT's gonna do $10 million dolares in sales. Es verdad? Is it true?"

Averill was an expert about implying truth without exactly saying anything. "Yeah, well I heard that number too."

Of course he heard it. From Pedro – just a moment before.

Nearly everyone on Averill's hit list wanted in. Each time Averill sold another prospect on the deal, he used a small amount of money in their account to buy ROOT shares and bolster the stock price. The stock increased a penny, and more investors clamored to get in before it went any higher.

After a week, the "ask" had risen to fourteen cents – Louie's number. On Friday, Averill's clients bought five million shares from Louie DiSosa. The trade showed on the NASDAQ OTCBB computer screen as twenty-five separate trades of twenty thousand shares. ROOT appeared on the daily list of most-actively-traded Bulletin Board stocks. Penny stock traders around the country took notice and clicked on the ROOT profile on their computer screens. *Who the heck is ROOT?*

Averill charged the firm's standard five percent sales commission for the purchase of DiSosa's shares. Again, LMNOP took their 50% house's cut.

His investors in the ROOT private placement couldn't believe their good fortune. Their stock was up 40% in just a few weeks. ROOT was all you heard during breakfast at Ben's Deli, during drinks at Tommy Fox's, and while buying breakfast buns at La Placita Bakery following Sunday mass.

Averill thought through his plan. This was only the first step. He had three large groups of shareholders to deal with. Oeno owned forty million shares and could slam the market as soon as the registration statement went effective with the SEC. The bridge note investors had been pretty quiet, but give them time. They might stay along for the ride, but they could dump their shares at any moment.

Then there were the old investors from the shell company. Their twenty million shares were spread around thousands of people. Most of them hadn't yet woken up to the fact that they owned something valuable again. One day they'd look at their account and be pleasantly surprised. Their $10,000 investment which had gone to zero was now worth $500. Some would sell. Some would double down.

Averill prioritized. Deal with Oeno first. Find buyers for their stock just like he did for the Shell King.

CHAPTER 124

MAY 28, 2012

Misty had no shame, but she still had fear. She had heard Ben was on vacation this week, but Miguel would be on the lookout for her after getting chewed out by his boss.

She hid in the dining area behind the partition while her only friend in the world, Miggie, snuck her coffee and a bagel. Miggie had an uncontrollable frizzy mound of brown hair and a flattened nose. Misty treated her like a mutt.

Bret was in Misty's rearview mirror. She had no time to waste. According to her clock, she needed a husband in the next twelve months. She needed a new quarry, preferably a wealthy one.

After the heads-up from JB, Misty snooped around town. Women gabbed about ROOT in her aerobics class. The overhead TV at the Fitness II gym aired a local news report about this upstart penny stock with the funny symbol. Bergenfield was becoming famous for something besides its high school band and championship wrestling teams.

JB was right – ROOT had raised $10 million, and this CRAB craze was making money for everyone. And Averill was on center stage with a half million in his bank account.

She'd have to swallow a lot of pride to settle down with Mr. Creepy. Misty ignored Miggie's chitchat while she studied Averill sitting two tables away.

He wasn't terrible looking, but he needed a new suit. And a new shirt. And the tie had to go. What do they call that pattern? Memories of childhood screaming? And who was the color-blind designer who made it? Ugh! And the shoes had never seen a coat of polish. And the socks were too short. Even his belt needed replacement.

He also could use a new hairstyle. And he needed to do something about the beady eyes and shady looks around corners. He ate breakfast like a two-year-old in a highchair. Crumbs flew everywhere. The moustache had to be trimmed.

Well, thought Misty, *at least he isn't fat.* Misty concluded she could mold this man into someone or something respectable. As long as he made enough money. Besides, she had a couple of months to kill until something better came along.

Misty left Miggie and stood in front of Averill while he was talking on the phone. It sounded like he was trying to sell somebody stock. She waited until Averill took a glimpse of her in her tight black stretch Capri pants and black silk blouse. After she was sure he noticed her, she sat and politely waited until the phone conversation ended. Unbelievably, Misty did know when to be quiet.

Misty swallowed her pride. "Hi. You're Averill, right? I'm Misty. I've been noticing you around here lately."

Misty was charming, sweet, and as always, beautiful. Averill looked up and momentarily eyed her. He wasn't accustomed to good-looking women sitting anywhere near him. Usually they moved away when he sat down. Then he realized why she was there.

He said, "Oh you must've heard about the new stock offering. I guess you want to open an account. It's a great story."

Averill brushed food crumbs from his handlebar moustache and began his ten-minute, prepared pitch about how great ROOT was. "Roots prospects are bright…the beginning of a great adventure…big plant…great management team. . . gonna blow away the numbers this quarter…how many shares do you wanna buy?"

Misty patiently sat through the sales show. "It all sounds very interesting, but I'm not sure I can free up my assets for another stock right now. Trust funds and all. But I'd be glad to talk about it over dinner tonight if you're buying."

Averill totally missed any sign Misty was interested in him as a date. He was confused. He had zero skills at reading a woman's advances because no woman had ever made a move on him. His radar detected something, but if she wasn't interested in ROOT stock, then what?

He said, "The market closes at four, but I cold-call until five-thirty. Do you want to meet at the diner at six?"

"Avy, the diner?" she cooed. "Come on. I'm a lady. Let's meet at Tommy Fox's and have a nice glass of wine and some dinner."

Misty glanced at her Movado. "My word. Look at the time. I have a client meeting in five minutes. Have to go. It was a pleasure meeting you, Avy. See you tonight!"

Averill had met his match in professional lying. Misty had no trust fund. She had no money. And she certainly had no clients. She was just heading to her job at the used car dealership. She smiled and gently touched his arm as she left. "Don't be late!"

Eight hours later, Misty sat in Tommy Fox's. He was late. In fact, he had forgotten about the date or meeting. Misty dialed Averill's cell phone number. She exercised full temper-restraint and dug deep to find a pinch of sweetness.

"Don't worry, Avy. Take your time. I'm just finishing up some calls until you get here."

CHAPTER 125

JUNE 15, 2012

Competition is the backbone of American commerce. It didn't take long for two hair product companies to announce they too had developed a formula to use the natural degreaser found in crabgrass.

Vital Beauty Products offered limited quantities online of its new Lori's Glory shampoo. Sadie Snookum's Shampoo said it had created a second brand of its "Yearn to be Free" shampoo with a formula free of sodium laureth sulfate. The product roll-out started in California, and the shelves quickly emptied.

It didn't take much to move the price for CRAB futures. Two weeks before the June delivery, the CRAB price had escalated to $58 a pound. The weekly trading daily volume exceeded the size of the June contract.

The price curve for future deliveries was temporarily inverted. Typically, longer future contracts traded lower than the current delivery price because of holding costs and the time value of money. The October ROOT contract was a full $5 higher than the June contract.

Eva called her team in for an emergency meeting at Pierre's Morristown headquarters. Olivier sat by her side. She asked for the chemical analysis of the competitor's products.

Albert said, "Ve purchased both zie products, but zhey vere very hard to find. Our preliminary tests show zat zhey are missing zie key additives to make zis vork effectively. Zhey haven't refined zie product enuf. And zere is still a trace of green in zere coloring. Zhey are very far behind us. It vorks, but not vell."

Steven interrupted, "Think of it as using sugar cane instead of sugar to make a cake. In other words, they have to use three times the quantity we use to achieve our results. They cannot do this for very long."

Eva responded, "Nonetheless, they are affecting the CRAB price. I have worse news. I received a call from the CEO of a national tooth paste company. The name's confidential, but it's one of the big ones.

"They want to know if we would share our formula with them under a licensing agreement. This sodium laureth sulfate is in everyone's toothpaste, and some people have a bad reaction to it. They're planning a small product launch for natural tooth-paste like Tom's. The all-natural market is tiny, but it could grow.

"The CRAB price is nearing $60 dollars. How much have we purchased?"

"We have about a two-year supply," Stephane answered, "but that's based upon the last sales projections."

Steven commented, "The problem is our sales are increasing rapidly. Every time I get a forecast from marketing, they send me another upward revision. If this keeps going, we may not have even a one-year supply by the end of the summer.

"The good news is Albert has reduced material usage, so I'd say we're doing okay. Our problem is over half of the commodity purchasers are by speculators. We cannot keep outbidding them."

"I wouldn't worry about having the wrong year on the futures," Eva said. "You could always store the stuff.

"Vital Beauty Products is owned by a big conglomerate, but some stupid product manager with an unlimited budget is making these decisions. Snookum's is a small public company. Maybe we should buy it and end their misery."

Olivier interjected, "It would take you a year to get by the Hart Scott Rodino anti-trust review. You could never buy it quickly enough to have an impact. Plus, once you owned ten percent, the market knows about it and they push the stock price up."

Eva said, "I know Ollie, but give a girl a chance to fantasize here. Stephane, keep buying next year's futures for now. I want to take physical delivery of every pound in our June contract. I want to make sure no one else gets a hand on enough CRAB to develop more uses in the lab. Competition from shampoo and toothpaste markets is more than enough.

"Guys, we're making a lot of money on the shampoo. The consumer feedback is incredibly positive. Not only does our shampoo contain no chemical degreaser, but the shampoo is improving our customer's hair. It's thicker and fuller. The blogosphere is filled with thousands of crazy positive comments. If this keeps up, we might cut back on advertising. . . Just kidding, Olivier.

"If this CRAB price keeps rising, we can raise the price to cover the costs. But first, we'd reduce the container size from sixteen ounces to twelve. I just don't think the mass market will go for anything over $25 dollars. Meeting adjourned."

CHAPTER 126

JUNE 25, 2012

The STCK-TV screen announced the next story:

CRAB GRASS FUTURES MAKING EVERYONE SNEEZE?

The news anchor, Jay McCall, said, "There's a short squeeze going on in the CRAB pits this morning. A month ago, the price of CRAB inexplicably rose over $50 dollars a pound. Today, the price is over $70 dollars and there's a war going on near the Chicago shore.

"What's causing this hyper-growth in the price? We know Pierre Beauty Products is the leader in the development of this natural product which replaces the degreaser chemical in shampoo. Last month, two more companies announced they too had adopted the ingredients found in this weed spun into gold.

"Den-Ken Commodity Brokers is leading the commodity trading on CRAB. They raised $5 million last year and quickly raised a second round of $50 million in a partnership called CRAB FUND II, LLC. We understand its investors include a number of institutions including state pension funds.

"So what caused the price spike? There was a big short interest growing in CRAB. A group of traders didn't believe the hype. But the short sellers hadn't anticipated the recent positive news. The short interest for the June contract has risen to forty percent of the open interest. The CRAB bid price jumped to $71 dollars this morning and there were no sellers. The price is limit up for the day. It looks like it's going to a hundred this week.

"Now a classic squeeze is on. The sellers who sold short the June delivery cannot close out their positions and they can't deliver. They had planned to roll to the next maturity, but got caught in a trap.

"This is reminiscent of commodity squeezes in the past, like the Maine potato scandal. You're all too young to remember, but sellers dumped truckloads of potatoes on buyer's lawns because the buyers wouldn't settle out the contracts.

"The Chicago MERC, now merged with the Chicago Board of Trade and part of the CME Group, announced it will hold an open meeting to discuss how to settle the contracts. Forcing the shorts to buy June deliveries to close out their positions would ruin more than a few brokers. The MERC suggested several solutions including forcing set-tlements or allowing the June contract to deliver though July and August. Newspapers estimated the short sellers might have to purchase CRAB for as much as $100 dollars a pound."

CHAPTER 127

JUNE 25

As soon as the story hit, Eva called Albert, Steven and Stephane into her office. Olivier was again by her side.

"This short squeeze is bad for us," Eva said. "On one hand, we want the speculators out of our CRAB supply. This will certainly ruin a few of them. But the long holders are winning big. If we let this go on, we'll encourage more speculation and further price increases.

"I received a call from the MERC an hour ago. They asked what we could do to alleviate the short-squeeze. I told them we'd discuss it. We're already up to $90 dollars. If we don't intervene, the price could be $100 dollars by tomorrow.

"Stephane, we're going to sell enough CRAB for June delivery so the shorts can cover. When the market settles back down, buy an equivalent amount of futures for next year's delivery."

Stephane replied, "I'll do what you request. You realize we'll be booking a large profit? We own about a million pounds for delivery in June. We only need half of that for production."

Eva said, "I'm fully aware you'll be booking a nice profit this quarter, but you need to reinvest in future deliveries after the price subsides."

Pierre took the pressure off the market for June delivery. The price declined steadily from the $90 peak until it reached $75 a pound. Commodity brokers were bleeding from the exercise, but they would live to trade another day.

The August contract resumed trading at $70 a pound and the MERC announced the squeeze had solved itself because of efficient market mechanisms.

Regardless, the intense trading and newspaper headlines attracted all sorts of potential new buyers for this strange commodity.

CHAPTER 128

JUNE 30, 2012

Averill visited Johnny no-longer True Value on Saturday at his office. It was the final day for delivery of the June contract, and the nearly-built plant was extremely busy. Fifty temporary farm workers processed the incoming crabgrass. A long line of vehicles waited their turn.

Johnny was beaming. "This plant is rockin' n' rollin'."

Even though it was a weekend, Averill still dressed for work. He wore an olive-colored cotton summer suit Misty had circled in a catalog. She had seen Bret wearing the same suit last summer. The Averill makeover had begun.

"Johnny, you're wasting your company's capital," Averill said with authority as the company's self-appointed financial advisor. "We didn't raise $10 million so you could put it in a savings account. You're missing the greatest investment opportunity of your lifetime, and it's right outside your offices."

"Oh no. What're you schemin' now?" Johnny said warily.

Averill gave the smile of a mischievous leprechaun. "Johnny, me lad, NBCI is authorized to buy CRAB futures to smooth its operations. CRAB is going bonkers. Pierre just sold some contracts to force the price down, but there's nothing to stop this from doubling.

"What you should do is take the $10 million we just raised and buy October futures contracts. There's a twenty-five percent margin requirement. That means you only need $2.5 million of equity to buy the contract."

Johnny protested, "Justin's not gonna let me do this without goin' to the board."

Averill laughed and said, "Justin is a bean counter. You're the president. You make the decisions. Justin counts the money. End of story. Besides, the money is still in the brokerage bank accounts. He won't know until October and by then you'll have made so much money he can't complain."

Averill returned to his office and purchased 2,000 October 2012 CRAB futures contracts at $58 per pound. Each contract equaled a hundred pounds. NBCI was now the proud owner of nearly $12 million of CRAB futures.

CHAPTER 129

JULY 3, 2012

The July Fourth week was wasted. The holiday was on a Wednesday, and Averill worked over the weekend denying Misty an extended vacation. She sat in the deli impatiently waiting for him to show.

Misty and Ben had finally called a truce. Ben agreed to ignore her if she sat out of sight. No face-to-face meetings either. Someone would have to purchase her breakfast for her, or she'd have to wait until Ben was away from the register. The terms of surrender would have to do. It was too hard a life to be exiled from Ben's.

She loudly drummed her fingers and played with her iPhone. Finally, at 10:00 AM, Averill entered and sat down with a black coffee. He was wearing the olive suit for the fifth straight day. You can dress him up, but…

Misty asked in an angry voice, "What took you so long? I've been waiting over thirty minutes in this godforsaken dive."

"I had to take care of some clients. I have to make money, don't I?" Averill retorted.

Misty snapped back, "Who's more important, me or them?"

Misty had made reservations at the Aztec Motel on the Seaside Heights boardwalk. It was a motel with a pool and a view of the boardwalk, ocean, and the Seaside Casino Pier. And it was conveniently attached to a popular bar.

Misty wasn't planning any holiday in an expensive Cape May inn this time. She wanted to be close to home in case this Averill expedition turned sour. She carefully planned her escape route just in case.

Her plan was to get Averill drunk on hard liquor during the day so he wouldn't pester her. At night, Averill was springing for a huge lobster dinner and expensive wine at a nice restaurant up Route 35. Then she'd return to the room and feign sleep. In two days she'd have a nice bikini tan line and go home.

Pierre no longer called emergency meetings to deal with CRAB. They now held a regularly-scheduled weekly crisis meeting, which allowed Stephane, Albert and Steven to plan their calendars.

Stephane began, "Eva, someone's accumulated a large position in CRAB. At first we thought it was another speculator. But this is a series of large trades, and the open interest has increased a lot. We don't believe it's just Den-Ken's funds.

"I spoke with marketing. They believe Lori's Glory and Sadie Snookum's Shampoo could use at most a hundred thousand pounds between the two of them. Apparently, the price spike spooked them a little.

"We asked ourselves, who else could it be? There's a good possibility EXXON and Chevron already are experimenting with it. If the toothpaste giants are interested, then so is Tom's Toothpaste. Or is it somebody from out of left field like Pep Boys or Palmolive?

"We looked hard at this. We concluded none of them would be purchasing large quantities for R&D. At most, they'd buy a thousand pounds or two for experiments. We think the buyer must be someone who intends to take delivery and use the product.

"Last point. Following your instructions, we reduced our August CRAB position to 800,000 pounds under the theory it would create a surplus and lower prices. Unfortunately, this unknown party or parties have purchased the available CRAB and put us right where we started. Prices will not be declining in August."

Eva tapped her pen on her notepad. "Thanks, Stephane. Now I need to hear from Steven about our local reconnaissance."

Steven placed a large map of Bergenfield on the projection screen. Thousands of squares were marked solid green, yellow or white representing every home in town. "As you can see from the map, at least 5,000 houses marked in green are prepared to deliver in August. The yellow boxes are homes we believe will convert over the next one or two delivery dates. By next June, we estimate 7,000 homes will be delivering CRAB.

"Also, an active crabgrass seed market has developed. NBCI has been separating the seeds from the plants during processing and selling them for $10 dollars a pound. Next year, if the last 2,000 homes convert, they'll need these seeds to plant crabgrass.

"Also, you asked me to investigate homes outside Bergenfield that might be able to grow this plant. It's a very small area below the brook on the New Milford border. The stream acts like a Maginot Line defense. We could add another five hundred homes in Dumont, but the quality of the crabgrass deteriorates rapidly farther north and west.

"You'd have to get the commodity listing changed to accept this new product. Right now, only Bergenfield crabgrass is eligible. It's safe to say Den-Ken would fight it because it would increase supply and lower prices. We can still try."

Eva pondered the data for a minute. "So what? We don't have to buy it on the exchange. We can go directly to those homes and offer them an option agreement. Although, that didn't work too well for us last time, did it? I'm sure NBCI would process it for us.

"Gentlemen, we tried choking this runaway pricing problem by cutting our demand. Apparently that didn't work. Also, we cannot prevent someone from researching and finding new uses. They probably can't get around our patents, but patents don't scare people much anymore. It takes seven years for the courts to hear the cases.

"So let's increase supply. Make sure there's enough for everyone. First, control the seed market and make it available to anyone who needs it. Steven, work with legal and negotiate a contract with NBCI to buy all of their seed. Give them more money if you have to.

"Next, get Gilbert and Vinnie to help us sign up the homes in Dumont. Let's not make the same mistake. Pay the homeowners a decent price.

"Stephane, tell legal to file a request with the MERC to amend the commodity-listing agreement. We want those 500 properties to become eligible, even if it takes two years and a few lawsuits with Den-Ken.

"I have one last idea. Let's try to increase the yield per home. Let's teach people how to grow more. We won't be able to do it ourselves. The town hates us.

"Albert, find someone in the agriculture community who can help people improve crop yields. I'd look in the state college Ag departments. I'm assuming that people have no idea how to grow weeds after spending a lifetime trying to kill them.

"This is all very perplexing. A dozen companies are buying small amounts to see if they can replicate our formula. That means we're still ahead of the competition. Now someone new is buying a big position. I'd make a big bet that they are a speculator, not an end-user. And if it's not one of the Den-Ken funds, who is it?

"Guys, keep your ears to the ground. Albert and Steven, visit that deli. The place is filled with gossip. Ask Gilbert if he knows anything."

CHAPTER 131

JULY 13, 2012

Averill stared at the abyss within his stock market realm. He faced the unequivocal truth about all micro-cap stocks. They had zero followers in the big brokerage community. Every once in a while, some tiny company would jump a level and become accepted by a Merrill or a Morgan, but most languished unloved in micro hell.

A few buyers scattered throughout the country had nibbled at ROOT's stock. They might be day traders working from home. They could be working at a small office in an isolated town. Perhaps they had decided to take a flyer after they saw ROOT hit the most-actively-traded list or saw it on STCK-TV.

However, none of these investors was going to backstop ROOT. They nibbled and dabbled. They wouldn't take the big bite. Like a remora attached to a shark, they'd enjoy the ride but leave the big chomping to Jaws. None would commit. ROOT needed more investors and brokers who would take the lead and promote it like Averill did.

In a few weeks or a few months, the SEC may or may not bless ROOT's registration statement. If they did, a huge block of shares could sell in the market. It was a potentially bad day for ROOT's stock price. Averill didn't have the firepower to buy seventy million shares hitting the sell button all at once. The Oeno partners, the shareholders who came with the shell, the bridge lenders – everyone could theoretically sell. Not to mention, his employer could dump the two million shares they received as commissions.

Averill realized he may have created part of the problem. He was too good at promoting the stock since its IPO debut. ROOT was now up 70%. People like to take profits when stock prices double. It was the oldest rule on Wall Street. Sell the stock, take your gain, and then play with the house's money.

The reality was simple. It's easier to make a stock price move when there was no "float" for sale. Demand exceeds supply – prices go up! Averill was about to face the corollary. When supply exceeds demand…

Averill went through his penny stock playbook. Johnny had to hire an investor relations firm to tout the stock. Nano cap IR firms were easy to find. The big PR firms wouldn't touch a company like NBCI. And Johnny would have to pay for a crazy-positive research report, too.

Then the management team would have to hawk the stock at the penny stock investor conferences. The next big conference was in October. They'd stand in a booth and call customers over to take a chance. "C'mon, young man. Show your lady friend how strong you are. Just swing that sledgehammer and make the puck ring the bell! You can do it, sonny!"

Averill also concluded he had to do something more immediate and much bigger than IR and investor conferences. Averill needed help from his penny stock brethren.

CHAPTER 132

JULY 13

Averill had five friends. Actually they were merely acquaintances, but they were the closest thing to friends Averill had. They shared a life experience which created an eternal bond. They had been fired together as stock broker trainees at 900 Wall Street, a small brokerage firm. Technically, street numbers only ran as high as 111 Wall Street. That would land 900 Wall Street past the FDR Drive, across the East River, and somewhere around Pineapple Street in Brooklyn, which was where its main offices sat.

Averill, Sticky Jones, McSorley Blain, Mickey Muirfield, Lefty Stonewall and Dicky Duckworth were let go due to unethical trading behavior. They churned accounts, lied to customers, sold to widows and teenagers, and took the phone off the hook after a stock tanked. This group did it all in less than one year on the job.

They split up, and for the next seven years, they moved from firm to firm. They found new clients, promoted a story stock, lost money, and found new clients. It was a tough living. The NASD had seen each of their faces in arbitration more than a few times. Usually, they moved to another firm after their Series 7 license was reinstated. Lifetime bans were a rarity in the securities world.

Averill organized a conference call on FreeConferenceCall.com. After the market had closed for the day, The Sticky Five dialed in. "We all have some piece of crap penny stock we're trying to promote," Averill pointed out. "I have a winner, but this one is legit. The market knows my firm is the buyer of most of the trades, which is hurting my plans. I could buy from discretionary accounts that I control, but they still show up as LMNOP."

"You have clients who trust you with their money? Wait until they find out." joked Lefty.

"Believe it or not, I've hit a winning streak," Averill insisted. "My customers made so much money, they think I'm Albert Freakin' Einstein. But back to my problem. I need to spread the buying around a little, and I'm gonna pay you guys to do it.

"In four weeks, the earnings number is gonna surprise everyone. That gives you a little time to get into the stock cheap. I'll let you know what, when and where. I also wrote up a tout sheet for each of you guys. Send it to your clients.

"If the market reacts, and I'm pretty sure it will, you guys win. If it doesn't, I'll buy the stock in my discretionary accounts and bail you guys out. Either way, you're still ahead."

"We're doing all we can to promote our own worthless stories as it is. Why are we gonna help keep your stock afloat?" McSorley said cynically.

"I told you I was paying you, didn't I?" Averill snapped. "I control a million shares of ROOT. The shares were issued to a fictitious name in the private placement. We just have to transfer them to you.

"I trust you thieves. If you screw me, I'll make you pay for it. I'm telling you, I practically control this company. Management will do anything I say."

Lefty asked, "If you issued the stock in a private placement, it's unregistered. What good is that to me? I can't sell it, and at fifteen cents I can't margin it. What am I supposed to use for money to prop up your garbage?"

Averill ignored the knock and said, "I need all of you to swear to secrecy. I never stamped the shares. There's no restrictive legend. The company just changed transfer agents, and it's total confusion. The new guys have no clue these shares are unregistered.

"The shares are sitting in an account at LMNOP in the name of Rockland IR. My compliance guys are bugging me for the corporate formation docs. One of you has to sign some forms and take over the account. Mickey, do you still have the prepaid credit card you used to cheat on your wife?"

"Yeah, I got it. What do I need to do?" Mickey said apprehensively.

"You're gonna have to set up Rockland IR as a real company in New York State," Averill explained. "Once I prove to my compliance guys the company exists, they'll let you trade the account and take the money.

"Guys, Mickey's taking extra risk, so he gets an extra piece of the pie. Everyone gets 180,000 shares, which is like thirty grand today. Mickey gets an extra hundred thousand shares.

"It'll take Mickey a week to get you the money, and then you'll have three weeks to buy stock. I'll put some pressure on the stock price so you can get starter shares cheap. Are we agreed?"

Everyone mumbled their assent. Averill didn't have to convince them to be dishonest. They were long past that issue. And no one objected to the scheme. However, they all thought the same thing: *I'll buy some of this stock, but there's no way I'm using my own money to back Averill.*

Lefty asked, "And we all get to throw one of our stocks into the mix, right?"

"Yeah, Lefty," Averill growled, "but you better not pump-and-dump me. Let's be fair. When you're about to dump, you warn us first so we all get out before your clients."

"Guys, trust me! ROOT is legit. You'll see."

Lefty laughed. "Sure it is. Fair enough, Avy baby. Our man's gone honest!"

A handful of chuckles could be heard over Averill's speaker phone. He said, "Okay, we're agreed. We need to develop a secret communications network. No office or personal phones. Go buy a prepaid cell phone. No emails from your personal account or your office. They can trace it. Open up a new email on Yahoo or Google and send mail from an Internet café.

"Listen up! I've established four identities on Yahoo! Finance. The names are Tektikker, Greenmasheen, Contrariologist and Biohzrde. When you see Tektikker use the word HUMONGOUS in capital letters, it means something big is about to happen within twenty-four hours.

"Good luck guys, and don't do something stupid and get caught!"

CHAPTER 133

JULY 27, 2012

Averill had just finished posting his daily comments on the Yahoo! Finance ROOT message board. He visited Johnny's offices. "Listen, it's your job to promote your company's stock to the public. It's time to begin your investor relations activity. You need to build a brand."

Johnny said defensively, "Averill, we're really busy 'round here. I don't hafta tell you we're tryin' to get the final permits. We have truckloads of crabgrass arrivin' every hour. I'm huntin' all over to find migrant workers. I don't have time for this. And besides, we already got our money."

"Yeah, but your stock options ain't worth a dime until we get the stock price up," Averill lectured. "Let those Chicago guys run the facility. You need to develop the image of this place. If you don't, you're gonna lose your job!"

"Okay, okay, Averill. I'm just not sure what to do. You gonna hafta help me," Johnny pleaded.

Averill got carte blanche, exactly what he wanted from Johnny. "You let me do the work. I just want you to allocate some money to promote the stock. In a few weeks I'll need twenty grand as a deposit to hire an IR firm. For now, I want to place an 'independent' research article in the Penny Daily News. All the small brokers read it. It'll cost two grand for a full-page ad."

"How can an article be independent research if we're writing it?" Johnny scoffed.

"You ask too many questions," Averill smirked. "This is how things are done when you're a small company. When you're a big company, Wall Street does it for free. When you're tiny, you hafta pay people."

CHAPTER 134

JULY 28, 2012

Averill was about to submit the full-page research report to the *Penny Daily News*. The paper made him admit, in very small type, the article was an advertisement.

Penny-stockbrokers are always searching for the next stock to promote. They aren't necessarily looking for companies with better business prospects. When they discover a company is about to spend money on hyping its stock, antennas go on high alert.

Avy read through his draft.

Seventy percent of the article was about the great returns on CRAB futures and the recent dramatic short squeeze for June deliveries. ROOT was there battling on the front lines.

Pierre Beauty Products was so frequently named a reader might think they were buying a perfume stock.

He wrote about the magical attributes of this miracle plant. He mentioned rumors about beauty product competitors entering the space. Would Big Oil try to buy the technology to keep competitors away?

He described the quality management team with decades of experience. Johnny was identified as a former CEO of an agribusiness supply company. The True Value hardware store was not mentioned as his employer.

The ROOT transfer station and processing plant was described as a state-of-the-art facility that would yield incredible operating efficiencies as production volumes increased. No pictures were shown of the construction in process and the small trailer used for temporary offices.

The report talked about the fully-automated logistics system. It neglected small details such as the dozen coalbins on railcar wheels pushed around the plant by hand.

The report went on at length about the large trained work force. It failed to mention the hundred seasonal workers, some of whom were local soccer moms and retirees who had become bored sitting at home.

Avy wasn't going to let the facts get in the way of prosperity. His job was to tell the dream. To sell the vision.

CHAPTER 135

AUGUST 10, 2012

Averill called The Sticky Five. "Don't use any real names while we're on these phones. Everyone, if you haven't already, get your buy orders in now. In two days, ROOT's issuing its earnings, and it's a really good number."

He hung up without any further discussion.

Averill sat in his brokerage firm offices with the shades drawn and door closed. He logged four iPads onto the Yahoo! Finance ROOT message board using the Wi-Fi signal from the middle school. Message boards are used by investors to ask questions and make comments about stocks. More often than not they were used for silly chatter and bashing other posters.

Averill had established four identities for posting. He needed four different computers and email accounts so Yahoo! Finance wouldn't be able to identify him as a single user. Tektikker, Greenmasheen, Contrariologist and Biohzrde each transmitted from their own iPad.

A month before, Averill had posted under these names on dozens of other message boards. Investors can trace comment threads, so Averill had to leave a trail of legitimate posts in a wide range of companies. He didn't want to be discovered as a shill for ROOT.

He posted positive messages about Qualcomm and GE. He trashed Dell and Hewlett Packard. Tektikker sarcastically posted: "Isn't a Packard an old car from the fifties? They went bankrupt too, you know!"

Finally, with a sufficient cover, his four pseudonyms posted for the first time on the Yahoo! Finance message board for ROOT.

Tektikker: "Root is going to $2! STCK-TV airs a story a week about CRAB. ROOT's gonna be the big winner. Earnings release soon. This is HUMONGOUS!"

Greenmasheen: "My Uncle Tio and I bought in the IPO. I'm up 50% in two months. I bought another 5K today at $.16."

Contrariologist: "Earnings should be big. I rode by the plant. Really busy. Should be a good quarter. I'm long."

Biohzrde, the teenager penny stock investor with a social conscience: "I bought 500 shares with my savings. I heard this bio chemical will replace the harmful carcinogens in our products."

Greenmasheen snorted: "You sound like a kid. Was that your whole allowance?"

Tektikker: "He is a kid. Leave him alone. He's learning. Reminder. Big earnings release tomorrow."

CHAPTER 136

AUGUST 10

NBCI filed its first Form 10-Q with the SEC since its IPO. It simultaneously issued a press release, which said:

> NBCI, or the Company, reported $3.0 million of EBITDA and $.4 million of earnings after taxes in the quarter ended June 30, 2012. Revenues were $5.5 million for the quarter based on the processing of 1.2 million pounds of product from six thousand homes under the CRAB contract. The Company expects to process from over 8,000 homes by June of next year.
>
> Revenue and income were substantially above Wall Street analyst estimates. The June results do not include profits from two thousand CRAB futures contracts which, at August 10, 2012, had an unrealized pretax profit of $3.4 million.

Averill had a small hit on his hands. His idiot friends tried calling to congratulate him on the supposedly-secret, prepaid-cell-phones. He warned them to hold calls for a few days. ROOT's stock price jumped six cents to $0.24 a share after the press release. Finally, Oeno had a reason not to sell so quickly.

CHAPTER 137

AUGUST 15, 2012

Florida has nothing on Bergen County's summer weather. The North Jersey temperature was 98 degrees, the humidity was 90%, and the air moved not a wisp. It felt heavy. Breathing was difficult. It was stifling. You could see the heat rising from the pavement. A few of the town's Asian women sought shelter with decoratively-colored sun umbrellas. Most stayed indoors.

Weed-growing was a new science. People had spent their lives trying to kill the darn things. In June, Auntie Ev and the Nanny Grannies started holding meetings at the Elk's Lodge on West Church Street to learn better ways to grow and sell CRAB plants. Husbands and a few friends joined in, and it quickly developed into a social outing. All included, the CRAB party had maybe a hundred unofficial members.

Today, they were going to learn how to hedge their crop sales. They had watched fast-talking commodity brokers convince everyone in town to sell their production on the exchange. The price went up, and someone else seemed to get a piece of the profit. They couldn't tell if they were getting hornswoggled because they didn't know the rules.

Sean Murray, Pat Gatton's childhood friend from Pawnee, Illinois, volunteered to give a primer about hedging. He and his partner, Jim, farmed wheat and corn for a living. Pat hooked his laptop to the large Samsung television on the wall and dialed into Skype to start the video conference. Sean and Pat were both handsome Irishmen with full heads of white hair in their sixties.

After a few minutes of small-town talk about how friends and family in Springfield and Pawnee were doing, Pat explained the CRAB business.

Sean interjected, "Patrick, I watch STCK-TV at the town diner after the farm reports are off the air. I saw your Easterner zaniness going on. It looks like those media guys are poking a little fun. Don't let them bother you. Anyway, we're not in the habit of telling other people their business, but we can tell you how we do it here.

"Having said that, we NEVER speculate in our farm products. We sell futures against our planned production, but we never bet. Hedging is the opposite of gambling. When you hedge, you take less money today as insurance against a possible price decline. The traders are the speculators. They're willing to buy your future today and take the risk that the price goes down.

"Sometimes, if the future price is good, we might sell some before the season starts. Wheat prices are usually pretty stable except in 2007 and 2008 when those Wall Street types started running the prices up."

Jim poked his head onto the screen. "Well, we made some pretty good money one year, but seed and fuel prices took most of the profits away the next."

"Good point, Jim. You have to cover your variable costs, especially seed, fertilizer and fuel. We use a lot of diesel during harvest. From what I understand, this stuff is a weed, and you don't need to feed it. That makes this pretty easy," Sean affirmed.

Jim piped up, "If I didn't have any incremental costs to grow or harvest or transport, I'd sell a percentage of my futures to lock in prices. But I'd never sell more than I could deliver. We use forty percent as a good number, but in 2007, we sold seventy percent. We didn't get the highest price, but I can tell you, there were a lot of new Ford pickup trucks in Pawnee and Springfield that year."

"The average house produces six-hundred pounds," Patrick said. "Some houses have a little more land, but not much. Let me try to emphasize your rules for everyone to be sure. When, if ever, should we sell seventy percent on the futures market?"

Jim continued, "Thanks, Pat. It's important to highlight this. We sell forty percent or a little bit more in a good pricing year. You never know when there might be too little rain or a natural disaster to ruin your crop. Who knows what bug invades town? Maybe a really cold winter destroys the seeds in the ground.

"You have to ask yourselves some hard questions with a new crop like this. What if they find a better substitute? Maybe a magnolia bush works too. If you sold futures and your crop gets wiped out, you'll get caught in a squeeze by those Chicago traders. They take no prisoners on the Exchange.

"And don't do what they did down in Texas back in the eighties. Oilmen were certain prices were going up. They didn't sell futures. They bought them. Then the price of oil went from $26 to $12 dollars a barrel. They lost fortunes. That's gambling, not hedging. In fact, traders now call it a Texas Hedge."

Auntie Ev spoke up, "Jim and Sean, thanks for your help on this. So, as a general rule, we can safely sell forty percent of our crop assuming we can grow that much with bad weather. But I don't know what bad weather is to this weed. The hotter it gets and the less rain, the better it grows. Back to my question. What if the price goes way up just before contract expiration?"

Jim thought for a minute. "Well, generally I don't want to pay broker costs. But I would also say none of you are big enough to affect the market. And these traders are a lot more sophisticated than any of us. As they say in the farmland: pigs get slaughtered. Make yourself some good money, but don't get too cute.

"But if you've already cut your crop, AND it's safely stored, there's no harm in selling your production before the end of a contract. But safely stored does not mean in the ground. It means in the warehouse."

"Okay, I understand the rules," Auntie Ev nodded to the members at her table. "Don't sell what you don't own. Forty percent sounds like a low-risk hedge, but if we go higher, we should make sure the crop is harvested and stored safely."

"So if we hedge our crabgrass futures, does that make us a hedge fund?"

Sean Murray laughed. "Well, I think a lot of Wall Street hedge funds don't hedge, they just gamble. But 'hedge fund' isn't a legal description. People just use it generically nowadays."

Auntie Ev said, "If it's a term of art, then I don't see why we can't call ourselves a hedge fund. Girls, I propose we change our name from Nanny Grannies to Hedge Fund Grannies. I'm a little tired of being called a nanny, anyway. All in favor, say aye!"

The girls laughed, and a chorus of ayes filled the room and transmitted across Skype to Pawnee, Illinois. Auntie Ev declared, "It's unanimous. We're officially a hedge fund. Thank you for helping us so much. It was wonderful to meet you both."

Auntie Ev led the Hedge Fund Grannies over to The Dangerous Knitter for a morning of strenuous knit and purl. The men left the Elk's lodge and walked down Church Street and pulled up a bench at Cooper's Pond for a morning nap.

The CRAB transfer trucks roared toward the processing plant. Two miles away at what was left of Prospect Park, a line of pickup trucks and cars filled with weeds waited their turn to drop off their precious cargo.

CHAPTER 138

AUGUST 20, 2012

The end of summer was approaching. When the beach crowd realized there were only two weeks until Labor Day, they quickly calculated their remaining vacation time at work. Last year, Hurricane Irene interrupted plans. Not this time!

The temperature was a constant ninety degrees. The ground was baking, which the crabgrass appeared to love. The hairy weed was spreading everywhere. So was the litter. Crabgrass blades formed a beeline to the transfer station.

Kids outfitted with knapsacks patrolled the streets on their bicycles scavenging for fallen weeds. The transfer station would only take deliveries from authorized sellers, so Billie Tucker converted an old lemonade stand and offered to buy loose weeds for $25 a pound. The kids were glad to sell the scraps to the young middleman at the discount price. The money bought a hundred hours of *Halo* online video game time.

Billie's father, William Tucker II, combined the scraps with his own crop and delivered the entire production to NBCI. The Tuckers made an extra thousand during delivery week.

Mayor Alvarez surveyed the area with the head of town maintenance. "Well, at least the children are keeping the streets clean."

Harold replied, "Unfortunately, the dirt is everywhere. These streets will turn brown if it starts raining."

CRAB farmers were finding outlets for their newfound wealth. The housing bubble and stock market crash had put a dent in discretionary spending. For three years, no one had an extra dime. Fear of another stock market crash gripped investors. With some cash to burn, it was time for some fun.

Some paid off credit card balances. Summer wardrobes improved. Even the worst of the farmers managed to sell enough to buy a few toys. New cars began to cruise the main drag.

A caravan of locals had visited the Raritan New Jersey Boat Show back in February. It inspired them to form the Bergenfield Yacht Club, even though the town was landlocked unless you counted Cooper's Pond as a navigable waterway. Why not? The New York Yacht Club wasn't located on the water either! Its members sailed in Newport.

The commodore and his yacht club cabinet used their June CRAB sales to pay the 20% down payment for new Wellcraft and Bayliner cruisers; the rest of the purchase price was financed at 12% interest. Barnegat Bay's Sea Tow service had a banner month rescuing boaters who had run aground. The yachters would have to study the inland water charts a little closer next time.

The more compulsive sort travelled down the parkway to Atlantic City and paid the $1,000 entry fee to a satellite Texas Hold 'Em tournament. They had practiced their skills online and were ready for the big time. Most lost badly in the first round. It was a lot different playing for real money. They moved to the craps tables where they lost even more.

A line formed at the bank to refinance home mortgages. With the added income, housing values had increased. Michael Li was always polite while telling customers no. His bank had no appetite for new mortgages. They considered the CRAB income fleeting. It could end quickly and harshly.

Homeowners shopped around and found bankers willing to lend. A mortgage broker convinced lenders to include the new CRAB income as a verifiable income source. Others obtained new home-equity credit lines.

People were enjoying their new prosperity and spending it freely. That is, everyone except the Hedge Fund Grannies, who sold their product and invested their profits in high-dividend-paying blue-chip stocks.

Not everyone excelled at harvesting. Bergen Development was an absentee farmer on its 35 homes and had no one to grow or cut the crop. Gilbert turned to his partners for a solution. Johnny and Howie were resentful they had to sell to Pierre for only $15 a pound. The rest of the town was selling for five times that amount. Chris and Trudy were sympathetic but didn't know how to contribute. Only Vinnie lent a hand.

"I can't get my guys to do dis work," Vinnie said. "They just ain't built for it. Anyways, I don't think dey make good farmers, ya know what I mean? We need ta find a better solution."

Gilbert and Vinnie drove to the Teaneck Armory and recruited a handful of day workers. Even though the workers made a mess, they managed to salvage enough plants to generate some modest revenue.

CHAPTER 139

AUGUST 24, 2012

Allie was a little mopey sipping on her second cup. The Jets were having a terrible preseason. She claimed that her now renamed store, Allie's Hardware and Home Center, was just having sympathy pains.

"JB, everyone in this town's makin' money 'cept me. Well, it isn't exactly true. I make money and pay it all to Jake's for junk I don't need."

"Crabgrass is all this town seems to talk about," commiserated JB. "The world is upside down when a guy like Averill becomes the center of the universe. He really hit the Crabgrass Lotto. Are you clearing enough to at least pay Jake's in October?"

"They're takin' every last cent I have," Allie said sadly. "The big payment next year is gonna be real tough. If I get lucky, I might have enough to pay half of what I owe 'em."

"A year is a lifetime away," JB said. "Something good is bound to happen. Uh-oh. Don't look at the TV. It's another CRAB news report."

A reporter appeared on Ben's television screens. He held a STCK-TV microphone as he stood in front of NBCI's processing center. Ironically, NBCI had landscaped its headquarters with real sod.

"The CRAB mania is taking over the small town of Bergenfield. The price of the CRAB commodity took a price breather after a very powerful short squeeze in June. At June 30, over 3,000 contracts had not yet settled either regular-way or under EFP, or the Exchange for Product rule. This could have been a disaster for CRAB shorts. The MERC claimed the problem solved itself, but traders in the pits believe Pierre Beauty Products intervened and sold contracts to cool the market.

"Now, here we are in late August, and the price of CRAB resumed its pace to over $70 dollars a pound. Traders are saying there may be hundreds of alternative uses for this miracle crabgrass. It's a natural degreaser. In addition to health and beauty aids, other companies might want to buy. It could substitute for the degreaser in your laundry detergent. Why not your dishwashing detergent? Why not hand soap? Are there any limits to the uses for this new bio-product?"

The host, Jay McCall, commented from the studio, "It's just soap, isn't it? How good can it be? Most people don't care about this as long as the shampoo works. I don't know about this fuel poured onto already speculative fire, but it's happened before. Is this a game changer? Is this disruptive bio-technology?"

Jay turned to his co-host, Betsy Sands. "Betsy, would you pay $50 dollars for a shampoo that's chemical free?"

Betsy laughed and said, "I'm required to shampoo my hair at work, so I guess I'm not a good judge."

"You're kidding me," Jay said, slightly teasing. "You have to shampoo here?"

"The clause is in my contract," Betsy said. "Apparently they value my hair. But I might buy it if I didn't work here. Women pay a small fortune for wrinkle creams and lotions. Why not shampoo? But the all-natural or chemical-free market has always been relatively small. I'm surprised this shampoo is so appealing to the mass market."

"This just isn't fair," Jay said. "I don't have a hair clause in my contract. I pay out of my own pocket. Maybe the station thinks my natural good looks don't require special shampoo. I think it's time to renegotiate!"

Cal Bonita laughed as a picture of Jay sporting a photoshopped mullet appeared on the split screen. The music from *Hair!* played.

Give me a head with hair, long beautiful hair. . .

Jay spoke with a slight wise-guy tone, "Even though I'm a Jersey boy, I never had a mullet. I'll admit my hair was long in college, but NEVER a mullet. I get a businessman's haircut on weekends. Victor Alarcon's been my barber for years. Shout out to the George Ryan Salon in Palm Beach Gardens!"

Cal Bonita quipped, "You go to Palm Beach to get your hair cut? The barbers in New York aren't good enough for you?"

"Not Palm Beach," Jay smirked. "You have to be deceased to live there. My barber is in the Gardens, home to the most upscale mall in America. Every Saturday, I play golf with my buddies at Bear Lakes, have lunch with my wife at The French Corner Bistro, and get a haircut. What's wrong with that plan?

"Enough about my good looks. We reported about a reverse merger stock a few weeks ago which was trying to attach itself to the CRAB story. NBCI, ticker symbol ROOT, went public at ten cents. Today it's still on the radar screen and has more than doubled to twenty-five cents. Is there any sanity in the world this morning?"

CHAPTER 140

AUGUST 27, 2012

Lofton Meriwether, the tall, dark and handsome banker from Mexican Charter Bank, knocked on the town treasurer's office door and peeked in.

Work had become considerably less stressful since the bond offering had been completed in December. Suzanne looked up from her *Wall Street Journal* and said, "Lofton, why are you here? Your client's in the northwest corner of town. Just follow the trail of grass clippings."

Lofton was impeccably dressed in a Paul Stuart handmade suit and a blue-and-white striped, broadcloth-cotton dress shirt with a solid white collar. His initials were embroidered on the French cuffs. The navy pin-dot tie was an intentional understatement. Even in ninety degree heat, he looked cool.

He said, "Actually, I came to see you. We have a proposal for the town, not the transfer station. We can hedge your exposure to the NBCI industrial revenue bonds at a very low cost right now."

Suzanne looked at the business card again. "When did you move to the derivatives trading group? I thought you were in institutional sales."

"Derivatives are where the action is these days," said Lofton taking a seat. "As you can imagine, the profit margins are a lot better than those in fixed income."

"I'm always willing to listen. Plus, things are a little quieter on this side of the Hudson," she said ruefully. Suzanne missed the power and prestige of her Wall Street days.

Lofton sat with his legs crossed and his hands quietly folded. He tugged on the shirt cuffs to make sure they showed. "We appreciate that your mayor is unhappy with the industrial revenue bond. While we believe the investment is a great deal for the people, the town is a guarantor and perhaps not getting a fair return for its risks. Am I right in our perception?"

"Well some would say the deal was a lot better for your bank than it was for anyone here," Suzanne said with a twinge of sarcasm. "You took 600 basis points on a bond which should have paid you no more than two-fifty. But your perception is correct. Are you here to tell me you're going to unwind the bond? That's a laugh."

"No," Lofton said slyly, "we have something better in mind. We created a derivative product with no upfront costs to you. Each unit will provide a credit default swap on $10 million dollars of your bonds. The CDS portion will protect you if the bond gets in trouble and you get called on your guarantee. It costs three hundred basis points today. That equals $300,000 dollars for a $10 million insurance policy. You can buy as many as fifteen units if you commit this week. I don't know what the cost will be next week.

"The interesting part is how to pay for it. The town owns acreage which has the CRAB plant on it. On principal, the mayor refuses to sell the crop. For each unit, we recommend you sell 4,000 pounds of the town's CRAB. This is a legitimate hedge. That's a quarter million to pay for the swaps. We also recommend you short the stock of NBCI. A million shares sold short today would generate another quarter million…"

"Okay, I understand the deal," Suzanne interrupted, "but you're generating $500.000 dollars of proceeds to pay $300,000 dollars for the CDS. Where does the rest go?"

"That's our fee," Lofton fired back. "Before you throw me out the door, please listen. You cannot accomplish this derivative hedge on your own. No insurance company will allow you to buy a credit default swap on your own debt. That's like letting a wife take out a double-indemnity life insurance policy on her cheating husband. You need us to complete this transaction for you."

"First, the obvious question," Suzanne said skeptically. "Are we allowed to buy CDS protection on debt we guaranteed? Second, if we're allowed, how will you hide our identity from the market? And third, assuming we're inclined to do this deal, how much can we buy?"

Lofton's face turned pleasant. "You are allowed to buy a CDS on yourselves, but not many have tried. There was a fellow in West Palm Beach who was near bankruptcy during the real estate collapse. Investors were ganging up on him and buying swaps to make money when he defaulted. He figured it out, bought the swaps on his own mortgages, and made a fortune. It's the only transaction I've heard of.

"I'd say most insurers would avoid this deal. However, you aren't buying a CDS on the town of Bergenfield. You're buying it on NBCI. So there's a subtle difference. You should confirm the legality with your lawyers, but we're certain it passes muster.

"As to your second question, the CDS is being purchased in a special purpose corporation. Your name will not be associated with it. Hounds Tooth Insurers of London is underwriting the deal for a reason. The current CDS for the industrial revenue bond is quoted at only a 150 basis points. They're charging you 300 bips. You can assume they're laying off some of the risk by buying a CDS on the town. They're carving an immediate profit.

"As to your next question, we can do $150 million at this rate. You don't need any more. The bond requires NBCI to keep $50 million in liquid collateral."

"Lofton, I'd take you to lunch, but Nobu Restaurant doesn't have an outlet in town. Leave the presentation with me. I'll give you an answer tomorrow. The timing is tight with Labor Day weekend coming up." Suzanne walked Lofton to the door and thanked him for visiting.

She studied the pitch book. Credit default swaps were at the heart of the collapse of Lehman Brothers and near destruction of the entire worldwide banking system. Financial institutions had bet increasing amounts for and against the financial life of companies, cities, countries and currencies.

Betting on a company's collapse had always been considered illegal gambling. Banks tried increasingly clever ways to hedge their credit risk on corporate loans, but they needed help from Washington to make it legal. In 2000, a senator had inserted a 262-page measure called the Commodity Futures Modernization Act into a $384-billion omnibus spending bill. The United States Congress legalized investing in CDS. It made betting a legal activity for financial investors. The meat of the bill said:

> PREEMPTION. This title shall supersede and preempt the application of any State or local law that prohibits or regulates gaming or the operation of bucket shops (other than antifraud provisions of general applicability) in the case of (1) a hybrid instrument that is predominantly a banking product; or (2) a covered swap agreement.

The legislation opened the barn door. It didn't require an investor in a swap to have a financial interest in the underlying debt. There was no limit on the size of the bet. If you wanted to gamble that Mr. and Mrs. Jones in Peoria, Illinois would default on their $200,000 home mortgage, you could bet a billion dollars on it. All you had to do was identify the mortgage-backed security that held the debt. And Wall Street knew where all of the mortgages were because they had packaged the securities.

If you thought about it, and were really evil, you could bet so much that it provided an incentive to force the borrower to default. Ask Lehman Brothers. The holders of CDS on Lehman Brothers had shorted Lehman's stock and drove it out of business. Or ask AIG insurance. They took a lot of those bets and needed a few hundred billion in federal bailout loans to survive.

Suzanne thought about the proposal. She was a muni-banker, not a derivatives expert. The bad press about CDS was related to the high risk gambles that banks made at the height of the stock market bubble. A few notable default swaps surfaced in the papers long after the collapse of Lehman. But a CDS was a legitimate hedge if the counter-party was a financially sound, substantial company.

Suzanne analyzed the transaction a step deeper. The purchase of CDS was expensive with a 3% risk premium. But can you buy a CDS on your own debt? It sounded suspicious.

Paying for the premium with a hedge on the town's acreage was a legitimate way to finance it. But Mayor Alvarez wasn't going to be happy. Shorting the ROOT stock appeared risky. The stock traded low volume and under 30 cents a share. The broker associated with NBCI was a known sleaze in town who was pumping the stock. She had to talk to Hector.

CHAPTER 141

AUGUST 27

Suzanne hustled upstairs to Hector's corner office at Municipal Hall. The town had finally purchased a working, window air conditioner, and Hector kept the thermostat at a freezing 65 degrees. Suzanne put on her cardigan sweater and tried to explain the CDS offering over the noise from the 5000 BTU Frigidaire.

Hector was unusually savvy about plain vanilla municipal bond financings, but this was different. Hector scratched his chin and said, "We need some help from friends who know Wall Street. I'm sure JB is on the golf course. Bret's at work. Let's track these guys down and ask them what they think. I'll see you tomorrow first thing at Ben's Deli."

The following morning, Suzanne and Hector sat with JB, Bret and Michael. Bret, usually circumspect, said, "The speculation in the CRAB commodity is getting way out of hand. Wall Street would say your VIX shot up in the last three months. I'm sorry, Hector. Let me explain. VIX is the volatility index of the S&P 500. It trades on the NASDAQ. A high VIX indicates high volatility and usually means high risk.

"The big banks wouldn't touch this deal. If it goes sour, the bad press would be expensive to their reputations. Also, Montauk's research analyst believes the chemical-free, beauty products market is more price sensitive than people think. If the price of CRAB continues to rise, Pierre's product will become unaffordable except to the luxury buyer.

"My analyst also believes there are alternatives in the works at several companies. The venture capital firms in Silicon Valley have funded two bio-engineering start-ups. Within five years this CRAB stuff could be obsolete. But my analyst also believes the Pierre product is very real. That means there will be speculative activity until alternatives or a bigger supply source is developed."

Hector said, "If what you're saying is true, then we should definitely protect our town's credit rating with this insurance in three or four years, but not now, right? Also, is it legal?"

Bret said, "The credit default swap is cheap now because you don't need it. Try to buy it in three years, and it may be unaffordable. As to legality, you can buy CDS protection on yourself if you can find a willing seller. AIG wouldn't buy it after what happened in 2008. I already checked on a no-name basis. Some insurers would, including Hounds Tooth. They're really a syndicate of rich individuals who make huge returns on insurance products."

"They know we're the buyer," Suzanne said. "That's why we're paying a premium. We'll never know who has the ultimate risk. But our counter-party is Hounds Tooth. They'll have to pay if this defaults."

JB counselled, "Hector, you've guaranteed a $200 million dollar bond you didn't want. Your town council overrode your objections. If NBCI defaults, Bergenfield is on the hook. The town could go bankrupt.

"I know everyone is excited about CRAB. People are making real money. But the town isn't getting any direct benefit. In fact, all you get are the headaches and costs for a lot of cleanup.

"I wouldn't say this is a boom yet. You never know a boom until after it busts. This definitely shows signs of speculative activity. Den-Ken has two commodity partnerships investing already, and you can be certain they're raising money for a third deal.

"So from a risk management perspective, which is what I often did as a CEO, I'd say you should mitigate your exposure now while the cost is low. You could have personal liability if the town goes Chapter Eleven. I'd also think about increasing your D&O coverage.

"You can always cancel the contract in a year or two if you think the risk has abated. I'd avoid shorting ROOT. It could backfire. Sell your CRAB production from the town properties. I know you object to it, but you may want to get past your principals on this one.

"It's not a moral issue, you know. It's indignant the way the town council treated you. I'd be mad too. But do what's right for the town. Sell the town's production in the market and pay for the hedge. And in the end, if the rest of the town hates you, you have a handful of friends at this table who know you did the right thing."

Hector pondered the advice. "Assuming I agree to get into this horrible business, the revenues wouldn't even be paying for town expenses like weed cleanup. They'd be paying for a hedge for a bond that I don't want. We need that revenue to pay the town's bills. Our tax revenues have gone down and we still have hundreds of houses not paying taxes. I need to close the tax gap."

Michael leaned forward. "I wouldn't worry about collecting those real estate taxes much longer. Investors are scooping up the houses for their CRAB income. Over a hundred houses in default were sold in the last three months. Our bank isn't writing the loans, but a lot of our defaulted mortgages were just paid off."

Ben overheard the conversation and sauntered over to their table. "You know, you guys are friends with someone here at the deli who's an insurance executive. Solomon Brown runs a corporate property and casualty insurance brokerage firm. He's over there having an egg sandwich."

JB called Solomon over and acted very palsy-walsy. "Sol, I don't see you much anymore. You too busy to stop by?"

Solomon laughed and sat down. He was a handsome, athletic black man in his forties. He dressed stylishly with a lavender tie and a tan worsted-wool suit. "JB, your table is always too busy. I need quiet in the morning before I go to the office.

"I don't know what you're talking about. We're usually a nest of church mice," JB kidded. "Anyway, this is on a confidential need-to-know basis. You cannot tell anyone outside our group."

Solomon retorted, "Don't ask me to do anything illegal. That's for the men and women in government."

JB chuckled. "It's not illegal, it definitely isn't government, and if this affects your company, you can warn them off without providing the details."

Solomon nodded. "Okay, hit me."

Suzanne explained the proposal. At the end, Hector asked, "Are we doing anything wrong or illegal?"

Solomon thought for a moment, then replied, "Whoever loses money on this deal is going to charge you with doing something unethical. But it's not illegal. It would be better if there was full disclosure, and you might want to consider that. In fact, if you went to someone like Lloyds of London and offered them a premium over the market, they might take you up on the same offer. . ."

"Actually," Suzanne interrupted, "our investment banker already cut the deal with Hounds Tooth."

Hector thought out loud: "Assuming we do this, and it appears your arguments are convincing me, how much insurance do we buy? Do we buy enough to cover the entire $150 million dollar exposure? We could sell crabgrass from the ball fields, the area around Little League and Memorial Park. There's also the high school football and soccer practice fields. Would it be possible to grow the first two crops and leave the October crop alone so the school kids can have their games?"

Suzanne said, "I can suggest two things. First, I'll go back to the banker and get them to cut their fees. This is over-the-top greedy. Second, if we're still short, you could sell next year's futures to help pay for this year's premium."

Hector winced, "It sounds like we're getting into even riskier territory. But, if we get through a few years, this may calm down and turn into a stable business. I think it's a good idea. But we're staying away from shorting ROOT. Those guys scare me.

"And buying all $150 million of protection seems like overkill. I've been told most bonds in default pay nearly fifty percent. Let's keep it to $120 million of coverage. I can justify that amount.

"Okay, we're going to do this." Hector rose from his seat and shook Solomon's hand.

"Hold on a second, Hector. You need to get legal counsel to okay this," Bret cautioned. "The last thing you want is personal liability for doing something the town charter doesn't allow. And don't use Howie. Ask your outside counsel."

The mayor returned to his offices and called Jonathon Prescott, his outside counsel in the Hackensack offices of McQueen and McQueen to discuss the plan. The deal was a go after Suzanne got Lofton to cut his fee. The Little League fields were saved from crabgrass invasion.

CHAPTER 142

AUGUST 28, 2012

ROOT filed a final amendment to its registration statement. To paraphrase the SEC, who wrote in long uninterpretable legalese, "Okay, you can sell now. But first add a risk factor to your prospectus that says if you all sell at once, your stock is going to zero." The SEC hated reverse mergers, but it couldn't really stop them.

When ROOT had gone public, Oeno's partners had to file a bunch of forms with the SEC showing their percentage ownership. Now that the shares had been registered with the SEC, any of the Oeno partners could sell. And they did… but to whom? The computer screen for the OTC Bulletin Board reported twenty separate crosses of two million shares each. ROOT was once again the daily volume leader.

Four hours after the registration statement went effective, twenty Oeno partners filed Form 4s and 13Ds with the SEC showing they had disposed of or otherwise gifted their shares and no longer had any interest, pecuniary or otherwise, in the NBCI shares.

Averill scratched his head. What the hell just happened? He was certain Oeno was going to sell and put pressure on the market. Then they disappeared from view. Forty million shares had just moved into the account of Depository Trust where all shares in "street name" were held. Oeno had gone underground.

The good news was that the sales had not affected the stock price. The high volume attracted a lot of attention, and ROOT continued its move upward. It was hovering around the price of a nice shiny quarter.

CHAPTER 143

AUGUST 28

The harvest was good, but could have been even better. The new CRAB farmers tried a variety of techniques to improve production. Had they left the crop alone, they might have grown more. Nevertheless, CRAB prices continued to move higher. Nothing seemed to dampen this story.

The cook at Ben's convinced NBCI to hire some of his Central American compadres to work at the plant. In their first week on the job, they discovered water leaking out the tailgates of some of the delivery trucks. A few creative sellers had been soaking their crops just before delivery to increase the weight. Some people seemed to have an endless imagination of ways to beat the system.

The more affluent residents began to cave in. They hadn't been seduced at $15 a pound. At $75 a pound, we're talking about a lot of money. The extra income would partially make up for the annual executive bonus no one would get this year. The wealthier families left their front yards well-manicured and worthy of a nicer home. But the backyards had been converted to CRAB farms. They hired O'Hara Landscaping to manage the crop.

Online media poked fun at the new industry. Agribusiness had been comically renamed Crabi-business. It parodied the mayor with a caricature of him wearing farmer overalls and a straw hat and holding a pitchfork over a clump of crabgrass. It was titled "Bergenfield Gothic!"

Bergen Community College added something new to its accomplished faculty, cutting-edge facilities and opportunities for cultural awareness, civic engagement and service-learning. It offered a MOOC, a Massive Open Online Course, to teach students how to grow and sell CRAB.

Students earned three credits for the night course. The syllabus featured agriculture experts who taught how to tend crops, fertilize, use precise watering systems, and create direct sunlight. The experts included professors from Purdue University, a former director from the United States Department of Agriculture, and commodity trading experts from MERC.

However, Auntie Ev stole the show. She gave the inside scoop about how to improve CRAB yields and how to hedge your crop sales. Auntie Ev warned, "Whatever you do, don't water the good grass. And don't fertilize it either. It'll only encourage it. And don't hedge more than you can deliver!"

Auntie Ev earned a nice framed certificate for speaking. Her advice was worth a million bucks.

CHAPTER 144

AUGUST 31, 2012

Who the heck chose the end of August for CRAB deliveries? It was too close to Labor Day weekend when the shore commanded the presence of all Jersey citizens.

It was hot and humid and the transfer station started to smell. There wasn't enough time to dry and bale all of the crabgrass to prevent it from composting. Tom McInerney would have to find a better way to run the plant.

The shipping dock was a bottleneck. The line of vehicles to the receiving dock stretched the length of Harrington Street to River Edge Road. Fifty-pound lawn and leaf bags were the primary method of handling the crabgrass. People had to wait until their delivery was inspected and approved. It took a good deal of time.

Most of the town didn't notice, but anyone living within two hundred yards of the transfer station got a good whiff at three in the afternoon. Neighbors complained to the mayor.

The road into the facility had developed a deep rut from the constant truck traffic. Neighbors complained to the mayor.

CRAB clippings and dirt littered the streets. And neighbors complained to the mayor.

Gilbert had his own problems. He called another partner's meeting to discuss how to harvest Bergen Development's CRAB crop. This time, Johnny and Howie attended rather than face the wrath of Vinnie.

Gilbert opened, "You all know we're counting on CRAB income to pay the mortgages. Our working capital is running low because we're not selling as much as we expected. We hired some locals to cut the crabgrass, but they're leaving half the stuff on the ground. The good news is Vinnie visited the tenants, so I don't think they're gonna be stealing anymore."

Chris kidded, "Yeah, but are they gonna be stealin' any less?"

"Stop the jokes, man!" Howie whined. "Gilbert, you brought me in for legal work. I did my job. Whadaya expect me to do – go clip weeds on the weekend?"

Gilbert held up his hand. "Easy, Howie! I'm not asking you to do anything except give me your approval. O'Hara Landscaping gave us a proposal to manage our mess. This is delicate, because they don't know we're behind the investment. Our Miami lawyer is acting as our go-between.

"Anyway, O'Hara can't make money cutting lawns anymore, so they went into the CRAB maintenance business. They're not cheap. They want $250 dollars a house to cut and deliver each crop. The good news is they'll monitor the homes so no one can clip us. Ha-ha! It'll cost us $25,000 a year for thirty-five houses. I guess we can afford it. If the homes start producing like they're supposed to, we'll clear over a quarter million a year which will cover the mortgages and taxes."

"Gilbert, this is a no-brainer. I recommend we approve hirin' O'Hara," said Trudy.

The vote would have been unanimous if anyone had bothered to count hands before they ran out the door. Never call a partner's meeting the Friday afternoon before Labor Day weekend.

CHAPTER 145

SEPTEMBER 4, 2012

Averill was angry. Or maybe he was jealous. Or perhaps he was experiencing uncontrollable greed. Whichever? His prefrontal cortex was in full gear grappling with the issue on this Tuesday after Labor Day.

He watched CRAB's price soar as his ROOT stock price was left in the dust. CRAB was $15 last year when Pierre first started generously giving contracts to the lucky thousand homeowners. The price on the MERC exchange had since quintupled.

Meanwhile, NBCI's stock price, the company which Averill declared critical to the future of this miracle crabgrass, was a mere 28 cents a share. ROOT had generated record earnings for the June quarter, yet its stock price still languished behind the CRAB gains. Granted, there were no prior records to compare, and it was the first quarter ROOT had ever reported anything, but it was a record nonetheless.

Averill ignored the arithmetic that his stock had nearly tripled. What he wanted was $30 dollars, not 30 cents. It wasn't that he hadn't made money. Averill had made more money in the last twelve months than he had made in the prior seven years combined. He just wanted more. He wanted to be a multimillionaire. He wanted to be Upper Saddle River or Far Hills rich, the closest thing New Jersey had to Southampton rich.

His customers were excited about their newfound prosperity. His penny stock buddies were ready to carry him on a litter. They wanted to build him a monument. They were originally skeptical, but Avy had delivered. A double was a double, no matter in what league you play. Their clients made money, too, but who was asking?

The Motley Fool emailed an article to subscribers warning about speculative fever. It used NBCI as an example of an overbought penny stock. They badly tarnished ROOT's good name.

All news was good news to Avy. He looked up "hello in Chinese" on Google Translate and called his customer. "Nǐ hǎo, Mrs. Chan. You know, Motley Fool talked about our stock today. Stocks usually go up after a positive mention in Motley. Are you sure you don't want another ten thousand shares? At today's price, it's only $2,800 dollars."

After his morning client calls, Averill visited the NBCI offices. Johnny was wearing the same farmer bib overalls he had often worn at the hardware store.

Averill greeted him derisively. "You better not be wearing that hick outfit if the reporters show up here. The stock price'll go back down to ten cents."

Johnny snarled, "I'm not gonna wear a suit in this barn!"

Averill said in exasperation, "Okay, Johnny. But can't you wear some Dockers khakis or something? At least it'll look nicer." He then said resignedly, "Forget it. I'm not here to give fashion lessons. I hear that all day long from Misty. Right now, we need to work the stock price. It's time to begin a public relations campaign. NBCI should hire an investor relations firm to manage its image. They'll develop a brand for the stock. This'll cost about $50,000 a year, but it's well worth it.

"Also, there's a green-tech conference in Vegas in a few weeks. We can get invited, but the fee is $5,000 dollars. A nice booth with good signage will cost another $2,000. And we have to prepare marketing handouts."

Johnny moaned. "Where am I gonna get the time and money to do this? Can't you see we're runnin' a business here?"

"Ask Roland to approve it," said Averill. "With his board stock options in the black, he has to be pretty happy. Tell him you're working on the company image and he might even give you a raise. Boards will approve anything to make the stock price rise."

Johnny recoiled at the math. "That's $60,000 a year just to get started. How many more conferences? This could be a lot of money."

Averill glared at Johnny and talked down to him. "You're out of your league here. I'm trying to be diplomatic, but this company needs to promote itself. I'm doing all of the work around here. You'd still be ten cents a share if it weren't for me. No one knows you exist. Do you want to be a tiny penny stock forever? Do yourself a favor, and listen up!"

Johnny offered no further protest. As he thought about it, Averill had raised the money, so he should know best. Johnny walked down the hall and asked Justin to cut the check for the conference.

When he returned, Averill asked, "How much of the August contract did Pierre buy?"

"Pierre? Only 8,000. You see those big trucks outside loadin' bales of CRAB? They ain't Pierre's. They're deliverin' to some silo in Pennsylvania. Some company named Buckstown Financial. I also got fifteen other truckers scheduled to pick up this week."

Averill looked shocked. "What? When were you planning to tell me this? How much is Buckstown taking?"

Johnny had been clueless about the importance of these buyers. He tried acting nonchalant. "Buckstown bought 2,000 contracts – 200,000 pounds. A coupla beauty product companies bought a few hundred each. The rest of the crop was divided equally. Buncha oil companies. Some Delaware chemical companies. I got the cargo manifests here." Johnny indicated his desk's top drawer. "I thought you knew. By the looks of it, I'd guess Buckstown's gonna buy a lot more. It's a big silo. Enough for a million pounds, I'd say. And someone else paid us to store a thousand contracts till next June."

Averill hopped around the office in excitement. "Johnny, these are the buyers everyone's trying to identify. Someone's been outbidding Pierre this summer. I gotta find out who these guys are.

"Listen, we need to buy more futures before this gets out. This is huge. CRAB is going to a hundred."

"I can't free up no more money," Johnny said in a pouty voice. "Justin'll never okay the transfer. He'll make me ask for board approval. Don't we still have money in the brokerage account?"

Averill quickly calculated. "You have enough cash and plenty of equity if we sell the October contracts and buy contracts expiring next year. They're twenty percent cheaper.

"After we get our orders in, we have to feed this Buckstown information to Den-Ken, unless they already know. Let me run. I got work to do!"

Johnny looked surprised. "Isn't tellin' Den-Ken insider trading? Are you allowed to do any of this?"

"Insider trading is only for stocks, Johnny. There's no law against insider trading in commodities." Averill spoke with the apparent authority of an attorney, which he wasn't.

CHAPTER 146

SEPTEMBER 4

Averill sped back to his office after the meeting with Johnny and went to work. Over the next three days, he carefully sold NBCI's October delivery contracts. The market was very active, and he managed to sell on an uptick. Traders in the pits weren't focusing on the 2013 deliveries. Trading the short-term contract expiring in October was where you made the most money.

Once Averill had liquidated ROOT's 2012 position, he bought 2013 contracts like a madman. Traders in the virtual pits looked surprised as 6,000 contracts were bought in one day at an average price of $60. NBCI was now the proud owner of $36 million of ROOT futures contracts bought with cash of $9 million and margin debt of $27 million.

He called The Sticky Five on their prepaid cellphones and told them about the Buckstown purchases. Averill yelled, "Listen, you idiots. If you want to make fast money, buy the futures. If you can't trade futures, at least buy the stock. You've got forty-eight hours. Then I'm taking a leak, or leaving one. HA! HA! HA!"

Tipping off Chicago about Buckstown was easy. Averill called his favorite grapevine leader. "Arturo. Como esta? I need you to do me a big favor. Call your broker over at Den-Ken. Ask him who this new buyer of CRAB is. Tell him you heard trucks loaded with bales of CRAB were headed to silos in Bucks County. They'll figure it out.

"And ask Pedro and the guys to make the same call. It's gonna help your CRAB price and your ROOT stock. Bueno suerte!"

CRAB hit $90 within a week. ROOT moved barely a penny to $0.29.

CHAPTER 147

SEPTEMBER 12, 2012

Two weeks earlier, Panama Blonde had received a surprise phone call at work and tried to keep it a secret from her friends. The person sounded like her missing husband. At first, she assumed it was a macabre prank call. But soon she realized Ned Mulcahy was alive, and she became excited. As the story unfolded, she preferred he were dead.

Ned pleaded for Catherine's forgiveness. And for plane fare. He was stuck in Orange County airport and had no money. Catherine hung up the phone mid-sentence. She had just spent five years of her life in anguish over her "deceased" husband while he was partying with teenage girls in French Polynesia. And he had faked his own death. Who was this man? She called a divorce lawyer.

Now, the press had picked up the story from a reporter who was friends with a highly-amused Customs Agent. Catherine was mortified. Ned had fallen astray. Four years ago, he anchored his sailboat in Cook's Bay on the Island of Moorea near Tahiti. He had only planned on staying a week. He stayed longer. He decided a sailboat in the South Pacific loaded with cases of rum would be a relaxing way to spend an eternity. It was time to enjoy the tropical life.

Ned had befriended another sailor anchored in Moorea who was cruising solo around the world. Ned gave the sailor his Emergency Position Indicator Radio Beacon and a case of rum. In exchange, the sailor agreed to drop it in the ocean on his leg around South America.

The EPIRB beacon sent a signal to the Chilean Coast Guard for a brief time as it sank in a thousand feet of water. The records showed Ned's boat had disappeared near known pirate waters.

After Ned had run out of money and rum, he tried to sail home, but encountered terrible storms. He jerry-rigged his main sail to keep moving until he found his way to Long Beach, California. Exhausted and emaciated, Ned tied up next to the Pacific Princess. Of all places, Mr. Mid Life Crisis had docked alongside the *Love Boat*.

Ned had lost his passport and wallet long ago. Who would need such extravagances in Moorea? It took two days for U. S. Customs to verify his story. They finally allowed him to call his wife to vouch for him. After she hung up, they finally believed him. Who could make up such a story?

Ned Mulcahy borrowed airfare from a friend in Los Angeles, but the ATF wouldn't let him board without a valid ID. He hitchhiked across the United States on Class Eight Freightliners and Mack Trucks until he reached Bergenfield two weeks later.

Panama let the ultra-tan playboy stay on the couch, but gave him one week to find a new place. Newspapers loved the story and tracked him down. The paparazzi parked outside Catherine's house hoping to get a picture of the famous sailor and his enduring wife.

A picture of Ned with six women, some bikini-clad, some topless, partying on his boat surfaced on the web. Ned was tan, blond, bearded, and muscularly thin. He was a small-town hero to many, but not to Catherine. She threw him out of the house after the neighbors complained about the media attention. The TMZ web site paid a thousand dollars for the video of Catherine tossing Ned's suitcase on the lawn.

Dr. Phil offered Catherine and Ned $5,000 to appear on an episode about husbands who disappeared and later returned home. Catherine declined the offer. Ned appeared on the TV screen alone and tearfully begged for her forgiveness. She didn't watch the show.

The laws in New Jersey required an eighteen-month waiting period before the divorce would be granted. Her lawyer filed for an exemption, which the judge allowed under the circumstances.

After weeks of media attention, Panama sat with JB, Allie, and the rest of the gang at Ben's Deli. She was telling the tale when Misty strutted by.

Misty looked directly at Panama and laughed. "I told you he left you for a hotter babe."

CHAPTER 148

SEPTEMBER 17, 2012

Misty sat with Averill at Ben's oblivious to the CRAB and ROOT mania reported on STCK-TV. All she knew was that Averill was making some big bucks, and her lifestyle was growing to accompany it.

Misty's hair and makeup were perfect as always. Lacquer kept the curls in place. The eyelashes received a heavy dollop of mascara. Today she wore a Mrs. Robinson leopard-pattern silk blouse and skin-tight black stretch capris pants. Misty certainly had the body to wear the outfit, but she did remind one of a 37-year-old divorcee still looking for Mr. Right.

Misty had wasted no time mourning the loss of Bret. She'd given herself one year tops to get remarried. Averill was a sure thing. He had no prospects and no one wanted him. Misty always kept one eye on the lookout for another suitor, but time might be running out.

Misty stood up and hovered over Averill like a turkey vulture eyeballing road kill. She stamped her feet and stabbed her finger into Averill's chest. Averill was cowering in fear of the 100 lb. New Jersey Devil.

Misty went to leave, but turned and yelled down at Averill, "It better be delivered tomorrow, or you can spend Thanksgiving by yourself!"

Misty flew out of Ben's but failed to slam the door. Ben had installed a new air brake over the weekend.

JB and Gavin shook their heads. JB said, "You know, there's not one redeeming quality about the kid, but you have to feel sorry. She's terrorizing him."

Gavin replied, "It's cause and effect, like karma. These two were destined for each other like no couple on earth."

CHAPTER 149

SEPTEMBER 18, 2012

Misty arrived at Ben's early and gave her best high school cheerleader entrance. She was gleefully obnoxious to Miguel as she paid for breakfast. *Rah! Rah! Sis-boom-bah!*

She looked dressed for a car rally. Misty wore a hot-pink designer tee shirt, black culottes, leather motorcycle riding boots, and a black leather jacket with huge epaulets. She finished off the ensemble with a white silk scarf trailing behind her. Snoopy was still hunting the Red Baron!

Her outfit mesmerized the table. Gavin asked, "Where does she buy this stuff? They can't be selling it at Macy's."

Decker grinned. "Maybe she's racing at Daytona this weekend."

JB chimed in, "My first thought when I saw the shoulder pads was *Wizard of Oz.* You know, the wicked witch's winkie castle guards. Try to say that three times fast!"

At that moment, a brand-new red BMW 525 IS pulled up in front of Ben's and parked illegally in the bus stop. The horn honked obnoxiously loud and long. The car hood was wrapped with a big silly red bow. It reminded one of the holiday TV commercial which said subliminally, *You're a real jerk if you can't afford to buy your wife a $60,000 car for Christmas!*

Averill jumped from the front seat and burst into Ben's as giddy as a teenager. He leaped across the room to Misty's table.

She innocently shrieked, "Oh Avy, I can't believe it. You bought me a BMW. Look everyone, Avy bought me a Beemer!"

Ben shook his head in amazement and flipped the juke box switch, playing *We Gotta Get Out of This Place* by The Animals.

Misty walked outside to show off her present. The Ben's crowd ignored her. Misty jumped in to take a test spin.

Shelly Greenberg was slowly walking her elderly mother across the street. Misty leaned on the horn for a full ten seconds, then sped around the startled grandmother. Misty cut into the opposing lane forcing oncoming cars to swerve. If you thought Misty was a terror before, she was going to be something else in this German ultimate driving machine.

CHAPTER 150

SEPTEMBER 25, 2012

Averill worked on the investor presentation with Alistair McClendon, who was a 28-year old, Little Ivy League English lit major. He was good looking, could write well, and had a great British accent. He also did all of the hard work at the investor relations firm while the 60-year-old owner sat around and blew smoke at everyone.

After a week working together, Avy convinced Johnny to hire Alistair full-time for $55,000 a year; then they fired the blowhard and his IR firm.

Alistair would have to present at the investor conference. There was no way that Farmer Johnny was getting on stage to represent NBCI. The same could be said for Tom and the rest of the management team. They were smart, but didn't have Wall Street savvy.

Averill handed Alistair his "research report" published in the *Penny Daily News*. He insisted, "This is what we should present in slide format. We want to catch the tailwind of this CRAB price boom. There's no reason why we shouldn't be going up just as fast."

On slide one, Averill wrote some gibberish about corporate strategy which he plagiarized from the annual report of a commodity trading giant.

On slide two, he dispensed with any unnecessary words. Pictures and graphs are what investors wanted to see. He inserted a picture of the new plant with its green lawn.

On slide three, he inserted a graph showing the trajectory of the CRAB futures if it kept growing at the same rate for five years. The arrow increased at a 45 degree angle toward the magical $1,000 target. It was only a matter of time.

Below was another arrow for the stock price of ROOT. In a cloud insert, he wrote, "ROOT Stock $10???" It was up to Alistair to convince the audience that ROOT was undervalued by 95% compared to the increase in CRAB.

Slide four showed the price movement for CRAB during the recent dramatic short squeeze for June deliveries and the more recent jump when Buckstown began buying. Again, ROOT was there battling on the front lines.

Slide five was the five-year stock price chart for Pierre Beauty Products.

Slide six showed pictures of several shampoos, Palmolive dishwashing soap, Tide laundry detergent, and Purell hand cleaner. The cloud asked, "How many more uses could this miracle plant have?"

Slide seven discussed the quality management team with decades of experience. No pictures were shown.

After they finished the slide presentation, Alistair asked Averill, "Shouldn't we send this to your SEC counsel for review? It was standard practice at our firm."

Averill sneered at him. "Are you kidding? If you send this to a butcher attorney, there won't be a slide left. This is close enough."

CHAPTER 151

OCTOBER 4, 2012

There were additional beneficiaries to the recent jump in CRAB prices. Downtown Bergenfield, whatever was left of it, was bustling again. The restaurants were full. Ben's was packed until closing. Local television and online media were looking for news scoops. How was the crop growing? Who was selling? Who was buying? What did Auntie Ev have to say?

The no-tell motel on Route 4 in Hackensack began renting by the day. No more hourly rates. They applied a coat of paint, purchased new mattresses and added outdoor window shutters to give it a quaint colonial look. It appeared near respectable. If the walls could talk!

The Star Ledger investigated the Buckstown Financial investment rumor. The crack investigative team discovered that Buckstown was owned by Intergalactic Bank. The behemoth, multinational investment and commercial bank someday would have ATMs on other planets. When Congress made it legal to bet on credit default swaps, they also dismantled the laws that kept commercial bankers separate from Wall Street. Now banks could invest your savings and checking accounts in risky, unregulated markets like silos full of crabgrass.

The reporter speculated that antitrust bad behavior was behind their moves. Intergalactic had recently gained control of the molybdenum and lithium metals markets by buying storage facilities and amassing huge positions in the metals. Were they doing it again with CRAB? The article asked – what else might they do? Will they buy NBCI?

The Hedge Fund Grannies and friends met at the Elk's Lodge to plan their CRAB-selling strategy. The early autumn weather was particularly nice. The evenings were cool, and the midday temperatures settled around 70 degrees.

Mrs. Hadley, the retired grade school principal, gave a presentation about weather patterns. October was usually tame. The precipitation was average. There was just the one exception – really bad flooding from Hurricane Floyd in 2005.

Auntie Ev walked to the window, symbolically stuck a wet thumb outside, and declared, "Girls, it's time to sell! Our crabgrass is already nice and bushy. It's not going to grow much more. Remember, big piggies get slaughtered! All in favor of selling for a tidy $100 a pound, say aye!" A chorus of voices sounded their approval. Ev announced, "The ayes have it!"

After the meeting, the core group began the trek to The Dangerous Knitter. When they reached the corner of Palisades Avenue, a WPIX Channel 11 news reporter and her cameraman burst from Ben's Deli and ran toward the ladies. Roseanna Danica-Danner, the easily recognizable six o'clock news anchorwoman, waved the microphone in front of Auntie Ev's nose.

"Auntie Ev, can you tell us your forecast for October?" Roseanna asked with feigned urgency.

Either it was a really slow news day, or any sound bite from the charming Ev was precious. Auntie Ev didn't shy from the camera. Her closest friends knew she had been a very successful businesswoman in retail management and was accustomed to media promotions.

She looked over her glasses and said, "I remember you from when you covered the evening course at Bergen Community. You know my answer already if you paid attention. I don't predict the weather, now do I? And I certainly don't have a bunion to help me.

"However, if you're asking the best time to cut your crop, the answer is now – this week. Why should you wait until the last minute and take the risk of inclement weather or some other bad thing to occur? Tsk-tsk!"

The ladies crowded behind Ev and bobbed their heads. They mugged for the camera as huggable grandmas. Roseanna was interviewing someone who was fast becoming a local celebrity.

"Auntie Ev, what do you think about Buckstown Financial trying to corner the market in crabgrass? Do you think this will be good for the CRAB market?"

Auntie Ev took a few seconds to compose a measured response. "What Buckstown does with their money is really no business of mine. However, I understand they are speculators, and speculation only benefits short-term traders. They wreak havoc on long-term stable markets.

"I'm still angry about Wall Street's misbehavior in 2008. Traders ran up oil prices and made us pay more for gasoline. They made wheat prices rise, and now we pay more for bread. Wall Street financed gambling in real estate and ruined the housing market.

"They affected the lives of everyone who lives in our nice town. Now, maybe we're benefitting today, but for every beneficiary, someone else is paying the price.

"So from my perspective, and the view of our little group, we'll sell our crops early and put the money in the bank. Someday, when things turn for the worse, we want to be sure that we're not exposed."

Roseanna had enough footage, but a group of 20 women pushed onto the scene and muscled their way to the camera. They were all similarly dressed – gray hair in buns, flowered long dresses, long pocketbooks on their arms, and glasses. All wore granny glasses. They looked remarkably young for the elderly.

The leader spoke in a nasally, granny falsetto. "I just wanna say old Auntie Ev is just a big know-it-all. She's no weather forecaster. She's no professional farmer, either. Auntie Ev is a big media hog. All she wants is to be on TV and be famous. Well, let me tell you sonny, Auntie Ev isn't the nice lady y'all think she is.

"We're the real grannies in Bergenfield. We've formed our own group, and we put a web site up so y'all can hear us. The site is Anti-Grannies.com. That's A-N-T-I, not A-U-N-T-I-E!"

Auntie Ev and the gals left the scene laughing. Ev said, "Who was that back there? I swear I've heard that voice before? Probably some college kids from Fairleigh Dickinson."

"Nevermind!" quipped Joan Fogarty doing her best Gilda Radner impersonation.

Roseanna had some great videotape. She saw through the costumes and the makeup and concluded she had just witnessed either a small flash-mob or smart-mob. Whatever their purpose, they would make the six o'clock news.

CHAPTER 152

OCTOBER 5, 2012

Bret joined the breakfast table for the first time in months. He was always exhausted from long hours at work. "I'm in full Misty-avoidance mode. If you see her, give me a signal!"

While JB was getting a refill, Bret said, "Allie, I'd like to make a deal with you. You owe Jake's some big money next year. If you didn't have to pay those guys, your business would be doing pretty well from what I can tell.

"Me, I want to leave Wall Street. I've had enough of the grind. I have a lot of savings. If you want, I'll invest in your business with enough money to make your next Jake's payment. You make me a financial partner. I don't want a job. I'll find a general counsel job somewhere. I can help out on weekends but only if you need me. I definitely won't interfere in management."

Allie said kindly, "Bret, my situation is worse than I'd wish on an enemy. I owe $300,000 next October and then two more payments of $135,000 dollars. The only way to fix it is to sell weed killer, which may never happen. I may even have to dump the stuff so I don't have to pay for storage.

"It's more, Bret. Even if I didn't have the Jake's situation, I'd make a decent living, but not enough to pay an investor a return on his money. Also, I really want to make it on my own. This store requires me to work the hours to make money. Please don't be offended."

As JB sat, Allie looked up and saw Misty walking into Ben's Deli wearing a smile from ear to ear. She was about to sit behind the deli partition in accordance with their armistice, but Ben called her over to the register.

"Your punishment's over," Ben announced. "You can come to the register when I'm here. But no more shenanigans, you understand?"

Misty smiled as sincerely as she could. "Thank you, Ben. It's hard living in exile. I'll be a good girl. I promise."

Misty sat with her breakfast no less than five feet from Bret. She was either taunting or teasing him. Either way, he wanted none of it.

JB leaned toward her. "What's up now, Misty? Or should I be afraid to ask?"

Misty gave a mischievous look. "Oh nothing much, JB honey. Avy just bought us a house down the shore. It's one block from the ocean in Ortley Beach. Next year we're going to trade up to waterfront property, but this'll do for now."

"Are you sure your boyfriend can afford it with the new car and all?" JB said wryly. "You know, he was broke a few months ago?"

Misty gave a huge, arrogant, beaming smile. "We're doing just fine. FYI…Avy's the senior investment banker for a public company. He's just a genius at these stock market things.

"Well, I gotta go. Can't get another parking ticket. Nice seeing you, JB. And don't be so shy, Bret. I won't bite you."

Bret cringed as Misty wiggled away and everyone laughed. Ben left the register and sat down at the board table. "JB, I hope there's no afterlife. I want this to be the end."

JB laughed. "Why is that, Ben? Don't you want a final resting place?"

Ben sighed. "Can you imagine spending the rest of eternity in heaven with that character? Or is that what hell is, living with Misty and that stockbroker?"

Michael Li spoke solemnly, "Perhaps she shall occupy the basement apartment of your afterlife. She shows no respect for her elders. She shows no respect for anyone."

Everyone smiled at Michael's wisdom.

Bret stood to leave. "The good news is they'll be spending more time at the shore. We won't have to put up with that phony puss of hers during the summer at least."

CHAPTER 153

OCTOBER 5

Averill sat in the middle school parking lot and opened his four iPads using the school Wi-Fi. The administrator changed the password regularly. Last week was PhysEd. Today's secret word was French.

He logged into the Yahoo! Finance ROOT message board and began posting.

Tektikker: "This stock is going to $20! Have you seen the technical charts for CRAB? Big winner."

Greenmasheen: "I loaded up on 20,000 shares today at $.30. Buckstown deal is big."

Contrariologist: "Pierre Beauty Products can't get enough of the CRAB stuff. ROOT's fortunes are going to be fantastic."

Biohzrde: "I hope they thought through the environmental impact of all of this dirt everywhere. I hope this isn't toxic."

Greenmasheen: "There you go. Another liberal teenager protecting us from the evils of Corporate America. Go buy a windmill!"

Biohzrde: "No, I like the stock. I own 1,000 shares now. I just want to make sure they are socially responsible."

Greenmasheen: "Kid, you spent $300. How many school lunches did that cost you?"

CHAPTER 154

OCTOBER 8, 2012

Roseanna Danica-Danner interviewed Tom McInerney on NBCI's receiving dock for Channel 11 News. There wasn't much of a story. His team had managed to reduce the chaos at NBCI down to an orderly state of confusion. Allowing early deliveries had reduced the bottleneck at the delivery dock. This interview was not worthy of nightly news.

The cameraman took b-roll video of the plant area for the archives, then they headed back to Ben's. That was where most of the action was. That was where the pastries were.

The news crew sat at a small table next to a group of eight middle-aged men who were having an animated conversation. Everyone at the table wore a different color plaid shirt. It looked like a lumberjack convention. The ringleader of the table had dark piercing eyes and jet black hair forming a widow's peak in the front.

He stabbed a piece of breakfast sausage and leaned over to Roseanna. "Hello, Miss News Lady. I'm Vladimir. All of us here seen your six o'clock news. Those ain't girls in them outfits. And they ain't from town."

The reporter smiled and continued sipping her coffee. She said with a wide smile, "Of course they weren't women. However, they were news. Ratings, ratings!"

Not to be dismissed, Vlad swallowed his forkful and said, "And the Grannies ain't the only people 'round here who know how to make a livin' sellin' crabgrass. I got a whole table here of guys who know better."

The town was split 70-30. Most had adopted the cut-and-deliver-early strategy. The remaining risk takers were holding out. The price was creeping up a dollar or two every day. Selling early left money on the table. Every day delayed meant another day of growth in the unusually warm fall weather. It looked like October was going to yield a bumper crop.

Roseanna told her cameraman to start filming. The lights blinded Vlad from such a close distance. "Okay, Vlad the Impaler, tell me your interesting story."

Vlad shielded his eyes and demanded. "Hey, stop that! You don't have the right…"

She was clearly messing with him. Roseanna signaled to her cameraman to cut. "Sorry, your eyes must be sensitive to light. Tell me how you hedge. If you're interesting, maybe we'll put it on the news."

Vlad composed himself. "Don't get me wrong. We all like Ev and the gals, but she's more wary than us guys. Always has been. She left ten grand on the table by selling early. You know why? Here's why: Because the price is already up another ten bucks. And we're growing almost a fifth more than her 'cause we're cuttin' at the end of the month. Look at the weather outside. It's prime growing season!

"So us guys got smart. We figures we're gonna sell an extra 50 pounds each if we wait. Now, a contract is only 100 pounds, so you might be askin' yourself, 'How am I gonna sell two-and-a-half contracts?' Well, we got together and every other guy's gonna sell one extra contract. We'll divvy up the winnings in November."

Rosanna was a big star in New York television. She was known for being sassy in the studio, but more popular for her tough, New York style, in your face, on the street interviews.

She was a pretty Latino woman with dark black hair and a beautiful face. She spoke perfect English with a slight Spanish lilt passing through ruby-red lips. The total package was extremely sexy.

"Okay, Vlad. You have a nice plan, but eight guys at the corner deli don't make a story, now do they?"

Vlad leaned back and said smugly, "Not eight guys, Rosanna honey. Eight hunnerd. Just 'bout every home down in the valley plus every fireman, policeman, garbage man, and shop owner is in on it. Didja know the homes at the bottom of the hill got the best growin' soil and the best waterin'? Specially near the pond.

"I guess that makes us a hedge fund too, right? You can call us the Blue-Collar Hedge Fund!"

Rosanna laughed. ""I guess you are. Okay, Mac, turn the camera on. A little dimmer on the lights. We're going to interview Vlad."

And Vlad got his five minutes of fame on the six o'clock news.

CHAPTER 155

OCTOBER 12, 2012

The price for ROOT stock moved into the $0.40 range. Trading volume had increased, which is always a good thing. Averill calculated his net worth, which he did every morning and at least two or three times during the day.

At $0.10 cents a share, he wasn't wealthy. At today's price, he was a multimillionaire. Averill stared at the number –$6 million dollars.

Averill controlled 14 million shares and 5 million warrants. He had legitimately earned 2 million shares and 5 million warrants as a commission on the private placement. He outright stole 2 million shares, now sitting in his Tuxedo Investments account. Everyone assumed they were owned by one of the Oenotropae partners, and Oeno had distanced themselves from the company after the reverse merger. Averill was pretty sure he got away with it.

The largest and most disputable issuance was the 10 million shares he had awarded himself in exchange for a $1 million note. He had expected some pushback from the board before the private placement had been completed, but never heard a word. He thought he would eventually settle for 1 or 2 million shares. He now was almost certain Johnny had never cleared them with the board.

He had a choice: Either bring the issue to a head early and compromise for a lower amount, or let the matter settle down until memories were foggy. He chose to wait. To cover his tracks, he made sure they had been described in the private placement memorandum and in the reverse merger documents. His strategy was to lay low. With sufficient time, the board would retire, forget, or pass away. Then nobody could dispute his claim.

Averill thought: *Okay, so I owe the company a million, but I'll provide "Investment Banking Services" and get them to write it off. That's what the big investment banks do. I got a lot of shares. A HUMONGOUS number. Ha! Trading volumes are picking up, but they're still low. I'll need million share volume days to dump my load on the market. I'm not ready yet anyway.*

I may have to sell a few shares to pay the Misty luxury tax. She's really starting to ratchet up her demands. Right now, I have to get back to work. Find some new buyers. Create big events. Spread the rumors and gossip. There's no shortage of stories with this company. I don't even have to make them up. I'm a millionaire on paper. Just stay the path and execute the one-year plan to cash in and then get out of town.

Averill walked light-footed to Ben's. He was giddy. The millionaire status made his day. He was in a fantastic mood. Then Misty sat at the table and sucked the life from his lungs.

Misty scolded, "I told you I need a fur coat. I want a real fur, not that crappy synthetic type. And I want it now. I told you over a month ago I needed it by October. Well October is here, and I want it now, now, now! And screw PETA. I dare anyone to try and squirt ink on my mink."

Averill cowered in his chair. A second ago he was fantasizing about his new role as a captain of the financial industry. Someday he may make the Forbes 500. Now he was getting browbeaten by a five-foot-tall hellhound.

Misty clicked a switch and changed personalities. "Now, Avy honey. You know what tonight is. You don't want to miss out on our Friday special date, do you? I'll wear the mink to bed with nothing else on. Wouldn't you like that, sweetie?"

Averill quietly fantasized about a naked Misty. He thought, *Well, at least it isn't as expensive as the BMW. I have to find a mink coat fast.* He then lied, "I just thought of something. Have to get back to the office. I already picked out the fur. Just have to pick it up."

Misty turned sweet. "Don't bother doing all of that shopping, Avy dear. I found the one I want. You just need to give me your credit card so I can pay for it today."

Averill handed his AMEX over to Misty. Later in the day, he received a call to authorize a large purchase. Averill sighed. Misty spent 60,000 shares of ROOT on a coat. Could she possibly outspend his first-and-only fortune?

Panama Blonde and Jonathon Decker were huddled at the far end of the board table. Decker looked worried. Panama looked concerned.

Bret asked, "What's up with the loners? Too good to sit with us?"

JB shook his head. "Decker's having problems with his bank. Gavin and I met with him yesterday. The prognosis isn't good, I'm afraid. This real estate market is years away from recovery. The home improvement market is the same. I don't envy him."

Decker was facing serious financial problems in his door and millwork business. It once was a service business where you made decent money by taking care of your customers. After the big-box home improvement chains took over, everything was about price. The little guys couldn't make money anymore. Then the real estate market collapsed in 2008. A rising tide lifts all ships; a low tide stinks, and the biggest keel gets suck in the mud.

Three of his biggest customers went bankrupt during the summer leaving him holding the bag on a half million of worthless receivables. He was stretching payables to stay afloat.

The stock market collapse slammed Decker's door closed. The company had a working capital loan from Starship Financing Group. Starship was owned by a hedge fund that had lost a lot of money when the market tanked. Its investors began redeeming their partnership interests, and the hedge fund was forced to sell its investments to pay them back. The media politely called the phenomena "deleveraging".

When Decker had applied for the loan seven years ago, the nice Starship brochures pictured a crew on a forty-foot sailboat in Greenwich Harbor. The caption read "Financial Freedom". What it didn't say was that the happy sailors were the lenders, not the borrowers. Starship wanted its money back.

For the last year, the bank officers had tightened the terms on the loan and reduced the borrowing base. Decker Doors was getting squeezed. Last week, the bank's auditors handed Decker more bad news. Over a million dollars of inventory had been reclassified as slow-moving and no longer eligible for borrowing. More and more customer receivables had moved into the seriously past due category. His customers weren't paying on time, and the entire supply chain was stretched to the limit.

The bank cut the loan availability. Decker Doors was losing over a $100,000 month. It only had a few months to live.

JB and Gavin had sat with Decker the prior evening. After hours of analysis, JB advised, "You can try to refinance with another bank, but it would be hard to borrow under these conditions. I recommend that you start preserving your personal assets and make sure you have an exit plan in case this doesn't end well."

Decker spoke with a cracked voice. "It's too late. They have a mortgage on my home, a lien on my family antiques and valuables and a personal guarantee from me. I'm doomed."

CHAPTER 157

OCTOBER 22, 2012

As a couple, Misty and Averill seemed happy in their misery. From afar, they appeared to be looking to their future. But their words were not planning eternal bliss. They were plotting revenge. All Misty talked about was all those horrible people who wronged her. The war against Panama and Allie was far from over. She said, "I know that those two were behind it. I saw Allie talking to the nuns at Mass."

"You're so right, Misty. They're so unfair to you." Averill had learned his lesson. If he disagreed, she'd snarl like a junk yard dog and scratch like an alley cat. Averill didn't have much choice. He hadn't had a decent looking date in years unless you counted escorts.

Averill appealed to the one thing that motivated Misty: spending money. "Why don't we go to Atlantic City this weekend and get away from this town?"

Misty brightened. "Fantastic idea! We can stay at the Borgata Hotel in one of their Piatto suites. I was there New Year's Eve. And I can use their spa during the day while you gamble. At night we can go to a show. Barry Manilow is playing this weekend."

Averill had the fear of a bad puppy in his eyes. What he was about to say would be met with a whack from a rolled newspaper. He took the chance. "I was thinking we could stay at my cousin's house in Egg Harbor. It's twenty minutes from the casinos, and we could have dinner there."

Misty had tired of browbeating Avy. This time she chose flattery, and cooed, "Avy dear, you're a big financial star now. You have to dress and live like you're successful. If you act like poverty, you'll live in poverty. If you act like you're rich, you'll be treated like the rich. Now, where do you really want to stay in Atlantic City?"

Averill knew only one answer. She had a million ways to humiliate, not the least of which was poking him in the chest or pulling his hair. She'd win eventually. Averill said, "I think you're right. We should stay at the Borgata in the Pizza Suites."

"Piatto Suites, you idiot!" Misty cried in disbelief. "And Avy, honey pie, I play hundred dollar slots. No nickel slots for your best girl, right?"

Averill thought, *I'm gonna need ROOT's stock to go to a hundred to pay for this lifestyle.*

CHAPTER 158

OCTOBER 24, 2012

On Wednesday, Misty drove her red BMW, top down, 90 mph on the Garden State Parkway. Averill held on for dear life, his moustache pinned back toward his ears. She pulled into the middle lane to let a caravan of cars pass her doing a 110. No matter what the speed limit was on the parkway, drivers added 20. The left lane added 40.

A weather alert interrupted the Lady Gaga tune on WQHT, Hot 97. "Hurricane Sandy has passed Florida and is moving northward up the coast. There's a strong possibility that the storm could reach the greater New York Metropolitan area by the weekend. We caution everyone to begin preparations now. Drinking water, batteries, all of the necessities you need are listed on our web site."

Averill listened, and said, "What're the chances New Jersey is going to see a hurricane two years in a row? There's no way we get hit, right?"

"All of those people are wasting their time getting ready for a storm that's heading to England," Misty cheerfully said. "We're going to the Borgata!"

She hit the radio scan button until it found Maroon 5's *Payphone*.

They reached Atlantic City at midnight, and the casino game room was quiet as church on a Monday afternoon. The desk clerk greeted them cautiously. "Welcome, Mr. Winthrop. I'm afraid your stay may be shortened. If this hurricane reaches the Outer Banks in North Carolina, we may have to close the casino."

Misty gave her meanest scowl and raised her voice, "You have got to be kidding me. Surely you guys can handle a little storm."

Wrongly assuming he wore the pants in the family, the manager stepped in front of Averill and said, "I wouldn't take this storm too lightly, Mr. Winthrop. First, we're very close to the ocean. More importantly, we have to worry about the safety of our employees. Many have to commute up to an hour away. They need to prepare for the storm, too.

"Right now the forecast is changing, but the latest says weather patterns in the Midwest are affecting the path and could draw the storm toward New Jersey. We're evacuating 48 hours beforehand if the storm keeps heading this way."

Misty ignored the manager and said, "Avy, stop arguing and check us in. I'm going over to the slots. Give me some money to get started."

Averill sighed and handed Misty a few $20 bills. Misty glared at him. He emptied his pocket and said, "I'll be down in a few minutes and get you more from the cashier, honey."

Misty charged toward the machines. Everyone else in the state was boarding up their homes. Misty was playing $100 slots.

CHAPTER 159

OCTOBER 25, 2012

Gavin pulled extra seats up to JB's board table. He and his URI Fiji fraternity brothers were rendezvousing in Myrtle Beach for their annual golf weekend. Jim Malachowski had organized the event for over two decades.

Gavin introduced his frat brothers to JB and the table. Tom Picarillo had been a Dumont soccer star and went on to be a successful pharmacist businessman. Jeff Gardiner flew in from Hollywood where he worked on production of a late night TV show. Tony Bale was a building contractor from Glen Rock. He had bought a storm-damage home restoration business last year just in time for Hurricane Irene. He looked at Sandy with divided loyalties. Sure, he wanted to play golf with his buddies. But if Sandy hit, he'd have plenty of business for months to come.

Gigs Croteau, Willie Montone and Bob Fulford drove down from Southern New England. Gigs played old-time rock 'n' roll piano when he wasn't running a real estate development company. Willie was an HR executive who needed a break after working nonstop on company acquisitions for the last ten years. Foo was the director of purchasing for a high tech firm on Boston's Route 128.

Maestro and Bruce Kaercher completed the entourage. Maestro was a retired hi tech software exec. Bruce had sold his steel pipe business and now played golf in Arkansas and wherever else he could find a foursome. When he wasn't playing golf, he was on the phone with the contractor who was installing a huge man-cave in his basement.

For over twenty years, the group descended upon Myrtle each October and reconnected. Most everyone had a nickname that had stuck since college. Choggie, Jo Jo White, Deuel, Roger and Riles, Stotty, Woody, Doc Holiday, Deuel, Swierk, Pita, Levin, Goose, Big Jon, Shorty, Straight-man, Tip, Robertson and Walsh would be waiting on the first tee.

The airport limousine pulled up to Ben's and the optimistic golfers departed for another memorable golf weekend. Suitcases bulged with extra rain gear. Hurricane Sandy was a big question mark. It had skirted Florida and looked like it might stay offshore. The group would decide when they got to Myrtle if the storm was for real.

CHAPTER 160

OCTOBER 26, 2012

By Friday evening, a third of the golfers headed home. The airports were closing. It was near impossible to find a flight. The storm wasn't as much violent as it was massive. Not to disrespect the hurricane goddess, but a Force One hurricane was relatively small, although it still did damage with 75 mph winds. Forecasters were more concerned about tidal surge and flooding than the wind because of the storm's size and the timing of the landing.

On Saturday, the Fiji golfers who stayed watched as the storm passed slowly 50 miles east of Myrtle. Eighteen brothers, tried and true, ignored the rain and played True Blue. It was one of the few golf courses that remained open during the wet weather.

A thousand-foot high wall of black clouds and water, barely offshore, headed north. Man vs. Nature. In North Carolina, it was a tie. This wasn't going to be good if it turned toward New Jersey. Well, it would be good for Tony's home restoration business, but not for too many others.

CHAPTER 161

OCTOBER 26

The Chicago MERC declared a state of emergency for several commodities affected by the hurricane. They delayed the trading close and delivery date of the October 30 CRAB futures until November 15. Trading could continue assuming you had power. NBCI shut its doors at sundown Friday evening with a hundred vehicles still in line.

Pierre had commandeered O'Hara Landscaping for their services well in advance of the hurricane and had harvested most of their crop. Fifteen hundred clients went to the back of O'Hara's waiting list.

People were triaging. Do I protect my home, or do I salvage the crop? Crab Babies had sold out. There was a trick to cutting the crabgrass properly to get the full plant. O'Hara was an expert, but they were behind schedule. So what if the grass gets a little wet. It'll still be there after the storm. Right?

CHAPTER 162

OCTOBER 27, 2012

Saturday evening, the Borgata management walked through the casino and quietly advised the remaining gamblers and hotel guests that the casino would be closing at 10:00 PM. Misty screamed at the pit boss near her card table. "I'm down $10,000. I'm staying until I win it back!"

The casino manager stood between the dealer and Misty. He said, "You can stand in that spot all you want, but there won't be any chairs or tables in two hours. We're closing for the safety of our employees and guests. We suggest you go home, too."

Misty was steaming mad and snapped back, "I'm betting until you close the tables, and we're staying here tonight. We're in the Piatta Suites, you know!"

The manager shook his head and walked away contemplating other career paths. Normally, he'd call security and have the gambler removed from the premises. After the games closed, hopefully they'd leave on their own.

Misty and Averill played the slots after the craps and black jack tables were closed. The hotel was moving the gaming equipment to higher ground. They left one machine for Misty to play until she left frustrated and beaten.

The hotel stayed open for the night to accommodate the few guests who couldn't get flights out of Atlantic City until the next morning. On Sunday morning at eleven o'clock, Averill went to valet to get his car. Sheets of rain swept in from the Atlantic. No one was working.

The manager walked outside and handed him his car keys. "You're the last guests in the hotel. Valet service is closed. Good luck!" It was an insincere wish.

A half hour later, Averill pulled to the front of the Borgata soaking wet with his hair a tangled mess. He cried to Misty, "It's a nightmare out there! The attendant parked the car on the top floor. I'll bet he did it to get back at us. We're never coming back here!"

Misty plopped into the passenger seat and yelled, "Stop whining, you big baby. Look at me, my hair is wet. Let's go home. Step on it!" He peeled out of the parking lot, fishtailing on the wet pavement.

Traffic was slow. Workers and residents were still evacuating the island. On the Garden State Parkway, they drove north at a snail's pace.

As they neared Exit 82 for Seaside Heights, Misty asked, "Avy, honey. Don't you think you should go to our new house and do something? You know. Put up some plywood or put towels by the doors to stop the rain. Maybe you should stay in the house until the storm passes."

Averill couldn't believe what he heard. "Isn't it a little dangerous out there? The winds are whipping up. Besides, the house will be fine. It's almost a block from the beach."

Misty snapped back, "The hurricane won't be here until Monday. You have a whole day to prepare. Now be a man. I'll drop you off at the Toms River bus station, and you can take a bus or cab over there."

Just two weeks ago, Misty had convinced Averill to name her as a beneficiary on a life insurance policy. Averill thought to himself: *She wouldn't kill me over money, would she? Nah, she'd have insisted on a much bigger policy.*

Averill uncharacteristically showed his temper. "Alright, alright. But I'm not taking a bus! I bet they aren't even running. Nobody's working except the cops and firemen. Even the toll collectors took off. Let's go home. I'll drive back tonight and board up the windows."

Misty wasn't accustomed to Averill standing his ground. She fumed all the way home changing the FM dial every five seconds. She complained, "All they talk about is this damn hurricane. I bet it doesn't hit here and heads out to sea."

Averill endured the petulant tirades until Misty fell asleep. Averill listened to the weather doomcast on the radio.

Meteorologists and news channels called the Halloween hurricane "Frankenstorm". The weatherman warned, "Hurricane Sandy is a Category 1 hurricane with wind speeds over 75 mph. It's expected to merge with a cold front and could create a large, dangerous "superstorm" that could be two thousand miles across. We expect the hurricane to land in the New York metropolitan area on Monday night. Excessive flooding is expected due to the presence of a full moon. If you live in a low lying area near the water, please heed evacuation advisories. The storm surge is expected to be very high and possibly even more dangerous than the winds."

Averill dropped Misty off at her parents' home so she could sleep off her bad mood. There was no way that he was heading back to Ortley tonight. He'd tell her Home Depot was out of plywood or the bridge was closed. He was a professional liar. He'd come up with an excuse.

CHAPTER 163

OCTOBER 28, 2012

Allie opened the store on Sunday for customers needing Sandy supplies. Pre-hurricane sales were brisk. Rope, chains, bungee cords – anything you could use to tie things down. You can never have enough duct tape. Coleman hurricane lanterns, flashlights and lots of batteries. Nails and hammers. Lawn trash bags. Brooms, shovels, rakes. Everything sold. The shelves were half empty in a couple of hours.

Shoppers dreamed up new uses for practically everything in the store. Except for Allie's Corner. People weren't thinking much about making their house pretty today. They weren't shopping for weed killer either. They were hunkering down. Man shall prevail over nature once again! With enough duct tape.

The $60,000 payment to Jake's was due on the 31st. Allie had mailed it Friday. If the USPS trucks were still moving, it should get there on time.

CHAPTER 164

OCTOBER 28

Gavin saw the Sunday weather reports from his hotel in Myrtle Beach. Many of his nephews and nieces lived near the line of danger.

Gavin texted: "Please stay safe and indoors. No heroism. Do you need a hotel?"

Jenna near Asbury: "Jersey strong. We don't need a hotel! BRB, goin' surfin'!"

Rusty: "BRB, goin' surfin'!"

Gavin: "You already msged that!"

Rusty: "Repetition is the soul of wit!"

Alex at FIT: "Just called Comcast. Told them my cable would be out tomorrow!"

Lindsay at Ramapo College: "Great priority. LMAO."

Samantha in Toms River: "Waterfront property soon. Send in the Marines."

James Donald: "I was Army; call my Navy friends for help!"

Terry Michael in NYC: "Armed with my camera. Ready to record this historic event!"

Dannie: "I'm in Frankfurt AGAIN! Always on the road. Missing all the fun!"

Riane: "New England is next. Good luck!"

Sharon: "I just fixed the shingles. Here it goes again!"

Kim in Manasquan: "Sandy aiming at bull's-eye on Main Street!"

Facing a crisis of Mother Nature, the greater New York area kept its sense of humor.

CHAPTER 165

OCTOBER 29, 2012

At 5:10 PM on Monday, October 29, 2012, New York City's Mayor Bloomberg, having already issued a mandatory evacuation order, went on television and said, "Conditions are deteriorating very rapidly and the window for getting out safely is closing. It's getting too late to leave."

Governor Chris Christie of New Jersey was less subtle after people ignored evacuation orders which had been issued for every Barrier Island from Sandy Hook to Cape May. He said, "This is no time to be stupid. This is a time to save yourself and your family."

Was it brave to defend your property, or was it foolish?

The center of Hurricane Sandy slammed Atlantic City at 8:00 PM. The daredevil news crews for The Weather Channel and the television networks stood in two-feet of water in the Atlantic City streets. Crews waded knee-deep in New York City's Battery Park to show the extent of flooding in just the first hour of the storm. It would only get worse.

Halloween was canceled. School was canceled. Electricity was canceled. Breakfast at Ben's Deli was canceled. Normal living was canceled as the storm surge flooded lower Manhattan, Queens, Brooklyn, Long Island, Connecticut, Staten Island, Hudson River towns and cities, and the Jersey Shore.

A few who stayed to protect their homes in low-lying areas didn't survive. An entire section of Queens burned to the ground as a fire spread during the high winds. Power went out for millions.

Ocean and river levels rose everywhere within 200 miles of Manhattan. The combination of tidal surge and storm surge raised tides 14 feet in downtown New York. In Atlantic City, the ocean rose 9 feet, flooding the coastal town and the main floor of the Borgata Hotel and Casino.

Some shore communities like Point Pleasant with higher land and protective dunes fared relatively better, but most towns were devastated. *The New York Times* ran a photo of the Seaside Heights Casino Pier which had collapsed into the ocean. Amazingly, the Jet Star roller coaster stood upright in 10 feet of ocean waves. Jersey Strong!

Two miles north of Seaside Heights, Ortley Beach became the intense focus of news media as a large number of properties were in total ruins. Many houses were physically moved from their foundations. Residents couldn't return to what was left of their homes after the storm passed. The area was declared a national disaster.

Soon after the storm, Republican Governor Christie took Democrat President Barak Obama on a tour of the damaged areas. Just two weeks before Election Day, the Republican Party was aghast at this traitorous act. But Jersey residents temporarily became nonpartisan as their governor pled their case for national assistance.

If there was a crisis that required tough decisions, Christie was "the" governor. Some might argue that that doesn't say much because New Jersey had a governor issue for most of the last fifty years. But Christie appeared to be different. There was talk of a presidency in his future. Tea Party leaders shuddered at the thought.

It was beyond description what happened in New Jersey and New York. It wasn't just the homes. Along the shoreline, businesses were destroyed. Boats were washed up onto parking lots and front yards. Thousands of cars were ruined after they filled with salt water. The storm surge pushed the beach sand inland. Miles of boardwalk were washed away from Belmar to Atlantic City to Cape May.

A construction crane hung precariously 74 stories above Midtown Manhattan. A ship ran aground on Staten Island. You would need a submarine to travel the Brooklyn Battery tunnel. Subways in lower Manhattan sat submerged. The basements of office buildings on Water Street filled with 20 feet of water. It would be a month before executives could get their lunchtime shoeshine in the American Express Building basement.

In the suburbs, no electricity meant no gas pumps meant no driving. Gasoline rationing was instituted in New Jersey and New York to reduce the long lines at the few stations that remained open. Cold weather was on the way. Thousands of residents became homeless and sought shelter with friends and relatives.

To add insult to injury, the National Hurricane Center downgraded the storm from a hurricane to "Post Tropical Cyclone Sandy" because the wind speeds were below hurricane status. Tell that to the 30 million survivors.

CHAPTER 166

OCTOBER 30, 2012

Denise DiPaolo Selleck, a happily married nurse and mother of two, kept a log during the storm while working extended shifts at Riverview Medical Center in Red Bank.

Worked the day before the hurricane and packed enough clothes to stay for 3 days in the hospital. Lucky enough to find a stretcher to sleep on in Same Day Surgery department. The hospital is on a river and the water entered the sub-basement at the storm's peak. Workers saved the equipment.

The hospital was on generator power for 3 days. The day after the hurricane, it was filled with local residents. I tried to find something to eat, but the cafeteria was wall-to-wall people (not hospital workers). The general public figured out we had a generator and we would have everything up and running. One patient complained because his TV didn't work. Every outlet in the hospital had a cell phone recharging.

Two of the nurses on my floor received calls that their houses were completely destroyed. Both stayed to work and help out. I finally got to leave the night after Sandy. My house had no power for 12 days, but no other damage. Mark, the children and I moved in with my in-laws up in Suffern who have a generator.

Over the next few weeks, the hospital was at greater than full capacity. We couldn't discharge people to homes that no longer existed. The army opened shelters so we could discharge them to a place where they could continue to get medical care. Several nursing homes suffered great damage and those patients ended up at the hospital or at the shelter.

In the end, we survived. Luckily, the loss of lives in this huge storm was minimal. People close to the water lost homes. Everyone sustained damage to one degree or another, but for most of us, it was just stuff. We're Jersey strong. We always prevail!

CHAPTER 167

OCTOBER 30

The television and radio news reports focused on the ocean flooding, the physical damage to homes, the lack of electrical power, and the loss of life. But Bergenfield's problems were different. It had its share of downed trees and torn off roof shingles lost to wind shear. Electricity was out. However, Sandy's greatest impact on Bergenfield was groundwater from the rain. The CRAB crop was in trouble.

The ground was soaked. Lakes formed on front lawns. Normally, water is good for a crop, but not at harvest time. The Hedge Fund Grannies had smartly sold their crop early. Vladimir's 800 were under water, literally and financially. Who would have thought that rain would be bad for crabgrass?

People dug trenches and French drains to route the water away. The water table was too high. The French drains never emptied.

A few diverted their basement sump pumps to their lawns, but the water had no place to go. If you drained your property, your neighbor's water spilled over. It was a Sisyphusian task. In Greek mythology, Sisyphus was compelled to roll a large boulder up a steep hill, only to watch it roll back down, and have to repeat the task forever. Likewise, CRAB farmers drained the water, watched it flood back in.

By 2:00 AM, it didn't matter. The electricity went out and the sump pumps stopped working.

Mayor Hector Alvarez toured the town with the chief of police and the heads of maintenance and sanitation. Four-way stop signs had been placed at main intersections until the traffic lights were working again. Town policemen were directing traffic. Overtime pay would be exorbitant this month.

Streets at the bottom of the valley became impassable due to flooding from the brooks that ran through the neighborhoods. Church Street was two feet deep in water. Maintenance laid down old railroad ties across the flooded area to let cars cross.

Clumps of dirt and grass that had fallen from delivery trucks formed a stream of brown water that ran through town. The mud tracked from the ROOT transfer station back to River Edge Road, down the hill past the One Stop Auto Spa, and emptied into Coopers Pond, which was now brown. They lowered the dam gate by the Old Mill, but it would take days for the water to run its course. It was good news for ducks. Their pond had doubled in size. They quacked their appreciation.

Hector looked at the river of mud and said, "Add silt removal to the clean-up budget."

Harold Worth, the head of town maintenance, said "Right now, our staff is busy removing trees and branches knocked down by Sandy. In a week, the crews may be free. The mud is mostly concentrated on the main routes through town and gets worse near the transfer station. Cleaning the streets now would be wasted money. The sewer system is filled to the gills with water and the sewer grates are clogged with debris, so we can't wash the mud away yet. But once this stuff dries, it'll be real tough to remove.

"We still don't have electricity, and it doesn't look like we'll have any for a week. Excuse the pun, but maybe you should change the town name to Brownfield?"

Hector managed a chuckle. "It's good to keep your sense of humor at a time like this, Harold. The town should get funds from FEMA to cover this, so it's not a money issue. Once this water subsides and the sewer system becomes available, we're going to give Washington Avenue and Main Street a bath. After your crews are free, run the street cleaners through the main roads in town and shovel as much as you can into garbage trucks. We might even use the fire department to hose the streets.

"For now, I'm using my powers to institute a local fine for littering one leaf of crabgrass or clump of dirt. A hundred dollars should do it. Chief, every truck transporting CRAB must be fully covered with a tarp. I hate this weed!"

CHAPTER 168

NOVEMBER 1, 2012

On Thursday, NBCI reopened its doors. It had no electricity and no power generator backup, but it could still accept deliveries. Workers pushed the rail trams with a pickup truck.

The commodity market continued to operate during the storm. Traders in Chicago who weren't affected by the power outage saw the problem with the CRAB contract and bet on it. Short sellers were out of luck.

A trader's best friend is volatility. And volatility's best friend is chaos. The commodity markets bowed to the Four Horseman of the Apocalypse – Pestilence, War, Famine, and Death. Tornados, hurricanes, blizzards, flooding, locusts, nuclear meltdowns, drought, assassinations, and plane crashes help too.

The CRAB price increased limit up three days in a row, and was approaching $140 a pound. Short sellers couldn't get out of their contracts. Sellers couldn't deliver what they had sold. Buyers held their ground and demanded delivery. Over a thousand homeowners wouldn't be delivering some or most of their crop. If they had sold futures, they'd be writing a check for the loss.

As the first post-storm truck began unloading its product at NBCI, Tom McInerney stopped the delivery and ran into Johnny's office. The general manager blurted, "Johnny, we have a problem. They're delivering crop that's soaked. We'll be paying for water. We have to stop accepting deliveries."

This was way over Johnny's pay level. He called Jack Barlowitz, the company's new outside legal counsel who had been hired to replace Louie DiSosa. Jack was an SEC attorney with little exposure to commodity legal issues. Jack brought in Manna, Craw and Grill, a law firm that was experienced dealing with the MERC.

Mary Ellen Grill, the managing partner of the New York offices sat with Jack, Johnny and Tom in NBCI's unlit offices three hours later. She carried a few too many pounds and dressed rather frumpy. Her hair was plain and flat without any discernible styling. She wore no jewelry except token silver posts. Makeup was undetectable. In summary, Mary Ellen didn't care much about *Elle* or *Glamour* magazine.

However, she knew her commodity law. "Jack, you don't technically take title except for any commodities that NBCI purchased for its own account on the exchange. I understand you own some futures contracts. If you took delivery, you have a different issue.

"Under your particular agreement with the MERC, NBCI is a bailee, like a parking lot attendant or dry cleaner. A bailee receives property and is entrusted for a specified objective by the bailor according to the terms of an express agreement. The agreement is the contract that you have with the MERC to ascertain that the product meets the specifications set out in the CRAB contract. Pierre originally set the standards in the agreement, but they can be amended.

"I called my contact at the Chicago MERC. He suggested you take the product and adjust for the estimated salvageable poundage. Use an estimate that's in your favor to cover any possible losses.

"They also suggested you're allowed to charge an additional processing fee to reduce the water content and make it deliverable to the buyers. Pierre told us they insist on a dried product. You might also set a limit for each seller based upon their historical shipments. That would protect you somewhat.

"If you think this is a good plan, I can put it into writing and have the MERC accept the amended agreement for this delivery date."

Tom said, "My guys have been weighing the first load and estimate the product is thirty percent water. It'll take us a month to dry out the deliveries.

"Our shaker capacity wasn't designed to process wet product. I'm guessing we have to build two more shakers quickly. They'll cost $20,000 apiece, but my guys can build them if we get an electric generator in here.

"I'll have to hire more seasonal workers to get this done. They'll cost me $150,000 for the month. So to be fair to us and conservative, we should charge a thirty-percent water allowance, limit every home to 180 pounds, and then charge them $10 per pound to process. We might make some money, but we won't lose any."

Mary Ellen responded, "That seems eminently fair and well thought out, Tom. Mr. Carrera, is that your proposal?"

Johnny was shocked someone called him by his real last name. *Everyone still calls me Johnny True Value, not that I mind getting my old name back.* He said, "The numbers look right. If it's okay with Tom and Jack, it's okay with me."

Jack took command. "We'll need to send a notice to all homeowners, send a press release to the wire services and file an 8-K with the SEC. The extra revenue is a material event that needs to be shared with the public. In the meantime, everyone needs to keep this confidential until the 8-K is released. Mary Ellen, can you prepare the paperwork for the MERC?"

Mary Ellen agreed and everyone stood to leave the meeting. Johnny turned to Jack and Justin and said, "You guys stay! We got somethin' to talk about."

CHAPTER 169

NOVEMBER 2, 2012

On Friday, Johnny sat in the NBCI offices hiding his glee. This would be a surprise. "There's more news, I'm afraid. You know the ten mil we raised in May? Remember we had some profits we reported in August?"

Justin had a look of terror. "Yes, we reported we had an unrealized gain of $3.4 million. I thought you were going to close out the contract. Don't tell me you blew the money!"

"No, Justin. I didn't blow the money," Johnny said smugly. "And we never actually agreed we were gonna stop hedgin'. We were gonna defer to the board, and we never heard back from 'em.

"Anyway, I did sell the October contracts. We made $6 million in September. Then I reinvested the proceeds into next year's contracts at $60 a pound. As president, I decided it was important to hedge our 2013 operations, too. That little hedge, guys, is now showing a $30 million profit. Thank you, Sandy!"

"How can you have done this?" Justin said in disbelief. "I'm the controller here! How can you act without my permission? Without me knowing about it?"

Jack tried to calm Justin with a hand motion, but Justin was incensed. "Johnny," Jack said with annoyance, "you're incredibly lucky. But Justin is right. This type of activity has to be approved by the board. And your controller has to be informed. Let's get past this. I'll add the information to the Form 8-K."

Johnny stood his ground and said defiantly, "You go ahead and ask the board if it's okay their president just made the company $30 million on a low-risk hedge. I'd like to hear what they have to say. While you're at it, I want blanket authority to keep hedgin'. They can establish limits, but I don't want my accountant second-guessin' me. Justin, I don't have to ask your permission for nothin'.

"Oh, by the way, when you ask their okay, tell the board their stock options probably quadrupled in value today."

Justin stormed out of the office. Jack contemplated his words carefully. "Johnny, this is not how it's done. Companies must have controls over spending limits. Public companies have to comply with Sarbanes-Oxley now. If every company president was allowed to go to Vegas and bet the house, we'd all be in trouble."

Johnny folded his arms across his chest. "Jack, someone dropped the ball, and it wasn't me. Everyone knew we owned futures contracts in August. You sent an email to Roland. I saw it. Why didn't he call a board meetin'? You know why? Because he thought we did a great job. He hasta be jumpin' outta his wheelchair.

"So, you wanna get past this? Fine. I'll get past this. I want authority to invest the money I just made. I got product comin' in here every day and I don't know till the week after delivery deadline who owns what. I hafta hedge!

"And another thing. My controller doesn't tell me what to do. He counts the money after I make it. He pulls this stunt again, he's fired."

"Johnny, you have some valid points," Jack said, "but you can't fire your controller without the approval of the audit committee. I'll get the board to act. Roland is getting a little old to be chairman. I doubt they'll give you $30 million dollars of authority, but I can see you need some room to manage your operations."

After Jack left, Johnny called Averill and told him NBCI was going to file an 8-K to report the unusual profit. Averill barked, "I already know how much you made, buddy. I'm way ahead of you. Looking at the account. Gotta go. Phones won't be working for long."

CHAPTER 170

NOVEMBER 2

Averill hung up the phone and quickly entered orders to buy ROOT stock for his personal account. The middle school was getting power from a loud, diesel, back-up generator and somehow had managed to keep its Internet service going, too. Averill hitched a ride onto its Wi-Fi. An English teacher with a sense of humor had chosen *The Ancient Mariner* as today's password. *Water, water, everywhere, nor any drop to drink.*

The market totally misunderstood the impact of Sandy on NBCI's operations. It had concluded ROOT would have a bad quarter because its processing fees would be lower. The stock price moved down as the storm passed. That was a mistake.

Averill had maybe two hours of battery power left on his laptop. Twice he had snuck into the middle school to recharge, but he nearly got caught. He couldn't use LMNOP's offices in Brooklyn; they had been submerged during the storm. It would be weeks before they were up and running again.

He had to hustle. Averill placed buy orders. He bought 50,000 shares at the bottom for $0.25 cents a share; 20,000 shares at $0.30; and, 30,000 shares at $0.45. In an hour, he had amassed a position of 200,000 shares. Then the sellers disappeared. The "bid-ask" spread had reached $0.20 cents, healthy even by penny stock standards. The market knew something was up.

After filling his own plate, he texted The Sticky Five. "HUMONGOUS! No time to talk. Chat in an hour."

In a moment of weakness or perhaps moral sympathy, he thought about his clients' economic welfare. He decided to let them in on the action. He couldn't reach anyone by phone, but bought stock for all of his discretionary accounts. ROOT's share price increased to $0.80 cents.

Then he grabbed his four iPads and drove back to the middle school parking lot. His pseudo identities posted on Yahoo! Finance:

Tektikker: "Something's up in ROOT. Stock plunged and then tripled. Heavy volume. Another HUMONGOUS opportunity!"

Greenmasheen: "Hurricane must be a bonus for ROOT. ROOT for ROOT!"

Contrariologist: "CRAB future price $140 a pound. ROOT gets a percentage fee for processing. BIG PROFITS FOR ALL!"

Biohzrde: "I hope they didn't hurt the environment. It's tough enough to breathe in New Jersey. Does anyone know if this has an impact on our clean water?"

Tektikker: "Wah, wah, wah, kid. You're in the way of progress. Sell your stock and let us playas make money!"

Averill's phone service read "No Signal" after the cellphone towers had finally lost battery backup power. He called The Sticky Five from Bergenfield Public Library's landline payphone. It was probably the last working phone in the county. It might also be the last payphone in the state.

Averill gave a two-minute update and said, "Guys, your cell phones probably only have minutes to live. Buy now. In a few hours, it'll be too late."

The boys joined the fray from their darkened midtown offices. Backup power was reserved for trading on PCs only. No lights allowed. Lefty Stonewall almost missed out on the action. His office on Water Street was literally under water. Dicky let him borrow an office to trade.

In the next hour, two million shares exchanged hands. All over Wall Street, ROOT was appearing atop trader's stock screens. It was leading the market in percentage gain. Something was definitely cooking in Bergenfield.

When the market closed at 4:00 PM, the stock had broken the magical $1 barrier. Averill smiled. ROOT finally had attracted some new investors.

CHAPTER 171

NOVEMBER 3, 2012

Jack Barlowitz prepared the 8-K and press release to disclose the financial impact on the quarterly revenues and profits due to Hurricane Sandy. Little ROOT was going to show an extra $11 million in CRAB processing fees. It also had an unrealized $30 million profit from commodity trading. It was one of the few companies to benefit in such a time of hardship.

Jack sent the press release and 8-K to the NASDAQ. At 8:00 AM, he would file it with the SEC before the market opened.

The NASDAQ market specialist called Jack and said they would halt trading on the stock until the market had time to absorb the new information. He also observed that a lot of activity had occurred the prior day and asked if Jack knew about any insider trading. Jack said he did not, but noted the CRAB price had increased considerably since the hurricane, and perhaps the speculation came from the news.

At 11:00 AM, ROOT trading resumed, and the stock price jumped to $1.20. Averill was beyond amazed. This was the first time that the stock went up without Averill pumping it. Parts of Bergenfield had their power restored. He started calling his customers until he realized that most everyone's phone was probably still out of service.

Averill thought, *It's too early for Tommy Fox's. I'll just go to Ben's Deli and gloat.*

CHAPTER 172

NOVEMBER 3

Ben's Deli reopened for business using a generator for power. All of the perishable food had to be destroyed. Deliveries wouldn't resume for days. Miguel drove to a Costco in Scranton, Pennsylvania to restock the food inventory.

Decker and Panama walked into the deli and sat down wearing huge smiles. "Hurricane Sandy did a number on my plant," Decker exhaled.

"So why are you so happy?" Allie asked.

Decker leaned forward. "So I'm having bank problems, right. Remember I told you my bank declared my screen door inventory was bad collateral. Well the hurricane knocked the roof off the outbuilding and destroyed everything in it. Our insurance is going to pay a half-million dollars. My business is saved!"

The table laughed for a full minute enjoying Decker's good fortune. Tears of laughter streamed down Panama's face. JB regained control and said, "It goes to show you. Well, congratulations!"

Averill entered Ben's, looked around, and thought, *Where's the standing ovation? The applause? These guys are clueless. Aren't they watching the stock price? Don't they know we had a great day?* He ordered a coffee and left the ungrateful lot.

CHAPTER 173

NOVEMBER 3

Word spread quickly around Bergenfield that the CRAB price would get a haircut because of the water saturation. Some deliveries might be rejected altogether.

Most of the town had sold and delivered before the storm. Fifteen hundred homes had sold their crop but not delivered. Some had managed to cut part of the crop and stored it in their garages. Bad idea. Everything at ground level was soaked. Wet or not, they still had to deliver the weeds in the next two weeks or write a check.

You really couldn't cut crabgrass if it was in standing water. Ingenuity took charge. The weeds were mush and fell apart during clipping, so the ground had to be dried first. A few tried using leaf blowers. Some dug trenches and used small buckets to bail the water from the foot-deep holes.

It was all to no avail. No matter what they tried, they wouldn't be able to deliver at least half of the 200 pounds they had sold in the market, 250 pounds if you were in Vladimir's trading group.

The post office was three days behind schedule. Den-Ken paid Chris at *The Bergenfield Valley News* to hand-deliver a flyer to the town. They were going to save everyone from crop failure.

Den-Ken hosted a meeting at the Teaneck Marriott at Glenpointe, which was near the entrance to the New Jersey Turnpike. They rented a van equipped with roof speakers and drove through town to announce the seminar. The van was last used for Hector's mayoral election campaign.

CHAPTER 174

NOVEMBER 5, 2012

Over a thousand people crowded into the hotel's main ballroom. Ken DeLong launched the presentation on the big screen TV. The title was a cartoon of a personified crabgrass plant yelling "Help!"

Ken said, "I'm assuming the people in this room didn't harvest on time and have a problem. If you sold and delivered already, you don't need to be here."

A handful of embarrassed people left the room.

"Homes on average produce 200 pounds each season. If you didn't sell futures against this production, you have no problems. This isn't a gardening lesson."

Another small group sheepishly exited.

"That leaves the rest of you – the ones with a problem. Each of you has sold futures and can no longer deliver. Either your production is short, or you sold more than 200 pounds, or the NBCI haircut is affecting your sales. Raise your hand if you are in one of those categories."

A roomful of unenthusiastic people half raised their hands.

"Okay, we have a solution that will ease your cash flow situation, but you'll be borrowing against next year's sales. If you prefer to write a check and take your loss, please feel free to leave."

No one left.

Ken smiled benevolently. "I'm guessing a lot of you are O'Hara clients. They're way behind schedule and may not get to your home. The gasoline shortage is hurting their efforts. Also, cutting the crabgrass is a problem in these wet conditions and taking much longer than usual. You only have about ten days to deliver your crop. Don't wait on O'Hara. We suggest you go outside and do your best to salvage what you can."

Sighs of disgust filled the room and many started to mumble.

Ken clapped his hands. "LISTEN UP! Stop trying to air out your crop. It's too late. The MERC gave NBCI a water allowance, so no matter how much you dry it, they're still lopping off 30 percent. Deliver it wet. Also, NBCI is getting $10 dollars a pound for water removal."

People moaned.

"NEXT! There's a 180 pound limit for every home. If you had a bigger crop, you won't get paid for it. Store the extra until next year!"

Vladimir screamed garbled profanities in a foreign tongue.

"Let's talk money," Ken continued. "We studied our customer accounts. Many of you sold the contract in September for $80 a pound on average so you already received $16,000. You're going to be short half of that. Hopefully you haven't spent it all."

The Bergenfield Yacht Club section cursed in English. Their new boats had turned to flotsam and washed ashore in Toms River. And now, they had to write a check.

"About 800 of you sold in the last week of October at an average of $110 a pound. You apparently sold an extra 50 pounds each in some sort of arrangement amongst yourselves. You're going to be short $15,000."

"It may not sound like a lot of money individually, but this room lost $20 million of equity. I can't be sure, but I'm guessing most of you don't want to write a check."

The crowd nodded and mumbled acknowledgment.

"We have a temporary solution for you. We recommend you sell your June 2013 crop now. That will give you enough in your account to cover your losses. We can guarantee this price today only."

The crowd broke into mumbled confusion.

"Listen up! I can't talk over the noise. You have two choices. Write a check to cover the losses today. Or sell a future for June delivery and use the proceeds to pay the deficit. But we have some advice for you. Make sure you harvest on time in June. Don't let this happen again. We have paperwork here for any of you who want to take option two."

The lines formed and six commodity brokers took orders to sell June futures from frantic CRAB commodity speculators.

Den-Ken was going to earn $1 million in commissions today on the orders. There's another adage in the commodity business. If you want to make money, don't buy commodities. Be the broker and charge commissions.

CHAPTER 175

NOVEMBER 6, 2012

The 35 homes owned by Bergen Development Company could have fared worse. Pierre had jumped to the front of the line and incentivized O'Hara Landscaping to cut the crabgrass on most of their properties before the storm.

Disinterested and financially unmotivated homeowners did nothing to save the crops at the few homes missing the cut. It was a small and manageable loss of revenues for Gil and his partners. The bigger problem was the storm damage to the houses.

Gutters and torn shingles would have to be replaced. The damage was less than $1,000 per home, so insurance wouldn't cover much after the deductible. Worse, the tenants were threatening to break their leases.

Gilbert and Vinnie toured the homes to assess the repairs. The other partners were worthless. Vinnie said, "Insurance companies got bigga problems than yer gutters. Dose guys insured homes dat was ocean-front and now have a super close-up view of the bay, if ya know what I mean. I'd bet every house on Long Beach Island is a total loss. Da Post Office is gonna get dizzy tryin' to figger out where to deliver da mail."

Gilbert forced a laugh. Vinnie continued, "Da claims adjusters won't visit here for a month. You can fix damage that exposes you to the elements. I'm pretty sure about dat. My boys'll come over. We'll tear some more shingles, pull some tar paper, ya know, make it look worse, like two grand of damages So, we'll get a grand from da insurers above da deductible, which will pay our costs. We'll take pictures for now.

"I ain't gonna charge the partnership nothin'. I'll work off da insurance proceeds. But if I were you, and I am not you, I'd hit dose silent partners of yers for two big ones each. They don't do squat 'round here. Except Trudy of course. Don't assess my cuz'."

Gilbert gave it a quick thought. Vinnie was going to make another thirty grand on this work. But he was right about the assessment. And he was providing a real solution, which was better than any of his other partners. He said, "It's a deal, Vinnie. Tell the insurance broker what we're doing. Make sure it's okay."

Vinnie looked askance at Gilbert. "Wha? You don't tink I done dat already? Gilbert, you offend me! Da adjuster's a not-too-distant cousin of mine."

Vinnie strutted to his black GMC Yukon with dark, black tinted windows. The vanity plate read "BADA BING".

CHAPTER 176

NOVEMBER 7, 2012

A Nor'easter snowstorm walloped New Jersey with a knockout blow nine days after the hurricane. The snow served as temporary refrigerators for people still without power.

The storm ended all hope of salvaging the crop for the last hundred homes. The damage was fatal. ROOT wouldn't accept delivery of frozen CRAB.

Hopeful news stories aired about homeowners in Ortley Beach who were rebuilding. It might take a year for the government to revise the building codes. It might take longer to get building permits. Ignoring the bureaucracy, Ortley residents along with their friends and relatives removed saltwater soaked sheetrock, insulation and floors.

Bulldozers moved sand from the streets back onto the beaches. Town crews sifted the piles to remove debris. Waterlogged mattresses, televisions and children's dolls were carted away.

CHAPTER 177

NOVEMBER 8, 2012

A STCK-TV reporter spoke as the b-roll video of NBCI's bustling plant ran on the screen behind him. "New Jersey Senator Alonzo Gruenfeld has added an unusual earmark of $2 million to the Department of Agriculture federal budget. The funds will go to Rutgers University to study the environmental conditions and growth requirements of the rare species of Sanguinalis plant native to Bergenfield. The senator's office issued a statement that the federal government wanted to find additional areas in New Jersey where the crabgrass could grow freely and benefit the local economy."

Following the report, STCK-TV's bond analyst Dickie Tribecca and economist Les Stevens resumed their onscreen battle over tax reform. Bond guys hate inflation, and deficits cause inflation. Economists hate recessions, and spending was needed to stimulate the economy. They were both right, and neither would win.

The arguments made interesting theater. It was the Wall Street ultimate fighting championship. Men in blue suits were throwing hard, powerful shots worthy of Ali and Foreman. Jay McCall watched with a Cheshire-cat smile knowing this battle was ratings nirvana. Betsy Sands tried to mediate, but the referee couldn't stop this one.

CHAPTER 178

NOVEMBER 12, 2012

Wall Street is notorious for gallows humor. Jokes launched from trading floors and within minutes reached all corners of the earth. Traders, brokers and bankers in Hong Kong, Paris, Singapore, Frankfurt, Sydney and London regularly joined New York for a quick laugh and then got back to work.

Very few world events, celebrity mishaps, and business failures escaped their reach. In December 1986, an alleged head of the Gambino crime family, "Big Paul" Castellano, was murdered gangland style at Sparks Steakhouse in midtown Manhattan. *What's the latest drink at Spark's? Six shots! What vegetable are they serving? Rat-tat-tat-a-touile!*

In 2008, the sovereign debt of European countries was in extreme financial distress. Traders created an acronym for the five countries with the biggest financial problems: Portugal, Iceland, Ireland, Greece and Spain became known as the PIIGS. *What's the capital of Spain? About twelve pesos!*

The wrath of Hurricane Sandy didn't escape the Wall Street wit. Lower Manhattan was under water. *What drink to do you get when you mix the Hudson and East Rivers? A Manhattan with a splash!*

Seaside Heights' boardwalk had been washed away and its roller coaster and pier collapsed into the ocean. It had been home to MTVs drunken reality show, *The Jersey Shore,* led by its star Jersey girl, Snookie. *Why didn't Snookie take a shower on the Casino Pier? Because she wanted to wash ashore!*

Jokes aside, in a moment of crisis and pain, New Jersey's and New York's greatest stars joined to raise money for the hard-hit. Bruce Springsteen, Jon Bon Jovi, Billie Joel, Jon Stewart, Jimmy Fallon and many others appeared on fundraisers immediately after the water receded and the sand had settled. It would take a lot more than a few charity concerts to fix the damage from this tidal storm, but the effort was appreciated by locals. The money couldn't come quick enough for people without homes.

CHAPTER 179

NOVEMBER 14, 2012

Misty demanded, "Averill, enough stalling! I want to see the damage to the house now! You better have done a good job putting up those shutters. The TV reports are horrifying."

Averill cringed. He had used up all of his excuses. No gasoline. Not allowed on the island. Too dangerous. It's snowing!

He had to get to the house ahead of Misty. The town wasn't ready for repopulation because of power lines and utilities, but contractors and residents were now allowed to enter with caution. The east side of Route 35 was still impassable.

The police formed a checkpoint at the Seaside Heights Bridge. Contractors entered the left lane. Residents with identification passed on the right.

Averill rented a van, bought some plywood, nails, a hammer and spray paint and drove down to the beach house. The Toms River policeman allowed him to cross the bridge. His eyes showed his shared grief.

When he reached the cottage, he couldn't believe it. The house was nearly destroyed. Parts of the roof were missing, the windows were broken, and most of the siding was torn off. Three feet of sand blocked the front door. He crawled through a window and waded through dead fish rotting in a foot of ocean water. The furniture was saturated.

He kicked the wall in anger weakening the sheetrock. A torrent of water poured from the hole. The insulation dripped putrid brine. It reeked like boat bilge. You could see the high water mark seven feet above the baseboard.

Averill thought: *Nothing to salvage. Total write-off. Thank goodness they didn't deliver the furniture and TV Misty ordered. The insurance will cover some of this old crap. Ha-ha! I finally found a way to stop her never-ending shopping spree. Call up a hurricane!*

Averill struggled to pull the plywood from the van. Mr. Home Repair he was not. The plan was to cover the windows and make it look like the house had suffered through the storm despite Averill's heroic attempts to protect the property. He covered a window with a piece of plywood. It didn't have the "I've just been through Sandy" look. He threw buckets of sand and salt water at it. Still too fresh.

A Toms River police car pulled up and two officers got out. Martin, the taller policeman said, "Sir, would you mind telling us what you're doing? It's a little late to be putting up shutters. That house is a total loss."

Averill concocted a series of stories, each one more ridiculous. First, he was preventing vandalism, but the cop observed there was nothing left to damage. Then he said he was trying to protect the house because he heard that the town was being declared a historic preservation. The cops laughed and said that was a new one for the books.

Finally, Averill broke down and told the truth. He didn't come down before the storm because it was too dangerous. Now, his fiancé would realize he'd lied. He had to make it look like he'd done something to prevent the damage.

The cops turned away muffling their laughter. They were sensitive to people's losses, but this story was just too ridiculous. Joseph, the younger cop, turned to Averill and said, "Okay, Mr. Winthrop. We get it now. Let's see if we can help you get out of here faster."

They helped him nail the last three pieces of plywood to the house and splashed the plywood with sand and water.

The police tried to leave, but Averill kept thanking them profusely. Martin said, "You know, Mr. Winthrop, they're rewriting the building code. If you don't build it to the new code, you won't be allowed to occupy the home. You really should hold off until they settle the rules."

Averill thanked them again and drove way in the rental van. Averill thought to himself as he crossed the bridge toward the Garden State Parkway, *There's no chance I'm rebuilding that mess. Give me my insurance money and I promise I'll never visit the ocean again.*

CHAPTER 180

NOVEMBER 15, 2012

"Give me the post mortem. How bad is it?" asked Eva.

Steven wore a suit for the first time since the storm. He was noticeably tired from the extra hours dealing with Sandy issues, particularly finding backup power during the day. He began, "Luckily, O'Hara was able to cut most of the crabgrass at the homes where we have option agreements. Of course, that doesn't include the homes that are suing us. They wouldn't let us enter their properties."

Stephane spoke up. "As far as the October futures market, we owned 10,000 contracts. Buckstown owned 3,000, and there were another 2,000 spread around a dozen small buyers. There wasn't enough to go around. In order to stabilize the market, we sold off 4,000 contracts at a nice profit."

"Buckstown is taking delivery. So is everyone else. It looks like they plan to fill up the silo – all million pounds of it."

"Do I have to raise my shampoo prices yet?" Eva said, unable to hide her exasperation.

Steven said, "Our breakeven today compared to using sodium laureth sulfate has improved to $90 per pound. Based upon our average cost, we're still ahead. If you consider our marginal cost on incremental purchases, you'd have to raise prices to keep the same margin. Don't forget we still have a thousand homes locked in at $15 per pound. So a quarter of our purchases are inexpensive. I hate to say it, but until Albert improves the yield, we should raise the shampoo price to maintain profit margins."

Eva scribbled numbers on her pad. "Well, we're above $90 dollars already. We're using average cost, Steven. If I were an oil refinery buying oil from Norway at $100 and Texas at $90, I wouldn't charge my customers different prices for gasoline. They get the average. For now, anyway. But if the prices increase substantially, then the incremental higher price might stop me from increasing production.

"Let's test the waters. Tell marketing to increase prices to $35 dollars a bottle. Let's see how the market reacts.

"Last thing. This hurricane temporarily scuttled our plans to add those 400 houses in Dumont. And I understand Den-Ken is opposing our amendment to include the town in the commodity specs. Let's redouble our efforts after this hurricane mess is past us."

CHAPTER 181

NOVEMBER 15

The 2013 CRAB futures approached $115 a pound. ROOT's stock held well above a dollar. Averill decided it was time to sell a little and get liquid again. The shares he bought in October were showing a pretty profit.

Avy thought, *I'll sell a million shares. That'll keep Misty in Dolce & Gabbana for another month or two. And it'll give me some cash to buy up shares if they get cheap. Then I'll be the buyer when the price is low and the seller when it's high! Imagine me – Averill Winthrop, the market maker. Besides, ROOT had a pretty good run, but it's going to be hard to repeat anytime soon.*

The hurricane was a stroke of luck. Well, maybe not for the victims, but it certainly was for me! Hurricane season's over, and I might have to wait until next August for another disaster to make money.

Averill took Johnny to breakfast. "Johnny, it's time to go on the NASDAQ. You meet the qualifications. You're big enough and certainly make enough money. Your market cap is over $200 million. Being on the NASDAQ will help the stock price, which is going to make those stock options of yours go higher."

Johnny washed his bagel down with a gulp of coffee. "Not sure what you mean, but aren't we goin' too fast? We're just recoverin' from Sandy. We're preparin' for next season's crop. Why do you wanna do this now?"

Averill said calmly, "There's never a good time when you're running a company. Look, the Bulletin Board is hell for small companies. It's where junk stocks trade. Companies on the BB are one step from extinction. If you want to run a respectable company, you have to go on a bigger exchange. To qualify, all we have to do is get your stock above $4.00."

Johnny protested, "But we aren't anywhere near that. And don't ask me to pay for any more cockamamie investor conferences to get the stock price up."

Averill laughed and said, "Easy boy! Down! Let me explain. It's legitimate and companies do it all the time. We'll do a one-for-twenty reverse stock split. Investors get one share of new stock for every twenty shares they own. Theoretically, the stock will be priced twenty times higher.

"You meet most of the requirements. You have enough shareholders. You trade more than a million shares a month. Your assets and equity are way above the standard. And you meet the market capitalization requirement.

"First, let's get you some more stock options now before it's too late. Give some to your management team and the board, too. You should get another million. Give everyone else a couple hundred thousand.

"There's a bunch of administrative details, like having committees and written charters and codes of conduct, but your outside counsel can write those easy enough."

Johnny sat overwhelmed. His head was spinning. "I dunno Averill. Sounds like a lot of work. I don't even know where to start. We should do this in March when it's slow around here."

Averill snapped, "Johnny, wake up! A million options. You want them priced today at a buck, or you want them later when they cost more? You're going to be rich, man. Just follow my lead.

"First, speak to Jack Barlowitz and have him call a board meeting before Wednesday. The board will approve anything that increases their stock option grants. Besides, going on the NASDAQ is a natural progression.

"Jack will prepare the application and paperwork. But before you do anything, I want you to delay the filing of your 10-Q with the SEC. Use the Hurricane Sandy exemption."

Johnny protested, "But we're ready to file. Why should we wait?"

Averill lowered his voice. "After you announce the reverse stock split, short sellers are going to come out of the woodwork and rip your stock price. We need ammunition to fight back. After we announce the split, the shorts will knock the price down. After the earnings press release, we'll buy and move the stock price back up. That'll stop them for a little while."

"You're tryin' to get this started Thanksgiving week after a major hurricane? Let's wait," Johnny pleaded.

"No, Johnny," demanded Averill. "You're going on the NASDAQ this year! The week before New Year's Eve! The waiting period is 40 days. If you file now, it'll be perfect. You wanna know why? Because the whole world takes Christmas week off. Even the short sellers go skiing."

Johnny was unsure. He meekly told Jack who thought the plan was brilliant. Jack filed the 10-Q NT to announce the late filing and issued a press release.

"NBCI (ticker symbol: ROOT) announced today that the filing of its Quarterly Report on Form 10-Q for the quarter ended September 30, 2012 has been delayed due to the effects of Hurricane Sandy. As a result of the storm, NBCI experienced a loss of power for ten days at its headquarters in Bergenfield, New Jersey. The

Securities and Exchange Commission recently announced that it would extend the filing deadline of any company that cannot timely file due to Hurricane Sandy until November 21, 2012."

CHAPTER 182

NOVEMBER 21, 2012

The NASDAQ quickly approved the listing application subject to achieving a $4.00 stock price. If everything went well, ROOT could begin trading on the famous stock exchange by New Year's Eve.

NBCI had to meet NASDAQ's corporate governance requirements, which weren't inconsequential. First, it had to add three independent directors. Roland agreed to retire as long as he was allowed to keep his options. Jack convinced Arthur Sterling, a retired executive from a Fortune 500 company, to join as the nonexecutive CEO and Chairman. Arthur would earn a nice salary of $250,000 a year plus a million stock options, which would convert into 50,000 options after the split.

NBCI announced the reverse split and NASDAQ application in the morning. They would issue the earnings release near the end of the day. In between, Avy implemented his plan. The Sticky Five were ready. They were liquid again. They had sold their ROOT positions when the stock hit $1.20, and had plenty of ammunition to buy after the stock crashed.

Averill pulled out his four iPads and posted on the Yahoo! Finance message board. Today's middle school password was Home-Ec.

Tektikker: "Going on the Nasdaq is huge for this little company. Plus they brought on an independent board. This is all good. Be patient."

Greenmasheen: "I agree, but it's always bad to reverse split. The shorts kill you."

Contrariologist: "I hope it goes down. I'll buy more. Every time the shorts try this, they get burnt in the end."

Biohzrde: "I only own 1,000 shares. After split, I only have 50. This is terrible."

Tektikker: "Kid, it's time to step up to the plate. You're up 80% from my calculations. Buy another 1,000 shares and you'll have an even 100 after the split. You'll become a man. Think of it as a stock market Bris. This is a HUMONGOUS opportunity."

After the announcement and before Avy could say boo, the stock dropped 20% to $1.00 per share. The shorts were hammering away. A million shares traded hands in the first hour. *That's okay. I expected worse*, thought Avy.

The shorts ignored the NASD uptick rule. No one knew how it worked anyway. They kept selling and pushing the price down. The stock went to $0.90 cents. It clipped $0.80. Two million shares had already traded. The stock had lost a third of its value in three hours. It stood as the day's largest NASDAQ's loser.

Tektikker went back online: "Did I mention this opportunity was HUMONGOUS?"

The battle had begun. Averill and The Sticky Five placed large buy orders at crazy low prices. Five million shares at ten cents. Twenty million shares at a penny. Then they canceled the orders. They were creating havoc. Hedge funds and brokers saw the activity on their stock screens.

Tektikker went online again: "If this hits $0.70, I'm going all-in!"

The Sticky Five weren't the only ones who read the message boards. Smart traders had figured out the pattern over the last month. Massive orders had been placed around Wall Street at $0.70. A floor had been set. The short sellers remained confident. They kept selling. Averill and company bought. So did many others. By 3:00 PM, five million shares had traded.

Technically, short sellers have to borrow the stock in order to sell it. Brokerage firms have full-time departments with employees who lend stock at a price. Availability of shares never stopped the shorts. In a week, they'd exit their positions. The arcane rules of stock loan were applied by trolls in the bowels of brokerage firms. It would be weeks before the NASD would become aware of the "fail-to-deliver" problem.

Averill called Johnny and told him to file the 10-Q and issue the press release. Wall Street monitors blared the headline:

"NBCI earns $5.7 million after taxes in the quarter or $0.03 per share. EBITDA was $11.2 million. Additional $30 million earnings boost expected in fourth quarter from hedging and $11 million in extra fees related to Hurricane Sandy!"

The shorts began covering their positions. A few locusts hung around to see if there was anything left to eat.

The stock moved back to a dollar, but the shorts had won part of the fight. They were up about $10 million dollars by Averill's estimation. How big was their position? Averill would see the published short interest announcement in a few days. Meanwhile, he had battled to a standoff. There would be more attempts on NBCI's life before they officially went on the NASDAQ.

CHAPTER 183

DECEMBER 3, 2012

Decker's good luck didn't last long. The half million of insurance proceeds went to Starship Financial to pay down the loan. A week later, they declared even more inventory was ineligible for borrowing. They were not letting any loan agreement get in the way. They wanted their money and had the right in their sole discretion to declare any collateral was garbage.

Starship demanded another meeting with Decker to discuss how he was going to repay his loan. Gavin and JB accompanied their friend to the windowless bank conference room. The nicer room with the windows, draperies and imitation impressionist artwork was reserved for new clients. Exiting clients got the basement wall view.

Four bankers entered the room. Decker passed a note to Gavin and JB: "I know the two on the right. Never met the others."

Joseph Sheller, the senior account officer, said, "Thank you for being here today. As our auditors informed you, your loan is currently under collateralized by $800,000. How do you plan on returning to compliance?"

Decker spoke eloquently for several minutes about the improving business prospects, the cost cutting efforts, the new customers on the horizon, and the strengthening economy. The bank wasn't listening.

Joseph cut Decker off mid-sentence. "While we appreciate your efforts to improve your business, we need a substantial payment to reduce the loan balance. What can you provide in additional collateral? What other personal assets or guarantees can you give?"

The bankers at the end of the table were scribbling notes to each other and chuckling at the proceedings. They wore mortician clothes – black suits, white shirts and black ties. Their behavior appeared intentionally rude and disrespectful.

Gavin raised his hand to stop Decker from responding. He said, "Decker, hold on. I want to know the identity of those two men at the end of the table and their position in the bank. I'm not accustomed to attending a meeting where people aren't introduced."

The banker with the grayish complexion and scraggly shadow said, "You don't need to know my name nor my title. I work for the bank."

JB asked, "In what department?"

The banker answered, "Forget the charade. My name is Mr. Blech, and I'm the senior vice president in charge of asset recovery."

JB asked, "I assume you mean workout."

"We prefer to call it asset recovery," Mr. Blech said. "We intend to have our loans repaid like you promised when you borrowed the money."

Gavin said, "Mr. Blech, seeing as we're in workout, it seems a little late to be giving you more collateral. Here is what we'll do. Decker Doors and Windows will work on a financial restructuring plan and refinancing. You already have all of our assets as collateral. We request 90 days of forbearance to find alternative lenders.

"If you agree to our plan, we'll begin an immediate reduction in inventory levels that will reduce your loan in the ordinary course of business. This is preferable to any other plan your workout bankers can deliver. We'll also reduce our work force and negotiate a payment plan with our vendors. That should move most of the vendor payments past the 90-day period we are requesting. You can provide an answer now, or at your own timing. The choice is yours."

Blech and his sidekick attorney left to confer for ten minutes and returned to the room. He said, "We're not agreeing to a formal forbearance. Go ahead and work your plan. If we see progress, perhaps we'll enter into something. Personally, we don't think you'll succeed.

"Meanwhile, we demand the following: First, the owner has to take a fifty-percent reduction in salary. He's overpaid as it is. Second, one of our collateral monitoring officers is moving into your offices full-time. Third, we won't advance any additional funds to buy inventory. No bonuses. No 401k. No consultants, lawyers or accountants get paid.

"But you will continue to make payments on Decker's $5 million dollar key man life insurance policy. You never know when we might get lucky. We want your plan in writing next week. Are those conditions agreeable?"

JB and Gavin side barred with Decker. Gavin answered, "The terms are not agreeable, but they are acceptable. We'll send you the plan."

They stood and left. On the drive back to Bergenfield, JB said, "Let's get some comfort food. I feel skewered."

He pulled into the parking lot of The Chit Chat Diner on Essex Street in Hackensack. JB ordered for the table. Road Side Sliders, Jersey Fries and a sampler of chicken fingers, Buffalo wings and mozzarella sticks.

Gavin turned to Decker and said, "I'm a workout consultant. But you shouldn't take my word on this because we're friends. Go see Michael Li tomorrow and ask him about the prospects of obtaining another asset based loan in this market. I think it'll be very tough. No one is lending these days."

Decker said optimistically, "Don't these guys realize that we're about to turn the corner if we just had a little more time and money?"

JB answered bluntly, "Decker, they live in a draconian world. They just want their money back. If you help them recover their loan, they'll be nice. If you don't, they'll wreak havoc on you. Now eat up. This is great food."

CHAPTER 184

DECEMBER 4, 2012

Hurricane Sandy was barely a month past. Awnings along Washington Avenue remained torn as a reminder. Shoppers at Allie's were still buying small items for repairs, but Christmas gifts were the furthest thing from most people's minds.

She had ordered her seasonal items six months ago, and customers were buying the more practical gifts so far. Allie's venture into specialty holiday decorations wasn't exactly taking off. Still, she wasn't panicking – yet.

Local content continued to rule. In October, Allie had brought up dozens of galvanized steel watering cans from the basement. She paid two high school art students three dollars a can to paint smiling suns and daisies. She had thought of moving the cans back to storage. Who the heck was going to buy a watering can after a hurricane? Then a few sold.

She hung a sign over the display: "PAINTED BY BHS ART DEPARTMENT STUDENTS!" The unpainted pails usually sold for $29 apiece. Allie marked the cans up to $40.

Barbara Lamanna, an old high school friend, saw the display and said, "Allie, they want $70 dollars for a vintage-like can online, and their flowers are stick-ons. Your cans are much nicer. You should raise your prices."

Afraid of being too greedy, Allie raised prices slightly. The pretty pails sold out in two days, and Allie rush-ordered more to meet the demand.

A teen Goth artist joined the painting sessions after school. She painted a pail with a scene of black suns and dreary skies over a graveyard. Her embarrassed but supportive mother bought the pail, and Allie kindly persuaded the teen to express her artistic ambitions elsewhere.

The Hedge Fund Grannies had created a line of knitted golf head covers with the high school logo. Then they needlepointed "I Survived Sandy!" on inexpensive canvas workshop aprons. They were a big hit!

Auntie Ev made another quilt – this time a New York Yankees theme using old team jerseys and tee shirts that her sons had left lying around the house. Allie hung the quilt in the front window. The highest bidder before Christmas Eve owned it.

First day bids exceeded $300. Customers offered to buy more after the bidding was complete. Auntie Ev begged off. She said, "Consider that one a gift, but it took a hundred hours to make it, and I'm out of material. By the way, you shouldn't sell it for less than a thousand dollars. It's one of a kind."

Marty found a better use for his time than spraying graffiti on the high school walls. He assumed the role of the store webmaster. He posted a picture of the Grannies in a circle making needlepoint on the store website. Under the photo, it read:

Hurricane Sandy Aprons – Available only at Allie's!

Allie thought, *Even if this venture fails, at least Marty is improving at school and a little happier. And he isn't getting into trouble now that he's busy. He's too tired at the end of the day.*

The elephant in Allie's store was the huge debt owed to Jake's. It was like the U. S. national debt. Everything was fine as long as you ignored the $20 trillion the country had borrowed.

CHAPTER 185

DECEMBER 7, 2012

Averill had to keep NBCI's stock price stable until the waiting period for the NASDAQ listing was official. He held an investor conference at the Clinton Inn in Tenafly, New Jersey. The event was disguised as a Retirement Planning seminar, but it was all about buying ROOT stock. Clients received a free dinner and drink if they brought along a prospect.

Averill was trying to upgrade his image. Tenafly was on the better side of the tracks geographically and financially. The eastern hillside of the town was home to the very wealthy and just a ten-minute drive to the George Washington Bridge and New York City.

A picture of Averill with his waxed handlebar moustache stared from the PowerPoint presentation. Underneath it described him as "Founder of NBCI – a seasoned financial executive born to a family hailing from three generations of Wall Street financiers."

Averill wore the latest version of his trademark brown vested suit and accompanying gold pocket watch. He pulled the watch out frequently to check the time and impress his clients.

The slide show mimicked the *Penny Daily News* advertisement. Why change a good thing? He talked about the great returns on CRAB futures, the Hurricane Sandy effect on prices, Pierre Beauty Products, the federal grant, the three new board members, and ROOT's longstanding good corporate governance.

Averill changed his tone and sounded like he had been born into three generations of circus barkers. He warned, "Don't buy CRAB futures. It's too risky. People lost family fortunes in October when Hurricane Sandy hit. When you buy futures, you're up against sophisticated and powerful commodity traders at investment banks with unlimited financial resources. In fact, you'd be trading against someone like me!

"Yes, I think the price of CRAB will keep increasing. It's a limited natural resource. It has the potential for many other uses. But an investor can lose money overnight and never get to see the ultimate dream of financial independence come true.

"No, I won't allow you to invest in CRAB futures. If you want to buy CRAB, I insist you trade with another broker. I'd rather lose the business than see my clients lose money to risky investments. No, my friends. The way to play the CRAB commodity is to own ROOT stock."

Averill had never fired a customer since the day he passed his Series 7 stockbroker exam. He had never refused an order considered too risky for a widow or orphan.

Averill cheered for ten minutes. ROOT was going on the NASDAQ in two weeks, which was fantastic for the company. ROOT was fabulous. ROOT was great. ROOT was wonderful. ROOT, ROOT, ROOT!

Averill opened a hundred new accounts at the conference. They all wanted to buy ROOT before it went any higher. The rumor spread around the dinner tables. Averill was close to management and had a pipeline to inside information. This was clearly a sure thing.

CHAPTER 186

DECEMBER 8, 2012

JB and Decker sat in Michael Li's banking office. Michael said gently, "I'm sorry. Our bank won't lend to any real estate or related industry. That includes building suppliers, lumber yards, electrical supply, anyone. I must admit, we'd call your loan too.

"Ten years ago, there were a number of asset based lenders who lent to turnarounds. They all were acquired by the big banks. The banks are in trouble, so the lending officers are twiddling their thumbs. This consolidation of the lenders has been a very bad thing for small borrowers.

"Here is what I would do if I were you: I'd develop a plan that raises the most money from liquidating your assets. If you manage to repay the loan, you may still have enough to restart the business someday.

"Unfortunately, you will be letting employees go along the way. The last person standing will be you and your accountant. Actually, he may be there after you leave."

After meeting with Michael, Decker gazed miserably from his office window at the plant floor. Most of his workers were idle but trying to look busy. He worked all night developing a plan to lower the bank's loans and save the company. He showed it to Gavin the next morning.

Gavin said diplomatically, "Why are you doing all of this work for the bank? They aren't giving any awards for sportsmanship, you know. Do you expect them to give you some bonus for paying back 80 percent of the loan? I doubt it."

JB offered, "It's worth a try. But the word 'lender' is now missing from their corporate mission statement. Those two characters that we met at the bank are not nice guys. We can try to get a release of your guarantee and some bonus for achieving your plan. Maybe they'll allow you to keep the company car for a while."

Decker requested a meeting with the bank. They declined in an email. "Just send the plan. Use regular mail. Don't waste money on overnight!"

CHAPTER 187

DECEMBER 10, 2012

Allie entered Ben's Deli and shook off the bitter December cold. The jukebox played *Cold as Ice* by Foreigner.

Allie called across the room, "Very funny, Ben. You know I'm not like that."

Ben gave his Rhett Butler voice, "Allie, my dear. Not every song is about you. Today, it's about the weather!"

Allied removed her New York Jets woolen cap and sat down with JB, Bret and Gavin. "Well, I learned another valuable lesson. Don't count on the mail during a hurricane."

Bret said with concern, "What happened?"

"Everything's okay now, but Jake's never got my check," said Allie. "You'd think they'd have called me, but no, they hired a collection agency who threatened to sue. Can ya believe it? I hand-delivered another check and made that jerk salesman leave his meetin' and sign for it. That'll teach him to harass me!"

JB asked, "How's the store doing?"

"I'm worried," Allie shrugged, "but I'm always worried. It's my first time around, and I just don't know what the norm is.

"Hardware did okay last month 'cause of the hurricane effect. I wish I had more power generators to sell. I'm still hopin' Allie's Corner picks up.

"It's the Christmas stuff that's not sellin'. I bought a lotta specialty decorations, lights, cute little Christmas village scenes. You know, the stuff you can't find at Walmart. It's just not moving. Any of you guys wanna buy a Charles Dickens streetlamp? C'mon Bret. Don't you need ten thousand bucks worth of bubble tree lights?"

Bret cowered in jest. "Um, I'm not decorating this year. Sorry."

"Bah, humbug! You Scrooge!" Allie laughed. "Well, if everyone's gonna be like Bret, I'm gonna be short. I already tried to clear out the rest of my 401k, but Avy's too busy doin' seminars to take my calls. Maybe he'll pick up the phone if I buy some NBCI stock…Not!"

"If you want, I'll talk to Averill," said JB. "He's probably just busy."

STCK-TV's Betsy Sands appeared on the overhead TV screen. The closed captioning read, "Apple is now down to $545 after hitting above $700 only a few months ago in September. Has Apple lost its luster due to competitive threats from Samsung and Rim? Is Apple's growth over and the growth stock is now a value trap? For an opinion on the trading activity, here is our own Cliff Lenihan."

Cliff sat next to Jay McCall and Betsy in the studio with a huge grin. Cliff was the loved-and-hated stock-picking personality on STCK-TV. He was revered by small investors who learned the inside story on stock trading principles. He was despised by jealous traders who thought he had far too much airtime. His cornball trading references were legendary and usually very funny.

Cliff said, "Apple is very volatile. It has dominated the news for eighteen months. The stock rise was almost unprecedented. But need I remind everyone about the Cisco rise just twelve years ago. In March of 2000, Cisco hit $147 a share and the market cap of the company was over $500 dollars. Sound familiar? Now Cisco trades for less than twenty bucks and everyone hates it.

"This might be what's happening to Apple. No one wants to own this anymore. Mutual funds want the stock out of their year-end portfolios. You should ignore this stock for another year. If you really have to own it, sell a put option. If the stock goes down, you own the stock at a cheaper price. If the stock goes up, you make money on the put. It's one way to make money on a stock sliding downhill."

Everyone was tired of hearing about the Apple demise. If you owned it and hadn't sold, you were panicking. If you never owned it, you had no sympathy for the people who didn't take their gains. Samsung had the audacity to air advertisements that Apple might not be cool anymore. It woke everyone up. The Apple glory days may have ended.

Averill watched Cliff's report. He still had customers holding onto their Apple stock. He began calling the remaining holdouts.

"Harold, Harold, Harold, listen to me. It's not going back up. I told you last week to get out of Apple and it's down another twenty bucks. You need to sell now. It's going to $300. Buy a good growth stock like ROOT and double your money in six months."

CHAPTER 188

DECEMBER 10

JB removed his gray herringbone fedora and unbuttoned his black cashmere overcoat as he entered the musty offices of LMNOP. Averill was surfing the web on his computer.

"Didn't you ever hear of porn shui?" JB bellowed.

Caught red-handed, Averill quickly closed his laptop and said defiantly, "You mean feng shui, don't you? My desk faces the door, which is how it's supposed to be. I read that stuff too, you know."

JB looked at the rickety chair and decided to remain standing. In a condescending tone, he said, "Feng shui is positioning your environment for positive energy. Porn shui is aiming your laptop so visitors don't see you trawling through disgusting web sites. I can see the reflection in the window, you moron."

"I don't know what you're talking about," Averill said sheepishly. "I'm researching a stock. Just clicked on the wrong site, that's all. They must have similar…"

JB held his hand up. "Averill, stop! I don't care. I'm here to help a friend. However, while I'm here, I think you and I need to have a chat. Maybe you can take my advice so you stop putting the whole town at risk. I've seen you hanging around with Johnny at Ben's lately. You guys have become pretty friendly, don't you think?"

"I'm his investment banker!" Averill said defiantly. "We have to stay in touch."

"Averill, you're an investment banker like I'm an astronaut," JB said with a smirk. "You're a broker. That's all. I saw how NBCI made its money last quarter. You guys bet the house on crabgrass, and got lucky with Hurricane Sandy. I'm guessing you doubled down this quarter. Am I right?"

Averill was perplexed. He didn't know where JB was going with the four headed conversation. "You're asking for material inside information. I'm not authorized to discuss the company's affairs with you."

"Why not? You tell everyone else in town. Besides, it's not illegal if I don't trade on it," JB smiled knowingly. "It doesn't matter. I already know the answer. Of course you bought more. You two clowns are risking the life savings of people in this town and putting Bergenfield at risk of a default. Someday your scheme is going to reverse and you guys are going to lose a bundle."

JB picked up a framed LMNOP certificate: *Broker of the Year.* "I guess this little award explains why your branch manager isn't watching you so closely.

"Let's get this over with. I have a simple request. Allie says you won't return her calls. She needs to transfer her 401k to a corporate account. I want this taken care of today. Agreed?"

"Is that it? I'll see what I can do. It's a lot of paperwork," Averill said dismissively.

JB growled, "Don't wise off to me, kid. You're not doing another thing today until you take care of this."

"Okay, okay. I'll do it," Averill cried in defeat. "She's not trading anyway. That it?"

JB leaned over Averill's desk with an intimidating glare. "I'm concerned about friends of mine in town. These are nice, older people whose life savings are invested in NBCI. I have nothing against the company, but no one should ever have their entire retirement fund in one stock, even an IBM or a Google.

"I don't care how you do it, but diversify their portfolios. No more than twenty percent of their assets go into NBCI. You understand? If any charity or church was stupid enough to trust their money with you, they go on the list too. Everyone else can make their own beds."

Averill asked, "What if some of them don't want to sell?"

JB shot him a steely stare, piercing through Averill's eyes straight to the back of his skull. "Just warn them. You send them a financial suicide notice that they are taking unnecessary risk. That'll make them think twice. If they don't sell, at least it was their choice.

"And stop this stupid insider information stuff. Keep it up and you won't be in business in three months. They'll repossess your girlfriend's BMW. They'll take your house. You'll spend your next summer vacation in Rahway Prison. Now, do as I say. I'd hate to hafta come back here. This place is a dump."

Averill didn't want to tangle with JB. He had been some hotshot at ITT and seemed to be everywhere and connected to everyone. "Okay, but it'll take some time to unwind the positions."

JB replied calmly, "It's less than fifty people. That's not enough selling pressure to slam the market. Just think of the bright side. You get paid commissions when they sell. And when Allie visits, you drop everything you're doing and take care of her."

Averill dreaded the work. He'd have to call customers and convince them to sell the hottest stock in their accounts. Luckily, they weren't large holders. "OK, I think you may be right. This is a prudent approach for the older customers. By the way, do you want to open an account with me?"

JB shook his head in amazement. "You've got to be kidding me. Not a chance. And stop watching porn at work. How old are you? Fifteen? And put some Qi on your door. You need more positive energy in this place. How you keep any customers is beyond me."

JB left and Averill immediately thought of a spin he could use. He called the first customer on JB's list. "Mrs. Kepler? Hi, it's Averill. I was talking with my buddy, JB, and somehow your account came up in the conversation. I have some ideas about how to diversify your portfolio, reduce your risk exposure and improve your returns..."

CHAPTER 189

DECEMBER 12, 2012

Decker heard back from Starship Financial. Their response was, in no order of importance:
Bonus for accomplishing the plan? No!
Keep the company car? No!!
Release the guarantee? No!!!
No, no, and no.

CHAPTER 190

DECEMBER 12

Allie walked briskly in the thirty-degree temperature up Washington Avenue and entered Averill's offices. Ready for a battle, she said sternly, "Averill, you've refused my calls long enough. I want my money!"

Averill said sweetly, "Of course Allie, I have a set of documents here to set up the transfer. I cleared this with my retirement fund department. I filled in the basic information for you."

Allie was surprised at how accommodating Averill was being. "If that wouldn't be too much trouble, I want the balance sent to my corporate 401k plan. I'm not withdrawin' it. I'm investin' it into my store through a 'rollover as business startup'. I think they call it a ROBS."

Averill said, "I understand. Just sign these few forms and you should have the funds by Monday."

Allie shook her head as she walked back to her store. She thought: *Who was that in there? It couldn't have been Averill. What a piece of work. There's not an honest thing about him. Doesn't matter. I have enough money to pay my vendors. I just hope sales pick up soon.*

CHAPTER 191

DECEMBER 13, 2012

Allie surveyed the store shelves with a dozen days to go before Christmas. It was clear what wasn't selling. The holiday section looked pathetic. Too much inventory. It scared customers away with that creepy "no one wants to buy this" look. Faced with adversity, Allie managed to crack a smile as she thought of a pun: *If you don't sell it before Christmas, yule regret it!*

Allie's backyard survey wasn't encouraging. Although Bergenfield wasn't as badly hit as the shore towns, Hurricane Sandy still took its toll. Friends and neighbors confessed, "The insurance deductibles ate up the Christmas budget." "My insurance company hasn't paid my claim." "I didn't carry flood insurance." "Allie, I'm sorry, but roof repairs are just more urgent than toys and gifts."

The big stores at the malls had conceded defeat just days after Black Friday. They could tell from their daily tallies that sales would be slow. They started Christmas clearance sales two weeks earlier than usual. It was time for Allie to take action, too. She couldn't wait for customers to change their minds. It was time for a big sale. Thirty percent off all Christmas merchandise! Fifteen percent off all electric tools.

There goes the profit margin, Allie thought as she hung the sale sign from the store awning in the freezing temperature. *Whatever made me think I owned a Christmas shop? Bubble lights? Never again!*

CHAPTER 192

DECEMBER 14, 2012

Averill was having a heated phone conversation with ROOT's controller. "Justin, those shares were issued to an investor relations company. It's 'cause of them that the stock went from a dime to a dollar! You think this happens on its own? Those guys earned that money!

"Come on! Be reasonable. We're going on the NASDAQ in two weeks. You can't bring this up now. You'll make the company look bad."

Justin was pacing around Johnny's office. He was hopping mad. No one on the board kept regular minutes, and Roland's memory had conveniently faded. Jack Barlowitz hadn't been the company attorney for the private placement. Louie the Shell King had papered the transaction, and he wasn't talking to anyone. Oenotropae wanted nothing to do with the company.

Justin argued, "There's no record of this Rockland company ever doing business. It's dormant. They don't even have an office. Who owns it?"

Averill was exasperated. He had reasoned for nearly twenty minutes, and the controller was relentless. Johnny had given Justin too much grief for the last few months, and now he was exacting revenge.

Averill said, "Listen, Justin. Those are payments to market makers in our stock. It's perfectly legal. I want to speak to Jack and Roland. They'll understand."

Justin responded sternly, "Sure, you can talk to Jack. Because I'm not signing another SEC filing until I get a legal opinion from him."

Now was the time to force the issue on the note shares. Averill asked, "Before you call, do you have my ten million shares and the $1 million dollar stockholder loan listed?"

Justin went ballistic. "I'm cancelling them, too! The board never approved them."

Averill knew this day of reckoning would arrive, and was prepared. "Justin, you're making a big deal out of nothing. The board approved my stock loan at the last minute. It was an incentive for me to help improve shareholder value. You saw the shares in the private placement document. Hell, you even disclosed them in your financials. I have a signed stock certificate. How can you say they weren't issued?"

Justin retorted, "If the board didn't approve them, then they don't exist. End of story!"

Averill knew that bad records were his greatest ally. He said, "I'm coming over. Let's call Jack and see if he can come up with a solution."

CHAPTER 193

DECEMBER 14

Jack, Johnny and Justin sat in NBCI's brand new conference room. It was large but sparsely furnished with a table, a credenza, four chairs and nothing else. Not even the standard tray of bottled water for guests.

Averill was kept in the lobby. Justin gave his animated version of the share issuances. "Yes, they were disclosed in the private placement, but Averill and Louie DiSosa drafted the document. Yes, they were disclosed in the 8-K, but I copied language from the private placement."

Johnny explained his version of the events, but he was clearly supporting Averill's side. "Besides, I wasn't invited to the board meetings!"

Jack called the new chairman, Arthur Sterling, to make him earn his pay. After explaining the different versions of the facts, he said, "Arthur, the new board of directors is going to have to approve this or fight it, but it needs to get resolved quickly. I wouldn't bet on the outcome, but I'm sure it would be a protracted legal battle. This is a lot of money to Winthrop.

"The only positive is that the share price has gone up substantially. The cost of this purported investor relations services is immaterial to the company. It probably can't be proved, but it looks like Averill paid someone in shares to support the stock price. It's been done before in less visible manners.

"There are also the Tuxedo shares. The company is offshore, and we can't identify the owners. Averill said the shares might have been issued to an affiliate of Oenotropae, but it could have been the shell lawyer from Florida. That guy stopped talking to us after our first inquiry. We can't force him to talk without a subpoena, and we cannot subpoena without a lawsuit.

"Let's put those aside for the moment. The largest and most troubling issue is the ten million shares issued to Averill for a $1 million dollar note, which he has in his possession. It's notarized by his secretary, for whatever that's worth. She does whatever Averill asks.

"I looked at her notary ledger to see if I could pinpoint the time. She notarizes so little that this transaction is actually the last entry in the ledger. The company recorded the transaction, which argues in Averill's favor. It was also disclosed in the 8-K and the quarterly financials. Justin is adamant that the shares weren't properly authorized, but Johnny and Averill claim he has a grudge against them."

Justin spoke up. "I don't have a grudge, but I object to these shares being issued. This is not right."

Jack said calmly, "I understand your frustration, Justin, but this happens to a lot of companies during startup."

Arthur said, "I'll speak for the board. There isn't a lot of evidence that those shares were granted except share certificates that were pre-signed by an 82-year-old former chairman who has conveniently lost recall of the situation. . ."

Jack interrupted, "The chairman signed a hundred blank certificates. I cancelled them, so they can't be used anymore. Someone could have given themselves a billion shares if they wanted. There's a note, I grant you that."

Arthur resumed, "My guess is that the share and note might have been discussed, but who knows if the board approved it? This guy Averill did a lot of work to get this company public, and the value has increased since then. But those Rockland shares are troublesome. I'd say we need to start distancing ourselves from this character over the next year." Arthur banked his head in the direction of the lobby. "Let's get this behind us. Chalk it up to the costs of starting a business. Maybe Averill got away with one. What I suggest is we compromise on the number of shares. Go back to Averill and tell him we are willing to sue him. Then offer him five million shares and increase the note to $3 million. Justin, are you okay with that?"

Justin was fuming, but he saw that Arthur was trying to minimize the damage. "I want it on record that I had no knowledge about these share issuances. At least this is something I can explain to the auditors."

Arthur added, "One last thing. Jack, I want you to hire Kroll Associates and investigate this whole matter. I want to know who owns Tuxedo Investments and Rockland IR. If someone did something wrong, we'll turn them in to the DA."

After the call ended, Averill was invited into the conference room and told about the proposal. Averill saw potential millions of profits washed away. He protested, "This isn't fair to me. I earned those shares. The stock has gone from ten cents to a buck. I raised all that money…"

"Averill," Jack interrupted, "if you want to avoid litigation, the only alternative is to compromise. The board is prepared to sue you. There's one additional thing. You agree to sign a release of claims against the company and its board and officers and directors. Arthur said that these are the last shares you will ever receive from NBCI."

Averill thought for a minute. The shares were worth $5 million today. He was still ahead. If he pushed this too hard, the board might start investigating further. He acted harmed but willing to deal. "It isn't fair to me, but I'll cooperate for the sake of the company."

Justin was still steaming over the deal, and Jack was trying to calm him down.

Averill returned to his office and thought: *Between the Tuxedo and the note shares, I still pulled seven million shares out without paying for them. I still have my two million commission shares and I still have my five million warrants. I'll be fine as long as Misty doesn't spend it all before sundown.*

CHAPTER 194

DECEMBER 22, 2012

Hurricane or not, the town managed to hang the holiday decorations, although later than usual. Antique Christmas, Chanukah and Kwanza holiday decorations tried to paint a festive downtown mood.

Appealing to its diverse ethnic constituency, the town placed Santa Harabujee, the Korean version of Saint Nick, dressed in blue, above the corner of Main and Washington. Down the road, a Filipino grocery shop offered large Christmas lanterns for sale. The traditional paróls were in the shapes of stars colorfully adorned with ribbons and bows.

Allie looked gloomily out her storefront window. She wasn't in the mood for a blue Santa. This just wasn't the season for frivolous gift giving. If she had stocked another fifty lithium ion, battery-powered chainsaws, she could have sold every one of them. The cute little Dickens' home with carolers and a horse drawn carriage? Humbug!

It wasn't tragic. Shoppers still visited. They just weren't buying the right stuff. Allie ruminated while she cut some ribbons: *I'll just have to tighten the belt. Tiny Tim will sell next year, if I can last that long. The big payment is due to Jake's next October. How the hell am I gonna find the money to pay that whopper? Forget it. It's Christmas, and no one's gonna ruin my holiday season!*

"*Fa-la-la-la-la, la-la-la-la!*" sang Allie as she wrapped the Black and Decker shop vacuum cleaner.

She thought, *Can you imagine getting' a dust buster for Christmas? The husband opens the festive wrappin' and weeps uncontrollably. 'It's just what I dreamed about. Oh, the joy!'*

"There you go, Mrs. Benson. And have a Merry Christmas!"

Tis the season to be jolly!

CHAPTER 195

DECEMBER 24, 2012

MERRY ROTTEN CHRISTMAS! Ho! Ho! Ho!

On Christmas Eve at 4:00 PM, Mr. Blech, Asset Recovery Officer of Starship Financial, personally delivered the formal notice of default to Decker. Blech wore a big smile.

He lit a cigar and said, "I wanted to make sure you got this notice in time for the holidays. Christmas spirit and all that jazz. You can stay at fifty percent salary and manage your inventory liquidation plan. Or you can leave and we'll run it for you. Either way, we don't care."

"You can't smoke in here. It's a fire hazard," Decker protested.

Blech flipped an ash onto the floor. "It's not your plant anymore, former rich boy. You don't make the rules.

"Here's a list of the pay cuts for the employees who get to stay. Everyone else gets fired on Wednesday. Terminate the 401k! And no paying the fees to administer the shut-down! It's time your employees paid their way. Empty the petty cash box into the bank account. No more frivolity. Nothing! I'm placing a monitor in the plant. We want to see every check."

Decker asked incredulously, "You're firing everyone the day after Christmas? Most of my people are on vacation this week."

Blech said, "Call them into the office and break the news. I'll do it if you can't handle it. I'm pretty good at this firing thing. Also, you have four weeks to repair that steel door inventory, and then those workers go too. And I have one last gift for you this Christmas Eve. Hand me the keys to the company car. That perk is kaput."

Decker fumbled with the key ring. He couldn't believe the heartlessness of this man. Minutes later, a security officer hovered over him as he emptied his personal belongings from the trunk. He stuffed the workout clothes and family photos into a paper bag.

Without a car, he walked slowly along the railroad tracks toward town. The old Christmas lights and decorations hung from lamp posts like a 1950's postcard. Decker wasn't living in a Norman Rockwell painting today. He was in a Steven King nightmare.

CHAPTER 196

DECEMBER 24

Panama Blonde was driving home when she saw Decker walking through town. Something looked wrong. She stopped and offered him a ride home. He said, "No thanks. I'm going to Tommy Fox's for a drink."

Catherine said, "Okay, I'll join you. It's not like I want to nuke a frozen dinner on Christmas Eve."

The bar was nearly empty. The regulars were home with family this one night of the year. They sat in a booth and ordered white wines. Decker told Catherine the story of his horrid day.

"I always cooperated with the bank. I just don't know why they enjoy demeaning me so much." Decker finished off his second glass of wine and signaled the cocktail waitress for another. "Maybe it's for the best. I've been working harder and longer hours. It doesn't make a dent. Customer loyalty only goes so far.

"My construction contractors are all going broke. They don't pay me…I don't pay my vendors. My workers haven't had a raise in three years. Morale is terrible. Maybe fighting this is a wasted effort. Decker Doors is a lost cause. Two hundred workers."

Panama tried to remain upbeat. "Decker, you're a good-looking guy. You're smart and hardworking. You've got great friends here. I always believe from every misfortune something good happens. Maybe someone is telling you there's a better opportunity on the other side of the mountain."

Decker gave a wan smile. "Okay, Miss Sunshine. Did someone take your car away today? He could've waited a day until I found a rental. He laughed at me as I walked out the door. Blech put on a Santa Claus hat and pretended he was firing workers sitting on his lap. He's just cruel."

Catherine touched his hand and said sympathetically, "I'll give you a ride home tonight, as long as I don't drink too much. Then we'd both be walking home."

Catherine let out an evil chuckle. "I have a great idea. You can use my husband's car until you get on your feet again. It's old, but it's cute. It's a 1979 Karmann Ghia convertible, but the heater works. It's a classic. You'll look cool in it!"

They laughed and ordered another round. She palmed the mistletoe she was going to use to cheer Decker up.

CHAPTER 197

DECEMBER 27, 2012

The board of directors and management team assembled early morning for a corporate photo at NBCI's headquarters. They would be ringing the opening bell the next morning at the NASDAQ Stock Market. Averill injected himself into one of the group photos despite Arthur Sterling's scowl. The chairman pulled Jack aside and said, "I'm not going to make a scene today, but make sure that last photo doesn't see the walls of our offices."

Averill looked positively slithery in his medium-brown vested suit. Misty had given up trying to improve his style of clothes. She had partially won the battle by forcing him to at least buy better quality versions of the same model. The suit and gold pocket watch made him feel like an original robber baron. He used extra wax this morning for his handlebar moustache. He wore a permanent press white shirt and a dark green striped tie he purchased at the town's discount men's store with some of his newfound wealth.

The NBCI management team wore imaginative sport coats. Tom McInerney had on a horrible maroon and gray checked jacket, a short sleeve shirt and a tie that was three inches above his belt buckle. Johnny wore a cloud of black: Black jacket. Black tie. Black shirt. Black socks. Everything was black except the fashionably incorrect brown shoes.

Justin dressed in accounting splendor – drab navy. Alistair McClendon was the only team member who looked respectable in his gray Savile Row wool suit and subtle pencil-thin striped tie.

After the photo session, the chairman called Johnny and Averill into the conference room and dressed them down. Or more appropriately, he told them to dress up. "Averill, Alistair is too busy planning the ceremony. I may regret putting you in charge of anything, but, albeit brown, you're the only other one around here who knows what a suit is. This team must wear appropriate clothes for such an important event. You and the team are driving into New York today to buy some respectable clothes. You're going public on the NASDAQ, for cripe's sakes."

CHAPTER 198

DECEMBER 27

Averill drove the fashion-challenged management team to the Brooks Brothers store on Madison Avenue and 44th Street in New York. Arthur had called the store in advance and requested concierge treatment. In an emergency like this, Brooks Brothers would find a way to tailor the pants and jackets the same day. Buy a suit, belt, shirt, tie, and shoes for three men. That's about $4,000 dollars.

The Madison Avenue store was worthy of landmark status. It's stately. It's old world. It's grand. Upon entering, you see tall ceilings and old wooden display cases, salespeople impeccably dressed, and a large floor of the best of everything. Brooks Brothers defined haberdashery for business men and women.

Averill took the three NBCI gherkins to the fourth floor "1818" suit section. Averill began to explain their situation to Mr. Samuel Benedict, who by his gray hair and demeanor appeared to have worked at the store for a very long time.

Mr. Benedict held up a polite hand to interject. "Arthur told me you were coming. As a favor to him, we will accommodate you. We have dressed over thirty U. S. Presidents and many CEOs around the world. Do you want to look around or do you want me to suggest something?"

He didn't wait for a response. "For the TV cameras, two of you should wear dark gray and two should wear navy suits. No striped shirts. No geometric tie patterns. They don't show well on television."

Averill tossed a thumb at his companions. "We only need suits for those three guys."

Mr. Benedict cleared his throat and said in a low voice, "Mr. Winthrop, I'm sure you feel comfortable in that suit, but you'll make a much stronger impression in something darker."

What he didn't say was, "Your suit doesn't fit, the lapels are too wide, the seat of your pants is baggy, your pants pocket is torn, the heels of your pants are dragging on the floor, they don't have cuffs, and the toes of your shoes curl like Santa's elves."

Averill at first was flustered because he thought he looked quite dashing. Then he thought, *I'm getting a free suit, so why argue?*

Mr. Benedict continued and showed suits for each executive that matched their personalities. "Mr. Winthrop, this charcoal gray suit is what we call the investment banker's special. Most Wall Street executives have at least one in their closet."

Averill beamed as he tried on the suit. *Hey! Look at me. I'm an investment banker!*

Mr. Benedict fitted the rest of the team with conservative suits and took the foursome to the first floor to shop for ties. "I recommend this red striped tie for the navy suit, this blue foulard for the pinstripe suit, and this gold striped tie for the other gray suit. Mr. Winthrop, may I suggest that you wear this grey and maroon wide stripe tie. The bankers at JC Montague wear this tie."

JC Montague! That was all Averill needed to hear. He was sold.

After the ties, everything else was standard issue. Blue or white button-down shirts. No stripes on TV. Winged tip shoes for the two operations executives. Cordovan loafers for Averill and Johnny.

Mr. Benedict said, "Mr. Sterling has already paid for everything. The suits will be ready for you at four o'clock."

As they left the store, Averill argued it didn't make sense to head home and then head right back again. They walked to Smith & Wollensky on Third Avenue and 49th Street where they waited an hour to be seated. Averill thought, *Maybe we won't have to wait next time if we wear our new wardrobes?*

CHAPTER 199

DECEMBER 28, 2012

It was the Friday before New Year's Eve. The NBCI board and management team assembled at NASDAQ's glamorous and spectacularly lit studios in New York City's Time Square.

Arthur Sterling would be ringing the opening bell, a ceremonial benefit for new companies listing on the exchange. The video was streamed live to audiences of STCK-TV, FOX Business and MSNBC.

Averill had no intention of missing out on the ceremony. He pushed his way to the front of the group and stood next to Johnny. He wanted to be sure that he could be seen on television. The NBCI corporate team clapped upon orders from the NASDAQ coordinator, and Arthur rang the bell at 9:30 AM. It was a great ceremony and a once-in-a-lifetime experience for the limited few.

The reverse split officially occurred at the opening of business. A little over 190 million shares magically turned into 9,725,000 post-split shares. The 6.5 million management stock options reversed into 325,000. Johnny's 100,000 options no longer looked so impressive.

The stock price had closed the night before at an even $1. Averill had successfully managed to keep the stock propped up during a difficult time for many companies. When the ROOT shares opened for trading, the opening price was a nice, round, trader-assisted $20. A perfect one-for-twenty reverse split.

After the bell-ringing, management photos were taken in Times Square. The NASDAQ electronic tickertape streamed the ROOT stock price across the building facade. Behind, the stands were being constructed for dignitaries to witness the New Years' Eve ball dropping ceremony on Monday. This was a big moment for Averill. He thought, *Life can only get better from here.*

CHAPTER 200

DECEMBER 31, 2012

On the morning of New Year's Eve, Averill strutted into Ben's Deli in his new "I'm a Wall Street Investment Banker" charcoal-gray, Brooks Brothers suit. He looked rather sharp, even though he was wearing the same shirt as Friday. Averill made a mental note: *Buy more shirts at Brooks Brothers. Maybe even a second tie.* He felt fabulous.

At first, diners barely recognized the well-dressed version of Averill. Ben was kind to him despite his love connection to Mean Misty. He said, "Avy, you guys looked great on TV yesterday. We're all proud of you. Breakfast is on me."

A shocked Averill thanked Ben and sat alone at a booth and waited. Misty arrived a half hour late in a hissy fit. She destroyed Averill's fifteen minutes of fame in fifteen seconds.

She lashed at him, "How dare you go to that ceremony without taking me! You ungrateful selfish jerk! After all I have done for you, you think only of yourself. At least I would have improved the appearance of you clowns in your boring dark suits. Who dressed you, the Grim Reaper?"

Misty stabbed Averill for another ten minutes with her caustically worded fashion dagger. She huffed out of Ben's and drove away in the BMW that the ungrateful, selfish jerk had bought her.

JB stopped at Averill's table as he was leaving. "Kid, don't listen to her. The first respectable thing you ever did was buy that suit and tie. The second respectable thing was not bringing her to the ceremony. It's not a cocktail party. It's business! May I suggest you keep the suit and drop the baggage?"

Averill shook his head. *I can't win.*

CHAPTER 201

DECEMBER 31

It was New Year's Eve. Evening was approaching and, once again, Bret was nowhere to be found around town. Well, he could be found, but it was in an office in downtown

Manhattan with a team of colleagues making final document changes to an investment which absolutely had to close before midnight.

Sometimes he had to prepare documents for an acquisition that had to close before year-end for tax reasons. More often, it was because the company wanted to book investment banking fees before year-end to pay banker bonuses. Whatever the reason, the lawyers worked every last minute of every New Year's Eve to get documents signed and filed.

At 5:30 PM, Bret walked into the offices of Chadwick Townson, the investment banker whose deal was so earth shatteringly critical. Chad wasn't one of the smart MBAs who knew how to structure corporate finance deals. He was a front man, a pretty boy who wooed customers for the investment banking area. He stood six-foot-four, had dark, Alec Baldwin gelled hair, and wore obnoxious suspenders with dollar sign decorations.

Bankers brought Chad along for client presentations because he was a good looking jock. He was mildly famous for scoring a touchdown in the final seconds of a football game memorable only to a Yale or Princeton alum. It didn't hurt that his family was wealthy and connected. The word around the office was that Chad was a dope and barely graduated in five and a half years. The real bankers asked him to restrict his conversation to football matters in client meetings.

Bret handed Chad the signature pages with Post-It Arrows indicating the John Hancock lines. "Sign here and we're finished!"

Chad looked askance at Bret and said, "Have you made all of the changes I requested?"

Bret said less than politely, "They're cosmetic and not necessary. Please sign this now so we are assured of closing today. I'll bind a closing book for you on Wednesday which will reflect all of your urgent and important changes. You'll have your deal."

Chad raised his voice. "I demand to see the marked changes before I sign. Otherwise, you won't be working here!"

"Then you won't have a deal tonight, will you?" Bret said sarcastically. "And you won't make your bonus check either. Now, either sign this page, or I leave and you have nothing."

Bret's bosses had left the executive offices hours earlier. There was no one for Chad to appeal to on New Year's Eve. He couldn't force Bret to stay short of physically tying him to a chair. He angrily scribbled off his signature and said, "Enjoy your next career, putz!"

Bret realized that he may have unintentionally just tendered his resignation. It would only be a matter of time. But he didn't care. Bret hadn't kissed a date at midnight on New Year's Eve in ten years. He thought: *This has to change. I'm making a ton of money and have nowhere to spend it and no one to spend it on. This year, my resolution is to have a normal life.*

CHAPTER 202

DECEMBER 31

Bret called Allie at the store just before closing time and told her what happened. She said, "Bret, you'll be happier leavin', trust me. Workin' for jerks is demeanin'. Buy a retail store like me. We can go broke together!"

Bret laughed and offered to buy Allie dinner. She said, "Boy, you really don't get out much, do you? You can't get a reservation anywhere tonight unless you're Donald Trump. Come over to my house and join Marty and me. I'm makin' poor man's Chateau Briand. I use sirloin instead of filet mignon, but it tastes great! You can bring the wine.

"I need another hour at the store. I just took delivery of the December shipment of 12,000 bags of worthless crabgrass killer. I had to rent a huge trailer to store the stuff."

Bret searched his credenza and found what appeared to be expensive wine that an M&A client had given him at a closing. Chateau Margaux Premier Grand Cru Classe sounded fancy enough.

He drove the familiar way home, the same route he took a little more than a year ago to meet Misty. He thought as he took the Degraw Avenue exit from Route 95: *This isn't a date, right? I mean, we're friends. Everyone's a buddy to Allie. She treats JB like a father, Michael like an uncle, and Buyout like a kid brother. Allie's just one of the guys. Romance is off limits because of her kid. She made that clear a long time ago.*

She's pretty and smart with a heavy dose of Jersey girl attitude. What the hell am I thinking about? We've known each other for five years. What? All of a sudden we're going to start dating? Nah, I'm sure we're just friends. Boy, leaving work early on New Year's Eve sure does get you into trouble.

Bret pulled up to Allie's little Cape Cod home on Dudley Drive. Marty opened the door wearing a tux shirt and clip-on red bowtie. Allie walked from the kitchen wearing a sleek black cocktail dress and high heels. She had let the work ponytail down and added a few curls to her shoulder-length hair. Bret thought: *Whoa! That's not the Allie I know from breakfast!*

Allie greeted him with a brush kiss on the cheek and handed him a drink. "Scotch, right? I got this Johnnie Walker Black when I bought the store. I thought booze with the name "Johnnie" had to be good karma, right? Ha-ha!"

Allie returned to the kitchen to prepare dinner while Marty showed Bret how to play tennis on his Wii Sports game system. Later, during dinner, Allie told long tales about customers.

She had nicknames for her favorites: Mrs. Cummerbunds who always wore a fanny pack; Suzie Sweet Lips with her fantastic daily choices of colorful lip gloss; and her favorite, Prissy Primrose Prickly Thorn. Prissy had a massive rose garden and the cuts on her hands to prove it.

There was no talk of problems selling Christmas inventory. There was no discussion of Chadwick the preppy banker. If it wasn't funny and entertaining, the topic was jointly vetoed.

After dinner, they channel-surfed the New Year's broadcasts from around the world. Allie finally settled on the ABC New Year's Special. Ryan Seacrest had taken over for the late Dick Clark, and Fergie and Jenny McCarthy were interviewing fans in the crowd. Marty sat in the den and played games and chatted with friends on his laptop.

Maybe it was the heavy dinner. Maybe it was the scotch and red wine. Maybe it was the relaxed feeling around people he liked. Around 11:00 PM, Bret dozed off on the couch. A few minutes later, curled up in the Queen Anne chair, her high heels lying on the carpet, Allie fell asleep holding the remote.

Just before midnight, Marty woke them to the tune of *Old Lang Syne* on a toy kazoo. On the TV, the ball was being lowered in Times Square while billionaire New York Mayor Michael Bloomberg watched from the grandstand.

They walked outside. Fireworks sounded from the neighborhoods. Families had roused their children from sleep and banged pots and pans on their front porches. Allie, Marty and Bret blew on horns and blowouts to welcome the New Year.

They returned inside and Allie popped a small bottle of Frexienet Champagne. After the toast, Bret said it was time to go home. Allie followed him to the door and said, "I hope you enjoyed your first New Year's Eve as a free man." She gave him a cheek kiss as he left.

Bret thought as he walked to the car: *What was that? Did I just get friend-zoned? Not quite a kiss. What does that mean?*

He was beyond clueless when it came to women.

CHAPTER 203

JANUARY 12, 2013

Mid-January was the customary cold, dreary, gray and wet. The country had survived December's threatened government shutdown, members of Congress agreed to continue to hate each other, Europe managed to stay solvent, Japan was devaluing its currency, and China was, well, China.

The NBCI management team was slightly deflated. One day, you're a rock star wearing Brooks Brothers' suits and ringing the opening bell at the NASDAQ. The next, you're back at work wearing overalls and sorting crabgrass.

The stock price had stabilized around $20 in early January after the one-for-twenty reverse split. Moving to the NASDAQ was considered a success. The board was happy. Management was happy. Congratulations went all around. Even Averill got a pat on the back from the chairman. There just aren't many opportunities in a lifetime to experience the big event.

NBCI was now a near-respectable company with revenues and profits. The market value of NBCI reached $200 million. Not bad for a former penny stock.

Averill did a double take as some very weird trading activity flashed across his stock screen. Thousands and thousands of buy and sell orders for ROOT flooded the market in a rapid-fire style. The transactions didn't move the stock price much in either direction, but something was up. Humans couldn't enter orders this fast. It had to be computer program trading. Someone was clearly trying to manipulate the market.

Two million shares exchanged hands during the hour – 20,000 orders for a hundred shares each had traded on the Frankfurt Exchange. Averill thought: *When did we get listed in Frankfurt? This can only mean something bad. If this were insider trading, I'd know about it. Heck, I'd be the one starting the rumor. No. This can only mean one thing. Someone is organizing a short on ROOT.*

Then several large sell-orders hit the market. Bids for ROOT usually were in 100 and 500 share lots. An occasional 1,000 share order would appear. Orders for 10,000 shares were rare.

Bigger and better market makers had begun to trade the stock since ROOT joined the NASDAQ. However, none were going to risk their capital defending ROOT from selling pressure. Buyers cleared out of the way as 50,000 shares were offered for sale at $19. The offer price slid. Another 50,000 shares were offered for sale at $18. A hundred-thousand teased at $17. A buyer would need $1.7 million to execute the transaction. Even at $16, no one bit. Within an hour, the stock price settled to $15, down 25%.

Averill's iPhone was pinging mad. Lefty Stonewall messaged: "WTF? You better check out ROOT's message board. Someone's spreading rumors."

Averill was aghast. He thought he had been clever using the Yahoo! Finance message board to post rumors to help the stock. The shorts had outdone him. The Internet was flooded with the three I's: insinuations, innuendos and insults.

Dozens of shills posted:

BreakingWater: "I heard a woman in Kansas lost her hair. Suing Pierre!"

BrokenUnsound: "She's not the only one. Heard feds are investigating."

SquareRootofZero: "This stock is plummeting. I'm selling my position."

GasBag: "Forget selling. I'm shorting! Stock is going to zero!"

NoProblemoPaco: "I heard fraud. They cooked the books. Numbers aren't real."

AdieuToYou: "Fraud makes sense. Ain't no way they made those numbers last Q!"

Me-A-Me: "Odd the way the chairman left the company. No press release?"

ShiftlessInChiffon: "Yup. Old man musta known sumpins up."

CHAPTER 204

JANUARY 15, 2013

The major frontal assault appeared to be over. The shorts had sold two million "borrowed" shares. Someday, once they were satisfied with their gains, they'd buy the shares back at a lower price and return the shares to the lender.

Now, waves of small rats would nibble at the stock, a little every day. Keep the selling pressure on. Break the hearts and spirits of the investors until they gave up all hope. Plant the seeds of doom. Scare the hell out of them. "Hey, you suckers. Better sell now and get out before it's too late!"

So far they were winning. By Averill's calculation, the shorts were $10 million in the black. The question was always the same. Would they exit the position, take their profits, and leave the company alone?

History had shown that they always wanted more. If the first attack had worked, why wouldn't another? It usually took months of selling and planting false rumors to make most stocks dive. They had done it to ROOT in a day.

Averill warily watched the activity. Worried customers had called. "Should I sell?" Averill lied, "Of course not. This is normal after you go on the NASDAQ. It'll come back."

Averill received a call from his head of commodities, Peter Pleasance, the "P" in LMNOP. "Averill, the June CRAB contract is limit down this morning. A lot of contracts sold quickly at the opening, and someone offered to sell a thousand contracts at $120 dollars. Trading is done for the day. Tell me what you know!"

Limit down is a magical number established by the MERC for every traded commodity. When the price declined a certain amount, trading was halted for the day. CRAB's magic number was $20 dollars.

"What?" Averill pulled up the commodities screen and read the chart. "How could this have happened? Didn't Pierre buy anything on the down dip? Who's doing this?"

"All of the selling came from overseas," Peter said. "I'd guess this trade and yesterday's attack are related. NBCI owns a bunch of CRAB. If CRAB declines, doesn't it lose money?"

"I gotta go. I'll let you know," Averill said in a frantic voice.

Averill knew he had a huge problem. Someone was organizing a short run on CRAB futures and ROOT at the same time. Someone who had a lot of financial resources and sophistication.

CHAPTER 205

JANUARY 15

Averill called Johnny. "Do you guys have any bad news you haven't told me?"

"No," Johnny said in a puzzled tone. "We got those profits from the last CRAB transaction. We booked the extra revenue in October, but we already told everyone. We just went on the NASDAQ. What's bad about that?"

Averill said, "If they don't have bad news, they'll make it up. Johnny, how much cash does ROOT have?"

"Oh no you don't," Johnny said defiantly. "We gotta keep that money in the company under the muni bond. Don't even think about asking us to buy back our own stock."

Averill feigned the sound of being offended. "Of course I wouldn't ask you to do that. But we could buy more CRAB. The stuff is cheap right now. It's going to $200 this year. You'll double your money. You can't lose. Trust me.

"Listen, you have stock options in this company. They're going to be worthless if you guys don't fight back. Here's the deal. If the CRAB price drops more than ten bucks, you can sell and we'll bury the losses in the Pierre contract.

"But if the price bounces back, NBCI will make money. The stock will go to twenty bucks again, and your stock options will be worth millions. Johnny, you need to do this. It's your retirement plan!"

Johnny replied, "Okay, maybe we'll do it. Wait until tomorrow. See how the market opens. Maybe it'll go down more and we can get it even cheaper."

CHAPTER 206

JANUARY 26, 2013

And down it went. For the next ten trading days, the CRAB price declined steadily, a buck or two a day. It was nothing as dramatic as the first $20 selloff, but nevertheless a serious downtrend in the commodity world.

Rumors can move markets for a few hours; sometimes even for a few days. After a week, investors prefer facts. Pierre had never stepped in as a buyer and had remained remarkably quiet on the untrue stories circulating about their product. Hair salons don't read Yahoo! Finance message boards. Pierre was finally benefitting from the drop in CRAB prices, and didn't want to stop the decline.

ROOT's stock price fell in tandem. Traders were tense.

Ask any MBA what makes a stock price go down, they'll say it is a change in the discounted value of the market's expectation of future cash flows from the company's operations.

Ask any stockbroker, and he'll tell you there were more sellers than buyers. It's a strange answer. Aren't there a buyer and a seller every time a share changes hands? Yes, but in a declining market, the sellers are more anxious.

The short sellers were driving the herd to the slaughterhouse. Make everyone want to sell. Beat the optimism out of every holder. Make them wince every time they check the price. Regret not selling earlier. If the stock price shows any sign of a comeback, whack it over the head. If you want to invest in any company surrounded by professional short sellers, you needed a strong stomach and a lot of patience.

CHAPTER 207

JANUARY 29, 2013

Another storm approached from the Midwest. North Jersey temperatures dropped to 18 degrees. A pod of walruses had swum into Ben's and sat for coffee. Small human faces peeked from large, black, quilted overcoats. *Barrrruuuupha! Snort, snort, snort!*

Standard-issue New Jersey winter wear is basically a comforter with sleeves and pockets. Warmth overruled style. Think *Pillsbury Doughboy* in black. Diners shuffled sideways through the aisles. Hanging up your coat was unthinkable. Too much effort. Besides, where the heck were you going to hang forty quilts in Ben's?

Averill sat alone, his cheap raincoat slung over the back of his chair. He looked up and read STCK-TV's Jay McCall's closed caption words on the TV screen.

"In an article this weekend in Barker's Financial Magazine, an analyst claimed the FDA was concerned with the health effects of the CRAB commodity. The article also reported a rumor that a United States Congresswoman requested an inquiry into the subject. We asked around and have not been able to identify such a person in Congress.

"It's a little suspicious that NBCI shares dove the last two weeks on large volume. Now there's a selling pressure on the CRAB futures, too. Futures prices for June delivery have dropped $40 dollars this month, and it looks like shorts caused the decline."

Cliff Lenihan, the energetic stock-picking host, entered the screen. "Jay, don't be so sure about the existence of a real problem. Short sellers have used Barker's as a mouthpiece for negative news, and this may all be an attempt to profit quickly. Notice all of the unnamed sources and rumors. There's not a fact in the entire article. I don't know how these things get in the press and find legitimacy."

Betsy Sands, the morning co-host, chirped, "Is shampoo something the FDA even regulates? We don't consume it. For more on that topic, here is a report from Vijay Tavata."

Vijay stood shivering holding a microphone in front of a Washington, DC building. "Yes Betsy, it turns out the FDA does regulate cosmetics under the Federal Food Drug and Cosmetic Act, or the FDCA. It prohibits the marketing of adulterated or misbranded cosmetics in interstate commerce.

"I'll read the rule to you. *Violations – whether they result from ingredients, contaminants, processing, packaging, or shipping and handling – are those that cause cosmetics to be adulterated and subject to regulatory action. Under the FDCA, a cosmetic is adulterated if it contains any poisonous substance which could injure a user or it consists of any filthy, putrid or decomposed substance.*

"None of these applies to the Pierre shampoo, so it appears someone is trying to spread some nasty, unfounded rumors to move the markets. To verify our story, we contacted the FDA. They say they have no ongoing investigation of any products made by Pierre. So the story in Barker's appears to be fabricated. Back to you, Betsy."

CHAPTER 208

JANUARY 29

Finally some good news, thought Averill as he ran back to his office. He placed a few small orders to buy ROOT, and the price moved up a few pennies. The gain was short lived. A sell order for 5,000 shares slammed the market and drove the price back down. The shorts were still outselling him. Whatever Averill bought, they sold ten times as much. He wasn't going to win this battle.

Some little thing like the truth on STCK-TV wouldn't stop them from selling more. They were sitting on profits and had more than enough money to fight this battle. Besides, the news show only had a million or two viewers. Over 300 million Americans would never see it.

Averill thought through what was happening to the stock. He was trying to plug a leak in a dam using a thumb and pinkie. He was losing and didn't have enough resources. The buy side had collapsed. Where was the support?

The major brokerage firms that had become market makers during the last six months weren't buying today. Averill looked at the quotes for ROOT stock. It was filled with "out of the money" bids that would never get filled. The bidding floor was disappearing.

In the old days, the New York Stock Exchange had "specialists" assigned to every stock. They functioned as a middle man. It was part of their responsibility to keep trading flowing and make shares available to buy or sell when the market dried up. They continued to make markets when there was unusual pressure on a stock.

If price swings became too much to handle, market makers could initiate a trading halt. The exchange would ask companies if there were any unannounced news affecting the stock price. After the market stabilized, trading would resume. Trading halts were a rare occurrence, but it was also at a time when stocks didn't increase and decrease two percent every day.

But nowadays, trading was electronic. Market makers sat behind computer screens. Selling pressure on stocks came in blitzes from computerized trading programs. The programs were based upon complex algorithms written by Princeton mathematics whiz kids. When their calculus computation saw a stock price reach an inflection point, the program automatically sold shares.

Traders had always controlled the short-term markets, but now they had more powerful tools than ever. Long-term investors had to drink Bromo Seltzer to get through the day as the fast money wreaked havoc on stock and commodity prices, particularly for stocks that had little liquidity. Investors using these tactics controlled billions of dollars of resources. They could move markets in minutes by using ETFs to trade baskets of stocks quickly.

No one was big enough or dumb enough to step in front of a runaway train. Market makers simply get out of the way and let a crashing stock fall until it bounced off the floor. If the specialist rules applied today, there would be trading halts every five minutes. Chaos would rule. Specialists would be bankrupt.

Averill plugged the $12 share price into his "net worth calculator" and saw the number shrink below $5 million. If this kept up, he'd have nothing. He reminded himself of two of the oldest investing adages: "The trend is your friend," and "Never catch a falling knife." He was violating both.

At noon, he reversed course and began selling. He'd get liquid again, then buy back in at the bottom. Without Averill's buying support, the stock quickly plummeted to $10. Averill managed to sell 200,000 shares.

His customers were less lucky.

CHAPTER 209

FEBRUARY 1, 2013

Averill was in customer avoidance mode. He stayed away from Ben's and took the three office phones off their hooks. Clients were calling frantically, but Averill didn't want to take any sell orders. More selling would make the price slide even worse. He needed time for the market to cool.

He looked up from his desk covered with pink "important message" reminders and saw a story airing on STCK-TV on the small television screen in the conference room. Averill turned up the volume as exchange floor reporters, Bartholomew Mathews and Sally Guerra, spoke while the b-roll video of NBCI's plant ran in the background.

STCK-TV always had one reporter in charge of tough interviews. Bartholomew had become the newly appointed pit bull following the departure of the long-reigning attack dog, Christina Barcelona. He was a Brit in his thirties with light brown hair and horn rimmed glasses. He was sharp witted and very challenging with guests.

Sally was a no-nonsense, intelligent woman in her forties who was more politically sensitive in her reporting. She could easily be mistaken for an attractive soccer mom on weekends.

Bartholomew began, "Well, if we didn't have enough CRAB commodity and ROOT stock news for the month, there's more. Grossinger Securities has established yet another ETF. This $200 million offering is based on everything CRAB-related. The ETF is named Shampoo and the trading symbol is POO.

"For our newer viewers, an ETF, or electronic trading fund, is a listed security that has underlying assets like stocks, bonds or currency futures. An ETF trades a basket of related securities in real-time which means prices change throughout the day. This is different than a mutual fund, which settles at the end of the day.

"For example, your mutual fund company may offer an index fund that tries to mirror the performance of the S&P 500 index, which is composed of the largest 500 stocks. Similarly, the ETF version of an index fund is the SPDR S&P 500, known as the 'Spider'. Its ticker symbol, SPY."

The camera panned to Sally who said, "The POO ETF is unusual because it contains stocks, bonds and commodities. One of the more interesting attributes is that this ETF presents an arbitrage opportunity because investors know the underlying securities in the ETF. For example, arbitrageurs can sell the ETF while buying the CRAB related investments until the prices merge. Or vice versa.

"A unit of the POO ETF has a blend of Pierre Beauty Products common stock, CRAB commodity futures, ROOT common stock, and the NBCI industrial revenue bonds. Those bonds financed the transfer station and processing plant for the CRAB commodity.

"It's priced at $100 per unit and goes effective at the end of today. If you buy 100 shares of POO, you hypothetically own 20 shares of Pierre, 200 shares of ROOT, 60 pounds of CRAB, and $2,000 of Bergenfield-backed industrial revenue bonds."

Bartholomew added with a laugh, "No longer do you have to invest in all four vehicles to lose your net worth. You can just invest in POO and double down all in one place. I guess it will make tax record keeping simpler. No jokes please about what to use the POO paper certificates to wipe after it becomes worthless, please!"

CHAPTER 210

FEBRUARY 1

Averill jumped from his chair and waved his arms in a faux cartwheel in the cramped conference room. During the trading day, the POO ETF would begin buying CRAB futures and Pierre Beauty Products stock. Best of all, it would have to buy $25 million of ROOT stock.

The shorts were going to get squeezed. If the price of ROOT started rising, the shorts would have to buy back shares at higher prices. Watching a short squeeze was a lovely thing.

Averill had just sold 200,000 shares. It was time to buy them back and more. First, take care of his portfolio. Then answer customer calls.

He bought ROOT for his own account and quickly rebuilt his position. Averill wasn't the only one buying. A million shares traded during the hour. The price moved up quickly to $12.

The CRAB futures were moving too. Chicago traders had seen the same announcement. Averill called Johnny and left a message on his voicemail. "Johnny, the June CRAB future is about to take off! I'm buying 2,000 contracts for the company. You can thank me later. I had to do this to make the quarterly number. Don't tell Justin yet."

Averill called The Sticky Five. They had already seen the news. He posted on the ROOT Yahoo! Finance message board.

Tektikker: "Big news for ROOT today. POO on you, short sellers. This is HUMONGOUS."

Greenmasheen: "SHORT SQUEEZE! It's better than squeezing lemonade from lemons. The SHORTS are going to have to buy stock and take a loss!"

Contrariologist: "There's nothing to stop ROOT from going to $30 this time. I'm doubling down again! GO ROOT!"

Biohzrde: "I was really worried the last week. You guys told me to buy more. Good thing I did."

Averill thought about calling individual customers, but it would take too much time. He arranged a conference call on FreeConferenceCall.com. Averill's book of business had grown to 2,000 customers. He mass-emailed the list.

After the customers joined the call, Averill began his pitch. "Many of you made a lot of money during the last year on my advice by selling Apple before it collapsed. You made a lot more buying NBCI. We had a little bump in the road in January due to some misguided short selling activity. Two weeks ago, the shorts planted a story that the government was investigating the CRAB commodity which the FDA denied. STCK-TV uncovered the fraud.

"But today," Averill said in a deep, dramatic voice, "a very important event occurred. A highly-respected brokerage firm has created an ETF that includes ROOT as a key component.

"This is an historic moment. It is an unprecedented achievement for this little startup company, and you, my faithful investors, were there in the beginning. You believed NBCI would be a great success. You trusted me. And today, it's about to happen.

"The reason I'm calling all of you on such short notice is there will be a large inflow of ROOT stock orders from the ETF. They have to buy a lot of ROOT stock in the next few days. The short sellers will try to buy back stock and cover their short positions. It's pure physics. The stock price has to go up!

"You need to get in now and buy ROOT, meaning today, to beat the rush. You're my most important and trusted clients. You've been at the forefront of this biotechnological break-through. Only you had the foresight to understand the greatness of this world changing technology. You all are pioneers. You all are entrepreneurs. You are heroes. You're leading the future."

Had his clients invented the wheel, built the pyramids, or just bought a little crabgrass? Next, would Averill be telling his clients they were the world's most precious resource?

Averill knew when to shut up. His phones were already ringing with orders. "We have a few hours until the market closes. I will now take your calls. For the next two hours, I will only accept orders in minimum quantities of 1,000 shares. If you want to purchase a smaller size, please hold your calls until 2:00 PM. No email or text orders. You must speak with a registered representative. Thank you."

Averill's clients bought nearly a quarter-million shares before closing. The short sellers were frantically buying to close out their position. The stock ran up to $18. Averill cashed in on half of the shares he bought before the conference call and booked a huge gain.

At the end of the day, after the market for ROOT stock was exhausted and trading volume had thinned, Averill put in a window dressing order to buy 1,000 shares at $20. He sent congratulatory notes to his customers for the excellent investment decision they had made.

ROOT was listed as the top performing NASDAQ stock for the day – up 100%.

CHAPTER 211

FEBRUARY 1

Decker drove Panama Blonde's Karmann Ghia through the streets of Bergenfield in the 28 degree windy weather. The canvas convertible top did nothing to insulate the antique loaner from the chill. Decker half-shivered, half-shrugged. *It's still wheels until I get back on my feet. Besides, I look good driving in a ski hat and gloves.*

Decker wasn't calling the shots at the plant. He had laid off half of the workforce the day after Christmas. Another 40 employees would be pink-slipped this week. They were prepared for this day and had been counseled on how to secure their unemployment benefits. The remaining crew was mostly customer service, accountants and shipping personnel. There wasn't much need for a receiving clerk or production supervisor.

Morale was low, but employees tried to maintain a cheerful environment. They felt for Decker. Dignity wasn't a concern of Starship Financial. Decker had to walk down the long hall to the bank monitor for approval of every decision.

Danny the banker had commandeered the former sales director's corner office. He was all of 25 years old with no operating experience. He barely had shaving experience. His main job was to make sure the collateral didn't leave the side door.

"Danny, the word is out we're closing," Decker said glumly. "A hundred-fifty people filing unemployment claims don't go unnoticed in this town. Our customers aren't buying much. We'll have to run daily specials to move the rest of the inventory."

"That sounds reasonable," said Danny, who pretended to have both business knowledge and authority. "What discount do you need to offer?"

"The customers are accustomed to weekly specials at twenty percent off. I think we need to give thirty. That means we're selling close to cost. Do I have your approval?" Asking permission from a boy barely out of college was extremely hard on Decker. He had been the president for ten years.

"We aren't trying to make a profit here," said Dan, unconvincingly repeating the Blech mantra. "We're trying to get our money back. Let's get the protocol straight. You manage the business. You suggest the discount. We veto if we disagree."

Decker thanked the kid and returned to his office to stare out the window. There just wasn't much to do when the plant didn't manufacture anything and customers stopped calling.

At the end of the day, Decker met Catherine Mulcahy at the Chapala Grill for some Mexican food and a margarita. Make that two margaritas with floaters. It was a tough enough day. No reason to stay gloomy at night.

CHAPTER 212

FEBRUARY 5, 2013

Misty's mysterious absence from Ben's for the last two weeks had barely been noticed. Her return to the deli caused a full-table, double take. JB, Gavin, Bret, Decker, Catherine, Allie, Buyout and Michael couldn't stop staring.

Misty had two new friends, and they were sitting inside a D-cup bra. Prior to today, Misty had been a small B-cup, and that was giving her the benefit of the doubt. The new additions looked oversized on her petite frame. Proud as a peacock, she strutted up to Ben bobbing her head.

Misty stood with her chest out and asked, "Ben dear, can I have a caramel latte with whipped cream? I know it's early, but could you do that for me?"

Ben said with a totally straight face while shooting a glance at the board table, "What size cup would you like?"

JB practically did a spit-take with his coffee, laughing and coughing. The whole table was giggling. What was more amazing was that Misty took the recognition of her new talking points as a compliment.

JB turned to Bret and said, "Tell me you don't miss that."

Bret shook his head. "Not one bit. That girl is crazy. I think Avy and her are perfect for each other."

On her way to her table, Misty stopped to say hello. She twisted her tiny frame and gave her new accessories a 180 degree tour of the table. They paused briefly in the direction of Bret. He averted his eyes.

As she walked away, JB said quietly, "Is it me, or are her headlights out of alignment?"

Allie nodded agreement. "My God. Did you see that, too? It's hilarious. She's gonna blind someone with those high beams."

Misty might need to revisit the surgeon. The left one was pointing at the oncoming traffic.

CHAPTER 213

FEBRUARY 6, 2013

Averill sat in Johnny's office. The management team had finally moved into the main building. The rented furniture would eventually have to go.

"Johnny, we got lucky," said Averill. "Let's not lose momentum here. We could have blown up the company last month. Our problem is we're undercapitalized. We need more money to hedge your CRAB position. You have to deliver more profits this quarter than last, and the only way to do it is to buy more CRAB."

Johnny had yet to win a point with Averill in their year-old relationship. So far, Averill had delivered. The stock was up. They had gone on the NASDAQ. They lived through a short-sale crisis. This time would be different.

"Stop right there," Johnny snapped. "You aren't allowed to buy CRAB futures without my express approval. You hear me?"

"You didn't answer your cell phone," said Averill. "What was I supposed to do? You want me to cancel the trade? Let's see, 200,000 pounds at $20 dollars. That's $4 million. I'll debit your account today."

Johnny backpedaled. "Stop bein' a wise guy. We're gonna get in trouble if the board finds out you're tradin' without permission."

Averill eased back in his chair. "Okay. Send me an email approving the buy. I won't do it again. Let's talk about the private placement."

"Averill, not to offend you," Johnny said defensively, "but the new board isn't lookin' to enter into more business with LMNOP. They explicitly told me to clean up the deals we got goin'. I think if Arthur Sterling wanted to raise money, he'd use a bigger firm."

"Good luck with that one, Johnny," Averill said snidely. "I have a tail agreement with NBCI for two years from the time that you give me formal written notice. You have to use me or pay me a big fee. You signed the deal. You should know.

"And Mr. Tonto Hi Ho Silver Hair may be the chairman, but he only has one vote on the board. You and I rescued those other four losers from old-age poverty. They were broke until they joined the board. They need us to keep this boat afloat."

Johnny stuttered and tried to end the conversation, but Averill raised his hand like a crosswalk guard. "Stop and listen to me! We're making money here. Your stock options are worth a bundle. This company can't grow from this small processing fee. The only way to make higher profits is to trade CRAB futures. And you need more capital to do it. I can raise that money for you.

"I have an idea. Go back to Arthur and the board. Tell them I'm willing to get rid of the tail if you let me raise another $30 million in a private placement. You need the money. My commission is eight percent, or $2.4 million dollars. My firm gets half, but I'll kick back some of my share. Fifty grand. What do you say?"

Johnny said weakly, "Let me think about it."

CHAPTER 214

FEBRUARY 9, 2013

After the morning crew left for work, JB sat in Ben's Deli leafing through *The New York Times*. Hurricane Sandy recovery efforts dominated the headlines. The federal government released about $10 billion of aid, barely a pittance toward the cost of restoration. The money mostly went to the New Jersey and New York shore areas. Rebuilding of the beachfront was finally beginning, particularly in the area from Seaside Park north to Belmar.

Jenkinson's Boardwalk in Point Pleasant reopened its arcades and gift shops. The Seaside Heights boardwalk reconstruction was starting in a week. The construction company said they could complete a block every two days, and the boardwalk should be open for business by Memorial Day.

It was doubtful the Himalaya or Jet Star rides would be rebuilt, but you never know. With New Jersey ingenuity, they might convert the sunken roller coaster into an underwater slide.

Was it possible to be hit relatively worse after a hurricane like Sandy? Across the bay from Ortley Beach sat Toms River and Little Silver. During the storm, houses had floated off their foundations as water rose nine feet above the bulkhead. The towns north of Ortley like Lavallette, Mantoloking, Normandy Beach, or Sea Girt were also badly affected. And below the Barnegat lighthouse, Beach Haven, Surf City and Ship Bottom all felt the blows.

Remember the board game, Monopoly? Sandy had landed on Boardwalk and Park Place. No rent was due. The houses were gone.

Even on a relative basis, Breezy Point in Queens was possibly the worst hit of all metropolitan communities and wouldn't be rebuilt so quickly. The community was leveled from a devastating fire during the storm. Amazingly, charitable support reversed course on the

Atlantic. The Irish dominated neighborhood received attention, support, manpower and money from the Irish government itself. Volunteers were bused to Breezy Point for "Irish Days of Action". The Irish Tenors serenaded local residents during Christmas and wished them *Erin Go Bragh*.

The prognosis wasn't good for the homes closer to Seaside Heights and Ortley Beach. Access to the island was still restricted to repair crews and residents, and the Toms River Police were a constant presence against potential vandals. But New Jersey was Jersey tough, if anything. The shore was part of every Jersey Boy and Jersey Girl, and it would be rebuilt, only stronger and better.

CHAPTER 215

FEBRUARY 12, 2013

JB said with a frown, "I think this is the last year for the Valentine's Day lingerie exchange. The spouses are getting a whiff of our scheme."

"JB, you're not kidding," said Michael Li. "I'm not joining this year. My wife is suspicious. Before, I just bought candy. Now she's getting exotic undergarments. The camisole that I gave her last year had the smell of perfume. I played dumb and said, 'Bloomingdales must've added the scent!' I never lie to Mama-san."

Walter said, "I cannot believe after all these years my wife went looking for that black thong. She must think I'm wearing her underwear."

Allie shook her head. "You guys are pathetic. You just have to be a little smarter this time around. Make sure you pick the right size in the raffle. Don't pick anything too tight or too big. Bart, you're ineligible. Your wife needs to go on a diet."

Bart the pessimist protested, "This year I have a one-size-fits-all purple silk robe. This is good stuff."

"Alright," JB said. "Bart you're in. But God help you if your wife accidentally sees someone wearing that robe. Allie, girls are allowed this year. I assume you don't want lingerie. What'll it be? Oil change kit?"

Allie pretended to be offended and said, "Hold on a minute. I might have a need for some intimate apparel. Size eight for those who need to know. Tags must be intact. No scent!"

The boys snickered and catcalled. Bret slunk down in his chair. JB snickered, "Might Allie be in the hunt again after all these years?"

Allie laughed it off. "Down boys, there's nobody just yet. But I'm not a nun, you know! In another year, Marty graduates from high school, and I won't have much of a say in his decisions anymore. I just might be in the market again. I think twenty years is enough to get over one bad husband."

"Okay," JB rubbed his hands in anticipation. "Everyone show your wares. This is our final event, so make it good!"

CHAPTER 216

FEBRUARY 13, 2013

Averill called Johnny. "I want to roll forward a few of the June contracts and buy August. We got lucky. I have a firm quote for 750 contracts of CRAB at $108 dollars. That's almost $4 million of profit."

Johnny protested, "That's not right! I can see the ROOT price on my computer screen. The ask price is between $112 and $115 dollars right now."

"That's only if you sell in size," Averill lied. "This order is small, and I can't get more. Wait a second. I just got a bite at a $110. Johnny, we need to get this done now before the price drops."

Johnny agreed to sell, but begged Averill to try to get a higher price. Averill bought the contract in his Tuxedo Investments account and immediately sold the contract in the market in 15 separate transactions at $115. He skimmed nearly a $400,000 profit and charged NBCI a $100,000 commission to boot. That was petty cash for Misty. She could spend faster than a Kardashian.

He thought about Johnny: *I think it's time for him to join the team.* He called and asked Johnny to visit his office. "I have a little gift for you. Come on over this afternoon."

When Johnny arrived, Averill said, "You were right about the price spread. My traders weren't being honest with me. I managed to get a credit of $150,000 but I haven't put it into the account yet. I have an idea, but I'll deny it if you turn on me. I think you and I should split it fifty-fifty."

Johnny said nervously, "Averill, that's stealin'. We're gonna get caught. Justin's watchin' like a hawk. He'll trace the check."

Averill waved him off. "Forget Justin. He'll never see it. This is between you and me. Do what I did. Set up a company and move the money there. Preferably in the Cayman Islands where no one can see the wires."

Johnny thought for a moment, then said, "Averill, we've done some iffy stuff. I mean, I pulled some fast ones on Allie, but it wasn't stealin' really. We're crossin' the line here, aren't we?"

"How do you think people get rich," Averill lectured, "by working for a salary and slaving their lives away? No way. Now, do you want $75,000 or not? Otherwise, I'll send the money to the company."

"Okay," Johnny conceded. "I'll do it just this one time. I own an LLC. JTV Enterprises. It's not offshore yet, but it's safe."

Averill and Johnny filled out the account documents, and Averill instructed his cashier to move the money. It was 4:30 and the market was closed, so the two walked down the street to Tommy Fox's for a beer. Johnny was celebrating the money that the IRS would never find. Averill was celebrating the half-million that he'd skimmed.

As Averill sipped his beer from a pint glass, Johnny said, "I spoke to Arthur about your private placement. The board said that they'd approve it if the tail was canceled. They left it up to me to decide."

Averill wiped the beer suds from his moustache and said excitedly, "That's great! Let's get started tomorrow."

Johnny raised his hand. "Not so fast. Now that we're partners, the deal terms hafta change. We're both gonna go to jail someday if this stuff gets out. I want more money for my work. JTV Enterprises is now in business."

Averill thought quickly. "It's easy. Increase the commission to nine percent, and I'll give you three hundred grand. We'll call the increase an unaccountable selling and marketing allowance. But you still trade the commodities through my firm, right?"

Johnny was never surprised at Averill's ability to find ways to steal money from a deal. He nodded. "Okay. Done. We raise thirty mil, you get a nine percent commission and you wire JTV Enterprise its fee. Let's drink to our new deal!"

They raised their glasses, and Averill only half-smiled. He was thinking, *Maybe I'm teaching Johnny too many tricks?*

CHAPTER 217

FEBRUARY 15, 2013

Bret was dressed in winter casual wear sipping coffee at Ben's. He wore a navy cashmere crewneck sweater under a Lands' End sleeveless vest. JB looked intrigued and asked, "What gives, barrister? Wall Street finally give in to casual Friday?"

Bret smiled and said, "That's ex-barrister to you. I officially resigned yesterday. I'm not retiring. Just taking a couple of months to look for a general counsel job. Something interesting that doesn't require more than 60 hours a week. Until then, I'll work two extra coffee shifts with you in the morning. I can mingle with the other customers, like the poker moms or Auntie Ev."

Allie strolled into Ben's as the juke box played *Misty* by Johnny Mathis. Allie scowled at Ben, and sniped, "How dare you? You, you, you traitor, you!" She flipped her ponytail, winked, turned and marched to the table.

Allie sat between Bret and JB and jabbed JB's arm. "I'm sure you had somethin' to do with that horrible song selection."

JB blurted, "Forget the song, which by the way was a brilliant choice. We have bigger news. Bret quit his job!"

Allie squeezed Bret's forearm with both hands and said excitedly, "I'm so happy for you! At least there's one man at this table, no disrespect to you, Michael."

Bret wasn't sure where to put his hands. Slightly embarrassed, he said, "My bonus check was even less than I expected and they paid it half in restricted stock. I'd have to stay another five years before I could sell it. Forget that. I could be dead by then. So I took the cash and resigned.

"The corporate bigwigs took me to lunch at Peter Lugers over in Brooklyn. Best steak in New York. Even Dave Fullerton, the head of convertible bonds, was there. It was a nice going away party."

On the TV monitor behind the table, STCK-TV reported that Den-Ken Commodities had just raised $100 million for CRAB FUND III. This fund was slightly different. It had the authority to hedge against the stocks and ETF related to CRAB, and was allowed to short-sell the CRAB commodity.

CHAPTER 218

FEBRUARY 21, 2013

Cliff Lenihan wore a Beatles' wig to open the hour-long *Stock Pickers* show on STCK-TV. He said, "Let's talk about Pierre Beauty Products, symbol PBP. Pierre has an ingredient in its shampoo, and it's raising a lot of eyebrows. Is this a game changer? Is this disruptive hair technology, like the beehive in 1960 or Beatles mania in 1965? Personally, I think Ringo Starr is the most underrated drummer in the history of rock and roll. But that's just one man's opinion.

"The blogosphere claims the shampoo is the greatest thing that ever happened to women's hair. Is this a one-year wonder? Or is it just another sad dream for lonely housewives?

"I say NO! NO! NO! This is the real deal, and it's, dare I say it, a 'biotechnology' that will lead to increased earnings and surprising results for Pierre. By the way, Pierre happens to be run by a very beautiful woman, Eva Marteen, but enough of my personal fantasy.

"So my staff studied Pierre. We think this shampoo could be a $1 billion dollar category. Could be, but can Pierre get its hands on enough of the miracle ingredient to make its product? So we studied their Form 10-K which Pierre files with the SEC. Anyone can get a copy. Just go to www.sec.gov and look under filings. You'll find it.

"Under the raw material section in its 10-K, Pierre said it engages in hedging activities. While it may have periodic fluctuations in prices of certain commodities, including CRAB, it believes that it has adequate supplies and futures contracts. Any shortages of product or increases in CRAB prices won't materially affect its business. That's a pretty heady statement.

"We believe Pierre has quietly played the commodity game on CRAB and won. We also believe Pierre has a two-year head start on its competitors and knows how to process this unique material better than others. There are now seven companies claiming to use versions of this CRAB stuff. But we believe that none of them yet has the intellectual property necessary to make big bucks by making big hair. And we all know that big hair is big business.

"This morning, Pierre reported better than expected year-end results. This shampoo product helped the top line by $200 million in its inaugural year of sales. However, Pierre's full company operating margins also improved $30 million beyond what is explained by the sales increase. Their gross margin expanded by three full percentage points. I would have expected their margins to compress with all of the trading activity on the CRAB markets. But the opposite has happened."

Lenihan stared at the camera bug-eyed and said, "I think Pierre pulled a Southwest Airlines. Our viewers may remember when Southwest bought oil futures a few years ago before oil prices spiked. They had hedged their fuel costs by purchasing jet-fuel futures contracts before the price increased. They were able to fly at a profit while everyone else lost billions.

"Perhaps Pierre has done the same thing. But the hedging of this commodity is small potatoes compared to the overall financials of Pierre, so it doesn't show up as a line item or even a disclosure item in the footnotes.

"Pierre wrote in its MD&A. That's Management's Discussion and Analysis of Earnings for those who don't know. Their gross margin percentage improved due to improved purchasing economies and futures hedging gains. They don't mention CRAB, but I have a sneaky feeling that the boost in gross margins is temporary.

"But I think this is bullish for Pierre, and it's bullish for CRAB futures. Usually, you can only game the system once and get that big profit. After that, you're hedging at a higher price. I believe Pierre bought more than a one-year supply.

"Everyone knows I'm a Jersey boy, like Bruce Willis, Jon Stewart and Danny DeVito. So I always root for the home team. Bergenfield, New Jersey is like Source Perrier for shampoo. You can only get Perrier water in one place in the South of France, and you can only get this shampoo ingredient in a small town in Bergen County. Once again, Jersey is the place to be. The hippest place used to be on South Street in Philadelphia. Now it's Washington Avenue in Bergenfield.

"One last point. We believe Pierre is the premium brand in this market and can pass on some price increases. This shampoo is the real deal. And women will go to any measure and spend extra money to remain beautiful.

"Let's talk about a closely related topic. As you know, I don't play penny stocks. The company that appears to have a stranglehold on the processing of this crabgrass is a little company in Bergenfield with the symbol ROOT. This stock has increased from $2 dollars post-split to over $20 dollars in less than a year. That's a pretty historic run.

"But this company hasn't been around long enough to prove it can run the business. Its market cap is nearly $300 million. It charges up to $10 dollars a pound to process crabgrass. That's a potential $50 million in revenues. You can see where I'm going here. ROOT is now trading at a multiple of six times possible sales.

"Here's the problem. The town can only grow a limited quantity of crabgrass, and the processing fee is capped, so there's no potential for new growth from the core business. The only way for ROOT to grow is to make more money from commodity trading, which is a very risky business. Which means, my friends, the business model has to change.

"I admit that so far they have done pretty well trading. The numbers are impressive, but they benefitted from one short squeeze and a hurricane that drove up prices. How many more strokes of luck will they enjoy? This earnings expectation is all built into the stock price today. At some point, they have to miss, don't they?

"In conclusion, this is an exciting stock, an exciting story, but it could end badly. If you want to own it, keep your exposure small. Don't bet your house on it.

"Let's hear from some callers about their stock picks. . ."

Averill turned away from the office TV. Lenihan was wrong on this one. ROOT was going to raise another $30 million and triple its commodity profits.

Averill put the finishing touches on a research article promoting the NBCI story on Seeking Alpha, the online free stock research site. The Seeking Alpha editors have final say over which stock market research articles are worthy of publication. They rejected the article because of excessive unsupported puffiness.

Averill then massaged an article that Alistair had drafted about the benefits of CRAB for publication on Wikipedia, the Internet encyclopedia containing 25 million articles.

Wiki's editors reviewed the submission and labeled it unverified. As an open-source web encyclopedia, viewers are allowed to make changes to any submitted article. Almost all of the claims, including the one that CRAB might one day cure illnesses, were stricken by the Wiki police. After editing, the only words left from Averill's submission were "CRAB is a comodity." The spelling for *comodity* was corrected to include a second 'm'.

CHAPTER 219

FEBRUARY 26, 2013

Decker and Catherine Mulcahy entered Ben's Deli laughing and gave a boisterous hello as they sat at the table. Decker had found love in the sawdust as he dismantled his family business.

JB asked, "How's the inventory liquidation going?"

Decker said dreamily, "Who cares? You're such a buzz kill. I'm enjoying myself this morning. Leave us alone.

"Just kidding. We moved six months of inventory in six weeks. We're the only supplier of wooden sash in the area. Also, we carried odd sizes for older homes that you can't get anywhere else. Customers got nervous about their supply chain and started buying.

"If this keeps up, we might pay off the loan and keep the company. Who knows, maybe we start up again when the real estate bust ends. The bad news is we're closing the plant in

April. Let's talk about something else… but not that stupid crabgrass. How did the undies exchange go? Give us the sordid details."

JB turned on his Mr. Charming voice. "While you and the lovely Catherine Mulcahy were underground, the lingerie exchange went very well."

As JB concocted funny untruths about the Valentine's Day tradition, STCK-TV's Betsy Sands appeared on the screen. The closed caption read:

"A group of pension fund managers have reacted to a *Newark Star Ledger* exposé that claimed they were speculating in commodities. The five funds defended themselves declaring commodities to be a legitimate asset class. They also said their commodity investments were in a diversified portfolio including oil, gold and wheat. When we asked them about the CRAB commodity, one New Jersey pension fund admitted owning CRAB both directly and through CRAB partnerships."

The story hadn't yet finished, and the CRAB price spiked another $10 a pound. Traders celebrated the new buyers. The more, the merrier.

CHAPTER 220

MARCH 3, 2013

The Hedge Fund Grannies had written a book about growing crabgrass. Last June, on a lark, Auntie Ev had sent a draft to John Wiley & Sons, the publisher of the *Books for Dummies* brand. Wiley had published over 1,600 *For Dummies* books around the world. Auntie Ev 3,000 thousand copies at twice the regular price if Wiley agreed to rush it into print.

Auntie Ev's sharp editorial staff researched all of the lessons about how to get rid of crabgrass. If you want a nice lawn, water regularly! Apply crabgrass killer! Make sure you aerate the soil! To grow healthy crabgrass, simply do the opposite. Turn off the sprinkler!

Mr. Grayson and Mrs. Wilson added a chapter about cutting crabgrass properly and promoted their Crab Baby scythe. O'Hara Landscaping gave a lesson on how to make crabgrass look attractive in a garden. The boys from Pawnee, Illinois gave advice about conservative CRAB futures trading.

The Grannies also wrote "Watching Your Crabgrass Grow" for the less serious reader. The chapter recommended knitting as a great use of your time while waiting for the crop to blossom. If you tire of knitting, try quilting, beading or crochet.

Wiley had rushed a delivery of the books with the distinctive *For Dummies* yellow soft cover. Remarkably, the first edition sold out almost entirely through online sales. CRAB traders in Chicago and investment bankers in New York thought nothing of spending $29.99 for information that affected their trading profits. For the locals, it was a collector's item. Someday it might become memorabilia. Would anyone actually read it?

Wiley printed and rushed another 3,000 books. Bergenfield was short a bookstore; they had become the dinosaurs of media. The new authors convinced Walter Harrigan to hold a sale and book signing in his record store. In return, Auntie Ev and her gals offered to autograph a copy for anyone who also bought a record. The line formed around the corner at The Bergenfield Record Store. Of course, around the corner meant a dozen patrons, but that was the longest line the town had seen unless you included the car wash on Saturday.

At 10:00 AM, Mike the Cop stood watch at the door wearing his blue policeman's uniform and carrying a nightstick. It wasn't that crowd control was required. Mike just didn't want to miss out on the big media event. Life was slow around town unless it was about crabgrass. CRAB was becoming a media sensation. Everyone wanted to be a part of it.

A few buyers requested photo opportunities with their iPhone cameras. Auntie Ev took control and started charging a dollar for a photo with the Grannies.

In January, the girls had sat for a group picture for a funny Christmas card. The photo showed them sitting around a circle knitting crabgrass sweaters. It was a total goof. The Grannies played it up wearing spectacles hung by gold chains and flowery print dresses with lace collars. Each tied her hair in a distinctive bun. Auntie Ev weaved a French Braid.

Chris at *The Bergenfield Valley News* was scheduled to print the cards for delivery in the fall. Auntie Ev called him and commanded, "Send those Christmas cards over to The Bergenfield Record store right away.

"Also, I know you can make posters over there. I want you to mock one up with the picture, and underneath put in a title, 'Watch Crabgrass grow with the Hedge Fund Grannies!' And hurry up. If we can sell ten of them, we can sell a thousand, but only if you get a sample over here in the next two hours."

By noon, Chris had delivered a box of Crab Grannie Christmas cards and a sample Granny poster. They set up a table and offered posters and Christmas cards along with the *Crabgrass for Dummies Limited Edition*. At $29.99 for an autographed book, $10 for a signed poster and $15 for Christmas cards, the price point was right. Buy all three and save five dollars.

Walter had lost control, and was visibly sweating even though it was thirty degrees outside. He said, "Ev, we can't keep this up. We don't have enough salespeople. We're selling stuff we don't have in stock."

Auntie Ev held up her hand and said, "Stop right there Walter, you sack of pillow stuffing. If you don't find a new way to make money in this antique record store, you'll go out of business. How much longer do you think people will be buying old scratched albums?

"Now just follow our lead, and the only thing you'll have to worry about is how to carry the cash register receipts to the bank safely. And Mike the Cop will help you with that, right Mike?"

Mike nodded his head. Auntie Ev turned to her next customer and said, "I was once head of merchandising for Blackman's seasonal department, you know. I ran all of the promotions for Christmas. My area made half of the store profits and yet they demoted me. They said that I was too old to keep up with the young kids with the new ideas. They tried to make me into a desk jockey. Fat chance!"

Auntie Ev gave Walter a cut of six dollars a book and a dollar per poster or box of cards. It usually took him months to earn the same amount he made in one day today. It was like Christmas in March. The CRAB economy was trickling down to the local businessperson.

CHAPTER 221

APRIL 16, 2013

As the days warmed, tulips and daffodils began to show. So did the crabgrass.

CRAB growers were learning what it's like to be a farmer. You do all this work; then you sit and wait. You pull some unprofitable rye grass. You trim bushes to provide more sunlight. For the most part, you stare at your crop. In the beginning, you check the crop daily. After a little experience you cut back to weekly inspections. But nothing much matters when it comes to growing weeds. If you leave them alone, they'll grow.

Allie hooked up an Internet camera at a neighbor's home and hosted a CRAB-cam on her store's web site. People all over the world could log in and watch. With a slight breeze, the grass might even flutter. It was meant to be humorous. Commodity traders in Chicago thought it was more than useful.

Allie wrote the third check for $60,000 to Jake's. She had no idea where she'd get the rest of the funds. CRAB this. ROOT that. Everything was insane. She couldn't find a way to profit from the mania. Everyone else was making money off of this craze.

Her store still sold a few Crab Baby scythes, but by now most people already owned one. A few homeowners on the Teaneck and Tenafly border were still fighting the CRAB craze, but most had given up. The money was too good.

She carried the *Crabgrass for Dummies* how-to book, but the book craze was over. Auntie Ev knew a fad when she saw one.

Somehow, Allie had to generate $300,000 by October and another $135,000 by December and next May to pay Jake's or she was out of business. Paint and hammers. Screws and latches. Watering cans and garden frogs. A half million dollars was an awful lot of garden frogs.

CHAPTER 222

MAY 1, 2013

A flash headline scrolled across the television screen – TRADING HALTED ON PIERRE BEAUTY PRODUCTS. Ben turned up the volume. Several diners moaned simultaneously, "This better not be bad news."

STCK-TV's Jay McCall turned to Cal Bonita on screen and asked, "Do I buy more shampoo, or is it time to sell?" Betsy Sands muffled a laugh, and Cal, considerably younger than Jay and the object of a lot of his teasing, forced a stoic look for the camera.

Cal said, "The NASDAQ issued a trading halt this morning on the stock of Pierre Beauty Products following a large order imbalance. There are an inordinate number of buy orders for the stock, which was up 20 percent in pre-market trading. Eva Marteen, the CEO of Pierre, stock symbol PBP, is here to speak with us live."

The diners stared at the TV screen as Eva entered the studio with the grace of a former high fashion model. She wore a dark green skirt a few inches above her knees and an India green Chanel hand embroidered jacket over a white silk shell. The jacket alone had to have cost at least $5,000. She stopped and posed for the camera before sitting across from the hosts.

Jay was giddy. His voice went up an octave. "Hello Eva, and welcome back to the show. You look magnificent, as always. You're doing such a great job running Pierre. Profits and sales are up. Your brand is strong. Something must have leaked to the buying community. What's in the works?"

How a CEO handles those first seconds of an interview can drive traders into a frenzy. Was she nervous? Defensive? Angry? Hiding something? Did she look tired? Was something seriously wrong?

Eva flashed a glamorous smile. "Jay, you look so handsome. You must be using our products. Now, if every…"

Jay interrupted to talk about his most important subject, himself. "Unfortunately, Eva, first I have to finish up a ten-year supply of Pantene hotel samples before I actually pay for a bottle of shampoo. Besides, your products are above my pay grade."

Eva again smiled, and said with the slightest French lilt, "Jay, your hair is fine, but it would be so much better if you used our product. I will send you some, and if you feel more comfortable, we'll ship them in those hotel-sized containers. You know, the Four Seasons and The Ritz Carlton provide our products to their guests. Anyway, back to your question.

"We report everything material about the company as required by the rules of the SEC. There are no acquisitions or talks about a buyout, and let me be clear, we are not for sale. However, as you and I speak, my CFO is filing a Reg FD disclosure on Form 8-K with the SEC. It's in reaction to the heightened interest in our all-natural shampoo product. We just announced that we are asking retail stores to limit sales of our Pierre Salon Shampoo to one bottle per customer until we can increase our production. We also increased our retail price to $75 dollars a bottle to cover the increased cost of our materials.

"I'm delivering a presentation this morning to a Merrill Lynch investor conference, and we're expecting questions from the audience about this issue. We felt it was best to disseminate this information so all investors have access simultaneously."

Betsy said, "Eva, I love your products. I use them regularly including here in the studio. This is surprising news. For our audience, Pierre created this new salon version of your shampoo which has rapidly developed a fan base. Last year, you replaced the sodium lauryl sulfate with a natural ingredient. SLS is a degreaser used to clean hair. You now sell a 100 percent natural hair product with no manufactured chemicals.

"Earlier this week, we reported your store shelves were empty. And this morning, your shampoo appeared on eBay for over $95 dollars a bottle, which is higher than your new price. What are Pierre's plans to solve this supply issue other than rationing?"

Eva's mood never changed. She was calm and collected. "We don't endorse or support hoarding or any black market for our products. We intend to keep our prices affordable and want to ensure that our loyal customers have access to our hair products. Until we can substantially increase production, we have asked our retailers to cooperate.

"I guess it's a good problem to have, but we most of all want our customers to be treated fairly and not become disenfranchised due to a temporary supply imbalance."

"Like Betsy, I also use your hair products," Cal quipped. "When we reported last year, you had just created a new formula using a chemical from the crabgrass grown locally in Bergenfield, New Jersey. The weed is now traded on the MERC and prices have increased tenfold since our last interview. This morning, they moved again to $140 a pound. How will these higher prices affect the price of your product, and how are you protecting yourself from competitors replicating your ingredients?"

"Cal, I can tell that you use our products," said Eva. "Thank you for your patronage. Yes, we use an organic chemical from the plant, and we prefer not to describe it as a weed when it has such beneficial attributes. It is just one of several ingredients that are very secret and not known to the public. We have filed for preliminary patent protection, but haven't yet decided if we will allow it to become effective. We are concerned competitors might be able to copy our formula. Consider it the Coca-Cola of shampoos. Our recipe might be intellectual property which is best kept secret."

"Only two employees know the entire formulation, and both are bound to us contractually, financially and through loyalty. But remember, there are other ingredients that make this work so well, and the precise mixture took us years to develop."

Jay asked, "Eva, would you consider this a disruptive product or technology? And if so, would you make your formula available to other hair care product companies?"

Eva said, "It's clearly disruptive to the normal way of cleaning your hair, but it's not an inexpensive method, and therefore not all hair care companies would choose this formula.

"The recent rise in the price of the CRAB commodity is having an effect on the cost of our product. We don't think pricing is totally inelastic. At some level, customers will stop buying. That is why we are doing everything we can to increase the supply of CRAB and finding alternative sources.

"What is disturbing is how Chicago traders have taken control and driven prices to unrealistic highs. They're hoarding the commodity in silos. We believe we are the only viable user of CRAB. Yes, we admit that dozens of companies are now experimenting with it, but the only effective product on the market is ours. Chicago is going to kill the goose that laid the golden egg if they keep driving prices up. At this level, we are being forced to find a cheaper alternative.

"Remember, we are a premium quality product, and our customers are willing to pay extra to have beautiful hair. As to your licensing question, it's way too early to discuss such activities. Shampoo companies, toothpaste companies, even big oil. They're all trying to replicate our formula with no success to date. Anyway, I must join the Merrill conference now. Thank you for having me on your show. We watch you religiously every morning before our daily meetings."

Eva stood to leave and Jay said, "Well, thank you Eva. I look forward to receiving your free samples assuming my producer will allow me to take them home. Where is he anyway?" Eva laughed and the camera followed her beautiful figure until she reached offstage.

"Did you hear that? Eva watches me every morning. Okay, let's see," Jay said as he studied the onscreen price chart. "It looks like the stock is finally opening at $130 dollars a share. That's up thirty percent on significant volume. It looks like forty million shares traded already in fifteen minutes.

"Cal and Betsy, if I heard Eva correctly, they have to increase prices, but believe there is a limit to how much customers will pay. So is this stock price increase deserved?"

Cal said, "We estimate this product can get to a billion in sales very quickly with a fifty percent gross margin. While it's a good result, hair care products are only twenty percent of the total Pierre business model, so this large increase in their share price appears excessive."

"I don't know, guys," said Betsy. "I think this is disruptive biotechnology. Eventually everyone will convert to this formula if Pierre will give them access. But this whole space is crazy right now. The commodity is up tenfold. NBCI, the former penny stock, has gone from $2 dollars to $20 dollars. And now the stock price of a big Fortune 100 company jumps on this news.

"It sounds to me like we need a reality check here. But I'm going to my salon on the way home and get my allotment before they run out. In fact, I already called and the girl stowed a bottle for me."

CHAPTER 223

MAY 1

After the interview ended, Ben turned off the volume and the deli chatter returned to normal. Averill was officially dazed, positively stunned. Over the last year, he had gone from broke, to eking out a modest living, to making great money. And now he was sleeping with Misty, arguably one of the hottest and hottest-tempered women in town. But this report from Pierre was too good to be true. Prices were going to infinity. The $30 million private placement was going to be oversubscribed!

Averill turned from the television and opened his laptop. When he was in money raising mode, his eyes became even beadier, if that was possible. Today, they looked positively crow-like. He opened his Latino clientele list and called. "Senora Casiano. Buenas Dias. Como esta usted? Muy bien. Y tu?

"Did you see the news just now about Pierre Beauty Products? That's right. They have to ration their products now because demand is so high. You know, NBCI owns all of the rights to process their secret material. The stock is $20 dollars this morning, but we think it's going to $100 dollars. I'm calling you to increase your investment, which is already up 400 percent this year.

"NBCI is raising $30 million in a private placement this month and you are one of the lucky ones who qualify as an investor. This is an insider deal. You buy the stock at a five percent discount to the market and you'll get one warrant for every share you buy. There's a lot of money in warrants, you know. You can't beat these terms.

"Thank you, Senora. I'll pencil you in for a $50,000 dollar unit until you speak with su marido.

"If you don't mind, can you provide me the names and numbers of five of your friends and relatives to let them in on this great ground floor opportunity? You know, your community has done very well with their investment in NBCI. I always put the Latinos first."

He also put the Filipinos, Koreans, Norwegians, Germans, Chinese, Italians, Kenyans, Greeks, Irish, Hare Krishnas and Martians first. And any other nationality, religion or alien species who had money to invest.

JB overheard Averill and turned to Bret. "You think we missed out on this one? It's probably too late to buy now, but this thing took off right in front of our eyes."

Bret looked up from his PDA and said, "Problem is, we know these critters. Would you put money in any deal that had Johnny and Averill running it? Not on your life. I'd bet on Allie before I'd bet on those two clowns."

CHAPTER 224

MAY 1

After the Merrill presentation, Eva hastily left the conference to return to her offices. Things couldn't have gone worse. The entire audience wore blinders and ear plugs. No one heard anything bad. Hedge fund traders were buying Pierre's stock from their seats while she presented. The stock was up another ten percent by noon.

She thought her warnings would ease the pressure on CRAB commodity prices; they moved even higher. She warned them Pierre was looking for cheaper alternatives. What they heard instead was Pierre had found nothing so far. Bullish news for CRAB traders!

Eva had been scheduled to endure one-on-one meetings with money managers and Wall Street research analysts. She canceled them all. This pop in the stock was never good. A long steady rise is wonderful. Anything that goes up quickly must by sheer gravity come crashing back to earth. And everyone who bought stock at the top is an unhappy investor after it falls.

Before today, Pierre Beauty Products had 500 million shares held by thousands of happy investors and hundreds of top institutions. Pierre was always a premiere holding at the Fidelity, Vanguard and Templeton mutual funds. By the end of the day, 100 million of those shares will have switched hands to hardcore speculators. Somehow, she needed to temper their enthusiasm. Or was it too late?

The town car worked its way through the Holland Tunnel, past Jersey City and toward her offices on Route 24. Eva thought through her choices. She called Thurston Hollaway, her investment banker at Silverheels & Penny. Silverheels was the world's most prestigious investment bank. They moved markets.

Thurston insisted they meet immediately. The driver reversed course though the side streets of Jersey City, through the Holland Tunnel again, and headed down the West Side Highway toward their spectacular offices on the Hudson.

She entered the eighth floor meeting room with the most fantastic views of the lower bay of New York City. To the left was the Statue of Liberty and Ellis Island. A Staten Island Ferry was making its twice hourly trip between the borough and the Battery Park Pier. If you looked hard left, you could see Governor's Island, at one time a base for the U. S. Coast Guard.

Across the Hudson was a low lying road in New Jersey that coursed its way along the river. The waterfront was once a horrible eyesore with old broken-down piers and sunken barges, but no longer. One had to wonder if Silverheels & Penny bought the property and had it cleared just to have a nice view. They certainly could afford it.

Thurston had his usual accompaniment of two analysts and two vice presidents from banking and trading. But there was another attendee, a person whom Eva had seen on television many times, most recently at the congressional hearings on Wall Street Reform. At the head of the table sat Laughton Grenoble, the Chairman of Silverheels & Penny.

Laughton was not the prototypical six-foot plus intimidator of banking. He was easily under five-foot-eight, slightly balding, but still quite handsome. The epitome of charm, chivalry and gentlemanly behavior, he politely introduced himself, then offered Eva Perrier water, soft drinks and a plate of raspberry cheese croissants. The most important banker in the free world was serving breakfast! The bankers refused to even glance at the pastries. A hungry banker demanded a trim waistline.

Eva was a powerful woman in her field, but Laughton was the captain of Wall Street. When he spoke, traders stopped and listened. Congress and the Treasury confided in him and asked his opinion. This man was the king. He and Joey Raffe at JC Montague had the capital markets locked up with a few scraps left for the other hundred banking firms.

Olivier joined the conference by phone. Laughton said, "Eva and Olivier, we've been Pierre's lead investment bankers for fifty years. It's at a time like this that you probably need us the most. Let me sum up quickly what's happening here. Your stock is under attack. Your shares are changing hands from friendly long-term holders to traders who want instant returns so they can profit quickly and dump your stock.

"The aftermath could freeze your capital market activities for years. Research analysts will change their buy rating on your stock after it jumps and then plunges. It will become too volatile for mutual funds and family investments. Your stock will be held by speculators who will trade your shares ten times a day. This is a CFO's and CEO's nightmare.

"I know you don't need the money, but now is the time to raise cash and put it away for a rainy day. Rates are low. Your stock price is high.

"Our analysts are always prepared with financial forecasts and modeling for Pierre's business. We saw the interview on STCK-TV and also saw a tape of your Merrill presentation. Thurston's team immediately went to work on how we can improve your capital structure. He will provide the details, but be assured that Silverheels is here to help you through this period. Thurston, please proceed."

An assistant handed Eva a spiraled ring "pitch book". Thurston began, "Eva, although your stock price is up substantially today, we do not recommend that you issue more stock under your shelf. Such an issuance would be dilutive to your shareholders.

"Instead, we are recommending that Pierre Beauty Products issue a zero rate convertible redeemable preferred stock with a fifteen-year maturity. The conversion rate will be at 110 percent of today's closing price, which we do not believe your stock will see again for a while. Therefore, you will be raising capital, have no annual dividend burden and won't have to repay the money for fifteen years, if ever. If buyers exercise the conversion feature, you'll never have to repay it.

"Furthermore, the 'delta hedge' on your stock is 40 percent. That's the percentage of a convertible stock that traders expect to hedge in your stock by shorting it at the time of the underwriting. The shorting of your stock will actually have the effect of stabilizing your stock price by supplying additional shares for sale to the market.

"The convert traders will thereafter begin trading your stock in a very narrow range. The reason they will buy this investment is that they expect to make money immediately on the short, and still have the protection of the redemption value. In fact, they will cover their short after your stock has declined, and then short it again if it rises too high."

Eva knew the financing well. She had been pitched the idea by every investment banker in the world for the last five years and had always turned them down. But the terms had been more expensive – a 4% dividend, 105% conversion premium and a five-year maturity. This proposal was downright cheap – more like a zero coupon long-term bond.

Eva thought a moment and asked, "Will there be a limitation on dividend payments or buyback of stock? Will there be any tangible net worth restrictions? And assuming we agree, how soon would you close the deal?"

Thurston replied quickly, "No restrictions, no covenants. Our team has already drafted the 424B prospectus with your counsel, and we can file tonight and be effective immediately. We've received indications of interest for three times the offering, so selling the whole deal will not be a problem."

Laughton counseled like a wise advisor. "Eva and Olivier, this CRAB commodity has taken on certain aspects that resemble a bubble. We appreciate that you have a need for this product and that it's in limited supply for the time being. But the available annual supply is changing hands almost weekly, and the prices have increased above all reasonable levels.

"We respect your need to secure your supply to produce your products, but we want to put in place some controls so that this capital isn't used to amass a large position in the CRAB commodity. This is rainy day money. Companies should raise capital when the timing is right and not be forced to raise capital when their fortunes are less favorable. Let's agree among ourselves that this new money won't be used to speculate. Agreed?"

Eva responded solemnly, "We're equally concerned about the speculative fever in the commodity and surrounding financial instruments. We aren't fueling this activity. We have contractual rights through purchase agreements and futures contracts to purchase enough to produce at sixty percent of our plant capacity for the next three years. We're not buying at today's prices.

"Thurston, the Den-Ken commodity funds are generating very high returns. They are attracting more capital and more investors to speculate in the commodity. However, anything that Silverheels or JC Montague can do to break this bubble before it ruins the market would be appreciated."

Olivier spoke up. "That's a good point Eva. What about JC Montague?"

Laughton answered, "I have already spoken with Joey. His team has worked with ours all day. We'll split the deal fifty-fifty. Our name will be on the left side of the cover, and we'll be the book manager.

"You'll need board approval. I'm friends with three of your seven members and have discussed the mechanics with them. You and Eva make five. You could call a meeting and approve this today. Your board members would have to waive your 24-hour notice requirements, but we're relatively certain that all of your board is reachable. Would you like us to place the conference call now from our offices?"

Eva said, "Olivier, we've been discussing a similar route for over a year. The timing is perfect. Also, this will stabilize our stock price. If you are in agreement, I suggest we do this today."

Olivier said, "Apparently the board is way ahead of us. I have three text messages asking me when the meeting will be held. Silverheels, as usual, you do thorough work. Set it up!"

The board met and approved the transaction to sell $500 million of convertible stock. The prospectus supplement was filed at 5:00 PM before the SEC electronic filing office closed for the day. The buyers of the preferred stock had already begun shorting the common stock to achieve the delta hedge target, and the market for Pierre stock retreated to finish up only 25% for the day. The Pierre Beauty Products balance sheet looked even more beautiful with an extra half-billion dollars in its coffers.

CHAPTER 225

MAY 7, 2013

NBCI filed its quarterly report on Form 10-Q with the SEC. It simultaneously filed a press release with Thomson Reuters news services which automatically sent the release to all of the major wire services around the world. The company then filed an 8-K with a copy of the press release attached just to make triply sure everybody read it.

The press release stated, "The company earned $5.6 million of EBITDA in the quarter ended March 31, which was substantially above Wall Street analyst estimates. These exceptional financial results were achieved even though the company does not earn any processing fees during the March quarter.

"We presently are giving the following range of estimates for the remainder of the year: Revenues between $70 million to $80 million and EBITDA between $45 million to $55 million. This would equate to earnings of $2.25 to $2.50 per share."

Of course, none of the large brokerages' research analysts covered ROOT, so there were no credible real street estimates. But there were plenty of paid-for research reports that were available on Yahoo! Finance for as little as $50. They all recommended ROOT as a screaming buy.

The guidance numbers were a staggering surprise to everyone. ROOT had been trading around $20 per share and moved higher after the news.

On *Stock Pickers*, Cliff Lenihan looked at the camera with a funny tilt to his head and said, "I may have been wrong on this one. Maybe not. I thought NBCI was just a CRAB processing center and transfer station. It turns out that they're a CRAB speculator as well. If you want a cheap way of speculating on CRAB, perhaps this may work, but we have to study it more.

"But NBCI still doesn't fit the profile of companies I want my listeners to own. You need to buy companies with a long history of solid earnings growth. Stay away from speculative fever, or you may get the flu. Also, this company has seen a meteoric rise. Don't invest here at these prices. If you own it, I think that you take your profits." He patted the studio's collie bobble head, and it barked. He screamed, "This stock may be cute, but it's a puppy soon to be a dog! Sell it!"

CHAPTER 226

Far below the rank of captain of finance, buck private Averill Winthrop raised $30 million for NBCI in a private placement offering in record time. It didn't hurt that the price of ROOT jumped following the Pierre Beauty Products news.

It was a hot deal. No need to cajole, arm twist or bully. Everyone wanted in. Moms and pops. Grandmas and grandpas. Ministers and rabbis. Arabs and Israelis.

Several mid-sized investment banks lowered their standards and asked the LMNOP brass if they could co-manage the offering and join in on the fun and profits. Averill told his bosses: no need, no thanks. He had already invited The Sticky Five into the deal so they could make a few bucks on commissions. Who would have thought knowing Avy would have been such a good thing?

Avy received tributes from his cabal including a bottle of 100-year-old Macallan scotch, a box of Cuban cigars disguised as Dominicans, a case of Veuve Clicquot champagne, and front row seats at the November Bruce Springsteen concert in Madison Square Garden.

Averill prepared the investor questionnaires with the answers pre-completed and ready for signature. According to the documents, every investor either had $1 million of liquid net worth or had income of $250,000 a year. If you believed Averill's investor files, Bergenfield had more millionaires per square mile than Monaco. The questionnaire said in small print:

"The information contained herein is being furnished to you in order for you to determine whether shares of NBCI may be offered and sold to you in a private placement which is exempt from registration under the federal securities laws pursuant to Section 4(2) of the Securities Act of 1933 blah, blah, blah. And, oh yeah, you're a millionaire! Sign below.

Averill's clients signed the twenty-page document without reading a word.

Averill also counted on earning as much in CRAB commissions as he did on private placement fees. He called Johnny and said, "El Jefe, we need to put this money to work. I recommend we spread the money out over the next six CRAB delivery dates. That way, we can show some profits in each quarter and help the stock price."

Johnny raised his voice over the speaker phone. "Hold on a minute. This is a lot of money. I don't want to gamble this away."

Averill said calmly, "Johnny, how many times are we going to have this conversation? It's tough being the president of a public company. It's lonely at the top. But as boss, you're riding a shark. If you stop swimming, you drown.

"You just raised a lot of money. The private placement document says the proceeds are going to be used to hedge CRAB futures, so you're authorized to do this. In fact, if you don't invest this money in CRAB, some crazy shareholder might sue you for not investing. You have to do this.

"I'm going to make one last point. Last quarter profits were okay, but people weren't expecting much because it's off-season. But now they're expecting a Sandy-type quarter in June. You guys aren't even close right now. If you don't find another $10 million in profits in the next sixty days, your stock is tanking! And so are your stock options! Let me buy a thousand contracts. That's $14 million, but only $3.5 million on margin."

Johnny paused and said, "Okay, I hear you, but Justin will go ballistic. Arthur is keepin' a tight rein on us, but he's also pretty happy with the gains. I only got the okay to invest thirty mil, and this'll bring it to thirty-two. How do I explain that?"

Averill said gruffly, "You'll only be a little over the board limits. By the way, I have JTV's share of my commissions. Do you want me to wire to the same account?"

Johnny picked up the phone receiver and whisper-yelled, "Shut up, you idiot! Justin might hear this. No one is suppose-ta know I got a cut. No one! You understand?"

"Easy Johnny," Averill said calmly. "Okay, I'll watch what I'm saying if you promise not to use your speaker phone."

They both laughed nervously in the spirit of mutual prosperity.

CHAPTER 227

MAY 22, 2013

For Decker, sitting in his office with nothing to do was torture. The remaining inventory just wasn't selling. The customers had moved on to other suppliers. An accountant, a customer service rep, and a shipping clerk were his last employees. Even the night watchman had been fired. What was there to watch?

Decker asked JB to help figure his next steps. JB suggested they meet away from the office to escape the potential eavesdropping by Blech's forces.

Cooper's Pond looked quaint. It was a beautiful day in May. Flowers and trees were in full bloom. A lovely, centuries-old mill and dam sat at the far end. A pedestrian bridge led to an offshore gazebo. Near the entrance to the park, a beautiful stone memorial stood dedicated to those who lost their lives in the terrorist attack on 9/11. And hundreds of citizens had purchased inscribed pavers to create a walkway through the park.

An old warming hut still guarded the entrance. It had once offered a fireplace to skaters during winter. The pond rarely froze anymore, which was a never-ending mystery to the town managers. Climate change probably wasn't to blame for this one. The pond had been formed long ago from the Long Swamp Brook as part of the Cooper Mill property. Silt buildup was inevitable and the pond had to be dredged every few years.

"The loan is way down," Decker told JB standing near the memorial. "I still have $2 million dollars of inventory, but I can't sell it without the retail stores. I don't know how to sell the rest. But we've done a pretty good job. We started with a $14 million loan. The bank should be happy, right?"

JB said soberly, "The bank will never be happy until every last cent is paid. You get no credit for B-plus.

"You have to stop thinking about saving the company. That ship sailed a year ago, and you're just acknowledging it today. What you should do is find a way to preserve your own assets, protect them from the bank as much as possible, and prepare for your new life."

"I told you," Decker said, "the bank guarantee is secured by everything I own. It's just a matter of time before they take my bed."

JB waved his finger. "Uh-uh! Actually they can't take your mattress, but I'm guessing the four-poster in the asset list is one of the antiques they get. Am I right?"

Decker looked amazed. "JB, you've only had a day to look at the documents, and you know them better than I do. Yes, there's a bunch of heirlooms and antiques that are like two hundred years old. Some paintings too. They don't have a claim on the regular stuff like dishes, coffee makers and whatever. My problem is I'm stuck here in the house. If I sell it, the bank gets the money. But I don't know where my next job will be. I may have to move."

"First, you need a fresh start, a clean balance sheet," JB counseled. "This is just stuff. Imagine you got wiped out by a fire and lost everything. It's over. Let's start anew.

"The bank clowns are acting like they have all of the cards, but you have a lot of leverage. Until you agree to sell the house and the contents, they can't collect, right? When these two workout guys inherited this loan from the good side of the bank, they were told to get as much cash out of the business as quickly as possible.

"Bad loans are like old fruit on a produce stand. The older a melon gets, the more it starts to stink. From their bosses' perspective at the bank, they have been doing a pretty good job so far. How much loan is left of the original $14 million?"

"The inventory loan is down to about $1 million dollars, but there's still a $2 million dollar mortgage on the buildings," Decker replied. "The building is worth much more than that. They should feel good about the real estate."

JB waved his finger again. "That's pretty good progress, but the bank isn't going to wait three years for the market to recover to collect on the mortgage. Gavin tells me your inventory is too low to attract customers. Selling in dribs and drabs will cost you overhead. You should hold a yard sale and sell everything in one weekend. Get this over with!"

Decker chuckled. "You want me to hold a flea market for doors and windows?"

"It's done all the time," JB declared. "The contractors will come out of the hills to buy this stuff at the right price. You have to convince the bank this is in their best interests. In the end there'll be some mortgage left, and they'll be looking at your home and antique collection as money they can't get until you vacate the premises.

"Let's add it up. If you sell your inventory, the house and the antiques for $2 million, the bank exposure will only be $1 million. They'd still be holding liens on your building and equipment. They should be okay with that."

"I don't want to give up my home. It's been in my family for a hundred years," Decker pleaded.

JB tried to be sympathetic, but he was seasoned in delivering tough medicine. "Decker, if you hold on, you'll get nothing. Right now is the time to get some money out of this mess while you still have leverage. I might have a plan that could get you something to start a new life. Do these guys have any clue what this stuff in your house is worth?"

Decker responded sourly, "They make a lot of snide comments and rude jokes about the 'valuable' antiques. They don't think much of them. Definitely nowhere near the million dollars they should be worth. They were appraised at twice that before the market crashed."

JB pondered the issue. "What you don't want is to be forced into personal bankruptcy. In bankruptcy, you might be able to keep your home, but they still keep the mortgage. What we prefer is that they agree to allow you to sell the house and personal property, and give you a cut of the proceeds to start over.

"If we got you $100,000 dollars of cash, would that work? You keep your 401k. You have a new home starter kit with the household stuff. Everything but the antiques. And you keep your credit rating."

Decker mulled it over. "I guess if I landed on my feet free and clear with a little money in the bank, I'm much better off than I am now. The family heirlooms are more important than the cash. I really want to preserve some of my family's heritage. It's not a money issue. They're paintings of my great grandparents. There's other sentimental stuff."

"Okay," JB said calmly, "if I get you $100,000 of combined cash and precious family things, would you be okay?"

"Yeah, I guess," said Decker sheepishly, "but I don't think these guys'll go for it. They're pretty ugly."

"In more ways than one," JB laughed. "Don't worry. I know how to get around them. Go to the bank and make them an offer. I'll write it out for you. Keep us out of the meetings, but bring a lawyer. Expect that Blech will reject your offer out of hand, yell and scream at you, demand you move now. Don't listen to him. He has to talk to headquarters and tell them the offer. Last thing. To make this work, we need to control the auction process."

Decker brightened. "Panama, I mean, Catherine works at Paramus Auctions."

JB's eyes lit up. "You're kidding me. I never would have thought it. I need to speak to her before you approach the bank. Ask her if she can meet us for lunch somewhere near her office. Better yet, let's meet at the Fireplace on Route 17 this Friday. You can smell those charcoal grilled burgers a mile away."

CHAPTER 228

MAY 25, 2013

On Friday, Catherine and Decker joined JB at The Fireplace in Paramus. She looked very professional in her navy Armani jacket and skirt, white pleated blouse, a string of pearls and gold hoop earrings. Was this the same Panama Blonde who was in a catfight at Ben's Deli?

JB took command. "If you've never been here before, follow my lead. Order the bacon cheeseburger, fries and a shake."

Decker laughed and said, "Who hasn't been here? I'll have the same."

Catherine noticed JB discretely sizing her up. "Chef Salad for me. Excuse the fancy outfit. We have a high-end auction this afternoon. This is what I wear to sell estates. When I sell inventory closeouts, I wear khakis.

"JB, we've never had a normal conversation." She looked him directly in the eye. "You hang with your Ben's bros and find some pretty mischievous ways to amuse yourselves.

Until I met Allie, I was scared to death of you guys. I never knew what was next. Now I realize you don't mean any harm, but you can be pretty harsh at times.

"Anyway, Decker asked me to be here, so here I am. I just want to be up front. I love Decker and I'll do what I can to help him as long as it's legal."

"Don't be afraid," JB winked. "We only tease people we like. You have to admit you were pretty aloof until the food fight with Misty. Anyway, I agree. We're here to help Decker, and you might be the missing piece of the puzzle. Do you actually conduct auctions, or are you like an administrator or assistant?"

Catherine took a deep breath. "How do I not take that question as an insult? Oh, I get it. You're an old man who's never been trained in office sensitivity. Yes, I'm a full, certified, top-notch auctioneer."

"Ow! That hurt. Easy tarantula!" laughed JB. "It's not an insult. Decker needs a 'friendly' auctioneer to help sell his personal assets. Has he explained his personal situation?"

Catherine said matter-of-factly, "Decker and I talk about everything. Go on."

"By the way," JB grinned, "we took bets on a Misty-Panama bout and I had you winning in three rounds. There's real interest in a celebrity match if you want some real revenge."

Catherine laughed and lowered her defenses. "No thanks. Besides, Misty's gone underground lately. I'm very happy for her and Mr. Creepy. Tee-hee!"

JB nodded, "Yeah, they seem to be made for each other. Okay, tell me about your experience auctioning antiques."

"I worked at Sotheby's long before I joined Paramus Auctions," said Catherine. "I was doing well there, but leaving was my choice. I wasn't excited about dealing with dilettantes willing to spend $10,000 on an old spoon.

"Paramus Auctions does very well and we serve a great need for our customers. Half of our work is getting rid of schlock for stores in Paramus. The other half of our business is estate…"

JB interrupted, "I believe you. I'm sure you know how to do this work. Next question. Do you ever sell with no reserve?"

Decker looked quizzical and asked, "What's that?"

Catherine answered before JB had the chance, "It means we take whatever bid, no matter how low. Final estate and bankruptcy sales sometimes go this way.

"Higher-end items usually have a reserve. In other words, the auctioneer has a minimum price and if the final bid is too low, he can withdraw the item and not sell it."

"Next question," JB said gamely, "assuming collusion is illegal…"

"I'm not sure I like where this is headed," Catherine said nervously. "I'm not doing something dishonest. Decker and I can start over. Why risk going to jail over a few family possessions? You know, Sotheby's and Christie's were investigated for auction rigging by the Justice Department. Rings were pretty prominent in auctions back then."

"Trust me," JB said seriously, "We're not going to collude. But, I have a pretty good hunch Blech might. In fact, my plan depends on it.

"The big banks have workout officers who are extremely careful about violating bank laws. On the other hand, Decker's bankers think they're below the radar and can get away with a lot. They act more like mobsters. Blech seems to take an incredible amount of pleasure inflicting the maximum amount of pain.

"And that's why I think my plan will work. We're going to let him do what comes naturally to a guy like that. Does your audience of bidders, how do I say this, get together and try not to overbid each other?"

Catherine looked uneasy. "The estate bidders know each other, and it's well known but not proved that they prearrange bids so they don't drive the pries too high. This doesn't happen on high-end stuff. It happens with items where the value isn't well-established. They also gang up on rogue bidders who may not be antique dealers.

"The bidders travel in packs like wolves. Your antique sale is their chicken coop. They're going to raid it and steal all your chickens for as little as possible. Sellers know it, and accept the losses as long as the assets are sold."

"It's not just the bidders who play games. The auctioneers have been known to put a few shills in the audience to keep the bids higher."

JB said assuredly, "Nothing illegal, Catherine. I'm trying to understand the dynamics. Next question. If you were auctioning an estate, would it be uncommon to include items from other lots or estates?"

"No," Catherine said, "it happens often. But it has to be stated in the offering circular. That puts bidders on notice to watch for cheaper items in the mix."

Amazingly, through this entire deep conversation, JB had managed to eat his lunch. Catherine never touched her salad. Decker sat mesmerized by his girlfriend's knowledge.

"Catherine, we're going to help Decker keep some of his family estate, the things that have the most sentimental value. We'll ask the bank to approve an auction and the sale of his house. Your job is to generate at least $300,000 from the sale of antiques to keep the bank happy. That plus the house sale will add up to maybe $1.2 million.

"The bank agrees to let Decker keep $100,000 of the auction proceeds. I'll advance Decker $25,000 to bid on the last tranche of antiques. I'm allowed to bid, right? Coincidentally, the last items up for sale will just happen to be the antiques he wants to keep. By then, all of the other buyers will have gone home by then if we play our cards right. So, Decker gets $75,000, the important family heirlooms, and a clean start."

They huddled closer. JB continued with a sly smile. "Here's what we do. We'll hold the auction in December when…"

CHAPTER 229

JUNE 4, 2013

It was just after lunchtime and a pleasant 78 degrees outdoors. Men wore aviator sunglasses and walked through town with their suit jackets slung over their shoulders. Women dared to wear skirts again after a weekend of tanning behind them.

Gilbert interrupted the early summer bliss and called an emergency meeting of the partners of Bergen Development Company at Vinnie Martini's house. Vinnie opened with, "I'm sure dare's no bugs. You know, dem electrical listenin' devices. I just had da place swept last month. Ha-ha!"

Vinnie had created a man cave deserving of an award. He had constructed a stage two feet above a dozen theater seats. Three microphone stands, an electric piano, an electric and bass guitar, a set of drums, and massive speakers stood ready for action. Overhead track lighting illuminated the room.

Vinnie handed out beers and sodas. "My kids and I got a rock band. They wanna play Zeppelin, so I soundproofed the place, which I'm guessin' is comin' in handy today. So Gilbert, wassup?"

Gilbert climbed onto the stage as Vinnie took a seat in the rear row. "First, David Elliot isn't here, but I told him what we're doing and he gave me his proxy. I have very good news. We have an offer to buy eight of our houses for a price of $6.4 million dollars. That's $800,000 a house, almost quadruple what we paid for them. The reason they're willing to pay so much is because the houses are contiguous."

Chris let out a big sigh. He was struggling with the printing business and had expected bad news. Trudy tried to contain her excitement. Johnny rubbed his hands and smiled. He was going to be rich.

Gilbert continued, "The buyer is a Chinese investment company. They're going to tear down the houses and build a CRAB farm. After they learn the business, they'll export the technology to China where they can expand it. It's what the Chinese do. Build everything to a bigger scale and then dominate the world markets.

"There's a small hitch. The houses are under contract with Pierre, which means the Chinese can't take the crabgrass, yet. They found a loophole in the option agreement. If the town council changes the zoning to agricultural use, the contract with Pierre becomes void. You guys have to hold a meeting and quickly approve this, like tonight."

"That should be easy enough," said Chris.

"Thanks, Chris. We have several decisions to make today, which is why I asked you all here. First, you should approve the sale as a formality. Next, we have to…" Gilbert caught movement out of the corner of his eye and turned his head. "What is it Howie?"

Howie was grinding his fist angrily. "How do you know this is the best price? How do we know we can't get a million each for these homes? At $130 a pound for CRAB, the houses could be making almost eighty grand a year. If they tear down the houses, they'll be making four times that amount."

Trudy said politely, "But our houses can only make $9,000 'cause of the Pierre contract. Am I right? I don't understand your thinkin'."

Gilbert waved his hands. "Howie, I misspoke. I'm not asking your permission to sell the eight homes. I already sold them. The Bergen Development agreement gives me full management authority, and after conferring with a couple of partners, we decided to take this deal quickly before it went away. I thought it would be nice to approve it formally."

Johnny had grown increasingly cocky around town lately, now that he was the big shot president of an important public company. He stood and said, "I agree with Howie. Why are you sellin' anythin' without my okay?"

Gilbert said politely, "First, we did try to get a better offer. Vinnie and I visited a couple of the landlords in town. They said tearing down the houses was a crazy idea, at least for now. Even after they cleaned up the property, they'd have to find the same topsoil to grow the crabgrass. They said it won't work. It's too big of a risk.

"But both of you bring up a good point. This was a good deal, but our interests might diverge going forward. Howie and Johnny, the decision has been made on the eight houses. We have to decide what to do with the money and what to do with the rest of the houses."

Howie snapped angrily, "You distribute the money to your partners. That's what you do with the money. Unless you want me to sue you!"

Gilbert stayed calm. "Let me understand this. You're going to file a public lawsuit that I unfairly sold houses that you basically stole from the owners? The same houses where you as town council members wrote off real estate taxes we owed? Wait until the media gets wind of that one. I think not. But let's keep this civil. No one is stealing your profits. We have a mortgage to pay first."

Howie and Johnny sat steaming in their seats. Trudy and Vinnie remained calm and said nothing. Chris was on the fence, not sure with whom to side.

"What I recommend," Gilbert said, "is we put all of the remaining houses up for sale, get this done in the next six months, and close down the partnership so we don't risk discovery. This is a one-time deal with the Chinese. We won't get the same money for the remaining homes.

"I think the best buyers for these homes are the landlords in town. They can keep renting them and still make money under the Pierre contract. On average, we might sell each house for $600,000. If we take that amount plus the money from the Chinese, the limited partners would make $6.7 million or about $840,000 per partner."

Howie said belligerently, "Those numbers don't add up. I calculate the partnership makes closer to $17 million. Where's the rest of the money?"

Gilbert let out an exasperated breath of air. "Howie, I don't understand how you can forget the history of the transaction. You were the lawyer and wrote all of the documents. Or are you just ungrateful?

"You put up $15,000 and are about to make over eight hundred grand. I'm the general partner. I organized the deal. I put up the first $100,000, seven times what you invested. I created all of the value. I negotiated the agreements with Pierre. I found the homes to buy. I convinced the bank to lend us the money. I watched over our investment. For that, I earned only a twelve percent general partnership interest on top of my 48 percent limited partner interest. I should have gotten more.

"Does anyone in this room have a problem with that? You didn't have a problem when we started."

Vinnie stood over Howie with his fists clenched like a bar bouncer waiting for a fight. He glared at Howie and said, "I personally wouldn't never renege on da deal we cut. Dat would be dishonest."

Howie was combative. "Well, maybe we don't think it's time to sell yet. This crabgrass mania is just starting."

"Maybe, or maybe it just ended. Howie and Johnny," Gilbert said, somehow maintaining a thread of civility, "if you want to hold onto your share of the houses and not sell when the rest of us sell, then we'll accommodate you. We'll pick a few houses as fairly as possible and deed them…"

Howie interrupted in an accusatory voice, "I think you're working a deal with someone."

Gilbert, while town mayor, had handled hecklers from the audience many times. He grabbed a drumstick and smacked a cymbal to get everyone's attention. "Howie, I'm not working a deal or getting a kickback. I've never done anything illegal. The Pierre offer at $15 a pound was a great price at the time. And it was the single, principal deciding factor that allowed us to buy these homes and get financing."

Johnny yelled, "Whadaya mean, you never got a kickback? What about scammin' the town council to forgive the taxes? What about the payments to Elliot to get the mortgages?"

Gilbert glared and said ominously, "Johnny, we've been friends a long time. You seem willing to risk our friendship over money, whereas I'm not.

"I didn't vote on the town council. You did. I was the founding partner of Bergen Development and offered you an opportunity to make a lot of money. How much I put up wasn't based upon tax forgiveness. Your contribution, however, was. If you didn't 'scam' the town, as you put it, you'd have to put up another $10,000 for your partnership interest. Why is it now you don't recall? I know Vinnie and Trudy remember it that way.

"Let me say one more thing. I didn't need your investment. I could have closed with fewer houses. The real estate tax write-off was a good deal for the town. As much as Hector and I have our differences, even he might not have turned down a deal to get those houses back on the tax role.

"The reason I brought you all in is because of the loyalty I've had for each of you since I was mayor. I also wrongly assumed you'd pitch in and help maintain the houses. The only one who helped was Vinnie.

"But let's get back to your accusations. If any of this becomes public, I'm innocent. You're not. As far as bribes paid to David to get the mortgage deal done, I'm not on the paper trail. Go and check whose name is on the wires and checks deposited into Elliot's account. It's you, Johnny, and you, Howie. And let's not forget. Trudy didn't vote in the town council meeting. She's in the clear. You want to go public. . ." he paused for emphasis. "Welcome to your own hanging."

Howie and Johnny were fuming and wanted to lash out, but they looked beaten. Chris moved away from Howie and stood next to Vinnie.

Howie said, "So we don't have any say in this? We do it your way or fry?"

"Let's keep this friendly," said Gilbert. "I said if you want to keep your houses and try to get a better profit, go ahead. We aren't going to stop you. But like it or not, we're breaking up Bergen Development in the next six months.

"I want to warn you. Real estate transactions are recorded in the county courthouse records. In today's Internet age, they're easily searchable. If we sell the houses while they are still owned by the LLC, they can't trace it to you. Once you take over the property, the deed transfers to your name.

"And here is my last point. You're both passing up pretty good returns. If you want more, I won't begrudge you. I'm now asking for a vote.

"If you vote yes, let's call it the 'Gilbert path', you agree that the LLC sells the remaining houses for the best price possible in the next six months. We first use the proceeds to repay the existing mortgages and then we pay out the profits. If you vote no, let's call that the 'Howie and Johnny path', you'll get some houses which will be mortgage-free after we repay First Second Third Bank."

Vinnie stood and stared down at Howie. "I'm votin' for da *Gilbert path,* and I got a few words of advice. First, Howie and Johnny, keep your freakin' mouths shut. I'd use the correct vernacular, but my cuz is in da room. Even if you ain't done nothin' wrong, you don't want no one nosin' around and causin' trouble.

"Second, I wanna thank my friend Gilbert for findin' dis deal and bringin' it to a successful endin'. You didden hafta let me in, and I hope dat I was a good partner. I knows my guys're very 'preciative of all da fix-up work you gave dem on da houses."

Johnny wisecracked, "Of course you're happy. You made more money than anyone."

Vinnie looked hard at Johnny and said threateningly, "You watch it, Johnny-boy. I WILL kick your ass, and dare won't be no witnesses 'round, ya hear me? Youse gotta big mouth. You and Howie are gonna get us in trouble if youse don't be careful.

"Here's my last words to youse, you bigmouth sonofabitches. In my business, if your boss gives youse a gift, you thank him and act grateful. Even if it ain't what you thought you shoulda gotten. Ya know what I mean? Den next time, dat boss'll tink of you again when dare's a good opportunity. You, Johnny, you're not grateful. You should be on your knees kissin' the ring on Mr. Gilchrist's hand for all he's done for youse."

Gilbert called for a vote. Howie and Johnny took ownership of three houses worth an estimated $1.8 million instead of cashing in.

CHAPTER 230

JUNE 4

Johnny hurried over to Averill's offices. He rocketed in the door, out of breath, and exploded, "The Chinese bought CRAB houses!"

"What?" Averill said startled. "You bought Chinese lab mouses?"

Johnny blurted out a quick version of how the Chinese "stole" the houses at a ridiculous amount of money. Averill leaned back in his chair, and said, "You can't make this stuff up.

"I can't believe it. I just sold the contracts from last October. We gotta buy them back and all of the CRAB we can get before this gets out. Second, we need to buy more ROOT stock."

Johnny threw up his hands. "We can't go over $30 million, Averill. The board won't allow it."

Averill glared. "Screw the board. Just say you misunderstood. Tell me. Did they say you could buy $30 million dollars of contracts or you could invest $30 million dollars? There's a difference."

Johnny thought for a few seconds. "They just said, 'You have $30 million.' They didn't get into the details."

"Perfect!" Averill exclaimed. "If you buy on 25 percent margin, $30 million gets you $120 million of CRAB. Besides, you don't have enough time to ask their permission. Either we do this today, or we miss it."

Johnny said warily, "I'm definitely gonna lose my job over this. And aren't we gonna get in trouble for insider tradin'? I mean, this information ain't public yet."

Averill said with great authority, "You're not going to lose your job when you just made the company a bunch of money. Also, this isn't inside information. It's information about a bunch of houses getting sold. We just connected the dots and guessed CRAB would do well."

Johnny protested, "But I'm an officer. Don't I have knowledge about a material event?"

"Stop it Johnny," Averill snapped. "I'm an expert on insider trading. You have safe harbor protection under the Maloney rule. You're fine."

Averill smiled as Johnny deferred to his expert legal knowledge. Of course, there was no such thing as the Maloney Rule. It was as useful as the Baloney Rule. Whenever someone argued, Averill cited the made-up infamous court ruling to shut them up.

Johnny left, and Averill bought 3,000 CRAB contracts for NBCI for $42 million. The price rose dramatically to $160 a pound. The market had quickly figured something was up.

NBCI now owned 4,000 contracts spending $26 million more than the board had authorized. Using margin loans, NBCI had only "invested" $14 million.

Averill turned his attention to the stock market and loaded up on ROOT stock for his own account. Then he used his discretionary authority to buy shares in his customer accounts.

He called The Sticky Five on their prepaid phones and told them the news. He then logged his four iPads onto the Yahoo! Finance ROOT message board and began typing.

Tektikker: "ROOT stock is moving again today. There must be good news coming. The stock is up $3. Trading near $33. This is HUMONGOUS."

Greenmasheen: "I knew there was more coming. This is the best management team of any public company. ROOT for ROOT!"

Contrariologist: "I started buying when the chart went nuts. This stock is going to $100!"

Biohzrde: "Glad to be along for the ride. Now I can pay next month's tuition bill."

Averill summoned his brokerage customers to an emergency conference call. He cautioned, "First, let's obey the rules here. No one records these calls. Next, I want to welcome our new investors, who are up ten percent already. Congratulations!

"Here's the news that's moving the stock. We learned from a reliable source that the Chinese have made a significant investment in CRAB related properties. This information will probably be out tomorrow. We urge you to act now. I'm taking orders to buy NBCI stock as soon as this call ends. Again, I will only take orders of a thousand shares or more from now until 3:00 PM. After that the lines will be open to everyone."

Averill hung up, and the phones started ringing. Everyone was buying. By 4:00 PM at the market close, the ROOT stock had risen 20% to $36 a share.

CHAPTER 231

JUNE 5, 2013

Ben's Deli was buzzing. News crews had displaced regulars from their favorite booths. Ben began posting "reserved" signs declaring ten tables off limits to invaders.

A cameraman complained to Ben at the register, "That stupid senior prom photo shoot at Cooper's Pond yesterday made me miss my deadline. They had the whole town bottled up in a traffic jam."

The town annually closed Church Street to traffic at 5:00 PM for the high school seniors. Dressed in tuxedos and prom gowns, they posed for pictures at the Coopers' Pond rotunda and bridges. Over a thousand family and friends joined in the festivities.

Ben told the cameraman, "The event was on the town agenda. It's posted online. Aren't you guys doing your research?"

The cameraman shook his head and headed to a booth. Great attention surrounded Pierre, NBCI, CRAB futures, the POO ETF and the Den-Ken partnerships. Network financial reporters were crawling around Bergenfield to find news stories.

Daytime television pity-shows tried to drum up stories for their audiences who loved tales about victims. It was hard to find someone hurt by the craze.

The conservative Fox network aired a piece criticizing Democratic Mayor Hector for interfering with free market principles. STCK-TV focused on the effects on the financial markets. CNN stuck with old hurricane footage. Their largest audience ratings seemed to be related to natural disasters.

Roberta Shamsky sat at JB's table which was unusual for two reasons. First, she never hit Ben's Deli before 9:00 AM. Second, she usually preferred the mayor's table. Roberta was a real estate broker for Century 21. She was always cheerful and dressed to show homes. She was a full-bodied fiftyish with blonde hair perfectly dyed and set at Trudy's salon.

She said, "JB, you're the first to know. I have hot news. The Chinese just bought eight adjoining homes on Summit Avenue. The homes were owned by some offshore investment group. They sold for $800,000 apiece, at least twice what they're worth. I was the listing agent and got half of the commission. How'd I do?"

JB asked, "Who was the buyer?"

The CNN news correspondent leaned over and asked, "Yeah, who was the buyer?"

Roberta said, "Xie Development Company, which means crab in Chinese. Pretty funny, huh? It's a company financed by CIC, the China Investment Corp. They didn't buy them to rent, I can assure you. They already filed permits to raze the houses."

By 10:00 AM, the story was on CNN. The news reporter related the details and added, "The site is slightly less than an acre, which must set some sort of record for land sales in Bergen County. Not even the homes of the ultra-wealthy in Alpine up on the Palisades would have land costs that high. Xie declined to comment. It's easy to presume that they intend to learn the secrets to produce crabgrass and export the technology to China."

By noon, outrage erupted from the halls of Congress. New Jersey Senator Alonzo Gruenfeld held a press conference. "This is another critical American technology that China is stealing due to their cheap Yuan currency. China continues to export goods at noncompetitive prices and use profits to buy foreign assets. We need to stop the exportation of any crabgrass, seeds or intellectual property. This biotechnology should be classified as an asset critical to our national defense!"

JB commented, "If this keeps up, the crabgrass will be worth more than the homes. They'll demolish the town and plant weeds in its place. Where will I eat? Where will I get my car washed? Ben, you won't sell out, will you?"

Ben answered with a huge smile, "Of course I'm selling. Who's gonna come here for breakfast if you guys move outta town? Anyone here wanna buy a diner?"

The surrounding patrons laughed but most were wondering, *What will life be like after Ben's?* Going to Ben's was a tradition. Before work. After the gym. After dropping kids at school. Ben's was a poor man's country club with no entry fee and no blackball committee. It defined affordable luxury – fine dining consisting of Starbucks and a fried egg on a bagel. Stuff a few fresh pastries into your briefcase for the office.

Having your regular table was an inalienable right. Sitting with friends and gossiping. And witnessing an occasional food fight between two hot women.

There was a moment of deep and profound thought in the deli. *Someone has to put a stop to this destruction of the eternal happiness. The town cannot let the Chinese take over. Don't turn this residential community into farmland. Where's our mayor?* Then the diners returned to their breakfast and the next topic on STCK-TV.

The CRAB futures had moved ahead of the Chinese news announcement. So did the stock. Information was reaching some traders earlier than others. Had someone spied the Chinese delegation on Allie's webcam?

CHAPTER 232

JUNE 7, 2013

Eva rushed into the conference room and cried out, "Shi-Shi-Shi. . . Chicago! I'm sorry. I apologize. I promised never to use profanity at work. How can the Chinese do this? We own the right to take the crabgrass from those properties! What's going on here?"

Olivier stood near the doorway with his arms folded. Steven, Albert and Stephane sat opposite Eva. Conrad, Pierre's general counsel, explained, "Their attorneys claim our option agreement only covered the land as residential properties. The Chinese somehow convinced the town council to rezone the six homes as agricultural use. They're already tearing down the homes. They paid the tenants to leave. We can fight it, but it means going to court."

Eva was uncharacteristically angry. "Somebody paid off the town council. What's wrong with these people?

"We'd better fix our option agreements now. Let's settle the lawsuits. Come up with a plan to give them more money but at the same time doesn't ruin us. Make them happy or we're going to have an insurrection on our hands. And sue the damn Chinese!"

CHAPTER 233

JUNE 11, 2013

You can only keep a secret so long. Traders in the pits saw everyone and anyone who was buying and selling. Virtual traders could see their identity on computer screens.

The top brokers were often associated with certain clients. ALF Commodity Brokers traded for the California Retirement Fund. If ALF was buying, everyone knew CALPERS was behind the trade. Bloomfield Brokers represented the Teamsters Pension Fund. If Bloomfield was bidding, the unions were increasing their stake. Pierre Beauty Products had spread its trades across a dozen larger firms, so it was a little more difficult to determine when Pierre was behind the trade.

The market hadn't expected a lot of activity during the last few weeks before June delivery. There was no bad weather, no extraordinary crop news. Clients had begun rolling their positions to August and October deliveries. It was going to be a very boring month end.

The CRAB futures market had traded quietly in early June when, *bang*, the price jumped $20 a pound. A single trader had bought just before the Chinese story broke – LITE Commodity Brokers.

At the end of the day, several competitors from the CRAB pit took Brandon Bigelow, LITE's trader, to Ceres Café on West Jackson Boulevard under the guise of celebrating his huge day. They got him drunk. Within ninety minutes and after a lot of booze, he revealed the name of his client. The $649 bar tab at Ceres was worth a million dollars in trading information.

Loose-lipped Brandon bragged that LMNOP was behind his trades. They were NBCI's investment banker and had just raised $30 million in a private placement. Better known as ROOT, NBCI was for now a potential whale that traders would be watching very closely.

CHAPTER 234

JUNE 22, 2013

Pierre announced an end to the class action lawsuit with the homeowners who had reneged on their option to sell their crabgrass. Under the settlement, they would receive $20 per pound for the first 500 pounds produced each year and could sell the rest of their production at market prices. The new terms were offered to anyone with a Pierre contract, litigant or not. Pierre paid the lawyer a nice $4 million contingency fee because he rounded up his clients quickly and convinced them to accept the offer.

At $150 a pound, "free market" homes were now making $90,000 a year. People under contract to Pierre had been making only $9,000. The new deal would increase their earnings to just over $30,000. It was a huge improvement, but there were always complainers.

After the news hit the tape, October CRAB prices climbed another few dollars. There was no such thing as bad news for CRAB. Everything was going up, up, up!

CRAB and ROOT prices continued higher the last few days of the month. By Thursday evening, CRAB had hit an historic high of $177 a pound. ROOT touched $40 per share. On Friday, the final day of trading for the month, a flurry of sell orders hit the markets for both the commodity and the stock. June CRAB dropped to $170 and ROOT collapsed to $33. Volumes were extremely high; ROOT alone traded more than a million shares.

Averill explained away his investors' concerns. "Just normal profit taking for skittish investors. Stay the course! Be brave!"

Vladimir and another thousand homeowners had already sold their production last November to pay off their commodity losses. They watched jealously as everyone else got rich. Maybe next quarter they would finally start making money. They just couldn't get ahead of this game. At least they were out of debt from the Hurricane Sandy fiasco.

Bragging rights at Ben's Deli now went to the person who made the most money. A few speculators bought futures in March and made a tidy profit, but Tubby Rodgers won the crown this quarter. He sold the entire year's crop of 600 pounds near the peak June prices. Tubby paid cash for a new Lincoln Explorer SUV with his gains.

Averill finally sold NBCI's June contracts. For the moment, the company's CRAB investment was down to $42 million of contracts, still well above the board's limit. Averill thought: *If I were the board, I'd look at those whopper gains and ignore the technical infraction.*

Averill was cash poor. Everything he had was tied up in NBCI stock, even the sales commission from the private placement. He had taken a quick weekend trip to the Cayman Islands and deposited 100,000 shares of ROOT stock and some cash into a brokerage account under the Tuxedo Investment name. That money wasn't coming back onshore.

At some point, he was going to have to get liquid. But when? The stock was unstoppable. The drop in price the last day of June was nothing. It couldn't be the shorts. There was no way they would return and attack NBCI. The operating results were too strong.

The news wasn't all out yet. NBCI still had a whopper of a June quarter to report. The company wouldn't be telling the public for another five weeks. By Averill's estimation, it had earned about $16 million of EBITDA.

Averill thought: *If I want to sell some stock, I should do it after NBCI releases their quarterly earnings. The stock will pop and I'll make the most money. It may be the last chance too. When the board discovers how much money we gambled, it might be the end for Johnny. And if Johnny goes, it'll be the end for me.*

Now that I think of it, the only one who's unhappy with our performance is that jerk controller. Even the chairman wasn't exactly upset the last time we made a good number. Okay. Here's the plan. Set up Justin to get him fired. Then report the earnings early in a Form 8-K. Sell the stock on the news. And if we're lucky, Johnny keeps his job and the new controller will be so worried about finding the bathroom, he won't have time to bust Johnny's chops.

CHAPTER 236

JULY 2, 2013

"No way! The board loves the guy. They think he's a financial genius. They'll never let me fire Justin," Johnny said. "But personally I can't stand him. He's like a professional tattle-tale waitin' for me to do somethin' wrong so he can run and tell Arthur."

Averill paced around Johnny's office. "You don't have to fire him. Just make him want to leave. Give him so much work he collapses. Complain he's not putting in enough hours. Tell him he's slow. Dream up stuff.

"Create a bunch of useless reports and make him deliver them every morning. Then call a lot of meetings to discuss planning so he doesn't have enough time to get his work done. Tell him you want next year's budget on your desk by the end of the month. Demand a five-year plan. Then a ten-year plan. A hundred-year plan! A capital budget. A corporate financing plan. A human resources plan. An IT plan. Nobody can get all of this done.

"Manuals, too. I guarantee you he doesn't have a documented accounting manual. Tell him to get it finished or he's fired. Write him up and put it in his personnel file. Tell him he's sloppy and his office is a mess.

"Then make him worry about his job. Make him feel excluded. Hold offsite management meetings, but don't invite him. Management lunches, too.

"Make him think you're looking for his replacement. Place an ad for a controller on Monster.com – 'Ag processing plant in Bergen County searching for competent accounting officer!' Don't use NBCI's name. He'll know it's you, but he can't prove it.

"Let's dream up stuff that eats up his time. Then when he's late delivering numbers, you complain to the board."

"Well, I can make up some projects," Johnny agreed. "First, I'll make him count inventory. That'll take days. How about an analysis of crabgrass production by property? A daily cash report. I'll create districts in town and make him report sales by district. Sales by customer. Pounds of seed per pound of crabgrass report. Overtime analysis. Productivity per worker."

Averill gave a sinister look. "Johnny, if anyone can create useless work, it's you! You're a genius!"

CHAPTER 237

JULY 2

Averill protested, "How can you be pregnant? Weren't you using, you know, like birth control, or something?"

Misty started weeping. "No, I wasn't using protection. Were you? I thought you'd be happy for us. Now you're ruining my day."

"I'm sorry, honey," said Averill. "I just didn't think about this. What do you want to do?"

Misty blurted through her tears, "What do you think I'm going to do? I'm having the baby, with you or without you." Her crying intensified. The tears looked real enough.

Averill had been too busy making money and manipulating markets. He had never thought about marriage. In fact, he never thought Misty would want to marry him. Half the time, he felt like she hated him.

He imagined for a second that Misty might become nicer once they were married. Maybe she was bitchy and mean because she was single. Having a child had to have some positive effect, didn't it?

"Okay, marriage it is. When do you want to do it?" Averill was trying to act understanding, but he wasn't quite familiar with the protocol. Do I smile? Frown? Shed a tear? Pat her on the head?

Misty slowed the tears and said, "You have to ask my father's permission first. He has to give his blessing."

The next night they visited her parents in Cresskill. The meeting downright frightened him. Misty was the spitting image of her mother. Between the two of them, they spent four hours a day on their makeup and hair. Like Misty, her mother had not one nice word to say about anyone.

Averill was hoping the meeting would be an exchange of pleasantries. Hi. How do you do? Where did you go to school? Where do you work?

Instead, it was a grilling worthy of an Ed McBain crime novel. "Who are your parents? What did your father do for a living? Did you serve in the military? How much do you make? What is your net worth? Do you have any debt? Have you sired any children out of wedlock? Have you ever been arrested? How often do you attend church services?

"We aren't giving our blessing without a prenuptial agreement financially protecting Giovanna, my poor baby girl," wailed Mrs. Francella.

Misty's mom soon realized Averill had made a small fortune during the last year. She switched from attack to kiss-ass mode. "Averill, you're such a successful young man. I don't know how you do it."

Misty's father was nice enough, but he clearly did not wear the pants in the family. After he had said a pleasant good-night and retired to bed, Misty's mother cackled, "God bless me for staying married to that spineless worm for forty years. I could have done so much better."

The good news was that, based on her mother's looks, Misty was probably going to be beautiful into old age. The bad news was she'd probably stay mean, too.

CHAPTER 238

JULY 4, 2013

The reconstruction of the Jersey Shore was slowly continuing. Houses were still unrepaired. Wide areas of beaches were eroded. Dunes hadn't yet been rebuilt. The aftereffects of Hurricane Sandy didn't keep beachgoers away on the Fourth. The towns cleared small areas for bathers and beach volleyball. Without many available rental cottages, most made the best with day trips.

Storeowners found a way to open despite the inefficient town permitting process. A bar owner who couldn't get an operating permit opened a tiki bar outside the boarded building. It was doing a brisk business. Joey Harrisons was still closed. The iconic bar on Ortley Beach was embroiled in a dispute with its insurance company. How would bathers survive without Joey Harrison's?

The main boardwalks were mostly rebuilt. The Casino Pier was a work in progress. They had finally removed the Jet Star roller coaster from the ten-foot waters.

Sonny & Rickey's repaired their stands and opened their carnival games for business. For a dollar, you had a chance to win a cupie doll or a stuffed bear.

FEMA paid Belmar $30 million to repair its beach area. They paid Seaside Heights and Park $400 million to build breakwaters and cement pilings to replace the pier that had collapsed.

Kohrs Custard maintained its Abercrombie & Fitch recruiting standards. They always hired the best looking teens from the area. The water slide park, which at the height of the storm theoretically stretched to Ireland, was back to its half block boundary.

Unfortunately, Hurricane Sandy may have unintentionally robbed the poor and given to the rich. Insurance settlements were disputed. Rebuilding at all was questioned by many. Building codes remained subjective. One block was rebuilt. The next was a mess.

Owning beachfront, waterfront or bay view property was always expensive, but there was so much of it in New Jersey that average families had managed to claim a small sliver since the sixties. Including its large bays and inlets, New Jersey had 1,800 miles of tidal shoreline.

The Jersey Shore had always been democratic. Everyone had access. The Garden State Parkway, Atlantic City Expressway and Route 195 were nothing more than big entry ramps to the beach. It was a quick hour plus ride from most of the state. Many planned their retirements around their small cottages.

Now, that inalienable right of a summer home near the water had been taken away. The combination of poor insurance settlements and increased construction costs made waterfront unaffordable for many. Homes had to be raised on pilings to meet new building codes. Rich carpetbaggers were combing neighborhoods for cheap waterfront lots.

Over the years, friends and relatives at one time or another had bunked at the Ortley Beach summer house. They repaid the favor and helped replace wallboard, insulation, electrical wiring and ducts. As long as you didn't have a bank mortgage dictating your choices, you could make the place livable.

If you had a mortgage, but weren't rich, rebuilding wasn't an option. Towns were not issuing building permits unless the owners met code. Homes in Little Silver on the Toms River side of Barnegat Bay had five feet of water in their living rooms during the storm. Houses rated V Zone on the water had to be raised 15 feet above the land.

Eventually, many reached a hard decision. They couldn't rebuild with the paltry insurance proceeds. Families watched as wreckers tore down their dream homes.

CHAPTER 239

JULY 4

Bret hung around Allie's store for the country's birthday party. The holiday provided a brisk business for everything Fourth. Allie applied American flags and eagles to water pails, rocking chairs and outdoor garden items.

Bret brought his Iowa charm and wit to the store and gave free horticultural advice. "You know, I was raised on a farm in Iowa, though we don't have any crabgrass where I come from. Just corn, pigs and chickens."

Up north, a million spectators stayed around to watch the Macy's New York City fireworks display from both sides of the Hudson River. The event had grown so large that it had gone network. Usher, Mariah Carey, Taylor Swift, Selena and Tim McGraw took turns entertaining the national television audiences. On the Jersey side of the Hudson, celebrators found their way to primo viewing spots. They watched from the Palisades Cliffs, River Road in Edgewater and the heights of West New York.

Misty and Averill sat in a plane on the tarmac. Their flight to Nevada had been delayed until fireworks from New York to Philadelphia ended. Naturally, Misty was furious at Averill for choosing such an inconvenient departure time.

CHAPTER 240

JULY 5, 2013

Las Vegas was 105 degrees outdoors. Avy had rented a white tuxedo with gold braiding for the wedding ceremony to be held at the King's Chapel. He was having a blast fooling around with the Elvis characters who were paid to be witnesses. Misty felt physically uncomfortable and wore a pantsuit with a loose top to hide the tiny baby bulge.

As soon as the ceremony ended, she hit Averill up for $5,000 and headed to the craps tables. Averill drank alone at the casino bar, bewildered at what had just happened. He was supposed to be happy. Even the working girls stayed away from him. He looked too miserable even to a professional who was paid to have a good time.

Misty turned in at four in the morning to a drunken husband who was still wearing the Elvis sideburns. She'd be sleeping with Averill every night for the rest of her married life, however long that lasted. The snoring was too loud. She curled up in the guest bedroom. It was a perfect, unconsummated wedding night.

CHAPTER 241

JULY 20, 2013

"I wired the company $30 million this morning. That should keep your bookkeeper happy," said Averill sarcastically. "I see his door's closed. How's Justin doing with our new executive training program? Has he cracked yet?"

Johnny wasn't accustomed to being on the front lines. He was battle-weary after barely a week. "This place is a war zone," he said. "This is a tough way to go to work. You shoulda seen the budget template he gave me. He hardcoded zeros into the budget line for income from hedgin' activities. Heh, heh. Like the board would go for that."

Averill laughed. "Do you know what CPA stands for? Certified Pain in the Ass! I got an idea. Fix the thermostat in his office and sweat him out. I know a guy who can do it. He'll block the air ducts too.

"Just keep working him over. Reprimand him every day for something new. Make sure you document everything in writing. This guy has to leave, or we'll never make any money.

"Speaking of which, we have to start buying CRAB again soon. If we don't buy now, the quarter will be over before you know it. The market's been real quiet for three weeks. It's in the doldrums. Everyone's on vacation. When they get back to work, we have to be fully invested. I'm projecting big gains in August and September. And you need Arthur's blessing, or Justin's going to stop you. Here. Look at this."

Averill handed Johnny a sheaf of spreadsheets plus a typed agenda. "It's a script. Ask Arthur to meet in person. We need to convince him to do a bunch of things. First, you want board permission to invest everything we earned so far in futures contracts. Tell him the market is expecting at least $40 million of gains in the September quarter or the stock price will be going down big time. He'll be screwed.

"Next, you need his okay to spend money on branding and advertising. We have to promote the crap out of this stock. And last, you need to get rid of the thorn down the hall. Justin's gotta go.

"As far as Arthur is concerned, you have to make this affect him personally. Tell him his stock options are going to tank if we don't continue what we've been doing. Also, tell him you accrued a big bonus for him and management in the June quarter. There's nothing like a cash bonus to get a chairman to see your point of view."

CHAPTER 242

JULY 24, 2013

The NASDAQ Short Interest reports for June 30 were released for all public companies. In April and May, the short sellers had left ROOT alone. Now they were back.

Stocks often have a small short position. They could be related to market puts and calls or executive option programs. They could be a hedge against a convertible bond investment. But the large sell-off of the ROOT stock on the last trading day of the month was more than profit taking. The million shares sold during the last hour of June trading had all been sold borrowed and short.

Averill dismissed the report and thought: *Anyone could have done the trade. Only an idiot would be crazy enough to attack us now. The trend's up. Trading volumes are high. Two research analysts at big firms are preparing to launch coverage. Yeah, the stock got killed the end of June, but it's held steady since the Fourth. This is summertime. Everyone's on vacation. I'm not worrying about this. I'll get out of the stock soon enough.*

CHAPTER 243

JULY 25, 2013

Johnny managed to get ahold of Arthur just in time. In a few days, the chairman would be heading to the south of France for a month-long vacation where he would be mostly unreachable. Johnny drove into the City and met him at 21, New York's famous restaurant for celebrities and politicians on West 52nd Street. Johnny dressed in the same suit, shirt and tie he had worn to the NASDAQ ceremony.

He was scared to death waiting for the chairman to arrive. After opening the menu and seeing the prices, he double checked his wallet to make sure he had his corporate American Express card.

Arthur sat in an incredibly good mood and all full of chitchat. He was being a gracious host and addressed Johnny like he was a seasoned and respected corporate officer. He talked about his upcoming trip. He was excited about the prospects for NBCI. All of his friends were impressed that he was the chairman of this high-profile start-up. Arthur was feeling grand, sipping his martini.

After Arthur ordered a second drink, Johnny said, "Mr. Sterling, I don't want to surprise you. We may have gone a little over your budget for hedgin' this Q. We made some money, but…"

Arthur sat up straight. "Johnny, keep your voice down. This place is full of reporters. How much over?"

"We earned $16 million EBITDA, and that's after we socked away a reserve for chairman and executive bonuses." Johnny was quoting from Averill's notes even though he had no clue what was so special about EBITDA.

"We learned 'bout the Chinese buyin' houses and bought contracts. We sold just before the top price of $170 a pound. There wasn't time to call you to ask permission. Problem is, sir, we aren't sure what the board had authorized. Was it $30 million of. . ."

Arthur interrupted in a whisper, "Johnny, that's a big number. You guys already did over $40 million in the last nine months, but most of that was because of Hurricane Sandy. No one is expecting this type of gain. Who knows about this? When are you releasing earnings?"

Johnny suddenly realized his boss wasn't angry. "Justin knows, but he's not gettin' along with the team. He's not happy with the tradin' stuff. The only other person who knows is the broker, you know, Averill.

"Justin's been late with a lot of his work. He's locked up in his office. I don't know, maybe he has a drug problem. I'm not sure when we're gonna release. I was hopin' to release numbers early so, you know, like we don't have a leak."

Arthur finished the martini and ate the olive. "Of course, we don't want any insider trading. So what do you want from me? To loosen up the reins a little? You guys proved you can make some money. I'll get the board to increase the allowance to... how about $40 million dollars? That lets you play with the money you made so far. On margin, you can buy, what, four times that number? Just don't go over the limit, okay? What else do you need?"

Averill had given him instructions. Always lead your request with something that Arthur wants for himself. A nicely furnished boardroom to show off to his cronies was a perfect lead-in. Stately leather chairs. Big table. Top-of-the-line video equipment. The works!

"Um, we need some money to furnish the boardroom," Johnny said cautiously handing Arthur a drawing. "Here's the layout."

Arthur studied the rendering of the new boardroom. It looked spectacular, perfectly fitting for important board meetings.

"We also hafta buy a couple of pickup trucks," Johnny said after Arthur finished admiring the sketches. "And we could use a little money for office furniture. We're rentin' now."

"And I need a budget to promote the stock more. We wanna hire a company to improve our image on Wall Street. You know, brandin', logos, that kinda thing."

Arthur was decisive and very chairman-like. "Done. Is a million enough? What else? This controller conflict isn't healthy for a company going through such rapid growth. Justin is getting a little old. You need a young gun. Use a search firm to find a CFO. In the meantime, I'll have a talk with Justin. We can't let accountants run the business."

"Last thing. Between you and me, I want a heads-up before you release those earnings. And tell Justin to get the numbers done now. Before month-end!"

After they finished lunch, Johnny was preparing to leave when several of Arthur's pals stopped by the table. After some manly back-slapping and guffaws, one of the men leaned over and said, "Mr. Carerra. You're doing a great job. I own a little of your stock. Keep up the good work!"

Arthur whispered to his friends, "Like I told you guys, NBCI has a great strategy. They really have an edge on this trading market because of their position as the transfer company."

The Star Ledger reported another unintended but positive outcome of Hurricane Sandy. When the power went out after the storm, couples looking for a flashlight apparently groped something else. Nine months later, the birth rate at area hospitals was up nearly 20%. There's a silver lining to every hurricane cloud.

Averill couldn't care less about the stork story. He had a baby on the way and no clue how to deal with it. He focused on what he did know. He called The Sticky Five.

McSorley Blain interrupted the beginning of the call. "Averill, the market cap of ROOT is getting too big. We don't have the capital to do all of this buying. I think we need to expand the group. I decided to invite a friend."

Averill said warily, "Man, that's not a good idea. We have to keep this very quiet. Tell him on your own time. The larger the group, the greater the chance we'll get caught."

"It's a little late for that," McSorley said unapologetically. "He's on the call. Meet Jean Jacques from Haiti. No last names, please."

"Avy, buddy," Lefty Stonewall said. "I got someone on the call, too. Meet Carlos from Columbia. In fact, we all have friends on the vine. How do you think this stock moves? From five small brokers?"

Averill heard another accent in the background which sounded Eastern European, perhaps Ukrainian. He couldn't tell. Averill sighed and said, "It's a little late to stop this call now. I hope you guys know what you're doing. Okay, here's the deal. You can each add one person to the group, but that's it. Same procedure. Untraceable prepaid cell phone. Don't use personal emails. Set up dummy accounts.

"I'm going to make this quick. And no recorders! NBCI made $16 million EBITDA in the June quarter. Trailing earnings per share are over $3.00 dollars. Trailing EBITDA per share is almost $6.00. That's the number you should concentrate on. Our depreciation is big because of the plant, but it was all paid with a muni bond. Stock is selling at less than ten times earnings and growing 200 percent. You guys know this is very cheap. Should be a double before year-end.

"If you look closely at the numbers, the company socked away $1 million dollars of reserves for a rainy day. Only rich companies can afford to do this. We're going out early with the numbers in a few days. Buy now, but be careful. Keep your trades small! Anyone buying large blocks or options will attract attention. Good luck!"

CHAPTER 245

JULY 31, 2013

So much for buying small lots and avoiding the options market. Whoever was on Monday's call had placed huge buy orders. The stock jumped $4.00 to $40 per share. ROOT was on the move again.

Averill thought: *These large share blocks and heavy options volume are bad. They're going to attract attention from the NASD or SEC. My guys have got to straighten out their new pals. Keep everything under the radar!*

Averill left his office before lunch and drove to the parking lot behind the Roy W. Brown Middle School with his four iPads in tow. Averill peeked through the school secretary's window. Today's password was "vacation". He posted on the ROOT Yahoo! Finance message board:

Tektikker: "ROOT was quiet in July, but yesterday it made a big move. Anyone know what's up? Is this HUMONGOUS?"

Greenmasheen: "CRAB futures near $190. Has to be the reason. ROOT made good money in March Q from trading. Maybe they did it again in June. Someone buying big lots. Must be institutional buying."

Contrariologist: "Looking at the technical chart. Volume building. 50 and 100-day averages all up. ROOT must have caught the Chinese price move. I'm long and going longer."

Biohzrde: "You guys are great. You're like stock uncles to me. I can't believe how much $ I'm making."

Tektikker: "ROOT could go to a $100. This IS HUMONGOUS!"

Just like he had planned, traders had caught on to the pattern of the encrypted messages. Every time his four ghosts chatted, the stock picked up a notch. Who knew who the buyers were? They could be dozens or hundreds of brokers buying on the tips themselves and then spreading the rumors. Occasionally, one would leave a tell that he had seen the messages and was buying.

Every hour, Averill monitored the chat room and scrolled through the banter. He read a hundred posts full of ridiculous garbage, mostly from angry teenagers screaming at one another to STFU, teen-speak for SHUT THE F*** UP! Then he noticed what looked to be an informed source. It appeared different.

MongoosesKillCobras: "ROOT is going to $100. They're gonna make a killing on CRAB trading. Kill the snakes!"

TheLanghorneInterloper: "You have it right, mongoose, but for the wrong reason. ROOT is up because it's a takeover target. Buckstown Financial is the buyer."

Averill looked at a Google map and reflected, *Langhorne is a town in Bucks County. It's maybe ten miles from the silo. That's not exactly a clever disguise. It has to be someone who works near the silo. Maybe someone who overheard a conversation. If Buckstown takes over NBCI, I just found my exit strategy.*

The message board wasn't really a chat room where people hung around and talked. It was rare to catch someone live in the room. Averill didn't have time to drive to the middle school. He had to speak to Langhorne before he signed off. Averill broke protocol and posted as Tektikker through his office Wi-Fi.

Tektikker: "Hey Langhorne. Welcome to discussion. I'm very long on ROOT. You?"

LanghorneInterloper: "Yes. Getting longer. Stock was cheap until yesterday. Now getting expensive. Time to buy call options."

Tektikker: "Which calls? Sep or Dec?"

LanghorneInterloper: "Dec to be safe."

Tektikker: "Do you want to speak? Do you have a Kik? My Kik is Tektikker."

LanghorneInterloper: "What's Kik? I think this was a bad idea. You guys figure it out. I'm signing off chat for good. Good luck!"

Averill was excited. *This guy is real. First, he wrote too well. He hasn't learned to disguise his text. Second, he talked about call options. You always buy options if you think a company is a takeover target. He might even be a stockbroker. He also doesn't know what Kik is, so he's not a teenager. Every teen in America has a Kik Messenger account. They use it to hunt for girls so they can sext. But the best thing is he got nervous. He didn't want to chat anymore and get caught. This guy's source was real.*

By mid-afternoon, Averill's euphoria changed to concern. The intercontinental members had blogged on the ROOT Yahoo! Finance Message Board. They weren't well-disguised.

CRABBabyDoc: "Reliable tip. ROOT caught the June CRAB. Heard they made $16 mil. Buy now before it's too late!"

PabloEsCRABar: "They raised $30 million in May and bet it all on CRAB. I think you're right BabyDoc. This stock is cheap. BTW, how is Papa Doc?"

IgorCRABinsky: "You chumps are missing it. Yeah, they made great $ in June, but they have a $100M war chest. Next quarter's going to knock your knickers off. I predict ROOT will be $100 by October. I'm betting on it."

The art of subtlety had escaped the new ring members. This was potential trouble. They directly quoted the financial numbers Averill had given them. This was how you got caught.

Averill called Johnny at his office. "Prez, we have a small problem. Somebody went public with your earnings number on the Internet."

"What the…?" cried Johnny. "Averill, you gotta keep this stuff quiet. It's you and me and no one else. What're we gonna do?"

"There's only one thing to do," Averill said dead serious. "You have to stuff the numbers with some reserves and make the Internet number wrong. Book some extra management bonus. Accrue the costs of the public relations project. I have a firm you can hire. She'll backdate the invoices for you. Just be quick. I want the numbers released in two days."

CHAPTER 246

AUGUST 2, 2013

The quarterly report on NBCI's Form 10-Q wouldn't be filed for another week. Averill was getting anxious. He was ROOT-heavy and needed to generate some cash. Even a week was too long to wait. He needed one last little push on the stock price so he could cash in. He told Johnny to convince the attorneys to release earnings early.

Johnny initiated a conference call with Jack Barlowitz. Justin dialed in from his locked office twenty feet down the hall. He refused to sit in the same room with the president, rank insubordination or not.

Johnny looked at the script written by Averill and said, "Someone in a chat room talked 'bout a profit number way too close to our real results. The stock's gone up ten percent already. I'd say they're tradin' on inside info. The only person I told was Arthur. Justin, you talk to anyone?"

You could hear Justin slamming his table. He yelled, "Only the auditors know the number. I didn't even tell my wife! Maybe it was your buddy, Averill. He controls the brokerage accounts. He knows the CRAB gains, right?"

Johnny screamed into the speaker phone, "He doesn't know the rest of the numbers, now does he, you insolent, insubordinate twerp. How did the market know the EBITDA number was…"

Arthur had warned Jack about the increasing animosity between Johnny and Justin. Jack interjected with authority, "Guys, guys, no finger pointing. Okay. We have a handful of auditors who know. Normally, I wouldn't suspect them, but they're not all angels. Just this month an audit partner at a big firm in Los Angeles was sentenced to three years for giving inside information to a golf buddy.

"And Averill definitely has enough information to take a good guess. Even if he only knows the trading gain, it's not hard to figure out the rest of your results.

"Johnny, you told Arthur in a public restaurant, for crissakes. Anybody could have heard it, even a waiter. The 21 Club is infamous, you know. They filmed a scene in the movie *Wall Street* there. Don't you remember Michael Douglas and Charlie Sheen having steak tartare while planning illegal trading?

"Okay, forget the pop reference. No more discussions at any restaurant and that includes Wendy's! After this settles, we're going to have a class on communications in a public company. Right now we have to deal with the problem. Justin, is the 10-Q ready?"

Justin answered defensively, "The auditors haven't signed off yet. I have a real problem with our trading gains. This is a violation of our SOX controls. Someone needs to inform the board!"

"Justin, the board is fully informed about the gains," Jack said dismissively. "In fact, they're pretty happy and already increased the investment limit for hedging activities. We can talk about this privately later. Have the auditors at least signed off on the numbers?"

"Well, sort of," Justin shrugged. "They have some questions about a million dollars of public relations payments and executive bonuses Johnny told me to accrue at the last minute. I need board…"

Jack abruptly interrupted Justin again. "The board has approved those too. I'll send a draft of the minutes to your auditors. Assuming the auditors are fine, we should do an early earnings release in an 8-K. I'll draft it. Let's file it after lunch.

"We have to keep a tighter ship. Somehow the number leaked. Let's get beyond this. Also, it's not my job to keep you two guys from killing each other. Either resolve your differences or at least one of you will have to go. Those are Arthur's words, not mine. Gentlemen, good day!"

CHAPTER 247

AUGUST 2

NBCI filed the Form 8-K with the SEC. The NASDAQ instituted a one-hour trading halt to allow the market time to assimilate the information. It didn't matter. There was a rush to buy stock as soon as the hour expired. The market had concluded NBCI had developed a magic hand at trading CRAB futures and was making tremendous profits. After trading resumed, the bid for the stock was $42 a share, up 15%.

Buy on the rumor and sell on the news! That's one of many old Wall Street adages. Averill dumped the shares he had been accumulating since May. The tickets totaled over $8 million, all bought on margin. He had netted $3 million of profits in three months.

He still had the commission shares, the "note" shares, and the warrants. And he still had the shares sitting in his Cayman Islands account. He was most proud of the Cayman shares.

Averill opened his net worth calculator in Excel and entered in the new share price plus the most recent gains. He admired the new total – over $28 million of net worth. When he reached the "100" club, he was calling it quits.

CHAPTER 248

AUGUST 2

CRAB trading had been relatively quiet during July. It moved up or down a buck on small volume. The LITE floor broker had been mostly absent from the pit. That meant NBCI wasn't buying.

Before the market opening, the traders in the commodity trading room of Fischbein and Morgenbesser were tossing a Nerf football, getting in shape for their weekend sports fest. Some would be golfing in Lake Forest. A few might be sailing on Lake Michigan. There were only so many days of warm weather in Chicago, and one had to make the most of it.

The market opened and a dozen contracts quickly sold. Computers flashed the trades; the Nerf was tossed behind a cubicle. Someone had scooped up a handful of sell orders above the market. The orders were executed at $175.

NBCI earnings flashed across the Bloomberg screens. Everyone knew they had made some money, but this was astounding. Orders came streaming to the floor. Pension funds. Charitable foundations. University endowments. The Den-Ken funds. Professional traders. Amateur traders. Everybody and their brother bought CRAB contracts. NBCI had caught the trading bug. They'd be back for more.

CHAPTER 249

AUGUST 5, 2013

Suzanne ran into Hector's office. She slammed the NBCI Form 8-K on the mayor's desk. "NBCI made $15 million from trading gains. This is not good!"

The startled mayor exclaimed, "How's that bad? They made money. Don't the profits provide added protection for our bonds? That's all I care about anymore. I've given up battling the town on this one."

Suzanne settled down just enough and sat across from her boss. "Hector, the NBCI bonds are now trading at $80. The credit default swaps are up to 2300 bips. This is junk territory! The bond market thinks NBCI is taking abnormal risks and could fail. So do I.

"If they were making profits from processing fees, it would be a good thing. Unfortunately, most of their earnings are from speculating. I looked at their footnote disclosures. I'm pretty sure they earned all of it in the last three weeks of June. They raised $30 million in May and bet it all.

"Let me phrase it in Wall Street terms. They substantially increased their beta. They amplified their risk profile. This is equivalent to playing roulette in Las Vegas. They're betting on an ever increasing CRAB price. At some point, this strategy fails. No price goes up forever."

"Try telling that to the town," Hector lamented. "They're all getting rich. But aren't we protected by the credit default swap?"

"Yes and no." Suzanne rotated her hands open and closed. "First, we only bought $120 million dollars of swaps, and the bond is $200 million. Also, credit default swaps always have counterparty risk. That means you hope the insurance company has the assets to pay off the default. This was the issue with AIG when the market collapsed a few years ago.

Also, if the total outstanding swaps in the market are a lot greater than the outstanding bonds, you might have to fight to collect the full amount. Technically, we don't own the bonds, so our swap is considered naked. Right now, the bonds are only $200 million, but the bets against the bonds are $2 billion and growing. If they don't settle out before the default, there's a whole process we have to go through. The price they pay out is determined at a special auction.

"Let's say we're protected. We would still go through a horrible media exposure that will affect our future ability to raise municipal debt. We prefer not to go down that path.

"A friend of mine overheard that guy Averill bragging to a customer in Ben's this morning. He said NBCI is going to triple the June results this quarter. The only way they can make that much money is to buy even more contracts, another $100 million by my estimation. They're betting the house on a higher price!

"This is risky stuff. We have to warn NBCI's board about the potential of default on their bonds."

Hector acted calmly. "Okay, walk me through this. What do I need to do?"

Hector and Suzanne composed a letter addressed to the Chairman of NBCI.

Dear Arthur:

I wish to advise you, in the politest manner possible, that NBCI's commodity trades are taking on incredible risk and endangering the financial condition of your company. As a result, you're putting our town at risk due to its guarantee of your bonds.

Your operating and financial staffs are no longer hedging. They are speculating in CRAB futures. While your company has managed to show some short-term profits during the last quarter, we believe this is an unsustainable model.

This month, the value of the industrial revenue bonds used to finance your plant declined by over 20% on the news of your activities. The rate for the CDS, or Credit Default Swaps, on your bonds increased to 23%. That is officially junk status. We hereby warn you that your company's actions could lead to its demise.

Also, I remind you that NBCI is required to maintain $50 million of working capital under the terms of the bond indenture. Speculative CRAB futures are NOT eligible collateral under the terms of the indenture.

Arthur, we implore you to increase the oversight of your organization's activities and curtail your exposure to potential trading losses in the commodity markets. If the town suffers any losses on its guarantee as a result of your trading activities, we will hold you and your board of directors personally responsible.

Proceed at your own peril.

Yours truly,

Hector Alvarez

Mayor of Bergenfield

CHAPTER 250

AUGUST 6, 2013

Johnny signed for the hand-delivered letter and tossed it into the chairman's already overflowing mail slot. He was sure the letter was just Hector still griping about the CRAB boom. *The mayor's just a sore loser.*

Johnny wasn't going to bother Arthur. His new favorite chairman was going to approve big year-end bonuses. Besides, Arthur needed his rest. He could read the letter when he returned from Bordeaux in September.

CHAPTER 251

AUGUST 12, 2013

NBCI had found plenty of uses for its newfound fortune from commodity trading. Johnny had become a true believer in the magic of corporate marketing. The booming ROOT stock price was direct evidence of great investor relation success. Avy told him so, and Johnny believed him.

Ten days before, Arthur had approved NBCI's public relations and furniture and vehicle budgets. Johnny wasted no time spending it. On day one, Johnny bought the four members of his management team new $54,000 Ford F-150 pickup trucks. They were purchased fully-loaded and customized with chrome steps, louvers and bug shields. And what would a company truck be without a hand-painted company logo?

On day two, he hired Averill's contact, Sarah Dare, a brand consultant. Her task was to create the image that justified the heady $500 million value of the company. Sarah was a thirty-five-year-old brunette, a slender, athletic beauty who had toiled as an actress unsuccessfully off-off-off, way-off Broadway for ten years. Her "creative skills" had been developed by hanging around artsy people in SoHo. She teamed up with a geeky website designer and together declared themselves "brand consultants".

The logo alone should have cost no more than $5,000. Pick a fruit other than an apple with a bite out of it and make a fuzzy caricature. Sarah had grander ideas.

Every day, she sat in Johnny's office preaching her mantra. "Johnny, everything today is about branding your image." She went on to explain what this meant. "We need to effectively communicate that image. We need to reinforce it constantly. This is a full time job!

"When Wall Street hears your name, they must think positive things – hyper growth, a soaring stock price. You're not a basic commodity made from an ugly weed. You're the future of disruptive, organic biotechnology. My $100,000 consulting fee will be a pittance compared to the $100 million dollars of extra value from creating your brand."

She spent hours hovering over Johnny's shoulder to explain the latest improvements to the logo design. Johnny was smitten by her attention, her youthful enthusiasm, her intoxicating scent.

NBCI's head of public relations, Alistair McClendon, had been on the road promoting the company stock to the investor community. The share price had been slipping daily in July until the recent jump on the earnings news. Johnny summoned Alistair to come home. "You have to spend more of your time internally on branding, not at some silly investor conference in Arizona!"

In less than a week, the branding project fully taxed Alistair's resources. He hired three readily-available recent grads who had managed to escape college without any thought of a career. They would be spending their days answering investor calls and attending Johnny's four-a-day brand meetings. Johnny finally had something to do with his time.

CHAPTER 252

AUGUST 12

A sneak attack works once. Thereafter, the enemy lies in wait.

The big players in the CRAB market could be counted on two hands and a foot: Pierre, Buckstown, the Chinese, the Den-Ken funds, two small shampoo companies, and an assortment of corporate R&D departments. Most were investigating uses in toothpaste, detergent and oil spill cleanup.

Until August, NBCI had been thought of as a one-hit wonder, the *Who Let the Dogs Out?* of commodity trading. It got lucky and made the pop charts when it purchased some contracts before Hurricane Sandy hit. NBCI wasn't considered a regular in the pit. It didn't trade often. One and done!

NBCI's August earnings announcement told a different story. They had broken open the piggy bank in June and bought big. It was also clear that NBCI had the inside track on special events. They were buying before news hit the wires, and they weren't shy about it. Chicago would be now be watching NBCI's moves more closely.

Averill had miscalculated. The early earnings announcement was meant to boost the stock price so he could sell some shares. He hadn't understood it would also have an effect on the CRAB price. He had originally figured he could simply return to the markets, buy some more CRAB, benefit from another as yet unknown huge real or unreal event or announcement, and make more money. He had done it before. Easy peasy!

For the last ten days, NBCI had been nearly shut out. It managed to buy a measly hundred contracts a day. It needed thousands. Every time it tried to buy in size, the price moved away. Averill knew better than to place a market order. He kept attacking the market trying to execute small trades. The pit traders were one step ahead and a lot smarter. CRAB prices kept moving up a buck a day.

On Monday morning, the bid was $177, the same as the closing price Friday evening. The LITE floor broker continued the chase, raising its bid a quarter at a time. No one bit. After an hour of cat and mouse, a contract crossed at $180; a second crossed at $182. LITE missed the trades while it was fighting over pennies.

This scenario repeated. LITE bought a few small contracts, but every time it tried to buy in volume, the sell side disappeared. The market was up $5.00 for the day. Volume was low. An increasing price on low volume was bullish.

CHAPTER 253

AUGUST 13, 2013

Tuesday started the same. LITE bid discreetly in small increments. The big players in the market ganged up on it. The price continued to move. Averill reconsidered his strategy. NBCI would never book enough gains in the quarter by nibbling at trades. It would have to pay a premium to build a big position.

Averill called Brandon, the floor broker, who advised, "If you want to buy in size, I can get you all you want at $193 dollars. Otherwise, we're not buying much today."

Averill bit the bullet. LITE threw buy orders around like it was a Yankee's World Series ticker tape parade down Broadway. At the end of the day, it owned 4,000 contracts and had blown half its budget.

The traders informed their institutional clients that a baby whale was swimming in the pits. The three Den-Ken Crab funds were already long and fully invested. The pension funds increased their healthy positions. Buckstown increased its insurance coverage of the silo to its new value, $200 million. Through all of this, no one had seen evidence that Pierre was active in the markets. Everyone was making money. Who cared about Pierre?

Averill quickly calculated that CRAB would have to increase to $250 in order for ROOT to make its magic number by September 30. This just wasn't realistic.

He studied the price of the commodity options compared to futures prices. The way-out-of-the-money call option for delivery in October was cheap. A futures contract at $200 a pound required $50 in equity. An option had triple the leverage. The CRAB price was in a steep uptrend; the options had to increase.

To finish the day, NBCI bought a thousand "CRAB $250 Oct 2013" options for two bucks apiece. Either CRAB reached $250 by the end of October, or the options were worthless.

CHAPTER 254

AUGUST 15, 2013

Mid-August was hot as Hades. JB tried to act outraged, but his mischievous smile betrayed him. He addressed the full board table at Ben's: "I know a lot about strategy. Some companies go for dominant market share. Some prefer market niche strategies. But there is one corporate strategy that deeply offends me."

Gavin said, "Okay, JB, I'll bite. Who should we arrest? Dollar stores selling things for $2 dollars? Knockoff Rolex salesmen? How about overpriced designer tap water? Who?"

"Hollywood!" JB said in exasperation. "I'm tired of sitting through ten minutes of previews and piracy warnings before I can watch a movie. The DVD won't allow me to escape to the main menu or fast forward it. I paid good money to see a movie. Then I'm forced to watch trailers of movies that were failures at the box office.

"It's a form of home imprisonment. It's like an electronic bracelet. I can't leave the living room. No one wants to bother with this issue, but it's huge!

"Last night, Wanda and I tried to watch a ninety minute comedy. We had to sit through eight two-minute tragedies first. We tried to beat the system by switching to the TV while it played through the previews. When we returned, they restarted. And that's after a full minute of the FBI warnings. And now they've added an INTERPOL warning in French. How many times do I have to watch the same warning? I've practically memorized it."

Bret was laughing. "JB, start the DVD. Go make yourself a scotch. When you come back, the movie's on!"

JB smirked. "It would take two scotches. And if Wanda and I watch the movie over two days, we have to watch the trailers a second time. It's an outrage!

"I'm worth a thousand an hour, or at least I was when I was an executive. So my time forced to watch previews is worth $200 dollars. I'm sending Hollywood an invoice!"

He turned to his Wharton MBA number cruncher. "Buyout, quick. Google how many DVDs are sold a year."

Buyout searched on his iPad, found the site, and began punching numbers into his calculator. "The top hundred DVDs last year sold 140 million copies. Assuming 150 million for the whole market, and if you consider the average DVD might be in service five years, there are an estimated 750 million DVDs in place.

"Anticipating your next question, using an estimated nine minutes of previews per DVD, viewers are watching almost seven billion minutes of unwanted previews each year. If the average watcher's time is worth $40 dollars per hour which equates to an annual salary of $80,000 dollars, the cost to the consumer is an estimated $4.5 billion a year. Every year, you can add another fifth to the damage claim.

"I have one additional interesting fact. *Beverly Hills Chihuahua 3* was number 99 on the list and sold 600,000 copies, if you can believe it."

JB said, "Thank you, Buyout, for that complete and thorough analysis. Save that work. I'll use you as an expert witness at the trial.

"If a class action lawyer saw these numbers, he'd file a suit tomorrow. At a minimum, the studios should be required to put a warning on the DVD cover. Here. I drafted my proposed language."

JB handed out a sheet of paper typed in ALL CAPS:

THIS DVD REQUIRES AN ETERNAL AMOUNT OF YOUR VALU-
ABLE TIME TO PREVIEW BAD MOVIES THAT WE COULDN'T SELL AT
THE BOX OFFICE. WE ARE GOING TO MAKE YOU WATCH THE PRE-
VIEW AND NOT ALLOW YOU TO FAST FORWARD TO THE MOVIE
EVEN THOUGH YOU PAID US GOOD MONEY FOR THAT RIGHT!

"If they warned you, no one would buy the DVD. Now, some movies don't have mandatory previews, like *The Big Lebowski*. But that's a cult film, and you have to believe that the producers were too cool to force me to watch crap. Disney usually allows me to escape to the main menu. And there are art films and PBS specials like *Downton Abbey* that are okay. So maybe our calculation of damages is a little high.

"Okay, who wants to join me in a class action suit? Come on Bret, you're not working yet. Buyout, find me a local congressman who isn't under indictment. I want him to propose a law."

Bret shook his head, and feigned interest in helicopters flying during a brokerage firm ad on STCK-TV. He wasn't going to argue. JB may be right, but who wanted to spend the time and money to fight it?

Henrik Jorgen interrupted the class action lawsuit presentation and sat down with a big smile. "JB, congratulate me. I have an empty nest."

"Don't tell me your son found a job and your daughter found a husband in the same month!" JB chuckled.

"No," Henrik said. "I sold the next two years of my crabgrass crop and gave them some money to move out. I have my lovely home again. Here, everyone have a Kringle. I'm so happy."

Michael gave Henrik a congratulatory pat on the back, and the table feasted on the sweet Norwegian pastry from Henrik's wife's kitchen.

CHAPTER 255

AUGUST 15

Smack in the middle of August, another big financial story hit the news tape. Buckstown Financial had filed a Form 3 with the SEC announcing it had purchased over 5% of the common stock of NBCI. The commodity trading subsidiary of Intergalactic Bank had a history of acquiring commodity storage facilities in order to control supplies.

The New York Times had recently published a scathing exposé on Buckstown, how they had intentionally disrupted supplies of molybdenum by delaying warehouse withdrawals by customers. During the last ten years, many of the prominent investment and commercial banks had purchased critical supply chain assets, apparently in an effort to disrupt the movement of commodities and force prices higher. It looked like Buckstown planned to do the same to CRAB.

All news was good news. STCK-TV interviewed a Chicago trader, who had to shout over the noise on the floor. His buddies stood behind him hamming it up.

He yelled into the microphone, "If Buckstown gets control of NBCI, the price of CRAB is going to $500 dollars. I can tell you, CRAB is no different than oil. It's a natural resource with ever increasing and critical demand. It has a limited supply located in a small region of the world. It's like owning oil in the Middle East.

"Right now, only the United States is a major consumer, but Europe is right behind. Then South America. Then the developing world is going to want their fair share. The Chinese just bought eight houses in Bergenfield and tore them down to grow this stuff. India will be buying next!

"Companies are discovering new uses for CRAB every day. Shampoo is just one small product. They're talking about using it in toothpaste, curing acne, replacing detergents for washing clothes, using it as a fuel additive to clean your engine. Major oil and chemical companies are spending huge R&D budgets on the product applications.

"Hedge funds are buying CRAB. Major state pension funds, universities and foundations own CRAB. I think CRAB can go to $1,000 someday. I'm long on CRAB for as far into the future as I can see."

CHAPTER 256

AUGUST 15

Sorry to burst your bubble, CRAB bulls, but somebody doesn't like you. Nor do they like NBCI, Pierre or the NBCI bonds.

Four hours after Buckstown had filed its Form 3, Oxford Collar Securities reported to the SEC on Form 13F that it owned 30% of NBCI's common stock. It also had amassed a large put option position in NBCI, Pierre Beauty Products and the POO ETF.

Oxford Collar Securities was a Florida-based quasi-bank/arbitrageur/hedge fund. Frankly, sometimes it was hard to tell what they did. However, they were required to report and report they did. An hour later, Oxford Collar filed an amended Form 13F; the put options were still listed but the shares of NBCI disappeared with no explanation.

They owned 10,000 put options. Each put provided the right to force the other party to purchase 100 shares. It was the tip of the shark fin. Underneath swam the company-killing predator. Oxford stated that it was a member of a group that, through ownership of 30,000 put options, effectively made a huge negative bet on 3,000,000 shares of NBCI. It was nearly 30% of the company's outstanding stock. The other members of the group weren't required to file because of their size.

Averill read the report after the filing flashed on his Bloomberg screen. He thought: *Who are these clowns? They're probably the same guys who shorted the ROOT stock back in January. They lost money then. It looks like they're failing again.*

Averill exited the SEC web site and returned to the more socially oriented web site, "Buxom Beach Bunnies from the Sixties".

CHAPTER 257

AUGUST 16, 2013

Eva hung up the call from her investment bankers. She was studying the Oxford Collar Form 13F when Stephane entered her corner office.

"Our brokers on the floor say the first Form 13F was a mistake," Stephane explained. "They were short 3,000,000 shares, not long. Some law clerk is going to lose his job over that filing. You aren't required to report short positions, not yet anyway. The SEC has been trying to change the rules, but they're in a political fight on the issue.

"We looked at the trades for the last six months. It looks like their group bought the December 20 puts in June when they cost a half a buck. The stock price was almost $40 dollars. Oxford is betting NBCI is going out of business. Why else would they be buying puts so far out of the money?

"The NBCI stock price has been down almost every day this summer except the few days around the time they announced the big quarter. The technical analysts think ROOT is going to $25 dollars or worse."

After a moment's thought, Eva said, "The July 31 short interest number for NBCI came out yesterday. It's safe to assume they all belong to Oxford and friends. We need to keep a close eye on this. Something's up, and these guys in South Florida are notorious vultures. Silverheels & Penny told me this morning that Oxford typically gangs up on penny stocks that need financing.

"A few small hedge funds join them in these raids. They drive the price down so the company can't refinance, and the company either goes bankrupt or dilutes the heck out of their existing shareholders. They attack stocks like a group of hyenas chasing an aging wildebeest. It's not a pretty sight."

Stephane warned, "NBCI isn't going to collapse on its own, I'd guess they must be planning to do something before year's end to make the puts valuable."

"NBCI doesn't fit their usual mold of prey," Eva theorized. "First of all, this is much bigger than Oxford's usual target. They typically go after microcap companies worth less than $100 million. Second, NBCI doesn't need money. And the CRAB fever appears unstoppable.

"Why are they picking on NBCI? What do they know that we don't? Who knows better than us about the future demand for CRAB? The value of the crop is now over $1 billion a year. But there's $4 billion of open interests for 2014 alone. NBCI's market cap is almost a half billion. Why are they attacking the small player? Because it's too overvalued? Too leveraged? Most susceptible to a sudden correction? Or is this a game of dominos and ROOT is the first to fall?"

"Maybe they're attacking the ETF?" Stephane suggested. "It owns a little bit of ROOT, CRAB, Pierre, and the ROOT industrial revenue bond."

Eva nodded. "It could be part of the plan. Our bankers said that the high frequency trading programs are heavily into the ETF. It can withstand heavy volume orders, too.

"Silverheels suggested Oxford Collar might be betting that NBCI is going to default on their bonds. The credit default swaps became very expensive in the last month – twenty-three percent.

"Of course, to me, that doesn't make much sense. The NBCI bonds are only $200 million, and the company put $100 million in the bank in the last year. They're nowhere near a default. But I'm told CDS rates don't lie. Also, these hedge funds have a big playbook on how to force companies into technical default.

"These vulture funds are tough characters. We haven't come close to anticipating what they're dreaming up next. We must monitor this constantly. Most importantly, I want to make sure Pierre doesn't sustain collateral damage from any attack on ROOT."

CHAPTER 258

AUGUST 20, 2013

New Jersey's August heat rose from the pavement. Breathing was difficult. The air was dense. Light, loose-fitting clothes were the fashion of the day. The ducks cooled their webbed feet in Cooper's Pond.

Rain hadn't fallen for weeks. Crabgrass was flourishing and growing to historic heights, or more accurately, new widths. Crabgrass grows sideways.

The air conditioner was going full blast. Ben usually left the front door open to let the morning air cool the deli. Not this week. Sweltering was such a perfect word to describe this oppressive heat. One might think the word was a merger of sweat and melt, which would have been a great coining. It wasn't. The origin was hundreds of years old, an English word for dying, which is exactly how the residents felt this morning.

Ben's menu tilted to cold foods on days like this. Fruit salad, iced coffee or tea, and maybe even an ice cream treat after lunch. It was a slow day. Bill Hart and Jack Cavarretta stood on line buying breakfast before beginning another long day rebuilding homes damaged by Sandy. JB, Decker, Gavin and Buyout were the only members at the board table. The door slammed open and startled the eatery. The table looked up to see Misty waddling in.

The reason she hadn't been seen in two months quickly became evident as she turned the corner. Mrs. Giovanna Averill Winthrop was visibly with child. At five feet, Misty was nearly half as wide as she was tall. Her surgically enhanced chest had grown to a double-D and looked uncomfortable at best. She sweated profusely and wore oversized clothes in a futile attempt to hide her state. Spiked heels had given way to sensible Sperry boat sneakers. Composure wasn't a word to describe Misty.

She dabbed the sweat on her brow with a soaked handkerchief and gruffly ordered a Chai Tea, which clearly wasn't available this early in the morning. "No double latte supreme today, Misty?" teased Ben.

Misty grumbled something unpleasant which couldn't be heard from the tables.

JB commented, "Ben really needs to install a microphone so we can hear this stuff. I hate missing a good line."

Ben shocked everyone by acting sympathetically. "Sit down at your table, Misty, and I'll bring you an iced tea and scone." She nearly toppled over from the offer of kindness.

Minutes later, Ben delivered breakfast to Misty and said, "I guess congratulations are in order. I see you're wearing a wedding ring."

Misty looked disgusted and said sarcastically, "Yeah, I guess I'm married. Avy and I went to Vegas a few months ago and got hitched in an Elvis Chapel. Life is just bliss."

Michael entered and gave a surprised look to Ben's former tormentor. Michael was wearing a summery seersucker suit, a navy paisley bow tie and red suspenders.

JB sized him up. "Are you travelling to the Deep South in that getup?"

"No, JB," Michael smiled. "I'm battling the heat. This weather isn't good for business unless you're a lifeguard. No one should go outside in this. You should either be at the beach or near an open door in the frozen food aisle."

JB asked, "Isn't this great for CRAB sales? The futures price is $200 dollars a pound. This smells like a bubble. Make that double bubble, toil and trouble."

Michael shook his head. "Overvalued asset classes are bad especially if you're lending. We're monitoring this from the sidelines."

The table watched Misty walk past without saying goodbye. The deli door stayed half-open after she left. A customer groaned. "Hey lady! Close the door! Were you born in a barn?"

CHAPTER 259

AUGUST 24, 2013

With all of the newfound attention from Sarah the brand consultant, Johnny became suddenly embarrassed by his digs. He had Sarah bring in an interior designer friend to improve the image of his office.

Johnny gave the design team an unlimited budget and they found a way to outspend it. They covered the office walls with expensive wood acoustical paneling. They custom-made Johnny's new desk, which resembled a Star Trek command center. A remote on Johnny's desk controlled a 72-inch flat screen television. Acoustical tiles hid $25,000 of Bang & Olafsen speakers.

STCK-TV aired on mute all day. The three widescreen computer monitors on his desk were tuned to the Bloomberg Network at a cost of $30,000 a year. Hundreds of green and red numbers blinked from stock, bond and commodity screens. Had Johnny found a job as a Wall Street trader?

Solid oak wood floors reflected the sunlight. One large and two small oriental rugs accented the working areas in Johnny's thousand square foot office. A green glass conference table was surrounded by four soft leather swivel chairs. A cozy chair and sofa sat across the room surrounding a distressed black wood coffee table. Tiffany lamps provided soft light. An antique original of Fortune Magazine from the 1950s sat on the table. Nothing was too good for the king of crabgrass.

Johnny proudly displayed two Lucite capsuled tombstones celebrating the private placements completed by LMNOP. It had been quite a while since Arthur Sterling had reason to badmouth Averill. Avy was the money man, the guy who moved the stock price.

Johnny loved Averill for everything he had done. He'd made sure Johnny was awarded his fair share of stock options, which were now worth nearly a million dollars.

He'd kicked back some generous fees to Johnny under the table. And the grandeur of Johnny's new office wouldn't have been possible had it not been for Averill.

It was good to be Johnny. It was great to be Averill's friend.

CHAPTER 260

AUGUST 30, 2013

At this rate, Averill would never get to $100 million in net worth. NBCI couldn't buy CRAB in quantity without paying top dollar. Since August 13, they had purchased less than ten contracts a day. They needed ten thousand. Would NBCI have to pay another big premium over the market price to build their position?

The futures contract was moving up one or two percent a day on heavy volume. The 30- 60- and 100-day moving averages had steeply upward slopes. There was no danger of the lines crossing signifying a price reversal.

Traders normally expected short term bursts to ease, prices to correct, then resume a healthy upward movement. CRAB wasn't correcting. The CRAB price had started its climb in June at $140 a pound, and except for a few minor detours, shot straight to $225, a 60% gain.

Averill thought: *Everyone thinks we're moving the market. But it's not us. And it's none of the big guys. Not Pierre. Not Buckstown. Not Den-Ken. They all have their plates full. China was active in June but they're not the force. The buyers are new players, pure speculators. A lot of this movement is coming from the online brokers where the day traders lurk. You can tell by the volumes. Hundreds of small trades. In and out. Closing positions before the weekend so they can go jet-skiing. Then there are the institutional buyers. Every time I see an order for a hundred contracts, some college just bought CRAB.*

NBCI has to buy at least $20 million more, but if this keeps up, they may need twice that. This is the month I have to make my move. I can't fly at this altitude forever. NBCI has to announce a big gain in October so I can sell and get out of here for good.

It's one of two things. Either we need some bad news now so we can buy on the dip. Or we have to bite the bullet, buy it here, and create some huge news to make it go even higher. I'm not waiting anymore. If nothing happens, we're buying big on Wednesday.

The ROOT stock price hadn't fared well. Averill traded in and out and lost a half million during August. He pulled out his net worth calculator. He had lost $4 million since the earnings announcement. He was down to $24 million. His luck had turned sour. He thought: *Okay, I get it. It's summertime and people go to the beach. But that's no reason to trash my stock. I can't wait until this stupid Labor Day ends.*

CHAPTER 261

AUGUST 30

Den-Ken Commodity Brokers had unique access to trading information because half of the homeowners in Bergenfield kept commodity trading accounts with them. They generally knew who was delivering in October and how much.

Last year, a thousand of their clients had been hurt by Hurricane Sandy. Now some of them were trying to recover their losses. A group of Den-Ken's accounts had gone "long" on the October contract. Instead of selling their expected production, they bought, betting prices would go higher. So far they were right. And if another hurricane hit in October, profits would be extreme.

Den-Ken sent the speculators a "financial suicide" letter. One such letter read:

Dear Mr. Greenbaum:

In the ordinary course of monitoring our customer's account activities, we noticed that you have taken a long position in the October CRAB future. As a customer who intends to deliver approximately 200 pounds in October, it would be customary that you would have sold some or all of the expected delivery rather than purchase an equivalent amount.

Please be advised that you are using an unsophisticated and risky trading strategy, and that your entire account equity is at risk. If you fall below the minimum equity requirements, you may be subject to a margin call.

The warning was ignored. They were up over $50 a pound in August. How can anyone think making an extra $10,000 is financial suicide?

Den DeLong began paring the holdings in the three CRAB Funds. He was going to keep a real close eye on the market. He wanted to be nimble and ready to sell more if it showed any weakness.

It was an old lesson learned during the market crash in 1929. Be wary when the shoe-shine guy starts giving stock tips. The modern version was, "When a homeowner doubles down on a crazy commodity, get out of the market."

CHAPTER 262

AUGUST 30

The bankers for Starship Financial seemed to pick particularly inconvenient days to collect debts. First, there was Christmas Eve. Now it was the Friday before Labor Day.

Decker called JB and cried in disbelief, "They're in my house. They're tagging my. . ."

JB stopped him mid-sentence. "What do you mean? Why'd you let them in?"

Decker took a deep breath and said, "It's in the loan agreement and guarantee. In the event of a default, they have the right to enter my house and tag the collateral. You cannot believe this."

JB and Bret drove east on Main Street toward Tenafly. Decker lived in a two-story brick pre-Civil War home on a half-acre of land. A huge willow tree guarded the long driveway entrance. JB saw a police car parked near the house. Mike the Cop stood on the front lawn between Mr. Blech and Decker, who was red-faced and visibly angry. Mr. Blech's team of inventory taggers was standing to the side waiting to finish their job.

"Decker, what's the problem?" JB asked, flicking his eyes at Blech.

Mr. Blech was wearing his funeral director special, a black suit and tie. He smoked the stub of a smelly, cheap cigar. "We have a right to enter the property at any time, and we intend to do so under the terms of our agreements!"

Mike the Cop was slightly uncomfortable mediating this mess. He could handle domestic disputes and even library takeovers, but this had to do with a written contract which he had not yet read. "Mr. Black…"

"My name is Blech, not Black," he spat out, "and you better get it right or I'm going to have your badge by sundown. You're required to uphold the law, and this agreement says I'm allowed to enter the property to protect my assets."

Mike the Cop was doing his best to keep order. "I apologize, Mr. Blech. But you appear to be creating a disturbance and I don't see you handing me a court order giving you the right to enter. I need time to read this before I decide my next course of action."

JB was six-foot-three and stood eye-to-eye with Mike. They towered over Blech at barely five-foot-eight. JB pulled papers from his bag and showed Mike a highlighted page, then addressed Blech. "It says here you're allowed to enter the premises, but you have to give 24-hour written notice which cannot be unreasonably refused, correct?"

Blech jabbered, "We attempted to deliver the notice, but he's not answering, he's not. . ."

"And an hour ago," JB interrupted, "you entered his house smoking that disgusting cigar and tried to ruin his home. Mike, Herr Bleucker wrongfully…"

"It's Blech. You want me to sue you too?" yelled the financial embalmer raising his fist.

"Calm down," Mike warned, "or we'll resolve this at the station."

Decker had become a minor figure in an escalating war. It was clear that JB knew his way around this type of banker and wasn't ceding an inch. But Mike the Cop had to defuse this quickly. "Okay, Mr. Blech, did you give 24-hour written notice?"

"We tried to deliver it a dozen times. He won't answer the door," Mr. Blech responded slightly calmer.

JB pointed to the controlling clause. "Mike! Written notice delivered in person and accepted. Not verbal. Not left on the door step. It has to be served! Decker's in the right. He should have refused the Dark Lord entrance. I think Voldemort needs to follow protocol, and Decker needs to have his attorney or at least witnesses present the next time the Spirit of Eternal Darkness wants to cast his dark shadow."

Mike the Cop shook his head and chuckled at the new nicknames as he walked away to make a call from his cell phone.

He returned a few minutes later. "Mr. Blech, I spoke to the chief. You're to leave the premises immediately. When you finally give proper notice, please file a courtesy copy with the Bergenfield Police Department so we can be on call for your visit. Is that understood?"

Cops didn't scare him. Mr. Blech said defiantly close to Decker's face, "We own this house and everything in it. It's just a matter of time before this unlawful occupant removes himself from our premises."

JB stepped between them and stared down Blech. "You don't own the property. You just got a bunch of liens. If and when Decker sells this stuff, you might get your money. We gave you an offer to do a controlled sale of the house and antiques. You haven't responded.

"Bret," JB called over his shoulder, "I want you to file a restraining order against the bank preventing them from coming within a hundred yards of Decker. Maybe then they'll come to their senses.

"Don't misrepresent your position here to the law enforcement branch of our local government, Mr. Blackass.

"And Decker, I'll witness your complaint so you can recover damages caused by Satan's cigar smoke."

Mike the Cop again restrained his laughter. "Decker, if you want to file charges, please visit the stationhouse tomorrow. Mr. Blech, it's time for you to go."

The banker said in a huff, "I'll be back with my lawyers so we can do this nice and formal. You'll have written notice hand-delivered within the hour. In the meantime, don't remove any of those tags. That's bank property."

CHAPTER 263

AUGUST 30

Mike the Cop grabbed JB's shoulder, whispered a few words, and left. JB laughed quietly. The three men entered Decker's home and viewed the wreckage. The bank had moved furniture against a wall and attached asset tags claiming ownership to most every piece of furniture in Decker's home. But these weren't small tags out of sight on the underside of a desk or chair. They were legal sized 15" x 8" placards that said:

THESE ASSETS ARE HELD AS DEBTOR IN POSSESSION BY THE STARSHIP FINANCING GROUP. DO NOT REMOVE THIS TAG UNDER PENALTY OF LAW

Bret began removing the tags. Decker asked, "Don't we have to leave those?"

Bret pulled a tag hanging from an antique chandelier. "They didn't enter your premises legally, so they aren't legal. I think you can get a restraining order. You have a policeman as a witness. I'll sue them for free. With the right judge, you might win."

"Listen to Bret," JB nodded. "Let's not make it easy for them. These guys are using the A-hole playbook. We have to do the same."

JB and Bret left and drove to town. They passed a patrol car flashing its blue lights against the late August sky. JB and Bret waved merrily to Mr. Blech, who stood arguing with the policeman issuing him a speeding ticket.

"Remind me to buy Mike breakfast tomorrow," JB said gleefully.

CHAPTER 264

SEPTEMBER 3, 2013

Eva had circulated a folio to her executive committee before the Labor Day week-end. The top document was a memo for discussion at the Tuesday morning meeting.

To: Eva Marteen, CEO and Olivier Gaillard, Chairman
From: Commodity Analysis Taskforce
Subject: Is the Crabgrass Market Entering a Bubble Phase?

Asset bubbles have certain elements in common:
* Large available capital willing to invest.
* Leverage in the form of cheap debt or margin loans.
* Unknown asset values during early stages.
* The perceived ability to corner the market.
* Multiple potential causes of volatility (e.g., limited supply, dislocation, weather, or political instability).
* Government action to support minimum prices (including tolling, loans, grants).
* Government policies creating excessive liquidity and cheap interest rates (current U. S. policy on monetary easing).
* At the market peak, a large presence of speculators.

One of the paradoxes of this type of analysis is investors rarely know they are in a bubble while it is taking place. If an investor truly believed it was in a bubble, he would sell. The alternative is known as the "greater fool theory". This occurs where investors know an asset value is inflated, but believe there is always another party willing to buy it (the greater fool) when they want to sell.

We have concluded that the latest crabgrass price escalation has all the trap-pings of many of the most well-known historical booms and crashes – the stock market in 1929, gold now and in the 80s, dot-com, technology stocks in 2000, and subprime mortgages, housing, oil, and various metal commodities from 2007-2009. In addition, economists are now theorizing the cost of a college education and the U. S. Treasury debt are both in a bubble.

Each of these asset hyperinflation phases has similarities as follows:

<u>Large available capital.</u> There is unlimited capital available to invest in CRAB. The Den-Ken funds are sitting on $140 million of invested capital and $300 million of profits. The hedge funds, pension funds, charitable foundations and other institutions that are known investors in CRAB have nearly a half trillion dollars in available assets. The Chinese Investment Corporation, or CIC, has over $500 billion to invest. Its purpose is to invest the foreign currency reserves of China, which now exceed $3 trillion. By comparison, the value of the next three years of crop is a mere $3 billion.

<u>Access to leverage/debt.</u> The margin for CRAB is only 25%. The leverage is a hundred times greater for CRAB options.

<u>Unknown asset values.</u> There is no prior reference value for this asset other than what Pierre initially established and the Chicago commodity community subsequently challenged. The untested constraint for price increases is the price consumers are willing to pay for products using the raw material, or in our case, shampoo. However, other as yet unknown applications may yield a higher and better usage of the material.

<u>The small market size invites attempts to corner the market.</u> Our market size is very small. Wall Street can "buy" the market with a few billion dollars, a small amount of capital by their standards. We would be particularly wary of Buckstown Financial, who has purchased a large commodity position and has begun buying the common stock of NBCI. Buckstown is already under subpoena by the CFTC for its role in a very similar situation – intentionally delaying deliveries from their molybdenum warehouses for the purpose of inflating the price of the precious metal. Despite antitrust laws prohibiting such behavior, the trading houses apparently either feel the laws don't apply, or feel immune to prosecution.

<u>Interests aligned for price increases.</u> Other than Oxford Collar and possibly one or two competitors in the shampoo market, no current participant in the trading market has any interest in price stability.

<u>No market is too large or too small for speculation.</u> Not all booms are in small markets. Oil is a $3 trillion annual market, yet speculators entered the market and drove oil prices to $147 a barrel in 2008. Wall Street banks, hedge funds and a large number of institutions all joined in. OPEC, big oil companies, and North Sea oil producers allowed them to drive prices higher through benign noninterference. They all benefitted from the increasing oil prices and did nothing to stop the speculation. Car drivers had little say in the matter.

<u>Entrance of speculators in the trading marketplace.</u> Speculators buy assets simply because they believe prices are rising. They neither need nor want the end product. In fact, they would be unhappy if they had to take delivery. We believe institutions already had made a significant move to buy CRAB (see February *NYTimes* article). Beginning in August, a large number of small-time speculators also entered the market. The open interest in the October 2013 contract is now four times the size of the crop. A single contract costs $20,000, or $5,000 using margin loans. It's still affordable for small traders. That explains why the number of trades is high but the size of the trade is low.

<u>Conclusion</u>

As can be seen in the accompanying charts, the rise in CRAB prices closely correlates to the percentage gains of commodity prices in 2008. Those commodity prices all collapsed in 2009 precipitated by a worldwide financial crisis, massive sell-off of assets, and financial institution deleveraging.

We are convinced that prices will continue to rise substantially during the next year. The bubble will not break unless a market participant takes action to force the price down. There is virtually nothing impeding another 50% further increase in prices unless we take action now.

CHAPTER 265

SEPTEMBER 3

Labor Day had ended. Store the Weber grill! Back to work! Back to school! Back to CRAB speculation and ROOT stock manipulation!

At 4:30 AM, Rural TV aired its daily television episode of *The American Farmer*. The news reporter stood in the predawn darkness outside the Rutgers New Brunswick campus and said, "Friday evening, a professor from the university's Department of Agriculture, Food and Resource Economics issued a study that concluded that the Bergenfield variety of crabgrass is a far better feedstock for ethanol than corn. The study suggested that corn should instead be used to feed pigs. Swine dining habits have suffered greatly while their favorite food has been diverted to make ethanol. This month's cover of *National Hog Farmer* says it all."

The reporter held up a copy of the magazine with a picture of Iowan farmers walking their prize pigs into the state capitol building in Des Moines.

"Corn prices have risen dramatically over the last ten years due to competing demands for ethanol production. Following the report, New Jersey Senator Alonzo Gruenfeld spoke from Washington. He now intends to introduce legislation to make CRAB-ethanol eligible for the Federal fuels tax credit subsidy."

Pierre's investor relations department picked up the story and immediately sent a transcript to Eva. She cried sarcastically, "Crab-ethanol! What's next? Crabgrass-apple drink?"

Stephane, standing by her office door, chuckled at Eva's pun. Even under fire, she kept her sense of humor. Purely unflappable. "Excusez-moi. La réunion est sur le point de commencer."

Eva smiled. "Oui, Stephane. I know the meeting is about to start. Use English in the hallways. We don't want to make our co-workers uncomfortable. They might think we are talking about them. Let's go see how our team wants to tackle this monster."

She walked into the daily management meeting where twelve executives were already seated at the conference room table. They were Pierre's functional vice presidents and division heads and represented the entire executive committee. The seats closest to Eva were dominated by the five international sales and marketing honchos and Albert from product development. Representatives from manufacturing, finance, treasury, legal and strategy occupied the far end of the table. Steven and Stephane grabbed seats at the perimeter of the room. Olivier remained standing by the door.

Eva looked professorial as she stood at the head of the conference room table. Her pretty assistant distributed the handouts.

"Ladies and gentlemen, we're dispensing with the usual operating discussion. Today we're going to develop and approve a plan to deal with our emerging crabgrass supply chain issue. I asked Stephane to work with our corporate finance and strategy groups to analyze if we are facing a bubble. It is our job to understand the ramifications and take action to protect our company's image.

"The folder in front of you contains their analysis and an assortment of supporting financial information and graphics. I hope you had a chance to read the position paper I sent to you before the weekend.

"I think it's time we did something about this phenomenon. Let's study and decide. At the conclusion, I expect each of you to voice an opinion on our plans, and the possible negative effects it could have on your functional area.

"Let us say upfront that we have a remarkable product. It's easy to understand why competitors are trying to uncover the secret sauce. Maybe the oil or chemical companies have a better use for CRAB, but I don't know any consumer product that can afford to pay these prices and make a profit.

"All of the factors such as small market size, unlimited capital, ability to leverage are all a given. Our market is prone to speculation.

"Buckstown Financial is clearly trying to corner the market. They bought and stored a million pounds of crabgrass and acquired five percent of the stock in the transfer station. It's all the evidence I need.

"We have to ask ourselves the question. Why are speculators entering the market in force today? They can't be betting on a hurricane. The odds are against them. What do they know or suspect? Our reconnaissance failed to detect the Chinese move. Is there some other new factor? Or is it because they believe asset prices are undervalued?

"Albert, explain to the team why we are certain that we're the primary users of this material. Has anyone else discovered our magic recipe?"

Albert said with confidence, "Ve are years ahead. Zere are maybe ten companies who claim to be vorkin on zie formula for CRAB. Ve don't belief zat any haf developed our technology. Zie reason I believe zis is true is because zhey are vorking too hard to steal vhat ve know. Headhunters haf been trying to poach me and my chemists. But, yes, I vould say zat ve are ninety-five percent sure zat ve are zie only legitimate user for zis material."

Eva said sweetly, "Albert, you'll never leave me, would you?"

"Never," Albert said proudly, "but zie offer vas pretty good. Besides, as soon as zhey extracted zie formula, I vould be unemployed."

"Good!" Eva said. "Anyway, back to the causes of the speculation. Our investment bankers learned the Chinese purchased a half-million pounds during the last six months. They believe the futures were for deliveries spread over two years, but some is expected for delivery in October. Let's assume that's true. This poses a problem. Stephane, explain the supply and demand imbalance." Eva shifted to the side and Stephane moved to the head of the table.

"The market can only deliver 1,800,000 pounds in October," said Stephane. "We control 300,000 pounds through option agreements with homeowners. We own another 1.2 million pounds of futures contracts for delivery in October. The small shampoo and toothpaste companies are taking delivery of an estimated 300,000 pounds. The R&D centers including the oil companies will probably take very little because of the high prices. Throw in the Chinese, and that adds up to 300,000 pounds more than the town can deliver.

"We don't know what Buckstown's planning. There's no room for them or anyone else. If I were to sharpen my pencil, I'd say prices are going much higher."

"Thank you, Stephane," said Eva, moving to the front of the room. "There are only two players who could fix the imbalance. Either Pierre could take less, or Buckstown Financial could deliver from their silo. At current prices, they have a $200 million dollar gain. It's against their nature to ease the crisis. If anything, they'll pour gasoline on the fire.

"We haven't bought a contract in three months. This froth is happening without our participation. Let's focus on NBCI. Steven and Stephane, where are they this quarter?"

"They earned $15 million of EBITDA in the June quarter," Steven replied from the side of the room. "They raised $30 million of new capital in May and bet all of it. Their stock price is back up to $37 a share. Wall Street seems to love the company. Institutions now own thirty percent of their stock."

Stephane jumped in. "They were out of the CRAB market in July, but no one seems to know why. They tried to buy in August, but the market kept moving higher. Mid-August, they finally conceded defeat and appeared to overpay for 4,000 contracts at $193. In hindsight, they did the right thing with prices now at $230. They also started buying option contracts. We don't think they're done.

"I calculated that they've been sitting on $100 million dollars of cash. The guys in the trading pits are calling them the penny whale."

Heather from marketing: "What's a whale?"

Kent from treasury: "It's a huge player in a small corner of a market."

Mario from European sales: "JC Montague had a huge whale in the bond market. The scandal was big news in the Italian newspapers."

Kent from treasury: "JC loaded up on a series of complex derivatives associated with a small sliver of the treasury market. A large group of traders ganged up on them and Montague lost billions. They call the trader the whale because he always takes huge positions in the market."

Kim from domestic sales: "Why does a whale…"

Eva tapped her folder on the table like a courtroom gavel. "Enough! We don't have a single whale issue. We have a pod of whales. Buckstown, the Chinese, NBCI, two beauty products companies, five oil companies, and don't forget us. Pierre Beauty Products has bought more than anyone.

"But we aren't driving the prices higher. Our problem is the speculators. The last $75 dollar price move happened after the big players had already bought their positions. Small speculators and the institutions did the rest. Hedge funds, pension funds, foundations, universities, mega wealthy families – they're the culprits. Let's get back to our analysis of NBCI."

Stephane returned to the head of the table and said, "The market thinks NBCI is trading on advanced intelligence. So far, every time they bought CRAB, some incredible news happened a few days later. First, there was the Sandy crop problem, then the POO ETF, and then the Chinese housing deal. Traders think NBCI knows something again, and they're joining up for the ride."

Eva looked perplexed. "If NBCI has insider information, why would the guys at Oxford Collar short them? These guys aren't stupid. And a thirty percent short position isn't cheap. Maybe they met NBCI's president. He's a former hardware store manager, for Pete's sake!"

Steven covered his mouth and coughed to hide a laugh. The vision of Johnny as a pivotal character in a multibillion dollar commodity market speculation was just too funny. Albert didn't get the humor.

"Yeah," Stephane said, "but Mr. Carrera didn't pull the strings on this one. Their banker at LMNOP is directing traffic. The word is the president heard about the Chinese home purchase before anyone else, but the banker did the trades. The word in the pits is he invested above their authorized limits."

"Right now, only one of us wants the price to go lower," Eva said soberly. "We alone prefer a stable market for this product. Buckstown and the hedge funds want a higher price. So do the institutions, NBCI, and the Chinese.

"As I think about it, it's not entirely true. If Oxford Collar is betting against NBCI, they'd want CRAB prices to collapse, too.

"I don't begrudge the small shampoo companies for trying. I don't mind the big R&D departments developing new uses. I'm not even concerned about the Chinese entering the market. They won't be here for very long. They want to grow this on their own farms.

"These players are not the cause of the steep price rise. Instead, we have Buckstown, a Wall Street fund with unlimited capital trying to corner the market. Then we have an enormous number of speculators entering the market. They're the ones driving the price higher. They have no use for the product. They're only into it for financial gain. They're following this pied piper transfer station because they think it has inside info. This is the worst rationale for making an investment.

"NBCI's purchases are transparent. Stephane has a good feel for their position. They only own 4,000 contracts. The open interest is 70,000 contracts, or four times the amount the town can deliver in October. The value of open October contracts is $1.4 billion. Only a bunch of rich hedge funds and institutions can afford that number. At $20 million apiece, that's like what? Barely seventy investors?

"On a billion dollar portfolio, $10 million is a rounding error to these universities and foundations. Twenty years ago, they all hired Wall Street top guns to run their portfolios. The money managers convinced the trustees that commodities are a legitimate asset class. Now, they're speculating on everything from oil to wheat to crabgrass.

"I care about having supply to meet our production needs. At the same time, I want to end this speculative fever. The town can produce 5,000,000 pounds a year. Pierre has option agreements with townspeople for only 900,000 pounds a year. Stephane has purchased 3,000,000 pounds spread over three years.

"If we wanted to enter the mass market next year, we would need every blade of crabgrass to meet our production needs. If we want to tackle this cost problem now, we'll have to retrench our marketing plans. Only the salon and specialty store markets could afford our product at these prices anyway.

"However, if we don't fix this now, our raw material will become so expensive that we will have no product at all."

For the following hour, the dozen executives discussed the pros and cons of reduced production plans. Kim, with her performance bonus tied to top line growth, wanted no part of it. Heather had just spent six months developing an advertising campaign ready to launch into the mass market. Kent wanted to fight the bullies on Wall Street. Manufacturing had just developed a plan to handle the expected new volumes.

Despite the negative effects on every area of the company, the executive team concluded that the product would become unsustainable if the price escalation wasn't halted now. They voted to support Eva's plan. Then they tossed around a dozen possible ideas how to prick, pierce, stab and impale the overinflated balloon.

Eva would have to adjust the executive compensation plan to face the new reality.

"Don't be so somber," Eva said with conviction. "We'll win this eventually. I have a little glimmer of hope for you. Steven, please bring us up to date on our European solution. How is our little experiment going?"

Steven approached the table and said in a low voice as if the walls could hear, "In April, we managed to get 300 pounds through customs after a huge battle. Albert has tested the plants and the results are promising.

"However, the land is in a flood zone. The Netherlands has changed their approach to tidal flooding. Instead of dikes, they are letting flood waters go their natural course. Our crop could go underwater several times a year. . ."

Eva interrupted. "I've thought about that. It's also the prime reason the land is so affordable. We already learned from Hurricane Sandy that the crop survives heavy floods. We'll just cut more frequently. The three-crop-a-year rule is something we decided for convenience. There's no reason we can't cut monthly."

"Our main concern," Steven continued, "is seeds. We've acquired enough to plant about ten acres. This plant is prolific. Once it germinates, the area could expand four times that number. Therefore, it would take a year to get up to the full crop capacity.

"However, we should spend more time testing the results and planning. This is not a good way to develop technology. Assuming the project is successful, we could have production in 2015 at the earliest."

"Great! 2014 it is!" Eva said enthusiastically.

The executive team gave an encouraging laugh. Eva had swiped a year from Steven's timetable. Eva winked, "This meeting is adjourned. Thank you all for your thoughts on this important matter. I want to meet with Olivier, Stephane and Steven now. I'll let you know about our decision later today."

CHAPTER 266

SEPTEMBER 3

After the team left the conference room, Stephane and Steven sat across the table. Eva turned to the chairman and said, "Olivier, I'm usually a coward when it comes to operating risk. I'm a marketing type. Our fortune is based upon our compelling brand of providing the highest quality beauty products. We're not Wall Street traders. However, unless we stop this craze now, it could go on forever and ruin a very important part of our company.

"What I am contemplating is that we sell our entire October futures position now except for the 300,000 pounds we buy through option agreements with the townspeople. Theoretically, it should force the market down. If it doesn't become affordable, we'll repeat the exercise next June. Then next August. Forever, if necessary. At least until this craziness ends.

"We will be delaying our entry into the mass market channel. At worst, we will generate significant short term profit from our hedging gains. If successful, we shake the speculators out of the market and bring prices back to normal.

"In addition to our Netherlands solution, we have one more arrow in our quiver. If this action doesn't bring CRAB prices down, we could announce in October that we'll make our product available to other beauty companies. At a fair price of course."

Olivier nodded. "I agree, but we must have board approval. They need to be informed in particular about selling to the competition. If I understand what you're saying, a million pounds of CRAB may not have a home in October, which is less than sixty days from today. This will be a hectic period."

Eva turned to Stephane. "I will confirm this with the board this afternoon. Over the next three weeks, I want you to sell in an orderly fashion all but 300,000 pounds of the futures for October delivery. Do the same for the 2014 CRAB futures. Don't collapse the market by selling too fast. We should make some decent money selling our position.

"We are Pierre Beauty Products. We set the price for the CRAB material. The $20 dollars that we pay our suppliers is generous. It's a good and fair price. After the dust clears, we will offer everyone the same deal that our current homeowners have."

Eva said with the slightest hesitation, "What do we do about NBCI? Don't we need their transfer station? You know, they're corporate cannibals. They're eating their own. By forcing the price of CRAB too high, they're killing the thing that makes them profitable."

Steven frowned. "We cannot possibly build another transfer operation very quickly. I doubt there's another location anywhere near our current site. The $200 million industrial revenue bond was basically a gift from Wall Street. If NBCI collapses, we won't see that cheap financing again. Except for the president, they have a very good management team. I can't say the same for their board. They seem a little reckless.

"In my opinion, we want NBCI to survive, but to stop speculating in the market. The mayor of Bergenfield feels the same way, but no one is listening to him. I saw a copy of a letter he sent to the NBCI chairman warning him about speculating. It was ignored."

"I agree, Steven," said Eva. "So how do we stop them from destroying themselves? We know something that nobody else knows. The price of CRAB is going down next month. If NBCI is betting the farm on CRAB, they could go bankrupt. Should I talk to their chairman and tell him what they are doing is wrong for their business?"

"Not yet," Stephane shook his head emphatically, "if you want me to exit our contracts in an orderly fashion and make money while doing it. I need a month."

Olivier added, "Ask legal if you can talk to them. We don't want to be accused of manipulating markets, especially in light of what we are about to do to the October delivery. Also, perhaps they need to eat a little humble pie before they learn their lesson. I'd wait a little before giving them warning."

CHAPTER 267

SEPTEMBER 9, 2013

Stephane methodically sold Pierre's CRAB futures. The price of October CRAB dropped $5.00 a day for five consecutive days as he exited his position.

The phone rang and startled Johnny. "We just bought 4,000 contracts at $219 last week, and the price is dropping, Johnny. This ain't good for business," Averill said half-sarcastically, half-worried.

Johnny picked up the phone receiver and whispered. "I don't know, but I can't talk right now. Meet me somewhere. Forget Ben's. And forget your dustbowl of an office. Where's the most desolate place in town?"

Averill laughed. "That'd be my bedroom! Just kidding. Okay, let's meet by the Little League field."

Fifteen minutes later, Averill sauntered up to Johnny who was already sitting in the small baseball stands. "What's up? Why the secrecy?"

Johnny looked worried. "Someone's watchin' my office. I think it's the Feds. There's a spy van in the parkin' lot. It's like twenty feet from my office."

Averill's mind raced. "How do you know it's the Feds? They wouldn't be stupid enough to park that close, would they? Besides, they'd just bug your office. What does this van look like?"

"It's a plain old white Ford van with New York plates," Johnny said nervously. "First, I saw a camera sticking out from a roof vent. It was takin' pictures of the loadin' dock. Next thing I know, some guy in the front seat has this satellite dish aimed at my window. He must be listenin' in! We're gonna get arrested!"

"For what?" Averill sneered. "Your stupid little kickback? Trust me, no one will ever discover it. Your name's not on the check, right? If you're so worried, give me the money back." Johnny let out a small gasp.

"You need to calm down," Averill said with a sigh of irritation. "The Feds wouldn't be taking pictures of your plant. But a trader or hedge fund might. They use investigators all the time. And they might want to hear what you're saying too. My floor broker heard the traders in the pit think we have inside info. When we buy CRAB, they conclude something's up. Someone's trying to get ahead of the rumor.

"Here's what we're going to do. First, we're going to test this baby. You and I are going to have a conference call. You're going to put your speaker phone on max volume. We'll plant some information and see if it gets to the floor. If it works, we'll buy a bunch of contracts and plant a whopper rumor."

"We shouldn't buy anymore," said Johnny incredulously. "It's getting' real expensive. And you're already over Arthur's limit."

Averill raised his hand. "Stop it, Johnny. Arthur is sailing in the Mediterranean and can't be reached. Once again you have a scoop that prices are going up. We didn't get in trouble the last two times. Why would he get mad when you made more money than ever? If you want to cover your ass, send him an email and tell him what you're doing. Just trust me on this. We can't go wrong."

SEPTEMBER 9

Johnny returned to his office. Out of the corner of his eye, he could see the van window opening slightly and the dish aimed at his office. The spy was listening in. He called Averill on his conference phone at full volume.

He read from the script: "I have to work late Saturday night. I can't believe it. The Chinese are picking up 400 contracts. They're doing it in the dark so no one will see them. These guys are really sneaky."

Averill and Johnny exchanged unimportant chitchat to keep the spy off guard, then hung up.

Johnny joined Averill in his office safe from spy watch. Averill kept calling his floor broker at LITE, but nothing was happening. At 1:30 PM, the broker called, repeated the floor rumor slightly embellished, and hung up. Now the word was that the Chinese were picking up 800 contracts at midnight.

"Bingo!" yelled Averill. "I have a personal megaphone to Chicago. This is fantastic. Let's get our CRAB order in. Then we have to come up with a doozy story. One that can't be disproved for at least a month."

Johnny sat bewildered shaking his head. This was too surreal. He thought, *I saw this happen in the movies, but that was made up, right? Spycams, insider tradin', spreadin' fake rumors. No one's gonna believe this!*

Averill studied the commodities screen. CRAB had finished at $214 on Friday night. It was flat for the day. He said, "I think we can fill an order at a discount. Someone's been selling for the last week. Here it goes!"

Averill entered an order to buy 3,000 October CRAB contracts at $209 per pound. He placed another to buy 4,000 October $300 options. Within minutes, he received a message from his broker, "Filled only 2900 contracts. Bought 4000 options at $10. Any more?"

Averill messaged back: "That's enough for today. THX!"

CHAPTER 269

SEPTEMBER 10, 2013

Johnny sat at his Star Trek command center trying to act inconspicuous. He waited until he was certain the spy dish was aimed at his office. He dialed Averill from his new Polycom speakerphone.

He read: "Hey, man. This is gonna be one hectic October delivery. It'll be the shootout at the NBCI corral! We're gonna hafta bring in the National Guard!"

"What are you taking about? The market looks like it's going the other way. CRAB is down every day for a week!" said Averill in his best attempt at sounding skeptical.

Johnny was getting better at his new career as professional liar. He was learning from the best. "The market can't know what I know. The French think they're takin' delivery of every pound the town produces. The Chinese sent me more paperwork. They're takin' a million pounds. The rest of the buyers sent me notices they're takin' a half mil. The whole crop is only a million-eight. This is crazy!"

Averill acted surprised. "You're kidding me. You didn't even mention Buckstown. This can only mean one thing. CRAB is going up again. The MERC will have to intervene, just like last year after Hurricane Sandy. CRAB doubled from \$75 to \$144 in 2012. This could be a repeat. I have to go. I have to buy contracts for you guys."

"Okay," said Johnny. "You can buy up to a limit of \$225. No more. I don't want a repeat of August!"

Averill hung up and watched his computer screen. The "ask" for CRAB had jumped limit up to \$229 per pound, conveniently above NBCI's best offer.

He called his floor broker. "Keep bidding below the market. I want everyone to think we want volume. If you catch a contract by mistake, don't worry. I'll eat it. But the goal here is to make the floor think NBCI is a big buyer. Just like in August."

Sarah, the sultry branding consultant, unveiled the rendering of the new corporate logo to the management team. There wasn't a trace of crabgrass in the design. There were no images of the sun, the moon, the earth, the oceans, or anything natural. The ROOT logo was a dodecagon. It was a twelve-sided polygon with varying shades of coloring. It was the latest thing in 3D images. From the front, it was a bluish polygon. From a side view, the shape turned tones of green.

Sarah advised Johnny, "You don't want a strategy that limits your opportunities. If you called yourself a processing plant, you could never have bought CRAB futures. The twelve sides depict a company looking at all opportunities from all angles. There's no limit to the strategies you can adopt with a logo like this."

Sarah convinced Johnny to spend another $20,000 to create jpeg and tif images of the logo. A flashy movie with logos soaring across the screen cost another $15,000. "Your investment bankers will be impressed," she cooed.

Sarah had ordered a 3D printer to laminate the logo on the corporate letterhead. It was beyond slow. After a frustrating day of jammed paper trays and a small fortune in 3D printer ink, the staff opted for the flat dodecagon on the old HP printer. It looked like a pizza pie with twelve slices. Yummy!

Sarah had also ordered corporate logo tee shirts, golf hats, coffee mugs, gym bags, fleece winter jackets, canvas beach bags, and computer backup travel drives all with the new distinctive logo. The management team and staff grabbed one of each.

The web site design was a separate project. Johnny paid Sarah an additional $80,000 to create web pages that reinforced the new dodecagon brand. Floating images of the 3D logo crossed computer screens and made research analysts go cross-eyed as they tried to view the site.

The management photographs from December were filed away. They weren't professional enough for Sarah. A new studio was hired, and an entire day was spent trying to improve the image of Johnny and his management team. Air brushing would be required.

Investment banks had recently begun crossing the Hudson River to visit ROOT. They pitched one convertible bond deal after another knowing they would be turned down. It didn't matter. The bankers were merely marking territory in the event that ROOT suddenly became a worthy client.

Today, Johnny hosted the second-tier investment banking firm of Holcombe & Dangerfield. Johnny posed as a CEO who knew what he was doing. He paraded his brand team into the meeting: beautiful Sarah, British-accented Alistair, and his IR team – Sophie and Celeste, the two cute debutantes from Simmonds College, and Buck, the lacrosse jock from Madison University. The conference room was overflowing; there was no room for the rest of the management team.

Alistair had prepared a corporate pitch book with noninflammatory factual data about the state of NBCI's business. Visitors ignored the presentation and asked how the latest bull run on the CRAB commodity was going.

CHAPTER 271

SEPTEMBER 16, 2013

Justin demanded a meeting. He stammered, "J-Johnny, your marketing spending is out of control. I-I'm getting invoices from people I have never heard of. A brand consultant? A logo design? An Internet design? This has got to stop. You spent a million dollars already."

Johnny waved a dismissive hand. "Justin, you're an accountant. Your job is to count the money after I spend it. I'm management. I make the decisions here. You're outta your league. All-a this is money well spent. We hafta improve our image to improve our stock price. We're a $500 million dollar company. We need to start actin' like one."

Justin said incredulously, "I know the board approved the dollar amount, but they have no idea how you're spending it. This is outrageous. I'm not paying these invoices until Arthur gets back."

Johnny looked at Justin crossly. "You'll pay 'em or you'll be lookin' for a new job."

Justin stood in disbelief. "That's it. I resign. This is insane. I'm giving you formal notice. I am exercising my 16,000 vested options today. I'll give you two weeks if you want it."

Johnny turned to his stock screen. Without looking at him, he waved and said, "You don't hafta hang 'round. Let's call this your last day. Ba-bye!"

Justin stomped out the door, grabbed a box of his belongings from his office, and left the building. One thing you could say about Justin. He was always prepared.

Johnny leaned back in his Star Trek Command Chair, turned up the volume on the TV, and said to no one, "Ah, it's lonely at the top."

CHAPTER 272

SEPTEMBER 17, 2013

Allie looked at her bank account. She had about half of the $300,000 due to Jake's Seed & Supply in October. She had no other source of funds. She was at the maximum borrowing capacity with Michael's bank. Her 401K was empty. She'd never ask for help from friends and relatives. If this ship sunk, she wasn't taking passengers down with her.

The weed killer was overstaying its welcome. Storing a few thousand bags in a trailer might be okay for a few months. Another winter and the chemicals would harden. She had to deal with Jake's.

She met with JB and Bret at Ben's Deli for a 6:00 AM financial workout session. Allie said woefully, "The day of reckonin' is near. I'm thinkin' of sendin' 'em what I have and beggin' for another extension. Whadaya think?"

Bret opined, "Never give the cash first. Possession is nine points of the law."

Allie looked confused. "I thought it was nine-tenths of the law?"

"Either one," said Bret. "The Scots say point. Most say tenth. But believe me, when you're negotiating with Jake's, cash is king. Use it as an incentive to compromise."

JB nodded. "Bret's right. If I put my Jake's thinking cap on, I'd say they aren't expecting much from you. They may even be preparing to exercise their rights over the collateral. The CFO knows it's due, and he isn't giving you an extra thirty days unless he gets something in return."

Allie said calmly, "Alright, guys, what do you propose? Except for the payments to Jake's, I'm makin' a livin'. I can't go bankrupt. That's gonna hurt Michael's bank. I won't do it. How do I get more time to breathe? I can probably pay Jake's $10,000 a month if Marty and I eat Alpo."

"Companies in trouble typically propose payment plans to their vendors," said JB. "In other words, you give them a little now with a promise for more in the future.

"You want Jake to believe you'll file for bankruptcy. Otherwise you lose your negotiating edge. I'd offer them $50,000 now, and pay them $20,000 a month for a year. But you have to find a way to sell this stuff or return it. There is no other answer."

Bret's eyes lit up. "Return it? That might be a good threat. You could claim the product is defective or doesn't meet specifications. Worst case, get the salesman to repackage it and reset the terms. Tell him the product is going stale."

"The CRAB price is ridiculous," Allie said broodingly. "There's no chance this is goin' away. If people were willin' to plant crabgrass for $15 a pound two years ago, they're spoiled rotten today at $280 a pound."

JB spoke in a comforting voice. "Call the salesman and arrange a meeting. Bret and I will go with you. A cash payment should be a big bonus to those guys if they are rational businessmen. But if they turn you down, you have a much better use for that money. Don't pay the vendor who is screwing you. Hire yourself a bankruptcy lawyer and then pay Michael."

"Okay, guys," Allie said less than cheerfully, "I'll give 'em a call."

Allie looked up and groaned as a dozen cable TV reporters and cameramen from CNN and FOX bullied their way into Ben's. Allie gave a Jersey girl welcome. "Don't you guys have somethin' more important to cover, like a war or a Kardashian sightin'?"

CHAPTER 273

SEPTEMBER 19, 2013

Two days earlier, NBCI had made one final bet on CRAB. The price for October delivery had gone limit up for five days, a dizzying increase of nearly $100. It had reached $289 a pound, then settled back a little. Someday this move would be declared legendary by financial historians. Even the frenzied gold and oil trading of the 80s had not witnessed such a quick rise.

Most traders had rolled forward to next year's contracts – selling October 2013 and buying June or August 2014. The biggest gamblers held steady, playing a game of chicken as the maturity approached. Word in the pits about the mysterious spycam only increased the drama. October demand would be twice the supply – guaranteed! There was going to be another huge mismatch, just like October 2012. Anyone who sold short was about to great creamed.

NBCI already had enough staked on next month's showdown. October CRAB was far too expensive even for Averill's taste. Averill convinced Johnny to authorize one last trade. "We have to establish our June position while it's still cheap, but I can't sell October yet. Give me a week. I promise!"

June traded at the normal $35 discount to the October expiration. NBCI purchased 2,000 contracts for June delivery at a price of $244 per pound – $49,000,000 of contracts paid with $12,000,000 of equity and $37,000,000 of margin loans.

NBCI now sat on a paper profit of nearly $90 million on futures and options covering 1,800,000 pounds of CRAB. Averill thought, *We were so close when CRAB touched $289. The magic number is $310. Then we'll sell. Release earnings early next week and NBCI can tell the market it made $6.00 a share. ROOT goes to $100. I cash in and retire. I can taste it.*

In addition to all of his commission and note shares and warrants, Averill had purchased 500,000 shares in the open market. He was barely halfway to his $100 million goal. The stock would have to climb to $94.00 a share. It still had a chance. This was going to be a big month.

CHAPTER 274

SEPTEMBER 19

Averill was caught between fear and greed. Greed sat on his shoulder and demanded, "BUY! You're almost there. Don't wimp out now! What type of buccaneer are you?"

Fear breathed a traitorous thought into his other ear. "Don't listen to that bloated oaf! Sell your shares! Cash in before you lose it all!"

Callings of greed always triumphed over whispers of fear for Averill. He took a deep breath and spread orders to buy ROOT at his five online brokerage accounts. By noon, he had added 200,000 more shares to his position. Nearly $10 million of stock, all bought on margin. He was now the proud and nervous owner of 14% of NBCI.

He needed help if he wanted to make the stock double. He called on The Sticky Five and their new extended family to work their magic. When five brokers share inside information, you might call it a club. When eleven brokers talk by secret cell phones, it's officially a ring. Jean Jacques, Carlos and Igor had been joined by three new voices. They had the world covered. Abu from Nigeria, Mai from Malaysia and Blake from Australia introduced themselves. The only continent not represented was Antarctica.

"As of last night, ROOT had an $89 million dollar quarterly gain on CRAB futures and options. That's five bucks a share for the quarter. This stock will be a hundred bucks in a few weeks."

Averill spoke with the authority of a stock brokerage CEO. Brokerage offices across America hosted daily morning calls to their salesforces over the "squawk box". The heads of research, sales, marketing and trading bellowed what to buy and what to sell through the old tech speaker systems. Averill had mastered the art of pumping by listening to these morning calls. He was an expert.

"As I requested last time, which you guys stupidly ignored, be careful with your trading. Keep your trades small. Anyone buying large blocks is taking a big risk. Good luck. Now go buy it! Then spread the word!"

Despite Averill's warning, the ring flashed their wallets and bought a million shares and 20,000 call options in the open market. Who knew how many more were connected to the tip line? Call option volume was the ultimate red flag on Wall Street and in the halls of the SEC. It meant someone had inside dope. When Wall Street saw call option volumes increase, it bought shares and options. When FINRA and the SEC saw big option volumes, they investigated.

Before the market closed, the ring posted on the Yahoo! Finance message board:

CRABBabyDoc: "ROOT had amazing gain this quarter. Buy now before it's too late!"

PabloEsCRABar: "NBCI will quadruple the June number this Q."

IgorCRABinsky: "You chumps are way short. CRAB is almost $300. I predict ROOT will make $150 mil!"

ShrimpOnTheBarbieDoll: "That's earnings of $13 a share. At a multiple of 20, ROOT should be trading at $260. Way undervalued."

ThaiOneOn: "Don't forget Buckstown takeover. $300 price target!"

The stock price jumped 20% during the afternoon and another 5% the next morning. ROOT had increased to $51 per share. The market capitalization of ROOT touched $600 million. Everyone was rich.

CHAPTER 275

SEPTEMBER 24, 2013

The Battle of POO commenced. POO was being slung from the floors of Wall Street to the pits on LaSalle and back again.

Wall Street hedge funds had perfected their algorithms to trade the ETF. Computers arbitraged POO against the basket of underlying financial stocks, bonds and the CRAB commodity.

Meanwhile, the MERC created their own product using a series of swaps and spreads on the CRAB commodity. Chicago computers arbitraged the new derivative against CRAB.

The result was all out war. Both the Wall Street and LaSalle Street derivative investments used CRAB as the swing product. Computer programs spit out buy and sell orders. The Wall Street algorithms hadn't yet accounted for the effect of the Chicago algorithms. Chicago and New York were playing a game of tetherball and CRAB was the ball.

Making it more complex, the algorithms no longer looked at the mathematical sum of the components. A hundred shares of the POO ETF represented the value of 20 shares of Pierre Beauty Products, 200 shares of ROOT, 60 pounds of CRAB and $2,000 of face value of Bergenfield-backed industrial revenue bonds. POO had originally begun trading at $100 a share. Now the combined value of the components was an astonishing $312 per share. The only nonperforming component of POO was the Bergenfield bond, which was trading at 65 cents on the dollar.

The algorithm didn't look at the present. It looked at the future. Using advanced calculus, the computer trading programs were searching for the inflection point on a curve of price changes. When a slope changed from increasing-at-an-increasing rate to increasing-at-a-decreasing rate, it was a sell signal. The computer executed the trade without any human intervention.

The Wall Street algorithm contained one other element that Chicago was missing. The MIT PhDs had run a regression analysis of the CRAB futures price versus the Pierre and ROOT stock price changes. Except for a brief period, there was almost no correlation of Pierre Beauty Products' stock price to the CRAB price. In fact, there were many months of negative correlation. That made sense. Pierre was paying more for CRAB, so an increased price should hurt their profit margins.

But the correlation of CRAB to ROOT price changes was very different. Until a year ago, CRAB prices had increased a month before ROOT did. Then, in January, ROOT started jumping two weeks before CRAB did. And almost always, there was a significant news announcement after the most pronounced movements. The programmers theorized that they may have discovered an insider trading signal.

During the trading day, the Wall Street and LaSalle Street computers often traded in tandem. The sum of the algorithms instructed the computers to buy CRAB. Then a signal changed. The Wall Street computers sold CRAB heavily. The Chicago programs bought. Prices went wild.

Within minutes, the programs reversed course. It was absolute chaos.

On the day that ROOT shot up 20%, the Wall Street algorithms used that information to predict that the CRAB price would rise within ten days. ROOT must have inside information. The computers entered orders to buy the POO ETF and CRAB.

Traders stepped to the sidelines at least once a day while the "quants" battled it out. Traders began betting on the hour of calamity. For twenty bucks, a trader could buy a fifteen minute slot during the eight-hour trading day. Whoever had the highest intra-minute volatility won $640.

Winning didn't pay off financially. If you won the pool, you had to buy beers at the end of the day. At least you had the momentary value of hero status.

CHAPTER 276

SEPTEMBER 27, 2013

Averill watched NBCI's stock open. Many on Wall Street still called it the ticker, although they stopped using ticker tape to report stock trades in the sixties. Now, stock prices scrolled at the bottom of sophisticated computer terminals reporting hundreds of points of market data every minute.

NBCI's stock price had a nice run in the two weeks since Averill had told the ring about the September gains. They had to be pretty happy with a 25% gain and more to come. In a week, NBCI would prerelease the earnings number. This was going to be huge. The stock could double. Averill had to maintain discipline. A million things could go wrong.

Averill picked up a few shares at the opening bell. Nearly every small broker was a trader by nature. While they made most of their money from commissions, they also added a few extra bucks day trading their pet stock. It was a habit…$100 here; a $100 there. Daily chump change.

By 11:00 AM, the market had settled in after absorbing the world news, local news, government inflation and unemployment reports, a couple of corporate earnings surprises, and a few catastrophes. ROOT was trading flat with low volume when ten small sell orders appeared on the screen. Averill bought the 1,000 shares at $50, down a quarter. Minutes later, another 10,000 shares were offered for sale. Averill watched. Let another market maker share the load.

By the end of the day, a half million shares of NBCI had traded. It was slightly above normal, but nothing to worry about. However, the sell orders appeared to come in 10,000 share blocks. After the market closed, Averill checked the Yahoo! Finance message board and saw familiar but unfriendly posters.

BreakingWater: "I think ROOT is getting dry rot. Lots of selling today."

BrokenUnsound: "CRAB price down 6 days. Rally is over. Time to sell!"

SquareRootofZero: "Their bonds are trading like junk. Since when does a stock trade this high when its bonds = bankruptcy? I'm selling today."

GasBag: "Credit default swaps are ridiculous. Higher than Greek debt. 4800 bips."

NoProblemoPaco: "CDS never lie! Should we short this sucker?"

AdieuToYou: "Already have, and I'm shorting more. Bought the December puts too."

Me-A-Me: "The CRAB fad is over. People are getting tired of it."

ShiftlessInChiffon: "Pierre is tired too. Very silent last 3 months."

Averill checked the names. They were the same characters who posted during the last two short attempts. He thought, *Are these guys back again? They haven't made a dime so far. They think the stock is high at $50, wait until earnings come out next week. Those Oxford Collar gangsters have to be licking their wounds by now. Sure, they made a little money during the summer, but now they're down $10 again. They shorted what, three million shares? That's a big loss for anybody. I can't worry about this. I have to get organized. Next week is going to be beyond busy.*

CHAPTER 277

SEPTEMBER 30, 2013

Monday morning was a repeat of Friday. Ten thousand shares were offered just below the market. The market makers had become wary. The stock had just reached an all-time high. By the Wall Street handbook, a price correction was in order. A 5% decline was considered healthy for such a high flying stock.

And 5% it was. Then six percent. Then seven. Eight. A million and a half shares had traded by 2:00 PM, and ROOT had fallen to $47. Healthy correction, indeed.

Averill thought, *This is Igor and those thugs selling. I knew I should have never let them in. Is there no honor among thieves? They saw a little drop in the price, took their profits and fled the scene.*

Not a second after ROOT had settled down, CRAB came under selling pressure. It could easily be a similar correction, but this was going to hurt NBCI's September earnings. Two weeks earlier, Averill had told the ring that NBCI would report a big trading gain. You didn't have to be a graduate of MIT to figure out the gain would be a whopping $25 million less.

Averill decided to put a stop to the crash. He drafted a press release and emailed it to Johnny. It read:

"NBCI (Symbol: ROOT) will report an unrealized gain of $65 million for the quarter ending September 30, 2013. At September 30, the Company held 12,900 CRAB futures contracts and 5,000 CRAB options."

It was simple and sweet. What the draft release didn't mention was that NBCI had $89 million in profits just two weeks before and that the CRAB price was still falling.

Johnny took a quick look at the headline and said, "Okay, Averill. You know, it looks a little thinner than your usual stuff. I'll send it to the lawyers and we can release it tomorrow mornin'. I gotta go."

Johnny returned to his Star Trek command center. He and Sarah were preparing for another investment banker visit. She bantered with Johnny about the placement of the dodecagon on the title page. Johnny loved it when she spent time in his office and challenged him about such important matters. This was what real company presidents did with their time.

CHAPTER 278

OCTOBER 1, 2013

The markets opened and CRAB was again under heavy selling pressure. It was down $5.00 a pound before 10:30 AM. ROOT fell in tandem to $45 a share.

The number of open contracts had declined, but was still out of balance by 3:1. There were three times as many contracts issued than the town could deliver. With 30 days until expiration, market players normally would have rolled their positions forward to next year. This looked like another Halloween showdown.

Averill called Johnny. There was no need for secrecy today. The spy van was long gone. "El Jefe, where's the press release? We have to put something out to stop this bloodletting."

Johnny whispered, "We got a problem. Arthur's here and so's Jack. They want you over here. Now!"

Averill raced across town running the red light in front of the high school on Prospect Avenue. He entered NBCI's foyer and saw worried faces peering from offices. Arthur and Jack were sitting at the far side of the conference room table conferring over some spreadsheets. Johnny sat opposite, alone and looking worried.

Averill reached across the table to shake the chairman's hand. "Hello, Arthur. How was your sail…"

Arthur stared Averill back into a chair and said sternly, "Who gave you couple of idiots permission to exceed our commodity trading limits? I thought I made it clear."

Averill had sat far away from Johnny like he was contagious. "There was a market opportunity. Johnny told me you were on a boat and unreachable."

"It can't be hard to understand," said Arthur. "It's a five letter word. L-I-M-I-T. There are no exceptions. Jack tells me we have a $208 million dollar margin loan. Are you out of your mind? I want to unwind our position today."

Averill paused a few seconds. His only chance to reach his personal $100 million goal was if NBCI reported a big earnings number. If Arthur sold the CRAB futures indiscriminately, the market would get hammered. Even though the CRAB price had slid in the last week, it could still come back.

Averill kept calm, but his hands sweated badly. "I wouldn't recommend that. First, the market is expecting a big move before month-end because of Buckstown. Also, traders have been watching us. Until now, they think we bought because we have insight on a delivery imbalance. If we start selling, they'll conclude we don't. You could precipitate a price collapse."

"And who planted that idea in their heads?" Arthur snapped. "Let me guess. It's you. So if we try to sell in quantity, we'll spook the market. Exactly how did you expect to close out your position, or didn't you think of that?

"A hundred people bought this stock because they believed in me. I convinced them you guys were good at this. Now I can't tell them about this horrible situation because I'm an insider. They're all going to lose a lot of money. These are my closest friends!

"Averill, you're fired. We don't have time to move these contracts to another brokerage firm. I want your supervisor assigned as broker of the account, and I'll work with him to unwind the position. While you're at it, give me the name of your general counsel. We're suing LMNOP as soon as we get out of this mess. You're dismissed."

Averill took a shot: "We were planning on releasing earnings early in an 8-K. It could calm the markets."

Arthur stared through Averill. "NO! Why are you planning on releasing anything? A stockbroker doesn't make these decisions. This is a company matter. Get out of here before I have you arrested. You're pathological."

Averill shook his head, shot Arthur a warning frown, and stood. "You're making a tragic mistake." He strode from the offices, head held high, vainglorious and defiant.

"What a piece of work," Arthur said incredulously. "Johnny, as of this moment, you are president in title only. No responsibilities. No authority. The only reason I'm not firing you today is because Jack tells me we'd have to report a change in officers to the SEC. That's bad for the stock price in a crisis like this. I'm running the company until we find your replacement.

"I fired the CFO, too. Justin is returning this afternoon. He's the only executive here with any common sense. I hope we can clean this mess up without losing our ass in the process.

"How much did you spend decorating this place? Justin told me last night you went fifty percent over budget. This is a weed processing center, not Disney headquarters." Arthur jabbed an angry thumb over his shoulder. "And whose girlfriend is sitting in the lobby?"

Johnny was facing humiliating ruin. He saw little escape. Was there anything he could do to retain control of his Star Trek throne? He said meekly, "Sarah is our brand consultant. She prepared a corporate presentation for you. You'll like what she has…"

Arthur's mouth dropped open. "Are you kidding me? Who taught you good judgment? Justin said you spent $400,000 dollars on a web site and a logo. Are you insane?"

Johnny wanted to crawl under the table. "We're still sitting on a $65 million gain. That's good, right?"

Arthur pointed his hand toward Jack, who said, "If CRAB goes down $50 a pound, the profit is wiped out. While we were speaking during the last 15 minutes, CRAB went limit down for the day. The commodity market is locked out. You can't sell anything."

CHAPTER 279

OCTOBER 1

Averill rushed back to his office. If Arthur was going to slam the CRAB market, he had to dump his NBCI shares quickly without spooking the market. Fortunately, the stock had steadied after Monday's drop. He scattered a dozen sell orders for a thousand shares at prices just below the market bid. Averill controlled 1.7 million shares of NBCI. It could take weeks to sell without killing the stock price.

After placing the orders, he called Victor Troubicky in New York, a fellow stockbroker. The two had started at LMNOP together, and occasionally had shared accounts and commissions.

"Victor, I've got a great deal for you. I'm handing you a very large commodity account which has to liquidate over the next few weeks. All sales will go under our old shared commission code. Split fifty-fifty. The only hitch is you're going to have to pretend to be the office manager if the client calls. They want white glove treatment from a supervisor. Blind-copy me on every trade. Use text, not email. Do we have a deal?"

Why would he say no? Selling the portfolio was worth a million in commissions.

After Averill transferred the accounts to Victor, he turned to his larger task. He was selling about 10,000 shares of NBCI an hour, a dangerously slow pace. The shares which he had purchased in the open market sat in a half dozen accounts at online brokerages. The Tuxedo shares were held in a Cayman Islands account. The rest of his NBCI shares were in his LMNOP account. He didn't have possession of the note shares just yet. He also owed $17 million on stock loans.

A large block bid appeared on his screen – 50,000 shares at $44 a share. Averill pounced on it. He was wired with energy.

At the end of the day, he looked at the tally of his sales – 200,000 shares; $9,000,000. He had a long way to go.

CHAPTER 280

OCTOBER 1

JB, Bret and Allie drove late afternoon to Jake's corporate offices in Parsippany, New Jersey. They sat with Benny, the same salesman who had negotiated the extended payment arrangement. Allie wore a navy skirt and white cotton blouse, the closest thing in her closet to corporate attire. JB and Bret wore sports jackets and slacks.

Allie said, "We wanna talk to you about returning some of the product. It's gettin' stale and just can't be sold. I think if you remix it and repackage it, it'll be fine."

"That material will not cross the threshold of our plant gate," Benny said stiffly. "If it does, I'd have to book a return. My CFO won't allow it."

Well, that didn't work, but no one expected it would. JB and Bret sat quietly and Allie said, "Then let's discuss a revised payment plan. This market just can't absorb this much product. It'll take eight years to sell."

"You're already on a payment plan," said Benny. "You owe me money in four weeks. Can I assume from this conversation that you're going to default?"

Bret touched Allie's arm and pointed to a scribbled note: *Anything you say could be an admission and allow them to start collection actions earlier.*

Allie nodded acknowledgment and turned to Benny. "I'm admittin' nothin'. However, I'm proposin' a new deal. I pay you $60,000 today and $20,000 dollars a month until the balance is repaid."

Benny replied, "Tell you what. Give me $120,000 today in good faith and we'll consider your proposal."

The tone was acrimonious. Benny was flippant. Working for a leveraged buyout group had worn away his customer relations skills. He had no intention to negotiate.

JB: "We'd like to speak to your CEO."

Benny: "Our CEO is too busy for this small amount. You can talk with me."

JB: "That's ridiculous. This is a lot of money to any company. You guys aren't big enough to write it off."

Benny, arms folded: "Your store is worth a million dollars. We have a lien on the assets and can collect one way or the other. Sell the store and you can pay us on time. If you don't, we will take ownership and sell it ourselves."

JB: "You cannot be representing the company this way. We want corroboration that the executives have reached this decision. I'm not talking with a salesman who isn't even a corporate officer."

Benny left the meeting and returned accompanied by a balding, round-bellied man of short stature. He grabbed a golf putter sitting against the wall and stroked a ball toward the practice cup. He turned to Allie and waved the putter at her.

"I'm the CFO of Jake's. You wanted an officer. Now you got one. And I am not talking to your cronies. I'm talking to a lady who owes me a lot of money. We aren't giving you any further extensions. We expect full payment or we will seize our collateral." He turned and left the room.

JB stood and said, "Let's go. We'll talk on the way home."

They drove away in JB's Mercedes. JB turned on the Sirius satellite radio and tuned to the Spa Channel. "Listen to some soothing music for your soul. It will help you think better."

Allie managed a small smile but said nothing. She had worked as a nurse in intensive care and daily saw patients fighting for their lives. She wasn't going to get rattled by this. It was just money…every single cent she had.

CHAPTER 281

OCTOBER 1

The defeated trio returned to Allie's store. They looked tired as they sat at the never-will-be-sold faux butcher block table. It had become the unofficial store meeting place.

Bret said, "We should do a few things to protect your assets. Jake's knows your bank account number. They're probably looking at an old canceled check right now. You should move your cash into another account at Michael's bank. That'll stop them from obtaining a court order and using a sheriff to seize your account.

"Also, don't pay any other vendors for a while. Maybe you can squeeze the rest of the payment from your operations. Your Christmas merchandise is arriving. Pay them after year-end. None of them individually is big enough to sue you."

Allie's son walked into the store. The table became suspiciously quiet. "The kid's here!" Marty joked. "Time to whisper!"

Allie put her arm around his shoulder. "We're not hidin' anythin', Marty, but we're discussin' some serious matters. There's snacks in the back room. Help yourself."

Marty removed his ear buds. "I heard what you're sayin'. You should do like Hollywood. Go viral. Hire paparazzi. Get on TMZ! Make Jake's look bad! It shouldn't be hard. They dumped chemicals in our parking lot. I have the video, remember? No company in America wants consumers hatin'!"

"Thanks, son," said Allie sweetly, "but this isn't like the movies. It's not Lyndsay Lohan flashin' her panties from a limo. I think we…"

"Hold on a second!" JB looked up brightly. "Your son might have an idea. I mean, it may not work by itself, but it could put pressure on them enough to bargain with us. What we need is time. Bret can stall them in court while the media campaign stops them from being bad boys. What do you think, Bret?"

Bret's face didn't register any enthusiasm. "I might be able to get you a few months, but their documents are pretty solid. I wouldn't count on this crabgrass fad ending soon. I think Allie should be acting to protect her assets and prepare for the inevitable."

JB was not to be deterred. "We'll do both! Marty, tell us about this viral thing? What do we do? Go on Facebook and Twitter?"

Marty swallowed a pretzel and gulped some Mountain Dew. He pointed to the can and said, "Caffeine and sugar, man. Ahhh!

"Facebook is for old people. You gotta be like twenty-five to use it. It's about as ancient as e-mail. Teens hate it. Who wants to chat when your parents are listenin' in? No offense, Mom. Kids use Instagram and Snapchat.

"But actually, it doesn't matter. We blast 'em all including Facebook for you oldies. First I'll set up a 'We hate Jake's' website. That's h-8, not h-a-t-e! We'll also do the whole Twitter, Tumblr, Instagram, Pinterest thing. I'll share with every bleeding hearts cause site.

"YouTube is huge 'cause it's video. If you get someone like Zoeller to support your cause – she has like four million followers. But they're mostly teens. She's into hauling, like hauling things from the store and opening 'em on film. It's how companies promote their stuff.

"But if you really want this to work, you'll need content. Jake's has to do something really bad to get people riled up. Tryin' to collect money they're owed may not make the cut."

JB remained optimistic. "Okay, it's a start. In the next month, we set up this viral thing, and if Jake's declares a default, we launch it. Marty, you go schmooze Zoeller. We're going to tell the world that Jake's is putting its vendors out of business. Maybe a newspaper will pick up the story. Get the other vendors involved. The home and garden trade association can give you a list of their members."

Allie said skeptically, "Sure, Marty can do this, but we only have thirty days. I just don't think we can accomplish much in so little time."

"Allie, you're the most optimistic person I know. Don't fail me now," JB flashed his pearly whites. "You have to try every angle. Right now, we should send a letter to their board. They may not know about this. Tell them we offered cash and the CFO turned it down. We'll send a warning letter to their D&O insurer, too. Bret, what legal actions can you take to stall this a few months?"

"Well, your documents aren't exactly cookie cutter forms from LegalZoom.com," said Bret. "Your fabulous lawyer, that would be moi, negotiated terms that would make them work to get your money. This is legal mumble jumble, but let me explain.

"There are three agreements. First, they have a financing statement which declares their rights and describes the collateral. Then they have a UCC, which is a filing in the county which 'perfects' their security, meaning they have first claims on the assets and the right to sell them at auction. And last, we signed a vendor restructuring agreement which spells out the order in which they take collateral.

"When we closed this deal, Jake's lawyers didn't want to fight with Michael's bank over an intercreditor agreement. Michael refused to share any first proceeds. That meant Jake's would have to wait until Michael was paid if there was a default. Michael was only lending a hundred grand against the weed killer, so Jake's lawyers decided it was the easiest collateral to secure."

"You mean Jake's can only go after the weed killer?" asked a surprised JB. "It's not worth anything."

Bret nodded. "It's their only 'perfected' security interest. And they have to sell it at auction or some other valid avenue. I'd bet they're going to argue in court the stuff is junk.

"Let's assume they win and they go to the next level. They have a right to grab Allie's ownership of the store and sell it at auction. They really screwed up on this one. The only way to perfect a security interest in Allie's store is by possession of the stock certificate.

"Allie never delivered it because she was waiting for the new certificate after the name change. They never followed up on it. The agreement says they have a right to possession, but I wouldn't hand it over at this juncture."

"You mean I can keep the store and not pay these guys?" Allie looked confused. "That doesn't make sense."

"No, Allie," said Bret. "You still owe the money. It just means they have to fight you for it. And if you declare bankruptcy, they become a general creditor. They don't get a priority on the proceeds. It's a card you can play. It might give you time.

"Then there's your guarantee. They have to sell all of the assets before they come after you personally. Hopefully, we never get there."

"Your last line of defense is the fraud angle. You could argue you were induced into this payment plan when Jake's knew the product was obsolete. Unfortunately, if you go this route, they pull out the corporate legal playbook and overwhelm you with expensive document requests, interrogatories, depositions. The works. You don't have the money to fund it, believe me.

"But if I were Jake's, I'd do it differently. I'd find a buyer for the business, have them refinance the working capital loan with Michael, and then go to court with a neatly tied package. Judges love neat. Then you lose.

"Add it all up, and you could fight for three or four months. What does that get you?"

JB said confidently, "It gives us time, a chance for a turn of fortunes, and if necessary, help from an angel. Maybe Allie makes enough money to pay Jake's while you're in court.

"For now, we have to work to do. If and when Jake's knocks on the door to deliver their default notice in November, we launch our legal and viral attack."

Allie said in a less-assured voice, "I'll do everythin' you say, but I don't have much hope."

"Chin up, Allie," JB said with overt cheer. "It's early! The next month is going to feel like a decade."

CHAPTER 282

OCTOBER 2, 2013

The street was dark except for the light shining from Ben's Deli. Averill could see the early customers at the register as he drove by. He arrived at his office minutes later at 6:30 AM, three hours before the markets opened. He had a big day ahead of him.

He didn't begrudge Igor and company any more than he resented anyone else. He just wished he had beaten them to it. When they saw CRAB go limit down, they had to have realized NBCI wasn't going to announce as big a gain. The stock was no longer going to $100, so they took their profits and ran.

But the volume yesterday had to be more than a few criminal traders from the Ukraine and Malaysia selling their positions. Someone else had dumped a million shares in big blocks. The market had traded a tenth of NBCI's "float".

Whenever someone like Oxford shorted a stock, they had to borrow the shares from a brokerage house. Averill called his stock loan department in New York who confirmed Averill's suspicion. They had loaned out 4,000,000 shares since June. While technically NBCI only had 10,000,000 shares outstanding, Oxford had sold shares that were already in the market. It effectively increased the tradable shares to 14,000,000. These extra shares could slam the market in the next two weeks if ROOT's price kept declining. It's what helps stocks collapse near the end.

Averill assessed his position. If he sold 300,000 shares today at $40, he'd be done with the margin loan. Everything sold thereafter would be profit. Averill entered premarket sell orders of varying lot sizes. Five hundred shares here. Four hundred shares there. A bunch of thousand share orders. He needed eight days to sell everything he owned. In two weeks, he'd be clear.

At 9:30 AM, the commodity markets opened for trading. It wasn't good news for CRAB. For a few brief moments, contracts exchanged hands down $10. Then the contract went limit down for the second day in a row. CRAB, which had hit a high of $299 on September 20, was now trading at $224 and heading lower.

Averill sold ROOT throughout the day. He was cautious not to spook the market, but managed to sell a few large blocks. Traders thought they were stealing shares at this new bargain price. If they only knew.

Averill thought, *Whenever people panic, the calm make fortunes. If ROOT is going south, then the put options are the place to make money. I may not get out of this stock if this keeps up. The puts will cover me.*

The "December 40" put was offered at $4.00. Each put gave you the right to force the seller to buy a hundred shares of stock at $40. If ROOT fell below $40, the put became "in the money". Normally a $4.00 premium on a stock trading near the strike price might be considered expensive, but when the market smelled risk, it made you pay for it.

Averill bought 10 put options at a time. Larger orders could move the market. It took an hour to accumulate 1,000 options. He switched to the cheaper "December 35" put option, which only cost a buck apiece. If you were absolutely sure ROOT was collapsing, the cheaper option was a better deal. He added 5,000 more options. The total cost was $1,000,000.

Exhausted at day's end, Averill checked the Yahoo! Finance message board. The board had been his ally on the way up. It worked both ways. He accepted that his fair weather friends had come and gone. The Sticky Five had been loyal for two years. The ring lasted less than three months. The lipstick was off the supermodel. ROOT had lost its gloss. They bragged about dumping their girl after a brief frolic. The board read:

JeanJacques: "I took my profits at $50. Now, I'm short. Bye-bye."

CRABBabyDoc: "I'm outta here, too. IMHO this run is over. I'm LT investor. Too wild for me. See you next September."

PabloEsCRABar: "Great run. Let's do it again sometime."

Averill tried to call McSorley and Lefty. Their cell phones had been turned off. More likely, they had been destroyed. He didn't bother trying the others.

Averill thought, *My guys helped, but they're all small-time players. They don't have a million dollars to play with. Except for Sticky Jones. He mortgaged his house and was $2 million ahead a week ago. He had to be heavily leveraged. I'm sure he got out like a stinking rat on a sinking ship.*

CHAPTER 283

OCTOBER 3, 2013

CRAB went limit down for the third day in a row. At $204 a pound, NBCI was now looking at a loss and still couldn't sell its position. Arthur hadn't listened. He had really screwed up. Averill was sure he could have managed the sale without causing widespread panic.

The most amazing thing to Averill was that investors in NBCI still had no clue of the calamity the company was facing. It wasn't shared information. NBCI had never disclosed to the public that it had a big CRAB position. The company certainly hadn't released any warnings either. Traders in the pits knew there was trouble. The only evidence that something was wrong was the stock price. It was falling fast.

Averill wondered, *Will NBCI ever get out of its contracts? If it doesn't, ROOT's stock price is going to zero. Bankrupt. Maybe Oxford was right. They studied the chain and found the weakest link. NBCI couldn't withstand a big drop in CRAB prices. The bonds would collapse. The credit default swaps would have to be paid by the insurance companies. Maybe they weren't trying to make money on NBCI. Maybe they had bet on the bonds!*

The opening bid for ROOT on Thursday morning was $34, down 15%. Averill gulped and sold 20,000 shares. The bid lowered to $32. Then $31. Averill dumped 200,000 shares on the market in a frantic morning selloff. He spent the rest of the day selling another

100,000. This was all profit, $9,000,000 of it. Twenty days earlier, it would have been twice that. At least the margin loan was paid.

Averill had seen more than a few accounts seized by the SEC and the IRS. Brokerage firms weren't shy about freezing employee assets either. It was a big bargaining chip. And there was always the court order protecting a future ex-wife. Insider traders stupidly left money around to grab. They thought they hadn't been noticed. They thought they were immune.

Averill's money was leaving town. It was leaving the country. And he knew just how to move it – David Elliot at First Second Third Bank.

"Speak up, Averill," David quipped, "I can't hear you above all of the customers."

The bank was on life support. It was now paying an 8% interest rate on six-month certificates, a clear sign that the depositors had fled.

Averill ignored the attempted humor and said, "David, I'm moving $9 million into your bank."

"Are you sure? The rumors about our demise are not greatly exaggerated," David warned with a laugh.

"Well, it won't stay there very long," said a serious Averill. "You have my Cayman Island bank codes. I want the money wired as soon as it hits your bank."

"Avy, baby," David said nonchalantly, "I'd love to help you, but these regulators are all over the place. A big wire will raise questions. I suggest you send a bunch of smaller wires. Like $100,000 each. And I also recommend that you open more than one account down there. You're entering dangerous territory here."

Averill said, "That'll take forever. Forget it. I don't have the time. Look, let's do three wires a day, three million apiece. I'll open more accounts down there this weekend. And your personal fee of one percent is a little high. I'm moving $20 million during the next month. I think a half percent is plenty."

David let out a bitter laugh. "If you think you can find another bank to move your sleazy money out of the country, go right ahead. There are new banking laws – Know Thy Customer! It'll take you six months to even open an account. You're lucky I don't charge you more."

"Alright, alright," Averill said in defeat. "I'll pay. But this is robbery."

The proverbial pot had called the kettle black. Penny stock manipulator and inside trader Averill accused money launderer David Elliot of robbery. It was like Ponzi schemer Bernie Madoff accusing the U. S. Post Office of mail fraud for delivering his fabricated customer brokerage statements.

CHAPTER 284

OCTOBER 3

Averill looked at the stack of messages on his desk while he cursed David for his ridiculous fee. At least a hundred phone calls had gone unanswered.

He opened his net worth calculator and entered the day's stock price. If it held steady, he could still clear $30 million before taxes. But who was going to pay taxes? Not Averill.

Two years ago, he had aspired to make enough money so he could occasionally eat at a nice restaurant. Now, he was a multimillionaire. Sure, a lot of people in town would lose money, but they knew the risks. Caveat emptor!

For the last week, Averill had trampled anyone in his way. He would survive. He didn't care about those left behind. There would be no remorse when the final tally was made.

Congenital greed is a tough diagnosis. Could someone be born this way? Is desire for money innate? Averill had thought about possessing other people's assets as long as he could remember.

He stole a bicycle when he was ten. It looked nice. He wanted it. He took it. After being caught, he fabricated an innocent sounding excuse. "The bike looked just like mine. I'm sorry. It was an honest mistake."

Averill had now polished his lying skills so well that sometimes even he couldn't determine the truth. Averill's career path as a penny stock broker was destiny. No other profession rewarded the craving for money like Wall Street. Greed was an awfully powerful motivator. High profile brokerage firms tried to weed morally bankrupt trainees from the ranks before they could do much damage. The top investment banks were wary of characters who were overboard in love with money. Still, bad characters slipped through the screening process.

Averill picked up the phone thinking Misty was calling. Instead, it was a customer who cried, "Shouldn't I sell my shares? The stock is down a lot from September."

Averill said charmingly, "This is no time to be selling. NBCI is having a great quarter. The stock will go back up. Why do you want to sell at the low? To tell you the truth, I just bought a bunch. You should think about averaging down. Buy more stock and your break-even will be lower!"

Averill didn't want his clients selling and driving the price further south. At least not until he sold first.

CHAPTER 285

OCTOBER 4, 2013

Ah! Relief! CRAB held steady through the morning. It had found equilibrium at $184 a pound after four consecutive days of limit down. Trading was active. Buyers concluded prices were finally a bargain. Sellers tabulated their losses, glad they had escaped.

Brandon, the LITE broker, had mysteriously changed employers overnight. The traitor had sold out NBCI for the price of a beer and a pretzel. He now wore the ID of Bloomfield Traders.

LMNOP scrambled through its ranks to find a replacement. They promoted Calvin, a junior corn trader who knew nothing about CRAB. He was being thrown to the wolves. Cal was brave. He was valiant. He pushed his way to the front of the throng of traders. It was times like these where being big and strong helped.

At the current price, daring holders still believed there would be an order imbalance at the end of the month. Cal managed to sell 4,000 contracts throughout the day for $74 million. He still had 8,900 contracts to sell and $135 million of margin debt to be paid. A profit was unthinkable. Recovering any of the $70 million in account equity would be declared a victory.

Trading volumes in ROOT lightened. Averill squeezed orders in as the market recovered midday. ROOT traders experienced momentary optimism. It didn't last long. Sell orders hammered the stock a few minutes before the market closed. Averill checked the price as he boarded the plane at Teterboro Airport. ROOT had fallen another ten percent in the final hour. It was near $25 per share.

He and pregnant Misty hitched a ride with four banker-lawyer types on a charter to the Cayman Islands for the affordable price of $10,000 paid in $20 bills. They couldn't risk taking a commercial flight and having their bags inspected before boarding. Not with $200,000 in cash and diamonds. Presumably, the other passengers had similar banking agendas.

Before he left, Averill had opened several bank accounts in the Caymans over the Internet. It had been remarkably easy. David Elliot introduced Averill to a "friendly" customs broker who promised to help him enter the country smoothly for a steep fee. This weekend was a test run. If it worked, he'd need five more trips to move the money out of the regulators' reach.

A weekend on a Caribbean island and no tan to show for it. On Saturday, instead of sunning on the beach, Averill established several safety deposit boxes to stash the diamonds and half the cash. He deposited the rest of the cash in his new bank accounts.

He and Misty took a commercial flight home early Sunday morning. There was no reason to pay big bucks for a charter when you're not smuggling.

On Monday, back in the office, Averill fought hard to sell his NBCI stock without driving the price lower. Dribbling out 100 shares at a time would take forever. Selling a block of 10,000 would require a big discount.

He looked at the CRAB market. It had finally settled down. Nice volume. Up a little. Down a little. Even for the day. Why the hell was NBCI down another 15% already?

At 2:00 PM, the bids disappeared for ROOT. There were some ridiculous way-off-the-market offers for a penny and a dollar, but nothing near the previous price of $21 a share. Averill tried to sell a block of 10,000 shares at $20 a share. Nothing. He lowered his ask to $19 a share. A counterbid for 1,000 shares at $15 appeared on the screen.

Something was seriously wrong. The entire support for ROOT had evaporated: the Sticky Five, the townspeople of Bergenfield, Buckstown Financial, Igor and the ring, the dozen small brokerage firms who had become market makers in the last year. All gone.

Those same people were now the sellers killing the stock price. Add Oxford to the cauldron, and you had a toxic stock. Averill called Brandon Bigelow, the LITE traitor trader.

Brandon spoke hesitantly, "I'm surprised you guys want to talk to me, the way I left and all. I had to protect my career. Rumor is LMNOP is closing their trading sub."

"I couldn't care less," said Averill impatiently. He just wanted info. "What's going on in the CRAB pits? I'm trying to figure out what's putting all the pressure on NBCI's stock."

"NBCI is wounded but alive," Brandon confirmed. "They're halfway out of their position from what I can tell. They sold another 4,000 CRAB contracts a tick under $184 dollars this morning.

"This locked market spooked everyone. This limit down of $20 dollars is way too small for a volatile $200 dollar commodity. The MERC's gotta increase the number. Rumor is they're gonna change the margin requirement to fifty percent instead. That'll make it worse.

"Some of the traders found another way to sell their exposure to CRAB, sort of. It's like a synthetic. They sell the POO ETF short and buy Pierre stock. Net-net, it's just like selling CRAB, ROOT and the industrial revenue bond. They all think NBCI is toast, so they aren't concerned about covering that exposure.

"Averill, we should get together for drinks. When you're in Chicago, I'll take you to lunch. Whadaya say?"

"Yeah, sure, Brandon. Let's do that," Averill said with as much politeness as he could muster while hanging up the phone. There was the smallest chance in hell he'd ever go to Chicago, and he had no further need for Brandon now that he'd extracted this vital info.

If Chicago was shorting POO, Wall Street computers would try to sell the components to match the trade. The programs spit instructions to sell CRAB, but a locked market meant no sales. If a lot of traders latched onto this synthetic hedge, ROOT could be in even more serious trouble.

Averill concluded that if he didn't sell now, he might never get out of this stock. He swallowed deeply and put a sell order for 300,000 shares at $20 a share. It was a steep discount to Friday's closing price. It was offered "all or none"; if someone wanted to buy at this price, they'd have to take the whole block. He tried again fifty cents lower. Then a dollar.

At $18 per share, Averill's order was filled. He had 450,000 shares left to sell, but half of those were the note shares and they were now officially underwater. He might never sell them. He thought, *Good luck collecting on the $3 million note, NBCI! That's what you get for screwing me, Arthur!*

Averill sat in his office exhausted. He thought, *Today's sales will clear in three days. I'll move $5 million to the islands this weekend. That leaves $8 million that will clear next week cash and $3 million in stock to sell. And no more traceable wires. I don't need you and your extortion fee, Elliot! NetJets, here I come!*

CHAPTER 287

OCTOBER 9, 2013

Stephane sat in Eva's office in the early morning. Her large green glass desk was clear of any annoying papers, as usual. Her credenza was host to a dozen picture frames with reminders of Paris. One photo was a selfie of Eva and a handsome man. La Tour Eiffel stood in the distance. This picture was the only evidence anywhere that Eva had a personal life outside Pierre.

Stephane spared Eva the commodity trader lingo, even though she seemed very savvy about the floor-speak. "I heard NBCI did a block trade. Someone bought the rest of their October contracts at $164. They have no more October contracts left, just some June, but those seem to be heading higher. Back of the envelope, I'd guess they lost $40 million. Pretty devastating.

"As for us, we already sold our excess contracts for 2014 and 2015 deliveries. I'm not sure what else I should do. Our trading gain is huge, but you know we won't have all the material we need. I hope this works. The month-end CRAB delivery is going to be pretty wild."

"Stephane, don't worry. I'm glad you're here," said Eva with unusual excitement in her voice. "We're having visitors in a few minutes. Buckstown is stopping by to chat, or so they say. They can only be here for one reason. Let's make sure they leave here scrambling to exit the CRAB market.

She winked. "This meeting should be fun. Stick around and follow my lead."

Three executives in their early thirties from Buckstown Financial sat in the conference room at 10:00 AM. Their suits were dark, their shirts were starched and white, and their ties were frivolously expensive. They checked on the market news with their iPhones and iPads while Eva made them wait.

Eva and Stephane entered the conference room a half hour later. Everyone exchanged business cards. Ralston and Raife were financial managing directors; Christian was a lawyer. The Buckstown trio tried to break the ice. Their small chitchat playbook didn't have a chapter on how to talk to a former supermodel. They couldn't talk sports with a woman, could they? "How 'bout them Yankees?" And surely she wouldn't understand their world of high finance.

Raife had conquered a few wannabe models in the downtown bars of New York. He talked knowingly about the Ford Models agency and dropped names of several near underage ingénues.

If Eva was insulted, she didn't show it. She remained polite but not engaging. Stephane kept quiet.

Failing at small talk, Ralston said, "Well, we find both of us in the same business…"

Eva interrupted, "I hardly think speculating in a commodity and cornering the market is our business. We are a beauty products company. What are you? What exactly do you manufacture on your Blackberry?"

So much for the sweet, glamorous and dumb model. Raife said, "We both invest in CRAB. We just use it for different purposes. We wanted…"

"Raife? Isn't that a German or Norse word for wolf?" Eva said with a cunning smile. "Did your parents have a premonition when they named you?"

Stephane held in a laugh. He had seen this side of Eva on rare occasions. She was a master at disarming men who assumed they were her superior.

Christian leaned forward and motioned to Raife and Ralston to be quiet. "Perhaps we should get to the point. As you well know, Buckstown has stored a million pounds of CRAB at a silo in Pennsylvania. We also control 5,000 contracts for delivery this month.

"We wanted to discuss a financial transaction with Pierre. We would consider selling our entire portfolio to you at a small discount to today's price. If we reach an acceptable agreement, we'll exit the CRAB market and agree not to trade for a period of five years. That's the purpose of our visit."

"Why would you want to sell?" Eva said coyly. "You aren't scared of this little price drop, are you? Let's see. It was $299 dollars on September 18 and now, look at that…" she held up her iPhone "the price is down $5.00 dollars a pound already today. A $140 dollar drop on a million pounds must be hurting your bonuses."

"For us, it's a matter of strategic asset reallocation and fundamental deployment," said Ralston in perfect business school mumbo jargon that Eva knew meant absolutely nothing. "We believe we have better returns available in other nascent markets. You wouldn't know about them."

Stephane watched as Eva absorbed the insult, yet another chauvinist assault on a female executive. She said with a slightly amused tone, "Another hit and run? We've hardly gotten to know each other. So, let's see. What's this slight discount to the market?"

"We think $150 a pound is a fair price compared to yesterday's close," Raife said in a condescending tone. "In effect, you would not be compensating us for the value of the noncompete asset. We are throwing that in for free."

Eva turned to her favorite French trader and said sweetly, "Stephane, What do you think? What's our average cost for CRAB? And tell the gentlemen the most we ever paid per pound."

Stephane tilted his head questioning the disclosure of the confidential data, but Eva nodded her okay. He said, "Our current cost basis is $30 a pound. The most we ever paid was $130 in May of this year. As for what I think, why would I pay you five times my cost?"

Raife glanced at Ralston and scribbled a note. If there was one thing Buckstown bankers could do, it was run complex numbers in their heads. If the Pierre team was telling the truth, then they hadn't been in the market for months. It meant the rumors in the trading pits were false. Worse, if Pierre's average cost was this low, they must have already sold their higher cost contracts. This was not encouraging.

Raife looked up from his notepad and spoke to Stephane in a lecturing tone. "Your historical cost is irrelevant. The reason you would pay our price is because it is below market. You are getting a discount and you get us to leave the business. That's why you would pay it!

"Ms. Marteen, we have presented to you a reasonable offer. It is more than generous. I can assure you that you will not appreciate our alternative strategy. Our offer is open for twenty-four hours."

The third insult was the charm. Eva closed her appointment book and spoke to the attorney, ignoring the bankers. "Christian, you're a lawyer. You shouldn't allow your bankers to threaten me so openly. You already have antitrust problems with your other commodity gambits.

"Here's my final answer. We will agree to buy your silo contents for $30 a pound if it passes inspection. You agree to leave the market forever. My offer is not open for twenty-four hours. You have five minutes."

The bankers were speechless. Raife moved forward. Christian restrained him with a hard stare and said, "We're sorry to have taken so much of your time. We thought there might be some interest on your part, but we were incorrect in our assessment. We'll see our way out."

The bankers gave Eva a smug smile that implied, *Wait until you see what happens next.*

After they left, Eva said, "I think that went rather well, don't you Stephane? I'll bet you a Euro they're calling their offices and giving sell orders right now."

CHAPTER 288

OCTOBER 11, 2013

Averill spent the week converting bank deposits into hard currency and diamonds. It was a full-time job.

He wasn't an expert. Most people had learned about money laundering from watching cops chasing drug dealers on TV crime shows. The kingpins got caught when they tried to move dirty cash back into the system. Averill laughed at the notion that he was doing the exact opposite – converting clean money in bank accounts into cash. He must be *un-laundering.*

There were only so many pawn shops and check cashing services, and they were only willing to convert a few thousand at a time at loan shark interest rates. Strip clubs were known for having high cash levels. Averill tried to talk to the manager of one club, but the bouncers physically threw him to the curb. This wasn't going to be easy.

Averill was exasperated; he didn't have time to learn a better way. He had at most two months to move as much as $30 million in cash. He'd never get there a thousand bucks at a time. He wired a million from Tuxedo's BreakTrade brokerage account to the Chase bank account. He drove to the Chase branch and tried to cash a check at the window for $25,000. The teller sent him to the bank manager who politely gave him a quick thumbnail of the Bank Secrecy Act.

Anyone who withdrew more than $10,000 triggered a form which was immediately sent to the IRS. He could have the cash, but he'd be investigated. If he tried to convert $9,999 at a time in a number of branches, known as "smurfing", they'd report the total of all withdrawals. And don't bother with the casinos. They report you too.

Local branches had a second more practical limitation. They rarely kept more than a few hundred thousand in the safe. Even if they were willing to give him the cash, they couldn't accommodate a large withdrawal. It was just really hard to get your hands on a lot of cash in America.

Averill decided he couldn't be concerned with the bank reporting requirements. By the time some Federal bureaucrat read the bank forms, he'd be long gone. In preparation for this moment years ago, Averill had opened multiple accounts in several corporate names in addition to his Tuxedo Investments accounts. Each company was named after a pair of the famous "robber barons" – Astor-Cooke Realty, Carnegie-Fisk Consulting, and Gould-Flagler Services. With properly filed state incorporation documents, the banks willingly let him open new accounts.

After spreading the money among his accounts, he then visited every branch of Bank of America, Wells Fargo, Chase, PNC, Hudson United, and Citibank within 20 miles. He withdrew the maximum allowed. He thought, *They're not reporting me. They're reporting Astor-Cooke Realty. Besides, by the time they figure this out, I'll be outa here.*

Bank branches had limited supplies of fifties and hundreds. The United States stopped printing larger bills long ago. A million dollars of paper currency was too bulky. There had to be another way.

For another outrageous fee, David Elliot introduced Averill to two diamond merchants on 47th Street in Manhattan. They agreed to sell him a million dollars of diamonds a week, for their customary markup of course.

Averill did his best to learn how to rate the cut, clarity, color and shape of diamonds. He concluded the best way to avoid getting swindled was to buy only white, round diamonds that were at least two carats. That would eliminate most of the poor quality stones. He had no idea how to identify imperfections or inclusions. Instead, he randomly rejected diamonds so the merchants would believe he had an eye. They weren't fooled.

Averill needed other ways to convert his funds. He had read about bitcoins, a virtual currency making headlines primarily because of its crazy price swings. Fighting for some legitimacy, bitcoins were also a known haven for moving illegal money around the world. Averill bought $100,000 in bitcoins to test the system. The problem he faced was how to convert them back into money when he needed it. It wasn't like there was a bitcoin ATM on the corner. He'd test the system once. If it worked, he'd buy more.

Averill only had 100,000 shares left excluding the note shares. Unfortunately, nearly $3 million of stock sale proceeds was pending in his LMNOP account. After it cleared, he'd move the cash in next week's run to the islands.

Averill stood alone at his desk with his door locked. He was rearranging the bundles of cash in his carry-on bag. He had stashed about half of the bills in the underneath shoe compartment. He was covering the rest of the money with clothing when his cellphone rang. It was Mickey Muirfield, the lead member of the Sticky Five.

"Mickey, why are you calling my personal phone?" Averill said nervously. "Are you crazy?"

Averill heard a bus passing in the background. Mickey was breathing heavily and sounded like he was walking fast. He said, "I had no choice but to call you directly, Avy buddy. You guys all killed your prepaid phones, didn't you? Nobody told me. What choice did I have?

"I'm near your office. I'm walking past some church on Clinton Avenue. Tell me how to get there. I want to come visit you."

Averill said suspiciously, "We really shouldn't be seen together. Anyway, I'm running out to an important meeting. Let's meet in the city next week."

Averill looked out his window and saw Mickey walking toward his office holding his phone in one hand and a paper sack in the other. He saw a glimmer of something metal pulled from the bag. This looked like trouble. It could be a gun. Averill swept a stack of twenties into his desk drawer, grabbed the carry-on bag, and scrambled out the rear door a second before Mickey entered the front.

Mickey sputtered into the phone as he walked into the lobby, "Where are you? Why didn't you tell me this thing was gonna collapse, you crook. I'm ruined. What happened? I thought we were friends."

Averill ran through the backyard of the dentist's office next door and crossed Washington Avenue. Over the phone, he could hear Mickey opening closet doors and searching the offices. Mickey yelled, "Why? Why didn't you tell me this stock was tanking. I'm ruined. They're gonna take my house. My wife's gonna leave me. I'm broke. I'm bankrupt. How could you do this?"

Seconds later, Averill turned and saw Mickey running after him. Averill slipped through the front door of the middle school and ran down the hall past a group of soccer players heading to practice. Mickey followed a hundred feet behind, closing fast with gun in hand.

Averill escaped out the northwest door into the teachers' parking lot. He squatted behind a large SUV. He could hear Mickey approaching. Averill crawled under the car. Mickey was still yelling into the phone, but Averill had hung up. He held his breath and texted Misty: "In trouble. Meet me west side of Clinton railroad tracks. ASAP!"

Mickey hunted up and down the rows of cars. When he neared the eastern end of the lot, Averill crawled from beneath the SUV and snuck through a hole in the chain link fence. He crossed the railroad tracks beating a freight train by seconds.

Misty had been sitting in Ben's when she saw the dramatic message. Her first thought was that someone was trying to rob her husband. And he had the diamonds. She jumped in her red BMW, tore down the street, sped midair across the railroad tracks, and screeched to a halt in front of the library.

Averill jumped in the passenger seat and Misty raced south on Front Street. Averill pressed redial on his phone. Misty could barely hear one-half of the conversation.

"Mickey, you gotta believe me. I didn't know. The other guys all sold out. They left me in the lurch. I'm wiped out too. Let me make it up to you. As soon as I get back to town. Monday. Okay? Keep cool, Mickey. That wasn't fun, bro."

CHAPTER 289

OCTOBER 11

Thirty minutes later, they sat in the waiting room at the Atlantic Aviation terminal at Teterboro Airport. Averill was still rattled, disheveled and sweating. His suit had small grease stains from crawling beneath the SUV.

Misty fixed her eyeliner and mascara while looking at a compact mirror. She complained, "You know, I barely made it across the tracks. That train almost hit me."

"I'm sorry, honey," said Averill. "He was a mad customer screaming about his losses. I had to get away or we'd miss the flight." He neglected to mention the gun.

"What's wrong with these people?" Misty said with a *tsk*. "They knew what they were buying. Don't let them get to you, honey. They should have sold if they thought the stock was going down. You did, didn't you? It's not your fault they didn't follow your advice."

Except, they couldn't sell. Averill had stopped taking client calls two weeks ago. The luckier customers had taken profits during September on the way up. A week ago, Arturo, fed up with Averill, called LMNOP headquarters, threatened a lawsuit, and demanded they send his shares to his Scottrade account. The word spread. If you were connected to the grapevine, you were fortunate and got out. For many others, it was too late. Young couples. Retired people. Widows. Hundreds had lost everything.

Averill carried the cash; Misty held the two-carat diamonds, all sixty of them, in her handbag with a makeshift false bottom. Even though their new "friend" would again expedite them through customs in the Caymans, they were taking no chances. Averill was betting they wouldn't search a woman who was six months pregnant.

CHAPTER 290

OCTOBER 14, 2013

Upon their return home from the Cayman Islands, Newark Airport's U. S. Customs agent wasn't as friendly. Their passports had the same Caribbean Islands stamp four weeks in a row. They had been flagged.

Averill endured twenty minutes of interrogation and lied his way through the process. He was on pleasure, not business. He had been shopping for a villa for weekend getaways. No, he wasn't carrying any currency into the states. And that was no lie.

They managed to get through the interrogation, but the heat was intensifying. They couldn't make many more trips.

Back in the office, he could see the cash in his LMNOP account. Last week's stock sales had finally cleared. Also, the put options sitting in his BreakTrade online brokerage account had tripled in three weeks. It was an unexpected bonus. He logged into the account and entered a sell order.

At 10:00 AM, Averill was about to contact headquarters to request a wire transfer when an official-looking sort walked into the foyer wheeling a large legal document case. He peeked into Averill's office.

"May I help you?" asked Averill slightly annoyed.

"I'm Marvin Gladstone from corporate compliance," said the gentleman. "I'm your new supervisor. Let's talk."

"Legal sent me to oversee your broker activities and help you clean up this mess. LMNOP has enough customer complaints about you to fill their calendar for a year. I guess I'll work from the conference room."

Marvin walked from the room and Averill shoved the pile of pink phone messages out of sight. He thought, *Corporate has to pretend they've been supervising me. It's litigation defense 101. I have to keep cool, act like I'm cooperating, and find a way to split. I've got money to move. How the hell am I going to convert that into cash and diamonds with a babysitter outside my office?*

I better move the $3 million in the LMNOP accounts this morning before they get any funny ideas. This guy plans on moving in here. My personal watchdog. A pit bull in a nice suit. He won't last a day in this hellhole.

Marvin walked back into Averill's office. "The place is a pig sty. I'm getting a cleaning crew in here this morning. How do you work in this pit? Oh yeah, by the way, your LMNOP accounts are frozen. You can't trade and you can't withdraw the funds until we settle these pending suits."

Averill said blankly, "I understand. I'll cooperate fully. This NBCI thing fell so fast. There was no way to handle the customer calls. I've been asking you guys in corporate for help for two years. Now look what happened. You guys should've listened to me. I'm the firm's top broker, and now I'm losing all my valuable customers."

Averill's motto: *Never defend. Always deny.* Make them doubt their words. Make them question their actions.

Averill pulled a phone message from the drawer and called the customer speaking loud enough for Marvin to hear. "Hello, Mrs. Edelstone. Yes, I know the stock has gone down. I sold your shares this morning as you instructed. I'm really sorry."

Averill had no customer named Edelstone. There was no one on the line. Marvin returned to the conference room.

At noon, Averill slipped out for lunch. He logged into his BreakTrade account from his car and initiated wire transfers to his five bank accounts. Converting into paper money wasn't going to be easy with Marvin hanging around.

CHAPTER 291

OCTOBER 14

Late Monday morning at the plant, Johnny opened the certified letter from behind his Star Trek command center. He didn't have much to do since being stripped of all duties. Sarah was no longer around to keep him company. Alistair's staff had been terminated. Johnny kept the TV on low volume.

He stared with disbelief at the 20-page epistle from the Securities Exchange Commission. It was a mere 18 pages if you didn't count the oversized embossed heading plus the intro-duction, complimentary close and list of 12 people carbon-copied on the last page. The SEC had conducted a review of NBCI's financial statements and reports on Form 10-K, 10-Q and 8-K and had a series of questions and comments.

Johnny slipped the letter under the controller's door. In the short time since his return, Justin had been professionally polite. Johnny had kicked him hard on the way out the door and was sure Justin was just waiting for the right time to exact his revenge.

Minutes later, Justin knocked on Johnny's door. "I just scanned this to Jack. We better call him together. From the conference room, not here." He glared at Johnny.

Johnny tried to wiggle out of the meeting. He knew nothing about the issues. "Arthur said I don't have no responsibility no more. Why should I be on the call?"

"Because you're getting paid a salary. Plus, it looks like some of our problems are because of your buddy, Averill." Justin snapped.

After dialing in, Jack said, "I see where they're going with this. You guys better make a quick assessment and fix your financials. A lot of this is technical accounting stuff, but if the SEC is right, you haven't fair-valued the warrants, you didn't follow the rules for reverse mergers, and you didn't properly account for the founder's stock paid to Averill.

"The biggest problem I see is we haven't adequately warned investors of the risks of commodity trading. And we're now facing a large loss that they don't even know about.

"Justin, you better talk to your auditors. You may have to restate your financial state-ments. In that case, the stock symbol gets a nasty 'E' next to it until you refile.

"For now, the company is in blackout. No officers or directors can sell shares or exer-cise stock options."

"I don't understand the warrant issue," said Justin, slightly perplexed. "We don't have a price reset on our warrants."

"Yeah, you do," Jack corrected him. "The warrant that Johnny signed is slightly different than the one you saw in the private placement. Averill must have added the reset provision."

Justin shook his head without saying a word. Johnny shrank in his seat. There was no end to the series of corporate offenses committed by Averill.

CHAPTER 292

OCTOBER 15, 2013

Justin and the company auditors spent the rest of the afternoon and late into the night trying to comprehend the letter. The SEC rarely told you what you did wrong. They criticized in rhetoric. It was truly an art form requiring a professional interpreter. They express their disgust with your filings with unanswerable questions.

SEC: "Did you consider the rules and regulations when you calculated the value of the derivative?"

Controller: "Well, I thought I did, but now I don't know, and based upon your comment, you think I didn't, but you're not telling me what I should do instead."

SEC: "Please explain why you did not consider the effects of blah, blah, blah on your reporting of blankety-blank."

Controller: "I didn't consider the effects of blah, blah, blah on our reporting of blankety-blank because I had no idea that such an obscure rule existed. Please tell me where to look. Oh, I forgot. I have to find it without any clues."

SEC: "Please explain why you didn't observe the double-secret obscure rule on page 9987 of the SEC Accounting Manual!"

Controller: "Um, we aren't allowed to have a copy of your secret accounting manual. Maybe if we had one, we wouldn't screw up so much."

SEC: "Please explain in great detail how you are going to account for your stuff if we adopt new rules that we're thinking about springing on you, but then again we may not."

Controller: "Huh?"

By morning, they had completed their assessment. NBCI would have to record a $10 million warrant liability and hit to stockholders' equity. Quarterly earnings would zigzag up and down millions each quarter in a confounding manner. Recording the reverse merger would affect the opening balance sheet two years ago. Wordsmithing would fix the rest of the problems. Jack would write an expanded section about commodity trading risks.

Gone were the days of the most basic accounting principle – using historical cost. In the old days, if you paid a dollar for an asset, a dollar went on the balance sheet. The SEC preferred fair value accounting. It wreaked havoc on small public companies. Cash-strapped start-ups had to double their accounting staffs to keep up with the never ending stream of new rules. They tripled their budgets to pay for CPA audits. It was a disaster.

Justin, Jack and the auditors met with the board and explained the bad news. By noon, NBCI had filed a Form 8-K with the SEC telling investors they could no longer rely on the previously issued financial statements. The company was technically in violation of its bond covenants. It had ten days to cure the problem or the bonds would be delisted. If delisted, the bonds would default and be callable. This would trigger a credit event under the credit default swaps. Hedge funds and institutions had bet billions that this would happen. It was a doomsday scenario.

NBCI advised investors in the Form 8-K that it had lost $45 million trading the CRAB commodity since the beginning of September. The only good news was that they no longer held any contracts. All of the added disclosures being drafted by Jack about the increased risks of trading would be for naught. They were already out of the speculating business.

The NASDAQ halted trading for four hours to give the market time to absorb the information. They added an "E" to the stock symbol indicating the company was delinquent on filing its financials.

When trading resumed at 3:30 PM, the stock opened down 40% at $8.00 per share. The vultures were circling above the plant. The 8-K disclosure was an open invitation to a class action suit against the company. It was a roadmap to litigators.

The credit default swaps on NBCI's industrial revenue bonds increased to an incredible 6300 bips. The $1,000 bond was bid $400. Traders were betting NBCI would be bankrupt in two weeks. Credit default swaps had been issued on $4 billion of bonds, even though there were only $200 million outstanding. You didn't need to own the bonds to buy a swap. You just gambled and won or lost.

CHAPTER 293

OCTOBER 16, 2013

It didn't take Oxford long to strike a blow. At the opening bell, they issued a press release.

Oxford Collar Financial, on behalf of itself and five private investors under the Carapace family of funds, has sent a Notice of Default to NBCI (symbol "ROOT") and its trustee for the $200 million industrial revenue bond.

Under its indenture, NBCI is required to prepare and have available at all times a set of financial statements prepared in accordance with generally accepted accounting principles. NBCI has recently withdrawn its previously issued incorrect, materially misleading and fraudulent financial statements. It is now in technical default of this requirement.

NBCI is also required to maintain a listing for its industrial revenue bonds on an "exchange". Trading was halted yesterday for four hours, which resulted in a technical default which cannot be cured.

We also hereby declare an anticipatory breach of the covenants that through the passage of time will cause a default. As a result, we demand that NBCI repay the bonds immediately in their entirety.

Oxford has also demanded payment by the town of Bergenfield, New Jersey under its guarantee of the bonds. Oxford has also notified the Hounds Tooth Insurance Company that the default has triggered an "event" under the credit default swap agreements underwritten by Hounds Tooth. We hereby demand that the insurance company make immediate payment of $750 per $1,000 bond under the terms of the credit default swaps.

It got worse. At midday, the NASDAQ released its September short interest reports for public companies. The short interest on NBCI had grown to 70%. Wall Street was joining Oxford Collar and ganging up on NBCI's stock, bonds, and credit default swaps.

Averill pulled up his account and sold the last 100,000 shares at $7.00 per share. He'd probably never see the money. By the time the sales cleared, he'd be out of the country.

CHAPTER 294

OCTOBER 16

Suzanne Pettigrew walked through NBCI's unmanned foyer and into the conference room. The tableful of auditors looked up surprised. Why would a pretty thirtysomething well-dressed woman be visiting a crabgrass processing plant? Hadn't they fired Johnny's brand consultant and PR staff?

Justin said, "Good morning, Suzanne. I guess we should've been expecting you. Jack, you know Bergenfield's treasurer."

Suzanne said, "Hello Jack. I'm here to represent the town. As far as we're concerned, the bonds didn't default and we intend to fight it.

"The NASDAQ issued a temporary trading halt. It didn't delist the bonds. They're still registered and they're still traded on an exchange, and that's all that's required. As long as you file corrected financials in ten days, we'll be okay."

Johnny ignored Suzanne and sulked in the corner staring at his iPad. Arthur insisted he sit through these miserable meetings even if he had nothing to contribute. It was meant to be demeaning punishment. Arthur had no intention of paying Johnny's severance package. He wanted him to leave under duress.

Jack said, "Nice to see you. We agree. The lawyers for Hounds Tooth say the same. We want to prepare a joint response. However, this won't be the end of it. This group of vultures has made a big bet. They aren't going away."

Johnny spit out from his corner, "This's ridiculous. You guys are gettin' pushed around like a bunch of pansies. Averill would never have stood for this. We should sue Oxford for wrongful litigation and RICO violations."

Suzanne. Sweet Suzanne. Professional Suzanne. Suzanne, wearing a string of expensive pearls, $300 Kenneth Cole pumps, and a red silk dress from Bergdorf Goodman, turned to Johnny and said, "It's malicious use of process, but they haven't sued us yet. They just filed a press release. You may be thinking of wrongful termination, which is what the company won't be guilty of when they fire your negligent ass."

Johnny said defiantly, "How dare you talk to me like that? I'm still president. You work for the town and shouldn't even be in this meetin'."

"Johnny, the board of directors asked Bergenfield to send a representative. Suzanne is here as our guest. Now muzzle it!" Jack swept his hand.

Johnny stormed from the conference room, finally having an excuse to return to the safer environs of his office.

"Let's get back to this default issue," said Jack. "Justin thinks we can file the amended financials within two days. I suggest we issue the press release now."

The following morning, NBCI, Bergenfield and Hounds Tooth Insurance issued a joint press release announcing that, after a careful review of the governing documents, a technical default had not occurred. No payment would be made on the credit default swaps or the guarantee.

CHAPTER 295

OCTOBER 17, 2013

Eva opened her purse and tossed a Euro coin to Stephane. She said, "I'll never understand what just happened. I was sure Buckstown would sell their CRAB position. I was absolutely certain the price of CRAB would collapse. Never underestimate those Wall Street guys. They always have another option in their hip pockets. And the price is going up now that everyone realizes NBCI has sold its position."

Stephane handed a Buckstown press clipping to Eva. "They did sell, just not into the market. Apparently they decided to get out of the physicals business after the government investigation. They sold the million pounds and the silo to Macedonia Vulture Partners.

"That explains why the June 2014 CRAB price was upside down. Everyone was rolling forward their expiring contracts. Macedonia executed a perfect arbitrage. They sold two million pounds for delivery next June and August. They bought Buckstown's position at a discount. They're renting some storage space at NBCI's warehouse for the excess.

"I wish I had lost the bet," Stephane allowed. "I hate to tell you this, but CRAB prices aren't collapsing anytime soon. If anything, Macedonia will make this worse."

CHAPTER 296

OCTOBER 18, 2013

The NBCI offices stayed lit late into the previous night. There would be no victory lap when the project was completed. No cheering crowds. No lighting of the torch. No wearing of the wreath. This was a thankless exercise.

Justin worked feverishly amending the company's two Form 10-Ks and six Form 10-Qs. It was a heavily administrative task once the numbers had been calculated. He'd hired consultants from Robert Half Accountemps to help rewrite the footnotes and SEC analysis. Secretaries hired through Kelly Girls typed the changes into the documents. Jack composed the delicate response to the SEC. Johnny napped in his office.

At 11:00 AM, Justin pushed the "file" button to post the revised financial statements on the SEC web site. An hour later, NASDAQ removed the "E" from the trading symbol.

Johnny sat in his office, percolating. *Justin controls the checkbook now. If I wanna get paid, I'm gonna hafta kiss his ass.*

Justin was preparing to leave early when Johnny entered his offices. "Justin, we should talk. I'm really sorry about how things happened between us. I must've misunderstood Arthur. I guess I wanna apologize."

"Sure. Yeah, I guess," Justin shrugged. He was exhausted; hadn't shaved or showered. He just wanted to go home. Thursday night had been a near all-nighter. He walked past Johnny toward the door.

Johnny stopped him. "This benefits you, too. You know, even though we lost money in October, the company still made some money last year. If you add it up, we're still owed our bonus. You accrued it, right? I think we should move the bonus money to a special account, you know, so the board can pay it in December."

Justin stared at him incredulously, "Is that it?"

Johnny said, "Well if it's okay with you, can we make the 401k matchin' contribution today? I mean, why wait till January? The board wouldn't take that away from us, would they?"

Justin sighed heavily. "Anything else? What about the health insurance? Why not pre-pay next year's health insurance, too?"

"That's a great idea," Johnny said eagerly. "Why not?"

Justin laughed derisively. "Johnny, I cannot believe how clueless you are. The whole management of this place is going to change, and that's only if we survive this Oxford assault. If they win, we're going bankrupt. And these financial restatements are on my back. I'm probably getting fired when this is over."

"My stock options are worthless," Johnny cried, "we're ruined! What're we gonna to do?"

"What's with this *we* crap?" Justin snarled, "*we* aren't doing anything together. I'm looking for my next job. Hopefully this place hasn't totally ruined my reputation."

Oxford ignored the NBCI press release and corrected financial statements. In their view, the default had occurred and couldn't be cured. They wanted their money, all $2 billion of it. On paper, shorting NBCI's stock and buying its credit default swaps was showing a ten-to-one return. It issued another press release.

> *Oxford Collar Financial, on behalf of itself and five private investors under the Carapace family of funds, has filed an action with The International Swaps and Derivatives Association, Inc.(ISDA) who will meet and determine if a "Credit Event" has occurred with respect to the default on the NBCI $200 million industrial revenue bond. We expect the ISDA Credit Derivatives Determinations Committees ("DCs") to rule in our favor within four weeks.*
>
> *The DCs make determinations that apply to credit derivative transactions on subjects including Credit Events and other issues. The determinations made by the DC are governed by the Determinations Committees Rules.*

This was no longer a war of press releases. Oxford was looking for swift action by the ruling body. If the DCs determined that an event had occurred, Hounds Tooth would have to pay on the credit default swaps. It would trigger a bankruptcy by NBCI and a call on Bergenfield's guarantee.

The bond price dropped another $5.00 following the announcement. The credit default swaps increased to 6800 bips, equivalent to 68% of the notional or face value. The CDS price would have gone even higher, but Bergenfield had been required to segregate $50 million of the original bond proceeds. That collateral was presumed safe by speculators. If the ISDA ruled that a credit event had occurred, the money would be used to mitigate the damages.

Archibald Smith, the general counsel of Hounds Tooth joined Suzanne Pettigrew, Arthur, and Jack at NBCI's board conference room, the grandest board room this side of the Hudson.

"I don't think the delisting issue will prevail," Suzanne said. "However, the company technically didn't have audited financial statements for a week. It could be construed as a default under the agreement. I'm worried about leaving this in the hands of the ISDA."

Archibald was dressed very British in his Saville Row suit and conservative dark tie. "Suzanne, our interests may not be aligned with the town's. You could benefit from a default because you own credit default swaps with Hounds Tooth…"

Suzanne interjected, "Trust me, Mr. Smith. We don't want a default on the bonds even if the swaps offset some of our losses. Remember, we only own insurance on $120 million dollars of bonds. We're still very exposed. Also, the aftereffect on our bond rating wouldn't be pleasant."

"My client is NBCI," said Jack. "We wouldn't take action to force ourselves into bankruptcy unless it was the last option. I think all of our interests are aligned enough to work together."

The group huddled for two hours analyzing defensive strategies, countermeasures, and media campaigns. In the end, there was little they could do but allow Hounds Tooth to argue before the ISDA that a credit event had not occurred. It was somewhat of a crapshoot.

CHAPTER 298

OCTOBER 21

Marvin Gladstone, Averill's new resident compliance officer, had watched his every move all day, every day. Averill was a captive without shackles, a prisoner inside a stale-smelling office. After years of freedom of movement, Averill couldn't stand the constant surveillance. Last week, he had managed one sick day to conduct his "banking" business, but it was nearly impossible to escape during office hours.

There was barely enough hard cash at the end of the week to risk a trip to the Islands. He travelled without Misty, telling her it was too small a deposit and he had to "sort out some bank stuff."

Back from the islands, Averill looked dejectedly at his LMNOP account. It held over $3 million, and he couldn't touch it. It was dead money he'd never see again. Last Friday, he had pleaded with Marvin to let him transfer $100,000 to Uncle Mickey, his terribly sick relative who needed the money for an operation. Hopefully, it would be enough to stop any more gun chases through parking lots.

Either Marvin bought the story, or he let Averill get away with one. More likely, Marvin needed Averill to cooperate with the LMNOP litigation team. The investor lawsuits were sure to come.

Early Monday morning, Averill expected to see Marvin when the office door opened. Instead, a frail-looking accounting type with a bad haircut and wearing an inexpensive suit and bow tie entered the foyer.

"We're not accepting any new accounts," Averill yelled from his office.

"Mr. Barry Winthrop," said the man. "Are you Mr. Winthrop?"

Averill shook his head extremely irritated that he was being interrupted. "That's me. What do you want?"

The man handed Averill an official looking document. "My name is Wallace T. Blankenship. I'm here from the New Jersey Bureau of Securities. We've received a number of complaints from customers about their inability to sell or transfer securities in accounts at this branch. This is a subpoena for your customer records."

Averill acted coolly and read the subpoena. This was only a state regulator looking into a dozen complaints. It was no big deal. They had little power except to slap his wrist or, at worst, take away his career, which he wouldn't need after next week.

"Okay, Mr. Blankenship. My supervisor is a little late this morning. Why don't you set up shop in the conference room over there, and I'll try to find the files for you."

Marvin had hired a demolition firm to clean out the offices. They had pulled the carpets, removed moldy wallboard, and applied three coats of paint. Marvin replaced the broken swivel chairs with rentals. A $40 Rothko knockoff painting hung on the wall. There was no reason to buy anything expensive. This office would close as soon as the litigation ended.

Averill scratched his head on what to do next. He called Marvin who told him to cooperate until he arrived. Averill found a few files which were woefully small and incomplete. He hadn't been very diligent about recordkeeping. Most of the papers sat unsorted in banker's boxes stacked to the ceiling.

Averill had planned to convert another million dollars this week. He was hopeful Marvin was going to ease up on his babysitting and find daily excuses to be in the City. That would be Averill's window to move money.

Every 15 minutes, Mr. Blankenship requested additional documents. It took time to find the files. At this rate, Blankenship could be here for a month.

Averill closed the offices for lunch and headed to the middle school parking lot. Today's Wi-Fi password was "onomatopoeia". He initiated wire instructions to his brokerage accounts. The money would be available by the next morning. That gave him three days to visit the branches and convert the cash. In between, he'd have to visit his diamond merchants in NYC and buy some more stones.

OCTOBER 24, 2013

It had been a very busy week for Averill and Marvin with far too many uninvited visitors.

On Thursday morning, a team of four men in suits entered LMNOP's foyer. Their leader handed Averill a document and said with exaggerated drama, "I'm Reggie Tupperman, senior investigator for FINRA, the Financial Industry Regulatory Authority.

"Barry Winthrop, aka Averill Winthrop, this is a subpoena for all of the records related to your trading accounts and any trading accounts of your clients who invested in NBCI. We demand that you turn the records over to us immediately."

Averill leaned back in his chair and smirked defiantly. "You can't have them."

"I'm not fooling around, Mr. Winthrop." Reggie came just short of baring his teeth. "I represent FINRA. Comply with the subpoena immediately or we will go before a judge and have you held in contempt of court!"

Averill said even more smugly, "Like I said the first time. You can't have them."

FINRA was the independent regulator for all securities firms. It disciplined bad boy brokers and firms who ignored federal securities laws. If there was a scent of insider trading, if there was unusual options trading, FINRA would be calling. If FINRA didn't get you, the SEC would.

The FINRA lawyer waved the subpoena at Averill and said angrily, "This is your last and final warning. We demand your records, NOW!"

Averill leaned forward, clasped his hands on his desk, and said obnoxiously, "This is my last and final answer. Like I said the first time, you can't have them.

"You see that conference room over there. The wimpy guy in the corner chair is Wallace T. Blankenship. He's from the New Jersey Bureau of Securities. He has first dibs on my files.

"You see the guy next to him. That's Carter from the Internal Revenue Service. Their subpoena is for all of our wire records and stock activity in NBCI. He gets them next.

"So, if you wait your turn, you can have the records after New Jersey and the IRS are finished. But I have a feeling it's going to be a long wait. Also, there isn't room for four of you. Two at most. Would you care for a Starbucks? I'm going over to Ben's."

Reggie refused to be ruffled. He said, "Fine. I'll sit with them and work out a sharing agreement. But first, where does Tektikker sit?"

Averill acted coyly. "There's only one person in this office, and that's me. Who's Tektikker?"

Reggie smiled. "Okay, if you say so, Barry. But I've got a feeling there's multiple personalities hanging around here. I mean, Averill isn't your real name, is it?"

"You already know Averill is a nickname," he said curtly. "My birth name is on your subpoena. It's Barry Winthrop."

"I've heard of nicknames like Billy or Joey or Buffy," scoffed Reggie, "but never have I heard anyone adopt a nickname from an esteemed figure like Averill Harriman. Why not call yourself Abraham Lincoln Winthrop while you're at it?"

"Funny, wise guy," snorted Averill. "What? You didn't steal your nickname from Reginald Owen, the guy who played Scrooge? Or did you take it from the Yankee's own Mr. October, Reggie Jackson? Cut me a break. You want coffee or not?"

Marvin entered the offices and saw the unexpected crowd. He reached Averill and said, "I'll take care of this. Do me a favor and clear out of here for a couple of hours while I try to smooth over the situation."

It was just the escape he needed. In two hours, he could visit at least ten local branches. That would add another $100,000 of cash to the money sitting at home. Tomorrow, he'd go "shopping" in the 47th Street diamond district.

CHAPTER 300

OCTOBER 25, 2013

On Friday morning, Averill kept his door closed and drew the shades while the subpoena party pored over his records. Marvin was politely answering questions and occasionally knocked on Averill's door to get an explanation.

Averill needed two hours to get into and out of the City. Merchants in the diamond district headed home early on Friday evenings to observe the Sabbath. The guests were watching his movements closely, particularly Reggie.

At 11:30 AM, Averill could see the investigators poring over documents in the conference room. He locked his office and quietly walked down an empty hallway and out the front door.

The trip took longer than expected. When he returned to the office, he kept the diamonds in his jacket pocket. He couldn't leave them in the car; thieves loved to steal BMWs.

He had to kill two hours within earshot of Marvin, who was upset with him for leaving the office during a time of crisis. He shut the door to escape the angry stare. He marked time by searching the web. The seconds were passing at an excruciatingly slow pace.

The plan was to pick up Misty at Ben's and head to the land of the Caribs. Two more trips and he'd be done. At 4:00 PM, his cell phone vibrated with a message. It was the signal: Go! Now! There was no time left. He had to move fast.

He signed into his bank's web site and initiated five separate wires to five different locations in the Cayman Islands. He cleaned out the domestic account except for a small balance. He erased his Internet file history and cookies, then turned on the smiley face screensaver.

At 4:15 PM, he stood and left the office, grabbing his jacket but leaving his laptop. He walked past his car in the parking lot. Instead of heading south on Washington Avenue, he walked east on Clinton. He passed the Clinton Avenue Reformed Church and turned on James Street. This was a parallel but slightly longer route to Ben's.

CHAPTER 301

OCTOBER 25

A woman and six men wearing FBI vinyl windbreakers burst through the front door of the LMNOP branch office. Marvin rushed to the small entrance area. The agents had their hands on the butts of their holstered weapons.

Three of the agents briskly pushed Marvin aside and began searching the offices. The group leader said, "FBI. I'm special agent Clarence Wyzlewski. We're here to arrest Barry Winthrop."

Marvin was shocked. "On what charges?"

"Money laundering and wire fraud, for starters," Clarence said.

The woman behind Clarence spoke up. "I'm Alisa Weiss with the SEC. You can add securities fraud, front-running client's trades, insider trading, and selling unregistered securities to the list. We have three of his cronies under arrest. Two have fled."

An agent returned from searching Averill's office and said, "He's gone. His computer is still on, but he's definitely not in the building."

"We'll get him," Clarence said. "He can't get very far without his car. The airports are locked down. He can't leave the country. Let's go find his accomplice."

The agents left the building running to the three parked black vehicles, a Crown Victoria and two Ford Explorer SUVs. Marvin, in all his years of experience dealing with and defending his brokers from accusation of some really bad behavior, had never witnessed such a high profile raid.

CHAPTER 302

OCTOBER 25

Misty impatiently waited in Ben's. Averill was late and wasn't answering his cell phone, which was very unusual. He usually came like a puppy dog when she called.

She had packed light for the weekend trip to the Cayman Islands. She had to make room for the bundles of cash stuffed in the bottom of a canvas beach tote. She hid a handful of two-carat diamonds in her makeup bag. Averill would give her the rest of the loot on their way to Teterboro Airport.

The agents walked into Ben's with their hands on their holsters. Diners backed away. Misty smelled trouble and started walking to the kitchen exit. Clarence hurried to catch her and grabbed her arm. "Mrs. Giovanna Francella Winthrop, you're under arrest…"

Misty pulled her arm away. The diamonds spilled from her makeup bag onto the floor. Alisa was close behind and grabbed the canvas bag. She pulled out a stack of fifties and said, "Going somewhere, Mrs. Winthrop?"

The crowd at Ben's craned their necks to witness the drama. Cell phone cameras flashed. The CNN news crew had been buying coffee at Ben's after taping uninteresting mop-up stories about NBCI. The cameraman flipped on his Alexa and recorded the action. He panned the faces in the crowd. This might be the new network's biggest scoop in a year.

A junior agent placed handcuffs on Misty while another scooped up the spilled diamonds.

Misty protested frantically, "I don't know what you're talking about. Those aren't mine. Averill handed me that bag at lunch."

Clarence grabbed Misty's arm and started escorting her from Ben's. "Speaking of which, your husband disappeared a half hour ago. Any idea where he might be?"

Alisa opened Misty's cellphone and pressed redial. Averill's phone was "out of service". She said, "Mrs. Winthrop, if you have anything to tell us about his whereabouts, now's the time to save yourself."

Misty couldn't wipe the stream of tears with her handcuffed wrists. "I don't know," she bawled. "We were supposed to leave from Teterboro in an hour. He…"

"We already knew that. What's his alternate escape route? He left his car in the lot. His cell phone is shut off. He didn't return to your house. Where is he?"

"I DON'T KNOW!" Misty wailed. They led her from the deli. Diners looked on in shock.

JB sidled up to Ben at the cash register. "What? No jukebox song to commemorate this special occasion? Perhaps a little Steve Miller and *Take the Money and Run*?"

Ben shook his head and said, "How tasteless, JB."

He paused until a customer had passed, then whispered, "However, if I were to play a song, and I'm not saying I would, it would be *Jailhouse Rock*. I mean, she did get married in the Elvis Chapel."

CHAPTER 303

OCTOBER 31, 2013

The October expiration of the CRAB contract was a nonevent. After all of the buildup, all of the suspense, the meteoric rise, the near catastrophic fall, October CRAB futures settled at $160 a pound. It wasn't anywhere near the high of $299 when the Hedge Fund Grannies had sold their crop. Nonetheless, people's lawns, or once-lawns, now farmlands, were still worth a pretty penny.

Macedonia Vulture Partners owned a fully-hedged, CRAB arbitrage with a locked-in profit of $60 million, $30 per pound on two million pounds. They had presold the futures for delivery next June and August. They owned the Buckstown silo and its million pounds of CRAB. They stored another million pounds in NBCI's warehouse. By August 2014, Macedonia would be out of the CRAB business, a one-year, extremely profitable trade.

Macedonia's partners never dirtied their hands with soil or fertilizer. They hadn't operated a Crab Baby nor even heard of it. They believed they simply performed the very important role of a middleman who made markets more efficient by providing liquidity to disrupted markets – for a handsome profit.

CHAPTER 304

NOVEMBER 4, 2013

The televisions at Ben's Deli were locked onto CNN for ten days running. Diners watched the footage again and again. Diamonds spilling on the floor. A Federal agent holding up a stack of bills. Misty wailing and unable to dry her tears as she was handcuffed and led away. The shocked looks of bystanders. "Hey, that's me on TV! How do I look?" cracked Bart the pessimist.

The story never got old. Averill was a mastermind. He vanished into thin air while being closely watched by the Feds. He had been seen walking two blocks from Ben's on Williams Street, but had never arrived at the deli.

How did he escape? Did he have a second car? None were registered in his name. Did he have an accomplice, perhaps someone with a Gulfstream? Did he have an alias? Many, it turns out. And the FBI wasn't the only group chasing Averill. More than a couple of unsavory characters who had lost money in Averill's deals would be looking for him, too. The CNN reporter speculated, "Maybe he really was a genius."

The airports had been closely watched. The borders had been warned. There was a good chance he was still in the country. He had lots of cash, but you couldn't even rent a hotel room in America without a credit card. A quick corporate search uncovered the handful of companies owned by Averill with robber baron names. Their millions were long gone, too.

Surely they would find him. And CNN would keep reporting to you every day until they did, or until a better story became available.

Misty quickly had to make a decision. Her husband had abandoned her; she was six months pregnant and caught holding the goods. Her court-appointed counsel was an inexperienced trial lawyer. If she had any money, she could have hired a better attorney who'd negotiate her freedom in exchange for valuable information. The district attorney gave her 24 hours to cooperate. She gave him the names of all of Averill's bank accounts in the Cayman Islands. The key account name was Tuxedo Investments, but there were many others.

Most people hiding money in the Cayman Islands think they're safe from the Feds, but the government has the right to seize deposits if the offshore bank was a branch of a U. S. bank. So much for bank secrecy laws. The IRS obtained a court order and looked at the accounts. All were empty. The cash had been wired to dozens of accounts in as many countries on October 18, a Friday. It was the day before Averill had visited the Islands alone.

They opened the safety deposit box. The diamonds were missing. The bank registry showed Averill had visited on Saturday.

It would take the IRS time to get court orders to seize the remaining accounts, but they were already convinced the money had left town. Averill had discovered the wonders of Internet banking and opened accounts in countries most people had never even heard of. He had wired and rewired the cash all over the world from a Starbucks Wi-Fi in Hackensack New Jersey. The IRS and Treasury Department would follow the trail, but they already knew the money was long gone.

Two years ago, Averill was known as a sleazy, penny ante con artist. Recently, a few people made money with him and declared him a financial genius. He directed the ascent of NBCI to a major public company worth over $600 million. Today, he was the great swindler, the king of criminal deviousness. He was diabolical. He was infamous. He was notorious. And *POOF!* He was gone.

CHAPTER 305

NOVEMBER 4

Allie stood behind the register watching Misty's arrest for the umpteenth time on CNN news. Marty sat in the back room pretending to do his homework. She was sure he was texting his friends, which was how most kids spent their study hours until the pressure to finish an assignment became past critical.

Jake's was required to deliver the default notice in person, no faxes or emails allowed. It would be any day now. Allie understood JB's plan. Delay Jake's with legal actions. Launch media attacks to stall them. Go to church and pray for a miracle.

In the end, she saw little hope. She was late making the $300,000 payment, and Jake's had the right to declare a default. The documents said so. She'd have to declare bankruptcy. Jake's would take ownership of the store and sell it to repay the debt. There was no way she could cover the shortfall even if she stretched every vendor payment. And there was another $135,000 due in December and May, although the goods hadn't yet been delivered. It was hopeless. She smelled doom.

She saw two men peering through the display window. She ran to the back and said, "Marty, hurry! It's Operation Grannie-Gate! Go man the register. Stall these guys until Auntie Ev gets here. And make sure the cameras are running!"

"Stop worrying, Ma," Marty said confidently. "I've got this covered." He moved to the front register and opened his school book.

Jake's diminutive lawyer and a burly companion entered Allie's store. The lawyer was wearing a medium gray suit, size 36 at most. The big guy was wearing a Jake's security guard uniform.

The suit offered an official-looking thick envelope to Marty and said, "I'm Mark Broadbent, general counsel of Jake's Seed & Supply. I'm hereby serving this notice of default. Please sign this…"

Marty raised his hands. "Whoa, dude! I'm not signin' for nuttin'. I'm just a kid. Can't you tell? You gotta wait till my mom gets back from the bank."

"Look, sonny," the lawyer said with slight condescension, "you're allowed to sign. You're a family member. There's no reason to delay this. It's inevitable."

"Call me sonny again and I'll show you what's inevitable, bud." Marty leaned forward menacingly. "Now wait until my mom returns and deliver it yourself."

Marty was a teenager, but had added a few inches and ten pounds of muscle weightlifting during the last year. He had learned the tough guy façade from Bruce Willis movies.

Allie called Auntie Ev and Chris Bloom from the storeroom. Ev was going to play the instigator. Chris was going to record the story for *The Bergenfield Valley News.*

Ev and a handful of Hedge Fund Grannies were ten doors away shopping at The Dangerous Knitter. They scurried down Washington Avenue and saw the two men at the counter as they entered Allie's store. Auntie Ev grabbed an item from the shelf and moved near the register. Chris arrived and began to browse the sandpaper section.

The lawyer wasn't the big imposing district attorney type. In fact, he rarely saw action at the front lines. Most of his dreary sixty-hour workweek was spent drafting vendor agreements and filing UCCs and security agreements. Today was his chance to get out of the office and in on the action.

Allie walked to the cash register, flipped her hair and asked innocently, "May I help you?"

The attorney was losing his patience. He had stood for five minutes waiting to serve the notice. Now the store was filled with a bunch of gray hairs. He said, "You know why I'm here. Jake's Seed & Supply is serving you with this. . ."

At that moment, Auntie Ev pushed to the counter, cut in front of the lawyer, and said, "You'll have to wait, sonny. Customers first."

Broadbent appeared flustered. He was surrounded. Most companies use a big and strong process server for a good reason. They were intimidating. He said assertively, "Your purchase will have to wait. I'm doing something important here."

He edged in front of Auntie Ev, who acted offended and said, "Well, I never…"

Broadbent said to Allie, "Let's make this simple so I can be on my way. Here's a notice of default and also a suit to take over the assets of Allie's Hardware and Home Center."

Auntie Ev was a full five-foot, ten inches, a tough Jersey gal. She stepped in front of the attorney once again. The other Grannies surrounded the lawyer. The security guard stood to the side. He was way out of his jurisdiction. Until today, he'd been working the gate to Jake's employee parking lot. He had no intention of breaking up a fight between a lawyer and a bunch of grandmas.

Ev said with the scolding tone of a schoolteacher, "You impertinent little boy. Let me see what's so important."

She put on the reading glasses suspended around her neck; then reached out and bent the edge of the notice so she could read it. The lawyer ripped the papers from her grasp and held them high over his head. He shouted, "Don't touch these!"

Auntie Ev cowered with her hands to protect her face as if she were in fear of being hit. The other Grannies stood in the background with mouths open and looks of shock. Chris snapped photos with the newspaper's camera. Broadbent put his hand up to block his face from the camera. It only made it appear worse. The store video cameras also recorded the event.

Broadbent was seething. The Grannies were clucking their displeasure. Allie waited a minute until the scene calmed down. Chris continued to take flash photos, which were further irritating the lawyer.

Allie said innocently, "It's okay, Ev. I'll take your purchase after the man leaves. Mr. Broadbent, you should be nicer to the people who shop here and help me pay my bills. This may be how Jake's treats its customers, but we do things a little differently."

Allie signed the receipt, and the Jake's advanced forces retreated out the front door. Marty turned off the cameras and grabbed the tapes. The Grannies took turns patting Auntie Ev on the back. "You were wonderful." "You were magnificent!" "You were gran-ificent!"

CHAPTER 306

NOVEMBER 4

Allie opened the envelope and read the default notice and the separate lawsuit. The notice simply demanded payment in full, even for goods that hadn't yet been shipped. Penalty interest of eighteen percent would accrue until payment was made.

The lawsuit claimed the weed killer collateral was worthless, and demanded that the court accelerate their right to sell the store immediately to the highest bidder. It wanted the keys to the door.

Allie had 15 days from the date of the notice to cure the default. In two weeks, she would be out of business and flat broke.

CHAPTER 307

NOVEMBER 5, 2013

The sight of Auntie Ev cowering from the evil lawyer was priceless. Marty captured the ten-second highlight and created a "gif". It was an endless loop: lawyer threatens with raised hand; Ev cowers; lawyer raises hand; Ev cowers…

Marty posted the gif on Tumblr and iFunny:). He edited the video into a ninety-second highlight reel and posted it on YouTube. He posted the links on his Facebook page and invited his 1,000+ FB friends to share the video with their friends. And share, they did. It went viral. The video was titled, "JAKE'S ATTORNEY ASSAULTS THE ELDERLY!"

Below the link on FB was a message: "Please Google Jake's Seed & Supply and click on the video. Make this atrocity the #1 searched item. Thx!"

It was a cause, a movement, an uprising, a revolution! Thousands of teens clicked and moved the video up the Google rankings. By dinnertime, the newly famous video had moved to number two on the search list. Number one was an advertisement sponsored by Jake's:

Buy Jake's seed and fertilizer. We love our customers! Get expert help from our friendly customer service representatives!

Chris rushed the new issue of *The Bergenfield Valley News* to press and delivered it to shops around town. A large, bold headline shouted:

JAKE'S ATTORNEY THREATENS AUNTIE EV!

Underneath the headline was a full-page picture of Auntie Ev striking her defensive pose. The paper would be on every doorstep by noon tomorrow.

CHAPTER 308

Bret filed Allie's response to Jake's suit at the Hackensack County Courthouse. There was no reason to deny the default had occurred. Allie hadn't paid the amount due. Instead, the suit demanded that Jake's follow the exact letter of the financing statement. Jake's had to attempt to sell the weed killer inventory first and obtain fair value before it could move against the common stock of Allie's store.

Jake's had already claimed in its suit that the collateral had become worthless. Bret argued that Jake's must conduct an auction to determine the fair value. It could take a month or more to sell assuming they could even find an auctioneer willing to try to sell it. If the court agreed, it would give Allie time.

Bret kept the real zinger in his hip pocket. Jake's didn't have a valid perfected security interest in Allie's common stock. If Jake's knew they had a problem, they hadn't brought it up. Bret didn't want to warn them of the issue so they could sue to fix the problem.

The Uniform Commercial Code set out specific rules to perfect liens. For an asset like inventory, the lender filed a UCC form with the county or state. But with cash or capital stock, it was different. The only way to perfect such a security interest was through possession. Jake's had to physically hold the certificate if and when Allie filed for bankruptcy.

For a final touch, Bret added a claim that Jake's Seed & Supply had caused irreparable harm to Allie's Hardware and Home Center and diminished the value of the estate. Remarkably, the amount of the claim was slightly more than the amount Allie owed.

Bret also filed for a restraining order against Mark Broadbent who had physically threatened one of Allie's customers. He appeared in front of a judge, who saw the photograph and gave temporary protection from the lawyer. It was a shallow victory. Anyone else from Jake's could still enter the store.

Judge Brunero set a preliminary hearing date on the remaining issues in two weeks on November 18. He glared at Bret and said, "If you've got discovery and interrogatories, get them done quickly. I'm not letting the value of the collateral diminish through stalling tactics, Mr. Wolfman."

JB greeted Bret as he exited the courthouse and handed him a copy of the morning edition of *The Record*. On the front page of the business section was the picture of a cowering Auntie Ev and the headline,

JAKE'S LAWYER THREATENS LOCAL SHOPPER!

JB said, "I'm buddies with the editor-in-chief. I owe him one."

Bret said, "I'm afraid that won't be enough. The judge just fast-tracked the hearing. He wants no part of a long trial. To him, this is just an argument over simple security interests. I'm afraid we don't have much time."

CHAPTER 309

NOVEMBER 8, 2013

Oxford Collar got its wish. The ISDA Credit Determinations Committee posted an announcement on its website in response to OC's request. The website links read:

Question: Has a credit event occurred with respect to the Bergenfield Industrial Revenue Bond resulting from the failure to have readily available audited financial statements at all times?

Question: Has a credit event occurred with respect to the Bergenfield Industrial Revenue Bond resulting from the temporary trading halt on NBCI common stock?

Question: Has a Bankruptcy Credit Event occurred with respect to NBCI?

In less than two weeks, the governing body over credit default swaps would make their ruling. Hounds Tooth Insurance, Bergenfield and NBCI would learn their fate.

CHAPTER 310

NOVEMBER 10, 2013

On Saturday, *The New York Times* ran a story in its business section about the new breed of leveraged buyout artists. Were these young MBAs destroying companies after they were acquired?

The article claimed that in the infancy of the LBO era, prominent buyers like William E. Simon and Ray Chambers nurtured and grew businesses. Today, the financial quants were running things with a calculator. Everything was measured in immediate financial satisfaction. Things like strategy, employee motivation, incentive systems, and human resources were given lip service. Only the bottom line mattered.

The article provided a case history on the buyout of Jake's Seed & Supply. Wall Street financial engineers were now running a merchandising company by the numbers. They were losing sales. Jake's had an itchy trigger finger and quickly sued its customers barely days after a payment had gone past due. There was no talk of working with the customer through their financial distress. *Pay us or we sue!* was their apparent motto.

A photograph of Allie with her shoulder length hair wearing a store apron headed the second page of the article. She was quoted in the interview:

> *I was a little naïve at the time. I thought the problem would solve itself. This buyout group had just acquired Jake's. It had to make a sales number to keep their banks happy. I had an open purchase order to buy this inventory that we now know cannot be sold. I got bullied into agreeing to take the goods. Now it's up to the courts to decide. But I do believe it's truly unfair that Jake's has already presold my store at below market prices to a related party and will make money on my misfortune. My son Marty and I will be fine. I'll just go back to nursing, but without any savings and a much bigger mortgage. I'll be like a lot of Americans today.*

Allie's web site received a staggering number of hits. Everyone wanted to know about the saga. The viral war was escalating, but Allie was facing a court date less than ten days away.

CHAPTER 311

NOVEMBER 12, 2013

Stephane, Steven and Albert sat with Eva at the Pierre conference room table. "This is absurd!" Eva said to her team. "NBCI collapsed, we scared Buckstown from the business, and we still can't kill this CRAB fever. The price is going back up. It was $222 last night. It's time to put a dagger in its heart. Stephane, tell me there's hope on the horizon."

"It's not going to happen on the trading floor," said Stephane in a discouraged tone. "There's nothing but euphoria down there. Traders are talking $300 by next June. When

Macedonia executed the arbitrage, they ended any chance to bring this price back to earth."

"Even though there's nobody to take the product except us. Albert, tell me how the Netherlands testing is going. I need good news," pleaded Eva.

Albert stood at full attention and removed his glasses. "Vell, zie tests haf been very gute, but ve need more time to be sure. Zere is no vay I can give full assurance zat ve are ready to use zis new plant. Vile most of zie Niederlande plants are much better zan zie Jersey plants, some are not so gute. It eez very important to determine zie cause of zis variance! I must haf at least a year."

Steven was argumentative and impatient. "Albert, the plants are better. You just had a few bad samples. But even if they're only just as good, we'd be ahead financially."

"Vell, zhey are vay better zan just as gute," Albert said proudly, "but I cannot guarantee ve vill be two times better."

Eva usually tolerated Albert's long analyses, but she was short of time. "Enough! We need to put a stop to this now. We need a kill shot. Even if it's not a perfect solution, this will send a message to these ridiculous speculators. These financial institutions have no business investing in our supply chain. We need to control our own destiny. No more of this crazy Wall Street behavior driving up our prices.

"Steven, the documents are ready to sign. Fly to Rotterdam tonight and close the deal. A thousand acres at $15,000 per acre. We'll use some of Stephane's trading profits to pay for it. In one way, we're lucky. This land would have cost twice as much a few years ago.

"Gentlemen, it looks like we have to go back into the farming business if we want to control our destiny. Steven, stay here for a minute. Everyone else, back to work!"

After Albert and Stephane left the conference room, Eva said, "Tell me about this woman in *The New York Times*. It says she may be losing her business."

Steven's eyebrows shot up in surprise. "You mean Allie Bertrand? She gave up a nursing career and bought the hardware store in Bergenfield from Johnny Carrera. He's now the president of NBCI. They used to call him Johnny True Value, but I've heard a few more appropriate names for him." Steven rolled his eyes. "When she bought the store, she became obligated to buy the weed killer designed specifically to kill the local crabgrass. You can imagine what happened to sales after this CRAB business took over.

"I'm afraid she only has days before she loses the store. It's a shame. A single mom with a teenage boy."

"Bertrand? Sounds French," said Eva. Her interest in the storeowner's fate appeared to be more than a passing curiosity to Steven. "Is there any way to help her? Maybe you can speak to Gilbert. We haven't talked with him in a while."

"Gilbert? He's gone," said Steven. "I heard he came into a lot of money and moved to Florida."

Eva considered this and said, "Well, just keep an eye on Ms. Bertrand's situation. If we beat this CRAB market, maybe she can too."

Steven said, "I don't believe there's enough time, but I'll see what I can do."

CHAPTER 312

NOVEMBER 14, 2013

Gilbert had indeed moved to Florida. After hiring a broker and selling the remaining homes, he had brought the real estate business of Bergen Development to a successful close.

Howie and Johnny had begged back in when they realized how much work it took to maintain and sell the houses on their own. Gilbert refused readmission. Once the deeds on the houses had transferred hands, he wanted no trace of ownership back to the partnership. Besides, Johnny and Howie had been a pain in the ass throughout the entire process.

Gilbert returned to town to distribute the winnings. At a small closing party in Vinnie's basement, Gilbert stood on the stage with a glass of chardonnay in one hand and a fistful of envelopes in the other. He handed a distribution check of $1.3 million dollars each to Trudy, Chris, Vinnie, and another to Vinnie for his crew.

"To say this was a successful venture would be a huge understatement." Gilbert beamed proudly at his partners. "We had our moments, but I couldn't have wished for better partners and such an incredible string of good fortune. I want to thank Vinnie especially for working so hard during this time. Without him, we'd never have done as well.

"Enjoy your profits and make sure they last. We may never see each other again. Let me restate that. I'd love to see you all in Florida someday, but I hope I've seen the last of Johnny and Howie. David Elliot, too!"

Everyone laughed at the shared sentiment.

Gilbert cautioned, "Everyone, keep your heads low. Enjoy yourself, but don't get flashy. Buy a BMW or Lexus, not a Ferrari. No excessive gambling in Atlantic City. And for Pete's sakes, don't ever tell anyone how big the check was and how we did this."

In its infancy, the partners had modest but real expectations. Buy twenty or thirty homes at distressed prices. Collect some rents to pay the bills until the Pierre news moved the market. Then sell the homes and everyone makes a hundred grand, two hundred at most. Instead, the market went berserk after the China deal. The partners got smart and sold out at the right time.

David Elliot hadn't been invited to the closing party. Gilbert had found a way to take a little out of David's hide. Over a year ago, David had held up the closing and greedily demanded three units. Gilbert had no choice at the time but to agree. Later, Gilbert quietly amended the LLC agreement and increased each of his "good" partners' shares to six units, double the ownership of David.

Gilbert wasn't worried about payback from David, Howie or Johnny. Gil hadn't broken any laws. He was certain of it. The town council members may or may not have violated some rules. In a few months, the two-year statute of limitations will have run out and they could stop worrying about it. David was most at risk, not just for bad behavior, but for a few felonies, too. But he was the most cunning and least likely to get caught.

Gilbert had used a chunk of his $9 million managing partner share of profits to buy a condo on the Florida Intracoastal Waterway. He lived a hundred-yard stroll from the Jupiter Pointe Marina. Gilbert bought his dream boat, a Jupiter 41 with triple 350 horse-power Yamaha V-8 outboards. He added a complete set of bells and whistles: a fish finder, depth finder, an outrigger and a tuna tower.

As the party ended, everyone shook hands and gave hugs. Vinnie jumped on the stage and said, "Hey everybody! Listen up! Dis is da last time I'm gonna say it. Pay your effin' taxes! And after you do dat, wipe da place clean. Dat means you get rid of any papers, notes, tapes, pictures, anything dat could be used as evidence. And get rid of da investment company too, however you do dat."

Trudy said with a laugh, "Gil, tell me you're not gonna miss Vinnie?"

Vinnie put his arm around Gilbert and said, "Wha? You kiddin' me? Gilbert and I are fishin' for marlin dis winter. Right, Gil baby?"

CHAPTER 313

NOVEMBER 15, 2013

It had been a grueling ten-hour session rehashing all of the permutations and combinations of the ISDA decision. There was a reasonable chance that the DCs would determine a credit event had incurred. If so, the credit default swaps would be triggered, Hounds Tooth would shell out nearly $4 billion, and Bergenfield would be called on its $200 million guarantee. There was little else that could be done. Their fate was in the hands of a three-man committee.

An exhausted Suzanne Pettigrew joined her husband for a late dinner at Le Bernardin on 51st Street, a stone's throw from the 21 Club. Just because Bergenfield was going bankrupt didn't mean she had to suffer.

While sipping on a glass of Margaux, her phone vibrated. It was Lofton Meriwether from Mexican Chartered Bank. She walked outside the restaurant to take the call.

"Are you calling for the casket viewing hours?" Suzanne said sarcastically. "We haven't officially died yet."

"No, dear," Lofton said smoothly. "I'm your personal corporate defibrillator. You have an ISDA hearing on Tuesday. I have a proposal. Can you get your team together tonight?"

Bankers have no respect for the clock. They call meetings at any time of the day or night if it meant getting a deal done. Christmas Eve, Passover, July Fourth. It doesn't matter.

Suzanne tried to round up the team, but finally convinced Lofton that Saturday morning at NBCI headquarters was the earliest they could all gather.

CHAPTER 314

NOVEMBER 16, 2013

At 8:00 AM on Saturday morning, Lofton Meriwether, in casual dress-up attire, stood at the head of the table with two young financial analysts to his side. The large screen television showed the first slide of his presentation: "Project Nehru".

Luckily NBCI had a large board room. Sitting on one side of the table were Suzanne, Mayor Alvarez, Arthur Sterling, and Jack Barlowitz. Archibald Smith and a team of three Hounds Tooth lawyers sat opposite. Justin had brought bagels and a three-gallon coffee urn for the table.

"Excuse the Nehru pun," said Lofton, "but my senior banker insisted. This deal will tear the collar off Oxford if we do this quickly. For those of you too young to remember, Nehru jackets have no collar. Hence, our project name."

Arthur grew impatient. "Enough! Show us your proposal. In seventy-two hours, this could be over."

The analyst advanced the presentation to the next slide. Lofton aimed his laser pointer at the TV screen. "There are approximately $4 billion dollars of credit default swaps betting for or against your financial health. There are only $200 million dollars of bonds outstanding. That means $3.8 billion of swaps are naked. They're pure bets on your bankruptcy."

"Yes, yes, we know all of that," said an irritated Hector. "What are you proposing that will stop me from writing a check on our guarantee?"

The next slide was a listing of 50 investors and amounts, the names hidden in code. Lofton aimed his laser pointer down through the list. He said, "This is very complicated and we only have the weekend to get it done. We know who owns three-quarters of your bonds. They're parked right where we sold them. During this last week, we acquired an option to buy their bonds at twenty points above the current price. That's $130 million of bonds. NBCI has $50 million of collateral sitting in escrow. We just need $20 million to fill the gap.

"If you buy back the bonds we control, you can call the rest at 105 percent. The ISDA can't rule that a credit event occurred if the bonds are called before their meeting. The credit default swaps will go to zero. Hounds Tooth escapes Armageddon. The town's guarantee goes away."

"Let me guess how you're coming up with the money to buy out your clients at fifty-five cents on the dollar? Bergenfield sells it CDS holdings in the market, right?" Suzanne smiled knowingly.

"Right," said Lofton, "If you sell your CDS, you'll net $81 million. However, you're still short."

"Why wouldn't the town just keep the money?" asked Hector.

"Because if you don't do this deal, the town will have to write a check for $70 million instead," Lofton said matter-of-factly. "Don't worry. You'll get the money eventually.

"Next, NBCI calls the remaining bonds at the end of the day on Monday. That gives my traders less than ten hours to sell everyone's swaps and execute our option agreements with the bond holders.

"At 105, you need $74 million to buy the remaining bonds. You pay the first $50 million with the money NBCI has in escrow. That leaves you $24 million short. Bergenfield gives you the surplus from the CDS sales. Hounds Tooth contributes $5 million so they don't have to pay $4 billion. After our fee, you'll still be short $16 million."

"It's a little outrageous that your bank is charging an $8 million dollar fee to get us out of the mess they put us in, don't you think?" said the mayor incredulously.

"Hector, we acted as a banker after your town council approved the deal," Lofton argued. "You and one other member were the only persons against the proposal. Now we're trying to fix this and make it right. But we don't do this type of work for free."

Justin said coolly, "So we're short. Who's writing a check for $16 million?"

"You've all signed confidentiality agreements," warned Lofton, "so you absolutely cannot trade on this information or disclose it to anyone. Pierre Beauty Products is your benefactor."

There was a collective "What?" "Huh?" and looks of bewilderment.

"That's right, Pierre," said Lofton. "They cannot make their product profitably at the current price of CRAB. They've found another place to grow the product. They're also unhappy with the chemical concentration in the plants in the outer perimeter of your town. They intend to reduce the circle of eligible suppliers.

"They're going to announce their new supply source in a few days. They'll also give notice to those homeowners where they will continue to buy, but only at their option price of $25 dollars per pound. This will effectively kill the CRAB commodity market.

"However, they still need NBCI's facility to process and store the plants. They have a proposal for you, Hector. If you approve this deal, they'll pay you the value of your CDS over five years. They'll also pay for a landscaping solution to improve the appearance of the 2,000 homes still growing crabgrass. And they'll also build a new entrance to NBCI's plant.

"Arthur, you have a part in this, too. Pierre has been buying NBCI's shares in the market since Thursday. They have ten days to announce their ownership. The way your stock is trading, they may accumulate as much as thirty or forty percent. A lot of people who own NBCI are selling their shares to get their tax loss.

"Pierre wants to buy NBCI and take it private. They think this has been a terribly bad exercise. After they buy whatever they can in the open market, they want to tender for the shares they don't own at $4.00 per share. They require an agreement with NBCI that if the tender is unsuccessful, NBCI will sell them sufficient shares to increase their ownership above 51 percent so they control the company."

Suzanne said while scribbling on a notepad, "If I got the numbers right, Pierre is getting a $200 million plant for $81 million it will owe to the town plus about $34 million they're paying for NBCI stock. That's a far cry from the $600 million market cap it had in September. But that doesn't matter to us, Hector. We're getting out of a $200 million guarantee and eventually we'll add a lot of money to our bank account."

Hector said with confidence, "I'll get the town council to approve this today if Hounds Tooth and NBCI approve their parts in the transaction."

"Don't count on Johnny being at the meeting. He quit NBCI yesterday and left town. Everyone else is available. I already checked," said Suzanne.

Archibald Smith said emotionlessly, "Hounds Tooth is prepared to write the check."

Arthur said, "I'll call a board meeting today. NBCI has no business being a public company under this scenario. It's better if Pierre owns it. NBCI has a $50 million D&O policy to cover shareholder suits. That's should be enough, but I don't want my board exposed personally after this ends. Pierre has to indemnify us. Jack, what's your opinion?"

Jack tapped a pencil on his notepad while in deep thought, then said, "It would be hard to decline this deal, Arthur. NBCI is getting out from under a $200 million debt.

You're facing class action lawsuits over the stock price collapse. You now have knowledge that your business is going to decline by half. I'd say you're fully protected under the business judgment rule."

Lofton clasped his hands together and said, "So we have a deal?"

The parties mumbled their reluctant assents.

CHAPTER 315

NOVEMBER 18, 2013

Love was in the air. JB looked around the table and thought he heard Decker and Catherine cooing. The guy was near broke yet still had time for romance. He watched Bret and Allie look like they were about to breach the lawyer-client relationship. Lately they had been spending their mornings in quiet little chats.

JB was losing his audience. Who was going to laugh at his jokes? Michael? He barked, "Snap out of it lovebirds. Mr. Blech could walk in here any minute."

The crowd had been huddling around Catherine and Decker for the last few months to shield them from the bank. Catherine held Decker's hand under the table. Decker announced, "We're getting married. Catherine's divorce date was moved up and we're going to tie the knot. You'll all be invited of course."

Congratulations went around the table. JB said, "Aren't you forgetting something? You need to get past this auction first. If Blech hears you're getting married, he'll suspect something's up."

Decker was giddy. JB couldn't burst his balloon. Decker cackled, "The heck with Blech. Hey, that rhymes. We should make tee shirts."

Gavin said, "Decker, We're glad for you. We all wish you a happy and prosperous life. Starting next year. For now, listen to JB. You need to pull off this auction first."

Catherine said, "Decker, it doesn't matter what day we get married. Listen to JB and Gavin. We have a lot of work to do, and we can plan a nicer wedding with the extra time."

"Okay, spoil sports," Decker said. "I'll wait. But I'm still making anti-Blech tee shirts. The Heck with Blech! And they'll be black, like Blech's dark soul."

JB thought he heard a distinctive chirping from Allie and Bret. They were goners.

CHAPTER 316

Four hours later, Bret walked into Allie's store wearing his Perry Mason courtroom suit. He wasn't smiling.

"I'm sorry, Allie," said Bret sadly. "Judge Brunero ruled against you. He didn't want to hear any of our arguments. He called them stalling tactics."

Allie looked around the store. It was empty on Monday mornings as usual. A pallet of Jake's useless weed killer sat in the corner covered in dust.

"It's okay, Bret," Allie said with resignation. "I wasn't countin' on a miracle. So much for viral attacks on YouTube, huh? So Jake's doesn't even hafta sell the inventory first?"

"No, I'm afraid not," Bret said. "Brunero bought their argument that the inventory was worthless. They still have to prove they already purchased the December shipment, but I doubt they would lie about it in court. If you don't pay them today, you lose the store."

"There's really only one thing to do," Allie said. "I'm headin' into Newark tomorrow and filing bankruptcy. I already hired a lawyer to draft the papers. I hope you don't mind I used someone else. I didn't wanna trouble you anymore. At least the bankruptcy filing will protect Michael's bank."

"Allie, please let me lend you the money," pleaded Bret. "You only need to make this payment to Jake's. It'll give you another month to find a solution to the December problem."

Allie said sincerely, "Bret, you're so sweet, but this is my problem. I just can't take your money. I couldn't live with myself. Not payin' Jake's is okay, but not payin' you, no can do."

"Just think about it. Please don't file until we at least talk again." He touched Allie's shoulder and walked from the store.

CHAPTER 317

NOVEMBER 19, 2013

Tuesday morning was chaotic. Lofton's bank was command central. Mexican Charter had underestimated the effort to execute all of the bond repurchases and credit default swap trades by the end of trading on Monday. The ISDA meeting would start in six hours. NBCI couldn't call the bonds until it was sure Bergenfield had sold the swaps to pay for it. Hounds Tooth refused to wire their contribution unless the bonds had been called. Pierre's money sat in escrow ready to be pulled if the deal collapsed.

Lofton, Suzanne, Jack, Arthur and Archibald kept the conference call line open. A trader yelled in the background, "Jalapeno is done! Five million. Book it." Traders had funny nicknames for their clients. Jalapeno could be a moniker for a trading account located near Mexico. Or perhaps the client just had a spicy female treasurer.

Jack's associate paced outside the ISDA offices awaiting instructions to deliver the redemption notice. Executives from Oxford Collar sat across the lobby greedily awaiting the decision that would earn them a billion plus dollars.

At 1:35 PM, Lofton read the final tally. "Bergenfield's swap sales are $6 million short." There was stunned silence on the conference phone.

CHAPTER 318

NOVEMBER 19

Allie had turned off her phone. Bret ran up the steps to the U. S. Bankruptcy Court at the Martin Luther King, Jr. Federal Building in Newark. He had parked his car illegally on Walnut Street.

He stopped and did a double take. Allie was in the arms of a man near the entrance. "What's up peeps? I didn't realize the marriage bureau was in this building," Bret said sarcastically. He wore the look of a hurt puppy dog.

Allie let go of the man. "Don't be silly, Bret. If you think that was a romantic embrace, well, really." Allie gave a flirtatious flip of hair.

"You guys should know each other. Bret, this is Steven from Pierre Beauty Products. He used to visit Ben's back in the day. Steven came here with a message not to file bankruptcy, but he won't tell me why. I'm afraid he's too late. I filed the bankruptcy papers ten minutes ago."

"Why does Pierre care about your bankruptcy filing?" asked Bret. "And furthermore, what's their big secret?"

Steven said cryptically, "My boss asked me to watch out for Allie. Until the news becomes public, I can't tell you. I guess it no longer matters if she filed already."

"Yes it does matter," said Bret. He hid his jealousy in a mask of lawyer arrogance. "Allie can walk back in and rescind the filing. It's done all the time."

"Bret, I'm done with this business," Allie said in exasperation. "All of this Wall Street big finance. Stock and commodity prices goin' crazy. A bunch of creeps at an LBO firm tryin' to steal my store. I'm forced to buy a junk chemical. Crabgrass is worth billions. This whole world is upside down. Isn't anyone legit? Isn't anyone honest?

"I can't stand it anymore. I've had enough. I'm just a hometown girl who tried to start a business and lost my life savings. I learned my lesson. It's time for me and Marty to start over."

"Just stay here for twenty minutes," Steven pleaded. "If something doesn't happen by 2:00 PM, you can walk away. In the meantime, let me buy you guys coffee."

Bret glared at Steven, the guy who had his arm around Allie moments before. He looked up and saw the meter maid in front of his illegally parked car. He ran toward her and yelled, "Hey stop! Don't ticket me. I'll move it."

Allie laughed. "He's so funny and doesn't even know it. I think he's jealous of you, Steven. Don't tell him you're married just yet. And I'll give you until two o'clock. Then you can tell me the big secret. It's not like I hafta get back to a jam-packed store or anythin'."

CHAPTER 319

NOVEMBER 19

Lofton said in a commanding voice, "In twenty minutes, this deal falls apart. NBCI has no money to help. It's either Hounds Tooth or Bergenfield. You both have a lot to lose. Talk it out. And you better hope my associate's phone doesn't die in the meantime. Which one of you is putting up the money?"

The minutes ticked away. Suzanne argued, "Hounds Tooth should put up the difference. You're going to lose billions if this doesn't happen. Besides, we can fight the guarantee. And we have the money in the bank to do it." Bergenfield was feeling rich now that it had sold its CDS.

Archibald spoke in his calm British accent. "It's Bergenfield's problem. The reason we're short is because you only sold the swaps for $75 million. It doesn't really matter. I don't have the authority to increase our payment. There's no way I can get approval from the London offices at this late hour."

They were both blowing smoke and everyone on the call knew it. Archie was a top executive at Hounds Tooth, the senior executive for all of North America. There was no way he didn't have the authority to add a few million to save a few billion. Bergenfield wasn't going the distance either.

Suzanne bluffed convincingly. She hung up the phone. At 1:50 PM, minutes before the ISDA hearing was to begin, Archibald flinched. "Call her back. We'll put up $4 million dollars if the town puts up the rest."

Suzanne was on a separate phone line with Jack. She agreed to the payment. Jack called his associate who ran into the ISDA meeting and handed the chair the redemption notice. A second associate handed the notice to the sales clerk at *The Bond Buyer*. It would be published in today's issue. The ISDA committee cancelled the hearing.

Jack filed an 8-K with the SEC. NBCI was redeeming their bonds at 105. Every $1,000 bond would receive a payment of $1,050. The filing noted that it had already purchased $130 million of bonds in the open market.

The market swallowed a gigantic $4 billion gulp of CDS losses. The money evaporated in seconds. The bid for the credit default swaps disappeared. Everyone lost money: colleges, universities, not-for-profit institutions, state pension funds, union pension funds, hedge funds, and day traders. The last speculators in the door who bought at 6,800 bips lost the most. They had bet $680,000 per million dollars of bonds that NBCI would default. It was technically classified as an investment loss, but in reality it was just gambling.

Minutes later, Pierre Beauty Products filed a Form 13D and Form 3 with the SEC announcing it had acquired a 53% stake in NBCI over the prior ten days. Separately, it announced its plan to tender for the remaining shares at $4.00 per share. NBCI announced its board had approved the sale to Pierre.

It was a whirlwind of market moving news. The NASDAQ halted trading on NBCI's stock to let the market absorb the information. Oxford's lawyers pleaded with the ISDA to allow the hearing.

You could almost hear Oxford Collar's Florida executives scream "AAARGH!" from Florida up Route 95, through the Holland Tunnel into the City and down the West Side Highway.

CHAPTER 320

NOVEMBER 19

Bret sat with Steven and Allie at the Starbucks on MLK Boulevard. It was deadline time. Steven slid the promised cup of coffee to Bret who pushed it aside and warily eyed his competition.

Steven logged onto the Starbucks' Wi-Fi and turned the iPad screen toward Allie. "There it is!" he proclaimed. "Pierre just announced it bought NBCI. They found another source for CRAB, and they're cutting back purchases in town to less than 2,000 homes. Everyone else will need your crabgrass killer again. I think you're back in business."

"Oh my gosh!" Allie said with both hands to her face. "Bret, isn't it too late? I mean, I missed the payment to Jakes. I defaulted already, right?"

"Allie, you just happen to know a great lawyer, and that would be me," Bret said as he jumped to his feet. "First let's get your bankruptcy filing back. I have a plan."

"Of course you have a plan." Allie stood, threw her arms around Bret's neck, and kicked one heel in the air. After squeezing him tight, Allie laughed and said, "Now this, Bret, is a romantic embrace!"

Bret's face became flushed but he held her tightly around the waist. Steven looked away slightly embarrassed.

Allie pulled from Bret's grasp, smoothed his suit lapels and straightened his tie. She said smiling, "Look at the two of you. You're both turning red!"

CHAPTER 321

NOVEMBER 19

Late in the day, Pierre made a series of announcements in the press and in SEC filings. First, it formally announced it was limiting its purchases of crabgrass to an area making up less than a quarter of the town of Bergenfield. It claimed the product concentration diminished greatly in the outer reaches. Second, it announced that it would no longer accept product purchased on the MERC. It would continue direct purchases like it had started two years ago, but only if the customer had an option contract with Pierre.

It further announced that it had acquired a thousand acres of low-lying tidal lands in the Netherlands that were suitable to grow the crabgrass. Tests had already proved a higher chemical density. And last, it said it would work with Bergenfield to improve the front yards of homes affected by the upheaval.

The market price for CRAB went limit down $20 per pound. No contracts exchanged hands. No one wanted to own this dead dog.

CHAPTER 322

NOVEMBER 20, 2013

At the end of the day, Allie wired the $300,000 payment to Jake's with the help of a little loan from Bret. Technically, it was a day late, but surely Jake's would overlook the slight discrepancy.

Allie signed a note and financing agreement with Bret and handed him the store's stock certificate as collateral. Perfecting its security interest in the store was something Jake's had neglected to do. Now, Jake's would have to fight Bret in court to gain a superior position.

At 10:00 AM, Manuel Velasquez entered Allie's store. His truck was parked by the loading dock. Manuel had cleverly adopted the O'Hara Landscaping name for marketing reasons. People just assumed Irish workers had green thumbs even though his entire workforce was Puerto and Costa Rican.

"Buenos dias, Senor Velasquez," said Allie in formal high school Spanish. "Como esta usted?"

"Hola, Senorita," smiled Manuel using the more casual form of greeting. "I have a big order for you. I need a thousand bags of your weed killer on thirty-day payment terms until Pierre Beauty Products pays me. Can you do this?"

Allie nearly fell off her chair.

Manuel said, "Pierre agreed to landscape the homes near the center of town to hide the crabgrass from street view. I have the exclusive contract. And 6,000 homes are about to re-sod their yards. My phone is off the hook. I can't handle all of the business. It'll take a year to do all the work. I may have to buy a bulldozer!"

After processing the order, Allie called Bret. "You're not going to believe this. I just sold a thousand bags of weed killer. I can pay you back in a…"

"Hold on, Allie," Bret said gloomily. "I have bad news. Jake's is going back to court today. They claim you were late and didn't include the December and May defaulted amounts. They claim they already own your store. I'm heading back to court at 2:00 PM."

"I'm coming with you," Allie declared. "I want the judge to look me in the eye when he rules against me."

CHAPTER 323

NOVEMBER 20

Macon Stone, Jake's attorney from the firm of Stone & Bradshaw, stood at the plaintiff's table. Superior Court Judge Brunero was becoming impatient. The black-robed judge peered over his reading glasses. "Mr. Stone, has your client purchased the 12,000 bags of weed killer for the next delivery to Miss Bertrand? It's a simple question I ask."

Judge Brunero sat behind the bench raised two feet above the courtroom floor. The Great Seal of New Jersey and the state flag hung on the wall behind him. It was the afternoon before Thanksgiving, and the judge was noticeably irritated he'd been called to court for this supposed urgent matter. So was the rest of the courtroom staff.

Bret had smelled a rat. He didn't have proof, just a lot of suspicion. There was no way Jake's would have ordered the next batch of chemicals knowing the state of the CRAB market. And Jake's didn't manufacture the chemical; they were just the middle man. Tooty's Chemicals, a company in Elizabeth, New Jersey made it.

Bret had tried to speak to Tooty's earlier. The president refused to take the call. His secretary had become very flustered. They were clearly hiding something.

"I believe my client has properly ordered the product," said Macon still standing.

"Objection!" said a calm and confident Bret. "Your Honor, we believe the plaintiff should be required to provide definitive proof that they've ordered and become legally obligated to take the product. The alleged debt of my client depends on this fact. Saying 'I believe' is not the same as stating for the record they ordered it."

Judge Brunero peered down at Bret and looked at the attractive, well-dressed woman defendant sitting beside him. She was polite, respectful and attentive. She certainly didn't look like a professional deadbeat.

"Sustained. I have to agree with you, counselor." The judge sounded more irritated by the minute. "Mr. Stone, you have one hour to provide me documentary proof that a debt has been incurred. You wanted a decision on this 'urgent' matter today. Decision you shall have. We will reconvene at 3:00 PM."

Elsewhere in America, turkey fixings were being prepared for tomorrow's feast. Wine was being poured for early guests from out of town.

CHAPTER 324

NOVEMBER 20

Macon Stone didn't need an hour to answer. Jake's general counsel had been sitting behind him in the gallery. When the judge reappeared, Macon stood and said, "I have conferred with my client. They have assured me that they have issued a purchase request with the vendor. In their view, they have satisfied the court's definition of an obligation."

Bret rose from his seat. "Objection, Your Honor. A purchase request is customarily not a legal binding obligation. It has to be a purchase order. Before you rule, Your Honor, I request that an executive officer of Tooty's Chemicals be called to testify."

"Sustained," the judge said as he gave a silent head nod to Bret. It meant for him to calm down. "Let me see the document, Mr. Stone. I don't need someone from Tooty's to be present to see if an obligation has occurred."

Judge Brunero ordered a fifteen minute recess and retired to his chambers. When he returned, he said, "This isn't a signed document. Do you have a signed copy?"

Macon kept his cool and said, "No, Your Honor. As a general business practice, they do not sign purchase requests, only purchase orders."

Allie was on the edge of her chair. This could go either way. Judge Brunero was undecided. Bret stood again. "May we approach the bench?"

Judge Brunero waved them forward. Bret and Macon stood in front. Bret argued, "Your Honor, rather than delay the hearing, may I suggest we call the chemical company and just ask them if they have a binding agreement to deliver goods."

"It's a little unconventional," said the judge. "I prefer to have them in court and sworn in. If the plaintiff's counsel doesn't object…"

Macon snapped, "We do object, Your Honor. The defense is trying to stall the proceedings, and…"

Jake's general counsel had made a slight noise from behind the railing and nodded to Macon to meet with him.

"Your Honor, may I have a few minutes to confer with my client?"

"Anything, Mr. Stone, to get me home to my family in time for the holiday," the judge said, exasperated.

Macon leaned over the railing and whispered with Jake's general counsel. The conversation was agitated and went beyond the requested time. Judge Brunero hammered his gavel. "Mr. Stone! I need a response."

Macon tried to recover his composure as he returned to the bench. "Your Honor, I've been advised that Jake's has withdrawn its claim that a purchase request created a binding obligation. The debt is not yet owed.

"However, we still contend that the payment was late and a default has occurred. We demand that the defendant turn over the stock certificate and ownership of the store to Jake's so it can sell the collateral."

"Denied," ordered Judge Brunero. "You've incurred no damages if she paid you, even if it was a day late. I'll go further, counsel. Your client has been less than honest with this court. You tried to deceive me today. I am awarding defendant court fees and costs. I will listen to their claim for damages. Mr. Wolfman, speak with your client."

Bret huddled with Allie for a quick two minutes. He stood and said, "Your Honor, my client is not looking for monetary damages. She believes the plaintiff would fight the award on appeal, and she would get nothing but a case of exhaustion. Instead, Allie… Ms. Bertrand simply requests that you consider freeing her from any further obligations to do business with Jake's including any obligation to purchase this chemical. She prefers to deal directly with the manufacturer."

Judge Brunero slammed his gavel. "So awarded. And Mr. Stone, if you want to fight my ruling, I will ask the district attorney to investigate the shenanigans behind this phony debt you claimed. Is that understood?"

Macon lowered his head and shuffled his papers into his briefcase. Jake's general counsel slipped out the courtroom doors.

Allie and Bret left the courtroom quickly. Outside in the hallway, she grabbed Bret, spun him around, threw her arms around his neck, and planted a long, deep kiss. Bret dropped his briefcase to the floor and returned the embrace. She broke away for a breath and said, "You're my hero."

JB walked through the front door of the courthouse and caught the end of the embrace. "What'd I miss? I mean except when he kissed you. I saw that. It's about time, Bret."

Allie laughed. "He didn't kiss me. I kissed him!"

CHAPTER 325

NOVEMBER 23, 2013

Saturday morning was unusually busy at Ben's. College students home for the holiday lined up for jumbo-sized, super-caffeinated, dark roast Starbucks. Manuel's landscapers were loading up on carbs for a big day of pulling weeds. A groggy Bret fumbled for change at the register to pay for his scrambled eggs and sausage special and two oversized black coffees.

"Congratulations!" said Ben with a huge smile. "Breakfast is free as long as you don't take a dessert."

"Thanks, Ben. We were lucky to get an understanding judge," Bret said as he playfully ignored Ben's conditions for a free meal and placed a cheese Danish on his tray. "It was a team…"

"Not the court case, dum-dum!" laughed Ben. "You finally kissed her!"

Bret turned slightly red and clucked his tongue as he turned and carried his tray to the board table. Allie was telling taller and taller tales about Bret's dramatic courtroom victory. He was Clarence Darrow and Perry Mason combined. He was better than Joe Pesci in *My Cousin Vinny*! JB, Michael, Decker and Panama Blonde sat gripped in the details.

Bret joined the table and said, pretending embarrassment, "JB, did you tell the whole town? Can't a man have any privacy?"

Allie laughed and flipped her hair. "It's okay, Bret. I won't kiss you again in public. You're just no fun now that you won a big court case."

Bret raised his hands in protest. "No, no. You can kiss me. That part I liked. I just don't want the whole town making a federal case out of it."

"C'mon Bret," teased Allie. "It was a special occasion. I'm not goin' to go all Misty on you and give you lap dances at breakfast." She threw down her napkin and jumped up. "I gotta go. Manuel is coming over to pick up a truckload of weed killer. Can you believe it?"

"Give me a sec. I'm coming with you," said Bret as he wolfed down a forkful of eggs. He put a lid on his coffee and followed Allie out the door.

CHAPTER 326

NOVEMBER 23

Bret and Allie walked past Fitness II on Washington Avenue where the early crowd was already working up a sweat on a row of elliptical machines. There was a commotion across the street in front of Allie's store. A small line of customers had formed in front. More people were hurrying across the street.

Allie walked to the loading dock at the rear of the store where Manuel and his landscaping crew were waiting by the O'Hara pickup truck.

Manuel greeted her and said as she unlocked the trailer, "Senorita, there's a rumor you are running out of weed killer. I think I might be responsible. I told my cousins that Pierre was paying us to buy the supplies, but the rumor spread that we're buying *all* of your inventory. I hope I didn't cause a problem?"

"No problemo, Manuel!" laughed Allie as she and Bret snuck into the rear entrance. "So that's why there's all of these people at my door. We better keep the store lights off till I figure out what to do."

They heard a loud knocking on the loading dock door. Allie took a quick peek and saw Auntie Ev and two other gray hairs. Ev pushed her way in and said, "Us girls were over at The Dangerous Knitter. We looked out the window and saw the crowd forming – figured you could use some sales help today. I have experience with big crowds. I worked a booth at Woodstock, you know. Don't ask what we sold. Ha-ha!"

"Bret can be the muscle. We'll handle the customers. You stay at the register. How much do you charge for a bag?"

"Fifty dollars, but that was two years ago," Allie said. "I was thinking about lowering the price to get rid of this stuff. I never want to see it again."

"Dearie, you just don't understand merchandising," Ev said with a playful *tsk*. She grabbed a white cardboard sale sign and a red magic marker from behind the counter and started writing. "The price is now $65 a bag. It's on sale for $55 if they buy a minimum of four. Where's your adorable son? We need him to carry bags to the cars."

Marty Bertrand, ear buds hanging from his neck and wearing jeans, sneakers and an untucked flowered Hawaiian shirt, walked through the loading dock doors. His eyes were half shut. He had been watching horror movies with his teen friends until three in the morning.

Marty said with his latest surfer accent, "Greetings! Dudes, *Psycho II* was awesome. So much better than numero uno. *The Shining* airs tonight at midnight. Hey, who's throwin' the rave?"

Allie laughed. Marty the surfer who now studied and went to classes was so much better than last year's model, Mr. Constantly in Trouble. "Marty, call three of your buddies and see if they want to work for the day. Ten bucks an hour and free lunch."

Marty began texting his friends. "Money and a luau! Double awesome! I'll start the dragnet."

Ev commanded her Grannies: "Open the doors. We have customers to serve!"

As Allie proudly walked to the front door, Marty turned to Bret and said, "Dude, you kissed my mom!"

Bret fumbled, "I-I'm sorry Marty, but…"

"Whoa, no, man. I ain't complainin'. It's about time, ya know?" He playfully elbowed Bret in the ribs.

By mid-morning, the rush had slowed to a steady stream. A woman wearing a tan trench coat, a head scarf and large dark designer glasses slipped into the store. She was about as inconspicuous as the Duchess of Cambridge strolling into a Home Depot.

"Can I help you?" Allie said looking her up and down.

"I'm so sorry to intrude during your busy time, Ms. Bertrand. I heard about your lovely store and was in the neighborhood," said the mysterious lady with the slightest French accent.

Allie studied her more closely. "I'm sorry, have we met before?"

"No, we haven't. My name is Eva Marteen. I work for Pierre Beauty Products. We ordered some chemicals through O'Hara. I was just checking. Oh, what am I saying? I don't care about the order. I really just wanted to see how you are. From the crowd of customers, you look like you're doing just fine."

"You're Steven's boss!" Allie said excitedly as she shook Eva's hand. "I'm so glad to meet you. Please call me Allie. You know, if it weren't for Steven, I would've lost the store."

A few feet away, Bret let out a low, jealous groan. "What happened to this morning? I heard you tell everyone at Ben's that your brilliant lawyer saved the day."

Allie turned to Bret and gave him a teasingly scolding look. "Stop it, jealous boy!"

She returned to Eva and winked. "I'm sorry, Ms. Marteen. He's my new boyfriend. I haven't properly trained him yet."

Eva looked Bret up and down. "Please call me Eva. Well, he's cute at least. Perhaps he's coachable," she said and they shared a laugh. "You know, we do have something in common. You and I were the only ones who hated this CRAB price escalation. I'm glad things worked out. We French girls have to stick together."

Allie grinned. "Bertrand is French, but I'm also part Irish and German."

"Don't tell anyone," Eva whispered, "So am I!"

Eva gave Allie an air kiss to each cheek. Bret and Marty leaned on the counter. They stared at Eva's long legs and swinging hips as she left the store.

"Hey, both of you, eyes back on your work!" Allie joked. She gave the Allie hair flip and tended to the next customer.

Bret elbowed Marty lightly in the ribs. "Did you hear that? Frenchie thinks I'm cute."

CHAPTER 327

DECEMBER 4, 2013

The SEC had opened an investigation into NBCI's role in the collapse of its stock price. They were particularly interested in the company's connections to Averill, fugitive from justice. NBCI's officers and directors spent days answering the SEC's long list of written questions. It was just a matter of time before they would be interrogated in person.

Lawyers copied computer and phone records and sent them to Washington. Johnny lay low at his Lavallette bungalow. The Feds were homing in on a series of his phone calls to Averill since May. They hadn't yet inquired about the checks from Tuxedo Investments to JTV Enterprises. Could they possibly connect JTV to Johnny? If they ever found Averill, Johnny's goose would be cooked.

The FBI led David Elliot away in handcuffs from First Second Third Bank. According to a STCK-TV report, the local banker had begun cooperating with the FBI after they traced the wires he had processed for Averill. Other arrests were expected.

Three small-time stockbrokers were perp-walked from their New York offices, raincoats raised to shield their faces from the media cameras. Two more were on the lamb. The Feds had traced Averill's wire to Mickey Muirfield. He folded like a cheap suit and ratted out The Sticky Five in exchange for limited immunity. The international ring members with aliases like CRABBabyDoc and PabloEsCRABar most likely would never be caught.

CHAPTER 328

DECEMBER 4

The price of CRAB had been in a free fall. There would be no dead-cat bounce. No buyers could be found at any price. After plunging limit down nine consecutive days, it settled at Pierre's quoted price of $25 per pound. There was still doubt that anyone could sell at the new posted price. Pierre had refused to buy any product through the commodities exchange.

It had been a zero sum game. You either won or you lost – everything. The few home-owners who had sold their 2014 production would be the last to make money trading CRAB through the commodity exchange.

At its highest point in September, the combined value of three years of open CRAB contracts was worth an astounding $17 billion. Nine thousand homes. Six hundred pounds of CRAB production each year. Contracts three years into the future. The peak price at $299 a pound. And open contracts equal to four times the estimated delivery. It had evapo-rated overnight.

The open contracts for June, August and October 2014 delivery were still owned by spec-ulators. During October, Macedonia Vulture Partners had sold two million pounds for 2014 delivery. Investors were now stuck holding the other end of the trade. Lawsuits were certain.

Fortunately for Den-Ken, they were closer to the action and had foreseen the coming collapse. They had sold most of the contracts owned by their partnerships before the wild finish. Den prepared a delisting application for CRAB. The MERC would consider it in their next meeting.

Mollusk Marine College on the lovely shore of North California was one of a hundred institutions who a year ago had bravely declared commodities to be a valid investment class. Unfortunately for Mollusk, its treasurer had bet the current year's operating funds on a complex Wall Street derivative. The instrument was composed of CRAB, NBCI credit default swaps, NBCI stock, treasury bond interest rate futures, a Chinese Yuan currency future, and the POO ETF. It was a bullish triple-leveraged bet constructed for maximum returns. Mollusk lost everything. Over students' protests, the doors were closed and the professors were fired. There would be no tuition refunds.

The largest of the country's educational institutions absorbed the CRAB investment losses and went about their business of educating the future leaders of the world. Portfolio returns would be lower. The annual plea for alumni donations would never mention CRAB's role in the schools' drastic need for increased contributions.

Luckily for the state and union pension funds, they didn't have to explain the line item loss to anyone.

Pierre hammered a twenty-second nail into the coffin. It announced a licensing and export agreement with the shampoo and toothpaste industries. They would make the degreaser chemical available to everyone at a fair price. They even cut a deal with Xie Development Company. They agreed to develop a crabgrass farm in China and supply them the chemical, but refused to transfer the technology. Xie would finance the entire project.

Pierre filed its tender offer for NBCI. In twenty days, it would be official.

The POO ETF liquidated its holdings and delisted its shares. The CRAB commodity was worthless. The Bergenfield bonds had been redeemed. The ROOT shares were about to disappear. The only thing of value left in POO was the shares of Pierre common stock.

Life was returning to normal in Bergenfield and on Wall Street.

CHAPTER 329

DECEMBER 7, 2013

The stage had been set. At 7:30 AM on Saturday morning, Mike the Cop picked up JB, Bret and Gavin at Ben's Deli and drove to Decker's home. A large "AUCTION TODAY!" sign pointed to the driveway entrance. There were several small moving vans near the garage that belonged to antique dealers. A hundred folding chairs were arranged on the lawn within four roped areas. The premiere seats were cordoned with a sign: "RESERVED FOR ANTIQUE INDUSTRY PROFESSIONALS".

It was chilly, but not the viciously cold weather JB had ordered. It bordered on freezing, and rain or sleet or snow could fall any minute from the gray clouds. Catherine Mulcahy tested a microphone on Decker's wraparound porch. A Paramus Auction Company sign hung behind her.

JB wanted the atmosphere to be uninviting except to the invited. There's no rule in auction law that required a comfortable seat for every bidder. He didn't want happy warm bidders unless they were part of the plan.

He had two objectives. First, he wanted to make sure the antiques and collectibles sold for enough money to keep the bank happy. JB had cut a deal with Blech's bosses at Starship Financing Group. Decker would receive 10% of asset sales in excess of $100,000. Otherwise, no auction. Blech was not happy.

JB was wishfully optimistic they would hit the number. Decker needed the money plus much more to start his new life. Catherine had recruited the best antique dealers from New Hope, Pennsylvania and placed large ads in the local papers.

The second and trickier part was to get the professional bidders to leave satisfied after Lots 1-21 were sold. With the New Hope crowd gone, JB's team would bid for the family heirlooms and paintings for Decker held in Lot 22. JB was advancing the money to buy the items, but only against what Decker earned from the auction.

JB had a devious plan to add money to Decker's bidding war chest. Would Blech cooperate by acting his usual greedy, miserable, suspicious, misanthropic self? JB had assured Catherine he would do nothing illegal. He wouldn't, but he was certain Blech would.

JB had recruited a legion of Bergenfield High School alumni and local townspeople to fill the audience. Section A was managed by Steve Stavrou and occupied by a few dozen former Bergenfield wrestlers and other athletes. Steve had wrestled heavyweight in 1970, the final year of Sal Cascio's hugely successful reign as wrestling coach. Sal's teams had won 65 straight matches in the sixties. Steve wrestled in the unlimited class in an era when heavyweights rarely weighed much more than two hundred pounds.

Section B was occupied by fifty alumni members of the Bergenfield Band and managed by Nancy, the blonde former lead majorette. Every year, 150 students intensely practiced and performed together as one of the most famous high school bands in the country. It had led the Macy's Thanksgiving Day parade and played halftime at the annual Jets-Giants football game. They were the pride of Bergenfield.

Section C seats were taken by civic and church leaders and Decker's closest friends. Mr. Blech and his banking assistant had been seated with the New Hope crowd up front in Section D. Latecomers were restricted to the standing-room-only section behind the ropes.

Mr. Blech browsed the area suspiciously. His radar was up. He smelled a bidding ring. Angela, Frank, Elsie, Robert, Joanne and Al represented six of the largest dealers in the area. He followed them and listened closely as they inspected the items one last time.

The bidding started promptly at 8:00 AM. The temperature wasn't warming. Auntie Ev manned the hot cocoa stand. Next to the stand was a wood burning stove for bidders to warm their hands. A cord of wood sat next to the stove.

The first item for bid was an antique low-boy. It was in perfect shape and appeared to be from the early 1800s. An experienced dealer would consider the item valuable and very saleable along Ferry Street in New Hope. Stavrou called out an opening bid of $250. Blech looked incensed. But a chorus of buyers followed with higher offers until the price reached $1,200.

Catherine hit the gavel and boomed, "Sold! Please proceed to the payment booth. Remember everyone, cash only today. The bank is not accepting any credit cards or checks. Their rules."

Al sent his assistant to pay for the transaction with a stack of $100 dollar bills. Blech checked his asset list. It was difficult to connect the assets on the list with the items being sold. The bank tags had been removed for the auction. But at this price, his attitude improved. An actual sale had occurred.

Providing warmth wasn't in the design of the standard-issue black trench coats worn by Mr. Blech and his associate. On a normal day, they rarely had to walk farther than a block or two to get from their cars to the office.

After several items had sold, and the auction appeared to be progressing, Blech crossed the yard and ordered a hot cocoa. Auntie Ev handed him a steaming cup. "That'll be five dollars," she said sweetly.

"That's ridiculous. That drink is worth at most a dollar. I won't pay it!" complained Blech vilely.

Ev grabbed the cup back from his hand. "I'm sorry, but the proceeds are going to the local church charities to buy toys at Christmas. There are a lot of unemployed workers in town. You should know. If you don't want to help the underprivileged, that's your choice. Happy Holidays!"

Blech mumbled an unpleasantry under his breath and moved to the wood burning stove to warm his hands. Ev admonished him, "The stove is for customers who buy cocoa, sir."

Blech left grumbling. He'd rather freeze than pay five bucks for a cup of cocoa.

The second item placed on the stand was a five-foot-tall floor lamp. The bronze finish had cracked; this was clearly not an antique. The same item might cost $150 new at Capital Lighting. Russ Dewitt, all six-foot-five inches of him, yelled from the wrestling section, "I bid two bits!"

Catherine restrained her laughter. "We only accept bids in U.S. paper currency, sir."

"Okay, I bid a buck and not a farthing more this cold Christmas season," Russ said with a huge smile.

The crowd laughed uproariously. The bankers stood numb. The auction would go on forever if they sold every little item. A breeze picked up. It was getting colder, not warmer. The sun would not be rising on this dreary December Pearl Harbor day.

The auction progressed for the next half hour. A mix of antique-looking furniture sold for anywhere from $300 to $1,500 apiece. A large oil painting caught the crowd's attention. Bidders in the SRO crowd battled it out until Catherine finally hit the gavel. "Sold for $7,000 to the gentleman in the cashmere overcoat. Pay the cashier!"

The iron was hot. Sales were moving more quickly. Bidder interest grew despite the increasing chill. Catherine's assistant brought out a weathered slant desk. New Hope Elsie offered $100. A voice from the BHS band section said $150. The bidding slowed considerably. Catherine chanted, "We have $325, going once, going twice and…"

Mr. Blech stood and tried to see the item from his seat. If it was on the asset list, it had to be worth at least a thousand. He wasn't letting anything sell cheap.

Blech had cash and was prepared to use it to keep the bidding honest. He wasn't going to be outmaneuvered by a band of shills. He nodded to his assistant who raised his hand and bid $650, double the prior offer. The crowd went "Oooh!" Mr. Belcher sat smugly and stared defiantly at his enemies in the crowd.

JB nodded to the athletic supporters. Eddie, the former BHS quarterback, bid $700. The bank jumped to $725. New Hope Elsie lost interest and turned away to chat with her neighbors. Others entered the fray. After a frenzy of increasing bids, Blech's aide yelled, "$1,500 dollars."

"Too rich for me!" Eddie declared and sat down.

"Sold, to the man in the black raincoat without a lining!" cried Catherine.

The bank had become the proud owner of an antique. Blech thought, *Fine, but at least that'll keep them honest. The bank can always resell that overpriced junk at another auction.*

The bidding continued. The New Hope group wouldn't pay top dollar for antique furniture. They had to buy at a good price to allow a 100% markup. The paintings were getting the highest bids. Catherine finally realized who was bidding on the paintings from the SRO section. She had known them from her days at Sotheby's.

In his concerted effort to "keep the bids honest", Blech and his bank were now the owners of a dozen assorted bulky items. He had plenty of cash to buy more. He had rented a small U-Haul truck to carry away purchased items at the end of the day, but he was already over capacity.

By 11:00 AM, Catherine was near the end of lot 21. Paintings alone had sold for $150,000. The artwork bidders were leaving the area. Decker whispered to JB, "That small drawing they just sold is a Winslow. It's not one of his better-known pieces, but it's still probably worth twenty-five grand. This is really sad."

It was getting colder. The New Hope contingent rose to leave and much of the crowd followed. The Starship bankers hovered with the remaining crowd. Catherine called out, "We are taking a thirty-minute recess."

A small group moved to the stove stand to keep warm.

CHAPTER 330

JB, Decker, Gavin and Bret met with Catherine out of sight. She said, "The total sales are about $350,000. Blech paid about $25,000 for your other items. JB, wherever did you find that stuff? They almost look like antiques."

JB laughed. "I bought those years ago at a closeout when they were liquidating a store in the mall. I guess they aged well in my garage."

"Anyway," said Catherine, "they aren't part of the liquidation estate. Thanks to your generosity, Decker gets that money.

"That means the bank will get about $325,000 less our fee of $32,000. They'll pay Decker about $22,000 next week. So far, so good. Starship should be happy until they discover your fakes. My boss will be pleasantly surprised."

JB said, "Decker, I suggest that you put the $22,000 into the bank. Let's just use the profits from today to bid on your family items. Besides, that's all the cash I have on me. Catherine, do you think $25,000 is a fair price for the last lot?"

"It's fair, but will Mr. Blech think so? The items have sentimental value to Decker, but they don't have any historical significance. So you have to decide. You can make an offer, but I'd need the bank's approval. Blech doesn't look like the kind and generous sort. He is also felling pretty proud of the auction, but isn't happy that he spent so much money to keep the auction honest."

"Or dishonest," interjected JB. "Technically, his bids were from an illegal ring. I don't believe he'll okay the sale if he knows Decker will get the goods. Now that he has all this money, he's no longer concerned with getting a fair price. He wants to inflict harm. He wants Decker to hurt.

"But you can try. You have a phone bidding line. Announce that you have an offer and see if he blinks."

Catherine returned to the podium and hit the gavel. "We have a bid of $25,000 for the remaining items in Lot 22. We need a bank representative who has the authority to approve the sale."

Mr. Blech was shivering and a deep red from the cold. When he heard the offer, he looked surprised. He had thought the auction was nearly over without much of anything of value left to sell. He looked at the auction sheet and realized buried at the bottom was a group of items described as assorted family pieces. Blech smelled a rat which was barely distinguishable from his own rodent odor.

He rushed to the front and demanded, "I want to inspect the remaining items."

Catherine maintained her composure. "We'll have another fifteen minute break. Everyone, please enjoy the cocoa on the house."

Everyone had had enough to drink, but no one was leaving the area. Steve and Maureen Stavrou rose from their seats to chat with Auntie Ev near the fire. A small BHS alumni meeting formed at the cocoa stand. Jim Bacci, Dave Saraceno, Jimmy Maguire, Rachel Skorstad Menna, Diane Engstrum Irwin and Jay Kernis stood together in the cold and waited for the drama to unfold.

Mr. Blech walked with Catherine behind the partition and looked around. He harrumphed, "So you thought you could pull a fast one on me. Buying for a favorite customer at a cheap price? Or are they for your boyfriend?

"Surprised? I have my spies. If Decker wants any of this stuff, he has to buy it at auction and outbid me. We'll see how much fee he has left after this next round."

"There'll be no Merry Christmas for this deadbeat. He still owes the bank money, and I want every last cent. Put them up for bid individually. And I want the cash from this auction turned over to me here and now."

"As you wish, Mr. Blech," said Catherine cheerlessly. Blech was having no part of JB's scheme to salvage a few items for Decker. "I'll need you to sign a release of claims which authorizes us to proceed and turn down this offer. It'll take a minute to print. My last advice to you is that these items won't sell for $25,000 if sold individually. This is a very good offer.

"As for the cash, we deliver that to the bank at their prearranged location in an armored car. We have no authority to hand the money to you here. This is the procedure. I don't write the rules, I just follow them."

Mr. Blech chewed on the small end of his cigar. He scanned the beginning of the agreement and quickly signed the second page.

CHAPTER 331

DECEMBER 7

The crowd had dwindled to about fifty buyers. Some were members of JB's legion. Some were bargain hunters still looking for a steal.

JB distributed the $25,000 in hard cash to his team. But how much did Blech have left to bid against them? It couldn't be a lot. It must be why Blech wanted Catherine to hand him the proceeds. Luckily, she had refused to fork over the money.

"Next, we have a late nineteenth century pine dining table. The starting bid is $250," Catherine said unenthusiastically into the microphone. Decker had eaten on this table his whole life. It wasn't a valuable antique.

One of JB's army bid the minimum. Somebody immediately bid $350. He had to be a Blech plant. The prices escalated, but JB gave the cutoff sign at a $1,200. He had lost the first bid. This wasn't going to be easy.

JB grabbed Buyout, who had just arrived, and said, "I want you to tail that guy and his buddy to the cash table. See how much money he has on him."

Buyout wore a Burberry's trench coat, but unlike the bankers, his had a lining to keep him warm. Minutes later, he reported, "I heard them talking. Must be ten grand between the two of them."

They could salvage some things, but at what price? JB and Decker began to triage, deciding which items were worth saving. Fifteen minutes and five items later, JB thought, *This is a war of attrition. I've spent half of the money and only have a few pieces of bedroom furniture. Blech has to be near the end of his cash. Does he have a printing press back there?*

At the halfway point, JB was out of resources. He decided to reserve the last $10,000 for two special items that Decker told him were the most important.

Blech saw resignation across the lawn. The next item offered was a beautiful antique china closet. It had been valued at $7,500 in the bank appraisal. This was one of Decker's special items. The bidding opened at $1,000. The banker raised to $1,500.

JB had seconds to make a decision. He was running out of money. If he bid any higher, he wouldn't have enough left for the painting of Decker's great grandmother. It may not be a valuable piece of artwork, but to Decker it was important. And if it was important to Decker, Blech was going to make him pay for it big time.

Blech smelled blood. He yelled, "$2,500 dollars." The small remaining crowd gasped. They had participated in a four-hour epic battle of good vs. evil. Evil was winning.

JB retreated from the bidding. He sat and looked despondent.

A woman's voice from the near-empty town section firmly said in a high pitched voice, "I bid $2,600." JB looked over. An elderly woman in a black wool coat with a gray scarf over her head had made the bid. This wasn't one of his troops. Someone else was going to get Bret's heirloom.

Mr. Blech was surprised. He was sure the war had been won. It was time for the losers to concede defeat on the battlefield and pick up their dead.

"Oh, really! Another of Decker's shills. Well, you can't beat me. $5,000!" Mr. Blech said defiantly.

The woman was praying and counting her rosary beads. She looked suspiciously like Sister Lucille, the third grade teacher at St. John's. Sitting next to her were two men whose faces were partially hidden behind wool scarves.

Father Flannigan from St. John's and Reverend White from the South Presbyterian Church rose from their seats and unveiled themselves. Father Flannigan said respectfully and politely, "Miss Auctioneer, can you verify that the bidder has the resources to pay for the item as required under the rules?"

Mr. Blech walked threateningly toward the priest and yelled, "Do you know who I am? I'm the bank that owns this property. And I have plenty of cash. This auction is over. Decker, you lose. And you, bud," he jabbed a finger at the priest, "I'll see you in hell."

Pastor White responded in a quiet and solemn tone, "Well, sir, I don't think we'll be crossing paths in the afterlife.

"However, auctioneer, the rules are clear. Does this gentleman have $5,000 on his person to buy the item?"

Catherine asked, "Mr. Blech. Do you or don't you have the money?"

Blech grabbed the cash from his two shills and counted the money. "I have most of it. I can get the rest in thirty minutes."

"Not good enough," Catherine said, restraining her joy. "You must have the funds on hand. You've violated the bidding rules and are not allowed to enter further bids. They're *your* rules."

"I'll sue you. You can't do this. I'll hold your firm legally responsible for this fraudulent sale," cried Blech.

Catherine said calmly, "You can't sue us. You just signed an agreement telling us to auction the last lot where-is, as-is. You gave all of us, including my employer, JB and Decker, a full release of claims.

"Now, I can't demand that you leave the premises because you represent the bank's holdings. However, you will have to move outside the gallery lines." She motioned to Mike the Cop to come forward from the driveway entrance to the auctioneer table. "Mike, please escort the gentleman behind the ropes. Let the auction continue!"

CHAPTER 332

DECEMBER 7

The mayor, police chief, fire captain and a handful of decades-old friends of Decker rose to their feet and gave light applause as Mike the Cop escorted Blech past them cursing, spitting and turning purple with anger.

As Mr. Blech passed through the crowd, a handful of friends opened their winter coats to reveal "The Heck with Blech" tee shirts featuring a caricature of Mr. Blech smoking a smelly cigar.

Mr. Blech yelled, "I'll sue you, too! You can't use my picture for commercial purposes!"

Bret said smugly, "It's a caricature, not a photo. But go ahead and sue. I'll defend them for free. I'm undefeated in the courtroom this year!"

Blech turned and started to leave. There was no reason to watch the ending. Besides, the bank had made enough money from the auction.

His assistants had loaded the valuable antiques into the moving van and left JB's faux antiques on the driveway. Catherine called to him: "Mr. Blech…what does the bank want to do with these other pieces you bought? You can't leave the items here."

Blech turned and looked at the varnished armoire and the heap of chairs, tables and boxes filled with sconces, china and smaller items. It was clear to him now that the goods were old, but not old enough to be classified as antique. He'd been had.

He said disgustedly, "That junk. I don't want it. Burn it for all I care." He had no intention of explaining to his bosses how the bank had purchased a truckload of old furniture that wouldn't make the cut on *Antiques Roadshow*.

After the banker left, the remaining items in Lot 22 were auctioned for the listed minimum bids. $50 for a silver tea set. $100 for the painting of his great grandmother. JB bought all of it and still had $3,000 left.

The crowd stood around Decker and Catherine and gave hearty congratulations. JB said, "I have a little money left here. I made a pledge to St. John's and South Presbyterian that if the auction went well, they could have the remaining proceeds and any unsold furniture. Blech doesn't realize it, but he just made a contribution to your parishes."

"You know, I was looking for spiritual assistance, but certainly didn't expect such active participation."

"First, let's say a silent prayer for the man's soul. He needs our help," said Father Flannigan as he lowered his head and made the sign of the cross.

He looked up a few seconds later and cheerfully said, "I know an Irish public house nearby by the name of Tommy Fox's that would provide some libations on this festive occasion. Care to join us? We're going to celebrate the engagement of Decker and Catherine and their wedding to be held at St. John's this spring."

"No, you don't!" Minster White said, holding his hand high. "Decker is a member of my congregation. The wedding will be held in our chapel."

Decker said gleefully, "Compromise. We can have a two-denominational wedding at the Cooper's Pond gazebo!"

Everyone laughed, and a large crowd made their way to Tommy Fox's. They had survived the Blech blitzkrieg.

At the pub, JB moved to the corner to hang out with a few Irish regulars who were born in the old country. A fiddler and guitarist played Irish Christmas ballads in Gaelic as JB and his friends sang along.

The out-of-the-closet couple had never been happier. Friends spent the night with never-ending toasts to their health and happiness. Watching Decker, you'd never have guessed that he had just lost both his family business and home.

CHAPTER 333

DECEMBER 13, 2013

After her arrest, the district attorney had argued that Misty was a flight risk and shouldn't be allowed bail. Even though she was seven months pregnant, they believed she had a secret stash of cash and valuables and had no ties to the community except her aging parents. One of the DA's compelling arguments was that Giovanna had no friends willing to vouch for her.

In early December, the legal team for the Treasury Department mysteriously removed their objections. Misty made bail after her parents borrowed money through a reverse mortgage on their home. Their entire retirement savings were at stake if Misty bolted.

It wasn't that the Feds felt Misty was no longer a flight risk – her jewelry now included an ankle bracelet, courtesy of the Justice Department, to monitor her movements. Rather, the investigators thought that if she were free, there was a chance Averill might try to rescue or at least contact her. They tapped her phones and email. They watched her house 24/7. They listened through satellite pickups. All they heard was sobs.

In the two weeks since being under house arrest, Misty never went outside. She was mortified. Her mother wailed to her rapidly dwindling circle of friends, "Giovanna, my poor girl. She's innocent. Those horrible agents set her up to catch that bastard. She'd never do anything wrong. My poor baby."

Would Averill risk getting caught to save his bride? Would he send her money?

Not a peep was heard from the perp.

CHAPTER 334

DECEMBER 14, 2013

Vinnie Martini and Manuel "O'Hara" Velasquez quickly formed a joint venture, "Martini & O'Hara". Vinnie had connections to the heavy construction business. His crew knew how to operate bulldozers and dump trucks. O'Hara Landscaping knew how to lay sod. Together, they signed up three thousand customers at $3,000 apiece "to restore the natural beauty to your front yard".

Mayor Alvarez overruled the ecology groups who wanted to compost the old crabgrass. "Burn every last scraggly weed and seed!" he ordered.

In less than two weeks, Vinnie's crews hustled to beat the winter freeze and had dug up ten square blocks. Following the bulldozing, Manuel's landscapers leveled the grounds and spread Allie's weed killer. The sod would be laid next May. By June, everything would return to normal.

CHAPTER 335

DECEMBER 16, 2013

Following the Pierre announcements, Bergenfield housing prices began plummeting. Six months before, speculators had been paying a large premium to buy homes because of the income from the annual CRAB crop. Now homeowners were lucky to find a buyer at any price.

Howie and Johnny, having ignored Gilbert's earlier advice to sell, were still the not so proud owners of three homes that were now in derelict condition. The renters had moved out. The crabgrass was so infested with foreign plant species that Pierre terminated their contracts.

Neither Howie nor Johnny wanted to spend one dime to fix the houses up for sale. In desperation, they hired Roberta Shamsky, the same real estate broker who had bartered the Chinese deal. They sold the three houses in a package deal to the only party willing to buy distressed properties in town.

Martini & O'Hara took particular joy squeezing Johnny hard during negotiations. "Dose houses are tear-downs!" Vinnie snarled at Johnny. "It's gonna cost me a hunnerd to fix each one of dem up. If ya don't wanna sell to me, you gonna hafta hire an arsonist. I told ya to take Gilbert's deal, but no. Youse guys were too smart for da man."

Vinnie paid the bargain price of $400,000 for all three houses. Howie and Johnny each had to pay taxes on their share of the phantom income from the sale of the houses to the Chinese. Then they had to pay taxes on the sale to Vinnie. After taxes and Roberta's commission, Howie and Johnny netted very little.

During the last two years, Johnny had pissed away most of the proceeds from selling his store to Allie, lost his job at NBCI, never cashed in a single stock option when they had been worth something, and now had less than $70,000 to show for his investment in Gilbert's real estate deal. Howie still had his law practice to return to, except the mayor had cancelled his $2,000 per month contract to perform legal work for the town.

CHAPTER 336

DECEMBER 24, 2013

Allie sat down with a full table at Ben's, none of whom would be going to work this cheery Christmas Eve. She unrolled a large poster and said "Look! I'm gonna be famous!"

It was a mock-up of Allie choking a cartoon image of a crabgrass plant with bulging eyes and a frightened face. Underneath in large letters was the title, "THE CRABINATOR".

"I'm rebranding my weed killer," Allie said. "Tooty's gonna pay for the new packagin'. Can you believe Jake's was makin' $15 a bag? And they never even handled the stuff.

"Tooty's had developed a much better formula, but Jake's delayed it 'cause it didn't want to kill the golden goose, or the golden weed. Whatever. Next season Tooty's is gonna use this new packaging. Whadaya think, guys?"

While everyone teased Allie, Ben pressed the Play button for the jukebox. At first, a Christmas song opened with beautiful violins. JB nudged Buyout. "Hurry, go get the record number from the jukebox."

After the opening bars but before Nat King Cole began to sing, the tune changed to the electric guitar opening to *Jingle Bell Rock*. Before Bobbie Helms could get a word in, the piano opening to *O Tannenbaum* from *A Charlie Brown Christmas* broke in. JB grabbed his iPhone and quickly turned on the voice recorder.

Ben had thrown a ringer into the juke box overnight. The last item in the annual Bingo contest was a medley.

A minute after the song ended, JB jumped from his chair and waved his entry form. He yelled, "Bingo! Buyout, give Ben the poster. I want it hung today!"

JB was as excited as a five year old on Christmas morning. Tables of diners groaned. Bingo entry forms were being torn to shreds. Neil Bailey, the senior partner in a securities law firm, yelled over, "I demand verification. There's no way you got the Christmas melody right."

Ben raised his arms and said, "It'll have to wait until my customers have been fed."

The jukebox Bingo contest was nearly a year old. JB's matrix was filled with the names of all hundred songs. To most of the regulars, it was an unofficial contest for fun. For JB, this was important. The winner would be accorded Customer of the Month credentials. His picture would be hung behind the register.

JB said, "Neil, the Christmas mix is thirteen songs. Ben should make a record and sell it. You'd never have to listen to Christmas radio again. Buyout, read 'em so they can weep."

Buyout stood and recited, "The Ben's Deli two-minute Christmas melody playlist is as follows:

Song one, *The Christmas Song*, Nat King Cole

Song two, *Jingle Bell Rock*, Bobbie Helms

Song three, *O Tannenbaum*, Vince Guaraldi

Song four, *Rockin' Around the Christmas Tree*, Brenda Lee

Song five, *Skating*, Vince Guaraldi

Song six, *All I Want for Christmas is You*, Mariah Carey

Song seven, *Christmas Baby Please Come Home*, Darleen Love

Song eight, *Wonderful Christmastime*, Paul McCartney

Song nine, *Happy Christmas (War is Over)*, John and Yoko

Song ten, *Blue Christmas*, Elvis Presley

Song eleven, *Little Saint Nick*, the Beach Boys

Song twelve, *Christmas Wrapping* by the Waitresses

And song thirteen, *Silent Night* sung in Gaelic by Enya

JB said gleefully, "The last song was tough, but they played that version at Tommy Fox's the night Misty was thrown out of the church. Who could forget it?"

Neil groaned and said, "I just didn't put enough time into this project. Work got in the way again."

Michael Li expressed remorse: "I only had ten songs, but I wrote the names in Chinese characters. Song 'Runaway' by Dion has strange meaning in Hunan, you know. It means criminal escapee." Laughter filled Ben's.

After Ben verified JB's card, he hoisted the oversized poster behind the register. JB had posed in full regalia, wearing a crimson velvet king's robe and crown while holding a scepter.

JB proclaimed, "As the king, I have the right to mint currency with my image. Buyout, distribute the coinage of our realm!"

The Wharton MBA handed out quarters pasted over with JB's photo. Neil called out, "No wonder the value of the dollar keeps falling!"

Customers would have to look at the poster for another month. Ben groaned, "I hope I don't lose any business over this."

CHAPTER 337

DECEMBER 24

Catherine Mulcahy waited patiently for her future ex-husband to arrive and sign the divorce and church annulment papers. In eight hours, she and Decker would be joining Bret and Allie for midnight mass. Decker hid out of sight to avoid an unnecessary confrontation. Just sign the papers so he and Catherine could marry.

Ned Mulcahy arrived in an obnoxiously happy mood. Even though it was December and cold, he wore a flowered shirt, shorts and sandals underneath his overcoat. He was permanently tan from the last adventure.

"You're late. Let's do this quickly. I have to get ready for church," Catherine said briskly.

"What's the rush?" Ned fired back. "You won't be seeing me ever again. You should be happy."

He signed the last pages without reading the documents and tossed them toward Catherine. She pushed them back. "You have to provide a forwarding address on the last page. The lawyers require it. I certainly don't need it."

"Sorry, babe!" Ned said sarcastically. "I don't have one, unless you want to mail it to my sailboat in the South Pacific. I'm going on another cruise and this time I ain't returning. I bought a sixty-footer. Plenty of room for my stockpile of Captain Morgan's rum!"

"Just write down a couple of harbors where you're going to anchor. Where the hell did you get money for a big yacht? My investigators said you were broke." Catherine eyed him warily.

"Oh, I didn't tell you? I have an investor. He's funding my trip providing I take him along. I gotta go. Have fun in crabgrass hell! My car's waiting. We're driving to the west coast!" Ned scribbled an address on the signature page and left.

Decker walked into the room and found Catherine looking at the signature pages in shock. He asked, "What's the matter? You should be happy."

Catherine showed him the page. "Look at this! Look where he's going!"

Decker thought perhaps she was feeling remorse or regret, and wanted to be supportive. "Forget it. You don't care where he is. It's you and me now."

Catherine started laughing loudly and couldn't control herself. Between gasps of breath, she said, "He's sailing from a marina in San Diego to the Cook Islands in the Pacific. Someone bought him a boat. Don't you get it?

"It was on *60 Minutes* last month. The Cook Islands are the latest place to hide your money from the government. That stock swindler crook must have moved his money from the Cayman Islands to the South Pacific. Hand me that FBI wanted poster."

The fugitive stockbroker's photo had become an instant collector's item. The post office kept a stack next to the priority mail envelopes.

"Jeez, I'm not so sure," said Decker. "Why was that Johnny Carrera character sitting in the passenger seat? Those two looked more like they're heading for a booze cruise."

"Johnny was in the car? I heard the SEC is closing in on him, too. That guy was Averill's only friend. I'll bet they're all sailing together. And if they're driving to California, it must be because they're carrying contraband and can't get caught flying.

"Averill can't get leave the country through airport security. They're watching all of the exits. But he can easily leave from a marina in San Diego. This is priceless!" Catherine wore an evil grin.

Catherine dialed the 800 number. "It's 4:00 PM on Christmas Eve. Will anyone be working? Hello, hello. Is this the FBI hotline? Yes, I'll wait."

She sang, "*Oh the weather outside is frightful...*"

"Hello. Yes. Is the reward still good for that guy Averill?. . . That was his alias. I mean Barry Winthrop. The stockbroker con artist who got away…It's still good. Fantastic! I know where he is. You'd better grab him before he leaves port. And I'm pretty sure he has two accomplices helping him...Fantastic!"

After she provided the FBI with the rendezvous details, Panama Blonde excitedly said to Decker, "I've gotta call Allie. She'll never believe this."

CHAPTER 338

DECEMBER 24

Allie laughed and said, "Tell me all about it later, Catherine. I can't talk right now."

Bret was holding steady on one knee. In his hand was a Tiffany's robin-egg blue, ring-sized jewelry box. He had popped the question and his romantic proposal was stalled in an infinite loop of poorly timed interruptions.

"I'm sorry, Bret," Allie said sympathetically. "I..."

Marty burst through the front door with his arm around Blondie Bondi, his tall, beautiful, tanned and freckled surfer girlfriend. Born Kelli, her friends nicknamed her after the famous Australian beach.

"Whoa, Bret! What're ya doin'? Look at the grey belly taking the drop. Continue on, your gnarliness!"

Marty and Bondi walked to the TV room giggling. Bret rolled from his knee to the floor with his arms splayed wide in a feigned look of defeat. The Tiffany box rolled from his grasp. Allie shut the door to the den and layed next to Bret on the floor, nestling into the curl of his shoulder.

She tugged on the white ribbon and began to open the box. She said teasingly, "Hey, this better not be one of the missing Averill diamonds."

She slipped the sparkling diamond ring onto her finger and whispered, "Oh, Bret, you're so romantic. Yes, I'll marry you, but you gotta get Marty's approval."

"Come on. Do you have to make this more..."

Marty yelled from the den over the roar of the surf crashing in the *Chasing Mavericks* video. "Permission granted. As long as I don't have to call you kahuna!"

Bret pulled Allie close, kissed her and said, "I love you."

Allie pulled away momentarily and said, "Love you, too, kahuna.

EPILOGUE

(SIX MONTHS LATER)

A handsome, extremely tanned and buff Marty Bertrand entered Ben's and sat next to JB. "Yo, dude. Just got back from dawn patrol. Big wave hangover from Hurricane Arthur. Ten footers with perfect curls. I'm so stoked."

Ben stood at the cash register giving the shirtless surfer a stern look while tugging on his apron.

"Oops! Sorry, Ben. Gotta put on the rash guard when visitin' the local food hut," he said, poking his mane of long curly blond hair through a red lifeguard tank tee shirt.

JB was infinitely entertained by Marty's new persona. "Kid, shouldn't you be finding a career now that you're out of high school? Or are you going to work at your mom's store for the rest of your life?"

"No way," protested Marty. "At the end of 'The Endless Summer', I'll be attendin' a highly esteemed, top-ten surfin' university. The noble and totally radical institute of Monmouth U. It's a short dune buggy ride from Manasquan Inlet, a perfectly fine place to drop in and ride the barrel before classes. An eighty percent 'swell ratio' in the summer plus some epic days like today."

"How did you get accepted there?" JB said in amazement. "I thought you needed better grades and high SAT scores?"

"I killed the SATs, man," laughed Marty. "But even a comeback senior year couldn't wipe out my bleak history. However, my application won kudos from the admissions dude. My essay was a draft of my short story about how Mom beat the crabgrass mania. He said I had an interesting writin' style and command of dialect, whatever that means.

"Well, gotta get back to work. They're lettin' the beach bunnies back into the surf at noon. There'll be lives to save today at Island Beach State Park. Me, four awesome dudes and three lady longboarders are totally responsible for the fates of swimmers caught in an endless riptide."

Marty took a bite of a bagel, a swig of Mountain Dew, then blew out the door. JB looked around a very quiet table. Michael Li was in deep thought reading the business section of *The Record*. Walter Harrigan yawned.

The media hounds were long gone from Bergenfield. Curiosity seekers had lost interest. The regular crew wasn't so regular anymore. Buyout had taken an assignment in his firm's Hong Kong office. Allie's time was presently consumed with interviews by the famous Joanie Steele for a documentary on women entrepreneurs. Bret's new general counsel job was in Mahwah, the opposite direction from Ben's, but he made a point to join JB at least once a week. Everyone else was too busy; they barely had time except to grab a coffee, say hi, and rush to work.

Ben sat next to JB. "You know, I had a huge offer to buy this place last year, but I turned it down. I figured after I paid taxes, I'd barely have enough to retire on. Besides, what would I do with myself all day?"

"Ben, I swear, if you put this place up for sale, I'm leaving." JB feigned a look of alarm. "Besides, who's gonna buy it after its most famous customer stops patronizing? Miguel? I mean, he's a hard worker and all, but he just doesn't get my sense of humor."

"Who does?" deadpanned Ben. "Speaking of humor, I haven't seen Auntie Ev lately. She used to motor by here about now."

JB gave yet another of his patented mischievous smiles and said, "Have you ever heard the story about a buncha guys who decided they'd been spending too much on booze, so they bought a bar to save money? Well, it looks like the Hedge Fund Grannies are trying to save money on yarn. They pooled their profits from CRAB trading and bought The Dangerous Knitter. I've never seen Auntie Ev so happy. She told me they were adding a whole bunch of product lines. Quilting machines, beading, the works. I guess now they'll be hedging wool futures. Ha-ha."

"By the way, did you hear Chris sold his newspaper?" Ben said. "NorthJersey.com bought it – the same guys who own *The Record*. They're changing back to the old name, *Twin-Boro News*. Chris is much happier now that he can spend his time on editorials and sales and not have to worry about production anymore."

"That's very good news," Michael said. His attention was drawn to the TV screen. "There they go again. A half year later and they're still showing it."

JB glanced at the TV screen, laughed, and said, "Michael, this will never get old. You hafta love CNN for replaying something so entertaining. Repetition is the soul of wit!"

The newscaster was showing a repeat of Averill's non-capture. The split screen showed the flotilla of Zodiacs filled with armed San Diego Coast Guard and FBI agents that had surrounded Ned Mulcahy's sailboat one mile offshore in December. Ned and Johnny were caught holding a small amount of the loot Averill had paid them to aid in his escape. But Avy was nowhere to be found.

Johnny and Ned had pled guilty and each received two-year sentences for their involvement in Averill's escape. The legal fees ate up most of Johnny's remaining liquid assets. The Feds seized Johnny's secret JTV Enterprises bank account and the bribe money. It provided a long trail of evidence against Averill.

Misty had been granted full immunity as the key witness. She knew nothing of Averill's insider trading, but saw firsthand the money laundering that could send him away for a lot of years if they ever caught him. In February, she had a baby girl, named Giovanna, who was as cute as her mother and fortunately hadn't inherited Averill's beady eyes. Misty seemed to be starting a new life, this time without the drama. Lately, she could be seen pushing a stroller near the Bergenfield Swim Club on Twinboro Lane.

JB turned to Ben and said, "You know, you'll probably never again in your lifetime get a front row seat to a boom and bust. I mean, they'll happen, but not here. I think our fifteen minutes of fame are over.

"Think about it. When you add it all up, the numbers are crazy. Nearly $20 billion was bet on the commodity markets. That dinky little processing plant became a $600 million dollar public company with $200 million in bonds. Credit default swaps bet $4 billion that NBCI would fail. The POO ETF was worth another $300 million. And don't forget housing values. Nine thousand homes in town were each suddenly worth a hundred grand more. Now, that's gone too. All of this money changing hands for a material that makes up at most a fifth of the ingredients in a shampoo with maybe a billion dollars of sales. None of this makes any sense.

"It's not just crabgrass. There's a flood of available money in the world today looking for huge returns that can only come from speculative investments. Today it's New York real estate, Spanish bonds and bitcoins. Five years ago it was housing, oil, gold and copper. Before that it was dot-com and tech stocks. You name it. Every one of them has experienced a bout of hyperinflation in the last ten years.

"Six months ago, it was crabgrass. Next year, it'll be something else. The speculators appear from nowhere like locusts. They swarm in, eat everything in sight, and leave nothing but dust."

"You're right, JB," said Michael in a resigned voice. "And it is a zero sum game. For every dollar that was made on CRAB, someone lost a dollar. That's close to $25 billion dollars that evaporated overnight. I'm so glad I work for a conservative bank. Many banks are exposed to this. A lot of people in town refinanced their mortgages. The bright spot is that most people in town were smart and saved their profits."

Michael stood and left the table to get a coffee refill. Ben said quietly to JB, "I heard what you did for Decker. Putting a million into his real estate venture was a nice thing to do."

"Nice nothing," laughed JB. "We're going to make beaucoup bucks on this deal. A coupla hundred homes in town defaulted on their mortgages because of the collapse of the crabgrass market. They're going cheap. How people could lose money speculating on crabgrass is just beyond me. All they had to do was let it grow, cut it, and sell it.

"Anyway, Decker needs to start over again somewhere. I had to twist Vinnie's arm, but I think they'll do well together." JB shot Ben a sidelong glance. "And I'm not the only patron around here. I heard about the trust fund you set up for Misty's baby."

Ben said softly, "You gotta keep this quiet, JB. His father may be a scoundrel, but the child is innocent and deserves better."

JB looked Ben in the eye, saw a tinge of guilt, and said, "C'mon Ben. Cough it up. Just the kid?"

Ben shrugged. "Okay, okay. I'm helping out Misty too, at least until she can start working again. The girl let greed and pride overrule common sense. She probably knew what Averill was doing, but chose to look the other way because she wanted the money. I think we have to give her one more chance."

Michael returned with his coffee. "Do you think Vinnie will be the best man at Decker and Catherine's wedding next week? I heard half the town is showing up."

"You mean double wedding, don't you?" JB said with a playful grin. "Bret and Allie moved their date up. The four of 'em are getting' hitched at the Cooper's Pond gazebo. Why do you think Mayor Alvarez rushed to dredge the muck left over from Hurricane Sandy? For the ducks? Not!"

"A June wedding! That's wonderful," Michael said affectionately.

The TV screen in Ben's flashed a grainy picture of Averill whose lizard-like eyes and ratty moustache portrayed the sinister outlaw he had officially become. The STCK-TV announcer Cal Bonita said, "Tonight at 9:00 PM on *American Avarice,* we'll be airing a one-hour special on the disappearance of the infamous Barry "Averill" Winthrop. This stock swindler extraordinaire was last seen leaving his Bergenfield, New Jersey offices minutes before the FBI arrived to arrest him. He was presumably headed to Ben's Deli, a popular local eatery, to meet up with his wife, Giovanna, also known as Misty. He never arrived.

"It was then believed he had planned an escape by sailboat from San Diego with two accomplices, Johnny Carrera and Ned Mulcahy. The alleged destination was a South Pacific island where Winthrop may have stashed his misappropriated millions. Carrera and Mulcahy were captured by the FBI in possession of a small bag of diamonds confirmed to be payment for abetting his escape. But once again, Winthrop was a no-show. And the big money has never been found.

"Averill Winthrop has been likened to a modern day D.B. Cooper, who vanished into thin air, too. For those of you too young to know the story, forty years ago, Cooper hijacked a commercial airline before takeoff, extorted a large ransom, and once the plane was mid-flight, he parachuted into the Northwest woods. They never found him or the money. The FBI case is still open."

The STCK-TV camera panned to Jay McCall, who laughed and said, "You know, this guy Averill is from New Jersey. Maybe he's buried with Jimmy Hoffa underneath the goal-posts in the old Meadowlands Stadium. Or perhaps we'll have another Averill sighting to report before tonight's show. This guy is slicker than an Alaskan oil spill."

"Watch tonight," Cal Bonita said, "as our investigative team explores the public's fasci-nation with Averill sightings. The speculation on his whereabouts is a never-ending tale of how elusive this character has become. People claim to have seen him in the Everglades, the Adirondacks, and even at Comic Con, but no one has been able to capture his face in a photo. Is Averill long gone and already sipping Coronas on a beach in the South Pacific? Is he still hiding in the States? Is he even alive?

"He has now earned a place on the FBI's Ten Most Wanted Fugitives list, and there's talk of increasing the reward. Who will be the lucky one to definitively answer the question, 'Where's Averill?'"

ACKNOWLEDGMENTS

I want to thank everyone, but in particular:
My friends from Bergenfield High School, URI and Harvard who cheered me on;
Tom Stitt, who created my social media infrastructure;
Ian Shapolsky, who gave great advice on how to convert my first draft into a novel;
The nuns at St. John the Evangelist who relentlessly taught me proper grammar;
Cliff Carle, my editor, who was remarkably understanding of my early creative writing flaws
and helped me convert perfect grammar (see above) into New Jersey dialect; and
Lisa, my wife, who encouraged me to write this novel.

Made in the USA
Charleston, SC
07 November 2014